❋ Acclaim for This Series ❋

"YOU CAN ALMOST SMELL THE LEATHER, THE SWEAT, THE BLOOD. Bunch's battle sequences are second to none. . . . Bunch manages to keep the tension high."

—*Portland Oregonian*

"A VAST AND INTRICATE TAPESTRY WOVEN BY A WRITER WHO KNOWS BOTH HISTORY AND WAR."

—David Drake, author of *Ranks of Bronze*

"BUNCH HAS A SURE GRASP OF MILITARY HISTORY AND ORGANIZATION."

—*Kirkus Reviews*

"WELL PACED AND FULL OF FASCINATING CHARACTERS . . . SUBTLETY AND SURPRISES IN AN EPIC SETTING. REMARKABLE."

—Michael A. Stackpole,
New York Times* bestselling author of *Once a Hero

"FAST-MOVING, WELL-PLOTTED FANTASY . . . A SOLID, THREE-DIMENSIONAL WORLD."

—J.V. Jones, author of The Book of Words trilogy and *The Barbed Coil*

"A GREAT SAGA . . . filled with duplicity, arrogance, magic, lust, and—best of all—honor. . . . A roller coaster of lust, revenge, power, breaches of trust, and courage. . . . The sorcery is sinister and everything you could fear. . . . The characters are alive and real. They are funny too, when they spout out observations that are so wry it sometimes takes a moment to catch their dry sense of humor."

—*Explorations* (Barnes & Noble SF/fantasy newsletter)

"FAST-PACED AND FEROCIOUS."

—Julian May, author of *Magnificat*

"BUNCH KNOWS HOW TO MOLD HEROES, HOW TO KEEP THE PACE FAST, AND HOW TO CREATE EXCITING SCENES OF BATTLEFIELD MAYHEM AND CONVINCING WEBS OF POLITICAL INTRIGUE."

—*Publishers Weekly*

"GRIPPING. . . . BUNCH ONCE AGAIN SHOWS HIS GIFT FOR TELLING TALES OF BATTLE AND INTRIGUE."

—*SF Site*

Also by Chris Bunch

The Seer King

And coming soon

The Warrior King

Published by
Warner Aspect

CHRIS BUNCH

THE DEMON KING

A Time Warner Company

WARNER BOOKS EDITION

Cover design by Don Puckey
Cover illustration by Tony Russo/Drew Blair
Book design by H. Roberts Design

Aspect is a registered trademark of Warner Books, Inc.

Warner Books, Inc.
1271 Avenue of the Americas
New York, NY 10020

Visit our Web site at
http://warnerbooks.com

 A Time Warner Company

Printed in the United States of America

Originally published in trade paperback by Warner Books.
First Mass Market Printing: January, 1999

10 9 8 7 6 5 4 3 2 1

for
Danny Baror
&
The Studwells:
Craig, Jan
Gillian, Matthew, and Megan

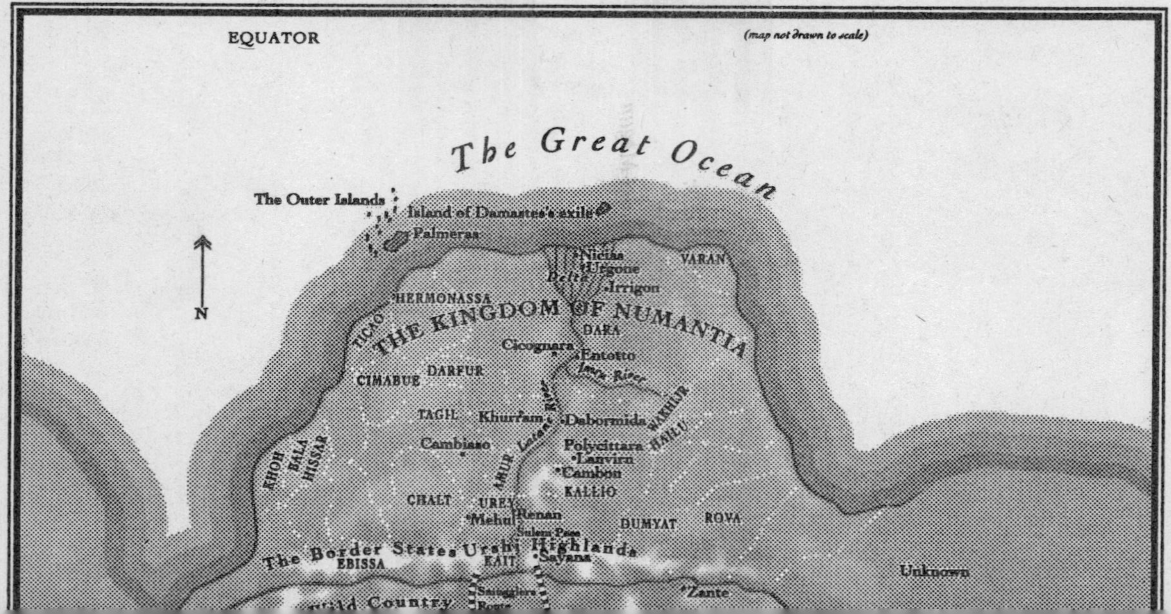

EQUATOR
(map not drawn to scale)
The Great Ocean
The Outer Islands
Island of Damastes's exile
Palmeras
N
Nicias
Urgone
Delta
Irrigon
VARAN
HERMONASSA
THE KINGDOM OF NUMANTIA
TICAO
DARA
Cicognara
Entotto
Imra River
CIMABUE
DARFUR
TAGIL
Khurram
Dabormida
WAKHIJR
HAILU
Cambiaso
Latane River
Polycittara
Lanvirn
Cambon
KHOH BALA HISSAR
AMUR
KALLIO
CHALT
UREY
Renan
Mehul
DUMYAT
ROVA
Sulem Pass
The Border States
Urshi Highlands
EBISSA
KAIT
Sayana
Unknown
Zante

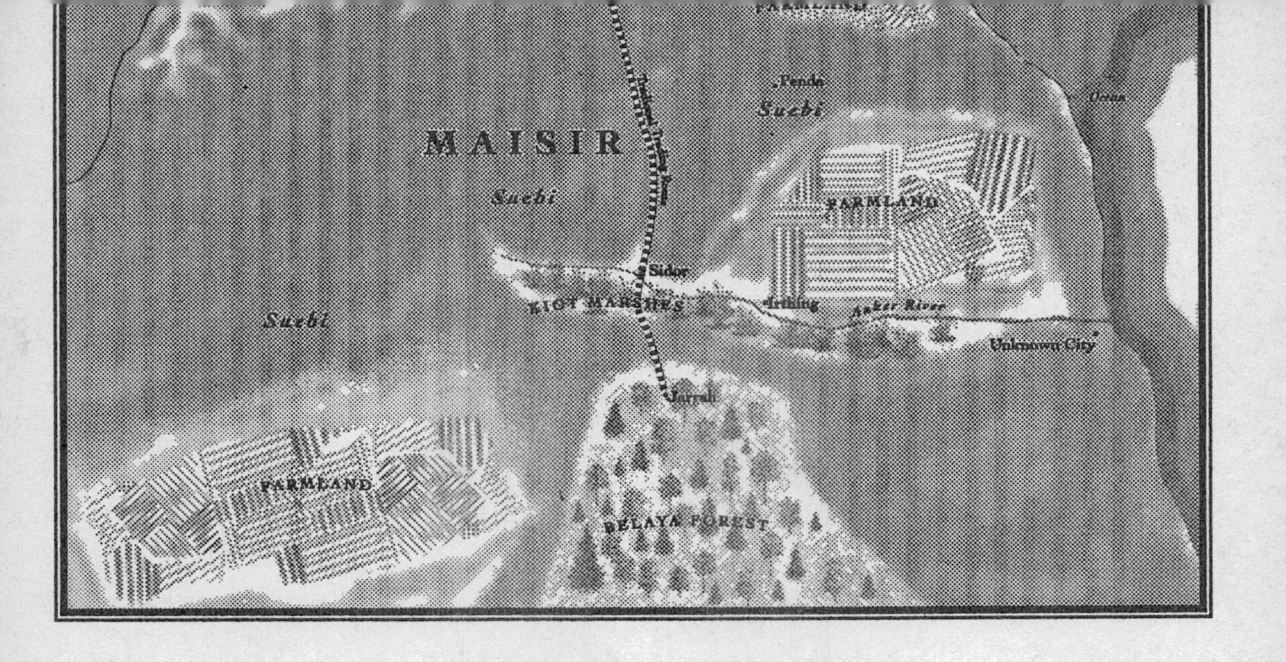

MAISIR
Traditional Trading Route
Pende
Suebi
Suebi
Suebi
FARMLAND
FARMLAND
Sidor
KIOT MARSHES
Irthing
Anker River
Unknown City
Ocean
Jarrah
BELAYA FOREST

ONE

THE GOLDEN AX

The postilion's sharp ears saved Marán's and my lives. He heard the cracking as the great oak above us broke and toppled, and yanked at his reins. The team, whinnying surprise, veered into the ditch as the tree smashed down in front of our coach.

Marán flew across the compartment into my arms with a shriek, and I sprawled backward as the huge carriage teetered and skidded wildly as a wheel splintered. There were shouts of men, screams of horses, and I slid from under Marán, kicked the door open and rolled out, reflexively drawing the sword that never left my reach.

But there was no one to fight, and nothing to see except my regal coach lying like a hulk, its eight horses plunging to be freed, and a sweltering mass of cavalry as my escort milled about in confusion.

On a far hillside I saw a plume of dust as a rider galloped for safety.

There were cries of "sorcery," "magic," "get the bastard," and Legate Balkh crying for volunteers to go after the would-be assassin, and behind that countermanding shouts from myself, Captain Lasta, and, against all rules, Lance Karjan, my bodyservant.

My wife peered out as her squealing maids ran up from their carriage behind.

"Are you hurt?" I asked.

"No," she said. "Just a little shaken. What happened?"

"Evidently," I said, "the Kallians know of our coming, and have expressed their opinion."

"But how did . . ."

"Come with me, and we'll see if we can figure it out."

I helped her out of the huge carriage that had been more a home for the last eight years than any of my palaces, and we walked to where the huge tree lay across the road. Magic was instantly and obviously the explanation. The tree's trunk had been cut through cleanly, not rotted and split. I spotted a glint in the grass. I picked up a tiny golden ax, no more than an inch tall, just as the regimental commander of the Seventeenth Ureyan Lancers ran to me and saluted.

"Domina Bikaner, send a patrol to that hilltop. Tell them to look for a small oak branch that's been cut in half."

"Yessir."

I continued examining the tree. "Look here," I said. Marán saw where a small limb had been neatly cut. I would never have noticed except symbols were carved into the bark, symbols oozing fresh sap.

"I'd guess that was how it was done," I said. "The wizard notched the tree trunk, put a tiny simalcrum of his sorcerous ax in the notch, then took the branch with him. The symbols on the tree make sure that the part can become of the whole, as Emperor Tenedos would say.

"He waited until the first troop of Lancers went past, knew our carriage for his target since it's the biggest and plushest, and commenced to cutting the branch. When it split, the tree dropped very neatly. All that can be slighted is his timing."

"I don't see how you can be so casual about this," Marán said. "The bastard could have killed us!"

"After the first dozen times," I said, " 'could have killed me' is quite as satisfying as 'never even thought about it.' "

"Why didn't you let the cavalry hunt him down?"

"Because I'll wager he had a hundred or so friends waiting over the first hill. Magicians don't scratch their butts without backup."

"Tribune Damastes, you are far too clever," Marán said. "Now . . . are you through being mad at me?"

The inn we'd stayed at the previous night had been vile, without question. The keeper had been surly, the rooms dirty, and the food so unpalatable we'd ignored it and eaten soldiers rations with the Lancers. Marán had summoned the keeper and told him, in some detail, what a worthless swine he was, and if it were hers to say she'd have the place razed as a health hazard and him whipped for general scalawaggery. The keeper was an incompetent and an ass, but he knew if Marán had been on her own lands she could, indeed, have ordered the building torched. The Agramónte name ran farther back in Numantian history than most laws.

Marán was behaving like an arrogant bitch, and I said so when the innkeeper had quavered away. That was foolish of me. When one is born to impossible wealth, and most of mankind exists as one's servants or underlings, it's not likely one will suffer fools, and besides her temper was almost as volcanic as mine.

"I am through being mad at you, madam," I said. "Are you through snubbing me?"

"Perhaps."

Men swarmed about our coach. Shouts came, and it was tipped upright and muscled back onto the road, and a spare wheel from one of the wagons in our support train was rolled up.

"Things appear to be well in hand," she said. "Would the noble tribune care to join me for a walk into the woods for a bit, to stretch our legs?"

"I would."

"Would the noble tribune mind departing from tradition and leave his bodyguards behind?"

"Would madam feel safe? After all, we are in Kallio now, and we've already seen what people seem to think of us."

"You have your sword, do you not? How could I fear anyone with such a brave man beside me?"

"Aren't you piling it a little thick?"

Marán giggled.

"I was wondering how long I could keep up that nonsense before you growled."

She led me into the small copse beside the road. Lance Karjan started after us, and I told him to stay with the carriage. It was the height of the Time of Heat, very hot, and very still once we were away from the road, except for the scuff of our boots, the whisper of her long traveling skirt against the dry grass, and the sleepy sound of bees. Marán leaned back against a rock slab that rose diagonally.

"I love this time," she said. "When I sweat it's like my body's oiled, all over." There was a film of perspiration on her upper lip, and she licked it away, slowly.

"Isn't that my task?" I said, my voice a little husky.

"It could be." I came close and kissed her, our tongues curling around each other. Her blouse unbuttoned like a military tunic on either side, and fell away, her breasts pointing up at me, nipples firm.

She lazily moved her legs apart and pulled her dress up across her smooth thighs. She wore no underclothing. She let her head fall back against the rock, lifted her legs about the backs of my thighs.

"Yes, Damastes. Do it to me now!"

When we returned to the carriage, pretending innocence and ignoring our tousled clothing, I took Karjan aside and reminded him rankers generally did not make officers happy by countermanding their orders, as he'd done with Legate Balkh.

"Yessir. Should've let th' pup ride off an' get hisself killed, an' a lot of better men with him. Sorry, Tribune. P'raps I'd be best takin' off th' rank tape an' bein' no more'n a horseman again, if th' tribune wishes."

I swore and told him I might be a tribune but I could still

take him behind the stables and be the only one to walk back, if he wanted to reduce things to that level. He looked unworried. Karjan, who served me indifferently in peace and perfectly in war—saving my life on half a dozen occasions—despised rank, whether held by others or himself, and when promoted found the nearest trouble to get him reduced to the ranks again. I'd made him a lance-major seven times, and demoted him eight.

But I counted him part of my luck, part of the trappings I had as first tribune. Some called me Damastes the Fair, which embarrassed me, although I admit I liked to dress colorfully and sometimes designed my own uniforms. They also knew me by my bodyguard, the Red Lancers, tough men who'd seen combat on the frontiers before volunteering for my service. Their horses' saddles and bridles were trimmed in red, as were their boots and helmets. Their lances were enameled red and, sorcerously, their armor was given a scarlet tinge, and their reputation in battle fit the name as well.

I also had the Seventeenth Ureyan Lancers, which I'd always think of as "mine," for they were my first assignment as a legate. The emperor had grumbled when I told him I wanted the Seventeenth withdrawn from the frontier, but the task he was giving me was so difficult I could've had anything and anyone I wished.

I'd asked Marán to come not only because we'd spent far too much of our marriage apart, but for her redoubtable social skills. I hoped I'd be able to keep Kallio calm enough for her to have a chance to use them.

When the emperor and I had raised the monstrous demon that destroyed Chardin Sher and his dark magician, Mikael Yanthlus, that ended the revolt. Everyone knew it was over—everyone but the Kallians.

Again and again they rose against the just rule of the emperor, sometimes in organized manner, sometimes in mere mobs. Worse, every man seemed to think he was his own rebel leader. Kallians had always had the reputation of thinking themselves superior to other Numantians, but they'd also been known for their respect for the law, sometimes overly so. No more.

It mattered little whether their imperially appointed governor was a tyrant or a weakling, whether he ruled by reason, law, the sword or caprice, or if he was an outsider or a native Kallian. The moment he suggested Kallio owed obedience to the emperor in Nicias . . . the killing began once more.

The cities had to be garrisoned by Numantian troops, the roads patrolled by cavalry, and a dispatch rider had to be escorted unless he wished to be found in a ditch with a second, red smile across his throat. Even civilian travelers or merchants who had no part in this feud of governments would be killed or held for ransom if they chanced the Kallian highways.

Four times ago, the emperor had named his brother, Reufern, as prince regent for Kallio, in the hopes that the province would have some respect for the name of Tenedos and settle down.

It hadn't worked, and now I was going to Kallio as military governor, with orders from the emperor to ensure his brother did not fail like the others and make the name of Tenedos laughable.

Tenedos's brother was older than Laish Tenedos and looked quite unlike him. He was tall where the emperor was stocky, slender where the seer was always struggling with a small potbelly, and handsome in a long-faced sort of way. The emperor's face had been round, boyishly good-looking when I first met him, but the strain of his office was already aging him, and he now appeared to carry more than the five years he had on me.

But the biggest difference was the eyes. The emperor's eyes caught and held you, blazing power and intensity. Reufern's eyes were pale, washed out, and shifted uneasily when you met them directly.

Marán and I had met Reufern on three or four court occasions, and had no more than polite conversations with him. If he had not carried the Tenedos name, I'm sure I would have forgotten him and whatever we talked about by the next morning.

This was the "leader" whose reputation I was to save.

But I was used to being the emperor's fireman, and never knowing much rest.

Eleven years ago, I had been a twenty-year-old legate in disgrace on the far frontier.

Three years later, I was first tribune, the highest-ranking officer in the army, and I stood in the greatest church in Nicias, Numantia's capital, and named Laish Tenedos as emperor of all Numantia, putting a strong, wise man on the throne and ending the incompetent vagaries of the Rule of Ten.

So why hadn't we found peace? Why, instead of being a cavalry commander in some dull garrison somewhere, or guarding my country's frontiers against the hill tribesmen, had I spent eight years dashing about the kingdom, ending food riots here, chasing bandits there, quelling peasant uprisings in a third and fourth place, ending a regimental revolt . . . I would have a hard time listing all of the places I'd ridden into, proclaiming I was "on the service of the emperor," and ordering instant obedience or face the cold steel of the soldiers behind me.

I'd seen the scorched land and ravaged civilians the marching songs don't dwell on, and had my own scars. Without realizing it, I touched the spot in my ribs where the sorcerously driven arrow had gone in, still tender after two years. That was but the visible sign of an utter nightmare, when I'd been sent, with three regiments, to subdue what was called a minor uprising in our farthest western state of Khoh, led by some village hag with a few spells. But she'd turned out to be a full-fledged sorceress, able to hold men's souls in their bodies after they'd been deathly wounded, and make them fight on.

Her ghastly minions had shattered my two regiments. I'd been carried from the field by one of my Red Lancers, treated by a village witch, and then tossed feverishly in a recovery tent for weeks, hearing the close creaking of the Wheel.

But I'd recovered, gone back with a dozen regiments, and she and her monsters had all died.

Still, there was a scar not just on my body, but on my soul, from that, and from other close-fought battles from one end of my country to the other.

Numantia should have been at peace, but was not. I wondered, then shrugged. Such thinking was beyond me.

Would that I had forced the thought, forced myself to ponder. Perhaps I could have changed things.

Perhaps I could have prevented the doom that was coming fast upon me, and all of Numantia.

TWO

DEATH TO THE EMPEROR!

It was a golden summer evening when we entered Polycittara. The city is quite old, and justly famed for being picturesque. Many centuries ago it was some fierce war lord's solitary castle, built of heavy stone atop a great mountain to stand against now-forgotten enemies. The castle was built larger and larger and then, with peaceful times, became a town and then a city, and sprawled down to the river and plain.

We'd stopped for a few minutes behind the last hilltop to brush off the worst of the travel dust to make a proper entrance.

We needn't have bothered. The gates swung open as we approached—Domina Bikaner had sent riders ahead. But, ominously, there was no cheering crowd. In fact, there was no crowd whatsoever. There *was* a small army band, tootling away as hard as they could. They were Numantian, as were the guards and a handful of civil servants, and they shouted greetings that echoed against the stone walls.

Nevertheless, we made our grand entrance—and then the splendor came to a rather embarrassing end as a regiment of cavalry, seven hundred horsemen, the two hundred men of the Red Lancers, plus some fifty carriages and wagons, my staff plus our household servants, tried to fit down one street.

I heard Karjan's voice from atop the coach, where he rode: "Goin' out of a city's like birdshit comin' out of a bird. Now we're attemptin' to put th' shit back in."

Marán and I laughed, and then everything ground to a complete halt. Officers bellowed orders, warrants screamed threats, and enlisted men muttered in their beards. I pulled on my plumed helm as I opened the coach door. The postilion whose keenness had saved us earlier dismounted, no doubt eager to further improve his reward, and hurried toward me.

I heard a scream of "Death to the emperor!" from above, and a huge chunk of rock, nearly the size of my chest, pinwheeled down from the roof of a house. I didn't have time to duck, but the boulder missed by inches—and crushed the postilion. The boy's head and chest were smashed, and he returned to the Wheel without ever knowing what happened.

"Get him!" I shouted, pointing up. Four Red Lancers jumped from their saddles and clattered up the house's steps, but Karjan had already leapt down and was at the door. He put his back against the railing and smashed a boot heel against the door, and it fell open. Saber snaking out of its sheath, he ran inside, the others behind him.

Captain Lasta was beside me. "I saw him, sir, after you shouted. He ran across the roof and jumped to the next building. Almost fell but recovered, damn his eyes. Young, black hair cut short. He was wearing light blue pants, tight, kind of dirty, and a white shirt. I'll know him when next we meet."

I nodded, knelt over the postilion's body, and whispered a silent prayer for Saionji to grant him the reward in his next life I had been unable to grant in this.

There was a scuffle and Karjan and the Red Lancers came out of the house, pushing an old man and two middle-aged women.

"This was all we found," Karjan said. "We missed th' shitheel. Stairs t' th' roof were blocked an' th' door was nailed shut. Took us forever t' break through."

"We'll take them, soldier," someone shouted. Ten men,

oddly wearing the uniform of Nician wardens, ran up. Then I remembered the warders of Polycittara had refused their duties, and so the imperial government had to import patrols from the capital.

The wardens wore helmets and breastplates and carried pikes, daggers, and heavy truncheons, more like riot soldiers than upholders of the law. The man who'd shouted wore the emblem of a sergeant and waved a sword about.

"Glad to be rid of 'em," one of the Red Lancers said.

"We saw what happened, sir," the sergeant said to me. "We'll enforce th' law without wastin' any of your time. Over against that wall's a good a place as any."

Three wardens muscled the trio against the bricks. The others took bottles of a colorless fluid from belt pouches and went into the house.

The old man moaned and one of the women screamed for mercy.

"You'll go first, bitch," the sergeant said. "By th' authority vested in me," he muttered perfunctorily, and drew back his sword.

"Sergeant!" My barracks-square bellow froze him. "What in Isa's bloody name are you doing?"

"Like I said, sir. Enforcin' th' law. Th' prince regent's orders're quite clear. Anyone attackin' a Numantian or a representative of the imperial government's guilty of crimes against th' state, and there's only one penalty."

"Sorry, Sergeant," I said. "But those three had nothing to do with what happened. The man that tried to kill me came and went over the rooftops."

"Doesn't matter, sir. My orders are clear. Aidin' or abettin' an attack's equally guilty, and their lives and property are forfeit. Soon as we execute these bastards we burn the house. I've already sent a man for the fire brigade, make sure the blaze don't spread, although it'd matter none to me if the whole gods-damned city burnt. Those are orders direct from the prince regent."

I hesitated. Orders *were* orders, and it was certainly not the brightest way to begin a new posting by breaking one of your leader's commands. But something begun wrong seldom rights itself. And what kind of peace was Reufern trying to keep? That of the grave? Marán was waiting to see what I'd do.

"Sergeant, I understand your orders. But I'm Tribune Damastes á Cimabue, Kallio's new military governor, and your superior-to-be. I'm countermanding that order to you right now, and I'll rescind it for the entire province before the morrow. You may release those three and return to your duties. Their home will go unburnt."

He hesitated, then his jaw firmed. "Sorry, Tribune. But, like you said, orders're orders. Stand aside, sir."

Again he readied his sword, and the woman, whose face had begun to show hope, whimpered.

"Curti!"

"Sir!"

"If that warden moves one muscle, shoot him dead!"

"Sir!"

"Captain Lasta, send a squad in after those policemen and bring them out. By force, if necessary."

"Yes, sir!"

The warden looked at Curti. The archer's bow was drawn to his ear, the four-cross warhead aimed steady at the policeman's throat. There was a small grin on Curti's face. They both wear uniforms and enforce the state's wishes, but there's no love wasted between policemen and the army. Perhaps being on different sides in too many drunken brawls is the reason, or perhaps most soldiers feel the police are little but poseurs at danger, and actually pass their days in cozy taprooms, inveigling the proprietors into letting them drink on the cuff.

The sergeant's fingers opened, his sword clattered to the street, and he flushed scarlet. I walked forward, picked the blade up, and slipped it into the man's sheath.

"Now, as I said, go about your duties."

He began to salute, caught himself, spun on his heel, and pushed his way through the watching soldiery. His men trailed behind him, pointedly not looking at anyone.

I heard a bit of laughter, broken off as men realized there was still a body sprawled in the street, a boy not many weeks off a farm who'd been pointlessly murdered by a cowardly dog.

"We'll bury him with the honors due a Red Lancer," Captain Lasta said. He unstrapped his cloak from behind his saddle and spread it over the corpse.

I got back in the coach and closed the door.

"This is not good," Marán said.

"No," I agreed. "Now, let's continue on to the castle and find out how much worse things can get."

"Did the sergeant of police inform you that those were my direct, *personal* orders?" The prince regent's voice quivered a bit, but he was trying to remain calm. There was no one but the two of us in the small private audience chamber off the main throne room.

"He did, my lord."

"But you still countermanded them."

"I did, sir. May I explain?"

"Go ahead."

"Sir, I'm to be your military governor. As such, I'll be responsible for enforcing the law. I know the emperor wants Kallio to return to normal as quickly as possible."

"As do we all," Reufern Tenedos said.

"If the law in Kallio is entirely different than that of the rest of Numantia, except on certain very special occasions, how can normal times ever come? We might as well be an occupying army."

"There are those who say we are that now," the regent said. He heaved a sigh, then forced a chuckle. It rang falsely. "I suppose I should find it amusing."

"What, my lord?"

"Well, here you are, Damastes the cavalryman. Damastes

the Fair, I've heard you called. Hero of a thousand battles, the emperor's finest soldier."

"I doubt that, sir. I can name a thousand better, and point out a thousand more whose names I've never learned but whose feats I'm familiar with. But what makes you find that funny?"

"Today there were two attempts on your life, both nearly succeeding, and you manage to maintain a peaceful air. Perhaps it should be Damastes the Kind, and you should serve a gentler god than the war god Isa, as a priest." There was no humor in his voice, but rather bitterness.

I said nothing, but remained at attention. He looked out a window into the huge courtyard where the Seventeenth Lancers and my Red Lancers were drawn up, awaiting his review. Then he looked back at me.

"Damastes, for so I wish to call you since I hope our service will be combined with the warmest of friendships, perhaps you're right. I'm assuming, though, that what happened was unique and you don't plan on questioning all my commands."

"I don't plan on questioning *any* of your commands, sir, not ever," I said firmly. "You rule at the wishes of the Emperor Tenedos, and I have sworn a blood oath to him. My family's pride and honor is that we have never broken our word or vow."

"Very good." Once more, he sighed, something I learned was characteristic whenever a situation grew too complex, which happened frequently. "Let us forget about it.

"Now, I'm most eager to renew my acquaintanceship with your lovely wife, the countess. Shall we return to the main room, then descend into the courtyard so I may welcome your rather impressive soldiery?"

I bowed, and we left the chamber.

"How was my brother when you last saw him?" the prince inquired.

"Healthy. Well. Working too hard." I didn't tell him how

concerned Tenedos was about his brother's inability to quiet Kallio.

"He's always been like that. And my sisters?"

I sought for exactly the right words, for they were also quite busy. Dalny and Leh, ten and twelve years younger than the emperor, seemed determined to ensure that the city of Nicias spent more time talking about them than about any other member of the family, including the emperor. They'd achieved this in a series of outrageous liaisons, from handsome young army officers to distinguished noblemen to diplomats both Nician and from the outer provinces. A goodly number of their lovers were married. It was hoped by half of the noblewomen of Nicias, Marán told me, that the sisters would soon marry, and cease poaching, although no one could wish on her worst enemy a bride like either of them would likely be.

"I don't have many dealings with them," I said truthfully. "But my wife tells me they've been quite successful helping others reach the ends they desire."

Reufern gave me a sharp look, and I realized I'd come a little close with my jape. He was, after all, a Tenedos, and couldn't be entirely dull-witted.

The castle atop Polycittara was enormous. But even the huge staff Prince Reufern had brought with him from Nicias hadn't been able to fill it. The Kallian administrators had vanished or, if tracked down, refused to return to their duties.

I thought, considering the way we non-Kallians were hated, the prince would have had trouble finding servitors, but the buildings swarmed with smiling hirelings eager to do the bidding of the humblest Nician. I shrugged, guessed there was little other work to be found, and forgot about the matter.

The prince told me to find quarters where I would, and it took Domina Bikaner, Marán, and myself most of the day to find an appropriate spot. It was a separate division of the castle that jutted out from the main complex on a rocky outcropping. It was a six-story polygonal keep, connected to the main buildings by a thick-walled spur. This spur had barracks built into its walls, which made it perfect for my Red Lancers and the Seventeenth Lancers. There was even a separate gate between the main castle and "my" section, which I had manned by sentries. I separated us in this way because I wished all Kallio to remember that they were governed by the prince and the Emperor Tenedos, and my soldiers and myself were only here temporarily, as outsiders, ensuring the laws of Numantia were obeyed.

Marán's and my chambers were gorgeous, with huge many-paned windows that looked over the city, the river winding toward the horizon, and the distant plateau that led toward Kallio's eastern border. The stone walls were warmed with thick tapestries and each room had its own fireplace and an attendant to keep the fire blazing on a dank day.

And, if nothing else, this keep was infinitely defensible. I had no wish to test my life on whether the old superstition about third attempts being successful was true.

Beyond the servants and the Nicians, there was a scattering of Kallian gentry in the castle, some of the oldest and most respectable names in the province.

Their noblest member was Landgrave Molise Amboina, every inch a grandee. He was tall, slender, and his silver mane matched his exactly curled beard. His mind and wit were keen, and he had the rare gift of paying exact attention to whoever was speaking. Marán wondered whether he was actually listening, or busy composing his next line of brilliant dialogue. He'd been widowed recently, for the second time, with a son and young daughter who spent most of their time at the Amboinas' country estate of Lanvirn.

Disbelieving in perfection, I determined to watch him closely, especially after I found that Prince Reufern trusted him completely and confided in him far more than I thought wise, although he appeared an absolutely loyal subject of the emperor's.

* * *

Our biggest problem was that Kallio was lawless. I don't mean that it was anarchic. It was worse. Prince Reufern ruled by caprice. One day a man accused of a crime might be sentenced to death, on the next another accused of the same offense would be let off with a reprimand, or a third would have all his property confiscated and himself sold into slavery.

I asked the prince how he determined the guilt or innocence of someone hailed before him, and he announced that he had a way of sensing honesty, of knowing whether he was dealing with a villain or an honest man. "An innocent man has a way about him that's easy to see, Damastes. I can sense truth in a man. Just watch what I do, and perhaps you can learn it as well." There was no proper reply to be made to *that*, so I withdrew.

I came to the conclusion that if law, an evenhanded merciful law, ruled Kallio, peace might return. And there was something I could do to bring this about. I proposed to use the army. The idea of soldiers being anything other than the bloody-handed enforcer of a tyrant's will sparks disbelieving laughter, with some justification.

Armies are hardly to be considered peace-bringers. Isa, god of war, is correctly a manifestation of Saionji the Destroyer. But armies, and soldiers, are very strange beasts. They can be impossibly ruthless, leaving a countryside in smoking ruin and the only landmarks the piled skulls of its people, but they can also be absolute purveyors of justice.

Many of us become soldiers because we wish to live in a world where there is right and there is wrong, with not much between them, and the military obligingly gives us a set of absolutes to live by. Soldiers are mostly young, and there's no greater thirster for absolute right than the young. Only with age does subtlety and the wisdom of respecting other ways of thinking and behaving come.

Give a soldier laws, tell him to enforce them equally, watch him closely so he doesn't become corrupted by his authority . . . well, that may not be a perfect system, but it'll be as good as most, and far better than some I've experienced. It certainly couldn't be worse than what passed for law in Kallio.

I already had the legal grounds to do almost anything I wanted, under the martial law that had been proclaimed.

On the frontiers of Numantia we already used roving tribunals, soldiers who went from village to village hearing complaints and settling them on the spot, or, in the event of serious crimes, taking the accused, accusers, and witnesses to a proper court, where wizards could determine the truth. The members of these tribunals were above the local corruptions and attempted to give the best judgments possible. I'd gotten some of my first—and best—training as a leader riding out on these justice patrols.

I had somewhat more than seven hundred men, six troops, and a headquarters element in the Seventeenth. Each troop was divided into four numbered columns. Bikaner, his troop commanders, and I considered each section leader of the Seventeenth. We ended with fifteen legates or warrants we felt could be trusted to provide drumhead justice—more than I'd expected. These fifteen leaders were given a two-day intensive training session in the law by my staff.

When all was in readiness, I offered my plan, of course as a suggestion, to Prince Reufern. He thought it capital, and hoped it actually might slow those damned rebels down a bit if they saw a Numantian soldier wherever they turned. He also hoped any traitor would be swiftly dealt with by my soldiery. I said that while my teams would be primarily concerned with enforcing the law, they would have no authority to punish capital offenses, such as rape, murder—and treason. Anyone accused of these sins would be brought back to Polycittara, to face high justice from either the prince or myself. He muttered that "it didn't take more than a ranker's judgment to know when a damned Kallian needed hanging," but looked away as he said it and didn't countermand my instructions. I almost sighed aloud in relief—having an eighteen-year-old soldier arbitrarily saber someone accused of cursing the emperor would hardly bring peace.

The next morning, at dawn, the heralds rode out. In each village and hamlet they shouted the people together and announced there would be a magistrate's forum within a week. All those with crimes to report, complaints of injustice done, disputes to be settled, were advised to be present. Broadsides were tacked to trees or glued to walls, and the heralds rode on to the next settlement.

But the Kallians also had their plans.

The first Ureyan Lancer to die was a new recruit who, we guessed later, had seen a young woman wink. A word, a quick promise, and he slipped away. We found him in an alley, stripped naked and mutilated. The Lancers growled threats, but they'd seen worse in the Hills, so I had no fear of murder gangs.

Three days after that, a patrol was nearly ambushed. It was the fault of the legate in charge—he'd fallen into the comfortable sloppiness of taking the same route back as he went out on. Fortunately his lance-major felt something untoward and was able to rein in just short of the killing zone. The Kallians were taking our measure.

Some action had to be taken. I could have done as my predecessors and ordered some hapless district to be cordoned off and any male whose looks I disliked cast into prison. But we were trying to end this nonsense, not prolong it.

The violence might have been anarchic, but there had to be areas, people, the disorders were centered around, just as a wildfire has hot spots that must be first stamped out. But I didn't know who or where they were. The intelligence provided by Prince Reufern's wardens and agents was useless.

As for sorcery, which most people think can know all and tell more, that, too, was nearly worthless. Prince Reufern had been given one of Nicias's more gifted seers, a cheery, bustling middle-aged man named Edwy. I asked what results he'd had from his magic, and he admitted to nearly none. Astonished, I asked why, and he awkwardly explained that his spells hadn't been "taking" here. Perhaps he hadn't as yet determined the proper methods or ingredients, although he said he saw no reason magic that worked well in Nicias wouldn't do the same in Kallio.

I set my own seer, an ambitious woman from Varan named Devra Sinait to work, although I wasn't sure what to expect of her, since she'd only been with me for a short time.

My previous magician had been fairly competent, and I'd grown use to his grumbling ways over the past five years. But old Maringnam had miscalled what would face me in Khoh, saying a mere witch couldn't be that much of a problem. It had been fortunate—for him—that he'd died in the wild flight before that "witch's" half-men.

It'd been Marán who suggested I might consider a woman for his replacement, saying, dryly, that a woman might fool a man, but not another woman, at least not often.

Sinait had been the fourth to interview, and I saw no reason to talk to another magicker. Sinait had been a buyer for one of Nicias's most successful milliners, somehow able not only to purchase no more than the quantities needed for a year, but also to anticipate what the rich and vagaried of the capital would find stylish. She'd never considered sorcery, until Tenedos's reign brought a fresh wind to the field, and someone suggested that anyone who could predict what foolish nobility would like should be able to predict anything—or make something desired come to occur.

She was, as I've remarked, ambitious, which was good for someone serving any high member of court. She was also very qualified, although she'd only discovered the talent in her thirties, and was still very much hot and cold in her capabilities. Sometimes she could cast a spell I thought the emperor himself would marvel at; other times she appeared the crassest beginner.

I might have found an older, male sorcerer, but he would no more likely have had experience with military magic than

Seer Sinait. Magic had changed and was still changing since Seer Tenedos had taken the throne, and too often older, more staid men found it impossible to accept these new ideas—starting with the principal that sorcery was every bit as important as any other military skill, no longer a by-the-way, while-you're-at-it thing that served, at best, to call up rainstorms to drench the enemy or send discouragement spells when the foe had already weakened.

But while Sinait learned her field, and explored the new arena of Kallio, I was fairly helpless.

I needed help, help from the emperor.

Back in Nicias, Tenedos had told me he wished to try something new in the event I needed to communicate with him directly, instead of using coded messages, couriers, and, from Kallio's borders on, heliographs.

He wanted to use the Seeing Bowl, which was the second magical ritual I'd ever attended in my life, long ago in Kait. Tenedos had told me this device depended less on equipment than on training. He wasn't sure if it would work or not, since one end of the link would be in the hands of a non-sorcerer, but it was worth trying.

"I'm hoping," he said, "proximity produces perfection. You've been around me, and my magic, long enough to hope there's been some fertilization."

I doubted that—the stupidest man I'd ever met was someone who'd spent half a lifetime cleaning the chalkboards at a great lycée.

"Be silent, unbeliever. Magic needs no skeptics. Remember you used my spell in the castle yard to bring up . . . that creature who destroyed Chardin Sher. That worked, did it not?

"Besides, what have we to lose? If this works, we'll save the life of more than one dispatch rider who would have been waylaid by those bastard partisans who interdict my highways."

He gave me exact instructions and had me rehearse them a dozen times. Twice the Bowl worked, but I still felt no confidence, since the seer was hanging over my shoulder. What would happen when some thousand miles separated us?

I had a separate room set aside in the castle, and guards set at the door, with orders to admit no one but myself. This was one of the emperor's orders. No one, not Seer Sinait, not even Reufern, was to know of this unless he ordered otherwise. I had asked why the prince shouldn't be told. Tenedos hesitated.

"I'll tell you the truth, Damastes," he said finally. "I want my brother to learn to govern, and if he knows he can call on my wisdom, such as it is, any time there's a problem, well, I might as well go to Kallio and rule those shitheels myself.

"I'll add, even though I don't think I need to, the caution applies to you as well. You're capable of reaching decisions without me, so the Bowl is only to be used in the event of an extreme emergency."

"If it works at all," I said.

"Damastes!"

"Sorry, sir. I'll not doubt its wonders ever again."

Yet I did just that as I took a bolt of black velvet from a case and unrolled it on the floor. The velvet had strange characters in different colors of thread woven into it. Onto it I placed the Bowl, which was actually a wide tray with a raised lip. Into the tray I poured mercury from a bottle until it covered the bottom of the tray.

I set up three braziers around the Bowl and sprinkled exact amounts of incense into each one, then lit them with a small taper. Three candles were set between the braziers and also lit. I unrolled a scroll, and read the few words that were written on it, then I put the scroll aside. Finally, I held my hands out, palms down with the fingertips curled over the tray, and moved them back and forth in a pattern he'd taught me.

Nothing happened.

I repeated the motions. There was still nothing but shimmering gray mercury. I muttered an oath, not surprised that magic wasn't for me, but still a bit angry at making a fool of myself. Of course it didn't work. It couldn't work. Damastes á Cimabue was a soldier, not a damned wizard!

I started to bundle the pieces up, then remembered a final suggestion. "If it does not work at first," the emperor had said, "try at night. Try within an hour or two of midnight. The skies will be clear, and for some reason the night favors magic.

"I shall not be sleeping," he said. "I find it hard to sleep these days," and for just an instant I heard self-pity in his tones, then he grinned. "If I'm not alone, of course, I'll be too busy to even know you were trying to contact me."

Once again I thought, What could I lose by trying? I came back after the castle was quiet and settling down for sleep. Again I lit the candles, found fresh incense for the braziers, said the words, and moved my hands in that certain pattern. Once, twice—it wasn't working—and then the mirror became silver, and I was looking at the emperor himself!

He was sitting at his desk, buried in papers, as I'd seen him all too often in the depths of the night. He must have felt my presence, if that is the correct way to describe it, for he looked up, then jumped to his feet, grinning.

"Damastes! It works!"

His voice came hollowly, then as clearly as if we were in the same room.

"Yes, sir."

"I assume," Tenedos said, "this is not an experimental use of the Seeing Bowl. You have problems?"

"Sir, it's a mess. From top to bottom."

"My brother?"

"He's doing the best he can."

"But it's not good enough?"

I didn't answer. Tenedos frowned. "So the situation is as chaotic as others reported. Can it be fixed?"

"I assume so. *Nothing* is a complete wreck."

Tenedos half-smiled. "One of your many virtues is your constant optimism, Damastes. Very well. I'll assume the problem can be resolved. My next question—can it be resolved with my brother still in charge?"

"Yes, sir. I think so, sir. But I need some help."

There was relief on Tenedos's face.

"Thank Saionji," he said. "Kallio *must* be pacified, and quickly. Now, what do I provide to make your task easier?"

I told him what I needed: a section of skilled police agents who could provide the answers we needed to strike to the center of the madness.

"I'll do better than that," Tenedos said grimly. "I'll send you Kutulu, and he'll bring his team with him."

He noted my surprise.

"I said Kallio must be brought to heel," he said. "The hour draws close."

"What is going on?" I asked, worried that something had transpired since I'd left Nicias.

"I cannot answer that directly," he said. "Magicians can hear other magicians. But I will give you a clue: Beyond the Disputed Lands lies the fate of Numantia. We must be ready to confront it."

I began to say something, and he held up a hand.

"No more. Kutulu will leave as soon as he can ready himself. I'll order a fast packet to take him upriver to Entotto. He'll go on fast from there, by horse, with no supply train."

"I'll have two squadrons of the Ureyan Lancers waiting at the Kallian border as escort."

"No," Tenedos said. "Post them along the main road, as a screening force. Kutulu will have his own troops. I'll send a heliograph at dawn to Renan, and have the Tenth Hussars come south to meet him at Entotto. They'll join your command as reinforcements."

I blinked. Like the Lancers, the Tenth was an elite border regiment. For the emperor to strip them from Urey, where their normal duties were keeping the rapacious Men of the Hills from raiding the province, reaffirmed what he said was the seriousness of the situation.

"One thing you must do, while waiting his arrival," the

emperor continued. "Find a local wizard, one who was high in the councils of Chardin Sher. Ask him why our magic is so unsuccessful at predicting what is happening in Kallio. I want that question answered, and I don't care how gently or harshly you ask it. Do you understand what I mean?"

"Yes, sir."

I heard the sound of a door opening and closing, and the emperor looked "past" me, beyond his Bowl. His eyebrows lifted in surprise, then he quickly controlled his expression.

"Is there anything more, Damastes?"

"No, sir."

"Then if you'll excuse me, I have a late conference that's very important."

I stood, saluted, and made the motions of negation. As the silvered mirror blanked to gray, I heard the ghost of a giggle across the leagues.

I had never heard a giggle from his wife, the Baroness Rasenna. Rather, she had a wonderfully sensual low laugh I'd always delighted in. Most likely I was wrong, for it took a remarkably evil imagination to think a man couldn't meet a woman other than his wife at a late hour in his private chambers without lewdness as the intent. On the other hand, I recollected Laish Tenedos's fondness, when single, for bedding every beauty within range, and I'd always marveled at how successful Rasenna had been in keeping him faithful since their marriage, after he'd taken the throne. Lately I'd heard gossip about Tenedos's displeasure with Rasenna for not having given him an heir, but I'd seen no such signs myself.

Not that it mattered whether the woman I'd heard was Rasenna or someone else—an emperor could futter whoever he wished, and it was none of my concern.

I was dwelling on this probably imaginary happening because I didn't want to think about the real surprise.

Beyond the Disputed Lands lies the fate of Numantia. Beyond Kait to the north was Maisir, ruled by the great king Bairan. Numantia had always been at peace with Maisir, although Tenedos had once told me "Kings always look beyond their borders. I do, so why shouldn't I expect that of others?"

But Maisir was huge, nearly half again as big as Numantia, with millions of people of many cultures and a great standing army. I didn't know which was worse—King Bairan having designs on Numantia, or the emperor Tenedos wishing to expand his own borders. What reason either nation might have for conflict was completely unknown.

I suddenly thought, or, rather hoped, I was seeing gloom in everything. First the emperor was being unfaithful, then there were problems with Maisir . . .

Pfah! as Tenedos was want to say when thoroughly disgusted. There is a time for thought and a time to shut off the mind.

Marán was sleeping, lying on her side in the high-framed bronze bed. She'd kicked a leg over the coverlet, and I admired the sleek curve of her calf and thigh on the silken sheet, lit by our bedchamber's two candles. She rolled onto her back as the door clicked shut. One hand moved down between her legs, and a smile came to her lips.

I remembered a game we'd played from time to time, a game she'd taught me, learned from her great friend Amiel, Countess Kalvedon.

I silently undressed, then crept to one of her trunks, made to sit on end like a bureau once we arrived at a destination. I found four long scarves and tied a loop in the end of each of them. I slipped one over each of her wrists and ankles, and snugged them.

Very gently I drew her arms up, until they were extended at full length. If Marán awoke, she gave no sign, but her smile was a bit broader.

Quickly I tied her hands to the bedstead, then seized one ankle scarf and lifted her leg straight up, until her buttocks were almost clear of the bed. I tied a quick hitch to the top of the headboard.

Now she allowed herself to awake, and struggled, thrashing about as I seized her other leg, lifted it, and tied that scarf to the opposite side of the headboard.

Her eyes were open.

"I have you now," I hissed, in my best imitation of a villain in a spectacle.

Her mouth opened.

"Do not scream, or I'll be forced to gag you."

Her tongue came out, slowly, to sensuously lick her lips.

"You can't move, can you?"

"No," she whispered. "I'm at your mercy."

"I can do anything I want, can't I?"

"Anything. I deserve your punishment in any way you wish."

I climbed onto the bed, pinched one nipple, then the other. She gasped, and pushed her breasts against my hands. I knelt between her thighs, ran my tongue up her sex, then into her. Her thighs tensed against my cheeks as I moved, and she groaned.

I kept moving in and out of her, as her gasping grew louder and quicker. Her hips began rotating. "Oh yes, oh yes, oh please yes," she moaned, but I paid no heed. Her hips jerked up, she squealed, and tremors ran through her body. I didn't stop caressing her with my tongue until the trembling slowed, then I rose over her.

"Now," I said, "*now* I'll make you really come."

I slid the head of my cock just into her wetness, then held still. She tried to move against me, but I moved back.

"Please," she said. "Please fuck me. Fuck me hard!"

"Like this?" I took her thighs in both hands, and pulled her to me, driving full into her, and she cried out again. I came back, then forward, moving hard, brutally, and each time she shrieked in near-wordless ecstasy, sometimes my name, sometimes obscenities. I held as long as I could, but at last let go, and with a great shout spattered inside her, feeling the Wheel's turning not far distant.

I was half-lying across her, braced on my hands, when I

came back to myself. Marán slowly opened her eyes.

"Let me taste you now."

I slipped out of her and moved under her legs until I crouched next to her head. She turned toward me, slipped her tongue out, and licked the head of my cock. "I am still your prisoner, Great Tribune," she said. "I demand more severe penalties," she added and took me in her mouth.

Between then and dawn, I cannot recollect having one coherent thought, especially about emperors and kings.

The emperor's command to find and interrogate a high-ranking magician became a wearying task. Most of the Kallian seers had died either in the civil war or when the demon brought down Chardin Sher's final redoubt. The survivors, as far as I was able to discover, had either fled the province or were hiding, and I suspected finding a sorcerer who didn't want to be found might be like looking for a black cat after midnight on a moonless night.

But eventually I found one. Much to my embarrassment, he was in my own—or, rather, Prince Reufern's own—dungeon. According to his file, he was less a practicing magician than a philosopher and teacher. But he had been a friend of Mikael of the Spirits, Mikael Yanthlus, Chardin Sher's magician, and might help me understand those who would rise against their rulers.

He was Arimondi Hami, a respected member of Kallio's highest intellectual circle. He was imprisoned because he refused to acknowledge Numantian authority and, worse, he'd been very vocal about his treason.

I'd often wondered how a magician, even a fairly minor one, could be held captive. Hami wasn't kept in some dank, slimy underground cell, but in a very clean, very sterile chamber directly below the citadel's guard room, and his cell was searched at unpredictable intervals, at least once a week. He had been permitted pen, paper, and any books he wished except those dealing with sorcery. He could have any visitor on the prince's approved list. His food was prepared by his own chef, and his clothing consisted of freshly woven woolen or cotton robes, without adornment. Any request was carefully examined by Seer Edwy, so he could never assemble the materials for an escape spell.

A mere scholar instead of a great wizard he may have been, but I still had two guards with drawn swords behind the chair I ushered him into, their orders to seize him if anything went awry, or kill him if that couldn't be done. He looked at the soldiers and trembled slightly. I asked him to be seated and inquired if he would care for a glass of wine.

"I would, Tribune á Cimabue," he said, and his voice had the mellow tone of a born orator.

I poured and handed him a goblet.

"You are not drinking with me?"

"I drink but rarely," I told him honestly. "I never came to favor the taste of alcohol, and its effects on me are embarrassing."

He looked skeptical. "I don't know whether to believe you or not."

"I don't understand," I said.

"Two men with swords . . . you won't share my wine . . . it would be easy to think that you've unwoven the skein that's puzzled Prince Reufern and those who came before him."

"I was never the finest student, Seer Hami," I said. "Too often my teachers were able to fuddle me, as often for their own pleasure as to bring home a point. I liked it little then, I like it less now. Please explain."

The scholar peered at me. "I assumed, when the guards brought me here, you'd decided to have me killed."

"Why would I do a thing like that? You may be a traitor, but you've done little except talk dissent."

"Which it's my understanding can get a man shortened by a head in these times."

"Not by me," I said. "Nor by anyone under my command. I need something else. But why do you think I planned to kill you? What is this skein you talked about?"

Hami drained his glass and smiled. "That is a good vintage, Tribune. Perhaps I may have another?"

I refilled his glass.

"The skein is the web of confusion about my fate. Consider it: I have refused to acknowledge the authority of the Seer Laish Tenedos, who's styled himself emperor. I hold the rightful rulers of Numantia are the Rule of Ten."

"*Those* incompetents?" I said. "Those that lived through the Tovieti Rising and the civil war have been put out to pasture. And why would you wish them to rule? They were as incompetent a group of dunderheads as ever sat a throne. None of them could pour piss out of a boot if the instructions were graven on the heel."

"But they were the legitimate authority."

"You think Numantia should have doddered down the path they were taking until we fell completely apart?"

"As a Kallian, I care little about what happens to the rest of Numantia. I found Chardin Sher's rule dynamic, progressive."

"How odd of you to say that," I said. "He was certainly as much a dictator in this province as you claim the emperor is now in Numantia."

Arimondi Hami smiled a bit. "That may be the case. But, to use language a soldier might, he may have been a son of a bitch, but he was *our* son of a bitch."

"Who happens to be very dead," I said. "Leaving, as far as I know, no heirs or relatives in the immediate bloodline. Would you have your kingdom ruled by any dolt who decides to seize the throne?"

The scholar laughed. I realized with a bit of chagrin that what I'd said could be easily misconstrued to apply to someone else who'd carved his way to a throne not long ago.

"I shall not further embarrass you and follow up on that," he said. "Let me only say that I think Kallio should be left to its own devices, as I think all mankind should. Perhaps you're right, and we'd end up ruled by some bloody-handed despot.

I'll freely concede that your emperor is far from the most unjust man I've ever read about.

"I chose to stand against him because I wish to see what could happen if the men of the sword were driven off. Perhaps other sorts—poets, saints, men of peace—would be chosen to rule instead."

"I doubt that would happen," I said. "Men of the sword seem predestined to succeed over men of words. The emperor himself needed the army to reach his throne.

"But we have gone astray. Continue explaining this web that you thought I was going to cut through."

"My apologies. You're right. I stand in implacable opposition to your emperor and am unwilling to hold my tongue as to what I think of his rule. Therefore, by his laws and lights, I am a traitor and should be executed.

"However, those who govern Kallio have had the sense to realize a murdered scholar also can provide an excellent martyr and rallying point. That is why I've been permitted to live and never even brought to trial.

"I thought, when I was summoned and saw these two, you'd decided on a soldierly solution of dealing with today's problems today and tomorrow's when they arrive."

"I think, Seer," I said, "you're being very naive about soldiers, at least those who command."

"Maybe," he said, and I could hear disinterest in his tones. "I've spent little time with them."

He drained his glass, rose, and, without asking, refilled it. I made no objection. If I could get him drunk, he might speak freely. I knew exactly what the emperor had meant when he told me to use any means necessary to get his question answered: There were torture chambers in the caverns below, and men, both Kallian and Nician, skilled at using the rusty-red implements in them.

"So I was in error," Hami said. "I'll admit, by the way, that I'm not terribly discontented with my lot. I'm well fed, I don't have to worry about a landlord or tax collector, I have access to almost all books I need, save those that deal with sorcery, and my theories had already passed well beyond what's in the grimoires. I'm well beyond finding my pleasures in a tavern or a wench's arms, so that doesn't matter. What, then, do you wish of me? I assume it has something to do with the fact we Kallians aren't knuckling under to your emperor as we should.

"You know," he continued without prompting, and I realized the wine was hitting him, "I was a friend of Mikael Yanthlus, Chardin Sher's wizard, at least as much as he allowed a friend. Mikael was a man who was only interested in power and sorcery, and anyone or anything who didn't add to his knowledge of either was a waste of time.

"I thought him the greatest sorcerer of all time. But I was wrong. The Seer Tenedos was his master. Although I wonder what price was paid."

"Price?"

"I've read accounts of what happened in that final siege, and even talked to survivors of that awful night when the demon rose out of the mountain to destroy Chardin Sher and Mikael. Where do you think he came from?"

"I don't think, I know," I said. "He was summoned by the Seer Tenedos."

"And at what cost?" Hami said, peering owlishly at me.

Tenedos had answered that before I volunteered to creep into Chardin Sher's castle with a certain potion. I decided to tell Hami what the seer had told me that storm-ridden night.

"The emperor said that the force, the demon, required him to show some degree of sincerity, that someone he loved had to perform a service," I said. "He said I was that someone, and so I did what was wished."

"He told you no more?" Hami asked skeptically.

Tenedos had also said there'd be a greater price, but one that didn't have to be paid for time to come. Perhaps I shouldn't have told Hami this, but I did.

"What do you think that will be?" he said, a debater's

smile on his face as he followed up on his opening.

"I don't know," I said. "I know as little of demons as you do of soldiers."

"Fairly put," Hami said. "I don't, by the by, suggest you remind the man who styles himself emperor about what we've been talking about, for horrors such as he summoned strike heavy bargains, and the magicians who strike such bargains generally don't wish to be reminded of them.

"And I'm running on, and this has little to do with what you called me for."

I asked him the emperor's question: Why was all imperial magic being blocked, as a man's vision is blocked by a fog bank?

He stroked his chin, picked up his wineglass, then set it down untouched.

"The war between Kallio and the rest of Numantia shook this world and beyond. There was greater magic used by man than ever before in history. Even I could sense this, with what small talent Irisu gave me.

"Before I was arrested, after the war ended, and brought into this dungeon I found great difficulty in working even minor spells. I assume I was in the backwash of greater energies than I can understand or evoke myself, energies, echoes if you will, from the confrontation between Mikael Yanthlus and the Seer Tenedos. And I can still feel them. The sounding of those days hasn't disappeared yet.

"That would be my primary theory," he went on, his dramatic tones fading into those of a pedant. "There might be another explanation, and this will shake your seer-emperor a trifle, and that is that there's another great wizard in the world who wishes him harm. Perhaps someone previously unknown, in Numantia, or maybe someone beyond our borders. I can't say," he said. "But if you wish to give me access to certain materials, I could experiment."

I laughed. "Seer Hami, I'm not so green-as-grass looking, so I'm most unlikely to let you work any spells of any sort." I rose. "Thank you for your time."

The man hid a smile of his own, then got to his feet, a little unsteadily.

"We should do this again. You have good taste in wine."

Contrary to what the Kallian advised, I told the emperor exactly what had happened. Halfway through my report, the mercury image blurred, and I thought we'd lost contact, but the emperor's image became steady once more. When I finished, he sat motionless, his face a blank. I cleared my throat, and he came back to himself.

"Hmm. Interesting," he mused. "So there *is* something out there. Very, very interesting. I'll wager it's in the present, not the dead past, though."

"You have a clue, sir?"

"I certainly do. But it's not within Kallio, so you needn't worry about it. That's for me to deal with in the future. The very near future."

After a time, I chanced it: "Sir, may I ask another question?"

The emperor's expression grew cold. "I assume about this price the Kallian spoke of?"

"Yes, sir."

"You may not. Not now, not ever. Damastes, you are a good soldier and a better friend. You are the last because you don't step beyond the limits of the first. Not that that bookish fool would know anything of what must be done, what must be paid, in the *real* world."

He suddenly stood and strode out of the chamber.

Perhaps I should have pressed the question, then or later. Numantia was my country as well as his, and as commander of the armies this was something I should have known. Instead, a little frightened, I put the matter out of my mind.

The gods failed me at that moment: Irisu the Preserver; Panoan, god of Nicias; Tanis, my family god; Vachan, my own monkey god of wisdom—they turned their backs.

The only god present was Saionji, and now, in my mind, I can see her gleeful capering as she anticipated the horror to come.

THREE

SKIRMISHING

I'd been in the field with one of my justice patrols, and been well satisfied at how the young legate handled matters, even though he was quite nervous with me in attendance.

It was a long and dusty ride back to Polycittara, and I was more than ready for a very hot bath, about three pounds of barely cooked beef, and six hours of uninterrupted sleep. The bath and the steak I could have, but there was paperwork waiting that would keep me awake until past midnight, so I wasn't in the best of tempers.

There were two surprises waiting. The first was Landgrave Amboina, sitting at ease in our reception room with a glass of wine, chatting amicably with my wife, and the other was a huge painting leaning against the wall. Amboina stood and bowed, while Marán gave me a quick and formal kiss on the lips.

"The landgrave has a present for us," Marán said, "and was kind enough to keep me company while I was waiting for you." She turned and indicated the painting. "Isn't it beautiful?"

I don't know if beautiful was the word for it. Awesome certainly was. It was about ten feet long by eight feet high, in an ornately carved wooden frame that was stained black and a very dark scarlet. I guessed I was grateful I was now rich enough, courtesy of the Seer Tenedos and my wife, to have several palaces with walls large—and sturdy—enough to hang the piece.

In the foreground was a moil of humanity, from peasants to lords, in marvelously tiny depictions of the life of Numantia and many of our provinces, from the jungles of the west to the high deserts of the east. Behind this landscape was the Wheel, turning, ever turning. To one side was Irisu, judging; to the other was Saionji, sweeping her taloned fingers across the landscape, bringing fresh deaths—and then rebirth—to the Wheel.

Behind all was a brooding, bearded figure that could only be Umar the Creator. Perhaps he was considering the splendor of what he'd created, perhaps about to destroy all and begin once more. Around these gods flocked many of their manifestations: the Guardians, with Aharhel the God Who Speaks to Kings in front, then the gods and goddesses of fire, earth, air, water, and many more.

I had to admire the hours, perhaps years, of work the artist had put into his work. But it, like other paintings and carvings, did little for me. If I am to love art, it should show something I am familiar with, perhaps a scene of a jungle farm in Cimabue or, better, a map from one of my campaigns. Such an admission no doubt brands me as a peasant, and so I am. Only music, of all the arts, has ever had power to move me.

I stared at this painting while dark thoughts grew within me. I turned back.

"It is very impressive, Landgrave. What made you choose to give it to us?"

Before Amboina could say anything, Marán spoke, and her voice was nervous.

"It's called *The Judging*, and it's by one of Kallio's most famous artists, a man named Mulugueta, who died over a hundred years ago. There are already two of his paintings at Irrigon. Damastes, isn't it wonderful? Won't it look nice with the others at Irrigon . . . or maybe at the Water Palace?"

I took a deep breath. "Excuse me, my dear. But I still don't understand. Landgrave, where did this come from?"

"From the estate of Lord Tasfai Birru," the landgrave said.

"I know him not," I said. "When did he die, and why did he choose to leave such a work to me? Has he no family or heirs?"

Amboina laughed tentatively, as if I'd told a poor jest. His laughter died when he saw I wasn't joking. I decided I didn't like him.

"He is still alive, Count Agramónte."

"You may refer to me as Tribune rather than Count, since that title has precedence over all, especially in Kallio at this time."

"My apologies, Tribune. As I was saying, Lord Birru is alive, although I predict he'll return to the Wheel within the next two weeks. At present he's held in this fortress's dungeon, charged with treason. There's only one verdict imaginable."

"I see. And this belongs to him?" I asked.

"Belonged. It, along with the rest of his estate, will become the property of the state. After a percentage is sent to the emperor, the remainder will be disposed of by an official chosen by Prince Reufern. Of late, he has been delegating this rather exacting task to me."

"Forgive me," I said, "for appearing a bit thick. But isn't it Numantian law that no man's property may be seized, whether land, slaves, or a painting, until he has been convicted?"

Amboina smiled, and there was more than a bit of gloating in his expression. "Such *is* the law, but the verdict is foreordained, as I said; Lord Birru was a close adviser of Chardin Sher. After Chardin Sher's death, he withdrew to one of his estates and refused several requests by Prince Reufern to attend him here in Polycittara."

"That makes a man foolish," I said. "And perhaps suicidal. But it does not make him a traitor. Is there any hard evidence to convict him?"

"May I speak honestly?"

"I wish you would."

"Lord Birru has—had—vast estates. These estates, Prince Reufern decided, would provide greater benefits for Numantia if they were in the proper hands."

"The hands of Prince Reufern?"

"I believe he plans on acquiring some of them. Others will be given to certain loyal members of his court."

"Such as yourself?"

Amboina colored slightly, but didn't respond.

"Very well," I said, and I heard harshness in my tone. "Thank you for the gift. But I must decline it. Would you please arrange to have it withdrawn from my quarters?"

"But I've already accepted it," Marán said in surprise.

I began to blurt something, but stopped myself. "My apologies, Landgrave," I said. "I don't think my wife understood the circumstances. We cannot accept this."

"Prince Reufern will not be pleased," the landgrave said.

"Since I doubt this gift was his idea, but rather your own, I would suggest, in the interests of *your* health, you not mention this incident. You should know two things, Landgrave, and know them well." I could feel anger building, and let it. I had been controlling myself for too long around these prancing fools. "Neither my wife nor myself are looters. Also, I was appointed to this post by the emperor himself. Does that not suggest perhaps this entire scene should be forgotten, at least by you?"

Amboina nodded jerkily, turned, made a sketchy bow to my wife, and hastened away. I went to a window and took six deep breaths.

"*How dare you*," Marán hissed from behind me.

That was all I could stand. I spun. "How dare I *what*, my lady?"

"How dare you embarrass me? First you deny the name of

Agramónte, which was old when your family was cutting trees for sustenance in your jungles, then you shame me personally by telling a nobleman like the landgrave you think he's some sort of grave robber!"

I could have responded sensibly, and explained that the landgrave had called upon me in my official position, then attempted to curry favor by calling me Agramónte. But I was tired, and I'd had enough of this nonsense.

"Countess Agramónte," I said, in my coldest tone. "You are the one who's overstepping her bounds. Let me remind you of something. You have no place or duties in Kallio. You are here as my wife. No more, no less.

"Therefore, when something like this occurs, you will have the decency to defer to the authority the emperor's placed in me.

"I'll add two more things, both personal.

"The first is how dare *you* decide something such as you did, which you aren't stupid enough to think was done because Amboina thinks we're the nicest people he's ever met, but rather to draw us into the prince's tidy little circle of bribed toadies?

"The second is that, yes, my family may have been cutting trees in the jungle and, probably, living in them sometimes. I admit I come from soldiery not much removed from a peasant farmer.

"But by the gods, Countess Agramónte, we are honest! Which appears to be more than can be said about some far older families, who perhaps achieved their prestige and riches as vultures!"

Marán's eyes blazed. "You . . . bastard!" She half-ran from the room.

I started to go after her, then realized I'd said more than enough. But I was still too hot to apologize, if an apology was, indeed, called for. I stamped out and went to the battlements. I'm afraid I snarled at the sentries, no doubt making them wonder if I'd have them brought up on charges for some imagined offense.

It took me a long time to calm down. I now guess it was because I was secretly angry at many things, from the incompetent prince I had been ordered to support, to nest-featherers like Amboina, to being assigned these murky diplomatic duties when I longed for the simplicity of the barracks or, better, the harsh realities of the constant border fights in the Disputed Lands.

Eventually I calmed down. It was late. One thing that Marán and I had been proudest of was that our fights were not only few, but they were always settled at the time. We'd never let anger work at us.

I went back to our apartments, to our bedroom door, and tapped. There was no answer. I tried the door. It was locked. I knocked more loudly. Again, no response came. I could feel anger build once more. But there was nothing sensible to do.

So I went to my office and worked until nearly dawn, then lay on the field cot I kept there. I had sense enough to put this night's paperwork in a separate place, knowing I'd best review it when calm. I managed to doze for perhaps an hour, then bugles woke me up. I went out on a balcony and watched guard mount in the courtyard below. The measured, never-changing routine of the army calmed me, knowing the same ceremony was being done at every barracks and post in Numantia. There was something larger than myself, than my petty problems, something I'd dedicated my life to.

I decided I'd spend the day with the troops, and hang paperwork and diplomacy. But not in the unshaven, rather disheveled state I was in. I had a spare field uniform in my campaign roll that always sat beside the door of whatever quarters I occupied, and I went to get it. I'd use the troop baths and have one of the men shave me. I didn't worry about what the soldiers knew or thought—what had happened between my wife and myself would have gone through the regiment the instant the sentries I'd snapped at were relieved.

As I passed the door to our bedroom, I tried it and shook my head at my foolishness. But to my surprise the handle turned. I opened the door and went in. Marán sat at a window, her back to me. She wore a black silk wrap.

"May I enter?" I said formally.

"Please do."

I closed the door behind me and stood in silence, not sure what I should say or do.

"Damastes," she said. "I love you."

"I love you as well."

"We shouldn't fight."

"No."

"Not over a stupid painting that probably'd get broken going back to Nicias."

I didn't answer for an instant. Marán knew that wasn't at all why we'd snarled. I considered correcting her, but thought better.

"No. That's not something to fight over," I agreed. "I'm sorry."

"And I'm sorry, too. I didn't sleep at all."

"I didn't, either," I said, lying but little.

She stood, and let the wrap fall.

"Damastes, would you make love to me? Maybe that'd make me feel better about . . . about things."

Without waiting for an answer, she came to me, and slowly began undressing me. When I was naked, I picked her up in my arms, and carried her to the bed.

Her passion was far greater than mine. Even when I was in her, part of my mind wondered if I should have said something else, if I should have insisted we talk about the real cause of our fight. A thought came and went that there was this wall called the Agramóntes between us, and sometimes I felt it was growing larger and thicker year by year. But I put the thought aside as foolishness and let the lovemaking take me.

Two days later, Kutulu and his staff arrived. They were surrounded by the soldiery of the Tenth Hussars, hard-bitten brawn from the frontiers. It was curious, and amusing, to see how carefully they guarded their charges.

Kutulu was as I'd last seen him: a small man, whose hair was now no more than a fringe around his polished pate, even though he was younger than I. But he still had the penetrating eyes of a police warden who never forgets a criminal's face, or anyone else he's had business with. Other than that, he was completely unremarkable, and would never be noticed in a crowd, which I'd learned is a prime virtue of a secret agent.

He was the emperor's spymaster now and wielded great power. Those who spoke ill of the emperor, his programs, or his intentions were visited by police agents and warned. Generally that sufficed, but a few were unwise enough to persist in their criticisms and were hauled into court, actually a secret tribunal. The charge would be "conduct inimical to the interests of the empire," and sentences ranged from a few days to a few years in prison. There already were two prisons especially built for these offenders, both located in the heart of the Latane River's delta, and there were dark rumors about what happened in them.

Kutulu had a staff nearly as large as the entire Nician police force, although no one knew how many agents there actually were, since they never wore uniforms or stood for the counting. Some were commoners, some were criminals, some nobility.

Kutulu was now known as "The Serpent Who Never Sleeps," and while I thought calling the quiet little man with the wary eyes a serpent rather romantic, the hours he spent serving his emperor suggested that possibly he did, in fact, never go to bed. If he did, it must have been alone, for as far as I knew he had no private life whatsoever.

He'd brought more than seventy-five men and women with him. Some looked like wardens, but most like average citizens or ruffians and whores. Many wore cloaks, hoods pulled up in spite of the heat, not wishing their faces to become familiar. Some were mounted, more rode in wagons. Most, city-bred, looked relieved to be in the safety of a city, behind stone walls, and no longer exposed to the unknown terrors of the open country.

I'd had quarters prepared for Kutulu and his force in my wing, across from the barracks the Lancers occupied.

"Good," he said. "There'll be few Kallians pass your sentries, so my agents can maintain their anonymity. But I'll also need chambers close to the dungeons that no one will be permitted to enter except my people. Other rooms will be necessary for my records, rooms that will always be guarded, where my reports can be filed.

"Finally, are there any secret ways in and out of this castle?"

I knew of none, and if I'd found any I'd certainly have had them bricked up.

"A pity," he said and sighed. "It would be nice to have some sort of rat hole for my terriers—and the rats we collect, both of their own free will and by our pressures—to enter and leave from at any hour without notice being taken."

He asked if I had a Square of Silence. Seer Sinait had cast such a spell in my office as soon as we arrived, to make sure no sorcerer could eavesdrop on my conferences.

"Good," Kutulu said. "Let us go there, then. I have certain questions I need to ask."

We went up the wide stairs toward the floor my offices were on. Halfway, he put a hand on my arm.

"Oh," he said, rather shyly. "I sometimes forget my graces. It is nice to see you, my friend."

I looked at him with a bit of astonishment. He'd told me, equally soberly, after I'd saved his life in an encounter with a demon guardian of the Tovieti, that I was his friend, but he had never used the word again. I became as embarrassed as he was, since I wasn't sure just what the word meant to the small man. I muttered thanks and tried to make light of things, telling him once he saw what a mess Kallio was in he'd probably change his opinion.

"No," he said. "I meant what I said. I know I am around one of the two people I trust absolutely." The other was the man he'd taken for his god—the emperor.

"I am glad to be away from the capital," he continued. "I'm afraid I like Nicias but little these days."

"Why?"

"The emperor is like honey," he said, "and there are too many flies buzzing around, trying to suck in as much as they can, and dirtying everything they touch. Sometimes I'm afraid the emperor pays far too much mind to these people, and not enough to those who supported him when it was a risk."

I managed to cover my surprise—I'd never thought Kutulu would have the slightest criticism of the Emperor Tenedos, even one as mild as he'd voiced.

"I'm sure the emperor knows them for what they are," I said. "Don't forget that, like you, he's got to use some fairly questionable tools to do what he must."

Kutulu looked at me for a long time, then nodded jerkily. "I hope you're right," he said. "Of course. You *must* be right. I should never have doubted." He attempted a smile, which his face found unfamiliar. "As I said, you *are* a friend. Come, let us dispose of our business."

In my office I set two chairs at the table the Square of Silence had been cast around and told him he could talk freely.

"Some of what I'm going to say comes from the emperor," he began. "But I'll have other questions as well."

"To which I must respond correctly, or face possible prosecution."

"What?" Kutulu was completely puzzled.

"Sorry. I was trying a small joke. You asked that question as if you were investigating me."

"Oh. I'm sorry. I'm afraid I concentrate too much on the task at hand."

"Never mind." Joking with Kutulu was like pissing into the wind—nothing much would get accomplished and the splatter was a bit embarrassing. Nevertheless, for some unknown reason, I sort of liked the little man, as much as it's ever possible to like someone whose passion and life's work is finding out yours, and everyone else's, business.

"I'll start with my own question. Are the Tovieti active in Kallio? I've seen nothing of them in your reports."

I gaped. The Tovieti had been a terror cult first organized in Kait, one of the Disputed Lands. They had been established by an unknown, probably dead sorcerer and given the crystal demon Thak to worship and obey. They spread across Numantia, murdering as they went. Their goal was to bring all society to an end, so their own rule could triumph. Their believers would be given not only the lives of the nobility and rich, but their gold, land, and women as well. But Tenedos had slain Thak, and Kutulu and I and the army had wiped out the Tovieti with drum patrols and the noose more than nine years ago.

Some must have survived our purging and fled. But we'd obliterated all their leaders, as far as I knew, and I thought the order no more than a bad dream of the past.

"I'm not mad," Kutulu said. "The Tovieti have risen again. Remember their emblem?"

I did—it had been chalked or scrawled on every wall in Sayana, Kait's capital—a red circle, representing the Tovieti, red for their slain leaders, whom they considered martyrs, with a nest of hissing serpents rising from it. Kutulu nodded.

"We cut off many of the vipers' heads. But there are still others."

"But who do they serve? Thak is dead, or at least I thought he was."

"No sorcerer, including the emperor himself, has been able to find the slightest trace of the demon," Kutulu agreed. "But the Tovieti have changed.

"I've arrested a dozen or more in Nicias. When questioned, right until death, they insist they have no master. Thak's death, and the deaths of those who were the organization's high council, proved they were following the wrong star.

"Now all members hold the same rank and are organized in small cells. They are to kill the mighty when they can, still with the yellow silken cord if possible, and are permitted to steal what they can to share with the others of the brotherhood.

"They say perhaps one day a new leader will manifest himself, but he won't be a demon, but a man, a man who'll lead them well, and they'll give up their bloody ways for peace, and all men and women shall be equal." He grimaced. "There's only a few, as far as I can tell. But they're troublesome. They've strangled at least a dozen people I know of, and I'll wager three times that number of killings have been done in other ways. I've been unable to find any central leadership to exterminate. Perhaps they're telling the truth, although I've never known a pack of dogs to not have a leader."

"This is all completely new," I said. "You know what sort of wardens we have here in Kallio, and that they're little better than door rattlers. As secret agents they make excellent chicken farmers. But I've heard no whisper of the Tovieti. Should I ask my seer to cast spells to see if she can find any evidence?"

"No. I doubt if she'd be successful," Kutulu said. "I had the best sorcerers in Nicias attempt such castings with no result, including the Chare Brethren, which the emperor has turned into a real force instead of a bunch of fossils creaking on about the theory of magic."

He glanced about, as if looking for eavesdroppers, then said, almost whispering, "Have you any evidence, or even suspicions, of any Maisirian activity?"

"None," I said, shocked—until I remembered Tenedos's words.

"The emperor wants to know if any of these vanished Kallian officials might have fled through the Disputed Lands and found shelter with King Bairan."

"No. Maybe a few tried," I said. "But I would find it hard to believe any official or magician who had more than a rag to wrap about his loins would have been able to convince the Men of the Hills to give him safe conduct to the Maisirian border."

"As would I. I believe that those who survived the war have gone to ground or fled into other provinces of Numantia. But that is not what the emperor believes." He shook his head. "Great men proclaim the truth, and we lesser beings can do little but try to make what we see fit into that vision.

"Very well. Let me see what I can discover."

The Time of Heat ended, and the Time of Rains began, at first with drizzles, then the full gush of the monsoon. It was still hot, but the gray, dank days matched the dirty business that had begun.

Without fanfare, Kutulu and his agents went to work. Strange people came and went at all hours, sometimes singly, sometimes in groups. Where they went, what they did, I didn't know, nor did I ask.

Others on Kutulu's staff were equally busy. I had to have the dungeon guard room moved up a level and thick carpeting installed on the floors. The screams from his torture chambers carried far.

I liked all this but little, but this is the way my country performs its investigations and enforces its laws. Prince Reufern seemed delighted and importuned Kutulu to visit the interrogation rooms. Kutulu refused, saying any interference from outsiders might destroy the pattern he was trying to create and reduce the flow of information his clerks were recording.

I had the comfort that my duties involved no such evil and that my magistrate's patrols were abroad, doing their best to provide justice in the broken land.

The man stumbled through the city's gates at midday, through the rain that blew in sheets across the sky. He still wore tatters of his uniform and to the sentries appeared quite mad. He was a horseman of Two Column, Leopard Troop, Seventeenth Ureyan Lancers.

He was rushed to the castle infirmary, and identified as Horseman Gabran. He'd ridden out with Legate Ili's justice patrol that morning, and his hysterical babblings made the watch officer send for me at once. He raved about snakes, huge snakes, people that became snakes, and they'd tried to kill him, but he'd run, run. Suddenly he became quiet, his eyes owl-like.

"They killed all of us," he said calmly. "All of the horses, all of the men. They tried to kill me, too. But I was too quick for them. I went into the fields, and then across a river. They couldn't track me.

"Now they'll come here. Now they'll come after me. But I'm safe now, aren't I? Aren't I? Aren't I!" and his voice rose to a scream. Two men held him, and a third forced a potion through his clenched lips. Again he quieted.

"That's to make me sleep, isn't it? That's all right. I can sleep. They'll not find me, when I'm asleep. Or if they do, I won't care. No. I won't care. I won't . . ." He collapsed, as much fainting as from the draft.

I ran out of the infirmary, shouting for the alert troop, for Domina Bikaner to attend me in the Lancers' ready room, and for a runner to summon Kutulu and Seer Sinait and tell them to make ready to travel. Sorcery would be needed if there was anything to Gabran's tale, and I planned to move fast, far faster than the Kallians believed possible.

Bikaner came at a run, buckling on his saber. His adjutant, Captain Restenneth, had told him about Gabran, and he'd served long enough with me to be able to tell what I planned.

"Legate Ili and his column went out at dawn with orders to hold court here," he said, tapping a spot on the ready room map. The village was called Nevern, and it sat in the foothills two hours ride from Polycittara.

"Very well," I said. "I'll have the ready troop . . ."

"Tiger, sir."

"Tiger Troop, and turn out my Red Lancers. I'll also have one company of the Hussars ready to ride in ten, no fifteen minutes."

"Yes, sir. I'll take personal command—"

"No," I said flatly. "This one's mine. But you can ride along if you wish."

"Yessir. Thank you, sir."

Kutulu hurried into the room as Bikaner ran out. I briefly explained what I thought had happened.

"We lack information," he said.

"We do," I agreed. "And if we wait for details there'll be nobody left to deal with. Are you riding with me or no?"

"I'll come."

"Good. I'll get you a mount." Karjan was waiting. My combat harness was beside him, and he wore helmet, breastplate, and greaves.

"Lucan's bein' saddled, sir."

"Very well. Take this man to the stables and get him mounted on a fast, dependable horse. Have another horse saddled for Seer Sinait. Go!"

Karjan ran out, followed by the warden. Captain Lasta clattered in, buckling on his gear. I gave him instructions as I fastened on my own weaponry.

"Sir? One question?"

"Go ahead, Captain."

"Supposing it's a trap? Supposing they've laid an ambush?"

I considered. No. They wouldn't be expecting a response this quickly. They'd think we'd wait until the morrow, when we'd have a full day, for no one chanced traveling the roads of Kallio near dark.

"Isa have mercy on them if they do. For we won't."

Seer Sinait was waiting in the courtyard, her robes rucked up so she could mount, holding a canvas roll with her magical implements. The troops formed up as I outlined what little I knew, their warrants shouting orders and instructions.

"Possibly," she said calmly, "possibly, Tribune, we should have found the time to discover further details, but I see you are intent on trapping whoever—or whatever—attacked your men."

"I am." Her words caught me, made me think. *Whatever?*

"Suppose it *is* a demon?" I said.

She shrugged. "I've never confronted one fresh from a kill. If so, it should make an interesting conflict."

I grinned tightly. One reason I'd chosen the Seer was her complete lack of fear. She was as much a warrior as any of us.

"Sir!" It was Bikaner. "Troops mounted and ready."

Karjan trotted up, leading Lucan. Beside him was Kutulu, astride a bay I knew to be a racer, but a horse I'd trust a babe on. I swung into the saddle.

"Lancers!" I shouted. "Ride out!"

The gates of the courtyard swung wide, and we trotted out, into the castle's main yard. The gates stood open, and the lamps of Polycittara were already glowing in the dankness beyond.

I saw Marán on an inside balcony. For just a moment battle anger left me, and I wondered what it was like to love someone who'd chosen a life as I had, when each leave-taking might be the last. But there was no time for anything behind. At a gallop we went into the driving rain and out of the city, with blood on our minds.

The rain stopped for a moment, and dying sunlight outlined the village of Nevern. It sat atop a hill and, even though it was unwalled, would be easy to defend, with only half a dozen streets, which wound past ancient stone houses. I heard the wail of a babe, quickly silenced, from one. But we had little attention for the village.

Twenty-five naked corpses hung on butcher's cutting tripods along the road, impaled on hooks through their rib cages. They were the missing Lancers. I looked at Legate Ili's body. Beyond the ghastly wound in its chest, it bore no signs of violence. But he had not died easily—his face, like the others, was twisted in a grimace of fear.

I remembered Horseman Gabran's babblings about men becoming snakes, and imagined Legate Ili's column a few hours ago, drawn up in the village square, about to begin the hearings, seeing the crowd pressed about them change, writhe, become serpents and slither toward them.

Very well. Those who dealt terror would experience it themselves. I shouted for the commander of the Tenth Hussars' troop, Captain Pelym, and ordered him to surround the village with the hundred men of his company. Kill anyone attempting to leave—man, woman, child. He saluted, and his company rode away.

"Your intentions, Tribune?" Kutulu was being formal.

"This village was responsible for the murder of twenty-five of their fellow Numantians. Under martial law, I intend to put it to the sword."

I saw Seer Sinait's eyes widen. For a moment, I remembered that police sergeant about to slay three elderly innocents, but shoved the memory away.

"Good," Kutulu said. "The emperor's rule can be just—but it can also be harsh to miscreants."

"Tribune," the seer said. "Will you give me a moment before you issue your orders?"

She dismounted, took the canvas roll from behind her, opened it, and took out a very slender dagger, the blade of which shone of silver, and the haft of gold.

"I would like to try something I've never attempted."

She touched the blade to her forehead, then to her heart. She walked to Legate Ili's body, touched the tip of the dagger to the gory wound in his chest, then went back to her roll. She took out a coil of string that shimmered in the light of the dying sun. Murmuring words I couldn't distinguish, she wrapped a figure-eight loop around the dagger's haft, then held it suspended in air. The perfectly balanced weapon hung level. Sinait chanted:

"There is blood
There was blood
Seek the Slayer
Find the man
Find the woman
Find the child
Blood seek blood
Point true

Point it well
Blood seek blood."

The dagger didn't move; then it swung, pointed toward the village.

"That's as I thought," I began, and then the dagger swung to the side. It moved back and forth, like a hound questing for a scent, then steadied. It pointed a dozen degrees away from Nevern.

"What does this mean?" I asked.

"Wait," the seer said. "Let me be certain." Again she chanted, and again the dagger behaved exactly as before. "These soldiers weren't slain by the people of this village. The dagger points to where the real murderers now are.

"I'd guess the villagers knew what was about to happen, but were afraid of giving a warning. The knife shows they carry some guilt. I felt this," she went on. "I sensed no threat, no enemies ahead. That's not a trustworthy feeling, all too often. But it's still worth considering."

"You said the villagers share guilt," Kutulu said. "That's enough."

Sinait didn't answer, but looked at me, waiting. That bloodthirsty warden came back, and a bit of my anger died.

"Tribune," Kutulu said, seeing my hesitation, "these people are admittedly guilty and must be punished. Should we ignore them, and chase wisps that will disappear in the hills?"

"Seer," I said, "the emperor's warden has a point. Can the ones who actually did it be brought down?"

"I don't know," she said honestly. "Is there a map of this area?"

"Domina Bikaner. A map, if you please!"

"Sir!" Captain Lasta pulled one from a saddlebag and handed it to Bikaner, who brought it to me.

"If you could . . . align it, I think is the word?" Sinait asked.

I dismounted and laid the map on the ground, using the village and a readily identifiable hillcrest not far away to orient it.

"We are where, exactly?"

I knelt and pointed. Sinait got down beside me, picked up a bit of muddy earth, and touched it to the map where I'd pointed.

"You are what you picture
You are what you show
Tell me true
Tell me firm
Jacini of the Earth
Limax of this land
One other who must not be named
But she knows, she knows
She knows I pray to her
Become what you show."

For just an instant, I swear the map became a tiny replica of the land, so Nevern wasn't tiny dots of ink, but small houses, and the hills around us rose up, like a sand-table model. But then everything returned to normal. Sinait took the dagger once more and held it over the map by the gold cord, muttering words I couldn't distinguish. The dagger hung level, dipped. She lowered her hand until the dagger's point touched the map.

"The ones you seek will be there."

I showed Captain Lasta the spot on the map.

"One hour distant, I'd guess," he said. "We can follow this trail . . . here. It doesn't look too bad, unless the map's lying to us or the rain's washed it out."

I stood. "Lance Karjan, ride for Captain Pelym, and tell him to bring his company back."

"Yessir."

Kutulu was frowning. "A word, Tribune?"

We stepped a few feet away.

"Do you accept her magic?"

"Not entirely," I said. "But I know damned well a group of farmers didn't come up with the magic to slaughter a quarter hundred Lancers, nor with the courage."

"But they knew," Kutulu said stubbornly. "Even the seer said that."

"So she did, and they'll be punished. But there are other ways of punishment than the sword or prison. I could order the village razed, but how many friends do you think that would win for Numantia in the towns around us?

"They'll be punished, Kutulu. Don't doubt that. Perhaps I'll order their marketplace destroyed, and all sellers and buyers to do their business elsewhere for a year. I must think on it."

"There is no place for weakness in the law," said the Serpent Who Never Sleeps.

"You might call it weakness," I said. "Perhaps I'll use another word. Mercy. Now, those are my orders. Obey them, sir."

Kutulu dipped his head and walked back to his horse.

Within a few moments of Captain Lasta's prediction, we reached the place Sinait had indicated our quarry would be. It was almost dark, and the rain had returned, but softer than before.

I'd already given orders to Bikaner, Lasta, Pelym, and Tiger Troop's commander, Legate Thanet, as the column wound through the hills. We'd leave the horses and close on foot. One man in four had been told off to hold them. The Lancers left their primary weapons behind. If I'd known we'd be fighting on foot, I would've had them draw shortswords and knives before we marched out. But their sabers would serve for the task I proposed.

I was properly armed, having learned years ago from my father that a saber is a single-purpose weapon, good only for a man on horseback, and so carried a straight double-edged blade whether afoot or riding.

I was at the head of the soldiers, and Domina Bikaner brought up the rear. Behind me was Karjan, then Kutulu and

Seer Sinait. We were flanked by archers, then Captain Lasta and the men of the Red Lancers. Before we started, I asked the seer if she felt any magic about, if the wizard who'd ambushed Legate Ili had laid out any wards. She cast two spells, said she sensed nothing, which puzzled her—was the unknown wizard that confident?

I noted a distinctive crest line just to the right of the direction we wished to travel in, outlined against the darkening sky, and we moved out through the night, not needing a compass. There was not a murmur from the men, and not a clink of weaponry or scuffle as we crept over the hills. Not far ahead, I saw the glow of a fire dimly reflected from the storm clouds above, and I moved in its direction. The ground climbed gently, and I stopped just below a hillcrest, and held out my hand, palm down. The soldiers flattened, weapons ready.

I touched Karjan, the seer, and Kutulu, and we moved to the top of the hill, keeping in a crouch. I was most impressed with Sinait—though she had none of the training of a soldier, and was hardly in the best of physical shape, she'd kept up without panting, and walked almost as silently as any of us.

There was a small valley below, almost a natural amphitheater. Fires burned smokily. There were no demons to be seen, but about fifty armed men crouched around the fires. Some were roasting meat, others sheltering under blankets or oilskins. They were talking animatedly, unbothered by the rain, and I heard occasional bursts of laughter. I saw no sentries.

We watched for some moments. I was about to return to the troops, but Kutulu held up a hand. He was waiting for something. One man stood and called names. Three others joined him, and they moved away from the fire to confer.

Kutulu leaned close. "Those four," he whispered. "Or, at any rate, the one in the center. He'll be their leader. We want him alive."

"If possible," I said, a bit of skepticism in my voice. There were no guarantees in close combat.

"Not *if possible*. I have some questions that must be answered." I saw the gleam in his eyes, reflected firelight. He drew on a pair of long gauntleted gloves, his favorite weapons—each had sand sewn across the knuckles and palms, ideal for knocking someone instantly unconscious. In his left hand he held a dagger he carried sheathed down the back of his neck.

We returned and I whispered final orders to Captain Lasta, and he went down the column, passing them along to warrants and officers. I wanted Tiger Troop to move around the valley to the left, and the Tenth Hussars to the right. They were to be in position by a count of two thousand from the time they left the column and, at my shout, were to charge.

I counted slowly as men slipped away. At one thousand, I motioned, and my Red Lancers went on line, crawling to the crest of the hill.

My mouth was dry, and I could feel my lips pull back in a humorless grin.

Time. I gave it another few seconds, then came to my feet. As I did, Kutulu bounded over the crest of the hill. I thought he'd not understood, or his nerves had gone, then swore as I realized what he was doing.

"Lancers . . . Attack!" I bellowed, and we went over the top in a rush down on the raiders. Kutulu was in front of us, and I saw him cannon into a man and send him tumbling.

There were shouts of surprise, screams. Men scrambled up, grabbing for weapons. Some tried to run, but saw the other two waves of soldiers, coming over the far crest. My cavalrymen smashed into the throng as if they were a phalanx of spearmen; sabers flashed in the firelight, and the screams were louder and now agonized instead of surprised. Some of the Kallians managed to break away from the swordsmen, but with no hope, for my archers stood at thirty-foot intervals around the rim of the valley, whipping down goose-feathered shafts.

A man was in front of me, open hands pushing, and my blade went between them into his chest. I booted him off my sword, then spun as someone cut at me with a scythe. I knocked the wooden handle up and put my sword through that man's neck.

Two men with clubs stumbled at me, and I danced to the side, sliced one's arm open, gave him an instant to howl in pain while I gutted his friend, then slashed, almost taking the first man's head off.

There was a man with a wide-bladed falchion, and he cut at me. I parried his thrust, struck, but he moved aside. He swung again, and I blocked his blade at the hilt, forcing his arm up, and our bodies slammed together. His breath stank of garlic and fear.

Before he could pull back, I jerked my knee into his crotch, and he screeched and doubled over. I crashed the pommel of my sword down on the back of his neck, cracking his skull, and finished him as he fell. Then there was no one standing except soldiers.

"Domina!"

Bikaner came toward me, limping a little. I saw the dark of blood on his thigh.

"I think I'm gettin' a little old, sir. One of 'em went down and I didn't stay to finish him. Bastard had th' brass t' cut me. What's your orders, sir?"

"Take their heads. We'll have something decorative for the walls of Polycittara come morning."

Bikaner's teeth flashed. "That'll give them something to ponder, sir."

The city would have more than just heads to think of. All Kallio would go into mourning for my fallen Lancers. Not that I expected them to do anything but rejoice privately, but they would mourn several things: the banning of all festivals and playing of any music for a time, and the shuttering of all public houses for the same. If I couldn't appeal to their sense of justice or their fear of the consequences, I'd instruct them through their guts.

Kutulu was two dozen feet away. A man lay moaning at his feet and, a foot away, a second was on his hands and knees. I went to him. "I thought you'd gone mad," I said.

"Not at all," and he looked about, saw no one else within earshot, "my friend. It didn't seem as if you could guarantee the safety of those I needed, so I thought I might make an early selection. One of these is the man we saw giving orders, the other's one of his . . . assistants, perhaps. We'll see what they have to say for themselves, once we return to the castle. I have many questions, and I'm sure they'll give me all the answers I need."

He neither smiled nor sounded angry, and his words were a simple declaration of fact. There would be no mercy from his torturers.

The skirmishing was over, and it was time for full battle.

FOUR

Casting the Net

"I never should'a played politics," the bandit who called himself Slit-Nose grumbled, and spat bloody teeth. "Thievin's never so dirty, an' worst it'll get you is a clean death."

"You'll have your death," Kutulu promised. "When you've told us everything—and we're sure it's the truth."

"There's naught more t' tell," the man Kutulu had taken said. "Th' man said he'd pay us good red gold, an' did. All we had to do was scrag those so'jers for him."

"Who was he?"

"I told you, an' I told that dogfucker who's been beatin' on me I don't know. He come to us, knew our hideout, knew th' places we'd been, knew me by name, an' was willin' to pay. A'ready had Oswy's people convinced, but needed more thieves. Wanted to make sure nobody got away. I asked what th' band thought. Pickin's been slender since th' war. Ain't none got coppers, let alone gold an' silver t' be thieved.

"We'd been thinkin' about goin' on east, into Wakhijr, an' tryin' our luck there. 'Stead . . ." Slit-Nose spat blood again and wiped his face. He looked distastefully at his shattered fingers. "Don't guess *those*'ll ever hold a blade again, now will they?"

I wanted to turn away and vomit, as much from the stink

of the chamber as what the torturers had done to this thief, but forced myself not to.

"I never had no use for you gods-damned Nicians anyway. Paradin' around actin' like you wouldn't say shit if you had a mouthful, so th' thought of puttin' you on th' long journey to Saionji sounded pretty right."

Kutulu's inquisitor raised his knout. I held up a hand.

"Let him speak on."

"'Sides, killin' sojers is good trade."

"Why? We seldom have money."

"Killin' a sojer makes th' dirt eaters think you're on their side. You know, like you're some kinda hero then, an' maybe they won't turn you in, first chance they hear of a reward."

I stepped back, curiosity satisfied. Kutulu frowned—I'd had no business breaking the rhythm of his questions.

"What did this sorcerer call himself?"

"Didn't give a name."

"What was he dressed like?"

"Rich. Dark brown breeches, tunic. Had a cloak in th' same color over it. Must've had a spell on it, 'cause it looked t' be wool, but cast off th' rain like it was oiled. Had two men with him. Rough-lookin'. Bodyguards."

"So he paid you, and you did his bidding?"

"We did."

"Did he pay the villagers, too?"

"Hell, no. Tol' th' menfolk t' get outa the village, an' hide in th' woods till th' next day. Guess they thought we wuz gonna tear th' town down an' take their women. Would'a, too, but th' wizard stopped us. Guess he put some kinda spell over us, 'cause when th' so'jers showed up, they treated us like we wuz no more'n peasants. Th' wizard said he'd give th' sign, an' he did."

Kutulu looked at me.

"Do you want any details of what happened next?"

"What was it like, being a snake?" I asked, somewhat irrelevantly.

A most evil smile came across Slit-Nose's face. "It was nice. 'Specially havin' all your thoughts wi' you, not like a dumb, real serpent. You could move like lightnin', an' th' swords never struck home. Mebbe," and he managed a chuckle, "mebbe when I reach th' Wheel th' goddess'll think bein' a snake'd be proper punishment for a rogue like me. I'd like that, I would."

The inquisitor saw Kutulu's nod, and the knout slashed down on the thief's gore-splattered back. He gargled a scream, and his head sagged. A bucket of water went across his face, bringing him back.

"You'll be respectful when you speak to the Tribune," the warden said.

"Was this the only task the sorcerer wanted of you?" Kutulu asked.

"You ast me all these questions a'ready," Slit-Nose complained.

"I did. And I may ask them another dozen times, to make sure you're telling the truth. Now answer me!"

"He said there'd be other jobs like this 'un."

"How would he contact you?"

"He said he'd know how."

"Could you find him?"

Slit-Nose hesitated, then shook his head. Again the whip ribboned his flesh. "No," the man moaned. "Not direct, anyway."

"Explain yourself."

"That ring I was wearin'? Th' one this bastard wi' th' whip stole?"

The torturer started to snarl something. Kutulu's hand came up, and the man's mouth snapped shut.

"Go on."

"Th' wizard took my ring for a bit, then give it back, sayin' he laid a spell on it. If somethin' came, an' I needed t' find him, I was to hold it to my forehead an' think of him. He'd come, or one of his men'd find me."

Kutulu stood. "You," he said to the torturer. "I'll have a word with you. Outside, if you please."

The burly man's eyes widened in fear. I followed them out, slamming the cell door. Behind me, I heard a low chuckle of evil glee from the bandit.

The torturer was twice Kutulu's size, but cowered before his master.

"The ring," Kutulu said.

The torturer started to protest innocence, but under Kutulu's hard gaze his hand went, as if self-willed, into his pouch, and came out with a heavy silver ring.

"I di'n't think," he started. Kutulu cut him off.

"Exactly. You did not think. This is the first time I've had to reprimand you, Ygerne. There isn't a second time. Steal from me, from the state, once more, and I'll put you on the road back to Nicias alone and on foot, with your trade branded across your forehead!"

Ygerne paled. He'd be lucky to make it out the gates of Polycittara alive with a sentence like that. Kutulu turned to me. "The tale of the ring is the only new information, Tribune, so I think we have all that man knows. Do you wish anything more?"

Only out of this terrible dank stone dungeon, away from its rusting iron and hopeless sobs and screams. I shook my head, and we went up endless flights of stairs, with guards at each barred landing, and at last came out into the great courtyard. I breathed clean air and thanked my family god Tanis for the rain that pelted across my face, washing away the memory of what was below.

Kutulu was examining the ring. "So what can we do with this?" he wondered.

"We do nothing," I told him. "We don't try to use it at all. If this wizard's as careful as I suspect, he'll have laid some sort of counterspell, so if the wrong person attempts to use it he'll either be alerted or possibly even send a demon against the interloper. Put that ring in a safe place. Don't wear it, don't try to use it for anything until I report what happened to the emperor. We may need far greater magic than we have access to in Kallio."

"I reluctantly admit your wisdom, although I don't like having to beg for help from Nicias," Kutulu said after consideration. "Shall I get a report ready for a courier?"

"No," I said. "There's something far quicker, if chancier." The emperor had said no one was to be told about the Seeing Bowl, but sometimes orders are made to be broken, and as I spoke I realized two others would now have to be told. "We'll have to take a chance this sorcerer may be able to eavesdrop on the sending, for we must move at once before he learns the killers are taken and flees."

"Very well," Kutulu said. "With the emperor's help, we'll give him a real surprise when he encounters a different sort of serpent." He smiled, and I laughed, for I'd not known he was aware of his sobriquet.

In bed that night I told Marán a somewhat edited version of what had happened in the dungeon.

"Do you think you'll find this seer?"

It was quiet and peaceful, with no sound outside our high window but the drum of rain and the occasional comfortable challenge of the sentries as they walked their post. She had her head on my shoulder, her hand cradling my cock.

"I don't know," I said. "I think it'll be a matter of magic against magic, and I know little in that area."

"But it'll be the emperor's magic?"

"I think so."

"Then we'll find him," she said confidently. "Maybe he'll tell you how to track down some other people."

"Like who?"

"Like all these elders and counts and so on and so forth that don't seem to be around. Don't you think something's very odd about that?"

"Surely. But there's been the war, and then we've occupied Kallio. Maybe those who lived through the madness have good reason to keep low."

"Of course they do. And I'll bet I can tell you what it is. Ruling, or at any rate being noble, is something I know something about."

"Go on." I was suddenly wide awake. Marán was right—she had generations of gentility in her bones.

"Start with something basic," she said. "A lord likes being a lord."

"Never imagined he didn't."

"I mean he likes it more than almost anything. Change that to a *lot* more than anything. So what made all these people suddenly duck into the nearest badger hole, instead of just changing lords to bow and scrape to and being able to keep on being noble?" Marán sat up quickly. Even in the dimness, I could see the excitement on her face. "The only way Lord Hibble and Lady Hobble would go to ground like the hounds were after them, instead of wanting to cut whatever slice of Prince Reufern's pie they could, is they've been ordered to keep low. Either they're afraid, or they've been promised something—and knowing bluebloods, it'll have to come quickly to keep them in line."

"But who could promise them—or threaten them—with something like that?"

"Maybe your magician?"

"Hmm."

She lay down again. "But probably I'm not making any sense, and just imagining things."

Marán was like that—a sudden burst of perception, and then a huge wave of self-doubt would strike. For a time I thought she'd been beaten down by that utter shit she'd been married to before me, but lately I wondered if maybe it came from her family. It didn't seem, from the little time I'd spent around her father and brothers, that a woman's ideas were especially welcome in the Agramónte world.

"Don't talk like that about yourself," I warned, and

slapped her bottom. She yelped in mock pain, and snuggled closer.

"Now, that's something we haven't done!"

"I didn't know there was anything left," I said.

"Let's see . . . silk ropes tying me facedown, spread-eagled so I can't move," she said, her voice becoming throaty. "I'm blindfolded, and gagged, so I'm utterly helpless. There's a bolster under my hips, and your cock is buried in me. I can feel your balls against me." Her breathing came a little faster. "Then you have a whip, and it's silk, too. You stroke me with it, then you hit me, and it stings. Then you move in me, hard, then lash me again, again and again."

My cock was getting hard, then, very suddenly, I remembered another whip, one wielded not in passion, and the broken face of the bandit in the reeking dungeons below us, and my passion died.

"Very well," I said. "Put it on our list." We had a mythical list of things we hadn't yet managed in bed—some of which would require more apparatus than a siege—that one of us had heard of and, giggling, told the other about.

I yawned and let sleep approach, listening to the rain.

"Damastes," Marán said, "can I ask you something?"

"Anything, so long as it lets me go to sleep pretty soon."

"How much longer will we be doing this?"

"Fucking like bunny rabbits? I hope forever."

"No, you loon. I meant you being a general and never having any time to be at home."

"That's the lot of a soldier," I said. "I go where the emperor wishes, when he wishes. That's the oath I took."

"Forever?"

"Oh, I suppose one of these years I'll get tired. Maybe have too many creaks and groans to take the field." I'd been about to say wounds, but caught myself. "Then you'll have more than enough time to get tired of me."

"I hope so," she murmured, then sighed. "Good night, my love."

"Good night." I kissed the top of her head.

For a time I lay awake, wondering what her last words meant. I'd known women who married soldiers not realizing the nature of their trade, and then grew hateful about it. But that wasn't Marán. She was far too bright, and her family had spent all too many years in the service of Numantia, as diplomats and governors. Besides, given the nature of my trade, it was highly unlikely I'd live to see retirement anyway. Some barbarian's arrow would keep me from having to worry about old age. Strangely comforted with the thought of dying in my prime, dying well, hopefully at the head of my soldiers in battle, and being commended by Isa to Saionji when I returned to the Wheel, although I couldn't imagine what a better life could be, I fell asleep.

The next morning I told Kutulu of Marán's thoughts about vanishing nobility.

"The baroness is even brighter than she is lovely," he said.

"*I* certainly know that. But what made you realize it?"

"One task when I arrived here was to examine the archives of Kallio. That, of course, is a task that'd take an army of clerks an eternity, but I set three men to checking events of the last ten years, which they're still at. Perhaps if we understand the history of this caterwauling province we might be able to rule it more effectively. What they've found is less impressive than what they haven't found. The records had been tooth-combed, and almost anything to do with Chardin Sher's court has been removed. I suppose, in time, we can find duplicates, or memoranda with court members' names on them in the central records in Nicias, but time is something we're a bit short of.

"My chief clerk thinks, interestingly enough, this destruction was done after Chardin Sher was first defeated beyond the Imru River and began retreating."

"That makes no sense," I said. "That'd mean that Chardin Sher knew he was beaten after the first battle, yet wanted his satraps to be able to go underground and fight on."

"Chardin Sher . . . or someone else," Kutulu said.

"Such as?"

"Perhaps our mysterious seer knows. I really wish to have converse with him, for your wife's contribution confirms what these files suggest by their absence—that there are two conspiracies here in Kallio. One is the mob, the spontaneous risings.

"The other is far more serious and is composed of the surviving members of Kallio's ruling class, who are hidden waiting the day and the signal to rise up and destroy every vestige of imperial rule. That is the conspiracy that really frightens me."

"Hold the object up so I can see it," the emperor ordered. "Just for a moment, though, in case we're being observed." I obeyed, turning Slit-Nose's ring this way and that over the Seeing Bowl. "I think your brigand was telling the truth," he said. "It's nothing innately magical. Probably the thief took it in a robbery and the person we seek then laid an incantation on it, to make it into a talisman. Now, if you'll move out of the way, so I may speak to your seers?"

I motioned Sinait and Edwy forward. Both showed considerable awe. Edwy probably would have seen the emperor in person, since he was part of Reufern's household, but I knew Sinait had not.

"Here is what we shall attempt," Tenedos said, sounding like the careful teacher he'd been. "A certain spell comes to mind that I learned in a village back in my youth, from someone who called herself a witch-finder." He held up a scroll. "Both of you write down, quickly, what is on this parchment. I must not say the words, for fear of being overheard."

The two wizards obeyed, their lips silently forming letters as they wrote. Sinait finished first, and Edwy a moment behind her. Seeing them look up, Emperor Tenedos put the scroll aside.

"Read what you have written now. I tried to make the instructions as clear as I could."

They did as told. "This one word," Sinait asked. "Meveern? Shouldn't it be Maverhn?"

"No," Tenedos said. "That would call, not send. You're attempting to reverse the incantation."

"I'm not sure," the older man said, "what, if this works, will be produced."

Tenedos looked exasperated, exactly like a lycée instructor trying to help a not particularly swift pupil, then caught himself. "You'll be drawn in a certain direction, toward the one who cast the spell on that ring."

"We'll be like a compass needle, Edwy," Sinait said. Obviously she understood quite well. Edwy looked embarrassed and nodded.

"Cast the spell as I told you, write down what it gives you, then break it instantly," Tenedos continued. "This incantation is an open path. Don't give this unknown one a chance to use it against you."

"I, at least, will move like the wind," Sinait said, smiling.

"Cast it once," Tenedos continued. "Then Tribune á Cimabue will escort you to another location, at least fifty miles from where you are now, and you'll cast the spell again. Lay those two directions out on a map . . ."

". . . and our villain'll be at the intersection," Sinait said excitedly.

"Exactly." Tenedos smiled warmly. Sinait blushed like a young girl just paid her first compliment.

"Now I wish to speak to the tribune privately," the emperor said, and the two seers and Kutulu bowed out.

"I'm not sure this is going to work," Tenedos said. "The man we seek is very careful. I'm already considering other things we might attempt if this fails."

"If it succeeds, what do we do next?"

"Take him alive," the emperor said.

"I've never tried that before," I said. "I understand trapping wizards is a bit like catching a serpent in your bare hands. You think you have him, but the question is whether or not he has you instead."

The emperor grinned. "I'll prepare incantations to be laid

by your seers on devices to make sure this particular serpent's fangs are blunted so he won't be able to slither out of your grasp.

"But he must be taken, and alive. I sense he's the linchpin, the key for many things that have troubled Numantia, things that must be ended at once!"

That night the spell was cast from a turreted room in one of the castle's towers. The bare room held only seven tall braziers of wrought iron and, between them, seven candelabra of the same material, in a large circle. Semicircles were drawn on all the walls, each figure about three feet in diameter. In each a different symbol was chalked. In the center of the room a large triangle was laid out, with an arc drawn at each angle. Along the sides words were written, in a script I didn't know. Herbs had been assembled: goldenseal, hyssop, rock rose, wintergreen, white willow, others, to be burnt in the braziers.

The incantation was quite simple, Sinait told me. The emperor's instructions said its potency depended more on repetition than length.

Edwy was clad in dark robes worked with silver and gold devices, representing star formations, magical tools, and such, tied with a spun-gold belt, very much the wealthy court magician. Sinait wore her usual brown.

I'd been greatly concerned with what Tenedos had said about danger. Sinait said she doubted they'd need help, but Edwy told me rather nervously, that it might be well to have soldiers ready, so I had ten men, including Karjan, standing by in light armor, weapons ready, on the narrow, winding stairs. What use they, or I, would be against a sorcerous opponent, I had no idea. But it was better than doing nothing.

The heavy oak door boomed shut, and we waited outside. And waited some more. None of us was bored, but we were increasingly ill at ease. I heard a wind building, and looked out a loophole. But the air was still. It was near dawn. The wind song grew louder and louder still, and I heard a man shout from within. My sword was in my hand as the shout became a cry of surprise and then pain. Sinait screamed, and I yanked at the door handle, but they'd barred it from within. I slammed against the door with my shoulder. The stout wood never budged. I hit it again, then was unceremoniously yanked away by Lance-Major Svalbard, a huge bruiser of a man. He smashed a great mace against the door twice, high and low; the hinges ripped and the door fell away.

Edwy sprawled in a sea of blood at one corner of the triangle. Seer Sinait was backed against the wall. Moving purposefully toward her was a huge warrior, far taller than I, wearing the armor of the Kallian Army of nine years before. He turned his head toward me, his eyes were pools of burning fire, his face a swirl of black.

A throwing ax whistled past and thudded into the being's armor with a clang. He was solid enough, at any rate. The spirit or demon turned away from the seer and rushed me, broadsword held like a spear. I parried, and felt solid steel. Then the warrior slashed, and I was barely able to turn his thrust aside.

I struck at his thigh, and my blade bounced off his armor as if it were a foot thick. Again he, or it, brought his sword down, and I sprang sideways as the blade smashed into the stone floor, sparks cascading.

I remembered a bit of what Tenedos had taught me of magic, and, instead of attacking the demon directly, I cut at the triangle's edge, slicing through the chalk line as the apparition rushed me.

Quite suddenly, as if a solid became smoke, I could see through him, see Sinait and the stone wall, and then there was nothing in the tower but soldiers, Sinait, and Edwy's corpse.

"So there *were* wards out," I said, stupidly stating the obvious.

Sinait shuddered. "But the emperor's spell worked before . . . before that whatever it was, came," she said. "I didn't have time to write, but we have one bearing to our enemy."

She pointed at Edwy's body. He may have been unimpressive in life, but in death he served Numantia well, for he lay with an arm outstretched, pointing not quite due east.

"Where he points," Sinait said, "is where that shade came from. One more casting, and we'll have that seer." She spoke without a tremor in her voice, and again I admired her courage. But a second casting would be almost impossible. This wizard had discovered our first attempt, and would be lying in wait.

The next day we held the death ceremony for Edwy and consigned his body to the flames. I gave the orders for three troops of Lancers to ready themselves as escorts for Seer Sinait, who was determined to make the second casting from the city of Cambon, about seventy miles to the south-southwest.

I'd attempted to use the Seeing Bowl to report to the emperor, but without success. Sinait wondered if our alerted foe might not have counterspells out against any magic we might try. "I don't know how powerful this wizard is," she said. "Powerful enough, for certain. And he'd need little energy to prevent your Bowl spell from working, since you have little talent and no training. I'd suggest you not even bother trying again."

This worried me greatly. Tenedos had promised additional spells to help trap this wizard, and now we'd be forced to battle without them.

We were less than an hour from departure when Kutulu found me in the busy bustle of the regimental headquarters. "I don't think we'll need any more magic," he said. "Come, and I'll show you."

We hurried to his office, which was cast in night, although it was a rare sunny day outside, for black curtains closed off the light. Spies abhor windows, unless they're the ones trying to peer in. A huge map of Kallio covered one wall. It was dotted with large-headed pins, each numbered in red. From the castle a line of yarn ran to the east, which was the direction Edwy's death had gained.

"I'll keep this very brief," Kutulu said with authority, and I felt a bit of amusement. Now I was in his arena, and he was very much in charge. "For we have our villain," and there was a flash of triumph in his normally calm, unexcitable voice.

"First, we have the yarn, representing the line from the seers' casting."

"I see it."

"Yesterday afternoon one of the clerk-drudges that I have shoveling through the paper ruins of Chardin Sher's empire found this." He picked up a piece of yellowing paper. "You're welcome to read it, but you needn't unless you wish. It's a requisition for carriages and soldiers to escort Mikael Yanthlus, Chardin Sher's magician, to the army's camp on the far side of the Imru River. By the date it would have been just before our army was so badly defeated trying to cross that river into Kallio.

"A paper of no interest to anyone but quartermasters," he said. "However, I found it fascinating, since it included the names of the three aides to Mikael of the Spirits. The first is unknown, as is the second, but the third has an interesting family name: Amboina. First name, Jalon. Only son of Landgrave Molise Amboina, Prince Reufern's most favored friend."

"Son of a bitch," I said.

"Indeed," Kutulu said. "Especially since Landgrave Amboina's made no mention of this reclusive Jalon's profession. I thought this was very interesting, so I determined to ask some questions of your friend the philosopher Arimondi Hami. I asked them in the company of Ygerne, who'll you'll admit has a certain presence."

I remembered what the torturer had done to Slit-Nose.

"I informed Hami that, unlike other Numantians, I had no particular interest in his continued well-being, and I wished to know everything about the Amboina family, and its relationship to Chardin Sher and Mikael Yanthlus. I told him it was utterly foolish to attempt either ignorance or vast bravery. Everyone will talk in time, especially when the questioner knows what queries to put.

"He was wise, and told me what I wished. Briefly, the Amboina family has served Chardin Sher, his father, and his father's father well, either directly as magicians when a family member had talent, or as go-betweens with other sorcerers, when those others used dark forces to accomplish their ends. The family's daughters married wizards as well, when they could and when they had a touch of the talent. Otherwise, it was perfectly acceptable for an Amboina woman to become a magician's concubine. Two of those girls, Amboina's daughters from his first marriage, accompanied Mikael Yanthlus when he fled to the citadel where he was destroyed, and evidently died there.

"Hami seemed proud that the Amboina family so gladly prostituted their women to be close to magical power, incidentally.

"Hami also said Jalon had a great talent and might have grown to become Chardin Sher's first sorcerer if the renegade Maisirian Yanthlus had ever left the office. I asked if Landgrave Amboina had any powers himself, and he said no, but he'd had an abiding interest in the art since Hami had known him.

"I wonder if this is another reason the traitor Hami hasn't been to the gallows. It could well be Landgrave Amboina interceded with the prince on his behalf."

I felt a bit ashamed at my kid-gloved questioning of Hami, but no more than a bit, which was why I was a soldier and Kutulu a warden.

"As soon as I received word of the sorcerers' casting, I laid it out on this map."

He picked up a long pointer, and ran it along the strand of red yarn, stopping about fifty miles from Polycittara.

"Just here is the seat of the Amboinas' holdings, their grand manor house, Lanvirn, where Jalon Amboina is supposedly resident. You'll notice it's exactly on the line, which, by the way, I had one of your officers check with a compass before we moved Seer Edwy's corpse.

"Another thing of interest. Look at the map. Those red pins mark anti-imperial incidents. You notice there are no such pins anywhere close to Lanvirn? The Amboinas were very clever, making sure their own lands and people were above suspicion. But, as you can see, once the problem areas are charted, this very absence of activity draws the eye."

I looked at Kutulu with admiration—he was, indeed, worthy of being the emperor's spymaster and chief warden.

"I think we should ride at once," Kutulu went on, "with a small detachment. Perhaps two score of your Red Lancers, and I have six or seven men who aren't unfamiliar with violence. Myself. The seer. Surprise can negate the need for large forces, which always broadcast their coming."

"Good. We'll be ready immediately," I said, eager for action. "But what about Jalon Amboina's father, the landgrave? I have to assume that he can communicate with his son, so we must keep him ignorant of what's about to happen."

"I have already told the prince of our discoveries, as my orders require," Kutulu said. "I asked him to have the landgrave seized and imprisoned. The prince was horrified, saying he could do no such thing without proof of the landgrave's involvement in this treason.

"I tried to argue, but . . ." Kutulu took a deep breath. "Instead, we invented an important errand. Amboina rode out of the castle two hours ago, with an escort of the prince's troops. The officer in charge had orders to keep the landgrave out of Polycittara for at least two days, regardless of what it takes. I don't like it, but that was the furthest Prince Reufern was willing to go."

Kutulu seemed to have thought of everything. Then a question occurred to me.

"What about Arimondi Hami? Would there be any advantage in taking him with us? Perhaps he could tell us more about this Jalon Amboina as we ride."

"Unfortunately," Kutulu said, "he died in the course of our conversation." Seeing my expression, the warden held up his hand. "No, not under torture. Neither Ygerne nor I laid a hand on him. He appeared to have died of terror. His heart simply gave out. I've already made arrangements for the quiet disposal of his remains, with a priest whom I can trust to keep silent."

I looked hard at Kutulu. The Serpent Who Never Sleeps' expression was bland, calm. To this day, I do not know if the warden told me the truth.

"This becomes interesting," Sinait observed, scratching her chin with a forefinger. "Taking a magician alive while trying to remain the same. Very interesting indeed. Now, let us assume he's a better sorcerer than I am, or at any rate is more familiar with the terrain, both real and spiritual; which I think is the best idea, since I've never yet sent a vengeful spirit against someone who's worked a spell against me.

"Kutulu has the correct idea. We must close with him as quickly as possible, and use surprise as our main weapon. You must not tell any of the soldiers what mission they will be on. Not that I think Amboina, or any other magician, can read thoughts, but if all these men are thinking of him, planning harm, that could create . . . vibrations might be a poor word for it . . . he could feel and respond to."

"As a deer can sense a hunter's presence if the hunter stares too closely at him?" I asked.

"A good example. Now, as I suggested, we must get close to this wizard as quickly as possible. I think he should be completely immobilized. Bind his arms and legs. Gag him so he can't begin any spells. Blindfold him so he can't determine where he is, and then get him away from his familiar surroundings.

"Perhaps I can sense any spells he tries and forestall them. It might be well to knock him unconscious at once and revive him once we've made our retreat."

I grinned wryly. "This, Seer, is going to be an undertaking. To break into a well-guarded castle without alerting anyone, especially Amboina, then bash him over the head and tiptoe away without anyone screaming blue murder."

"A task," Sinait agreed. "But something I've noticed thugs accomplish all the time. Since we're much brighter than any criminal, it should be easy."

That was the only laughter the day gave.

"Of course you're going to lead this raid yourself," Marán said.

"Of course."

She shook her head, tried to smile. "When you first asked if I wished to accompany you on this posting, I was delighted, for we've spent too much time apart. But maybe I was wrong. Before, when you were miles and leagues distant, I always imagined the worst could happen to you, and was always afraid.

"Now I've found that the truth can be so much more frightening. I'm concerned, my Damastes, my love, that you're too peaceful a man."

I lifted an eyebrow. "That sounds a trifle strange. Very few would consider a man who makes his trade as a warrior peaceful."

"Oh, but you are. If you weren't you, you would have sent out both regiments and ordered them to strike hard at this estate called Lanvirn, and take no prisoners, not peasant, not lord."

"The emperor ordered Amboina to be taken alive."

"The emperor, although I revere him as almost a god," she said, "is not the one who'll have to creep into a magician's chambers. Sometimes what my father called bloodyhandedness is a virtue."

"Sometimes it is," I agreed. "But not here. Not now. I truly believe that one reason Kallio is in shambles is that my predecessors and their superiors were too quick with the sword and the rope."

Marán got up and went to a window. "We've had this argument before," she said. "I have no interest in going through it once more. Not with you planning to leave me within the hour.

"Come, Damastes. Let's make love. Put some of your

courage into me with your seed. And give me something to be glad about, and think of while you're gone."

She wore a simple silk frock and quickly pulled it over her head, stripped off her undershift, then went to the nearby couch and lay down.

"Leave your tunic on," she said. "I want to see you make love to me as a soldier, so I can always remember what you are. Come to me, my Damastes. I need you so!"

A few minutes later I left our apartments. Standing outside was a calm Karjan and a irate messenger wearing the prince's livery.

"This babbler says th' Prince wants you," Karjan said. "I told him you give me orders to leave you alone. He wanted t' go in anyway. I didn't have t' slam him one, but it was close."

"How *dare* you," the man hissed at the lancer. "I speak for the prince."

"You!" I barked. "You have a message for me?"

"Yes. Yes, of course. Just what this idiot said."

"Then stop yammering, and take me to Prince Reufern."

"But aren't you going to do something to this, this . . ." The messenger read my expression well, clamped his mouth shut, and scurried off, his legs twinkling to stay ahead of my long strides.

"I told your domina I wished to accompany you on this raid," the prince said. "He acted surprised, then told me I'd need to tell you my desires." He pursed his lips. "Sometimes I feel less a ruler than a prisoner in this damned castle! Damnation, but I promised my brother I'd do the best job I knew how, and I am trying! I have no desire to be a peacock on a throne!"

He glared and I stared back. I was surprised when he didn't look away. Instead, his jaw firmed, and I saw a glimpse of that innate power his brother held in such great measure.

"My apologies, Your Majesty," and I meant what I said. "We became so busy in this matter we didn't take account of your feelings. It won't happen again."

"I'm not concerned about that greatly," Reufern said. "Forget about it. I always prided myself on appointing managers and stewards in my businesses and leaving them alone to manage.

"The point is that I propose to go with you. Don't worry, I know I'm not a general, so I won't try to interfere. But the people of Kallio will never respect me if I sit on my ass surrounded by my pack of pet fools and whores and let the real task of governing go to others."

"I'm sorry, Your Highness—"

"Stop!" Reufern barked. "Tribune, I told you what I propose to do, and I shall do it. I am giving you an order. Obey it, or I'll summon the guard and have you placed under arrest!"

By the withered balls of Umar, there was some fire to the man!

"I cannot obey that order, Your Majesty," I said. "Arrest me if you will, but I would like to have a chance to explain."

"I have no interest in your explanations! Dammit, my brother told me that you tried to keep him from going with you once, back in that shitty border town you both almost died in! But he insisted, and he went along. I'm doing the same."

I maintained my silence.

"Well?" he said.

"I asked if I was to be permitted an explanation. If I'm not, then you must do what you will."

The color receded from Reufern's face, and he rapped his knuckles twice on the table he was leaning on. "All right," he said finally. "I'll listen."

"Thank you, sir. Your brother did insist on going with me back in Sayana, and he was right. We sought magic, and he was—is a magician. This is different."

"Maybe I'm not a seer," Reufern said. "But I can use a sword, and ride as well as any of your Lancers, Tribune. Don't you understand," and his tone became pleading, "I've *got* to feel I can do something, for Irisu's sake! You don't understand what it is. Laish was—is my younger brother, and I grew up taking care of him.

"Now it's the other way around. Now he's the one with the power, and sometimes I feel as if I'm not much more than a hanger-on, kept around more for pity than because I can serve well. Sometimes," he said, and his voice was not much more than a whisper, "sometimes I wonder if I didn't like it better in the old days."

I almost let pity take me, but stiffened my resolve. "Sir, we're after a magician once more. A very powerful one. Somehow who knows everything that happens in Polycittara. I'll pose a question, sir, and you answer it as best you can, and if you still think it's wise, then we both ride within the hour:

"Don't you think that this Jalon Amboina would know, almost instantly, if Prince Reufern Tenedos, ruler of Kallio, left his palace for any reason at all, especially without warning and in the company of a band of armed men? Don't you think that might make him at least take alarm, and maybe even lay a trap for us?"

There was a very long silence. The prince sighed, and his shoulders sagged. I felt relief wash over me—I'd hoped the shrewdness that had made Reufern a successful trader was still in him.

"You're right, Damastes," he said grudgingly. "But I feel no warmth toward you as I say that. I'll stay, as you wish. But don't expect me to just smile and shrug this off as no more than a prince's momentary caprice, easily cast aside. I was serious about every word.

"You're dismissed, Tribune. I wish you good hunting." Without waiting for a response, he went out, and the slam of the door behind him was very loud.

I waited for a few moments, then left by the same door. I was very contemplative. Prince Reufern was a better man than I'd thought, and I reminded myself to not be so quick to judge. Perhaps the emperor hadn't been completely wrong in making him prince regent.

We rode out in groups of threes and fours, in mid-afternoon. The civilians left first, then the soldiers, wearing dark civilian garb, our weapons hidden. It was a squally, chill day, perfect for our purposes. We met on an agreed hilltop five miles beyond the city. When dusk came, and travelers grew fewer, we clattered down to the highway, and rode for Lanvirn.

Five of us sprawled on a muddy hilltop, staring down at Lanvirn: Captain Lasta, Sinait, Kutulu, Karjan, and I. The rest of my raiders were hidden in a rickety barn behind us. It was not long after dawn. We'd ridden all night, stopping briefly for a meal from the iron rations in our saddlebags and one small flask of wine. Seer Sinait had improved our meal by casting a small spell over the flasks to heat them, so there was some warmth in our bodies when we rode on.

Lanvirn, like Polycittara, had sprawled beyond its walls. The fortress itself was a rectangle, with four-sided towers at the corners of the seventy-five-foot-tall keep and one on either side of the main gate. A small river had been diverted from its course for a moat around three walls, and there was a swamp to the rear. The Amboinas had built beyond the gates as their farms and ranches prospered, and a clutter of outbuildings had grown around the central structure, on the far side of the three-arched fixed bridge that bestrode the moat. There were peasants working here and there in the mucky fields, and wagons creaking along the narrow dirt roads. Unless this was all an elaborate deception, Jalon Amboina didn't know we were coming.

We took it in turn to examine what lay below. The rear of the castle was one large donjon, and a flag flew over it, suggesting the Amboinas were in residence.

Sinait hesitantly suggested she could attempt a small seeking spell, but would rather not, for fear of alerting Jalon. I agreed—we'd find him by brute force.

First, we had to enter the fortress. It would've been possible for one or two to scale the outer wall, and we'd brought grapnel and rope, but we were after more than the family silver. I had an idea. I beckoned Captain Lasta to crawl over and pointed to where I thought Lanvirn might be vulnerable.

"Chancy," he whispered. "Very chancy. I assume we'd wait for someone to open our way?"

"Just so."

"Mmm. Four—no six men," he mused. "Put the rest of us . . . where, back in one of those sheds? The closest one to the moat?"

"No," I said. "That one over there. Let's not get too close to the moat."

"Chancy indeed," he said. "But I have nothing better."

We looked at each other, shrugged, and the plan was set.

A thin moon had risen, obscured by scudding clouds, when seven of us slid from the byre toward the moat. We were Svalbard, who carried bonds, gags, and blindfolds for the magician; an equally large bruiser named Elfric, who was one of Kutulu's men; two archers, both from the Red Lancers (Manych and a longtime comrade and possibly the best bowman I've ever known, Lance-Major Curti); Kutulu; myself; and my shadow, Karjan.

All of us except the archers carried swords, but we'd slung their sheaths across our backs. We'd need them after we made entrance to Lanvirn, but not before. I hoped. Our main weapons were long daggers and padded rolls of sand to quietly silence anyone we encountered. Karjan and I carried four-inch lead pigs, which could be held in the fist to improve a blow's quality, or thrown, as I'd done when I killed the Kallian landgrave Elias Malebranche. The archers' bowstrings were silenced with tassels.

There was no one about, nor were there sentries outside the barred gate of the castle, but lights gleamed from the tower on each side of the bridge, so watch was being kept from a more comfortable spot than a sentry-go.

We moved slowly, crouching, so many dark huddles in the night, until we reached the moat. River-fed, it wasn't the foul swamp most are, but it was deathly cold. I went first and had gone but a half dozen steps when the bottom dropped away and I was swimming. The current tried to sweep me under the bridge, but I kicked hard and made it to the first arch, where I was held by the current. Six heads bobbed toward me and we clung to the rough stonework.

We went from arch to arch, until we were against the dank stone walls of the fortress. Three slipped under the arch to the far side of the bridge, three others stayed with me. There was a slight ledge just underwater I hadn't been able to see, so we were able to sit.

I took steel tent pegs from my belt pouch and tapped them into crevices in the wall, using a lead ingot for a hammer. Svalbard gave me a hoist up, and I pounded in more, until we had crude steps to just below the parapet. I heard a clink or two and the scuffle of boots against stone, and knew Kutulu and his two fellows had done as I had.

Then we waited. I spent the time numbly trying to decide which was colder, the sodden part of me above the waist in the chill breeze, or what was still underwater. I guess we sat for an hour, maybe two, although it could have been several lifetimes.

Over the soft rustle of the river I heard horses' hooves. The stones of the bridge rang to iron horseshoes as riders approached the gatehouse. There were at least half a dozen, too many for us to overpower. A shout came, a challenge was answered. Harness creaked, and men muttered, then the great gate boomed open, and the riders entered Lanvirn. The gate closed, and there was no sound but the plash of the waters.

More time passed, and we heard more horsemen approaching, and it sounded like two, no more than three, riders. I clambered up the pegs. Karjan, then Svalbard were behind me. Again the challenge came and was answered. The shout hadn't died into the night before I rolled across the parapet, dagger in hand.

There were three of them. One still bestrode his horse; the other two had dismounted. They had their backs to me, but heard my boots. One turned, gaping in surprise, and my dagger's hilt thudded against his ribs, point sticking out a handspan beyond his back. The second's mouth was open, but a sandbag took him, and he was down. The mounted man's horse reared, someone grabbed the rider's leg, and tore him from the saddle, and Elfric dropped across him as he went down. I saw his dagger go up, then down, three times in the dimness, and the gate was opening. Svalbard grabbed the gate in two hands and pulled hard, yanking the astonished guard behind it out onto the bridge. Karjan dropped him with a sandbag, and we were inside Lanvirn.

The Red Lancers came out of the darkness across the bridge, Seer Sinait in their midst, and were with us in the courtyard. There was a winding staircase into one of the towers, and boots thudded as another sentry came down. Curti had an arrow drawn, and as the man came into the open his bow thwacked and a war arrow went through the man's throat clean and clattered against the stone.

Svalbard and Elfric ran up the steps. They were gone a handful of minutes, then came back. Svalbard shook his head and held his palms flat. No one else was on guard.

I marveled at the arrogance of Amboina. He had such confidence in his craft he felt untraceable, as if no one would, could, find him.

"Kutulu," I asked. "Should you be in command?"

"No," the spymaster whispered. "I want him taken by military law. He'll have less right of appeal then."

I half-admired a man who could think of such legal niceties in these circumstances.

"Seer," I said, "do you detect any traps?"

"I do not," and her voice was worried. "Either this Amboina is a far greater wizard than I thought, and can produce undetectable spells, or else he's unbelievably complacent."

"Let's see which," I said, and motioned my men forward. We ran along the wall, large rats scurrying, toward the double doors that were the entrance to the donjon. They were heavy wood with iron cross-bracing, and could have stood against a sizable ram. But they were unlocked and unguarded, and we drew our swords and burst through them.

The great hall could have kept harvest home for several hundreds, but there were only a dozen men and women inside, sitting at the remains of a late supper, with an equal number of servants.

At the head of the table was a man I instantly recognized, although I'd never seen him before. Jalon Amboina was his father's image. His face was that of a brooding dreamer, a poet.

Beside him sat a young girl I supposed to be his sister, whose name Hami told Kutulu was Cymea, at the most fourteen. They were richly dressed, as were their guests.

"Jalon Amboina," I shouted. "I have the emperor's warrant!"

A serving maid screeched and threw a tureen at Karjan, and he knocked her spinning. I drew my sword and ran around the table. The man sitting at the foot came up, and I smashed his temple with the iron pig in my left hand, and he sprawled across his dinner partner's lap.

Kutulu was beside me, and a man pushed his chair into his path, waving an eating knife. Kutulu's loaded glove thudded into his face, and he fell motionless across his dinner plate.

The gray-haired man next to Amboina's sister came out of his chair, unsheathing a slender sword. I lunged at him, and he parried, then cut. I smashed his sword aside, and ungentlemanly of me, kicked him in the stomach, then spitted him.

But he'd given Jalon Amboina a few seconds, and that was all the magician needed. There were ten yards between us, and in that space grew a shadow, then the form of that monstrous warrior I'd fought in the tower in Polycittara. This time it had a sword in each hand, and its fire-eyes glittered.

It cut at me, and I blocked its swing, and the shock sent my sword spinning away. I dropped to the flagstones as the creature slashed over my head. I scrabbled for my blade, got it in my hand, and back-rolled to my feet.

Behind his creation, Jalon Amboina was backing toward stairs at the rear of the hall. I heard him muttering his spells, and his monster attacked once more.

From nowhere an arrow sprouted from Amboina's eye, and his head snapped back with the impact. He tottered, then fell. The demon howled in agony, a matching arrow buried in its eye socket.

Cymea Amboina screamed and threw herself on her brother's body, and Amboina's monstrous defender vanished as if it'd never been.

"No one moves," Kutulu shouted. "You are all arrested, by the order of the emperor Laish Tenedos, on the charges of murder and high treason!"

There were squawks and shouts, and one man reached for a sword and was clubbed down by Elfric.

I paid no mind to them, nor to the servitors who poured into the hall, then stood indecisively, stunned by their master's death.

All I could see was the sprawled body of Jalon Amboina, gore soaking the skirts of his sister as she cradled his corpse and keened wordlessly.

FIVE

REVENGE

Jalon Amboina's body, trussed to a blood-hardened gelding, jounced along just behind me. His face, with the gaping wound where an eye had been, was open to sight, as were his trussed hands and feet. Also, a crude gag had been stuffed in his mouth as if he yet lived, and Legate Balkh assigned to watch the corpse closely.

This was at the instructions of Seer Sinait. She'd attempted a minor casting after we'd secured Lanvirn, and announced Amboina's spells were still in place—her magic had no effect, and she, as the emperor had, could still sense a dark force hanging over the land.

"This makes no sense at all," she said. "He's dead, so his magic should have vanished with him. Unless he was a far greater magician than I thought, with legendary powers. If that's the case, I want to know if that corpse suddenly shows signs of reviving."

We had seven prisoners—the survivors of the dinner party, including Jalon's sister. She was fourteen, and would be a raving beauty when grown. But it was most unlikely she'd see another birthday, nor would a long life be probable for the others who were at that table. Perhaps they were just friends discussing plans for the spring planting. But I doubted imperial justice, as administered by Prince Reufern and overseen by the emperor, would show anyone the slightest mercy, and I refused to think of what would happen to Cymea at the hands of Ygerne and Kutulu's other torturers.

I'd freed Amboina's servants, even those who'd fought us. Kutulu had argued, but I told him, flatly, it would be a poor servant who refused to defend his master, even if he was a traitor.

Our casualties had been very light—one Lancer with a broken arm, and two of Kutulu's men with cuts.

Kutulu rode amid the prisoners, carefully examining them, trying to see who should be questioned first, and who would be the first to break. Cymea looked at him once, a cold stare from green eyes, and somehow I knew she'd die without giving him satisfaction.

Strangely, I felt no sense of victory, as I should have, but I ascribed my gloom to the gray rain-dripping weather around us. I stopped my brooding by starting an argument with Karjan, telling him he was promoted lance-major, and this time, by the sword of Isa, he'd keep his rank slashes or I'd send him back to the Lancers. He merely grumbled, instead of becoming enraged. Perhaps the wretched day was affecting him, as well.

Prince Reufern said he'd hold a public tribunal in two days and show the citizens of Kallio how swiftly the Emperor Tenedos dealt with those who wished him harm.

"I'd like to suggest otherwise," Kutulu said, in his calm, emotionless voice.

"Why? I want to see these swine done away with as quickly as possible," the prince said, and then a slow, not pleasant, smile came. "My apologies, Warden. I wasn't thinking. There may be others in this conspiracy. In fact, I'm sure of it."

"I'm sure of nothing, Your Majesty, which is why I wish to question the prisoners closely."

"You have my full permission," Reufern said. "Any methods you choose are acceptable. Even if we . . . lose some of these traitors in the process, there'll be no recriminations."

"None will die," Kutulu said. "I won't let them."

My skin crawled.

"Your Majesty," I asked. "What of Landgrave Amboina? Has he returned yet?"

"No. But when he does, he'll go straight into the dungeon with the others," the prince said. "I'm chagrined that I allowed that smooth-tongued rascal into my graces." He shook his head. "I thought I'd encountered every sort of villain when I was a trader. But someone like Amboina, who could lie, and lie, and lie, as he did—never! I suppose he'll try to convince me that he wasn't aware of what his son was doing, or was under some sort of a spell.

"But I promise you, Damastes and Warden Kutulu, he'll suffer the same fate as the others. I'm not sure what method of execution I'll choose. But it will be one that will make every Kallian for ten generations shudder at the tale of how these dogs died!"

"Now I feel like a total ass," Marán complained. "I fill myself full of worries, seduce you before you leave as if I were never going to see you again, and you come prancing back with all of the evildoers in a sack."

"At least the seducing part wasn't a waste."

"You're nothing but six-and-a-half feet of lust, you know that?"

"I'm not quite *that* big," I said, waggling my eyebrows like a sex-crazed maniac.

"Big enough," she said. Her mood changed. "Damastes, could we try again to have a child?"

Marán had been pregnant with our child when we married, but had a miscarriage not long afterward. We both wanted children and had consulted seers and chirurgeons. The last, and most expensive, told us he doubted if we'd ever be able to have any. He thought the stillborn infant had taken with him Marán's ability to carry a child.

I was disappointed, but not destroyed. Since I was born to be a warrior and assumed I'd most likely die in service, I'd always thought that the family line would be continued through my sisters.

But it was terribly important to Marán. I wondered if her father and brothers were at her to produce an heir, but it was a subject I stayed well clear of. In any event she told me she didn't believe what the sorcerer had said, and how often they were wrong about other things, and refused to give up.

"Of course we can," I said. "Right now?"

"No, silly. I meant . . . you know what I meant. I've consulted with the seer, and she thinks the next few days might be ideal for conception."

"Hmph," I hmphed. "Next you'll have her in the bedchamber, suggesting in what manner we should be making love."

"That," Marán said, "is something I'm already quite familiar with." She echoed my eyebrow waggling. "Just wait until you come to bed tonight."

Seer Sinait straightened, shaking her head. The mercury pool was gray, featureless. "Still nothing," she said. "And I can *feel* being blocked when I reach out."

I'd had no luck with the Bowl spell at all, and thought I might be able to contact the emperor if a proper magician said the words.

"So who is stopping us?"

"I don't know. Who . . . what . . . Maybe it's just the placement of the stars," she said.

I knew she didn't believe that for an instant.

As dusk approached, I decided to attend guard mount. I'd ordered Domina Bikaner to double the watch, since Molise Amboina should be arriving momentarily, and I wished no slip ups. The officer of the watch was Bikaner's adjutant, Restenneth, and the domina and I were standing behind the formation, half-listening to the comfortingly familiar commands, when trumpets from the main castle blared.

"That'll be Amboina coming back now, and we'll be needin' to make sure he doesn't get a chance to run," Bikaner said. "Captain! Prepare the guard to receive a prisoner!"

"Sir!"

I went out of our keep, across the castle's huge center courtyard to the open gates, and looked down into the city. Two castle buglers stood on either side of me, about to play another fanfare. But instead of seeing Prince Reufern's escort and the landgrave, I saw a huge mass of soldiers, wearing Numantian uniforms, marching in orderly formation toward us. There must have been a thousand of them, a regiment and more. The emperor must have decided we needed further reinforcement and ordered another unit to Kallio, although I wondered how he'd been able to move soldiery in such a short time.

I was peering through the growing dimness, trying to see what device was on the banners so I could name the unit, when I heard a shout. It was Seer Sinait, running hard toward me, robes hiked up. "No!" she shouted. "They're not ours! They're Kallians!"

I blinked, looked again. She was wrong—I could see the men's uniforms distinctly. Their officers, in full dress, marched in front, to the steady thud of a half dozen drummers. Music wailed, and I recognized the tune, a standard marching song. I was about to reprove the seer for her unfamiliarity with the army, but she seized my arm.

"Rub your eyes hard," she ordered, "till they water!" I hesitated, then obeyed. She moved a finger across my forehead, I suppose tracing some symbol, then began chanting:

"Look well
Look hard
See truth
See what is
See beyond

Beyond the veil
See the truth
Look well . . ."

My vision blurred, then blinked clear. Instead of Numantian troops, a mass of Kallians now swarmed toward us. They were townsmen, artisans, peasants, nobility, armed with everything from spades to spears and swords. They were even organized into rough formations. On either side of this mob were men in armor, men with conventional weapons. The hidden conspirators Kutulu so feared had chosen this moment for their great rising!

Instead of music playing, they were chanting:

"Death to the Numantians
Death to their servants
Kill them all
Kill them all
Kill them all."

At their head, holding a spear high, was Landgrave Molise Amboina, shouting more loudly than anyone. On the spear was a small banner, which I recognized from the civil war—Chardin Sher's old flag!

"Close the gates," I shouted, and ran toward the huge windlass. One bugler stood, bewildered, the other followed. "Sinait," I shouted. "Get the Lancers out!"

She pelted back across the courtyard, into our keep, shouting for Domina Bikaner.

I put all my strength onto the windlass, and slowly, reluctantly, it creaked into motion. "Come on, man!" I ordered the bugler, and he threw his weight onto another stout wooden bar, then shouted in agony as an arrow buried itself in his side. He clawed at it, screaming, and thrashed down. I pulled my sword and hewed at the arm-thick cable, but I was too late, and the attackers were pouring into the castle. A spear clattered on the cobbles beside me, then another, and I ran for the Lancers' keep.

A man waving a bill broke from the mob and raced toward me. I turned suddenly and knelt, both hands bracing my sword, and he spitted himself on the blade. I kicked him free and ducked as another spear flew past.

"Take him!" the landgrave shouted. "That's their damned tribune!" I ran harder, through the gates into our own keep. Behind me came the mob, howling for blood. Bewildered men and women poured out of doorways into the courtyard like ants when hot water's poured down their hill.

I sheathed my sword, grabbed a bow from a downed archer, and slung his quiver over my shoulder. I nocked a shaft, scanned the onrushing crowd, saw someone in richly worked half-armor, aimed carefully, and he screeched and convulsed, my shaft half-buried in his groin. Other bows twanged and arrows hummed, and spears arced toward the Kallians. Men and women were hit, and went down, some lying motionless, some writhing, screaming. But their screams seemed to add fire to our attackers. I saw Amboina, shot at him, missed. By the time I found another arrow, he'd disappeared into the throng. I saw a big man shouting orders and killed him instead.

Outside the entrance to our keep, in the main courtyard, other soldiers were coming into action, some armored, some with no more than a sword and shield. I saw Prince Reufern, easily distinguishable in a red tunic, a long sword in hand, rush out of a doorway, flanked by a dozen or more soldiers. He plunged forward, into the fray, and I saw his sword rise and fall.

The Kallians slammed into us, and there was no time for anything except killing the man who was trying to kill you. A man swung a flail, and I lashed him across the eyes with my bow, crouched, and body-blocked him into two others. That gave me a chance to draw my sword, and I sent one down, then saw another man drive a pitchfork at me. I shrank back, just as that peasant gasped and whirled, and Kutulu pulled a long dagger from his back. Kutulu was bleeding heavily from a slash along his ribs.

He shouted something to me, and a dirty-faced woman clubbed him to his knees. She pulled a butcher knife from her leather belt and was about to finish the warden when my sword took her head off. She fell on Kutulu, who went down and stayed there.

There were too many of them, pouring like the tide into the castle. I heard the shout. "Back. Back and re-form." The voice was Bikaner's, and other officers echoed the command. I parried a spear thrust, killed the spearman, grabbed Kutulu by the jacket, and dragged him backward into our keep. Three Kallians saw my helplessness, but Karjan and another Lancer came from nowhere and took them down.

"Stand clear," came a cry, and I heard the grating of iron plates and the huge portcullis dropped, spear points impaling an enormous woman swinging a pruning hook. Just behind the portcullis the iron-barred gates slid to, and it was quiet. But only for a moment, until the wails and shouts of our wounded rose. From outside came answering howls of rage.

Bikaner brushed blood from a gash across his forehead without knowing he'd done it. His breath came in gasps, and his sword was red to the hilt. "There's windows into th' court-yard," he began. "We'll put archers in 'em, drive th' bastards back from our gates. We'll reinforce th' gates with timber balks, and—"

"No," I said sharply. "They think they've got us pinned. They'll finish the others in the castle and then lay siege to us."

Bikaner thought, then nodded jerkily. "Aye. That's what they'll do."

"So we'll not do what they want, Domina. Drag the wounded out of the way and form the men for a charge. Right now. On foot, open ranks, Lancers in the lead, Hussars to follow. Make sure the men in the front ranks are wearing at least breastplates. And I want the buglers. All of 'em!"

"Yessir."

Other officers had gathered around. "You heard what I said," I ordered. "Make it so!" They, too, ran off.

There was no time to treat the wounded now. I saw Kutulu among them, lying motionless, and hoped that slut hadn't killed him. We'd been hit hard. There must've been thirty or forty men motionless, more who were wounded. But some were forcing themselves to their feet, and into the battle lines. Now the merciless discipline of the frontier regiments was paying off, denying men the right to moan or die.

I saw Marán at a balcony. She wore dark leather trousers and a vest, and held a small crossbow we'd used for target shooting. Beside her was one of her maids. She saw me looking up, waved, and pointed. I saw a Kallian sprawled faceup, with one of the weapon's foot-long shafts in his throat. Good! The Agramóntes may have been harsh, but they'd won their lands with courage and the sword, and their blood ran true in my wife.

Seer Sinait found me. "Now we know," she said.

We did. The magic that created the grand illusion of Kallians appearing to be Numantian soldiers had been cast by a master magician. It was now clear both Amboinas were wizards and the boy had been a mask for the older man's skills. There had been no leavings from the dead Mikael Yanthlus to cloud the emperor's and Sinait's powers, but a living master sage working in our own camp.

If we died this day, he would be able to continue his masquerade, claiming to be utterly loyal to the throne. Such reliability, when the emperor moved against the rebels, would place him close to Tenedos, and that would complete his plan.

It was a cunning scheme, indeed, and, if Landgrave Amboina were able to gain the emperor's confidence, the Kallians would need no support from outside. Far more than our lives was at stake here—the emperor and all Numantia was at risk!

"We surely do," I said. "Can you cast a spell against him?"

"I have two ready," she said. "But I'm afraid his powers are greater than mine. I'd prefer to wait and see if I can't produce a counterspell once I feel him out."

"As and when you decide. Magic isn't my province."

The soldiers had regrouped, and I ran to their front. "Lancers! Hussars! They fooled us once and think they've got us trapped. But now it's our turn to determine who's on which side of the trap.

"Soldiers," I cried to the men on the gate pulleys. "Lift the barriers! Buglers! The attack!"

The main courtyard was a scramble of madness. Inside the buildings shouts and screams of battle continued, but the mob outside were already rewarding themselves. A dozen were rolling barrels out of one of the stronghold's wineshops, and several of the casks were upended and smashed open. There were screaming women, clothes torn away, men holding them down as they ripped at their own garments. Kallians scurried around with every sort of loot.

They saw us then, a thousand strong, shouting defiance louder than our trumpets. There was a great wail of surprise and fear, and we smashed into them. Swords, axes, rose and fell, and arrows spat into the throng. Some fought, some ran, and again the courtyard was a boil of killing and slaughter. Kallians inside the buildings burst out, some trying to flee, more ready to fight on, and we obliged them. I shouted orders, and the Hussars broke away from the hand-to-hand melee and circled behind the mob—and we had them.

I heard something, a deep musical tone, except it reverberated through my very bones. The air shimmered and Molise Amboina grew from nothingness, rising full fifty feet against the sky. His hair and beard were wild, disheveled. There were bloodstains on his face, and his hands clawed into talons. He was no longer the smooth nobleman, but a murderous, deadly seer, a greater demon than any he could raise. His words in an unknown tongue boomed against the walls, and I thought the stones themselves might burst.

Arrows whipped toward and through him, but he paid no mind, as his hands moved back and forth, up and down, arms curling sinuously, and the onrushing mob were no longer human, but transformed into slithering, hissing serpents. They moved toward us, a tide of green, brown, and black. Amboina was sending the same spell against us used to destroy the justice column. I slashed one serpent in two, and it became a blood-soaked corpse, but there were dozens, hundreds, more. Some of us were fighting, but others were hesitating, about to flee. Men were down, serpents' fangs buried in their flesh. The Kallians hissed in glee and rushed us.

Wind roared, and I glanced back, my guts clenching, knowing Amboina had sent a second spell to complete our destruction. There was another huge figure in the courtyard, as tall as Amboina. But this one, I realized, was quite familiar.

When I was a boy, in my jungled province of Cimabue, we had a village rat catcher, since we were frequently troubled with the pests, particularly when the rains came and they sought shelter in the farmers' huts or even in the buildings of my family's estates. The rat catcher knew a few simple spells to drive the rats mad with fear and make them rush into the nearest water and drown themselves. Adults thought him not quite right, and perhaps it was so. But to children, he was a sort of hero. He always treated us as if we were equals, and delighted in taking us into the jungle, where he'd tell us to sit and be silent while he whistled. We never knew what sort of creature would come. Sometimes it would be a sambar, once it was a crocodile from the nearby stream, sometimes a family of voles, or a flight of birds would circle and land amid us, as if they were our friends. He told us never to touch them, for man's scent would make them outcasts to their brothers and sisters, but we should watch, and learn how they behaved, for we were all animals together, and who knew but the soul of a gentle marmot could be one of us, sent back from the Wheel to pay penance for evil in a previous life.

The rat catcher was my apparition. But none of us saw the same man, I found later. One saw a nursemaid, who chased away nightmares, another a shopkeeper who'd run off a dog that terrified him as a babe. Karjan said it was a peasant from the small holding next to his family's, who'd rushed into a pasture and saved him from an angry bull.

My rat catcher picked up one snake, which grew to be ten feet long. As he did, he seemed to pick up all the snakes. He lifted the long snake close, examined it as it hissed and twisted in his hand, then cast it away. But the reptile never landed; it vanished, with the others, and the cobblestones were bare.

Amboina roared in rage, hands moving differently as he chanted a spell. I felt weakness in my guts and heard the crash of great winds. The rat catcher stumbled back and put out a hand to steady himself. He winced as an invisible blow struck. He staggered, and I heard Lancers moan—we were doomed.

But the rat catcher straightened, and spoke, and when he spoke it was in Seer Sinait's soft voice:

"O little man
Full of hate
You have no law
You have no good
Is there one
Who speaks for you?"

The rat catcher paused, as if listening, though I heard nothing. Then he went on:

"A dying voice
A dead voice
That is the past

There is none
O man so small
I ask Aharhel
But there is none
Not Varum
Not Shahriya
Not Jacini
Not Elyot

Not Water
Not Fire
Not Earth
Not Air

There is no one

No one but She
I must not name Her
She will welcome you
She will shelter you
She will let you come to her
She will return you to the Wheel."

The rat catcher picked up Landgrave Molise Amboina between thumb and forefinger, and the magician was suddenly his normal size. Sinait's apparition held the Kallian close, examining him curiously, as if looking at an insect of an unknown species. Amboina cursed and flailed, but couldn't escape. The rat catcher cast him away. But Amboina didn't vanish; he whirled through the air and smashed on the cobblestones, his body exploding like a burst melon.

The Kallians held for a frozen moment, then a moan of despair went through them.

"On them," I bellowed. "Charge!"

My Numantians attacked. Only a handful of the Kallians tried to fight, and then mainly when they were trapped. Mostly they ran, clawing, overrunning one another looking for safety. We killed and we killed, and then, at last, there was no one left to kill.

I stood in a room I'd never been in before, somewhere deep in the castle, over the body of a man who'd tried to fight me with a saber he had no idea how to use, and I did not know how I'd gotten there. I made sure the man was dead, then found my way back into the central courtyard.

Captain Lasta, of my guard, came over and saluted. "We've secured the castle."

"Good," I said. "Now we must find Prince Reufern."

Lasta began to say something but stopped himself. "Come with me, sir."

Prince Reufern's body sprawled outside the entrance to his throne room. A sword lay not far from his hand and ringed around him were the corpses of five Kallians. Sinait and Domina Bikaner were beside me.

"He died bravely and well for a merchant," the domina said.

"He died well," I corrected. But words after this catastrophe were meaningless.

"Very well," the emperor said. His voice was calm, his face quiet as he stared up from the Seeing Bowl. "You will continue as Prince Regent in his place."

"Yes, sir."

"Whether more could, or should, have been done to preserve my brother's life is a matter for future times. I shall be sending full and complete orders, along with the necessary troops to enforce them.

"But here are three immediate tasks: You said the Amboina child, along with the others you captured when you killed the traitorous bastard's son, escaped in the chaos. I want all of them found and executed. I'll determine the manner and will send it with Kutulu's replacement. He will live, I assume?"

"So Seer Sinait has told me. He's still delirious from the blow to his head, but he'll return to normal in time. And the spell on his knife wound is already working."

"Take no chances with him," the emperor said. "The moment Kutulu can travel, I want him returned to Nicias. He'll have the best seers in the land to make sure his recovery is full and rapid.

"Now, to return to these miserable Kallians. They hurt me

deeply, and they must realize what they've done. I want your drum patrols to ride out once more. They'll be reinforced with infantry elements I'll be dispatching within a few days. I want two leaders in every hamlet, every village executed. If they cannot be found, or if the Kallians will not surrender them to you, twenty men and women are to be killed in their stead and the village put to the torch.

"My final order is for Polycittara, where the snakes had their lair. Polycittara will cease to exist. Its name will be stricken from all records. I shall dispatch special units of masons in time to tear stone from stone and sow the land itself with salt.

"As for its citizens, they are to be decimated. One in every ten—man, woman, child—is to be killed. The manner of their death does not matter. All others are to be sold as slaves. No family is to be left intact. Those once known as Polycittarans will be scattered to the corners of my kingdom, their names, their homeland forgotten.

"Those are your orders, Tribune Damastes á Cimabue. Now carry them out."

I had been expecting that the emperor would want to punish Kallio, but not this terribly. I took a deep breath.

"No, my emperor. I will not."

"What?" It was the hiss of the snake.

"Those are orders against the way of gods and men. I cannot obey."

"You swore an oath to me!"

"I swore an oath to you," I agreed. "My family's principle is 'We Hold True.' But your orders are evil, and come from the heart, not the head, and it's my duty to keep you from evil as best I can. You swore an oath of your own to rule wisely and well, and to never treat your subjects with cruelty. I placed the crown on your head when you said those words."

"I am the emperor, Tribune!"

"You *are* the emperor," I said. "I shall obey any wish you have, including killing myself if that's your desire. But not those commands. I am sorry, sir."

Veins pulsed at the emperor's temples, and his lips were a thin line. "Very well," he said. "If you will not obey me, I shall find someone who will. You are relieved of your duties, Tribune Damastes á Cimabue, and I order you to return immediately and directly to Nicias. You are to issue no orders of any nature to anyone formerly under your command, is that clear?"

"It is, sir."

The emperor's eyes gazed into mine, a black glare of demoniac intensity, then the Seeing Bowl was blank.

I was ruined.

SIX

The Water Palace

The nymph giggled lasciviously and dove into the seething pool. She swam to where the waterfall cascaded, then climbed the sheeting water as if it were a ladder. She was very lovely, very naked, and had white-blond hair. She also had Marán's face. Near the top of the waterfall the nymph stepped onto a half-hidden, moss-framed ledge. She crooked an inviting finger at me, then vanished behind the waterfall, into her cave.

The nymph, or rather the foot-tall sorcerous illusion, had been a present from Marán when we'd been married for two years, one time, and forty-two days. I'd asked the occasion, and she'd said "Just because." *Just because* seemed like an excellent tradition to establish, and so it was.

I sat on a stone bench, heedless of the drifting mist that cloaked the garden around me. The nymph's slightly bawdy antics, which never seemed to repeat, generally cheered me. But nothing changed my mood, which remained as dark, as empty, as the season.

We'd left Polycittara five days after I'd been relieved, as soon as Sinait decided Kutulu could travel.

Domina Bikaner assumed my duties as well as those of

the prince regent until a replacement arrived. He tried twice to bring up what had happened, but I refused to allow it. We were both soldiers, oathed to obey the lawful orders given us. He ordered the Red Lancers to escort Marán, my staff, and myself to Nicias. Once the capital was reached, I'd no longer be entitled to my bodyguards, nor any of the staff allowed by the emperor. Karjan, however, announced he'd remain in my service. I said that was impossible—he was carried on the rolls of the Ureyan Lancers and should return to the regiment and normal duties. "I said what I said," he told me. "Y'll have me as a so'jer or a deserter. I don't give a shit which." Once again Bikaner provided a solution. Karjan was detached for "special duties" to me.

Prince Reufern's corpse, held in a stasis spell, was wrapped in dark silks, and the black-draped hearse traveled at the head of our column, behind the point riders. Behind Reufern was the ambulance carrying the still only semiconscious Kutulu.

I'd intended to ride out without ceremony, to avoid embarrassment, but that wasn't possible. The Seventeenth Ureyan Lancers and the Tenth Hussars, in full dress, were drawn up in the main courtyard, and when Marán and I came down to our carriage, the men cheered as if we'd won a great victory, cheered and cheered again.

I swallowed hard, then went to Domina Bikaner and told him to call for a cheer for the emperor. His lips tightened, then he nodded and gave the order. The men obeyed, although I won't praise the lustiness of the response.

There was no one on the streets of Polycittara as our wagons and carriages went down toward the city gates. The Kallians were cowering indoors, awaiting the lash they knew was coming.

The fast river packet *Tauler*, a ship I'd been aboard in better times, was waiting at Entotto, its usually gay bunting replaced with black mourning. We were its only passengers. We carried Prince Reufern's corpse aboard and then sailed north, down the Latane River, for Nicias.

There was a great procession waiting at the docks in Nicias for the body of the emperor's brother, and the whole city was draped in black. As for Marán and myself—there was no one at all. There was no representative from the emperor, no honor guard such as a tribune was entitled to, none of the friends we'd thought we had.

We had two palaces in the city—the one on the waterfront that was Marán's, a family gift when she married her previous husband, and the enormous Water Palace granted me after I'd crowned Tenedos emperor. I was for going to our house, but Marán shook her head. "No," she said. "Perhaps they think they can shame us like this, but the sons of bitches can't take away what the emperor has given us! We'll go to the Water Palace!"

I didn't bother reminding her the "son of a bitch" was the emperor—Marán knew that full well, and if she wished to think otherwise, what mattered it?

The journey through the streets was eerie. All taverns were closed, and few people were abroad. Nicias is a city of lights, laughter, and music. But not now. As Tenedos mourned, so would his kingdom.

At first when we reached the Water Palace, I thought Marán had been right in her decision. Our staff was still at the sprawling manor and greeted us as eagerly as if we were returning heroes. If they'd heard of my disgrace, no one then or afterward gave any sign. But after a few days, I began to think Marán had been wrong.

The Water Palace is monstrously large. It was built for the amusement of the Rule of Ten. Water from the nearby Latane River was pumped into an artificial lake atop a great hill. The water coursed down in a hundred or more creeks and rivulets, over falls, up fountains, and into ponds, surrounded by huge gardens. The gardens were planted with many herbs, flowers, and trees, from the mountainous jungles near the Disputed Lands, to the hothouse orchids of Hermonassa, to the river plants of the Nician delta. Those that did not thrive naturally were kept alive by sorcerous spells, tricked into believing they were in their native land. Statuary was scattered throughout, in every style from sacred to eyebrow-raising profane.

The palace was always thronged with the beautiful ones of Numantia, eager to see and be seen. But now it appeared abandoned, the only people on its winding paths were servitors or gardeners keeping the grounds in their always perfect trim. Unpeopled, in this autumnal time, it was the ideal place for glooming.

Actually, this time was harder on Marán than on me. Disliking the vast country estates of the Agramóntes, she'd come to Nicias searching for knowledge, freedom, and new ways of thought. Since the Agramóntes were one of the most ancient, most respected of the aristocratic families, and Marán was both beautiful and witty, she'd become the talk of the town. Now, no one came to the Water Palace, and when she went calling, those she visited were out, or so their servants said, or the occasion was short, stiff, and formal. Even her dearest friend, Amiel, Countess Kalvedon, was supposedly away from the capital with her husband at one of her river estates. Marán wondered if Amiel had heard of our disgrace and turned away like the others. I said that was ridiculous—Amiel lived her own life, caring little about what others said or did. Marán looked skeptical.

I shared some of her hurt, not just for her sake, but for my own, for my warrior friends were also conspicuously absent. I wondered how much longer we'd remain in this gray world of nonexistence. A time? A year? Forever?

The nymph peered out and smiled. I smiled back, and suddenly realized how wet my ass was. A laugh came, not the tinkle of the nymph's invitation, but a harsh, grating sound. I was on my feet, hand reaching for a sword that wasn't there as a swarthy man stepped from behind a high ornamental fern. He had wild curls and beard and a nose that had been bent at birth and further mutilated in a dozen brawls. He was dressed like a border brigand. He had a sword sheathed on one side and, just behind it, a dagger.

"Ah, Cimabuean," he growled. "Sitting there feeling sorry for yourself, eh? Serves you damned well right, trusting kings and shit like that."

It was Yonge, perhaps the oddest tribune of all. He was a Kaiti, a mercenary guarding our embassy in Sayana when the Seer Tenedos and I met him. Like most hillmen, he was an instinctual killer, but unlike many, he knew how to command and, as importantly, how to follow.

"I heard none of your brothers-in-arms have the balls to pay a visit, for fear the never-to-be-sufficiently-kowtowed-to emperor might smack their little bottoms, eh? A long time ago, I said I wished to learn more of honor. Perhaps I've learned all there is to learn in Numantia. Perhaps it's time for me to return to my hills. What say you, Cimabuean? Perhaps you'll give up this shit, turn your back on Numantia, and become a proper warrior in my band?"

Yonge had chosen a hard way to learn about honor, marching with us on that terrible flight from Sayana, and then done this and that in Nicias, with some equally disreputable friends, until the Tovieti rose and Kallio rebelled. Then there was a place for his sly talents, and he took charge of the army's skirmishers. He was made general and then, after our victory over Chardin Sher, Tenedos named him one of the first tribunes.

Authority hadn't changed his ways. He'd been given a palace, as had the other tribunes, but refused it, not wanting anyone to think he was part of this damned tropic marsh that was Nicias. Sooner or later, he'd return to the mountains, he said. He lived in the barracks with his men, although he spent as little time under a roof as they did. The skirmishers were always in the field, if they weren't fighting bandits or on the frontiers.

When Yonge was in Nicias, he was a constant scandal. Why so many women were so fascinated with the rogue no one, least of all their husbands, fathers, or brothers, could fathom. He'd fought half a dozen duels without ever taking a serious wound, and now his loves went unchallenged, Nicians preferring horns to the funeral pyre. If he were anything other than the best, no doubt he would have been cashiered. But he was Yonge, and so served on.

The smile the nymph had brought to my face firmed and grew broader. As always, I was glad to see him. "Are you drunk?"

"I'm never drunk, Damastes. I'm just drinking."

"How'd you get into the palace? I do have guards, you know."

"Guards? I could wear a pink skirt, have drums and bugles, and walk past them without their dull cow eyes seeing me. Guards! Your brain is going! You need a drink!"

I took him to one of my libraries and bade him wait. He slumped onto a worked-leather couch, without regard for what his drenched garments would do, and said I'd best summon a bottle, for everyone knew a Man of the Hills grows cranky when denied his pleasures. I asked if he wished to clean up, and he said, "Why? I already bathed this year," and chortled happily. It would be a long evening.

I found Marán and asked, knowing the answer, if she wished to join us. She made polite noises. It wasn't that Marán disliked Yonge—I think he frightened her. She was comfortable in the presence of warriors. But as I said, Yonge was a simpler breed, a pure killer. She said she thought not, but she'd at least come in and say hello.

My majordomo, Erivan, brought a wire-sealed flask of Yonge's favorite tipple, the raw, clear brandy made from grape skins the Varans never exported, but let their peasants swill instead; and a bottle of chilled mineral water for me. A serving man carried a tray of pickled vegetables, several varieties of olives, goat cheeses, and tiny, burning-hot olives.

Yonge waited until the door closed, then growled, "Damastes, I do not like what is going on these days."

"I'm not very fond of it myself," I said.

"Everyone knows you were in the right in what you did. Don't look surprised. Of course what happened in Kallio's all over the army and everywhere else. It makes quite a story. I think our emperor's mind has gotten soft. Perhaps he can't think on anything but his inability to breed a baby emperor on anyone who comes close."

"Careful," I warned, knowing one and most likely several of my servants would be spying for Kutulu.

"Piss on care! I say the emperor is acting like he shat his brains out and is trying to think with an empty arse, and I'd say it to his face if he were here." Yonge was telling the truth. "An idiot," he went on, "or some kind of primitive asshole in the hills. Like Achim Fergana. You know he still holds the throne in Sayana?" Fergana was king in Kait and held the capital of Kait by cunning and violence. He was the one who'd forced us out of his city on the death trek through Sulem Pass.

Yonge saw the gleam in my eyes. "Now, there would be a task for a dozen, maybe two dozen, good men," he said. "The emperor won't know you're gone. Why don't you and I and some others slip across the border and call on Fergana? We would gain long-overdue revenge, and maybe even take the kingdom. Now, wouldn't that be a blow to that little magician you serve, if he had to treat you as a fellow monarch?" Yonge bellowed a humorless laugh. "Don't look so worried, Cimabuean. I know you'll hold to your oath, even if Tenedos lets you rot in this swamp you think is a palace."

He got up, tore off a piece of cheese, and stuffed it into his mouth while pouring another drink. "I said I didn't like what was happening, Damastes, and I meant more than just what the emperor is doing to you."

"Why? What's going on now? I've been busy lately."

"You should take a look at the flitter-tits who've joined his court. I've never seen a bigger pack of gold-plated fools who do nothing more than prattle the emperor's praises and try to pry into his treasury. What worries me is that they're succeeding." I remembered Kutulu saying much the same thing. "But more," Yonge went on, seeing my almost imperceptible nod. "Look at the army. Have you seen any of the new commanders? Nilt Safdur, for instance, who's now got your cavalry. A blowhard and a fool who could lose his way behind a plow horse. Tenedos will take an officer who's done no more than beat up a few bandits, and make him a general. Worse, he's named a dozen, maybe more, new tribunes from their ranks. I'd piss on 'em, but none of them are worth the water. They aren't like we are, Damastes."

"We" were the first six the emperor had named tribunes after Chardin Sher's defeat: myself; Yonge; Herne, whom I liked but little for his ambition, but respected for his ability; Cyrillos Linerges, a former ranker, a patriot who'd left the army to become a peddler, a man who led from the front and had been wounded many times; Mercia Petre, humorless, dedicated, a student of war who'd devised the reorganization of the Army that gave Tenedos victory over the Kallian rebels and his throne; and Myrus Le Balafre, a swordsman, a brawler, and the bravest of the brave.

There'd been others appointed in the years since, some I knew well, others only by reputation.

"What's he trying to do? Give more work to the gilt-makers?" Yonge complained. His voice dropped to a whisper. "I fear he is getting ready to go to war, and needs more sword-wavers to holler 'Charge' for him."

"I think both of us," Yonge went on, his voice still low, "know who it might be against." He shuddered, a grimace of real horror. "You've never seen what lies beyond Kait. Maisir goes on forever beyond my mountains. Forests you could lose all Dara in. Swamps with creatures—and the sorcerers who control them—such as none of us have ever dreamed of. Plains that go to the horizon so far away your eyes hurt trying to reach it. I fear, if that's where the emperor's dreams lie, we might all find our doom."

I hope I managed to cover, remembering the emperor's words: *Beyond the Disputed Lands lies the fate of Numantia.*

Yonge took an olive, then put it back and drained his glass. "Do you remember, Damastes," he said, seemingly irrelevantly, "after Dabormida, when I came to your tent, drunk?" I did. "Do you remember what I said? That I thought my men were thrown away, were slaughtered, for a reason I didn't know then—and don't know now?"

"Yes."

"Think on that, Damastes," he said, suddenly gloomy. "If we march south, march into those wastelands of that king, whatever his name is—"

"Bairan."

"Whatever . . . if we march against him, what will happen?"

"Tenedos will become emperor of both countries," I said firmly.

"Probably," Yonge said. "But where will you and I be? Bones, forgotten bones, scattered by the wolves of the desolation."

A dark wind whispered across my soul. I forced a laugh. "What else happens to soldiers?"

"Especially," Yonge said, "those who are fools enough to trust kings or seers. Double fools those who believe someone who is both!"

"I truly want to thank you for coming here, Yonge, and cheering me so thoroughly," I said sarcastically. Before Yonge could answer, there was a tap at the door and Marán entered.

"Ah, the beautiful one," the Kaiti said. "Your appearance is at a perfect moment, Countess."

"You've run out of brandy and want more."

"Well, not quite, but soon. No. It is time for us to talk about other things than war and such, and perhaps you'll lead the way."

Marán looked at Yonge skeptically, not sure he wasn't making fun of her, but she realized he was serious. She found the pull. When Erivan appeared, she told him what Yonge wanted and added, "And bring a bottle of the green Varan first spring pressing for me." She saw my lifted eyebrow. "Since none of my friends seem to think I'm worth visiting, the least

I can do is cultivate yours. Yonge, start by calling me by my name."

"Ah! That is good, Marán. You are right to want to be friends with men like myself. We are not only charming and handsome, but entirely trustworthy."

Marán grinned. "I've heard stories."

"Mostly lies. I shall tell you, Count— Marán, a Man of the Hills can be trusted in all ways, at all times, as long as there is not a woman, a horse, gold, pride, or plain boredom involved. Then no one can tell what might occur."

Marán laughed loudly, and I realized it was days since I'd heard that silver cascade of happiness.

Two days after that, Amiel rode up to the palace. She had, indeed, been away, and Marán's fears ill-founded. Countess Kalvedon was my age and very beautiful—tall, well built, with dancer's muscles and black hair cascading down about her shoulders. The two greeted each other and burst into tears, and I found business in my library, having, like most many men, not enough understanding of women to be skillful with their problems.

I found out what was wrong that night. Amiel and her husband had withdrawn from Nicias to deal with a problem—her husband, Pelso, was having an affair. I puzzled, since the two had an open marriage and went to bed with anyone who caught their fancy, with no guilt or blame. Marán told me, though, that their understanding was based on an agreement: They could take any lovers they wished, so long as the attraction was purely physical. Pelso had shattered the arrangement by falling in love with his current bed partner. She was the sister of the governor of Bala Hissar, a coastal province to the far west, and was unmarried, with a lineage almost as noble as the Kalvedons'.

Amiel and Pelso had spent two weeks together, the situation getting more and more grim, then had a blazing row. He'd returned to Nicias and gone straight to the other woman's apartments. Marán said Amiel tried to make light of what had happened, saying no doubt Pelso would come to his senses, and refused to talk about it any longer. They spent most of her visit trying to figure out what they could do to slap the faces of these Nician bastards who'd dropped Marán. I admired the woman, as I admire anyone who can set aside his own problem to help another.

Amiel became a very frequent visitor, often spending the night at the Water Palace. I thoroughly approved, since it seemed to help Marán's feelings. At any rate, her smile came back, and her wonderful laugh was no longer a stranger to me.

"Damned if I'd let a coward into my house like you're doing," Tribune Myrus Le Balafre growled.

"I'd hardly call you that, sir." Le Balafre had arrived at the Water Palace in a carriage quite fitting for him—a practical, high-wheeled vehicle like an ambulance that had been gold crusted and enameled. With him was his wife, Nechia, a quiet, rather plain, small woman, who looked as if she should be minding a sewing stall at a town fair.

Le Balafre had tied his own sash of rank around me when I'd been promoted to domina and given command of the Seventeenth Ureyan Lancers. He was a hard and brilliant general of infantry, who'd led the right wing of our army in the Kallian war and, since then, had led expeditionary forces against the always-raiding Men of the Hills.

"But I am," Le Balafre went on. "You came limping back into Nicias with your colors reversed, the emperor ignoring you, and what do I do? I listen to my gods-damned aides about how it'd be impolitic for me to go calling on you, for fear the emperor'd think it amiss. Fuck the emperor! I'm his servant, not his gods-damned slave!"

Marán looked shocked.

"Myrus," his wife said gently. "Such talk is not gentlemanly."

"Nor terribly safe," I added, trying to hold back a grin, remembering Yonge's snarl of a few nights before. The emperor's best followers didn't seem very good at bending their knee.

"Safe? Pah! Safe is not something I've worshiped in this life. Well, don't just stand there, young Tribune. If I'm not a craven, invite us in!"

In a few moments we were sitting in one of the solariums, looking out over a small wind-rippled lake, while servants fussed around serving small sweetmeats and herbal teas. Le Balafre drew me to one side, while Marán chatted with the tribune's wife, who busied herself with what I thought to be a sewing sampler.

"As I said, Damastes, I'm not proud of myself. Will you accept my apologies?"

"What is there to apologize for?" I lied. "I just thought you were busy."

"I am that," Le Balafre said. He waited until the servants withdrew. "As are we all. The emperor's built up the garrisons in Urey and Chalt, and he sent your friend Petre off to recon the pass into Kait half a time ago." That explained why I hadn't seen Mercia—I may have been the humorless strategician's only friend, and knew he wouldn't care a lout's curse for who was in or out of favor. "And we've got over five million men under arm or about to be sworn."

I whistled. That was more than double the number of troops we'd had at the height of the civil war against Kallio.

"But let me return to something I said earlier," Le Balafre went on. "About this matter of cowardice. I like it little that I hesitated before coming here. This army of ours has changed, Damastes. It's gotten so . . . so damned political! We might as well be speechifiers and arm wavers as soldiers."

I thought of my assignments over the last eight years, and how few of them had to do with real war or soldiering, even though most ended in blood. But the plowman is always the last to notice the spring flowers. "You're right," I said. "But I don't see how the army could be anything else than political."

"I don't follow."

"We put Tenedos on the throne, didn't we?"

"Better him than those idiots who drooled around it before!"

"Agreed," I said, very unsure of where I was going, since politics was always a mystery to me, "but I'm afraid, Myrus, our political virginity vanished when we stayed in Urgone after the fighting, and stood with him against the Rule of Ten."

"Perhaps you're right," Le Balafre said grudgingly.

"I think I am. Another thing. I remember what the army was like before Tenedos. I was with one of those gods-damned parade units here in Nicias when the Tovieti rose. Remember those days, when it mattered more how polished your helmet was and how well connected you were to some lard-assed aristocrat than how well you soldiered? Remember going to the field with the generals and their whores and aides and servants and cooks and bakers? Remember how we changed all that?"

"I don't think you've been around the army lately," Le Balafre said grimly. "At least not in Nicias."

I hadn't, of course.

"It's changed yet again, and this change is back to the bad old ways. There're a lot more parades these days, and more than a few spit-and-polish soldiers who do nothing but prance nobly about the streets and bang boot heels together guarding imperial offices that don't need guarding. Our emperor is getting very fond of flash and filigree," he went on. "As are the people he's got dancing attendance on him.

"Another thing," he said, looking at me carefully. "Did you know the emperor offered me your post in Kallio, after you refused his orders and he relieved you? You know what I told him? I said you'd done the only right thing, and I wasn't a butcher any more than you. He could name me to the post if he wished, but he'd have to relieve me even faster than he had you if he gave me the same orders. He got red in the face, then told me to go about my duties."

"Who ended up with the hot potato?" I asked.

"It wasn't a soldier. That warder of his, Kutulu, who's up

and about again, more's the pity, had him name somebody named Lany, who used to be chief warder for Nicias. Word has it he went out with very different orders than the ones you had, and is supposed to try to settle the situation, instead of slaughtering everybody in sight. Wonder who talked sense into the emperor. Sure as hells couldn't have been the Sleepless Snake, now could it?"

I'd never known Kutulu to feel mercy for anyone or anything.

"At any rate," Le Balafre said, "don't get your guts in an uproar about what's going on. The emperor's no fool. Sooner or later, he's bound to take his head out of his ass and realize you saved him from himself."

"I surely hope so," I said fervently.

At that moment, Marán squealed in delight, and Le Balafre and I craned to see. In Nechia's lap was a circlet about the dimensions of two hands joined at forefinger and thumb. But it wasn't a sampler, it was a living diorama of a forest scene. I saw a tiny tiger hiding behind brush, while three gaurs grazed, not aware of the lurking death, in the glade in the center. I peered more closely. Now I saw minuscule monkeys, silent, waiting for the drama to play out, and heard the chitter of unseen birds. "I . . . can only keep the spell going for a second more," Nechia said, and then all she held was a hoop with brown cloth attached to it. There were arcane symbols on the cloth, and, between them, tiny fragments of hair, fur, and leaves. "This is a new one," she said. "Our son's a wandering priest, and sends me things I might find of interest. He wrote me about witnessing this in his travels, and gathered a bit of tiger fur stuck on a thorn, monkey fur, mud where the gaur scraped against a tree, flowers, and so forth."

I was amazed. "It reminded me of things I've seen in the jungles beyond Cimabue," I said, suddenly homesick for my homeland.

"When I get the little spells stabilized," she went on, "then I cast another spell over the entire thing, and I can hang it on the wall, or in a cabinet, and whatever action I chose will repeat itself over and over. I have street scenes, some boating displays, but this is the first time I've tried to do something I've never actually seen. Of course," she said primly, "the tiger never gets the oxen. A monkey gives the alarm, and they run off before he can charge. He swats at the monkey, then pouts away."

I marveled again, as much at Nechia herself, who was the last person anyone would imagine as a tribune's wife; and Le Balafre's son, whom I'd never been told of and, if I had, wouldn't have imagined to be a mendicant priest. Truly, none of us are as we seem.

The evening went late, although from then on we talked about inconsequentia. After his visit, I allowed myself the hope Le Balafre was right and my banishment wouldn't last forever.

One visitor became thoroughly unwelcome shortly after arrival, a young domina named Obbia Trochu. He said he'd served under me, as a captain of the Lower Half, at Dabormida. I rather sheepishly confessed I didn't remember him at all. I've always admired those great leaders who, so the story goes, see someone on the street and remember the man as a private they once shared a meager meal with twenty years ago. Admired, but never quite believed . . .

At any rate, I invited him in and asked his business. He looked about mysteriously, then closed the doors to the study we were in. "I decided to call on you, Tribune, because I'm utterly appalled at how you've been treated."

"By the emperor?"

Trochu inclined his head slightly.

"Sir," I said coldly, "I don't think it's your—or my—place to question what the emperor chooses to do. Both of us have taken his oath."

"Meaning no disrespect, or insolence, sir, but you *did* question your orders, didn't you?" I didn't answer. He was right. "I represent a group of . . . of concerned citizens, shall we say. Perhaps some are in the army, perhaps more are among the best thinkers of Nicias and Numantia. We've followed what's happened to you very closely."

"For what reason?" I asked, a bit angrily.

"All of us are completely loyal to the emperor, of course, and were among the first to applaud when he took the throne. But we've become increasingly concerned with the events of the past two years or so."

"Oh?"

"At times it seems the emperor's policies aren't as clearly defined or carried out as they once were."

"I've not seen any hesitation," I said, thinking of how overquickly he'd moved in Kallio.

"Of course not," Trochu said smoothly. "You've been his strong right arm, very close to the events of the day. But sometimes, when people are a bit removed from the tear and turmoil, they can get a better perspective."

"True," I said.

"The group I represent believe it might be time to offer their services to the emperor, in the hopes he might see his way clear to letting them advise him. There is the old cliché about the more minds the better on a problem."

"There's also the one about the ship with too many captains," I retorted.

"I don't think that would be the problem in our case," Trochu said.

"What good would I be to such a group of great thinkers?" I allowed a bit of irony to creep in.

"Frankly," Trochu said, "most of us are not well known, and have spent little time in the public eye. We all know that, ultimately, the masses must have their idols—men to respect, men to follow. That is where you would be of service to Numantia."

I kept my expression bland, mildly interested. "Let me pose another question," I said. "Let us say your group decides a certain policy would be beneficial to the country, and then let us say the emperor violently disagrees. What then?"

"I would hope we would have the same courage you have, and stand up for what we know to be right for Numantia. There is the advantage to our group. You were but one man, so when you did what you did, the emperor could brush you aside easily. But if there were ten, a dozen, a hundred or more of the Empire's best standing firm . . ."

I was on my feet. Anger boiled within me, but I tried to hold it back as best I could, which was not very much. "Domina, you had better hold your tongue. I'll remind you once more of your oath. What you've just suggested is ignoble. You, I, all of us, exist to serve the emperor. Not to 'advise' him, not to override him if he happens to have his own plans. Your words smack of treason, and your own behavior is dishonorable. I must ask you to leave this house immediately and never appear in my presence again.

"Perhaps I should notify the proper authorities of you and your little group. Perhaps I shall not, for I mightily despise a tale-teller. I don't think the empire or emperor is in jeopardy from a pack of fools such as you, however. You remind me all too much of those yammering do-nothings I was proud to help the emperor overthrow.

"Now, get out of here, or I'll have you tossed into the street by my servants!"

Strangely, Trochu showed no sign of anger. He rose, bowed, and left unhurriedly. I fumed for a time, then, when I thought I'd calmed myself, I sought Marán and told her what had happened. She exploded, and I had to calm her, feeling my own anger return through her.

"That little rat bastard! We ought to call Kutulu's warders and report this pissheaded domina and his shitheels! The emperor's got enough troubles without having dungeaters like them plotting."

My wife was noble, but could swear as well as the hardest drill master. I repeated what I'd said to Trochu about not being, or liking, a tell-tale.

Marán's lips pursed. "I know," she said. "I don't, either. But this is different. This is the emperor!" She broke off and looked at me strangely. "Damastes, a thought just came. A very odd thought. I'll ask it slowly, so you don't get angry. Right now, the emperor is mad at you, correct? Maybe even wondering how loyal you are?" She waited, probably expecting me to snarl something.

"Go ahead" was all I said.

"Maybe you're wondering just as I am. If I were the emperor, and I had someone who's known as the Serpent Who Never Sleeps at my beck, someone who's supposedly got an agent in every tavern, eating place, and public spot in Numantia, and another agent to watch the first, would I maybe have my serpent send to see if my disgraced tribune could be tempted into foolishness?"

"Such as joining a conspiracy that really doesn't exist?" I said.

"Or maybe it does, but only to keep track of possible betrayers?" Marán said.

I shook my head, not in denial, but in perplexity. "I don't know, Marán. I just don't know."

"Nor I. But Laish Tenedos and Kutulu are more than subtle enough to come up with such a scheme."

"So what do we do about it? Even if he is a double agent, I still don't like the idea of informing."

"We'll have to think about it," she said.

But we didn't have to. The next morning Kutulu came calling.

He was even shyer than usual and clutched a paper-wrapped parcel as he perched on the edge of a leather couch. Marán greeted him, then said she'd join us later in the green study. That was a code between us—that particular room had a secret alcove with a spyhole, entered from the neighboring linen closet, and Marán and I used it when one or another of us wished to hear something our presence might prevent being said.

Kutulu refused refreshment and said that he could only stay a few minutes.

"I see your wounds have healed," I said.

"Yes, at least partially," he said. "I still have some stiffness in this side. But my brain has returned to working order. For a long time I kept going in and out of fogs, and wasn't able to remember things, and lost track of conversations. I think . . . I hope . . . that'll never happen again. My memory, being able to add things together, is my only real talent." He might have said weapon.

"It probably won't," I advised. "Most people think a clout on the head just knocks you out. In reality, it takes a while to come back to normal."

"Who did it to me?"

"Some woman, who then tried to cut your gullet."

"I hope you dealt with her."

"Cut off her head, in fact."

"Good. I'd wondered. I was told you dragged me back inside our keep, but no one said what happened to my assailant. That's why I'm here," he went on. "To thank you, once again, for saving my life. I suppose it's become a habit."

I was slightly astonished. "Kutulu, are you making a joke?"

"Oh. Yes. I suppose I did, didn't I?"

Now I really began laughing, and a smile came and went on his face.

"At any rate," I said, "it's certainly good to see you. And I'm quite surprised you're here."

"Why? You're one of my few friends. I'm just sorry I was laid up for such a long time. Why wouldn't I visit you?"

"For one thing, the emperor isn't thinking fondly of me."

"What of that? I know—and so does he, really—you're not a threat to the realm, in spite of your differences in Kallio."

"I wouldn't think he'd be pleased to see you visit anyone who's in disgrace."

"Perhaps not. But I didn't choose to serve a man who's ruled by his emotions. If the emperor uses a moment of logic, he'll dismiss the matter."

"Well . . ." I let my voice trail off, then slightly changed the subject. "Does he still have you chasing thus-far-invisible Maisirians?"

Kutulu frowned, nodded.

"And have you found any more evidence than you had before of King Bairan's evil plots?"

"None. But the emperor persists in his belief." Kutulu shook his head. "Now, does that make what I said a few minutes ago, about imperial logic, meaningless?"

"As you said once before, the emperor's mind moves in ways we're not privy to," I said.

"I did, didn't I?" Kutulu hesitated. "Actually, there was another, more important reason I came. And even though it's somewhat threatening, I think your wife should be aware of what I'm going to say."

I went to the door.

"Never mind," Kutulu said, with that wisp of a smile. "I'll call her."

He walked to the waterfall painting concealing the spyhole and spoke to it. "Countess Agramónte, would you join us?" There was a hiccup of surprise from behind the picture, and I turned red. Marán's face was even redder when she came into the room a few moments later.

Kutulu shook his head. "Why you should be embarrassed is quite beyond me. Why shouldn't you have, and use, a device such as that? I would."

"Because," Marán managed, "it's considered the height of rudeness to eavesdrop."

"Not in my world," Kutulu said. "Not in my profession. At any rate," he went on, "I don't know if Damastes told you that our friends the Tovieti are on the rise once more."

"No . . . Wait, yes he did." Marán remembered. "In Kallio. But I didn't pay much attention. We had . . . more pressing worries, as I recall."

"Well, they're as active now as they were when the emperor sent me to Polycittara," Kutulu said. "In fact, busier. That's what's worrying the emperor. He's had me drop my other concerns to concentrate on them, specifically whether they're being financed by Maisir." Maisir again! Kutulu saw my expression. "He's wondering if King Bairan is their paymaster, just as Chardin Sher was for a time. By the way, of course everything I'm saying must not be repeated. I haven't found any evidence yet. But it would be logical."

"I don't see why this pertains to us," I said.

"Two weeks ago, I arrested a cell leader, and she had greater knowledge of the organization and its plans than any one I'd interrogated before. She told me the Tovieti's offensive is divided into two prongs. The first, and longest-ranged, is to continue murdering in the hopes that the emperor will tighten the screws and enact repressive laws. That will anger the populace, the anger will feed off the repression—back and forth until there is another rising, which won't fail.

"Their second, more immediate plan is selective assassination of the emperor's leaders. I asked her for names, and she said the campaign was still being discussed. But she did say the Tovieti targets would be men like, and I'm quoting her precisely, 'that gods-damned yellow-haired devil Damastes the Fair, the one who rode us down before and helped the emperor slay Thak. He's one, and so's his, pardon me, countess, solid gold bitch of a wife.'"

"But . . . but why? Why us? Why me?" Marán said, trying to keep her voice from shaking.

"Because you're better, richer, smarter than they are, maybe? I don't know. Doesn't the peasant always hate his better?"

"Not necessarily," I said, remembering the peasants I'd labored with as a boy, not much richer and at least as hungry as they were.

"I wouldn't really know," Kutulu said. "My parents were shopkeepers, and I don't remember anyone hating us, or us hating anyone.

"But that's another matter. I thought I'd best warn you. I wish the emperor would change his opinion of you and restore your Red Lancers. This palace is hard to defend properly."

"We have watchmen."

Kutulu was about to say something, but I shook my head

slightly, and he kept silent. "Be careful, both of you," he said, instead. He got to his feet, then realized he was still clutching the parcel. "Oh. Yes. Here's a present. For both of you. No, please open it after I've left." He seemed in a hurry to leave, and we escorted him out. He had only two warders to escort him.

"Kutulu," I said, "perhaps I should return the warning. You're a finer target for those madmen than I."

"Of course," he said. "But who knows what I look like? Or remembers my face?"

"A question for you," I said. "Have you ever heard of a certain Domina Obbia Trochu?" I described him.

Kutulu's face blanked, and he furrowed his brow, as if in deep thought. "No," he said blandly. "I don't believe I have. Should I?"

"Not necessarily," I said dryly. "Not unless you want to."

Kutulu didn't ask for an explanation, but climbed into the saddle. "I really like your home," he said. "Perhaps, one day, if the emperor decides . . ." His voice trailed away. He tapped his horse's reins and went off down the winding road to the street beyond the gates.

"That is a truly odd little man," Marán said.

"He is," I agreed. "Shall we see what present an odd man buys?"

It was an expensively worked wooden box. Inside were a dozen differently scented bars of soap.

"Oh dear," Marán said. "Has he *no* social graces? I've known men challenged to a death duel for such an insult."

"Would *you* challenge the Serpent Who Never Sleeps?" I asked. "Besides, perhaps he's right. Maybe we do need a bath."

Marán eyed me. "I suspect you, sir, of having ulterior motives."

I rounded my eyes and tried to look innocent.

One of the more secluded parts of the Water Palace was a series of falls, ponds, and rapids running through small glades and mossy gardens. Some of the ponds were icy cold, others sent steam roiling into the chill night wind. All were lit with various-colored lamps, hidden in glass-fronted underwater alcoves.

"Why do we start up here, instead of where it's warm?" Marán said. "This is arctic!"

"Sybarite! Do you want to always do things the easy way?"

"Of course." Marán wore a soft cotton robe, and I had a towel around my waist.

"Ah, my love, you're *such* an ascetic sort," she murmured. "Here I am, freezing my tits off, and you have nothing but that towel." She opened her robe, and, indeed, her dark brown nipples were standing hard and firm. "See?"

I quickly bent and bit one. She squealed, then took a bar of Kutulu's soap from the pocket of her robe. She'd had one of her maids drive a hole in it, and tied a silk cord through the center. She hung the soap around her neck. "Now, you filthy creature, you'll have to work for your bath," and she dove into the pool. An instant later, she surfaced. "Shit, it's even colder in here than out there," she yelped.

I plunged after her. It was cold, as frigid as any stream cascading through a mountain valley in Urey. I surfaced, shivering and treading water, and slowly moving closer to her.

"Ah-ah. I see your treachery," she said and dove, swimming hard. I went after her, following the foam and the flail of her feet. I was reaching for her ankle when I realized she'd made it to one of the falls, and then the current took me and sent me tumbling over the lip. I fell five feet and splashed into another pond, this as warm as the other was cold.

I let myself drift to the bottom, then languidly swam back to the surface. Marán floated on her back, looking up at the sky. The hard diamonds of the stars shone down. The steam from the water twined white serpents around us.

"I guess . . . most times . . . this isn't that bad a world," she said softly.

"There could be worse," I agreed.

"Are we possibly doing something wrong?" she asked.

"Not yet."

"I'm serious. Maybe we shouldn't be mewed up, here, sulking as we've been since we got back from Kallio."

"That's what Yonge accused me of doing. Do you have a suggestion?"

"Well, the Time of Storms begins next week. Should we have a grand party? Invite everyone who's anyone—including the emperor?"

I thought for a moment. "I don't know. But that's one way to take the battle to the enemy."

"Let's try it, then. Stupid soldiers," she added. "They can't find any other analogy besides whacking people with swords."

"That's not true. I've got other whackers around."

"Oh?" She swam to me, and we kissed, friendly at first, then our tongues twined together. Finally I broke away, swam to a submerged rock, and sat on it, the water coming to mid-chest. Marán lazily followed, and put her head on my shoulder, the rest of her body floating.

"Sometimes we let the world be too much with us," I said.

"I know. I love you, Damastes."

"I love you, Marán."

Words that had been said again and again, but always sounded new.

"Come on," she said. "Otherwise we'll just sit here until we melt, and never get around to serious fucking."

I waded after her, then we slid down a narrow chute into a small lagoon, this one blood-warm with a mossy ledge, illuminated by small tapers. Marán handed me the soap, and I began lathering her, first her back, down her legs, then she turned, and I slowly soaped her stomach, her breasts. Her breathing came faster and she lay back on the moss, her legs parting.

I turned her on her side and put her right heel on my right shoulder. I soaped my cock, then slid it into her. She sighed, and I began moving, slowly, deeply inside her, as my hands caressed her soap-slippery breasts and back. She arced back and forth, her leg trying to pull me down on her.

She turned, until she was lying on her stomach, pillowed her face on her arms, and I bent over her, feeling her soft buttocks move against me, her feet on the ledge, pushing up, as we moved in a common rhythm, harder, faster, and the small tapers blossomed into twin suns.

SEVEN

THE YELLOW SILK CORD

The card read:

Dear Baron Damastes & Countess Agramónte,
My thanks for your gracious invitation. But pressing affairs of the greatest import will not allow me to attend your beguilement. My most sincere apologies.

T

Marán studied it carefully.

"Well?" I finally asked.

"I'm not sure," she said. "It's not good that he didn't refer to you as tribune or Damastes, but on the other hand it's good that he didn't call you Count, but used the title the state gave you, even though it was the Rule of Ten's actual doing. It's not good that it's a printed card, but it's good that he seems to have signed it himself." The emperor had recently begun signing his missives with a single initial. "But it's not good at all that he waited until two hours before the party before sending it."

I shook my head. These elaborate dictates of etiquette were quite beyond me.

"At least he didn't just ignore the invitation," Marán said thoughtfully. "But then I wouldn't expect him to ignore anything from any Agramónte. I guess we just wait, and see what comes next."

I felt several species of a fool, standing in the great hall of the Water Palace, flanked by stone-faced retainers in the Agramónte family livery of plush dark green coats and breeches, with vests of bright red whipcord, with gold buckles and buttons. I was in full dress uniform and decorations, but without arms.

Marán wore a white lace top, V-necked, with pearls worked into the fabric in a triangular pattern. Her skirt was flaring black silk, with black pearl panels in the same pattern. Her hair was coiled atop her head, and she wore a black lace headdress over it. She wore no jewelry except a necklace of precious stones, each a slightly different shade, the whole a dazzling color wheel. She looked about the grand ballroom, frowning.

"So far," she said, "it appears a disaster."

"It's early yet," I said. "Not much more than an hour after the time on the invitation. You taught me no one but a bumpkin, an ancient, or a fool ever materializes on time." Marán tried a smile, but it was a poor attempt. There were, so far, only a handful of people here, and those the sorts who'll attend any event, so long as they're given food and drink, plus the usual knot of hangers-on who judge an event by the prestige of who's putting it on, no more.

Amiel bustled up to Marán. Not knowing anything of the dressmaker's skills, I thought her dress was two garments in one. They both clung tightly to her dancer's body and were cut high at the neck and ankle. But if this makes Countess Kalvedon sound modestly clad, she was anything but. The first, inner dress, was made of deep red and clear silk. Over that was a sea-green and clear second garment, the clear patches almost but not quite congruent with the other. She wore nothing underneath them, and each time she moved a flash of tanned naked flesh glimmered. Like Marán, she shaved her sex, but unlike Marán she lightly rouged her nipples. In a different mood, and if she weren't my wife's friend, interesting thoughts might have come.

"Who did the illusion?" she said.

"Our own Seer Sinait," Marán said, a spark coming into her voice. "Isn't it marvelous?" It was. Marán had held to her idea of a party celebrating the beginning of the Time of Storms. The weather was cooperating, and a tropical monsoon had swirled down from the northern sea. To match it, Sinait had created a storm within the ballroom—drifting clouds, some dark with rain, others climbing high with the threat of great winds; occasional flashes of lightning and barely audible clashes of thunder. But this storm rode across the ballroom at waist level, so it was easy to imagine oneself a godling, or perhaps a manifestation of one of the greater gods, floating through the heavens.

"I especially like—" Amiel broke off as her husband, Pelso, came up. She smiled tightly, then excused herself for the punch bowl. It was most clear the two were here solely because of their liking for Marán and myself. If either had his preference, they would have been on the other side of the city, and perhaps the world, from each other.

Count Kalvedon bowed. "May I steal your wife, Damastes? *She* might be willing to dance with me." Without waiting for a response, he took Marán's hand and led her off. There were no more than half a dozen couples on the floor.

I decided anything was better than standing here, and found Seer Sinait, who wore her usual brown, but now her garb was hand-loomed lamb's wool. I danced with her, and complimented her spell. "I wish I could do something more," she said. "Such as cast some sort of spell that'd work on Nicias's lords and ladies as honey does for ants. I despise seeing your lady feeling as she does."

"So do I," I agreed. "Any suggestions?"

"My only one would involve a certain someone who's behaving like a spoiled brat, but I won't chance your vows by using his name."

"Thank you."

"Not at all."

I danced with two other women, then with Amiel. She danced well, as if we were one, and very closely. Pelso had disappeared, having made as much of an appearance as politeness required. "Pity that bastard left," she whispered.

"Ah?"

"If he were still here, maybe I'd try to make *him* jealous."

"How? With whom?"

"I don't know," she said. "Maybe with you. Remember, there's many in Nicias who think we had an affair anyway." Amiel, when I'd first fallen in love with Marán, had done us a wonderful service, acting as what she called an "apron," so everyone would think I was carrying on with her. "I could start dancing with you like . . . like this." She slid her leg between mine, and moved her hips back and forth. "Sooner or later, someone would notice."

"Stop that!"

"Why?" she said. "It feels good."

"Maybe too good," I said, feeling my cock stir a bit.

She laughed, a bit forcedly, but did as requested. "Poor Damastes," she said. "Madly in love with his wife, and a man who keeps his vows. You don't drink, you don't use any herbs . . . you two will probably end up being the longest-married in all Nicias."

"I hope so," I said.

"How utterly dull," Amiel said. "But I suppose we each have burdens to bear."

I admired her for trying to improve my mood, but it wasn't working. I was about to try some half-witted sally, when the orchestra finished a number. In the momentary hush a laugh brayed across the room. I didn't need to look to see if a donkey had wandered into the room. The laugh could only belong to Count Mijurtin, perhaps as useless a being as Saionji had ever let return from the Wheel.

At one time, his family had been among the noblest in

Nicias, even having two members on the Rule of Ten over the centuries. But that was long ago. Now the count was the only survivor of the line. He'd married a commoner—the rumor was his laundrywoman, to avoid having to pay her bill. The two lived in a few rooms of the family mansion that had once been in a fashionable part of Nicias, near the river, that was now a slum. The rest of the house was abandoned for the rats to glide among the rotting family memories.

Not that anyone ever felt pity for Mijurtin. He was arrogant enough to be an Agramónte, thought himself clever when he was merely rude, was a tale-teller and a false gossip. No one ever invited him to anything, but there he'd be, in the finery of ten years ago, from dusk until the last servant yawned him out at dawn.

His voice was as annoying as his laugh, and now it rasped across the room: "It's like the Wheel, don't you know. Last year, they were riding high, this year . . . Well, mayhap it'll teach a bit of humility." Mijurtin suddenly realized how his voice carried, and looked about wildly. In one of his hands, a biscuit dripped unnoticed sauce.

My temper snapped, but before I could stalk across the room Marán was there. Her face was white, set. "You. Get out. Get out now!" Mijurtin sputtered. I was halfway across the floor. He saw me coming, his eyes widened, and he squealed and ran like a terrified hog seeing a hunter.

The orchestra hastily began another melody, but Marán held up her hand and there was instant silence. "All of you. Out! The party's over!"

Marán, blind in her rage, took the white linen tablecloth under the punch bowl in both hands and pulled. That crystal bowl took two strong serving men to carry, but it weighed nothing against her anger, and the bowl skidded across the mahogany, crashed to the floor, and exploded. Red punch like blood shot across the polished wood dance floor, and the few guests scurried for their coats. The storm beyond could never match the one here.

Marán spun to the orchestra. "That's all! You can leave, too!" The musicians gathered their instruments.

Suddenly the thought came.

I held up my hand. "No," I said quietly, but my voice carried across the room. "Play 'River-Swirl, River-Turn.'"

That song was the one played by a luxury ferry's band the night Marán and I first made love. It had taken some gold, more work, and a great deal of listening to discover the name of the tune, but it had been worth it when I'd had it played at our first anniversary by the same nautical musicians.

The musicians looked at me awkwardly. One, then another began playing. Marán stood motionless next to the red pool. Servants with towels hovered nearby, but were reluctant to approach.

"Countess Agramónte," I said, "would you honor me with this dance?"

She said nothing, but slowly came into my arms. As we began to dance, I could hear the last guest hastening away; then there was nothing but the music and the scuff of our feet on the floor.

"I love you," I said.

The dam burst then, and Marán began sobbing uncontrollably against my chest. I picked her up, and she weighed nothing, and I carried her out of the ballroom and up the stairs to our bedroom. I pulled the coverlet back on our huge bed, laid her on it, and slowly removed her clothes. She lay motionless, her eyes fixed on mine. I undressed.

"Would you wish me to make love to you?" She made no reply, but lifted her legs and parted her thighs.

I knelt over her and ran my tongue in and out of her body. Her breathing came a little faster, but there was no other response. I kissed her breasts, then her lips. They were unmoving.

Not knowing what else to do, and barely aroused myself, I slid my cock into her. I might as well have been making love to a sleeping woman. I withdrew. She still said nothing, but rolled on her side, away from me, bringing her knees up almost to her chest.

I gently placed the comforter over her, then crawled into bed. Tentatively, I put one arm around her waist. She was motionless.

After a time, I suppose I slept.

I awoke, and it was close to dawn. Rain spattered on the window, and the room was cold. Marán was at a window, staring out. She was naked, and seemed not to feel the chill. Without turning, she sensed I was awake.

"Fuck them," she said quietly. "Fuck all of them. I—We don't need them."

"No."

"I've had enough," she said flatly. "I'm going back to Irrigon. Come with me or stay, whatever's your pleasure."

Somehow, that pronouncement seemed to calm Marán. She allowed me to lead her back to bed, and almost instantly went to sleep. But I could not. I lay awake until gray light illumined the room. Should I go with her to Irrigon, the great castle on the river that ran through the vast family estates? Anger grew at the thought. No! I'd not run from a fight or a battle yet, and wouldn't this time. I'd stay here, by Isa, by Vachan, by Tanis! Sooner or later the emperor would come to his senses. Sooner or later, he *must*.

I dressed and went down to eat. The servants must have worked the night through, for there was no sign whatever of the disastrous carouse.

Marán woke around noon, called for her servants, and ordered them to pack. She kissed me farewell hard, telling me I was a fool and I should come with her. But I didn't feel any sincerity in her words. Perhaps it would be well for us to be separate for a brief time. Perhaps she blamed me for what had happened.

I watched her carriage, and her outriders, vanish into the hard-blowing storm, and tried to convince myself these problems would quickly pass, and all would be as before. But my thoughts were hollow, and my heart was as empty as the palace.

* * *

I thought of writing Tenedos directly, requesting a meeting, a hearing if he wished. I tried composing the note, but threw half a dozen drafts away. My father had taught me the soldier's old credo: Don't complain, don't explain. So I wrote nothing.

I did not, however, sit sulking. Since boredom is such a large part of a soldier's lot, it's good there are hundreds of ways for him to stay busy. One of the less comfortable realizations I had in Kallio was how poor a shape I was in. So I rose an hour before dawn, did setting up exercises, then ran for another hour. I breakfasted on fruit and grain, then took instruction in one or another fighting skill for another hour—bow, spear, club, dagger, sword, it mattered not. Karjan, grumbling, trained with me.

Then I went to my study, laid out maps of famous battles, and refought them, generally from the side of the loser. I hated this, just as I hate most exercises that stretch the brain more than the body, but if I was in fact still a tribune, I'd better be able to think like one.

My midday meal would be meat, barely cooked, or fish, frequently raw, and green vegetables from one of my greenhouses. After lunch, I'd saddle either Lucan or Rabbit and ride for an hour or two, out from the Water Palace to Manco Heath, where I allowed my mount a gallop. The pounding of the hooves cleared my brain and took my thoughts away from my troubles. At dusk, I'd swim for an hour, then have a simple dinner—bread, cheese, and pickled vegetables my general choice. I would go for a walk to digest, then to bed.

If I'd worked hard enough, sleep came. But all too often I'd toss and turn for hours. I'd never had trouble sleeping before, and in fact was proud that like any good cavalryman I could sleep anywhere, including the saddle. I was desperately lonely, but couldn't bring myself to flee to Irrigon. Not yet.

Several weeks passed like this. I had visitors—Yonge twice, Kutulu once, then a stranger.

Erivan, my majordomo, came and said Baron Khwaja Sala awaited my pleasure. Most people think a majordomo holds his position because of his ability to run a great household without his employers being aware of his silent, efficient mechanisms; plus an appropriate cold arrogance toward the unwanted. But there's a third, most important talent: knowledge of almost everything. If a guest wishes a certain exotic fruit from his homeland, the majordomo should know which marketplace might have the item. As a better example, he should have known who in the hells this strangely named baron was.

"He is the Maisirian ambassador to the court of the emperor." I raised an eyebrow, not afraid of showing ignorance, or any other failing, to a man who probably knew my weaknesses better than I. "He refused to state his business, sir."

"Please take him to the green study, see if he requires refreshment, and tell him I'll be there shortly."

That would make it easier for Kutulu's still-unknown agent to spy on us, since I had no intent of meeting with any Maisirian without witnesses.

"Very good, sir."

"Do you know anything more of the man?"

"I only know that he has the reputation of being one of King Bairan's shrewdest counselors, and reputedly is his closest adviser."

"I see," I said, although I certainly didn't, and thoughtfully made my way to the study.

Baron Sala was tall, almost as tall as I, in his sixties and very slender. He wore long mustaches and had the most sorrowful eyes, as if he'd seen every evil, every bit of duplicity the world could offer, and nothing could surprise him any longer. Once the amenities were finished, I asked why he'd come.

"I am representing not only my king, but our army's high command," he said. "One of the earliest posts you held was in the Kingdom of Kait when the Seer Tenedos was the Rule of Ten's ambassador there, am I not correct?"

"Such is common knowledge."

"My master and his officers need to know *everything* you remember about Kait. Those bandits raid south into Maisir as often as they trouble Numantia, and it's King Bairan's mind to put an end to their nonsense for good and all. That's why he requested I visit you and inquire about your interest in bringing peace."

"What form," I asked, "would King Bairan like this advice in? I'm neither a historian nor a scribe, and for me to labor out an account of what happened, let alone the 'everything' he evidently wishes . . . well, we could both be quite aged before the work is complete."

The baron smiled. "Such was my thought when the courier arrived with my lord's wishes, and so I requested further elaboration. Ideally, he would be delighted if you could somehow attend a conference with our high command on the problem."

"Where? In Maisir?"

"I doubt," Sala said dryly, "if your emperor would be thrilled to have an enclave of our generals arrive here in Nicias."

"Let's begin with the easiest of problems," I asked. "How would I get to Maisir? The commonest route lies through Kait, and since that murderous bastard Achim Baber Fergana still sits the throne in Sayana, and would be delighted to see me, preferably impaled on a stake, I doubt that's a feasible route."

"That, as you said, is the easiest of problems. There is a longer route that your army already knows of, that goes through Kallio and crosses into one of the other Border States. It's desert, and there are bandits, but it's passable for small units, if long abandoned. We could have a contingent of Negaret—those are the soldiers who patrol what we call the Wild Country—meet you at the border."

"That's one problem solved," I said. "Now let's address a bigger one. Do you think the emperor would allow one of his tribunes to travel abroad?"

"I don't know. But, if I may speak frankly, I understand your star is a bit dimmed in the emperor's eyes, so he might not object too strongly. I could make subtle inquiries, if you're interested."

There were advantages to the idea, not the least being I'd be out of this beautiful trap of a palace and away from the whispers and snickers accompanying any nobleman's fall. It would also give me time to puzzle out just what was going wrong between Marán and myself and determine what I should do to change.

To take the field, to be away from all of these words and buildings, into the hard, clean wilderness and the company of men who said and lived what they believed . . . I smiled a bit wistfully. The baron looked politely inquiring.

"I was just thinking," I said, "how I envy your officers and your prospective campaign. There is a grudge between myself and the Achim Fergana I'd like to resolve."

"That *is* interesting," the baron said. "King Bairan added a note that the ideal solution would be for you to join our campaign. We'd arrange proper recompense, both for you and the emperor, since he'd be deprived of your services for, oh, perhaps a year, perhaps longer, and of course you'd serve at your present level of authority, perhaps as a rauri, a commander of the advance guard."

"That's an idea I can't even think of. In fact," I said, "I'm probably coming very close to violating the spirit of my oath in discussing the matter at all."

"My apologies," the baron said, rising. "I'm very glad I took the time to meet you, Damastes. I expected little to come of this, and was a bit afraid you might be angered. I'm delighted you're at the least interested. Should I request an audience with Emperor Tenedos?"

"Not yet," I said. "I've got to consider things most carefully."

"I surely understand that," Sala said. "I'll wait until I hear further from you before taking any action. Feel free to discuss this with your wife and fellows. We don't want anyone to think King Bairan is considering anything even vaguely unacceptable to your emperor."

"Of course not."

After Baron Sala left, I went into the green study's spy chamber, to see, from simple curiosity, who Kutulu's man—or woman—was. The chamber was empty, although I touched my hand to the wood around the spyhole, and found it warm, as if someone's forehead had pressed against it.

I went to my library and made notes of exactly what had happened, word for word, while it was still fresh. Then I took out a fresh sheet of stationery:

> *To the emperor Laish Tenedos, and for his attention only.*
> *From his Most Loyal Servant, Tribune Damastes á Cimabue.*
>
> *Sir, I greet you, and offer my deepest respects. I am reporting on a meeting that took place this day between the Maisirian ambassador, Baron Khwaja Sala, and myself . . .*

Since I'm hardly a master of the written word, and wanted my report to the emperor to be precise, it was late when I sent my report off to the palace. I thought of eating, but wasn't hungry, my mind a roiling mass of questions and wonderments. I drank a glass of warm milk, hoping it would make me sleepy, but it didn't.

I listened to the wind roar across the treetops of the palace grounds, and watched the lashing branches, then decided I'd lie down, and perhaps the proximity of pillows, soft cotton sheets, and warm blankets would bring solace, though I knew I was deluding myself and rest would be a long time coming this night.

Sleeplessness saved my life.

The man should have killed me the quickest way he could. I'd been taught the fine art of killing an enemy with any tool that presented itself. The teacher, a scarred infantry color-sergeant, said too many soldiers fall in love with a single weapon. It could be a particular sword, or even a style of weaponry, and truthfully I've known men who nearly panicked if they were told to use a spear instead of their favored saber, or a dagger instead of an ax.

The man used the wind's blast to cover his springing the window catch of my bedroom. Barely opening the window, he slipped inside. If he'd had a sword, knife, or even a throwing-dart, and attacked the moment he found his footing, I should have died. Instead, he took the long yellow silk cord from around his neck, the cord the Tovieti stranglers loved, and crept toward the lump under the bedclothes.

He had had a second to realize the lump was nothing but hastily bundled pillows when I came from behind, hands clenched, smashing sideways across on the nape of his neck with all my strength. He contorted backward against me, and I smelt his bowels emptying as he died.

I spun out of the way, toward where my sword belt hung, and saved my life a second time, for I hadn't seen the strangler's backup come into the room. She was very good, slender blade burning across my ribs. She recovered and jump-lunged toward the naked man in front of her.

She was good, she was fast, perhaps faster than I, but she wasn't a back-alley brawler, rather she was used to the refinements of the fighting school. She yelped as I kicked a chair into her, sending her stumbling. Then she heard the dry whisper as my sword came out of its sheath. I lunged, and she parried. We both recovered, circling, eyes and minds on nothing but our blades, which reflected the flickering light from wind-blown torches outside.

I heard, but didn't let myself to respond, shouts, screams, crashing, coming from other places in the palace.

Circling, circling. Her blade darted, and I smashed it aside and struck, pinking her thigh above her knee. She grunted and flicked her sword's point at my eyes, and I barely ducked back.

She stamp-lunged forward, and I went low, under her thrust, and was nearly spitted for my bravado.

Again we parried, moving back, forth, looking for the opening. I heard her muttering, paid no mind. Her silhouette shimmered, and I realized magic was in the arena. She wavered, almost became invisible, and I snapped her concentration with a high cut toward her head. The spell broke, and I faced a solid, slender figure once more, moving, always moving.

She dropped her guard, but I was too wise, ignoring the feint and lunging under her blade, her guard, and I felt resistance as my sword slid into her chest, just under her rib cage. The woman said "Oh," in a mildly shocked voice, and dropped her sword. It clattered on the floor. I freed my blade.

She touched a hand to her side, lifted it, and even in the dimness we could both see the blood staining her fingers. She said "Oh" once more, but this time as if she had finally understood something obvious, and there was no strength in her knees, her legs—they buckled. Before her body thudded to the floor, Saionji had taken her back to the Wheel.

Another window smashed, and two men, both wearing black, jumped into the room. They saw me, shouted, and ran forward. Both were armed with short stabbing spears. I brushed one spear aside with my blade, and shoulder-blocked that man into his mate. They stumbled backward, flailing, and I ran the first through.

A door crashed open behind me, and I thought I was doomed, but had no time for anything but the man with the spear. He died with my blade through an eye, and I pulled my sword out, spinning toward the new threat, but too late, too late . . .

Karjan was there, saber in hand, and flanking him were half a dozen others from my household, armed with everything from candlesticks to a seaman's cutlass I'd never seen before. "Fucking Tovieti," he shouted.

"How many?" I forced calm.

"Hells if I know," he panted. "We must've killed four, five on th' stairs comin' up here, sir. Dunno how many others there are."

"We'll fall back on the armory," I decided. There'd be proper weapons there, and the barred room would be easy to fight from. I grabbed the ring of keys from where it hung on my wall, and we went into the corridor. There were four bodies there, and at the stairs were Erivan and another servant. Shouts came from behind, and I realized there must be more attackers coming through my bedroom window. "Go on," I ordered. "I'll hold them here for a moment."

"I'll fight here with you," Erivan said.

Karjan started to object, and I shouted, "Go on, man! We've got to have a rally point!" He nodded, and he and the others clattered down the steps.

There was only Erivan and me. He was armed with an ancient sword pulled from one of the displays hanging along the hall. "Now we'll see what they're worth," I said.

"We will," he said, and I heard a strange note of glee, strange for a man who wasn't supposed to have any of the bloodlust of a warrior. I glanced at the bedroom door, to see how many Tovieti we'd face, but saw no one. As I realized more magic had been spun, a yellow silk noose came about my throat, tightened, and I smelt Erivan's clove-scented breath hot against my ear as he throttled me.

The best way to successfully strangle an alert man is to use a very thin garrote, perhaps a wire. This will either crush or cut through the windpipe, and the victim will fall unconscious and die quickly. But the Tovieti loved their sacramental cord, nearly as thick as my finger, and the way it killed slowly, letting the red grasp of death gradually close on its prey.

I was vigilant, trained, and strong. Erivan should have yanked the cord tight about my throat, then turned his back and pulled, cord over his shoulder as if he were trying to lift me, as a laborer shoulders a sack of grain.

My fist smashed back like a hammer into his groin. He wanted to scream, but his wind was gone, keening like the tempest outside. I turned, inside his guard, not wanting my sword, rage at his betrayal shaking me as a terrier shakes a rat, wanting his death with my claws, my fangs, and I drove my fists into his ribs, his guts.

He stumbled backward against the balustrade. He was a big man, almost as big as I am, but I felt no strain as I picked him up by the belt and hair and bent him back over the railing. His face was close to mine, eyes wide in terror, and then I snapped his spine like a twig, and let him drop away, down the stairs, pinwheeling lifelessly like a rag doll a child tosses away.

I had my sword in hand and went down the stairs, looking for Karjan. Now we'd arm ourselves and hunt the Tovieti as if we were hounds, hunt them to their death. I heard cries from outside, shouted orders, the clatter of running feet, and guessed the Tovieti knew their trap had snapped empty, and now it was their turn to die.

It was. It took only a few moments to pass out weapons and divide my men and not a few women, angry as any at the invasion of their home, into teams.

As we burst into the drive, a company of cavalry, hard, battle-scarred men of the emperor's bodyguard, galloped to the palace, and their captain said the company was to obey any orders I gave.

Within the hour several companies of Kutulu's uniformed wardens reported. The grounds were sealed and surrounded and they were at my command.

We went systematically from room to room, building to building. My orders were simple: Kill them all. Perhaps I should have ordered a few prisoners to be taken, but I was as enraged as any of my servants, the sanctity of my refuge despoiled. Besides, I somehow knew the two leaders of the attack had been the woman who almost killed me and the traitorous Erivan.

We found only four Tovieti—one woman, three men, cowering in nooks. They died, and their bodies were dragged into the central drive in front of the main house with the others who'd died, in the first attack. None of us felt the wind or the rain that lashed down.

The storm died as dawn came, a gray, sodden, sunless time. There were fourteen bodies on the cobbles, and another nineteen of my own people, whose corpses were handled gently, carefully, laid with honor on the great tables of the main hall. They'd died in my defense—and, ultimately, the defense of Numantia—as bravely as any soldier on any battlefield. Their bodies would be burned with the greatest ceremony and I'd make many sacrifices to Saionji, to the gods of Nicias, and to their own gods and godlets if they were known, hoping the Destroyer and the Creator goddess would give them great advancement in their next life.

I heard more horses and saw a second group of cavalry, again from the emperor's bodyguard, ride through the palace gates. Behind them were four long black carriages with tiny window slits, no doubt intended to carry any Tovieti prisoners. They'd return to the dungeons empty.

At the front of the riders were Kutulu and someone I vaguely recognized as one of my servants, a woman I'd thought barely smart enough to handle her duties as a candle trimmer. Even in my grief and rage, I reminded myself yet again to never judge someone by his or her expression or behavior, and I knew Kutulu must've enjoyed giving her orders to play the dunce. Now she looked as she was in fact, a keen-eyed, sharp-witted police agent, and she half-smiled when I nodded to her. I wasn't angry, felt no betrayal—Kutulu and the emperor spied on everyone. Besides, it had obviously been she who'd gone for help.

"Good morning, my friend," Kutulu said. "I'm happy you're alive."

"As am I."

He dismounted carefully. "One of these days," he said, "I shall find a way to never ride a horse again. Murderous beasts!" The horse nickered as if it had understood him. Kutulu went down the row of bodies, staring carefully at each face, memorizing it. Four times he nodded, recognizing, even in twisted death, whom he was looking at. He came back and drew me aside. "Fascinating," he said. "Some of them I knew."

"I thought so."

"One was a criminal, a man who specialized in stealing jewels from the houses of the rich. I suppose he showed the others how to gain entry to your palace.

"But the others are—were more interesting. They were longtime apostates. They hated the Rule of Ten and have managed to transfer their treason to the emperor. All were from reputable, if dissident, families.

"You know, if they weren't traitors, you might almost respect them for their dedication to a cause."

"Fuck them," I snarled. "I don't respect anyone who tries to stab me in the back."

Kutulu shrugged. "Would you have them put on a uniform and propose open battle? That would be foolish, and the Tovieti aren't fools."

He was right, but I was in no mood to think logically.

"Now, Tribune Damastes á Cimabue," Kutulu said, suddenly formal, "it is my duty to issue the following order, which has been approved by the emperor: You are directed to leave this palace as quickly as it's possible to gather your belongings."

I felt as if I'd been sandbagged. Nearly murdered, and now the emperor chooses to disgrace me still further by ordering me out of this palace I'd been given? It was his right, but hardly honorable. Again, hard rage grew within me.

A voice came: "That is my personal order, Tribune, and must quickly be obeyed." I spun and saw, standing in the doorway of one of the carriages, the emperor, Laish Tenedos!

There was a gasp from my servitors, and a rustle as they knelt. I bowed low.

"Stand, Damastes, my friend," he said, and now my surprise was greater than any of my servants'. "We gave this order," the emperor went on, "because you are the best and most trusted of all my servants, and I can little afford to be without your services, especially in these troubled times." So my disgrace was ended. "Come, Tribune," he ordered. "Walk with me to the garden. We have matters to discuss."

I obeyed, rather numbly. Tenedos waited until we were out of everyone's earshot and had passed through a gate into one of my smaller glades, then said, calmly, "As I said, these are perilous times."

"I think last night brought that to my attention," I managed to say.

The corner of his mouth quirked. "Indeed. First, as to this matter of the palace. Kutulu said he warned you about its indefensibility before, and I think the Tovieti proved it rather thoroughly. When we've taken care of them completely, you may, of course, return. I intend to wipe them out to the last man and woman, and then extirpate all record they ever existed. Their treacherous heresy must not be allowed to propagate itself, even in dusty tomes only scholars consult. But there's a greater enemy to deal with first."

"Maisir?"

"Of course. There have been some . . . unusual incidents on our borders. There've been reports of Maisirian patrols crossing through the Border States and spying on our outposts, and also that spies and saboteurs have been entering Urey and moving north toward Nicias. As yet, Kutulu hasn't been able to arrest any of these Maisirian agents, but I'm sure he'll be successful, and then we'll find out exactly what King Bairan's plans are.

"I was impressed by his attempts to hire you away. I read your report this morning, immediately after hearing the news of the attack. Needless to say, I knew you'd penetrate Baron Sala's words and find the true meaning—that he wishes you, and your ability and popularity, out of the equation in the days to come."

"Thank you, sir," I said. "Much as I'd like to deal with that damned Fergana, things didn't feel right."

"I admire you, Damastes, and your absolute oath of loyalty."

"It keeps life simpler, sir."

Tenedos chuckled. "And it's been exceedingly complicated lately, hasn't it?" That was as much as he ever said in the way of apology for my and Marán's humiliation.

"Yes, sir."

"Now, on to the future. I was not speaking idly when I said I have a great task."

"Which is?"

"I'm not sure of the precise posting. But I want you to go somewhere safe . . . perhaps your wife's estates. I doubt if any Tovieti has courage enough to intrude on the Agramónte lands."

"Yes, sir."

"Those other carriages contain papers, maps, and reports I want you to be familiar with. All of them deal with Maisir. Let no one else read them or even know of their existence. Study the documents well, for they'll be the greatest weapon you'll have in the days to come. For Maisir is a mighty enemy, the greatest Numantia has ever faced."

"You're saying war is inevitable?"

The emperor looked somber. "I fear so. And if it happens, Saionji will be given blood sacrifices beyond even a goddess's dreams."

EIGHT

IRRIGON

I almost didn't spot the two faces peering through the brush, but a soldier's eye, like a hunter's, is trained to catch any movement. The men were bearded and wore crudely tanned conical leather caps with ties. I clicked my tongue, and Karjan, dozing in his saddle, snapped awake. I thought they were hunters, but the way they reacted suggested otherwise. One moment they were there, the next the leafy spaces between the brush were empty.

I gigged Lucan into the brush and up the slight hillside as my escort belatedly came alert. The two men were running hard, dodging from tree to tree, toward a low butte. They were armed, one with a bow, the other with a short stabbing spear. I saw the flash of a sword at one's waist. No one hunts anything, not even tigers, with a sword.

Karjan was beside me. "Take them," I snapped, and we kicked our horses into a full gallop, drawing our swords. Branches whipped, and we ducked behind our horse's necks. We were closing, less than thirty yards distant, when the two dove into a thicket. I pulled Lucan up, slid from the saddle, and pushed after them. Possibly I was foolhardy, but I doubted they were bait for an ambush.

The thicket grew out of the side of the butte, cracked gray stone that rose almost sheer. Nothing. The two had vanished. Karjan was beside me, blade ready. I nodded left, and Karjan slipped over. We needed no orders or discussion—we'd gone into cover after armed men many times, and the skills were pure muscle reflex. We close-combed the thicket and around it, but found nothing. We clambered to the top of the butte. By then, the rest of the Red Lancers had ridden up and were helping.

No one found anything—not the men, not their footsteps, not a single trace of anyone having ever trod this soil. I heard someone whisper, "Magic." So it might have been. Or merely that the men knew this ground and had an escape route that left no traces.

We remounted and returned to the road. An hour later, the road from Nicias came to the Penally River and followed the curvings of the windswept water. We were only a few miles from Irrigon. Irrigon and Marán.

Irrigon sat like a mailed fist across the lands the Agramóntes had ruled for generations. It was built as a fighting stronghold on the rocks above the Penally River, which secured two sides of the castle. It was five stories tall, and the roof was machicolated. On the roof remained hearthstones and iron cook pots for the oil the lords of Irrigon used for a last resort in primitive times. There were two four-sided towers on the river side, and a large round tower on each of the landward faces of the structure. In front of one tower spread a verdant park, and scattered not far from the other were outbuildings and stables, while the road meandered on toward the nearby village.

Irrigon had been given to Marán when her father passed away, which technically meant it was mine as well. However, I never felt comfortable in or near the brooding stones, and once thought on the matter, wondering if I were foolish enough to be jealous of Marán's wealth, far greater than even the Tovieti riches the Emperor Tenedos and his tiny demon had given me.

I decided I wasn't. I was all too aware there'd been too much force wielded by the Agramóntes over the centuries, too much usurpation of others' Irisu-granted rights in casual arrogance. I noted the ways the peasants looked at their masters—Marán's two brothers and the lesser if still mighty members of the family—hiding both terror and hatred. Only Marán was granted honest respect, although I thought it was wary, as if the workers were waiting for her to become like the others.

If I always felt a bit on edge at Irrigon, it had been worse when her father was alive, and almost as bad when her brothers, Praen and Mamin, visited. Fortunately they had their own manors a day or more away and spent little time at the family seat.

I once wondered if they felt the dark resonance of the blood and tyranny, but I was utterly foolish. The two were utterly unconcerned for anything but their own wishes. It took very little time to understand why Marán had fled to Nicias. The Agramónte men, and the other country noblemen I'd met, weren't dumb, but they had no interest in anything that didn't directly concern them. Their women and children took that behavior as a guide.

Realizing the two brothers were thick as rocks, I then embraced the obvious: They didn't like Irrigon because it was a dank, depressing fortress that would've made a good prison. As new owners of Irrigon, we should have had the lord's quarters, but we viewed that prospect with horror. Marán said it would feel incestuous, and I that countless generations of Agramóntes would be hanging over our shoulders, clucking in shock and dismay when they noted Marán and I liked to disport in original ways.

We took a tower on the river side for our own. The stone walls were fifteen feet thick, with never an iron bar or brace to be seen. Supposedly these towers had been built with wizardly assistance and the finest stonecutters in Numantia. The rooms were old-fashioned, tiny, with high ceilings. The windows were arched, coming together in a gentle V. We had the old, discolored, warped glass removed, and double layers of cleverly stained and tinted panes installed. Each pair of windows was connected with cunning rods and levers to open easily.

We decided on the upper floors for our living quarters, the lower ones for a warming kitchen, storerooms, and a tiny armory. Masons smashed through stone walls, keeping only the ceiling arches to maintain the building's innate integrity, and turned twenty or more rabbit-warren rooms into half a dozen spacious chambers. We had false walls built of wood, and the six inches or so between the walls and the stone filled with woolen yardage. Everyone thought this was odd, but I thought if wool around my body kept me warm, why wouldn't it do the same for a room? I was right, particularly after we'd lined the fireplaces with steel to reflect heat.

Most of this was done while I was off on the emperor's bidding, so I always had something new to anticipate when I returned to Irrigon.

I found it possible to enjoy Irrigon twice a year—when harsh winter storms slashed down and the trees shook and bowed around our snuggery; and again in the stillest, sweatiest days of the Time of Heat, when I was grateful the searing sun didn't penetrate the stone.

Another change made Irrigon more livable: The Agramóntes still ruled by the whip and the club, which was their right, but there were tales even harsher methods had been used without recourse to the imperial courts. I never doubted these stories, although I'd had no proof, for hard country justice was and still is common throughout Numantia, particularly in districts where the ancient nobility is the only real law. We told our overseers things would change, that no one was permitted to strike anyone else unless defending himself or herself, took away the brightly painted bamboo lashes they'd used as badges of authority, and promptly discharged those who didn't believe we meant what we said.

Those laborers and farmers who thought we were foolish and to be taken advantage of were turned out as quickly. In some ways that was a harsher punishment than a dozen lashes, for there was no employ other than the Agramóntes for many miles. Sometimes I wondered if we should have left the system alone, and a couple of times Marán had snapped at me about it, though she'd been as much in favor of change as I. But what I am, I am, and I cannot tolerate one who feels violence is his to deal out merely because he's larger, or has a better station in life and feels beyond the law.

I'd wondered, long ago when I'd first seen a painting of Irrigon in a museum, how many people were required for the lord and lady of the manor to be properly cosseted. Now I knew too well: 347, from gardeners, to kitchen sweeps, to guards, to musicians, to the girl whose sole duty was cutting and arranging the flowers for the castle, to the pair of silent men who moved from room to room replenishing the fires, with never a nod given to their presence. I knew well, because I paid them twice a year. Marán and I had the services of four bankers, working full-time handling our money. Once I thought I'd inquire just how much money we spent each time, but realized my heart might not handle the strain. Besides, as Marán said, there was no way anyone, no matter how profligate, could dent the Agramónte fortunes, so why concern myself?

My thoughts were drifting thus as we rode toward Irrigon. There were twenty-four of us: myself, the Seer Sinait, and twenty-one members of my hastily reformed Red Lancers, under the command of Legate Segalle. Captain Lasta, who would normally ride beside me, was in Nicias bringing the Red Lancers back to full strength. There was also Karjan. I'd decided to attempt a new tactic, and so he glowered at the slashes of a troop guide now, and I had every intention of making him a regimental guide in a time or so. I was determined to win this battle of wills that had lasted over nine years. Secretly I feared I was no more likely to win this round than any of the others.

Behind the quarter hundred of us were the three document-carrying carriages. I shuddered thinking how little I liked books and studying. But things might be different this time, for I'd tried magic. I'd had Seer Sinait prepare a spell, using bits and pieces of the material I was to study. The conjuration was an extended version of our standard Spell of Understanding. Now I could read any of the six Maisirian languages, and more importantly speak nineteen of the forty-odd dialects used in the vast kingdom. I'd need no interpreter if the emperor's fears of war came true.

My wandering mind snapped back to the present as we reached the long, sweeping drive that led to the castle, and I saw, at the foot of the steps, someone waiting, a cloaked someone who could only be my darling Marán.

Slowly, very slowly, I returned from the stars.

"Great gods of Numantia with a dildo," I managed. "Where did you learn that?"

Marán looked back at me over her shoulder. Both of us were sweat-soaked, in spite of the winter winds outside our tower.

"I'll never say," she whispered. "Let's just say that you learned to exercise certain muscles while I was away—and I did the same."

"You'd better tell. Or I'll become insanely jealous."

"Oh, all right. Amiel, last time she was here, brought some . . . devices with her. One was a bladder you inflate, and put where you are right now, and try to pump the air out of it with your muscles. She said you're supposed to do that twenty times a day. There wasn't anything else to do after she left. So I practiced . . . Did you like it?"

"Mmm," I said nuzzling the back of her neck, and biting her gently. "I definitely think Countess Kalvedon is a wonderfully bad influence."

"Oh she is, she is," Marán whispered.

The next day I sought our chief bailiff to see who the leather-capped men might have been. He was a scarred villain named Vacomagi, one of the few overseers left from Marán's father's time. It wasn't that he was any less brutal than the others we'd dismissed. But Marán noted he was scrupulously fair in his brutality, and that he worked at least as hard as any of the men and women he drove, particularly during harvest and haying times. She suggested we keep him on, and I agreed.

I'd privately had a rather nasty thought of my own: It's not bad to have a convenient culprit around, someone whom everyone blames for any necessary evils, instead of the kindly, benevolent lord. After that thought, I wondered if I were changing, if I were starting to think like the callously bestial autocrats I so despised.

I asked Vacomagi who the men in the bush were.

"We calls 'em th' Broken Men," he said. "Though there's women, an' younguns as well out there. Mayhap half a hunnerd, mayhap more."

"Who are they?"

"Some are ones we drove off from th' estates. Others're wanderin' outlaws. Some of 'em are just th' landless, th' ones who'll wander th' roads, al'as hopin' somehow somebody'll give 'em a real job, other'n some quick fill labor at harvest or such. I've even heard . . ." Vacomagi let his voice trail away as he glanced about.

"Go ahead."

He was still hesitant, until I pressed him.

"Some could be Tovieti," he said, in a low voice. "Or so I've heard. Like th' ones you an' the emperor put down."

"*Here?* On the Agramónte lands?"

"That's th' talk," Vacomagi went on. "Course, nobody'll talk straight about 'em. Not round me, anyways."

"Have they killed anyone?"

"You mean strang'lated? Like I heard they do with those cords they got? Nossir. Not yet, anyway. But there's been some disappear on th' roads. Nobody proper, yet. Nobody what counts. Just some peddlers who never come around anymore, or folks who were dumb 'nough t' go about th' roads wi'out bein' armed or wi'out an escort. But there's nothin' for you t' worry about. Th' Broken Men're too far down for even th' Tovieti."

He spat. "Seems like there's more 'n' more of 'em, every year. One of these days we'll have t' run 'em down, like we do foxes an' badgers. Sweep th' country, an' put those to the sword or torch that don't have the sense t' flee. Not t'worry, Lord. Th' Agramóntes know how to deal with such as them. Like the name says, they're broke, twisted, like a stook a' grain that's been blown over int' th' muck. All the soul's been beat, or feared, out of 'em." That was the end of the matter for Vacomagi.

But not for me. I'd seen too many "broken" men rise up to strike hard with swords, knives, clubs, or cobblestones to dismiss these outcasts from my mind.

I wondered why there were more of them each year, as Vacomagi had said. Times were far better for everyone under the emperor than they'd been under the Rule of Ten, weren't they? And the Tovieti were, or so Kutulu had told me, less an influence than before.

Broken Men here and there, and in other places in the kingdom I'd had to stamp out different rebellions. What was going on in Numantia?

I had no answers, not even questions, and so put the matter away.

I began my studies, hoping I'd never have to apply them.

Maisir was an ancient monarchy, its symbol a twin-lion-headed dragon, black on yellow. Its population was, and this was estimated, for the kingdom was not fully explored even by its rulers, 150 million. That was 25 million more than Numantia, but my land was more densely populated. Maisir covered more, or so the estimates have it, than 6 million square miles; Numantia, which I'd previously thought unimaginably huge, was no more than a million square miles.

Numantia stretched from just below the equator into temperate regions, and Maisir reached from the southern temperate region into the arctic. Its most prominent features were the vast deserts they called the *suebi*, wastelands whose terrain changed seasonally from ice to mud to dust to mud once more.

The land, I read, was truly vast, so large one traveler said it hurt his eyes to try to pierce the horizon, and made him want to cower like a tiny mouse hunted by an eagle. There were mountains far higher than anything in Kait, lakes one would think seas, rivers whose far bank could not be seen, farming districts as big as some of our states.

Travel was a nightmare. Outside the largest cities, roads were either dirt or nonexistent. During bad weather, they became impossible morasses. The great rivers wouldn't help our army, since the navigable ones ran west to east, across the country.

Maisir's capital was Jarrah, three hundred leagues south of the border, hidden in the depths of the Belaya Forest, protected to its west by *suebi*, to its north by the huge Kiot Marshes. There were some other cities, not all known to us, but none as big as Jarrah.

The enormity of Maisir also made communication between our two capitals difficult. Coded messages could be sent by heliograph south to Renan on our border. Then messages would go by heavily escorted courier into Sulem Pass and through Kait. On the Kait-Maisir border, the messages would be given to the Maisirian border guards, the Negaret, and ridden through the Wild Country until they could be passed to normal couriers, who took them on to Jarrah.

Maisir's king was named Bairan, and he was considered a good ruler, at least by the standards of the Maisirians. One report on the thousand-year history of his family was as fascinating as any salacious broadsheet.

"The only choice to give a Maisirian," one family proverb went, "is between the noose and the knout." It was a proverb they obeyed exactly. Some of Bairan's ancestors were as bloody-handed a set of demoniacs as any in legend. One, offended when a certain province didn't offer sufficient obeisance when he journeyed through it, had his sorcerers rouse demons, and ordered them to kill every man they encountered. Not content with that, he sent a second set of nightmares against the women of the area. The children, those who hadn't starved, were treated more kindly. The army was given a special mission: round them up for the slave markets. Finally, the province was given another name and repopulated by peasants forcibly uprooted from another province.

Another tale, and this one I had some trouble believing, was of a queen who was insatiable in her lust. She went to a great deal of trouble to select a hundred men, the handsomest and best-built of the entire army. She had them lie with her continuously for one week, and at the end of that time ordered them all returned to the Wheel, for "no one who's experienced joy such as they must have would wish to continue on in the world."

Bairan, in contrast, ruled well and thoughtfully, if harshly. I read of no horrors he'd yet committed, at any rate. The nobility around the throne was no better than could be expected, but Bairan seemed to have selected his advisers and cronies more for capabilities than corruption, unlike his father.

I wondered how Maisir could have existed for so long with such villains on its throne. One philosopher, who'd spent ten years in Maisir as a tutor to the royal children, offered an explanation I'm not sure I understood or understand now: "There are, for the most part, only two classes of people in Maisir," he wrote. "There are the rulers, and there are the ruled. Those who are ruled have no rights whatsoever, and even the aristocracy, in their various stations, have no more rights than the king might temporarily grant. No man is permitted to rise above the station he has at birth. Thus life is nothing more than a struggle for power, for only with power can life continue. All power belongs to, hence may be granted by, the king. No one would ever dream of blaming the king himself for society's injustices, since it's obvious to them he speaks with the gods' approval.

In another place, the man wrote: "While it appears both countries have the same religion, that commonality is purely a masquerade. It's said we Numantians are too stoic, too accepting, feeling that our unnoticed benevolences, like our sins, will be rewarded or punished when we return to the Wheel. If this is a belief in Numantia, it is a fixation in Maisir. Their only rewards come after death, when one is judged by Saionji. Any other pleasures must be seized quickly and guiltily. Therefore, it is right to flog a peasant, for his or her sins were undoubtedly terrible in his previous life, or else he would have been born to a higher station. A nobleman, on the other hand, is not only permitted but encouraged every indulgence as a reward for a pious prior life. If he sins, that is the way of the world, and he will be punished in his next life.

"Not only do the Maisirians worship more fervently than the most wild-eyed Numantian monk, but they also build great temples and have a vast host of manifestations unknown to us. Their magic, like their worship, is dark and death-worshiping, and I avoided their sorcerers as much as I could."

Sorcery was considered one of the state's main supports. Young men and women who showed signs of the talent were noted early and trained in secluded institutions. Then they'd choose, or have chosen for them—no one seemed to quite know—specific assignments. It sounded as if Maisir's magicians were as organized as soldiers. The closest thing we had, really no more than a mutual protective society, was the Chare Brethren. The Maisirians' master magician was a shadowy figure ironically known as the *azaz*, or master of ceremonies. Who he was, even his name, let alone his powers, was unknown.

As for the army itself, reports were quite contradictory. Their army was double the size of ours. However, this was a false cause for worry. Most units couldn't be assigned to new locales, since they were required to keep the peace in their garrison areas or to defend the frontiers. There were legends Maisir had been conquered in the dim past by lands to the west and east, countries yet unknown to Numantia, and the Maisirians were deathly afraid of further invasions.

The cavalry and guard regiments were elite and officered by noblemen, but these were in the minority and generally used as parade formations in the cities. The infantry was considered to be poorly led, and their badly and brutally treated soldiery thought not much more than rabble. Their officers were poorly educated, capable of little better strategy than attacking frontally, in mass. In battle the Maisirians might fight bravely, or as easily flee or surrender.

I puzzled over that one.

Their battle magic was another cipher. Maisir hadn't fought a major war in decades, so most information was legendary. But these stories were of the most awful sort, and suggested their mages could call up dark forces at least as powerful as those the Emperor Tenedos could summon.

There was one large difference between Maisir and Numantia. We recruited our soldiers with cash, with promises of gold, loot, glory. The Maisirians used the age system. Each man owed his king ten full years of service, and might or might not be called to the colors, along with everyone else his age, depending on the king's needs. Sometimes he served a full term, sometimes he was hastily trained and released from service. This wasn't dealt with very thoroughly, since analysts felt it was an impossible system, given the enormity of the country, the slow communication, the weather, the probability of corruption and evading such an onerous duty, and so forth. Again I wondered.

I read on, about the country's cities, built of stone and wood, wildly colored; their spicy food; their wild music; even a bit of their poetry and tales.

I wanted to go there, to learn more about this fascinating land—but not as a warrior, for as I read I felt a crawl in my guts. Maisir could be the final doom of Numantia.

Another reason I fled to my books and reports was Marán.

Something was dreadfully wrong. Wrong with me, wrong with her, wrong with our marriage—I didn't know. I didn't even know how to ask the questions, or how to ask them the right way. I asked her several times if she was happy, if everything was all right. She said she was as happy as she could be expected to be.

We slept in the same bed, and we still loved, our bodies twining frantically as if they as well were in search of something lost.

I noticed the way she looked at me, particularly when she didn't think I was paying attention. There was no softness, no gentleness, but rather a cold intensity, as if she were studying someone she'd only just met and was deciding if that person was a friend or enemy.

I felt there was a sheet of glass between me and the woman I loved. I looked desperately for an answer, but found none.

The winter was waning, and the last time of the year, the time of Dews, was almost upon us when the riders trotted up to Irrigon. There were ten of them, remounts tied to each rider's saddle, wearing the dark earth-brown and subdued green caps and cloaks of Yonge's skirmishers. Their officer, a young man whose dark complexion and hawk face suggested he might have been born somewhere not distant from the Border Lands, saluted, introduced himself as Captain Sendraka, and handed me a trebly sealed envelope. I invited him and his men inside, and he shook his head.

"No, Tribune. We're under orders. And I was told to have you open that packet immediately."

It could only have come from one man. I tore the envelope open, and the drizzle misted the single sheet inside. It was handwritten:

Come at once.

T

* * *

As I read it, the paper curled and smoked, and I dropped it into the mud as it flamed into nothingness.

"We dropped off relays of horses as we came, sir. For the return. You'll be ready—"

"We'll be ready in an hour," Marán's voice interrupted. "For Nicias?"

"Yes, lady, I mean Baroness, but there was no mention . . ."

"Is there any reason for a tribune's wife not to attend her husband?"

Captain Sendraka wilted at the stare I knew he was getting. "No, Baroness. At least . . . but we'll be riding hard. And, well, I don't know if a woman . . ." His voice trailed off.

I almost laughed. The good captain was about to have his opinion of women's stamina changed. I turned. Marán's eyes held mine. For an instant, they had that cold, assessing look I hated, then they softened.

"May I come with you, Damastes? Please?"

"Of course."

Thirty minutes later, we rode out of Irrigon on the emperor's command.

NINE

SHADOWS IN THE PALACE

Captain Sendraka had said we'd ride hard for the capital, and he wasn't exaggerating. I thought I was in decent physical shape, but relearned the lesson that nothing prepares you for hard living except hard living. My ass was sore within half a day, and got sorer.

At the first stop, an inn just at the edge of Agramónte property, one man was left behind, and Marán took his waiting remount.

The skirmishers noted Marán with admiration. She never complained, and when anyone looked at her, no matter how mud-spattered, how weary she was, she forced a smile.

We moved in the regulation forced march pattern: trot for an hour, walk your horse for an hour, walk beside your mount for half an hour, rest for half an hour, then trot once more. Since we were not in hostile territory, we started an hour before dawn, and ended an hour after sunset, more or less. More or less because, in consideration of my rank, each day's journey ended at an inn, where fresh horses waited. The inns were all outside of a town, and quiet. Since the emperor didn't want to advertise my coming, we ate in our chambers or in a snug, if the inn had one.

At our first stop I saw broadsheets that screamed the reason for the emperor's summons:

Numantian soldiers massacred!
A Maisirian ambush!

TREACHERY IN THE BORDER LANDS!

NO SURVIVORS!
200 of Our Bravest Cavalry Butchered Without Mercy!

EMPEROR REQUIRES EXPLANATION!

Harsh note sent to King Bairan

NUMANTIA DEMANDS REVENGE!

I scanned the broadsheets for details. There wasn't much more than what the headlines yammered. One sheet at least told me where the tragedy had occurred: "not far" from the city of Zante. It took some moments for me to remember where Zante was. I'd expected the catastrophe to have taken place in Kait, or the Urshi Highlands, where fighting was common. Zante was leagues to the east of Kait, just across the border from the mostly desert Numantian province of Dumyat. What were our soldiers doing there?

Another question I had was how was it known, if there were no survivors, the killers were Maisirian? All the Border Lands had adequate supplies of homegrown bandits. I guessed imperial sorcery must have given that answer.

Another question came to me: A normally sized troop (not company, as the always inaccurate broadsheets would term it) of cavalry was around a hundred men. This unit must have been specially augmented. I sought in vain to see what unit had been involved in the action. Naturally, the broadsheets either thought this didn't matter, or their scribes had been too lazy or ignorant to ask the proper questions.

If the facts were slight, the stories running around the inn's taproom beyond our snug weren't: Of course the Maisirians had done it . . . probably tortured any wounded . . . Someone had it on good authority that the most evil magic had been used to spring the trap . . . just like Maisirians, treacherous sons of bitches that they were . . . The emperor ought not to screw around with diplomatic notes but send the army across the border—ten, nay a hundred, for every one of our brave lads . . . Cheers and set up another round . . . Probably the same conversation, or more correctly mindless raging, was going on in every inn of Numantia.

I asked Captain Sendraka what he knew of the disaster, and he said very little—his regiment had been alerted after the disaster and he'd been immediately sent to Irrigon.

Marán wondered why I hadn't been summoned by heliograph, and Sendraka replied that the weather had been too chancy around Nicias to depend on those devices.

"What happens next?" she asked.

"I couldn't say . . . but all the first-line regiments were on stand to when I left Nicias," Sendraka said.

"Will it be war?"

Sendraka shook his head. I didn't know, either, but feared the worst, and reading my face, Marán knew my thoughts. Then I understood, perhaps, why she'd wanted to come with me. If I was to go to war again, she wanted our love rebuilt, until it flamed as high as it once had, and I loved her for that.

We rode on, and each night heard more anger, more rage, from the people around us. As we drew closer to the capital, we passed army posts. They were at full readiness, gates guarded by squads instead of single sentries, parade grounds alive with drilling men.

We rode into Nicias after nightfall. The streets, as always in the City of Lights, were alive, but there were so many uniformed groups galloping about we went unnoticed.

We went directly to a rear entrance to the Imperial Palace and were met by Emperor Tenedos's aide, once-Captain, now-

Domina Amer Othman. I thanked Captain Sendraka and let Othman lead us through secluded passageways to private apartments.

A lavish meal was already laid out, and beside it was a note from the emperor:

Welcome. Please wait until summoned.

T

As if we had any choice. Marán had gone to the closets, muttering what she'd do about clothes. She opened one and gasped. On the racks hung two dozen of her favorite garments. In cupboards were undergarments and everything else she'd need to appear at court.

Another closet and cabinet held clothes for me: all dress uniforms. I would not be presenting myself as Baron Agramónte.

"How did he know what to pick out?" she wondered, holding up the sleeve of one dress.

"He's a magician."

"But he's also a man," she protested. "Men *never* know things like that."

"Maybe emperor-type men do?"

She just shook her head and went into the bath chamber. I heard the sound of splashing. I lifted dish covers until I found something finger-sized and, munching a small, spiced, meat-filled pastry, wandered around the apartments. All was gold, silver, cut gems, or the richest, hand-rubbed woods. I could have quartered a company of infantry in these rooms, and wondered just how long we'd be kept in seclusion. There were several bookcases, and I examined their contents. Unsurprisingly, all of the volumes dealt with Maisir. There was no doubt whatsoever why the emperor had summoned me.

We spent four days in these apartments, seeing no one except smiling, faceless servants. We ate, slept, and grew increasingly nervous. Early on the morning of the fifth day

Domina Othman requested we be ready for an imperial audience after the noon meal, and for me to wear my medals. At least an hour before they came for us, we were ready. They escorted us to the main entrance of the palace, as if we were just arriving.

Trumpets blared, flunkies clamored our names and ranks, and we entered the great hall, which was packed with the nobility of Numantia. The entrance was on a higher level than the main room, a huge circular chamber on several levels with the throne at the far end. We started down the sweeping staircase. The crowd surged toward us, smiles spread as carefully as facial powder and rouge. Obviously Marán and I were once more in imperial favor. A lackey bellowed an imperial "request"—that our "friends" hold their welcomes until later, for imperial business of the greatest import was about to begin.

The court yammer stilled for an instant, then grew louder and louder as the court speculated on what could be happening. I noted the Maisirian ambassador, Baron Sala, in the throng, waiting with an utterly impenetrable expression.

I saw the emperor's sisters, Dalny and Leh, one with a handsome, foppish army officer barely out of his teens, the other with a bearded dandy who'd come to the end of four marriages now, each time having improved either his title or wealth. Both women wore black, but their gowns were reveal-ingly cut and suggested the sisters were no more in real mourning for their brother Reufern than if they'd been naked with kohl rubbed on their nipples.

What the broadsheets had termed the "Maisirian Emergency" appeared to have made no impression at all on these fools. I remembered how I'd despised the wastrels who'd buzzed around the Rule of Ten, and realized they now thought the emperor was an even bigger jar of honey. Was this why we'd undertaken treason and overthrown that pack of imbeciles?

Marán leaned close. "If we were brought to Nicias in such secrecy, why this?" she whispered.

I didn't know, but assumed the Emperor Tenedos, a man

of infinite subtlety and deviousness, had a reason. Once again trumpets blared, and this time the fanfare was twice as loud and lasted twice as long. The noblemen and -women, recognizing the voice of their master, stopped chattering in mid-syllable and, as one, turned to the throne. A door opened, and the emperor entered.

Seer Laish Tenedos wore something that might have been a uniform—a simple collarless raw silk tunic in dark green, black flaring riding breeches, and black knee boots, with a matching belt. His crown wasn't the simple, traditional badge I'd ennobled him with almost nine years earlier. This was new, elaborately figured and worked, with gems of many colors. Perhaps he needed a more ornate symbol, since he'd made Numantia into a greater kingdom.

Perhaps.

He seated himself on the throne, picked up a tall scepter that was also new, and rapped three times. Then he rose, and his voice, magically enlarged, boomed: "You all know of the outrage committed by the Maisirian Army against an innocent party of Numantian soldiers on a routine peacekeeping task well within our claimed borders.

"I told you I sent a sharp note to King Bairan, ruler of Maisir, protesting what his army has done and demanding a full apology and reparations for shedding the blood of our finest young men.

"This morning I received a reply, a response so shocking that I spent some hours considering what I should do. His reply, in essence, mocked me and all Numantia, saying he had no knowledge of any such event, and if something of that nature had occurred, no doubt the response was quite justified, in keeping with the recent warlike posture of Numantia!"

Tenedos's voice dripped scorn. I saw, but didn't understand, the shocked expression on Ambassador Sala's face.

"Warlike posture?" Tenedos cried out. "The man is a villain, a base villain of the worst sort! Time after time I've ordered our soldiers to ignore provocation from the Maisirian

Army on our borders. I've even kept from you, my own people, clear evidence that Maisir has had agents operating within our frontiers and has been agitating and fomenting unrest!

"For this I apologize, and beg understanding, for I wished to prevent turmoil from your own breasts, hoping I could maintain order and peace. But no more. This last outrage pushes our two kingdoms close to confrontation.

"As I thought about what I should do in this matter, I remembered that our finest soldier, the first tribune himself, Damastes á Cimabue, Baron Damastes of Ghazi, Count Agramónte, has recently returned from his estates, and so I summoned him to the palace. We spent some hours discussing the problem and are in full agreement.

"I . . . we all . . . wish peace for Numantia. But the shield of peace can only protect when there's a strong arm, well armored and armed, behind that protection. I've therefore commanded our army built up, and for our forces to be ready for any development. Strong times require strong measures.

"I have chosen First Tribune á Cimabue for a special command, a command I cannot at present detail, but which supersedes all other ranks in our army. First Tribune á Cimabue now has call on any unit, any officer, any man for whatever is needed in these extraordinary times."

I was grateful that the emperor's first statement had given me a few seconds to mask my face. Now, as the cheering began, no doubt encouraged by the emperor's toadies in the throng, all I had to do was bow deeply.

"I have prepared a reply to King Bairan's insolence," the emperor went on. "It will be given to the Maisirian ambassador within minutes.

"I request Tribune á Cimabue join me in my chambers, since information vital to our strategic position has just been received. That is all!"

Trumpets thundered and the crowd bellowed approval. Tenedos stood watching for a moment, an odd, small smile quirking his lips. Then he pivoted and strode off.

* * *

The door to the emperor's reception rooms came open, and Baron Sala stalked out, face tight with anger. He saw me, and his expression smoothed into blankness. He didn't speak, but nodded as he stalked past.

The emperor's aide rose from behind his desk, but the door opened again, and Tenedos stood there. "Come in, my friend. Come in," he said, his voice hearty. He closed the door, and indicated a seat, far across the huge room, on a divan. He sat beside me. On the end table was a decanter of brandy and glasses. He toyed with the stopper, then sighed.

"They never tell you about the times when you'd better not drink, do they?" He smiled wryly. "Sometimes I wish I had your discipline and never wished alcohol."

"It isn't discipline, sir. To me it tastes like shit."

He laughed. "I suppose," he said, "I should apologize for those slight falsehoods out there."

"You don't have to apologize for anything."

"No," he said. "I don't, do I? So instead of an apology, would you like an explanation?"

"Gladly."

"I summoned you at the same time as I sent the note off to King Bairan because I knew his reply would be sharp. It was the only possible response to my message. Actually, we still haven't received his answer. That was why Baron Sala stormed out of here, after using every diplomatic term for liar." He shrugged. "Lies in the service of your country are hardly sins. I know what Bairan will say, and I realized I had to provide the masses with an immediate answer."

"I don't understand," I said.

"Peasants have short attention spans," he said. "Now the people are worked up over what happened. A week goes by, and they maintain their indignation. A week later, there's less fervor, less ire. Two weeks beyond that, and the matter's likely forgotten while they babble about the latest scandal from the capital."

"Cynical, Your Highness."

"The hells it is. I call that realism." He stood and began pacing. "Now, for your ears only, here is what happened out there in the Border Lands. I'd become increasingly concerned, because Maisir is settling the lands just on the other side of the border, bringing in farmers and creating new units of those frontier guardians they call the Negaret. Guardians . . . or scouts for the invasion.

"Maisir attacked a reinforced troop of the Twentieth Heavy Cavalry, which I've relocated from Urey. The reinforcements were wagoneers, mapmakers, and so forth, for that district is little known." That explained the extra men. "They were on direct orders from me, so there was a magical link between us. I sensed something wrong, something to the north, used a Seeing Bowl to search the area, and my senses drew me to the terrible scene.

"My vision showed nothing but bodies. Bodies and the carrion kites picking at them. They'd camped in a hollow near a spring. I don't know if they were lax, or if their attackers silenced the sentries before they could sound alarm. A few appeared to have wakened, and fought back. They took a heavy toll of the Maisirians, but they were badly outnumbered. The troop was cut down to a man. The wounded were toyed with before being allowed to die. When 'I' came on the scene, the soldiers had been dead for two days, perhaps three.

"I used more magic to scan for their murderers. A day's ride further south, my all-seeing 'eyes' found tracks, and followed them across the border, to a Maisirian outpost. Since the bodies had been mutilated, it was obvious the Maisirians were reinforced by native levies from the Men of the Hills.

"I summoned spirits," the emperor went on, "and caused the bodies of my soldiers to burn with sacred flames. I sent a whirlwind sweeping across the area, so now there is nothing remaining, nothing but endless rolling hills of sand.

"I've ordered great sacrifices made to Saionji, and promised even greater, so our soldiers will be treated well on the Wheel and, because of their sacrifice for Numantia, given preferential treatment in their next lives. The men's families will be granted generous pensions."

Tenedos stopped, waiting for some response. There wasn't much I could say, other than to thank him for what he had done. "What happens next?" I asked.

"We wait for King Bairan's real response," Tenedos said. "We proceed with building up our army and move toward the Maisirian frontier. If they attack, I assume it'll be along the traditional trading route, through Kait, down Sulem Pass, into Urey.

"Which brings us to your role. I assume you've studied the materials I gave you?"

"Thoroughly, sir."

"Do you think a war with Maisir is inevitable?"

"I don't know," I said honestly. "I didn't find much in the reports to make me think Maisir wants, or wanted anyway, to invade us. At least they didn't before Bairan inherited the throne."

"There's the change I've sensed," Tenedos said. "I'm afraid he's now seeing our lands as being ready for harvest. Perhaps he still thinks we're as badly led as in the days of the Rule of Ten." Tenedos smiled tightly. "If so, he's misjudged things more than somewhat."

"What's Kutulu's analysis?" I asked.

The emperor's mood changed. His lips pressed into a thin line and I saw a vein throb at his temple. His eyes caught and held me with his searing gaze. "Kutulu," he said harshly, "is dealing with other, internal matters. I've been using different, perhaps more qualified, people to assist me in understanding what's happening with Maisir."

If I hadn't known the emperor for as long as I had, and hadn't therefore thought him a friend as well as my master, I would never have pursued the matter.

"What happened with Kutulu, sir? If I may ask?"

"Kutulu presumed," he said. "I'll tell you this once, and

request you never repeat it. Kutulu is in disfavor, although I assume as time passes, I calm down, and he returns to his senses, he could resume his former importance. I praised the man recently, in private, and said he could have any reward I could offer. He said he wished to be named a tribune.

"The fool!" The emperor's pacing grew quicker, boot heels slamming against the parquet flooring. "Spies aren't generals, aren't tribunes. Not ever!"

I remembered Kutulu looking up at the Water Palace, admiring it, and saying *Perhaps, one day, if the emperor decides* . . . and not finishing his sentence. At first I thought, *The poor bastard.* How could he imagine a warden could ever hold the army's highest rank? Then my foolishness and arrogance vanished. Why not? Hadn't a magician assumed he could become emperor? Hadn't I, a subaltern of cavalry, reached the summit? Hadn't Kutulu served the emperor as well, perhaps better than I? Who would have cared, anyway? Perhaps seven or eight old farts who would've muttered about tradition being once again despoiled by the usurper. But who listened to those creaking monsters these days, with the winds of empire blowing fresh?

I thought of defending Kutulu, but caution took me, and I said nothing.

"Now, we have more important matters," the emperor went on. "We'll start with your new assignment, the importance of which I was *not* exaggerating." An impish grin came. "But I'm not going to tell you what it is."

"I beg pardon, Your Highness?"

"You heard me clearly. By the way, I've changed my mind. Pour me a drink from that other bottle, the one shaped like a rearing demon, over by my desk. In the cabinet below it, you'll find various mineral waters."

I obeyed. Tenedos sat down, leg hung over the chair's arm, and watched, still smiling. I decided I could outwait him, and did.

"You won't ask, will you?" he said.

"No, sir. I figure you'll tell me when it's important for me to know."

The emperor laughed aloud. "Sometimes I suspect you know me better than I know myself. Do you ever find yourself missing the old days, Damastes? Before we had all the power and gold? Back when we wanted, instead of having?"

"Not really," I said. "I can't think of ever wanting to be somewhere, or in some time, other than where I am. Unless it's really shitty, like Sulem Pass. Then I want to be anywhere."

"That *was* horrible," he said. "But on the other hand, it was glorious. I remember that infantry captain . . . what was his name?"

"Mellet, sir. I make sacrifice to him, and his men, every year on the anniversary of that last stand."

I was amazed he could have forgotten Mellet, and the others of the Khurram Light Infantry whose bravery enabled us, and the Numantian civilians we escorted, to escape the doom planned by the Men of the Hills.

"Yes," Tenedos went on. "I remember him, and all the others, very well. I think it's well we remember men like him, and even brave beasts like that dying elephant that tried to rally to the trumpet when we first met at Ghazi. For that's the part of war that makes us all great, worthy to stand proud in front of the gods."

But I shivered, thinking of bloody times and the black wasteland war dragged across the world. I should have marked what the emperor said, but I merely thought it the romantic words of a man who'd known little of real war, and that almost always victorious. The emperor seemed to want no response, thankfully.

"Yes," he went on. "Glory still must be sought and won, or men grow lazy, weak, and stupid and are dragged down by those who are stronger and more brutal than they." The emperor sipped brandy and stared at me. Strangely, I thought he was seeing through me, or seeing me at the head of another great army, caprisoned for battle. I remained silent until the emperor's reverie came to an end.

"Great times," he mused. "But there shall be greater ones to come." He drained his snifter. "I still won't tell you what your next task shall be. But I'll tell you who shall. Seek your friend, Tribune Petre. For it's all, or everything beyond my initial idea, his doing."

I'd met Mercia Petre when we were misassigned to the Golden Helms of Nicias. Petre was a completely earnest sort, whose only life and interest was the military, its history and ways. In the long, dull weeks of parade-ground duty, we'd done what many young officers do and dreamily designed our very own army. But then the Seer Tenedos had given us the chance to make it real, and so the trudging, bloated divisions of the past became the swift-striking sabers that slashed into Kallio and ended the civil war.

Petre had been in charge of the dragoons during the war, then, as tribune, was given the nominal duty of commanding the army's center. But our full forces hadn't assembled since we'd destroyed Chardin Sher, and so he took charge of reforming the army's moribund training. To make sure he didn't stale in his post, Petre made periodic visits to the frontiers on "tours of inspection," where he threw himself into the heat of the savage little skirmishes as eagerly as any freshly named legate hungry for glory. Somehow he'd taken only the most minor wounds and had become legendary for his luck, just as tribune Le Balafre was known for always winning, but somehow always taking hurt as he did.

I was probably as much a friend as Petre ever allowed himself or wanted. All but one, and I met him on that day. Since the war, we'd both been busy on imperial business and met only half a dozen times, generally in distant, tiny outposts. I'd never been to his house. I imagined it would not be large, for Petre was a man of simple tastes, not much more than a bachelor officer's quarters, probably with a library the size of a lycée's attached.

Petre's mansion swept up the side of a hill, in the heights

with Nicias's richest. It was utterly beautiful, a series of sweeping curves, stone with marble facing in gentle hues that never seemed to reach a corner or a straight line. There was nothing stark, nothing harsh. Even the plants in the gardens were soft and tropical. Two smiling men, wearing unobtrusive livery in pale colors, took Lucan's reins and led him away. A finely dressed woman, about ten years older than I, greeted me, and said Tribune Petre awaited me in the library. The servants, mostly young men, were dressed in the same uniform as the footmen.

The library was big, open, airy, with many skylights and windows between the endless shelves. There were maps aplenty rolled on racks.

At least Petre hadn't changed. He wore a plain dark gray uniform with no medals, and the sash of rank around his waist was sloppily tied. His uniform looked like standard quartermaster issue, about half a size too big. Also Mercia was barefoot instead of wearing cavalry boots.

"So what am I to do next, then?" I asked. "What scheme have you devised this time? And by the way, you could always offer me something. It's still brisk out there."

"Oh," Petre said. "Oh, yes. Uh . . . some tea? Yes, we'll have tea."

"That would go well," I said.

Rather than signaling for a servant, Petre went to the door and called. After a time, the door opened and a tray was brought in by a very slim, almost uncannily handsome young officer.

"This is my aide," Petre said, and perhaps no one but myself would have caught that slight hesitation before the word "aide." "Legate Phillack Herton." He looked at me almost challengingly. If he'd expected to see disapproval, he was sore disappointed. If Herton was more than Petre's aide, what of it? My province of Cimabue might be backward in some respects, but unlike Nicias it didn't much care whom one chose to partner with. My only hope was that he made Petre's life a little less lonely, although I'm not sure that strange man knew the meaning of the word. Herton served tea, then, unbidden, curled catlike on a sofa, eyes intent on Petre.

"You and I are going to create a series of elite divisions," Petre went on. "I called them strike forces; the emperor decided they'd be named the Imperial Guard, and numbered. There'll be half a dozen at first, more as we raise the men. They'll be big units, at least ten thousand men, maybe more."

He went to a wall and pulled a curtain aside, revealing a chart: two Heavy Cavalry regiments, 1,000 men in each; two Light Cavalry regiments—lancers, 700 men in each; four dragoon regiments—mounted infantry, 1,000 men in each; one regiment of skirmishers, 500 men; one pioneer unit to cut roads, build bridges, etc., 500 men; one of a new unit, what Petre called gallopers—messengers who'd enable the Guard commander to maintain a sort of order in the march and, in battle, to hopefully have some idea of what was going on, 250 men; one unit composed of the quartermasters, farriers, animal nurses, 1,000 men; what I privately called the odds and sods—military warders, bandsmen, heliograph operators, stretcher bearers, chirurgeons, 300–500 men; and finally the command staff. Petre said there'd be at least fifty to a hundred in this unit, and I whistled. He shook his head.

"No. That's a bit small as it is. The way the Guard will be fought, its commander will need to subordinate all the authority he can, just to keep his mind clear for the greater picture. The staff won't be standing around admiring its medals for sycophancy."

"All right," I said. "I've got your Guard unit—call it a corps, perhaps—in my mind. How will this unit be fought? How'll it operate differently from our present tactics?"

"Not a great deal," Petre said. "Our cavalry's already trained to strike for the heart of the enemy. The Guard will only be an extreme version of this. Right now our cavalry can fight ahead of our lines for how long?"

"If they stay mobile, maybe two or three weeks," I hazarded. "Far less if they're pinned and brought to static battle."

"The Guard will fight like that—but if a corps is stopped by a superior force, it'll be able to continue the attack. The Guard's objectives will be what the cavalry's are now—fortresses, commanders, the enemy's capital—but they'll be able to stay out, stay moving, longer. Essentially they'll be an army within themselves, so when we're fighting on the *suebi*, they won't have to worry about when the rest of the army—the quartermasters, the magicians, the bakers—will catch up. If they have to, they can take an enemy city and hold it as their winter quarters, although we can't allow ourselves to be doomed by campaigning through the Maisirian winter.

"You'll have noticed," he added, "no more war elephants. They're slow, require infinite fodder which the *suebi* won't be able to provide, can't carry that much, can be killed by any infantryman who can dodge their trunks and tusks, and don't scare anyone but the greenest troops."

"Good," I added. "Plus they scare the whey out of horses."

I studied his chart for many minutes.

"I like it in a number of ways," I finally said. "I'd add two more units. First archers. Give me, say, five companies, a hundred men apiece. Let them train together, then break them up in detachments to be used wherever necessary."

"Good," Petre said, making a note.

"And one other, smaller unit. Magicians. We need battle-trained sorcerers who can feel for the enemy's magic and lay counterspells and spells of our own."

Now it was Petre's turn for surprise. "And what god is going to teach magicians to get along with each other for a common good?" he said skeptically. "Aharhel? He can talk to kings, but I think sorcerers would be beyond his capabilities."

"The god will be Emperor Tenedos," I said flatly. "If he can bring you and me to battle, then he can damned well horsewhip his brethren into the same harness."

"It's a good idea," Petre said. "And I'll very cheerfully leave that to the emperor, as you suggest. What problems do you see?"

"First," I said, "it'll take time to train these units if they've got to be able to fight in great bodies, and we'll have to have a lot of space to practice in."

"The emperor is already building training camps in Amur," Petre said. "Room there to maneuver whole armies."

That province was secluded, barren, yet close to the Latane River for swift communication with Nicias. The gold our army would spend there would be welcome.

"What about time?"

Petre shrugged. "As soon as you tell the emperor you're ready to implement my— I mean his idea there'll be a decree issued and we'll send men, each corps's future cadre, to every post looking for volunteers. If we can't get enough of them fast enough, or if we get stuck with slackers, then we'll use an imperial edict to draft the troops we need."

I thought again, then nodded. "Maybe your idea takes away some of the worry I've had about all those leagues and leagues of Maisir."

"There's only one real problem remaining," Petre said, and I thought I caught a flash of amusement in his eyes. "We'll need some sort of uniform for them. I suppose you'll find the time to design something?"

I looked at him hard, but his gaze was innocent. Herton was examining a nearby tapestry. I'd achieved a certain amount of . . . well, I suppose notoriety is the word, for my rather flamboyant taste. Marán had designed some; sometimes I'd had an idea of my own.

"Is that joke yours?" I asked.

"I'm afraid not," Petre said. "The emperor came up with it, and when he finished laughing he ordered me to repeat it—exactly—to you."

"Thanks, Mercia," I said. "Maybe first I'll ask his permission to redesign the battle garb of my fellow tribunes. Something in reds and greens. Floor-length robes. In velvet."

Marán and I didn't return to the Water Palace, but to our

own mansion on the riverfront, five stories that could have served as a blockhouse. I had no time to worry about the Tovieti, so I ordered my reformed Red Lancers to be quartered in the mansion, using two ballrooms for the men. There were more than enough disused rooms for the officers. Marán, by now, had become quite used to having soldiers garrisoned in our home. At least, she said, this place was big enough so we could keep them on the first floor and have the upper stories to ourselves.

Then Mercia and I set to work building an army for the emperor for the second time.

"Ah," Kutulu said, showing a trace of surprise, "this is a true turnabout. I visit you when you're in disgrace, now you have done the same. You *are* a friend." He picked up a box of the omnipresent yellow cards I thought he had every citizen of Numantia logged on, and was about to set it on the floor of his tiny, cluttered office. He plucked one card from the box first, though. "I must remember to deal with that man," he muttered to himself. "I doubt, though, if your visit is completely social," he added.

Actually, it was mostly that. I had a couple of questions, but didn't know how to tell Kutulu that, yes indeed, I remembered when he'd come to call some time earlier, and how it had heartened me.

"I wanted to know," I said, "if you'd been able to find any hard links between the Tovieti and Maisir."

"None, which is another reason for imperial ire."

Quite suddenly the small man's face twisted, and his lips worked. I was reminded of friends whose loves had betrayed them, and how they could be unexpectedly reminded of the catastrophe and their control would shatter. Tenedos had been the sun, moon, and stars to Kutulu, and to be in eclipse must have been as awful as any ruined love affair.

I looked away, then back, and the warder regained his rigid control. "My apologies. Perhaps I'm overworked." Kutulu's life was nothing but work, but I nodded yes, so it must be.

"Speaking of the Tovieti," I said, slightly changing the subject, "what wainscoting are those rats wandering in? Or are they no longer your responsibility?"

"I'm still pursuing them, and every now and then I trap one or two. I think they're getting larger—there's more and more signs of them. But I've still been unable to find their leaders, their central organization. Perhaps the emperor is right. Perhaps I'm working beyond my capabilities."

"I doubt that," I reassured him. "Come on, man. You told me the emperor would come back to his senses about me, and so it happened. Don't you think he'll do the same for you? He just has many things to worry about now. Particularly Maisir."

Kutulu began to say something, but caught himself.

"Yes?"

"Never mind," he said. "What I was about to say might be taken as disloyalty." I snorted disbelief. "I thought once," he said, in a very low tone, "that I could serve two masters. It appears I was wrong."

"You puzzle me."

"I should say no more, but I'll add that I became a warder because I wanted to serve the truth. Perhaps I made it my first god."

I had a sudden inkling of what Kutulu's mysterious words might mean, and did not want to pursue the matter. "Back to the Tovieti. Have you heard of this phenomenon called the 'Broken Men'?"

"I have," Kutulu said. "Numantia's always had a problem with the landless, called by assorted names. I suppose any country with a rigid system of place will have the equivalent.

"It worries me, though, that they're on the increase. And I've picked up some linkage between these drifters and the Tovieti."

"Should we be worried?"

"You shouldn't," Kutulu said. "I should, just as I worry about anything that threatens the stability of Numantia. As you said, rats in the wainscoting."

"Another question," I said. "Should I still consider myself a target of the stranglers?"

"Absolutely," Kutulu said. "Especially with the emperor having named you to command his Imperial Guard."

"You may be in disgrace, but it appears your ears aren't stopped," I said.

"Of course not," Kutulu said. "I'm not dead."

"Good. I think your talents will be needed in the near future." I stood up. "My real purpose in coming was to convey an invitation from my wife to dine with us, perhaps tomorrow night?"

Kutulu looked amazed, and I wondered if anyone had ever asked him to a completely social event. "Well . . . I normally work late . . . No. Never mind. Of course I'll be there. At what hour?"

"Two hours after sunset would be ideal."

Our driveway was filled with a dozen or more expensive carriages. On one I saw the Agramónte coat of arms. Wondering what this portended, I tossed Rabbit's reins to Karjan and hurried inside.

My new majordomo met me at the door. Marán's brother and some fourteen other noblemen were in the upstairs library, waiting. I shed my cloak, helmet, and sword and went to meet them in the circular meeting room.

Praen, Marán's oldest brother, stood just inside the entrance. It was sometimes hard to believe this big, bluff man was related to my delicate wife, or rather that she was a true Agramónte, since Praen and her brother Mamin looked exactly like their late father.

The other men in the room were older than Praen, but they were all of his class: well-fed, richly dressed countrymen of power and confidence.

Marán was the only woman present. I kissed her cheek and raised a curious eyebrow about what was going on.

"I'm sorry, Damastes," she said. "But Praen sent me a

note only this morning, after you'd left for the Palace of War. I sent a messenger, but he couldn't find you."

"I had some problems to deal with outside the palace," I explained.

"Praen said it was very important for him, and these other gentlemen, to meet with you as soon as possible," Marán said. "I told him you generally arrived home around this time, and the best I could suggest was that he could wait. He's told me what it's about, and I agree that it's very, very important."

I turned to Praen. "You are welcome in our house, as always. Some of these gentlemen I don't know. Would you do the honors?"

Praen introduced me around. Count this, Baron that, Lord this, and so on. Some were old riches, some new. I knew most by title. They were rural, very conservative in their beliefs, among the last to give the emperor's new reign more than lip service. I noticed few were drinking, although there were decanters and bottles aplenty.

"Gentlemen," I said. "I know you're all quite busy, so please let me know how I might be of service. We needn't bother with niceties."

"Would you ask your servants to leave the room, please," Praen requested. I obeyed.

One man, Lord Drumceat, stood, holding a leather saddlebag. He took four small icons from it and positioned them at equidistant parts of the round chamber. "My seer enchanted these this morning," he said. "Supposedly they should keep anyone, even the emperor's Chare Brethren, from being able to overhear what we discuss."

I felt a flicker of alarm—these men weren't about to propose anything the emperor would disapprove of, were they?

Praen cleared his throat. "What we've come to discuss, Damastes, is a serious problem for Numantia. These are perilous times, and we think we might be able to help the emperor, who's terribly busy with other matters."

I said nothing.

"Have you heard of the landless ones?" he asked. "They've got various names, but around Irrigon they're called the Broken Men."

"I saw two when I last traveled to Irrigon."

"There's always been a problem with the bastards," someone said. "People who know no law, no gods. Escaped slaves, a lot of them."

"The count's right," Praen said. "And it's getting worse. They're not content to huddle in their warrens and thickets. Now they're setting themselves up as bandits, in armed bands."

"The shitheels had the temerity to seize one of my villages," another nobleman said. "Rousted out two of my overseers, put their houses to the torch, and told 'em they'd have but a day to flee or they'd be for the flames, too."

There was an angry mutter around the room.

"It's common knowledge," Praen said, "that the emperor's concerned about . . . well, let's say external matters. But something's got to be done about these damned criminals, and done immediately. Let the rabble get the idea they can rise above their station, and Umar himself can't bring them to their senses."

"Like what happened ten years ago," another lord said. "With those damned Toveeti or whatever they called themselves."

"You know about them better than any of us, Damastes," Praen said. "You . . . and the emperor . . . put them down."

"There were some others involved," I said dryly.

"But you were at the heart of the affair," Praen said. "That's why we came to consult with you."

"I still don't know what you want me to do," I said.

"Nothing at all, sir," Drumceat said. "But you're the First Tribune. We want you to know what we're proposing, and would like for you, when the time seems appropriate, to explain matters to the emperor."

"I'm listening."

"What happens if one of these Broken Men is caught on

our lands?" Praen said. "Generally he's just driven on, or perhaps taken to the nearest town, and the local magistrate deals with him."

"Which is generally no more'n a taste of the whip, if that, and he's hounded on to the next village, and then the next," a man grumbled. "Steals a chicken here, guts a calf there, maybe finds a back door unlocked somewhere else. Sooner or later, he'll run into a maiden, or a child—and what happens then? I say," the man went on, "these people, although they're more beasts, should be dealt with early on, and swiftly."

"Yes," Praen said, his face coloring with excitement. "Swiftly is the catchword. For our loyal villagers see these sons of bitches, and if nothing happens to them, why, they think how interestin', being able to live a life with no duties, taking what you want when you want it, and never a thought for the plow or the hoe. We propose, Damastes, to deal with these men, and their equally monstrous women, as they should be dealt with, the minute they're found on our lands."

"Without involving the law?"

"Law," Drumceat snapped. "We know the law, the real law, better than any yokel of a magistrate with sheepshit on his sandals. Hells, Tribune, look around. We *are* the law of Numantia, really. Just as we're the backbone of the country itself."

There was a rumble of agreement. I looked at Marán. Her lips were pursed, and she nodded slightly, evidently in accord.

"Let's see if I understand," I said, feeling my pulse start to beat harder. "You want to set up what, private warders? Where would the men come from?"

"We'd use our best, most loyal retainers. Men who aren't afraid of direct action. If we need more, well, there're enough men out there who've been ex-soldiers we could hire, men who know how to obey orders."

"All right," I said. "What happens when your warders find one, or a dozen, of these Broken Men?"

"We search them," Praen said. "If we find anything stolen, or if there's been complaints in the district, we deal with them then and there."

"Even if they've got nothing," another man snapped, "we drive 'em away from settled lands. Into the wastes, where they belong. Let 'em stay there and breed, or die, or whatever they want, away from us, and away from our peasants we're sworn to protect."

"And the law—the warders, the magistrates—they won't enter into this?"

"We don't need them!" Praen snapped. There were a couple of half shouts of agreement.

I sought Marán's face, but couldn't read it. I waited for a few moments, out of simple politeness, for I could make but one reply.

"Gentlemen," I said, keeping my voice calm. "Thank you for keeping your proposal brief. I'll be equally polite. Numantia is a kingdom of laws. When those are ignored by anyone, a 'Broken Man' or a count, we have anarchy."

Of course what I was saying was somewhat foolish, since I was hardly innocent enough to think a slave or peasant ever receives the same justice as a nobleman.

"Let me put things simply," I went on. "There shall not be any of these 'warders' allowed on any lands I am responsible for. If any intrude, I shall take all of them, *and those who command them*, into custody. I will take these prisoners to the nearest magistrate and prefer charges against *all* of them, charges they've violated imperial justice and committed low treason, which the law punishes most severely.

"I will not report what went on at this meeting to the emperor. As you said, he has more than enough on his table at present. At least, I shall do nothing unless I am forced by circumstances to take action.

"That is all I have to say, or want to say, on this absurd matter, and I advise you to forget about this idea, for your own sakes. I thank you for thinking of me, and wish you well."

I swept the room with my eyes, willing anyone to stand, to meet my eyes. Praen did, for an instant, then looked away.

Only Marán gazed back calmly. In silence, the men rose, were given their coats, and left. Praen was the last to go. He looked at me, as if he wished to say something, then went out.

Marán had not moved. I waited for her to say something. Long moments passed, but all she did was stare, expression unreadable. Finally she rose and walked out. I felt a sudden chill, and a feeling that this house was not mine, at least not this night.

I returned to the Palace of War, ate a bowl of soup in the guard room, and slept on my office cot.

The next day, it was as if the meeting had never happened, at least from the way Marán behaved.

That night, Kutulu came for dinner. Instead of coming on horseback, he arrived in a coach. I don't know how it was outfitted within, but from the outside it looked like just another prisoner transport carriage.

Marán had thought she might play matchmaker and had invited one of her acquaintances, a very pretty blond frothhead named Bridei dKeu. But Bridei, usually a great babbler of cheery nonsense, seemed struck with terror in the presence of the Serpent Who Never Sleeps, and he took little more notice of her than one of the servants.

Marán and I tried to keep the conversation going, but it wasn't until I thought of talking about crime that Kutulu warmed up. He told us about some cases he was familiar with. He wasn't a storyteller, but rather a reciter of cold facts, as if testifying in a law court. Thank Tanis we'd finished dinner before he began, for his stories were utterly compelling, if for no other reason than that they were of the bloodiest and most subtle murders.

Marán and Bridei drank a little too much wine as they listened, and Kutulu himself had two glasses. He was no more a drinker than I, for the drink had an instant effect on him, bringing color to his sallow cheeks and further unloosening his tongue.

Suddenly he stopped. "It is late," he said, "and I have much work on the morrow. I shall leave."

Bridei said she, too, must be going. Their carriages were

brought around. Bridei started toward hers, then stopped. "Oh dear," she said to her man. "I promised Camlann I'd stop by after dinner, but it's far too late for that. Kutulu, could I trouble you to take me home, while I send my carriage to my lady friend's house to offer my apologies?"

"Ummm . . . yes. Of course," Kutulu said.

Bridei turned to her coach driver. "Very well. Tell Camlann I'll be sure to stop by tomorrow. Then return home."

The coachman looked utterly bewildered, as if hearing all this for the first time, then nodded. "Yes, Lady dKeu. Certainly."

Bridei went to Kutulu's coach, and waited. It took a moment, but then he realized what she was waiting for, held out his hand, and helped her into the carriage. He was about to follow her, but stopped.

"Thank you, Countess Agramónte."

"Remember, I'm Marán?"

"Yes," he said. "Marán. A very pretty name for a very pretty woman."

I was astonished.

"Damastes, my friend," he went on. "Let me give you something to think on. Something you might find useful in time to come. You remember what happened at Zante?"

Of course I did—the massacre of the imperial cavalry.

"Let me give you something to think on," he said. "I must be most circuitous. It was said, you'll recall, the incident in question happened 'near' Zante? 'Near' was not quite how it was put in the first reports," he went on. "It was, in fact, more than ten days' travel south of that city."

He didn't wait for a response, but stepped into the carriage, and without waiting for orders, his driver tapped his reins and the coach pulled away.

"What was that about?" Marán wanted to know.

I wasn't sure.

She shrugged and turned to look after Kutulu's carriage. "I thought I was a failure," she said. "But . . . do you think bloody murder is the way to Bridei's heart?"

I put what Kutulu had told me aside for the moment. "I don't know if it was her heart that was taken," I said.

"Thank Jaen she can't keep a secret," my wife said. "For Kutulu will never tell us what happens between now and dawn."

Marán started giggling and took my arm, and we started inside. "What tale do you think it was that so excited her? The one about the woman who poisoned three husbands and then her lover? Or the ax that seemed to have a life of its own?"

"More likely the poor bastard who was beaten to death with his own dildo."

She laughed. "Well, *I'm* not at all aroused. But if you'd care to come upstairs with me, perhaps we could remedy the situation."

"Gladly, my love. But give me five minutes first."

We kissed, and she started up the stairs. Normally I would have watched her buttocks bob as she went, but my mind was elsewhere. I hurried to my library, unrolled a map, and sought far south and east from Nicias until I found Zante, deep in the Border Lands. I held fingers together, approximately the distance a cavalry troop would travel in a day, then moved them ten times that farther south. Cold shock ran through me. I checked my estimates against the map's scale. Ten days' journey south from Zante was well across the border into Maisir!

What in the name of all the gods was a Numantian patrol doing violating the border accords? The Maisirians had been well within their rights to attack them.

What was going on in those wastelands? Why was Tenedos lying to everyone, including me?

Another question that wasn't answered was what happened between Bridei and Kutulu. All the woman would tell Marán was that she was very, *very* glad she'd come to dinner.

Two days later I put the last orders for the establishment of the Imperial Guard in the emperor's hand.

Numantia took one more step toward war.

TEN

CHANGE IN THE TIME OF DEWS

The coming year whispered change, and there were many listening.

The first was the emperor. Unofficially, he set his wife, Rasenna, aside. He hadn't ended the marriage officially, but he'd ordered her to make an extended tour of the Outer Provinces.

There was still no heir, male or female. It had been whispered before that Tenedos was trying to solve the problem with any woman available, although of course one sufficiently noble to carry an emperor's son, and I remembered the giggle I'd heard in Kallio. The rumor was now confirmed, and the number of women coming in and out of his quarters was a mild scandal.

The first to become pregnant, another rumor suggested, would be the emperor's new bride. I wondered if there were women foolish enough to attempt to fob another's work off as the emperor's, and shuddered, knowing Laish Tenedos would use every sorcerous test to make sure the child was truly his, and bring the most terrible punishment on anyone trying the cowbird's game.

The next change came early one morning. My household guard was drilling in the courtyard, and I'd just finished my daily morning exercises. Marán was drowsing awake, alert enough to watch my press-ups and murmur "Very sorry, Baron, but the lady appears to have moved," when I heard a carriage in the drive. I pulled a towel about me and went to the windows. The carriage's door opened and Amiel Kalvedon got out and hurried up the steps. I wondered why she was calling on us at this hour. She, even more than Marán, loved the midnight times, and seldom rose before midday.

There were hasty footsteps in the corridor, and before I could reach my dressing gown, the door came open and Amiel was inside. Her eyes were red, and she wore no makeup and a heavy cloak. She saw Marán, burst into racking sobs, ran to the bed, and threw herself in my wife's arms, not even noticing my near nakedness. I wondered what in the hells had happened, and determined, uncomfortable as any man when a woman cries, to slip away and unravel the catastrophe later. But Amiel saw my cowardly move.

"No. Please, Damastes. Don't leave."

So I didn't. But I did put my robe on, and sat, uncomfortable, until Amiel brought herself under control.

"He threw me out," she managed to sputter. "Out of my own house. That bastard! That lying, opportunistic, bed-wetting son of a bitch!"

Marán made soothing noises, and little by little, between outbursts of crying and swearing, Amiel told us that Pelso had come home at dawn, more than a little drunk, and said their marriage was over and for her to be out of their house within the hour. He'd have her things sent wherever she wished, but he said "he could stand this farce no longer and had to be with the one he truly loved."

I'd often wondered if it were possible to maintain a marriage like Amiel's and Pelso's, and cynically had thought not. In fact, I'd wondered why, if they wanted to sleep with anyone they met, they'd bothered to take vows at all. I'd asked Marán once, and she said that they really liked each other's company and were the best of friends. More than evidently the "friendship" was over.

We got Amiel calmed, and I had soothing teas brought up, and we found out the final blow had been struck when Pelso's lover's brother, the governor of Bala Hissar, had let it be known he wished his sister married and was willing to settle a large sum in gold on her groom.

"So the shitbutt cast me aside. All I'll have is what he's good enough to give me," she said through gritted teeth, torment now turning to rage. "All that my father gave as a dowry, all that we've gained through our investments—all that will be his and his alone. I'll have nothing."

"I think not," Marán said. "I know some people who'll have a talk with him. I consulted them when my own marriage ended. I doubt he'll want this matter to become as big a broadsheet scandal as I might arrange."

Amiel started crying again, moaning about having no one and nowhere to go.

"Don't be silly," Marán said. "You'll stay here now. With us. Isn't that right, Damastes?"

Certainly she hadn't needed to ask me, when I remembered how good a friend Amiel had been, from our very beginnings. I sat down on the bed and began stroking Amiel's shoulders.

"This is your home now," I said gently. "From now until you die, if you wish."

So it was that Amiel, Countess Kalvedon, came to live with us.

The emperor sat motionless at his desk, the top of which was made of various colored woods forming a map of Numantia, sealed in a clear glass. Behind him on the wall hung an ornate sword and, beside it, an equally flamboyant wand. Two braziers, taller than a man, sent red flames swirling up toward the chamber's high ceiling, flames that never smoked or emitted heat.

The emperor's face was stern, hard. "Sit down," he ordered, and I obeyed. There was only one thing on his desk, a standard heliograph message form, some pages long. "Here. Read this. It came from King Bairan yesterday near dusk."

I read it once, then again, more carefully. The document was amazing. Bairan opened with a greeting using all of the emperor's titles. He had finally received word from the frontiers about the terrible incident in question, the unfortunate fight between soldiers of our armies. He said various explanations had been offered, and he was satisfied with none of them. He'd ordered a royal commission of inquiry, which would provide a true and complete story within a time, perhaps two. But in the interim, he wished to extend his fullest apologies to the emperor and to the Numantian Army. The Maisirian unit had been restricted to barracks and would be dissolved. Its men would be broken to the ranks and sent to other units. The three officers in command had been hanged as common criminals. As for the native auxiliaries, he'd have them tracked down.

He'd further ordered all border units to withdraw two full days' march back of the frontiers, to make sure another terrible occurrence like this wouldn't happen. He promised to make generous restitution to the widows and children of the slain Numantians and would hardly object if reparations to the state of Numantia were required.

I whistled. "Sire, your diplomatic note must've been incredible. I've never heard of any king being this humble."

"That's what you think, eh?" the emperor said coldly.

"What else could there be?"

"Read the end of his message again."

The last two paragraphs said the king was tired of the bickering about the border between Numantia and Maisir and would like to arrange a conference between the two rulers to settle the lines. In addition, it was time to consider the Border Lands, long a prickle to both countries, and devise a solution that would make everyone, except perhaps the bandits of those regions, content. It was time, the letter said, "for absolute peace to reign."

"My congratulations, sir," I said.

"You believe all that?" His tone was a sneer.

"Well . . . I don't have any reason not— Yes, sir. I do. Shouldn't I?"

"Now we see," the emperor went on, "why sorcery is given to but a few who are capable of piercing the veil and seeing beyond words, seeing truth, seeing what is real."

I blinked, wondering why I'd been rebuked.

"King Bairan sends this message, and might as well have crawled from the borders on his knees. He abases himself," Tenedos said. "Why?"

"Maybe he's afraid of provoking you?"

"Perhaps," the emperor said coldly. "Or perhaps he's trying to buy time to build up his army. Or perhaps he's planning a surprise attack. My magics have sensed something building, something coming, something from the south. Or perhaps his hidden dagger lies in this prattle about a conference. It wouldn't be the first time that a kingdom was betrayed under a flag of peace, would it?" Tenedos was barely controlling rage.

"No, sir," I said, my voice neutral.

"Very well," Tenedos said. "He chooses to hide in silk. We shall do the same. For the moment. Damastes, you remember that the post of general of the armies was never filled after General Protogenes's death?"

Of course I did. It was gossiped about in the officers' messes, and everyone wondered if the emperor were keeping that title for himself. Older officers said this was more important than it appeared, for a king who attempted to be all things would end by being none of them. It mattered not at all to me—the emperor controlled the army with or without the title, for we'd sworn an oath to serve him, and there were few fools in uniform who wished to return to the old days of puffery and nonsense.

"Tomorrow morning you shall be named to that post," the emperor said. "I shall be studying this matter of Maisir even more intently than before and will need to spend a great deal of time in other worlds and times to touch the heart of this matter. I want the army to continue to be a smooth, fine-running mechanism and know you, as first tribune, will guarantee that."

I knelt.

"Get up, you damned fool," the emperor said, a smile pushing across his face. "All I've done is create more work for you . . . although I still want you to concentrate on building my Imperial Guard. I believe we shall need them sooner than ever, and more of them then I'd planned."

Obediently I rose, saluted. The emperor nodded dismissal. I walked backward to the door, reached behind me, and opened it. As I went out, I glanced back at the emperor and saw his face darken. He held the heliograph transmission in both hands.

"You bastard," he muttered. "You cowardly bastard! Trying to ruin everything!"

The delowa may be the only sausage ever banned for immorality. About a hundred years before I was born, the always-incompetent and generally laughable Rule of Ten looked around for something to be outraged about. The Festival of the New Year caught their eye.

Numantia has always celebrated the New Year with the first glimpse of spring. For one full day all work ceases, and most laws are ignored. Traditional customs are suspended or reversed. Lords dress and act like peasants, and peasants become ladies. Men become women, women men, and frequently they let their dress dictate their behavior.

One symbol of the festival is the delowa, and the first time you see one you realize the Rule of Ten wasn't utterly foolish. It's made of white chicken meat, egg yolks, bread crumbs, salt, pepper, parsley, chives, thyme, and savory. These ingredients are well mixed, then carefully stuffed in casing about ten inches long by two inches in diameter. The casing is string-tied flush at one end, then at the other the meat is patted into a taper, and finally the casing is tied off at that end with just a bit protruding. It looks very much like a man's cock. The sausage is boiled, then smoked for a short time, then grilled by sidewalk vendors. The image is further encouraged by the special bun the delowa is served in, a cradle closed on either end. For spicing, a hellishly hot white sauce made from Hermonassan peppers is spread, and then the sausage is ready for the lascivious eater.

The Rule of Ten tried to ban not only the festival, but its symbol as well. The result was that the nobility were mostly forced indoors with the wardens and officials and ignored what was going on around them, while the masses ran riot, doing vast amounts of damage. After that year the ban was never mentioned again, and things returned to happy anarchy.

"We are," Marán announced one evening after dinner, "going to celebrate Festival three days hence as it's never been celebrated before."

A smile came to Amiel's lips, something that was very welcome. She had been trying hard to be her usual cheery self, but with infrequent success.

Marán had followed through on her promise, and the men of the law had attacked Pelso like rabid weasels. He must have been surprised at their ferocity, for he and his ladylove fled the capital for the temporary anonymity of Bala Hissar.

"I'm game," I announced, then reality struck. "But there'll be a bit of a problem."

"Problems exist to be overcome," Marán said, in her most royal manner.

"Excellent. Attack this one: There are certain people in Nicias who do not wish either you or I well."

"The Tovieti," Marán said.

"Yes. So if we go out, we'll have to have a great clanking set of bodyguards with us. I'm sorry."

"Hmm," my wife said. "Well, what had you planned?"

"Not much," I said. "I thought I'd work until dusk. Then maybe we could invite half a dozen friends in for dinner and watch the fireplay and apparitions on the river afterward."

"How *fascinating*. Lady Kalvedon," Marán said, "bear

you witness to the fact my husband, once in the forefront of frolic, has turned into a pooptitty."

"A pooptitty?" I snickered. "What, pray, is that?"

"Look you in the mirror," she said. "Come, Lady Kalvedon. We women will, as usual, save the day." She took her friend's hand and stalked out.

I thought wistfully of the festival, and how I'd only once been in Nicias at Festival with my wife. But no one ever said, as the soldiers put it vulgarly, generalling was all bangles and blowjobs.

That night Marán announced, quite smugly, that she'd solved our problem. She refused to say how. I thought I'd subvert her and find out from Amiel, but all her friend would do was giggle and say I'd see, and it would be even better than Marán had predicted.

"Oh ye who lack faith in the true magic," Seer Sinait intoned, "now ye shall weep bitter tears."

"And then carouse until dawn," Marán put in. They were behind my seer, trying to stay straight-faced. Sinait carried a small case of instruments and a tiny flask. She set both on the table, opened the case, took out chalk, and drew on the library floor.

"This is not a spell," Seer Sinait said, as she marked figures inside a strange triangle with curving sides, "so much as an anti-spell. We use hyssop, slippery elm, squaw vine, yellow dock, goldenseal, and others. But where these herbs are generally beneficial for vision, we will cast a spell of polarity. If you three would now stand at the points of this figure . . ."

We obeyed, and Sinait stood in the center. "The words I use have power," she chanted, "power of themselves, power to give, power to take. Let not your ears hear what I say, lest these words take power over you," and as she spoke I was suddenly deaf. Her lips moved, but I heard nothing. The sound from the crowds already thronging the riverfront outside was gone. I remained deaf for several moments, then she took a small, leafy branch from a belt pouch and swept it in measured gestures at us, and hearing returned. "Now, each of you come here, and let me touch you with this ensorcelled branch. First you, Damastes." I obeyed, then she summoned the other two. "That's that," she said briskly.

"What's what?" I asked.

"That's my protective spell," she said. "Quite a good one, too. It'll take a master magician to see through it, and he'll have to be concentrating. I think you'll like its effects. When someone looks at you, they'll not recognize you, even if they're a close friend. They'll think, dimly, you resemble someone they know, but of course it can't be you. A stranger will not be interested at all, and his or her eye will seek to pass on, to more interesting sights. Of which I doubt not there'll be plenty on this night," she went on. "Now, however, if you do wish to be seen, all you have to do is whisper 'Pra-Ref-Wist,' preferably without laughing at the silly words, and the person you're looking at will recognize you."

"I told you, Damastes," Marán said, "I'd figure out a way to not need bodyguards."

I grinned. "It'll be as if we're children again, and our parents are away for the night."

"Exactly," Marán said. "But even better. Do your second marvel, Seer."

Sinait walked to the table and picked up the flask. "I'll need three drops of blood," she said. "One from each of you."

"What does this one do?"

"This is what I'm proudest of," Marán said. "Something Amiel said made me come up with the idea. She told me once she was sorry that you can't drink."

"Won't, actually," I said. "Tastes like dung and then my head's the source of the dung for the next day."

"But there's something to be said for wine," Amiel said. "It loosens the mind and gentles the senses. Some, anyway. Others it makes more acute."

"Then you're throwing up in the gutter," I said.

"So what we want," Marán said, "is something that'll give

you all the good that drink can bring, but none of the evil. I consulted Devra, and she said such a potion was possible. Amiel suggested we should all take the same potion, so we're on the same level."

"What's in this potion?" I asked suspiciously.

"A bit of a lot," the seer said. "Nothing that magical, other than that I said an efficacy spell when I mixed the potion, like a cook sautéing his spices for greater effect. As to what's specifically in it, mostly herbs from the Outer Islands. Some you might recognize, like Carline thistle, lovage, water eryngo, gelsemine, centaury, sweet flag root, three or four varieties of mushrooms—the usual witch's hellbroth, in other words."

"Do we drink it or pray to it?" I asked skeptically.

"First your finger," Sinait said, and there was a needle between her fingers. It darted, and a drop of blood welled on my fingertip. She held the flask under it and the blood dropped, further discoloring the murky solution. "This, and some things I did earlier, will seal the potion to you." She did the same for Marán and Amiel. "Now drink," she said. "Share it equally."

We obeyed. The mixture was bitter, tangy, but not unpleasant.

"Now what do we do?" Marán said.

"Whatever you wish," Sinait said. "The potion will be quite long-lasting, well into tomorrow morning."

"When will we know what its effects are?" Amiel asked, a bit nervously.

"You will know when you will know," Sinait said. "And there's certainly nothing to fear. All that I put in it is natural."

"So are nightshade and fly agaric," Amiel muttered, but appeared a bit reassured.

"Have a good time," Sinait said, and I swear she was about to add "children," but caught herself and bowed out.

"That is that," Marán said. "Now, what do we wear? I didn't have time to plan a costume."

I went to the window and opened the shutter. For once the sages were right in their weather prediction, and I felt spring rushing on the land. A warm, gentle breeze blew off the river, and I thought I could smell the sea, miles north of us, about to awake to Jacini's gentle touch.

Marán and Amiel looked at each other. "Come," my wife said. "Let's raid our closets. Damastes, meet us downstairs in two hours. Dress sensibly, for we're going to be the peacocks this night."

I bowed obediently. This night was to be entirely Marán's show.

I chose a flowing silk tunic in the deepest blue, black pants and kneeboots, with a matching cloak treated to be waterproof, remembering how quickly Nicias's weather could change. Even though Sinait said it wouldn't be necessary, I took a simple black domino. I opened one of my arms cabinets, but decided I'd be in no jeopardy this night. I considered how seldom I'd gone unarmed over the years, but put the thought aside as possibly depressing.

A few minutes after the agreed time the women came downstairs. Both were dressed very simply. Amiel wore a lavender silk button-front dress. It was strapless, and she had the top two buttons unfastened, so it was quite beyond me how it stayed up, barely covering her jutting breasts. She wore matching sandals with leather straps curling up around her lower leg. The silk was very thin, and I could glimpse her rouged nipples. Around her neck she wore a matching scarf, and a simple eye mask in the same color was atop her head.

Marán had chosen a dress of knit red cloth that fit her body like a sheath from her ankles to just above her waist, where the material came to a point under her right arm. A gold catch held a triangular cloth of the same color that ran over her left shoulder, then down her back, leaving her midriff and right shoulder to just above her breast bare. Her shoes were slip-ons and, like her feathered mask, matched her dress. Each carried a cloak over her arm.

"And aren't we gorgeous?" Amiel said. "The prettiest threesome in Nicias." Her mood changed suddenly, and she looked sad. "Isn't it a pity the four of us never went out more than we did? Perhaps . . ." Her voice trailed off, and she shook herself. "Sorry. I'm being dunce-ish, aren't I? We don't need anyone but the three of us."

"No," Marán said softly, seriously. "We don't."

We went out into Festival.

The riverfront was thronged with people laughing, drinking, eating. Some wore costume, more did not. We marveled at a man and a woman dressed as cowled demons, who must've spent an entire year working on their outfits, then a goodly sum on the sorcerer who animated them, for in place of the monsters' fearsome faces were mirrors, but instead of merely reflecting they showed the faces, magically warped into evil, of those who peered under their hoods.

We started for the artists' quarter, where Festival was celebrated with the greatest dedication.

There was a ten-piece band, earnestly playing a song that had been on everyone's lips last year. In front of each musician was a mug. But instead of holding money, it held alcohol, and any passerby with a flask was invited to pour a measure into it. I wondered what the always-changing concoction tasted like, and winced.

There were about twenty dancers weaving about the band, and as they spun, each shed a garment. Some were already naked.

"What," Marán wondered, "will they find to do in twenty minutes? They'll all be bare as babes by then."

"Maybe put everything back on and start over," I hazarded.

"Or maybe they'll find some other way to pass the time than dancing" was Amiel's guess.

I felt myself grinning, without any particular reason. My body was wonderfully, comfortably warm, and the night was alive with wondrous scents. The people around us were marvelous to behold, whether they were rich, poor, ugly, or handsome. I looked at Amiel and Marán, and knew there were no two more beautiful women in all Numantia, and no one's company I'd prefer. Everything was soft, gentle, good. My cares about my duties, my worries about Maisir—all were meaningless. I was in complete control, my senses heightened, not altered. All that mattered, all I should concern myself with, was this moment in time that would last forever, when everything was permitted and no one could mean anyone harm.

Amiel smiled at me, and I knew she was thinking the same as I.

Marán hugged me. "I think," she said softly, "there was some potion in that potion."

Hunger came, and we found a line of stalls, and then tried to decide which delowa vendor had the tastiest wares. We settled on one, and he took three of the sausages from the grill, their aroma floating around us, and slid them into their obscene buns. He ladled the fiery white sauce over them and passed them across.

Another stand sold drinks. Neither Amiel nor Marán wanted wine, so we bought three fruit punches, found a quiet corner, and sat on a stone wall.

Marán took her sausage from its holder. "I always start like this," she said, protruding her tongue and licking sauce from the meat, looking at me as she did, tongue curling around and back.

"I prefer getting straight to the heart of the matter," Amiel declared and took a crunching bite of sausage and bun.

"Ouch," I said. "So much for sensuality."

"Not so." Amiel used her tongue to scoop sauce from the bun, stuck it out at me, then curled it back into her mouth. "Some prefer it before, some after," she said.

My cock stirred, and I concentrated on my own meal.

We were in a many-angled square, and in its center were perfume trees, still without buds, but the trees' aroma drifted over me like a curtain. There was a street magician with a small stand and quite a large crowd around him.

"Look ye, look ye," he bellowed. "Let me take you beyond

this time, this place. Let me show you the terrors, the wonders of another kingdom, the evil kingdom of Maisir."

His wand swirled, and red fire dripped from it, fire that vanished before it could reach the ground. Above us stretched a foreign sky, and there were vast snowy deserts, then plains that went on forever, then a huge city unlike anything I'd ever seen. It was built of wood, wood painted in a thousand different colors. There were towers, some conventional, some shaped like elongated onions, others in more subtle geometric shapes. I knew it instantly from my reading—Jarrah!

"This is the heart of evil, the Maisirian capital," the sorcerer announced. "See its riches," and we were outside a palace. One wall vanished, and everything inside was gold, silver, riches.

"Ripe f'r th' lootin'," someone shouted.

Another image came, and we saw a young girl, in peasant woolens, screaming in silent fear, as a ruffian carried her away from a burning hut. We saw her again, and this time she was nearly naked, her body clad in translucent silk. There was still fear on her face, especially as a fat man, wearing fantastic garb, stood nearby. He beckoned, and she shook her head. Again he motioned, and this time she went after him, slowly, reluctantly, dread on her face.

"That's what th' king a' Maisir does wi' his virgins," someone shouted, and I realized, perhaps with the heightened awareness of the potion, that the same man had shouted both times. I looked closely at the magician, and recognized him. It took a moment to pull his name from my memory. It was Gojjam, and I'd last seen him years ago, giving a rousing speech to the soldiery before Dabormida.

He was no more a street magician than I, but was busily keeping the emperor's agenda alive. I wondered whose gold he pocketed—Kutulu's, the emperor's, or perhaps the Chare Brethren. But this was no night for thoughts like these.

Nicias is named the City of Lights for the enormous gas deposits under its rock, gas that's been channeled until the meanest house has free light for the striking of a match. At Festival the valves are turned up, so Nicias is aflame from one end to the other. Here are pools of light, there pools of darkness. Some seek one . . . and some the other.

A fortune-teller, old, with a white beard almost to his knees, had a stand. We admired its elaborate woodwork. He looked up at us, but said nothing, waiting.

"I already know my fortune," I said, and so I did, having had it told at my birth when my mother consulted a wizard and he'd said, "The boy will ride the tiger for a time, and then the tiger will turn on him and savage him. I see great pain, great sorrow, but I also see the thread of his life goes on. But for how much farther, I cannot tell, since mists drop around my mind when it reaches that moment." I didn't understand the prediction, nor did my parents, but those dark words kept me from ever consulting another seer.

Amiel shook her head as well. "I don't want to know about tomorrow," she said. "If it's good, then I'll be surprised; if it's bad, I don't want to worry."

Marán asked me for a silver coin. "What do you examine, seer?" she asked. "My palms?"

"I've already made my examination," the old man said quietly.

"So what is to come?"

The fortune-teller started to answer. Then he looked at all three of us, shook his head, and tossed the coin back. "Not at Festival" were his only words.

"What does that mean?" Marán demanded.

But the man was looking down at his table.

Marán's face darkened. "How in the hells can he make any money, being like that?" she demanded. "This is a complete waste of time!" She walked away quickly. Amiel and I exchanged glances, then followed.

In a few minutes, my wife's good spirits returned. It may have been the potion, but just as likely the laughter, the music of many bands, from official orchestras to neighborhood groups to the piping of a cheery drunk on his tin whistle.

A man stood in a deserted square, his arms moving as if he were conducting a full orchestra. There were no musicians to be seen, but music swelled, flared around us.

A column of bears moved past, as if part of a show—mountain bears, tropical jungle bears, even the huge black bears of Urey. But there were no keepers, no chains, and the bears disappeared into the night.

We reached the river, and now the walkways were packed. Every small boat in Nicias had been decked with flowers, ribbons, and multicolored torches, and drifted up and down the Latane River. Above them in the sky were other ships. These were made of the lightest paper and carried torches filled with oils that burned with variously colored flames. The hot air lifted these small ships of the heavens high. Every now and then flames would reach paper, and fire would cascade into the water.

We kept moving toward the Emperor's Palace, where there'd be a real show.

Festival was the time for Numantia's magicians to parade their skills, and their wizardry filled the sky as we approached the Imperial Palace. This year the wizards seemed to outdo their previous attempts. Lights from no known source or any earthly color flared, vanished. Strange beasts, some known, some fabulous, pranced along the walkways. Trees grew, changed, took on animal life. Huge fish broke water and leapt high into the air, fish no man had ever hooked. The crowds cheered and laughed when one creation, something half a lion, half an octopus, pranced from a balustrade into thin air, then shattered as its creator became flustered and lost control of his fantasy.

Then the images vanished, and there was nothing but the starry night, and the Grand Illusion was to begin. Nothing happened for long minutes, then Marán gasped and pointed. Slowly, very slowly, the stars were winking out. The crowd saw what was going on, and the murmurs of excitement changed, became fearful. Then there was complete blackness. Children started to cry. A woman screamed.

High in the heavens a tiny light was born. It grew brighter, larger, and became a swirl of colors, spreading from horizon to horizon. The colors massed to one side and a huge image formed, a bearded face, an old man, who gazed down, not angry, not pleased.

"Umar," someone exclaimed, and the apparition *was* him, creator of the universe. A great hand appeared, and on it sat a world. The world began spinning, and the hand set it in the void.

Another god appeared, this one black-bearded, long-haired, and this was Irisu, the Preserver. He moved behind the world and held his hands protectively over it.

We looked at that world and saw everything on it, great and small, near and far. We could see mountains, seas, rivers, plains, and the animals and men peopling them. Only the Emperor Tenedos would have had the skill—and the temerity—to duplicate before the gods their own work.

Umar's visage faded, was gone. Now there was only our world and Irisu. But there was something wrong, a rot, a fungus spreading, and I knew our world was aging, dying. I heard a harsh wind whistle, although there was nothing around me but the soft breeze bringing the Time of Dews and the New Year.

From nowhere came a horse, a pale, spectral horse. Its saddle and bridle were red leather, red like spilled blood. On the horse was a woman, naked to the waist and wearing a necklace of skulls. She had four arms, one holding a sword, another a knife, the third a spear, and the last the tiny torn corpse of a man. Her hair was wild, uncombed, and her face was the glaring countenance of chaos.

It was Saionji, Goddess of Death, the Destroyer, the Creator, the god Tenedos worshiped over all else, the god few had the courage to even acknowledge above a whisper.

Now there were screams from both men and women, and

people began praying as terror seized them. But the terror lasted for but an instant as Saionji's horse turned, and she swept her spear toward Irisu, and he fell back. She cut at the world, our world, with her sword, and as she did, the rot, the sickness, fell away. Lights grew around the world, and all was wonderful, all was living, growing. Then Saionji was gone, and an instant later there was nothing.

There was just the quiet flow of the river, the gentle breeze, and the star-filled sky. There were a few cheers, but not many.

This was too great an illusion to applaud. If, I thought, it had been an illusion at all.

The sentry peered at me, and I remembered to whisper the counterspell. He saluted hastily. "Sorry, Tribune, but it's dark, and I must be tired, and—"

I waved aside his apologies, and the three of us entered the Imperial Palace. The emperor's party had been going on for some time. We heard music from the main audience chamber. Two drunks were snoring happily in the long hall, one lying in the arms of a sculptured demon towering above us.

There should have been at least two guards outside the chamber, but there were none. I noted the slightly open door of the nearby guardroom, asked the women to excuse me for a moment, and ever the proper soldier, went to see what the problem was and to do some minor ripping and tearing.

Fortunately, I pushed the door open a bit before beginning my tirade. There was a woman stretched across a table, wearing only the top half of a costume. One guard, pants around his ankles, moved between her legs, which were wrapped around his waist, and two others waited their turn. A fourth guard was also half-naked, buttocks toward me, his cock buried in the woman's mouth. He pulled it free for a moment, teased her with its head, and I recognized the emperor's sister, Leh, a smile on her lips.

I closed the door very quietly. It was of little real concern if this inner guard post went unmanned, after all. And even

First Tribunes are vulnerable to the calumny of sisters interrupted at their pleasures.

Amiel asked what I'd seen, but I just shook my head, and we went into the main chamber. It was packed with the lords and ladies of Numantia. The human debris was more pronounced here. The orchestra still played perfectly, and some dancers maneuvered skillfully around the sprawled bodies of those fallen on the field of drink. Others had found different pastimes in the alcoves around the huge room.

"A little sloppy," Marán said, but she didn't seem disturbed.

Neither was I, the potion making me view everything calmly, contentedly. I saw the emperor, holding forth to a throng near the tall bay window he used to proclaim great announcements onto the palace grounds. His face was flushed, in drink or triumph at the success of his illusion, and his voice was louder than usual. Beside him, wearing only a wisp of silk, was a tiny blond woman. I knew her, fortunately not well. She was the Lady Illetsk, widow of Lord Mahal, one of the Rule of Ten murdered by the Tovieti during the madness nine years ago. She'd been a shopkeeper's daughter when Lord Mahal married her, and was admired for her extreme patriotism—and other talents.

I'd met her before her husband's death, when I was a newly promoted captain of the lower half. I'd been invited to an unfamiliar house, which turned out to be Mahal's, and encountered my hostess at the entrance. Her perfect body was naked, she was inebriated, and she greeted me with a childlike smile and asked if I'd like to come between her tits. A bit shocked, I'd made a hasty departure.

After a sedate period of mourning, she'd continued her sociable ways in various arrangements with various sexes.

Oh well. Festival was supposed to be a time of abandon, which was evidently Tenedos's thought when he chose his companion for the evening. The emperor's eyes swept the room, and fixed on the three of us. I could see him frown, then his magic pierced Sinait's spell, and he recognized me.

I bowed, Amiel and Marán just behind me, and he acknowledged us with a nod, then turned his attention to Lady Illetsk. "Shall we join them?" I asked.

Amiel shook her head. "I don't think so, unless you really want to. How do sailors put it? A stern chase is a long one. We'd have to do some massive drinking to catch up with them, at least from appearances."

"And I, for one, don't feel like drinking," Marán said. "I feel absolutely perfect as I am. Let's go find another party."

"Or make our own," Amiel suggested.

Marán laughed. "We could do that," she said. "Where? Back at the house?"

"That sounds wonderful . . . No, wait," Amiel said. "I know another place. I just found it, and it's close to hand. Come on."

Amiel led us out the back, past sentries into the Imperial Gardens. They were mostly deserted, since it had grown a bit cool. Marán shivered and started to don her cloak.

"It'll be warm where we're going," Amiel promised.

We walked along a winding path through the sprawling grounds. Exotic trees, plants just coming into season, rose around us.

"Let's see," Amiel murmured. "From this white stone it's . . . here." She turned from the path into what looked like a solid patch of brush. But it was an archway of boughs, somewhat. "I wonder if the gardeners even know this is still here," she said. "I found it two weeks ago, when I dropped a bracelet and, when I bent to pick it up, saw through the gap in the shrubbery."

We followed her down the tunnel of boughs. It came to an end, opening into a perfect natural grotto. Stone steps led down to a glade. We went down them, and our feet sank deep into the moss. There were huge stones set here and there. A tiny stream purled from a fountain carved out of the solid rock near one side, and ran along one face, pooling from time to time, then vanishing underground.

It should have been dark and chilly, but light shimmered across the moss from a gas jet somewhere behind this garden. Out of the wind, the glade was no more than comfortably cool. It was a tiny world out of time.

"Isn't this perfect?" Amiel said. "We have comfort, we have water if we thirst, we have light, we even have music." The palace orchestra's music came faintly. I spread the cloaks on the ground, and we sat together, silent, enjoying the night, enjoying each other. Amiel put her head on my shoulder, and it was warm, comfortable. Marán snuggled close to her friend. We sat in contented silence for a time, feeling the potion soothe our minds, our bodies.

"I want to dance," Amiel announced. She rose gracefully, without using her hands, and moved into the center of the glade. I'd noted her dancer's body before, and she in fact had studied the art before marriage.

She faced us, bowed, and ran her hands up her body, then extended them out, offering herself. She began to move slowly, attuning herself to the distant music.

Her body became the music, a shimmering light purple icon, swaying, turning.

Marán breathed a little faster.

Amiel's hands went to her chest and moved slowly down the line of buttons. She tossed the dress away and continued dancing, sinuously, gracefully, naked but for her sandals.

My cock was painfully hard. Marán ran the tip of a fingernail the length of it. She smiled at me, eyes half-closed, then turned back to her friend's dancing.

Amiel beckoned, and Marán got up and stepped toward her, graceful as a young deer. They moved as one, never touching, only turning, eyes intent on each other.

My pulse was pounding, and I felt as if I, too, was the music, the dance.

Amiel touched Marán, and she stopped dancing. She stood motionless, eyes closed, waiting. Amiel ran her fingers down my wife's sides, then up, fingers caressing Marán's face.

I remember few more beautiful sights. Amiel's fingers went to the clasp at Marán's side, and her dress fell away.

Amiel stood motionless, her arms out. Marán came very close, and they kissed long, deeply. Marán kissed down Amiel's neck, to her breasts, teasing Amiel's nipples with her teeth.

Marán knelt, lips and tongue moving across the other woman's stomach, then touching her sex. Marán cupped Amiel's buttocks, kneading them, her finger slipping between them, then she ran her tongue between Amiel's legs.

Amiel moaned, throatily, and her legs melted, became liquid, and she flowed to the moss, legs opening.

"Damastes," Marán whispered, but her voice was as clear as if she were beside me. "Damastes, my darling. Take off your clothes, my love."

I obeyed her, fingers moving surely over clasps, buttons.

"Now, my lover, my life. Come here. Come to us. Make love to us, as we've talked of and dreamed about."

Very slowly I went across the moss to them.

ELEVEN

TRIAD

Amiel came to her knees. She gently caressed my balls, took my cock in one hand, then leaned forward and kissed its tip. Her tongue darted across my foreskin, then ran down to its base.

I knelt, kissed her lips, and slid my tongue into her mouth, moving it about as her tongue met mine. A thought touched me—how strange: *This is the first woman I've kissed besides my wife in more than nine years.* She made a deep sound in her throat, and her arms came around me. I laid her down on the moss, kissed her lips again, then the softness of her throat.

Marán lay down on Amiel's other side. "I've dreamed of this," she said once more, then lifted herself on her elbows and kissed me. Her tongue swirled in my mouth, then was gone. She kissed Amiel as I had, kissed her throat as I had done, then her lips moved down again, over the flatness of her friend's stomach, across her smooth sex.

Amiel moaned, and her legs parted. Marán unstrapped Amiel's sandals, moved between the woman's legs, and parted Amiel's sex with her fingers. Her tongue moved up and down, then slipped into Amiel. Amiel lifted her legs around

Marán's back and pulled her close as her hands went around my head, twined in my hair.

I kissed her long, deeply, her kisses becoming more frantic as her body responded to Marán's tongue and she began twisting. Her mouth was wet, open, gasping. I got up, touched the head of my cock to her eyelids, then moved it in and out of her mouth.

"Now," Marán gasped. "Now, my husband. Come love her." She stood, holding Amiel's legs far apart, lifting them by the ankles until her buttocks were off the ground.

I slipped between her legs, and looked for a moment at the beautiful woman, her head moving back and forth on the pillow of her hair. Her eyes opened, held mine. I drove hard into Amiel. She shrieked, and her hands pulled at me.

I took myself almost out of her, then hard in, again, and again, and I felt her body pulse against me, trying to turn, trying to twist, but Marán held her firmly. Her hands clawed at the moss. I jolted, spasmed inside Amiel, and a moment later she came, whimpering.

Marán released her friend's legs, letting them drop to the ground. I collapsed limply across Amiel, still draining into her.

Marán lay beside us, dark eyes serious as she looked us up and down. "I love you," she whispered.

"I love *you*," I said.

"And I love Amiel."

"Then I must learn to do the same," I said.

"Oh, Damastes, I hope so," she said.

"Now," she said. "Come love me as I loved her."

Amiel protested wordlessly as I slid out of her. Marán's legs parted and my tongue entered her wet softness. I tongued her clitoris as I put two fingers in her sex, another in her anus, and gently moved them in unison. Marán rolled under me, but I moved with her until I was lying on my back, and she lay atop me, rhythmically pushing her pelvis against me and crying aloud.

Amiel told me to look in the pocket of her cloak, and take out the tiny vial there. I unstoppered it, and the rich scent of strawberries filled the glade. The oil also tasted like strawberries.

Marán lay beside her friend, limp from our love-making. I poured a bit of oil on my palm and began rubbing it on Marán's ankles, then up her legs and on her inner thighs.

The vial never emptied, and I guessed Amiel must have had a spell cast to make it bottomless. For a second the always-watchful soldier part of me wondered if it were possible for that incantation to be used on soldier's canteens. I sneered, and let my fingers rule as they slid easily in and out of Marán's body. Her breathing quickened once more.

I massaged Amiel as well, and their bodies gleamed in the light from the gas flare. Marán rolled onto her stomach and began nibbling, then biting sharply, on Amiel's nipples, and they were hard as tiny fingers. Amiel arched her back, pushing her breasts upward into Marán's mouth. Marán slid two, then three fingers into her friend's sex, curling them, caressing the inside of her body. Amiel moaned and gasped her friend's name.

I moved behind Marán, parted her legs, and pushed my cock into her.

"Ahh," Amiel gasped. "That hurt."

"S . . . sorry," Marán managed to sputter. "Didn't mean to bite. But you don't know what he's doing to me. Oh, Damastes!"

Her fingers worked more swiftly as I ran the head of my cock in and out of her sex. Blood pounded harder and harder against my temples and I yanked myself free and spattered across Amiel's stomach. Marán, breathing hard, got to her knees, her hair sweaty, pasted to her forehead. She touched a drop of come, and then drew a horned circle, the ancient symbol of union.

"This," she said, "will seal the three of us together." She rubbed my come across Amiel's stomach, then lay atop the other woman. Their lips met, and they moved together. Amiel lifted her legs around Marán's hips and moved them up, down. Marán turned end for end, and lay across Amiel's body as the woman writhed, legs wide. Marán's tongue went deep into Amiel, as her friend loved her the same way.

I was hard once more, found the vial, and oiled myself. I gently turned the two women onto their sides, and they reflexively lifted their upper legs, never stopping their movements.

I held Amiel's buttocks apart, oiled two fingers and slid them into her, moving them back and forth, lubricating her, and then her own body added to the slickness.

I pushed the head of my cock against her rose, felt only an instant's resistance, then entered her tight warmth. I moved slowly, steadily, each time going deeper into her, and she gasped at each stroke. Marán's tongue caressed my balls as I moved, and my arms were around Amiel, pulling hard against her breasts, and then her body swallowed my soul and I remember no more.

It was false dawn when we limped back to our house beside the river, and I was very glad for Sinait's spell of nonrecognition, since I did not particularly want the sentry to note our condition. We made our way upstairs, undressed, and washed, and then the three of us fell into the huge bed in our bedroom and were instantly asleep.

When I woke, it was almost noon. I'd expected to feel muzzy-headed, but my brain was perfectly clear, and I felt rested, peaceful, happy. The potion's effects had vanished as quickly as they'd come.

Marán's head was on the pillow beside me, her hand curled around my balls. She had a tiny, private smile on her lips, the smile of a little girl the night of her birthday.

Amiel slept on her other side, one hand around her friend's waist. As I sat up, her eyes opened, she smiled at me, and then her eyes closed again.

I slipped out of bed and stretched hugely. I thought about what had happened. I should have felt as if I'd committed some sort of sin, I suppose. Or that one or another of us had, at any rate. But I didn't. I wasn't sure what all this portended, what it would mean to our marriage, but decided that was for the future.

I yawned and wandered into the bathroom. I'd determined to install a bath as lavish as the one in the Emperor's Palace, but hadn't had the time as yet. The bath, or baths, we had, though, were quite luxurious, two seven-foot-long tubs of green nephrite, shallowing at one end. Marán and I could each lie in one and talk, or, as often happened, share one. I brushed my teeth, tsked at my long hair, badly straggled from the night's adventuring, and laboriously combed it smooth while both baths filled. I waded into one, soaped and rinsed myself, then drained it, intending to soak in the clean water of the second.

Amiel walked into the bathroom, naked. She stretched, her breasts standing firm, and I felt my body respond a little.

"Good morning," she said.

"More likely afternoon."

"What of it?" she said. "Did you have any plans for this day?"

I did not, knowing Numantia would either be sleeping off the excesses of Festival, still celebrating, or else in the various temples praying in apology, and this would last for the next two or three days.

She brushed her teeth and rinsed with one of the washes we kept. "I suppose," she said, making no move toward the door, "I should borrow one of Marán's robes and go back to my own rooms to bathe."

"You could," I said. My mouth was a bit dry. "But who would wash your back if you did?"

"Ah. A definite problem." She went to the open shelves where we kept a variety of soaps, sniffed at them and chose one.

I reached over and turned on the tap of the second tub as Amiel stepped down into my bath. "First," she said, "we should wash my front." I obeyed, moving the soap in long, languorous circles around her chest, over her hard nipples, then across her stomach. I ran a finger in and out of her navel, and she smiled.

"Now, why," she wondered, "should that make a woman feel so good?"

"Perhaps it's a suggestion of things to come?"

"So it's Damastes the Wise now, not Damastes the Fair?"

It was Amiel who'd given me that name, which somehow had been picked up by the broadsheets to my considerable embarrassment.

"Things to *come*," she said. "How interesting."

My fingers ran lower, and slipped into her for a moment. Her stomach muscles rippled as her body responded.

"Now . . . Now it's my turn," she managed to say.

"But I've already washed."

"I see a place you missed."

She soaped my chest and stomach, slowly, gently, then she lathered my cock. She ran a ring with thumb and forefinger down its length.

"Just the right fit," she said. "Perhaps a bit longer than some would prefer, but one capable of getting to the . . . bottom of things. Now, sir, you may wash my back and whatever else you wish."

She turned, and I began soaping. As I moved lower, she spread her legs and leaned forward over the edge of the tub, on her hands. Her behind was perfectly curved, sleek. I put a soapy finger in her, and she wriggled against it.

"I see," she whispered, "you are making sure I'm very clean."

"It's my duty."

"And I know you always do your duty, don't you, Count Agramónte?"

I slid two fingers in her, and her muscles relaxed, then clenched tightly about them.

"It is," I said. "And I happen to have a specially built cleaner for this exact place."

"Perhaps you'd care to demonstrate it to me?"

"I think I should," I said, soaping my cock. I but touched her, and she relaxed her muscles, opening to me. I pushed into her, and she gasped, and moved back against me. We moved together, my hands caressing her breasts, she forcing me deep inside her, as she clenched and loosened her ring. Then she moaned, jerked twice, and sagged. I was still hard, and kept moving, gently, slowly, and once more she became aroused. She bent forward, until her stomach was flat on the deck around the tub, then reached back and pulled her buttocks far apart.

"Now, Damastes," she moaned. "Now, as hard as you can. Hard and fast. Tear me now."

I obeyed, cock steel-hard, driving into her to the root, and she let out a small shriek as we came together.

Some time later our breathing quieted.

"I like loving like that," she whispered. "Sometimes it hurts a little . . . but it's more intense. Sometimes I like it better than the other way." She moved against me. "But that's good, too. I don't know a bad way to make love."

"Poor Marán," she whispered almost inaudibly, and I knew she hadn't intended me to hear her spoken thought. I pretended I hadn't, slid out of her, and busied myself draining and filling the tub, remembering Marán's first husband, the contemptuous way he'd treated her, and how little love there'd been in her life. But that was the past, and so I set it aside, and watched Amiel's grace as she stepped out of the bath and slid into the other tub.

We were lolling in the warm, scented water when Marán wandered in, rubbing her eyes sleepily.

"You two make a lot of noise," she said. "You woke me up."

"I didn't know anything could," Amiel said. "You were snoring like you were trying to swallow your nose."

"I don't snore!"

I laughed. Marán sat gracefully down on the edge of my tub, kicked water in my face, stuck out her tongue, then turned to Amiel.

"Did you leave anything for me?" she asked.

"You'll have to see for yourself," Amiel said. "If not, I'll make suitable amends."

"Yes," Marán said, her voice becoming husky. "Yes. I'd like that."

She reached out with a foot and caressed my limp cock.

"There's nothing here but a noodle," she said, ignoring my response. "You'll have to handle my problem."

She spread a towel and lay back on it. Amiel, oiled, sleek, lifted herself from her bath and began stroking my wife's inner thighs. Both women's eyes were on me, waiting for approval or shock now that the potion's strange effects were gone.

"You know," Marán said, "Amiel and I have been lovers for some time. Not always. But when you're gone . . ." She stopped and opened her thighs. Amiel caressed her clitoris with her thumb.

"I wanted Marán the first time I saw her," Amiel said. "Before she met you. But nothing ever happened."

"Nothing much, anyway," Marán said. "I think I let Amiel kiss me once or twice, and pretended I was drunk and didn't remember it. I was afraid. The first time we made love was after I lost . . . lost our baby. When you were at war."

I remembered well. For weeks after the miscarriage I'd heard nothing but two brief notes, then a sudden apology, and I remembered how she'd said she would "always be indebted to our dearest friend Amiel," who'd given Marán "the greatest comfort since our son died."

Perhaps I should have been angry, should have felt threatened. I would have if it had been a man my wife had taken for a lover. But I felt nothing but gladness for Marán, and also for her friend.

"You know," Marán said, "Amiel was only the second person I'd ever fucked who could touch my soul, could make me come? Getting you in bed with both of us is something we've talked about, schemed really, since we've been lovers," she went on. "To tell the truth, we hoped this is what would happen when we went to Seer Sinait for the potion. I felt like I was cheating on you every time I made love with Amiel and wanted to change that. The only way I could see to do that was to do what I did. I know I can't give Amiel up."

"And I couldn't stand to be without you, Marán," Amiel said. She giggled. "Not to mention that we've only been able to make love three, maybe four times since then," Amiel added. "Not nearly often enough for me."

"Oh yes," Marán said. "It wasn't enough. Now I know that. Oh, Amiel, don't stop. Don't ever stop."

Amiel's head lowered, and her tongue moved against Marán's shaved sex, inside it. Marán clasped the back of her knees with her hands, lifted her legs, and spread them.

"Let me do that," I said. I stepped out of the bath, knelt over Marán's head, and took her legs in my hands, holding them far apart, as Marán had done Amiel's.

Marán was twisting, moaning as Amiel loved her. My cock, stiffening, touched her lips. "Put it in my mouth," Marán managed to say. "I want to drink you. Oh, put it in me, Damastes."

We made love throughout the day, and had meals sent in. The servants bore completely bland expressions, as befitted professionals.

At dusk, we were lying on the bed. There were pillows on the floor where we'd loved, sheets and covers were everywhere, and there were open vials of scent and unguent on the bedside tables. Amiel's head was on my stomach, and Marán lay between her friend's legs.

"I could stay like this forever," Amiel said.

"Then you shall," Marán declared.

"No," Amiel said. "I guess we shouldn't arouse any greater scandal."

I chuckled.

"What's so funny?" Amiel wanted to know.

"I just realized something," I said. "No doubt everyone in the city knows you've come to live here."

"Of course," Amiel said. "There have been stories about the end of my marriage, and I've seen mention that I've taken shelter in your company."

"Well then, what do you think everyone is thinking anyway?"

"Ah," Amiel said.

"I've already got the reputation of a crazed goat," I said. "So it matters not at all to me. Marán?"

Marán sat up. "We can't . . ." Then she broke off. "Who said? Why can't we? I don't give a shit what anyone thinks except maybe my family, and they don't read the broadsheets anyway. Damastes is right. I guess we'll have to maintain proprieties in public. More or less. But this is our home. Here we do what we want, when we want, as we want. Amiel, this bed is yours as well. Such as it is," she said wryly, looking at the shambles.

Amiel's things were moved from her bedroom into ours. Marán emptied one of her two dressing rooms out, and that was that. No one in the household said anything, ever. Once I noted Seer Sinait looking at me speculatively, a concerned expression on her face. I asked if she wanted something or had a question, and she said no.

In spite of my resolution, I did wonder what the future would bring, what this meant and would mean to our marriage. But I had no answers.

Amiel's dark moods came to an end, and she was content in our mutual passion. I learned now why she was so prized as a lover—she acted as if love were her only concern, and those she loved the only reality.

Another thing had changed: Marán was happy, smiling. I didn't see that cold, apppraising expression any longer.

So I was happy, too.

But no idyll can last forever.

TWELVE

GAMES OF EMPIRE

Our raptured time was steadily eaten away by my duties. Men were streaming into the army's Nician depots, and being sent south to the new training grounds in Amur.

Some were veterans, others new enlistees the recruiters felt had mettle. Naturally, some commanders had played that old army game and sent us their worst and most laggard, and these were quickly sorted out and booted back where they came.

Something that niggled was the officer chosen to command the First Imperial Guard. He was a mounted infantry—dragoon—domina named Aguin Guil. He'd been picked by the emperor less, I feared, for his abilities than because he was wooing the emperor's sister, Dalney, and was so favored she'd given up her other flames. Myrus Le Balafre said Guil was brave enough, but had a slight tendency to become excited under extreme pressure.

At least nothing appeared to be happening in Maisir, in spite of the emperor's suspicions. King Bairan held to his promise of keeping his soldiery two days' march from the frontiers. The spies we sent across the border reported no sign of troop buildup, either.

Not that the frontiers were quiet. The emperor ordered half of Yonge's scouts broken into small detachments and sent to Dumyat to serve as border patrollers. The rest of the Twentieth Heavy Cavalry went to Dumyat and set up a base camp to the north, as a reaction force if the scouts were attacked. There was constant skirmishing, but this was with the Men of the Hills rather than Maisirians.

Lany, Kutulu's nominee for regent in Kallio, was keeping those unruly people quiet, so the emperor ordered the return of the Tenth Hussars and my own Seventeeth Lancers, reinforced with the elite Varan Guards, back to their bases in Urey. They were built to full strength and ordered to patrol aggressively south, into Kait.

Officially the emperor wished to ensure the peacefulness of the Men of the Hills and ensure Sulem Pass, the traditional path between Numantia and Maisir, remained clear. These reasons were true. But there was another. The trade route was the only possible invasion route into Maisir, striking straight across the mountains and wastelands to Jarrah. I wasn't much impressed with the emperor's subtlety—surely King Bairan would realize what the troop buildup in Urey was intended for.

Another move he'd made against Maisir must've been more subtle, since I saw no sense to it. To the west of the Urshi Highlands was another border kingdom, the backward region of Ebissa. Numantia had little interest there, since the land was nearly as mountainous as the Highlands or Kait, and thickly jungled as well. Ages ago, the Ebissans had been fierce warriors, for they conquered deep into Maisir before being driven back to their fastness. They still claimed sovereignty over the land they'd held for only a few years. It was just another of the inflated arrogances of the little bandit areas of the Border Lands. Yet suddenly the Emperor Tenedos announced he'd investigated the matter, felt there was justice and truth to the

Ebissan claims, and he was prepared to act on their behalf. Other than to anger King Bairan, I saw no point to this whatsoever. But he was the diplomat, and I was but his soldier.

I saw the emperor infrequently in these days. I was very busy, and he was busier. He'd chosen the tower we took refuge in during the Tovieti rising as his private sorcerous retreat, and had it surrounded with high, glass-topped walls, handpicked guards, and, it was said, the most devilish of magical wards. I sometimes rode past the tower, late at night on my way home. Once I saw flames roaring up, higher than the tower itself, flames in colors I had no words to describe, yet I felt no heat. Another time I saw a tiny dot atop the tower's roof, bellowing an incantation into the heavens. I heard the emperor's words clearly half a mile distant, though I knew not the language. What was terrifying was that his ceremony was what the priests name Call and Response. Each measured chant from the emperor was met with a louder, deeper response, and that response seemed to come from inside the earth itself.

Lucan whinnied in fear, and I let her trot off, pulling her back from a frenzied gallop.

If we went to war, there would be even more deadly demons on our side than the horrors the emperor had raised for the fighting against Chardin Sher. I shuddered, remembering a forest come alive, clawing at Kallian soldiers, and the primeval demon from underneath Chardin Sher's final fortress—and then I thought of Seer Hami's question of what reward that demon sought for his services.

I lay on the bed, watching Amiel brush Marán's hair, admiring the way the firelight cast shadows across her black diaphanous silk gown, and allowed myself lazy lustful considerations of what might happen when they came to bed in a few minutes. Amiel turned to me.

"You know, since Festival," she said, "I've felt no draw to anyone else. Your Captain Lasta, for instance, is a fine sort of man. Before, I might have blinked at him, backed him into a corner, and let him think he was seducing me. But I don't feel any desire for anyone, anything, but what we have. Why?"

"My sixteen-inch tongue," Marán said.

"You stole that line from me," I complained.

"You, sir, have other long things to brag on," my wife said. "Leave me what I have."

"Now," Amiel said seriously, "does this mean Pelso couldn't give me what I need, from the first day of our marriage to the last? Or does it mean I'm in love for the first time in my life—with both of you?"

Marán looked up at Amiel. "I can't say," she said. "But I know I love you. And I want a kiss."

Their lips met, clung together. I wondered exactly what I felt for Amiel. And for my wife.

Marán came into my study one evening with a parcel. "This doesn't pertain to Amiel," she said. "Only to us. It came from my brother Praen this afternoon." She dumped the contents of the package on my desk. There was a one-page letter and three yellow silk cords I recognized instantly—the strangling cords of the Tovieti. "Praen found these on our land," she went on. "Their former owners will have no further use for them. He also said that twelve of their friends were rewarded as these three were."

I felt anger. So Praen had paid no attention to my warning, and he and the others had hired their warders.

"Something I don't think you understand, Damastes," Marán went on. "I may be angry with my family, with my brothers, and sometimes they drive me quite mad. But that doesn't mean I'm not an Agramónte."

"I never thought it did," I said.

"Very well. Then do you understand what it means to me to have swine like this on *my* land? Corrupting *my* people?" Her cheeks were flushed, her gaze intense.

For once I thought before I spoke. "Did it ever occur to you," I said, in as mild a tone as I could manage, "that maybe

Praen could make a mistake? That perhaps one, or maybe more, of the people he judged and executed, might have been innocent? That he stepped on their rights as much as any tyrant?"

"*Rights,*" Marán exclaimed. "I also have rights. I have the right to peace, I have the right to my life, I have the right to my land. Anyone who tries to take those from me . . . I'm sorry, but I'm going to strike back as hard as I can. As my brother and his friends are doing."

"You didn't answer my question."

"No," Marán admitted. "Praen could be wrong, although I wonder what a magistrate would've done if he found the fifteen with these horrible cords. Would the emperor's justice have been any more kindly?"

I remembered the door-to-door, block-to-block patrols that had killed men, women, sometimes children on the strength of a cord or an unexplained bit of loot when the army pacified Nicias.

"No," I answered truthfully. "But the emperor's justice is a system, a system that works, a system that's in writing, not in somebody's mind and sword arm, and one most people agree with. If it weren't, Tenedos would never have reached, let alone held, the throne, with or without the army behind him."

"Damastes," Marán retorted, "we Agramóntes ruled our lands as we saw fit, as kings, as queens, for centuries while the Rule of Ten stumbled around. Do you think we bothered to bring evildoers all the way to Nicias for trial? I remember my father sitting in judgment outside Irrigon, bailiffs and swordsmen behind him, ordering people into exile, to be whipped, sometimes, sometimes to be taken away and I never saw them again. What's the difference between that and what Praen's doing?"

There was none, which was exactly my point. But I didn't want a fight.

"Marán," I said carefully. "What angers me the most, to be completely truthful, isn't what Praen and the others seem to be doing. But why does he insist on rubbing my nose in it? Does he want me to go to the emperor, as I threatened?"

"Of course not," Marán said. "Perhaps he wants you to wake up to what you are, dammit. Damastes, you're not just my husband, but you're Count Agramónte. Sooner or later, we'll have sons, and you'll have to teach them what the name means, what it's worth, how proud it is.

"You'll have to teach them they *do* have the power of life, of death, no matter what the law of Nicias, which is a long way from our land, says. Praen's trying to show you what you must become!"

I looked at her, and saw a great gulf, a gulf of years, of riches, of ideas, of tradition, of power, a gulf of life and death I would never be able to understand, accept, or cross. My anger died and, very suddenly, very strangely, I felt like crying.

There were rumors about the Maisirians: how they brutalized their poor; how any land they conquered was ruined under the boot heels of their soldiers; how they'd distorted our common religion into human sacrifices and the despoliation of virgins; the utter perversity and evil of their ruling class, particularly King Bairan; and so on and so forth. None were worth repeating or chronicling, and all were the usual crap that floats around about an enemy just before the start of a war.

Disaster struck the thickly peopled coastal state of Hermonassa, the next state west of Dara: plague. A man or woman would wake up coughing uncontrollably. Then a burning fever would set in, and paralytic stomach pains. The victim would begin bleeding from every orifice, go into convulsions, and be dead before dusk. Anyone around the victim would be infected, and almost all died as well. A few survived, but before they recovered they wished for death many times over.

The plague would strike here, then the next day ten leagues away, then the day after on the far side of the state. Nothing seemed to stop it. Hermonassa panicked, and the panic spread across the border into Dara, through Dara to Nicias. The plague would be here next. Many people fled the capital, going anywhere they imagined to be safe. But the disease never came; it seemed content to rage in the borders of Hermonassa.

A worse epidemic came with it: a plague of stupidity and incompetence. The governor of Hermonassa and his staff had died in the first days, almost as if the disease had an ability to strike at our most vulnerable points, and their replacements were confused and inept. The medicines Tenedos ordered sent were lost or stolen. The wizards and chirurgeons were delayed by rains or by wagoneers who refused to enter Hermonassa, regardless of bribes or threats.

Numantia responded with all its heart, sending food, clothing, and workers to the distressed state. But nothing seemed to reach the stricken area. Grain rotted on the docks or was ruined in transit. Clothing was misplaced in warehouses, not to be found for many times. Even the emperor's decrees were ignored or unenforced, and Tenedos raged in futility.

Disorder and mob rule spread throughout Hermonassa, and I was forced to declare martial law. Even the army was hit by this scourge of incompetence, and trusted units broke as if they were untrained recruits on their first battleground. Officers misunderstood orders, obeyed them poorly, or refused them.

I sent in handpicked dominas, men with hearts that could shatter the hardest stone, with orders to straighten out the army, no matter how. Eventually their savagery took effect, and chastened soldiers moved into Hermonassa.

Slowly the plague faded, and then was a memory. But more than half a million Numantians were dead. We sacrificed to all the gods, including the dreaded Saionji, but no seer could find why we'd been cursed, what Numantia and Hermonassa had done to deserve such punishment.

No one knows to this day. No one but me, and the terrible reason took long for me to discover.

A story came that wasn't a rumor: Three members of the Numantian Embassy in Jarrah had been expelled by King Bairan for spying. The emperor responded by ordering the entire Maisirian Embassy closed, and its officers escorted by armed soldiers to the border.

Curious, I rode past the shuttered embassy as the Maisirians were departing. The last to leave was the ambassador, Baron Sala.

He stopped at the small flagpole and personally lowered the Maisirian flag. His staff bowed their heads as he did. He meticulously folded the flag in military fashion, then turned toward his carriage.

He saw me, and we stared at each other. His face was worn and tired. He didn't greet me, nor I him. Baron Sala climbed into his carriage, and a footman closed the door and jumped up on the running board as the coach moved away.

The drums of war were getting louder.

"I expect," the emperor said jovially, "to be inspired, nay overwhelmed, by your Guard." It was warm, the Time of Dews almost over, the Time of Births about to begin, and a breeze ruffled his beard and my loose-hanging hair.

We were on the foredeck of the newly launched imperial courier ship *Kan'an*, sailing at speed toward Amur, where the emperor and I would witness the first full-scale battle game of the First Imperial Guard Corps.

"*My* Guard, eh?" I said.

"Of course it's *your* Guard right now," Tenedos said. "I'm assuming the worst. If things go well, and the unit runs like a clockwork soldier, then it'll become *my* Guard. Aren't you aware of how rank works, and in which direction shit flows? By the way, who is to play enemy against the Guards?" he asked.

"Half-trained recruits that we've formed into temporary units," I explained. "For officers and cadre, Yonge's given me two regiments of his scouts."

"I don't see these rapscallions providing much of a threat against trained soldiers in formation."

"Frankly, sir, they're not supposed to."

"Oh?"

"You don't bloody a horse's mouth when you first put a bit on him," I said. "I want these new Guardsmen to come away proud, feeling that they've learned something. Then Petre's instructors will show them how much more they've got to learn."

"Good. Very good," the emperor said. "Then real battle will make them learn they know absolutely nothing after all."

I smiled ruefully, and nodded agreement.

"So then there should be no reason whatsoever *your* Guard won't become *my* Guard three days hence," the emperor said. He laughed and stretched.

"Ah, Damastes, my friend. It does me, does both of us, vast good to get away from that scrabbling nonsense of Nicias. I vow it was nothing but courtiers nibbling at me like rats, or listening to myself drone spells night and day. Sometimes I wondered if this was why we told the Rule of Ten to pack their ass with salt and piss up a rope."

In this humor the emperor reminded me of the charming rascal I'd vowed to serve years ago.

"Nothing but courtiers and spells?" I asked in my most innocent manner. "Gods, but the nights must have been *dreadfully* dull."

The emperor lifted an eyebrow. "Peering through bedroom windows ill becomes you, First Tribune. For one thing, it gives you bloodshot eyeballs. And from what I've heard," he said slyly, "you have little reason to be sanctimonious about what anyone does when he retires."

So the emperor had heard of our affair. I shrugged, and he clapped me on the shoulder.

"Speaking of court," he went on, voice turning serious, "I gather some people think my palace has become decadent. I'm encouraging too many scoundrels in gold lace and whores in silk. But I know just what I'm doing. The people love spectacle, and I think it's important to give it to them. Besides, I rule the greatest empire of all, and I think splendor must be part of that empire. Should we be mousing around in gray homespun and living in hovels?

"No," he said. "Noblemen and -women, living nobly, are an inspiration to all, especially those who aren't as favored. It's much the same as the sound of marching boots and drumrolls. Anyone whose blood isn't stirred by the sight of soldiers on parade is dead of soul, and should be returned to the Wheel as a favor."

It was fortunate Domina Othman, Tenedos's aide, bustled up with some question, or I might have had to respond to what the emperor had said. I might be a warrior, but I knew that most heard the drum snarl with fear and dread, seeing the dark blood to be spilled, the roaring flames that were now peaceful cities, the women left without husbands, the children without fathers or mothers, that Saionji's manifestation, Isa the war god, brought.

My emperor, I feared, had forgotten the reality and, true to a worshiper of Saionji, had fallen in love with war.

The war games were an utter disaster—for the Guard. The plan was simple: The Guard Corps was to advance with three elements in line until it made contact with the "enemy." Conventional tactics would have had the forward element hold the enemy in place while the second and third attempted to envelop the foe and destroy him.

But I had devised a different strategy, one more suitable for fast, mobile warfare in the vast, open reaches of Maisir. The first element was indeed to keep the foe pinned, but the second and third were to circle the struggle and strike hard for the rear headquarters. That would either make the enemy surrender, break, or form a defensive circle that the battle could move past. The Corps following the spearhead could pause to obliterate the stronghold.

But the first element fell back instead of holding firm. The second got entangled in the first, and the third swung wide but never returned to the ordered axis of advance.

The emperor and I stood in Corps General Aguin Guil's command tent, and watched him lose control of fifteen thousand men. Our out-of-date maps were covered with symbols no one could understand, runners dashed about, staff officers shouted, and General Guil stood in the middle, mouth opening and closing without any words coming out.

He should have shouted silence and gone outside the tent for five minutes, breathing deeply, calming himself. Then he should have pictured the battlefield in his mind, imagined where his forces were, or should have been, and gone back inside and brought order.

But he just stood there helplessly, mouth moving as if he were a stranded fish. I wanted to help, but knew I must not. If the general was to become a general, he must learn I'd not be there to save him when matters went out of control—which is invariably what happens five minutes after a battle commences.

But the emperor didn't realize that. "Silence," Tenedos bellowed, and stillness spread like a wave, save for one wide-eyed captain who babbled on for a few seconds until he realized his voice was the only sound. "Now," the emperor said, "we must try to save the day. Send for . . . Who's the domina in charge of the First Wing?"

"Tanagra, sir."

"Very well. You. Galloper. Ride down the road until you see Domina Tanagra's battle flags. Tell him . . ."

What the emperor wished to have Tanagra do went unknown, for shouts, bellows, and screams rang, and fifty horsemen thundered into the camp, sabers slashing tent ropes, guards knocked spinning, and men running in all directions. Their leader slid from his horse, ran into the tent, and shouted, "You're all my prisoners! Surrender or die!" It was one of Yonge's legates. Three archers ran up beside the "enemy" officer, blunt arrows nocked.

"The hells we are," Guil snapped, reaching for his sword. An arrow thunked lightly into his chest.

"Sorry, sir," the legate said, no sorrow at all in his voice, "but you're dead now." He turned to the emperor and me. "Now, you two. Don't—" His voice went into a squeak as he recognized his emperor. For an instant, he almost knelt, then he remembered his role. "Your Majesty! You're captured. Don't move!"

Tenedos's face reddened. His gaze lanced out. "This," the emperor began, his voice like thunder, "is truly absurd! I . . ."

He must have seen my involuntary head shake, for he caught himself. He had his temper controlled instantly. The snarl on his lips became a smile, and a laugh came. Possibly I was the only one who knew how false it was.

"Absurd," he went on. "And a fine piece of work, Legate. You seem to have won the battle and, I'd suppose, the war. Damned few armies fight on when their emperor's in the hands of the enemy. Was this your idea?"

"Yessir."

"You're now a captain. Of the Upper Half."

We lost a battle and the war game, but the emperor won the day.

"Men of the Guard, listen to your emperor." Tenedos's voice boomed across the plain. He stood on a small reviewing stand, ten feet above the drawn-up First Guard Corps. "I came to see what sort of soldiers you are," he went on. "And now I know. You think you have done badly, and, in a manner, you have. But the blood that was shed was not real. The lives that were lost have not gone to Saionji.

"This battle can be replayed and won, if we so choose. What you should have gained in the past few days is knowledge of who you are. You are young, you are strong, you are learning. None of us—not you, not I—learn without making mistakes. Yesterday a mistake was made. Laugh about it, for it is worth laughing about. But learn from it, for it's also a great lesson.

"You are the first to carry the name of Guards. There will be others that will come after you. Now you must train harder, work harder, so that so long as there is an army in Numantia, so long as there are Corps of Guards, any soldier will know that the greatest duty he can perform, the highest honor he can reach, is to fight as well as you will fight. I salute you, Numantians, Guardsmen. You are mine . . . and I am yours.

"This day is the beginning. Ahead there is nothing but glory and honor."

He saluted, and the Guard Corps cheered him until I thought they'd rupture their lungs, as if disgrace would be buried in the wall of sound.

I'd seen another reason why the emperor was the emperor. This silly defeat in a war game in a desert state might steel the First Guard even more than a victory.

"I should've turned that limp-dick into a toad," the emperor growled.

"I didn't know you had that kind of power," I said.

"I don't. But I'd find a spell somewhere."

"By the way, who are we talking about? The legate?"

"Him, too. But I meant Guil. I hope Saionji toasts his foreskin on a very hot fire when she takes him back to the Wheel!"

"Do you want him relieved?" I asked.

There was a long silence. The emperor sighed. "Do you think he should be?"

"I don't know," I said. "He lost his feel for battle. But I don't know anyone who hasn't done that. He just did it at a time that was a little embarrassing."

"Embarrassing, my left testicle," the emperor said. "Damned humiliating."

"Especially for me," I said. "Showed me what happens when I start following people like you into tents."

The emperor glowered, then his mood broke, and he started laughing. "No. Don't relieve him," Tenedos decided. "My sister owes you a debt. But make sure he learns. I don't want there to be a next time."

"There won't be," I promised. "Not for him, not for his

whole gods-damned Corps. I'll have Mercia and his instructors drill them until they're bleeding through their eyeballs and toenails. I'll get an order out as soon as we get back to Nicias."

"No, you won't," the emperor said. "You're on two weeks' leave."

"Why? I'm barely back from the last one."

"It seems a certain lady came calling before we left. A certain Countess Agramónte. She wished a boon. She said her lands have a certain feasting when they plant the corn. She said it's a custom that goes back before there was an Agramónte, and the people feel it's the worst of luck if their lord is not present."

This was the first time Marán had ever asked a favor of the emperor. "That's sort of the truth, sir," I said. "But I've missed it three times since we've been married, off rooting around the frontiers for you."

"Terrible," the emperor said. "Custom is what binds the peasants closer to the lords. You'll not miss it this year."

"If you say so, sir."

"Besides, I promised Marán. And Jaen knows your wife is very beautiful, and I've never broken a promise yet to a beautiful woman." He stared out at the Latane River, and once again his mood changed. "So the First Guard isn't as ready as I hoped it to be," he said gloomily. "Which means none of the other corps can even think about full-scale maneuvers."

"I'm afraid not, sir," I said.

He said something very odd: "Thank Saionji that I've bought us all some time."

"I beg your pardon, sir?"

"Nothing," he said, hastily changing the subject. "Look. Out there. Is that child on the world's tiniest raft, or is she walking on water, in which case we should begin worshiping?"

Amiel and Marán were waiting at the dock when we disembarked—our departure from Amur had been signaled to the capital by heliograph. In spite of the weather—a light spring mist, almost a rain—their carriage was open except for an overhead canvas. Marán had a merry expression on her face; Amiel looked angry. I wondered what had happened. I looked closely and saw a thin film of sweat on Amiel's face.

"Here," Marán said, holding something out to me. I unrolled it, and saw it was a pair of women's underpants.

"Your wife," Amiel hissed, "is a hussy."

"This is true," I agreed. "What made you realize it?"

Marán started giggling, and said, "We've been good little girls while you were gone. Two whole weeks without doing anything with each other or even ourselves."

"If you had to do without, we should do the same," Amiel said. "So we did. Until this morning."

Their outfits were as seductive as could be imagined, barely permissible beyond the bedroom. Marán wore a flaring skirt that hardly went below her crotch, and revealed matching underpants of the sheerest silk, and a single-button black jacket, its button between her breasts and navel. She wore nothing beneath the jacket.

Amiel wore a dress that buttoned high on her neck, then opened daringly in a crescent to below her cleavage. It clung close to her waist, then was slit high on one side.

Marán explained—she'd arranged to have a light rainproof robe in the carriage, "in case the weather worsened."

"Liar," Amiel put in, then took up the story. "As soon as we left our house, she pulled the robe over our laps. Then she ran her hand up my leg, under my dress, and began rubbing me. I, uh, well, I let her. It *has* been almost two weeks. Somehow she got my underpants off, and got her fingers in me.

"I was trying to keep from yelling, trying to keep from squirming and keep the damned coachman seeing what was going on. I told her to stop, but she wouldn't. So I told her to go ahead, to help me finish. Just before I came, she did stop. The bitch!"

"I read in one of the books you loaned me," Marán said, "that sex is always better when you've been anticipating it for a while. I'm just being helpful, and wanted to make sure we wouldn't disappoint Damastes."

"Then for Jaen's sake, let's get back to the house before I explode," Amiel said plaintively.

Candles flickered on either side of our bed. Amiel half-lay on her back, propped against pillows, legs lifted and parted. Marán lay on her back, against Amiel's sex, as Amiel rubbed Marán's breasts hard. Marán's legs were on my shoulders, her heels on either side of my head, and I held her buttocks in my hands, lifted clear off the mattress.

Marán cried out, twisted against me, then went limp. Her legs thumped down on the bed. Still inside her, still hard, I lay down across her body and Amiel's legs, and found a pillow to support my weight.

"This," I said when my breathing slowed, "may be the best welcome home I've ever had."

"I'd say you should go away more often," Amiel whispered. "But we don't like doing without you."

"What are we going to do if war comes?" Marán said. "You'll have to smuggle us along. I can get a close haircut and pretend to be a drummer boy, maybe. But what about Amiel? How can she hide her titties?"

"I'm sure you two will devise some scheme," I said. I yawned. "I can't tell you how nice it is to be home."

"But not for long," Marán reminded me. "There's the Feast of the Corn. We're to leave tomorrow."

"Marán," Amiel said, and her voice was very tentative, "I don't think I'll be able to come with you."

"What?" Marán said in surprise. "You must! We've had everything set for weeks now!"

"What's the saying?" Amiel said. "Man proposes, Jaen disposes? Yesterday a seer confirmed what I already knew.

"I'm pregnant."

THIRTEEN

THE FEAST OF CORN

Marán spun, sitting up, and I slid out of her, unnoticed. "You're *pregnant?*" she said, in rigid shock.

"A time and thirty days now. The seer and I calculated, and it happened on Festival night, the first night the three of us were together."

Marán stared at her friend, and for an instant what might've been unutterable hatred flashed across her face, but it was gone so quickly I wasn't sure I'd seen correctly in the candlelight. She took a deep breath.

"This *is* a surprise."

"I hoped I was just late," Amiel said. "But really, I knew better. Isn't it funny, Damastes, all the times Pelso and I tried to make a baby, we failed. Then you succeed on the first attempt. I guess your seed is strong."

I hid my wince. Amiel had said exactly the wrong thing, considering all the times Marán and I had tried to create a child.

"So," Amiel said after a time, "that's why I won't be able to go to Irrigon."

"I don't follow," I said. "You're not that pregnant. Did the seer say there was some problem?"

"Oh no," Amiel said. "My health's excellent. But I'd like a few days to recover from the chirurgeon's ministrations."

"*What?*" Marán said.

"I'm already an embarrassment," Amiel said. "This would make things worse." She shrugged. "So I'll deal with it. I had to once before, long ago when I was a girl."

"You mean . . . have the baby aborted?" Marán said.

Amiel nodded. I started to say something, but held my silence hard.

"Don't you *want* the child?" Marán said sharply.

Amiel smiled, wistfully. "Of course I'd like a babe. A child of Damastes the Fair? A man who's welcomed me into his house, treated me always as a friend, and loved me better than anyone I can remember? The seer said she's certain it's a girl. Who wouldn't wish such a baby? I've wanted one for the last few years, feeling my time was running short."

"Then have the baby you shall," Marán said firmly. She recollected my presence. "I'm sorry, my husband. I didn't even think of asking you."

"You didn't need to," I said, and was honest. We'd have the child we'd both wanted now, and I didn't give a rap for what anyone said or thought. Not that I had any choice, not if I wished to look at myself in the shaving glass.

"Amiel, we told you once you were welcome here," I said. "Welcome now, welcome forever. We shall go on together. As three." I stretched out my hand to Marán. Amiel clasped our hands in hers, tears running from her eyes.

"Thank you. I didn't dare even think . . . Thank you. Thank you, Jaen, Irisu."

"The emperor sealed Damastes and me in marriage," Marán said. "He prayed to the gods and goddesses our union be blessed. I pray to those same gods for the three of us."

"As do I," I said huskily.

"And I," Amiel whispered.

"Now let us secure our alliance," Marán said. She tenderly took Amiel's head in her hands and kissed her, long, deeply.

The two lay down, their legs twining, rubbing against each other as their passion grew. Marán took her lips from Amiel's.

"Damastes, come love us. Love us both. And when you come, come in us both. Now we are three for all time."

The two women rode behind me, talking excitedly about the decorations for the nurseries in our three palaces, whether it would be better to have them all the same, or do them in different styles so the child could learn variety.

Karjan was beside me, and flanking us were twenty of my Red Lancers, again commanded by Legate Segalle.

I was feeling a little hungry, a lot thirsty, and was looking forward to our midday meal. We'd been traveling for some days, and had crossed onto Agramónte land two hours ago. It'd become Marán's and my custom to stop in Caewlin for a meal. It was a wonderful little village, with maybe a hundred or so people, just a few days from Irrigon. There was one merchant—who sold everything from spices to peas, generally on credit against the harvest—a village witch, and an excellent tavern known for its country ham, its fresh-baked bread, ales brewed on the premises, and its salads, spiced with herbs grown by the owner. We'd helped build her garden with exotic herbs from the capital, and now it threatened to devour the tavern.

I should have noted something wrong as we came around the final tree-lined bend, for I saw no playing children, nor heard the lowing of cattle or the gabble of geese. But part of my mind was on my stomach, and the rest on how I could further improve the Guard Corps.

Then we rode into desolation. The village had been utterly destroyed. The neat thatched roofs were gone, and torn brick lay open to the uncaring sky. Caewlin had burned, and then rain had drenched the fire. The windows of the tavern were shattered, and its door had been pulled from its hinges and lay in the yard. Men had torn down the nicely painted fence around the garden, and then horses had trampled the plants. Bodies were scattered about, some animal, more human. They'd been dead about a week, I estimated, long enough to bloat and blacken into thankful unrecognizability.

Amiel gasped, Marán swore, but it might as well have been a prayer.

My soldiers' lances were down, ready, although there was nothing to fear, nothing at all but death and the dry buzz of flies in the spring silence.

"Who . . ." Amiel's voice trailed away, then came back more strongly. "Who did this? Why?"

Legate Segalle pointed at a tree that had a wide stone bench around it, a tree that had been the communal meeting place. Nailed to it was a battered, swollen head, barely recognizable as human. I couldn't tell if it had belonged to a woman or a long-haired man. There was a dagger driven into the tree below it, and around the dagger's grip a yellow silk cord was tied.

"Tovieti did it!" he said.

"No," I said. "The other way around. Somebody thought *these* people were Tovieti. I suspect I know who the murderer was, or rather who ordered these deaths."

Marán looked away, then boldly met my gaze. "If they were Tovieti," she said, "then they got what they deserved."

"Tovieti, mistress?" It was Karjan. "Y' think *she* was Tovieti?" He was pointing at the corpse of a baby, facedown in the dust. The top of the infant's skull was crushed, and there was a dark stain against the tree.

Marán's face flushed with rage. "You," she snapped, "be silent!" She spun on me. "Can't you keep your retainers in hand?"

I looked pointedly at the child's body, then at Marán. She stared back, then her eyes dropped. We rode on in silence.

The rest of the journey was quite different from the first part. Marán and I spoke only when necessary, and Amiel also held her silence. When we stopped at an inn, we slept in separate chambers. The trip seemed interminable, but at last we rounded the curving river road and saw Irrigon.

There were thirty horses tied to a rail in front of the main house. They were still saddled, and showed signs of hard riding. One was a sleek thoroughbred I knew. There were cased bows on most of the saddles, quivers tied to the skirts. Some had spear cases under the stirrups, and many had bulging saddlebags, bags, and rolls that held obvious loot. My temper snapped.

"Legate!"

"Sir!"

"Dismount the Lancers for action! Kill anyone who threatens us! Four men, seize those horses!"

"Sir!"

Two men in armor peered out of the main entrance, saw my soldiers, and, shouting the alarm, ran out, pulling swords.

"Legate!"

"Fire," Segalle shouted. Bowstrings twanged and the two skidded down the stairs, feathered shafts sprouting from their chests. Other men ran out of the house, shouting. My voice rang over all.

"Silence!" And silence there was. "All of you," I ordered. "Lay down your weapons or die! You have a count of five! One . . ."

"Those men are mine," another voice bellowed and Marán's brother Praen came out. He wore riding gear, a steel waistcoat, and a sword belt.

"I ordered silence," I shouted. "Count Agramónte, do not interfere with my men, or be prepared to face the consequences! Two! Three!"

Swords thudded to the ground, and men unbuckled their belts and let them fall.

"Your hands in the air," I ordered.

"Damastes," Marán said.

"I ordered silence!"

She obeyed.

"Legate, escort these men to that stone barn. Remove all animals and anything that can be used for a weapon. Secure and guard all doors until we can have them nailed shut."

"Yes, sir."

"I said, those men are under my orders," Praen shouted. "You have no right—"

"Count Agramónte," I said, "I am an officer of the emperor. These men have committed a series of horrible crimes, and I propose to escort them to the nearest city, turn them over to the warders, and prefer charges, as I once promised you I would."

"Charges of what? Killing vermin?"

"Murder, sir."

"You can't do that!"

"I assuredly can and shall," I said. "Further, I may well choose to prefer charges against their leader."

"The hells you will! These brave men are soldiers, and they've been helping me rid the land of traitors! Tovieti! Don't you realize the good they're doing? Or are you one of the yellow-cord men yourself?"

"Legate," I said, "this man is clearly disturbed. He is on property he has no right to be on without my leave. Take two men and escort him off these grounds."

Segalle hesitated, then said, "Yes, sir."

"You have a choice, Count," I said. "Leave Irrigon of your own will—or tied across the saddle of your horse!"

"You son of a bitch!" Praen said. But he came down the steps quickly, and took the reins of the thoroughbred from the soldier holding them. He pulled himself into the saddle, then glowered. "You'd better rethink your decision, Cimabuean," he said. "For you don't know the hornet's nest you're bashing around!"

He didn't wait for a response, but spurred his horse into a gallop.

"Legate, assist your men," I ordered, then dismounted and went inside, not waiting to see what Marán and Amiel were doing.

Marán found me in the library. "I can't believe what you just did," she said. "Treating my brother . . . my own brother, like he was a common criminal."

"Exactly what he is," I said, trying to hold my calm.

"So you feel free to do as you wish, ignoring any promises, any oaths you might have made," she snarled.

That did it.

"What oaths, my lady?" I shouted. "Are you assuming that because I married you, I'm under some sort of obligation to kiss the ass of anyone who carries the name Agramónte? Or that I'm supposed to ignore any crimes your thug of a brother chooses to commit? An oath? The only oaths I can remember taking are those to the emperor to serve him well, and a vow of marriage to you.

"I've never broken either, nor thought of breaking them. I'll remind you of my family's motto: We Hold True. What's yours? We do whatever we want? Is that what it is, Countess? Is this what you call honor? I piss on your honor, your dignity, if you think the name Agramónte somehow entitles you to kill anyone you wish.

"Do you remember that baby, Marán? Remember the baby you lost? Do you think that baby's mother had a moment to mourn, to scream, before she was cut down by your fucking brother?"

Marán's eyes were cold, hard. "Praen called you a son of a bitch," she hissed. "And you are!" She stormed out.

I had to go to our tower for a change of clothing. The door to our bedroom was closed. Amiel was huddled on a couch outside. Her eyes were red, her face drawn. I said nothing to her, nor she to me. I went into my dressing room, and got what I'd come for, and came back into the anteroom. Amiel gazed at the closed bedroom door, then at me, and her eyes welled once more. The door clicked shut behind me.

The next day the Feast of Corn began. The small village beyond Irrigon was packed, and tents were set up for a league on either side. Every village in the Agramónte reach had sent at least one representative, plus there must have been a hundred hawkers and merchants with trays or booths. The first day wasn't a feast, since the elaborate dishes and dancing could only begin after the corn was planted. Before the seed was sown, we would eat only unleavened bread, no meat, and raw vegetables without salt.

When the seeds were in the ground, and seers had cast spells to notify other village wizards to begin planting, the real merriment would begin—five days of feasting, dancing, and celebration.

Our duties were quite simple, in spite of what the emperor seemed to think. We would merely offer a prayer for the success of the sowing, then stand by and look noble and approving while a respected seer ordered a maiden, chosen for her virginity and beauty, to sow the first seed. The Agramóntes were expected to mingle with their people for the whole of this day, and so, about two hours after dawn, we left Irrigon for the village and the midway.

Marán behaved as if I didn't exist, I reciprocated, and a miserable Amiel brought up the rear. We wore gaudy finery and were expected to be unarmed. However, it was absurd to go into that throng without any weapons, so I had a sleeve dagger hidden, and, in my belt pouch, a particularly nasty little device Kutulu had given me. It was a knuckle-bow, with a slender, spring-actuated dagger in the grip, locked in place by a stud worked by the thumb. In addition, I had Karjan; Svalbard, a monstrous Lancer who'd been with me since Kait; and two other Red Lancers. I'd considered having them wear Agramónte livery, but my stomach roiled at making honest soldiers wear the garb of murderers, and so the four wore undress uniform, with hidden knives.

We reached the midway and strolled down the line of tents. I was examining a bauble, a cleverly made carving from a root, that quite accurately represented Irrigon, when I heard shouts. I craned to see what was going on. It was Praen and two of his flunkies! I swore—I'd assumed Praen would've had sense enough to be invisible on this day. But here he came, in bright regalia, bluff, arrogant face gleaming, no soldiery at his beck.

The outcry grew louder, more enraged, but Praen appeared to take no notice. He pushed his horse into the throng, intending, I guessed, to ride down the carnival way to the sowing grounds. A melon arced through the air and burst against his green silk vest. Praen realized the crowd's temper and, being Praen, did exactly the wrong thing. "You dirty pig-fuckers," he bellowed, waving a fist.

There was a roar of laughter, and then a rock thudded against his side. He shouted in pain, and another rock struck his horse, and it reared, neighing in surprise. Praen scrabbled for his sword. He had it half-drawn when a man darted up and grabbed his leg. Praen kicked, but couldn't free himself. His blade flew through the air as he fought for balance, then he was pulled from his mount into the crowd. The mob growled pleasure and closed in. I saw fists, then cudgels, rise and fall.

"We've got to help him," Marán shouted, and started forward. I grabbed her arm.

"No! They'll get you, too. Get back to Irrigon," I ordered. She fought with me, not listening. "Karjan," I shouted. "Take her! We've got to get out of here!"

There was a rearing, shouting mass where Praen and his retainers had been, but I paid no mind. There were angry faces much closer, glaring at us. My dagger flashed into my hand, and I kicked away the merchant's table in front of us. His eyes were wide in horror. I shoved him aside and pushed my way out the back of the tent, Lancers and the women on my heels. Tents from the next row were almost back-to-back here, forming a maze of ropes and piled merchandise. I slashed the ropes of the tent we'd gone through, and it collapsed limply, keeping anyone from coming after us for a moment.

We ran down the cluttered way, leaping ropes as we went. Amiel tore away her skirt to run faster, and Marán did the same. At last she'd realized our desperate jeopardy. We reached the row's end, and I held up my hand.

"Now," I said, "into the open. But walk. Try to look calm. Maybe the craziness hasn't spread down here yet."

Breathing hard, the seven of us walked out, trying to pretend nothing had happened. All eyes were on the screaming mob around the bodies of Praen and his lackeys, and no one noticed us at first. We hurried out of the midway, onto the road back to Irrigon.

I looked back, and saw Praen's horse, blood-drenched, rearing above the throng, hooves lashing. A man wearing a butcher's smock, waving an already-bloodied ax waited his moment, then swung, burying the ax in the animal's neck. It screamed like a woman, then went down. "Run now," I ordered, for I knew where the blood on that ax had come from, and the murderers would soon be looking for other victims.

For precious moments we had no pursuers. Irrigon was in sight when I saw, coming toward the mansion, a group of forest workers, carrying their tools. They saw us and exploded into screaming rage, unlimbering their axes and brush hooks.

Now it was a race to see who could first reach the yawning gates of the castle. We were first, but only by moments. The guard dropped his lance, ran to the ropes that slid the gates closed, and fumbled with their ties. "The tower," I shouted, then cried for the Lancers to turn out.

One forester, a rustic wearing ragged homespun pants and no shirt, ran through the still-open gate, waving a rusty, ancient sword. He saw me, shrieked hatred, and charged. He swung, and I parried his blow with my dagger. Its blade snapped clean, just at the hilt. The forester shouted in triumph, recovered clumsily, and came in again. I ducked inside his guard, smashed his face in with the knuckle-bow, flipped the blade out, and slashed his throat as he stumbled back—then I had his sword.

Two men charged the man at the gate ropes, and his panic grew worse, as he tried to defend himself, tried to free the ropes. One forester smashed a shovel blade into his neck, almost cutting his head off.

The Lancers boiled out of their quarters, buckling on their gear, fumbling with their weapons. There was no chance to close the gate, as more landsmen ran into the courtyard. A peasant cut at me with his brush hook, and I slashed its wooden handle in half. He gaped at the stub he held, and I ran him through, then booted his corpse into another, turned, and fled.

Marán and Amiel disappeared into our river tower, and Karjan and the other three held at its entrance.

"Fall back," I shouted to the Lancers. "Fall back into my tower!" I ran hard for its doorway. Our only chance was to barricade ourselves inside it, hand out the weapons in the small armory, and prepare for a siege. I don't know if Segalle misunderstood my orders, or if he had ideas of his own, for there was no one behind me when I reached the tower. Instead, the Lancers were going on line in the middle of the courtyard. Perhaps Segalle thought the mob would break against his thin line, and he could drive them out of Irrigon after that. Perhaps he could have, with a hundred men instead of a bit more than a dozen. Fifty, a hundred, peasants crashed into the courtyard, saw the handful of soldiers, and roaring black madness, charged. My Lancers were good men, experienced, trained soldiers. But fourteen men and one officer can't stand against a hundred. The wave roared over them, dissolved into knots of battling men, and then I saw no more scarlet uniforms, just the screaming mob.

"Inside," I ordered, and Karjan and the others obeyed. There were two huge crossbars inside the door. We heaved them over the heavy iron brackets set into the stone walls, and the only entrance was secured. We blocked off the internal passageways out of the tower with foot-square pieces of firewood and were safe for the moment. There were no windows on the ground level, and those above had heavy iron bars. Men slammed into the outside of the door, and I heard shouts of anger. "One man stand guard here," I ordered, and a soldier nodded.

We went up the winding steps to the second level. Here was a small warming kitchen and storage chambers. One held an assortment of weapons. I found the keys in our bedroom and opened the armory, and we took out bows, arrows, and swords, then went on up into our living quarters.

Marán had found a dagger, and held it ready. Amiel was

close to panic, looking about wildly. "Come now," I said, trying to sound calm. "We're safe now. They'll never break through fifteen feet of stone." She nodded nervously, and forced calm.

Marán took a bow and arrows from Svalbard, and strung the bow. She went to a window and cranked it open. A rock clattered against the wall below, and she drew back.

"Open them all," I ordered. "Break the glass. If something shatters the window, flying splinters could blind you." The panes smashing drew howls of glee from outside.

The courtyard was a seething mass of people, shouting, screaming, staring up. An arrow arced, and I moved away from the window. The ledges were machicolated, so I could peer through the slots without becoming a target.

The mob screamed delight as five men appeared on the main building's inner steps. They held two struggling, naked women. I recognized both—young peasant girls Marán had trained as maids. A man lifted one and cast her spinning, screaming, into the crowd, and the horde closed around her. The second landed nearby. Their screams tore through the rabble's cries, and I looked away. I hope they returned to the Wheel quickly.

I spotted three people—two men, one woman—shouting orders, trying to bring the crowd under control. All three had yellow silk cords looped around their necks. An arrow whipped into the woman's rib cage, and she cried agony and fell. "Die, you fucking bitch," Marán shouted, and I grinned tightly. But there were more Tovieti down there, and they kept behind others while trying to bring order.

But the mob remained out of control. It swirled back and forth, going in and out of Irrigon, smashing, looting. Other servants died, or else, sensibly, joined the chaos. The rabble found the barred barn, tore away the barricades, and discovered Praen's homemade warders. The people knew them for what they were and tore them apart. Those I hope died very slowly. Minutes later, they dragged Vacomagi, our bailiff, out of the main house, and didn't allow him to return to the Wheel for a long, terrible time.

It grew quieter, and I had a moment to take stock. It didn't take long, and wasn't heartening. In addition to Amiel, Marán, myself, Karjan, and the three other soldiers, there was a scullery maid and one of our candle lighters in the room. Neither of them knew anything about weapons, so they wouldn't be of any use.

"What now?" Marán said, voice tight, controlled, again proving herself an Agramónte.

"We have food," I said. "And arms."

"For how long?"

"We'll have to use our supplies carefully."

"What'll they try to do next?" Amiel asked.

"Probably find ladders," I said. "We'll shoot the climbers off when they get closer."

"Then what'll happen?" she asked.

"They'll try again, and we'll stop them again."

"Will they win?"

I considered and decided honesty was best. "They could," I said. "It'll depend on whether anyone gives a damn about us and rides for help. Or maybe a passing boat might see what's happening." I glanced out a window that overlooked the water, and then down. The course was smooth, deserted.

The scullery maid moaned. "Twa, three days gone 'fore anyone notices? They'll be gnawin' our bones."

"Not mine," Marán said, touching her dagger. "I'll go to the Wheel without their help if it comes to that."

"Good," I agreed. "None of us will give them any pleasure." I went to Marán and hugged her shoulders. I felt her body stiffen, and quickly took my arm away.

There were shouts outside, and I chanced peering out. A man stood in the center of the courtyard.

"Agramóntes," he shouted. "See what we have?" He waved something. Marán came up beside me, but I pushed her back. I'd seen what the man held—a cock and scrotum.

"Guess th' count won't be takin' no more of our women f'r a lark, eh?" the man went on. "Now it'll be th' other way roun'. Wonder how many men your titty countess'll handle 'fore she goes mad? An' what about her friend? Mebbe she can take *all* of us on!"

I heard a grunt from Svalbard at the next window, and a spear arced out. The man tried to roll away, but he was too slow, and the weapon drove through the small of his back and pinned him, screaming, to the ground. I could have finished him with an arrow, but I let him die slowly.

"Now they'll attack," I said grimly.

But I was wrong. They came with fire.

The first fires might have been by accident. But once Irrigon began burning, no one tried to put the fires out. The cheering, laughter, and shouts grew louder, and I saw men and women tossing things into the flames.

Some of those "things" still moved . . .

Sooner or later, the flames would provide inspiration, and they did. Svalbard saw them first—men carrying lashed-together bundles of wood toward the tower. We shot them down, but others came, moving more stealthily along the walls.

Now I became ashamed of my lack of faith in the scullery woman. "Ah don't want t' burn," she whimpered and hurried downstairs. I thought she'd gone to find a hiding place and wished her well, hoping that when and if the doors burned through, they wouldn't winkle her out.

She shouted for the candleman, and he reluctantly went down the stairs. A few minutes later, the two tottered back up. They had a large pot, hung on a fireplace poker. The pot steamed and bubbled, and I remembered the ancient oilpots on Irrigon's roofs.

"They'll burn us," she said, almost cheerily, "an' we'll boil them first wi' laundry lye." She went to the window overlooking the door, peeped out, then she and her assistant dumped the pot over the window ledge. Screams of pain racked the gathering twilight, and the woman beamed happily. "That'll hold 'em back."

It did. For a time. Then I felt hot, as if I were an ant trapped in a sunbeam focused through a malevolent child's glass. I smelt smoke, and saw, in our fireplace, the always laid firewood begin to smoke, curl, and blacken. There was more smoke, coming from above, from the wooden chandelier, from wooden fretwork on a wall, then from the paneling itself. They'd found a seer, and his spell was attacking every piece of wood in the tower.

I shouted for the soldier guarding the door to come up, and we hurled furniture down the stairwells.

Karjan grimaced at me. "Y'know, sir, I could've stayed wi' th' Lancers in Urey an' none of this'd be happenin'. At least not t' me."

"Cheerful bastard," I hissed at him.

I went to Amiel and gave her a hug. She, at least, welcomed the affection. "Do we have any chance?"

"Of course," I said. "Nothing's ever for certain."

I looked at Marán, but her gaze was still chill, unforgiving. But I had to try. I went to her. "If the worst happens," I asked in a low tone, "will we go to the Wheel as enemies?"

She began to say something, then stopped and took a deep breath. "No, Damastes," she said finally. "You're my husband. We'll die together." She was silent for a time, then coughed. The smoke was growing thicker. "Maybe, in our next, when we return, maybe . . ." She didn't finish. I waited, but she just shook her head and stared out the window.

Amiel soaked handkerchiefs in water, and we tied them around our faces.

"The stone won't burn," I said, my voice muffled, "and their magic isn't good enough to make fire from the air. We'll wait until the doors burn through, and they come up, then see how long they can keep coming." I hope my words sounded less futile to the others than to me.

Then an idea came. "Who can swim?" I asked.

No one needed an explanation. Marán swam, like an eel, and the soldiers had damned well better, since that was part of their training.

"I can," Amiel said, "after a fashion."

"I'll swim with you," Marán said. "Don't worry."

"Or I can," Svalbard said. "You'll have no worries."

"I wager I c'n float," the scullery maid said. "Better'n fryin', no matter what."

The candle lighter just bobbed his head.

"All right," I said. "Marán, go through our wardrobe. Try to find dark-colored clothing. Everybody should wear pants, some sort of shirt. No shoes. We'll jump as soon as we're ready. If you think you can take a weapon with you, take a knife. But throw it away if it's a burden. Jump feet first, and keep your hands over your head. There shouldn't be anything in the water to hurt you, and it's deep under the tower.

"When you land, swim for the far shore. I'll be the last to jump, and I'll try to help anybody who's in trouble. Try not to splash and draw attention."

We hastily changed clothes, trying not to think about the long drop, and what terrible things could be at the end of it.

"I think," Amiel said, "I think I want to pray. Does anyone else?" All of us did, all except the scullery woman and Karjan. I prayed not only to my own gods, but to Varum, god of water, and hoped someone, anyone, would be listening.

The smoke was thicker, and flames flickered around the room. All of us were coughing. I peered out a river window and couldn't see any sign of life below or on the water.

"Now," I ordered.

The two soldiers went first, and hit the water cleanly. They surfaced and swam for the opposite shore, less than a hundred feet away.

Marán took Amiel's hand and led her to the window.

"Ready?" I said and kissed her lips, then Amiel's.

"Go," my wife snapped, and the two leapt into darkness. I heard a little yelp, and winced. But it evidently went unheard. Next was the scullery woman, then Karjan and Svalbard. As they jumped, I heard screams of joy, and the roar of flames. The outer door must have gone down and the rush of air was feeding the fire.

I waited for a count of three, time enough for anyone below to swim clear, then jumped. I fell for an instant, splashed into cold darkness, and swam away hard. The flames of Irrigon made the water a dark mirror, and I could see bobbing dots moving toward the far shore.

I was about halfway across when a dark bulk clambered out of the river. One of the soldiers, I guessed. We were safe—but my hope vanished as I heard a shout. Two men ran out of the darkness, and a sword gleamed as it slashed into the man's body. He cried out and fell.

"Downstream," I shouted, and saw splashes as my people heard and swam away from the bank, back into the swift current. Torches flared up both banks. I tried to stay low in the water, keep my hands and feet below the surface. The current took me and swept me along.

I don't know what the peasants thought, but none of the torches moved up- or downstream, but remained in tight knots on either side of the river, their fires dwarfed by the roaring cataclysm that had been Irrigon. Arrows, spears, rocks rained out, but splashed into emptiness.

The river narrowed about half a mile downstream where there was a ford. Once ashore, we could follow the road east, keeping under cover, and find safety in perhaps four days, beyond the Agramónte lands. I knew enough woodcraft to elude any pursuers, even foresters or hunters. We'd build mantraps to take care of them.

Perhaps, I let myself think, perhaps we wouldn't all return to the Wheel this night. I swam strongly, looking around, looking for the others. I held to the center of the river, and then saw, ahead of me, the twin brick islands that had been built one on either bank of the river. The space between had been dredged for small boats. When someone wanted to cross, there were heavy planks with ropes on either end to pull across for a footbridge.

The current quickened as the river narrowed, and I swam out of it, felt pebbles and sand under my feet. I waded toward the bank until the water was waist-deep, and scanned the night.

I saw a drifting head, waded to it, and pulled the scullery maid to me. She was nearly done, said she'd tried to help the candle lighter, but he'd flailed at the water, made a sudden sound, and vanished. She waded to shore and collapsed on the gravel. Then came Svalbard and Karjan. They'd seen no one else.

I heard splashing, faint cries for help, and swam toward the sound. "Help me. Help me." It was Marán. She was in water over her head, but only chest-high for me. She was pulling a limp Amiel. "Thank Tanis," I gasped and then Karjan and Svalbard were beside me.

I looked for the other soldier, but never saw him. I don't know if he was killed with his mate, or if he drowned.

I pulled myself through the water after my wife and Amiel. "Be careful," I heard Marán said. "There's something wrong with her."

I put my arm around Amiel, and she gasped in pain just as I felt the broken stub of an arrow between my fingers, just below her right breast. We carried her to shore. There was a thicket nearby, and we moved into its heart and laid her on the moss. I unbuttoned her shirt and saw the wound in the dimness. Blood was seeping slowly around the arrow.

"Damastes," Amiel said. "I hurt."

"You'll be all right," I said.

"Damastes, I don't want to die."

"You won't." I tried to sound sure.

"I don't want my baby to die. Please. Help me."

"I'll start now, sir," Svalbard said. "I can make the edge of your land in two days, running hard. Bring help back. You travel slow, move mostly at night, and it'll be all right."

That was as good a plan as any.

"Take care, sir," he said. "We'll get our own back." That was the most I'd had from Svalbard in the years I'd known him. Without ado, he vanished into darkness.

"Amiel," Marán whispered, "I remember a witch. She's two villages from us. I know she wouldn't join these bastards. When it's light, I'll go for her."

"Good," I said approvingly. "And Karjan'll go with you."

"I'll stay wi' your lady," the scullery woman promised. "Me an' th' tribune'll keep her safe."

Amiel's lips quirked. "All right," she whispered. "Now I feel like everyone's going to help me. Now I know I'll live. And my baby'll live, too. Won't she, Damastes?"

"She will," I said.

"Good," Amiel said again. Her hand fumbled out, and I took it. "Marán," she said, "take my other hand." I felt my wife move up beside me. "I love you," Amiel said. "I love you both."

"I love you," I whispered, and Marán echoed me.

"I think I'll sleep now," she said. "When I wake, maybe the witch will be here, and help me stop hurting." Her eyes closed.

Marán was crying silently. "Why in the hells do any gods let things like this happen?" she whispered fiercely. I shook my head; I had no answers.

Amiel, Countess Kalvedon, died an hour before dawn without waking.

Flames roared high into the cloud-whipped sky, taking Amiel's body into its embrace. Nearby a second pyre crackled, consuming what little we'd found of Praen's body.

There were three hundred soldiers around the field, all in full battle dress with arms ready. Svalbard had been lucky, and encountered an army patrol less than half a day's run from the river. They'd gone at the gallop for reinforcements, then ridden back, following the river road, and we'd joined up a day and a half beyond Irrigon.

We'd returned to Irrigon, and the soldiers had combed the countryside. The prisoners they took were penned in a hastily fenced compound, more and more as the days passed. I didn't give a rat's ass about them and would cheerfully have freed them all and rewarded them with gold if Amiel could thus have been with us.

Marán and I stood between the pyres. Behind was the smoldering ruin of Irrigon.

"It's over," my wife whispered.

"What?" I said.

"Damastes á Cimabue," she said, and her voice was firm, without a quaver. "I declare it finished between us. What was once, is no more, and will never be again.

"It's over," she said again.

FOURTEEN

To Speak for the Emperor

There were still the mechanics of dissolution, but Marán had spoken the truth, and there was no saving our marriage, our life together.

At least I still had my honor and my duty as a soldier. When we returned to Nicias, I immediately had those few things I wished to keep moved out of her house on the riverfront. I went back into the Water Palace. One of Kutulu's emissaries came, and said the Tovieti were more active than ever, and I might be considered foolish to dangle my coattails in front of them. I smiled, a tight, hard grin, and said I wished them well, and they were welcome to try once more. He eyed me, the sword at my side and the dagger sheathed across from it, bowed, and withdrew.

I went to Kutulu and told him all of what had happened, including the meeting I'd had with Praen and his cronies, and the murder gangs that had resulted from it.

"I suspected something besides the traditional estate goons was occurring," he said. "But you've given me the first clue these gangs are organized by a central group. I do wish you'd come to me when your brother-in-law—pardon, former brother-in-law—approached you."

"I'm not a tell-tale."

Kutulu inclined his head, didn't respond.

"What about these Broken Men?" I asked. "Now there's proof they're being run by the Tovieti."

"Within the past month I've had several confirmations of that information," the warder said. "There's been more than one outbreak of violence in the countryside, all of course appearing spontaneous.

"But there is a problem."

I waited. Kutulu squirmed.

"Everything must be paid for," he said finally. "Even spies and assassins. Perhaps them before anyone, since they work best for red gold.

"And there is no funding for any further investigation into the Tovieti. All secret service funding goes to working against Maisir. *All* of it."

"At the orders of the emperor," I said.

"Of course," he said, and I read helpless rage in his eyes.

I tried to pretend Marán, and our marriage, had never existed, and so avoided Nicias' polite society, where I might encounter her friends or her. Tales of what she was doing, saying, came, and I tried to ignore them, even though I was drawn, with a horrid fascination. Thank Irisu, Jaen, and Vachan I heard no stories that she'd taken a lover, for I don't know if I could have handled that.

Now the only thing that mattered was the army, particularly the new Guard. I frequently journeyed upriver to Amur, to oversee their training. And there were always paperwork and intelligence summaries on Maisir to study.

I saw the emperor more frequently now, and he never brought up my marriage, for which I was grateful. Once or twice I saw him looking sympathetically at me, but he said nothing.

The Time of Births ground past, and the Time of Heat began. I tried to convince myself my wound was healing, but someone would inadvertently mention her name, or I'd glance at a broadsheet and read an account of the Countess Agramónte's plans for the upcoming social season, and the scab would be ripped away once more. Marán didn't return to her old ways, when she had scorned the butterfly whirl of court for intellectual pursuits. These days no court occasion or ball was complete without the countess, her hangers-on, her latest imaginative dress, and so forth.

I dully knew only time would end the pain.

Once it was discovered that "Damastes the Fair" was available, my post was filled with offers—some subtle, some most appallingly direct.

Even more obscene were the hints from brothers and fathers who'd have liked nothing better than to make such a high connection, either through marriage or in a far less formal relationship. I availed myself of none. I felt no desire, no lust. My appetites had been burned with Irrigon, had died with Amiel, had withered when Marán turned me away.

The bad news came to Renan in the person of a small, friendly little Maisirian. He was one of Kutulu's agents and had been set up as a wandering sutler, dealing mostly in illicit alcohol, who moved from camp to camp of the Maisirian Army. His discovery was so important he chanced taking it across the border and through deadly Sulem Pass in person, rather than by the usual covert messengers.

King Bairan had called up three "classes," or age groups, to serve full terms in the army, which hadn't been done for at least thirty years to our knowledge. Also, the current class had been ordered to remain in service rather than being discharged. Maisir was mobilizing, and there could be but one cause, one potential enemy.

A day later, another, possibly worse report came, this one from our embassy in Jarrah. King Bairan had summoned a conclave of the highest-ranking sorcerers to the capital for a special conference. Ominously, the topic of the conference was considered a state secret.

I ordered Petre to accelerate the Guards' training schedules, with never a break in the schedule or between training cycles, and sent more recruiters out with the promises of greater rewards for the most successful.

War grew ever closer.

One night thunder rode the sky in a night-long drumroll, as if the cavalry of the gods were galloping past in review. Lightning flickered, then flared, not in comfortable white light but in reds, greens, purple—shades that no one could remember having heard of. It was a great storm, but during that long night, not one drop of rain fell.

A day after the storm, near midnight, I was summoned to the emperor's palace. I'd been finding it easier to sleep if I worked myself into exhaustion, and so was still at my desk when the call came. I pulled on my sword belt and helmet and galloped hard for the emperor's castle, Lucan easily staying ahead of my escort.

The Emperor Tenedos looked demon-haunted, as if he'd slept but little, and then his dreams had been more evil than reality.

"Damastes, this meeting must forever remain a secret," he began, without preamble.

"If that's your wish, sir."

"I mean *forever*, no matter what happens."

I was a little irked. "If my word isn't enough once, what will make it stronger a second time? Sir."

Tenedos began to get angry, then caught himself. "You're right. My apologies."

Even now, even with things as they are, even after all the betrayals, I still find it hard to continue, to break that now-meaningless promise. But I must.

The emperor paced back and forth, holding his hand near his heart, as if swearing an oath of his own. "That storm the other night was my magic," he started. "I won't . . . I can't . . . tell you who or what I summoned. I was attempting to reach into the future, for some inkling of what comes next for Numantia. That sort of thing generally isn't wise," he said. "Those demons . . . or gods . . . who might have the power to look beyond this moment aren't happy about being asked to help nonentities like ourselves.

"Nor is the future graven in stone, obviously. Everything can change in an instant, as a result of the most minute events. A child, for example, might take a different way to the market and, instead of seeing something marvelous that sets his curiosity aflame and leads him to become a great wizard, he sees nothing but the dusty road and dull people, and grows to become no more than one of them."

I waited, patiently, realizing the emperor was gathering himself. He looked at me hard, as if reading my thoughts. "Very well," he said. "I'll go directly to the matter. We must not go to war with Maisir."

"Sir?" I blurted the word in utter surprise.

"Both of us thought such was predestined, that there was no other road for our nation," Tenedos said. "But if we do declare war, all is doomed. Maisir will completely destroy us. That is what I was told by those demons, spirits, whatever, I consulted.

"We are still fated to march against Maisir, for there can be but one great nation in this world. But we must not do it for at least five years, until our country is far stronger and our army much greater than it is now."

"May I speak frankly, sir?" I asked.

"Of course."

"It would've been easier if you'd learned this back when King Bairan sent his reply to your first note, after that troop of the Twentieth Cavalry was butchered."

"I know," Tenedos said, showing no anger. "I overstepped my limits. Damned little good it does me, any more than regretting the past helps anyone. The question now is what to do next. What can we do to recover, to stall for time?"

"The king asked once for a meeting between you two," I suggested after a bit of thinking. "If you reminded him of that, would that be a possibility? Or, perhaps, if you went to Renan and then asked for such a conference?"

"I can't do that," the emperor said flatly. "That would appear as if I were begging, and Bairan would see our weakness at once, and almost certainly strike hard. Let me correct myself. I can't do that without preparing the ground. That is what I need you for. Damastes, I've asked you to go on some extraordinary missions since we've been together. This is the most dangerous."

"Worse than creeping into Chardin Sher's castle with a potion and a piece of chalk?" I half-joked. "I wasn't supposed to even live through that one."

"Yes," Tenedos said. "Far worse. Because I'm asking you to take on a task that has nothing to do with a soldier's skills and talents. I want you to go to the court of King Bairan as my plenipotentiary."

"Sir, I'm no diplomat!"

"Exactly why I'm asking you to go. I've half a hundred men who can talk for an hour and you'll be convinced you're no longer Damastes á Cimabue, but a goat. And King Bairan's got his own corps of smooth politicians. If you go to Jarrah, representing me, the king will realize my seriousness. If *his* most famous general showed up at my doorstep wanting to talk peace, I'd certainly listen."

I considered. Tenedos was making sense. "But what would I say, what could I offer?"

"You'll have complete powers to do whatever is necessary to stop the war from happening. Make any trade concessions that are asked for. If it's necessary to concede part or all of the Border Lands, do that. If King Bairan wishes to press those ancient claims Maisir has for parts of Urey, very well. *Everything* is on the table, Damastes. We must have peace and keep this war from starting.

"I have it," Tenedos said excitedly. "Return to your idea of my going to Renan. Once matters have been discussed, and it seems peace is reachable, then tell the king I'll meet him in Renan . . . or even across the border in Maisir, given sufficient guarantees for my safety.

"Damastes, you must go, and bring back peace. What I'm asking—no, demanding—is the most important job any Numantian has been given since I took the throne."

His eyes burned into mine, and I felt the truth in them. "Very well, sir. I'll go . . . and I'll do my best."

Tenedos sagged. "Thank Saionji," he whispered. "You've just saved our country."

But how in the hells was I going to get to Jarrah? The only practical route I knew was through Sulem Pass, past the Kaiti capital of Sayana, and then across the border into Maisir, and along the traditional trading route to Jarrah.

But Achim Baber Fergana still sat the throne in Sayana, Kait's capital. He'd have every warrior in his kingdom sharpening his sword in front of my image, and every *jask* atop mountains muttering spells to put a lightning bolt in my breeches.

I was trying to decide which was the quickest and safest method to travel—escorted by a full regiment of cavalry, probably the Ureyan Lancers, or traveling fast and incognito, as I'd done before.

I sent for maps, which was my mistake. I had had barely two hours to study them when a visitor was announced. Tribune Yonge. It was imperative I see him at once. I hastily covered the maps and opened an innocent folder. Yonge came in, barely nodded at me, then went to the covered table, and sneered. "You think you're clever, don't you, Numantian?"

I was in the dark.

"How are you planning to cross Kait?" he asked.

"How the hells did *you* know?" I stammered, hardly the finest way to divert an inquiry.

"You are a fool even if you're a tribune," Yonge said. "You

forget I am Kaiti. I serve Numantia—for the moment—but I am from Kait. I know *everything* there is to know about my country, and about anyone who's interested in it. When the First Tribune, General of the Armies, asks for maps of Sulem Pass and the trading route past Sayana to the Maisirian border, and I happen to hear of his request, what do you think I'm going to think?"

"Yonge, no one is that sneaky."

"Ha!" was his response. "And just because you're a barbarian who can't handle strong waters doesn't mean you shouldn't learn how to be a proper host."

"Third cupboard from the window," I said. "There are glasses on that sideboard."

Yonge poked through the assortment of liquors, found one to his choosing, tore the wax seal off, pulled the cork with his teeth, and spat it onto the floor.

"I assume you're planning to drink it all."

"Of course," he said. "What other payment would be proper for a man who's about to save your life?" He poured a glassful, drank it back, and grunted. "Good. Hog swill. Triple-distilled. You could clean rust from a sword with this shit." He poured another glass. "Poor baby," he crooned, going back to the table and pulling the cloth from the maps. "Trying to decide how he's going to go through my country, all tippy-toe or with banners and bugles, eh?"

"Nobody lets me have any secrets," I complained.

"With that stupid cowlike expression you carry around, you don't deserve to have any. I think both ideas suck goat shit," he said. "If you go with soldiers, unless you take a whole gods-damned army, Achim Baber Fergana will hunt you down with a bigger force. I understand that man, because I've taught myself to think like a pig. A clever pig, like Fergana, eh? He'll do anything to put you in one of those little cages outside Sayana and watch you rot. After he finishes pulling off all the stray parts he can get away with.

"That first way is stupid," he finished. "Pah." He drank.

"Next is to go a-secret, of course. Like the way we went into that demon Thak's cavern and killed all those Tovieti. Dress like country droolers and pray a lot. That's your other idea, isn't it?"

I nodded.

"Pah," Yonge said with even greater emphasis, and shoved the maps to the floor. "Now here is what you're going to do, Numantian. You're going to cross the border, but you're not going to go near Kait."

"I'm going to fly," I said.

"No. You're going to go where a mountain goat gets the drizzling shits just thinking of going. You'll be so far above the clouds you can piss down through them, and your water'll be frozen before it touches the ground. I, Yonge, know a better way. A secret way. A way that'll take you into the heart of Maisir."

Evil pleasure shone on his face.

"*Now* can I keep the bottle?"

It was an hour after dawn, and the river street was deserted. I sat astride my horse, looking up at the five-story mansion that used to be my home.

On the top story, behind a balcony, in the room that had been our bedroom, a curtain moved slightly.

I thought I saw a figure behind it.

The morning breeze moved the curtain again, then the wind died. All was still, all was silence. No one came out onto the balcony.

I waited for a time, then clucked to my horse. He nickered, and I rode away, not looking back.

An hour later, I sailed for Maisir.

FIFTEEN

THE SMUGGLER'S TRACK

The *Kan'an* made swift passage upriver toward Renan. Coded heliographs had already gone to Renan, and couriers would speed the news to Jarrah, so I could be met at the appropriate point by the Negaret, Maisir's border guards.

I took five men, with Captain Lasta as my aide and section commander. I thought of taking Seer Sinait, but Tenedos said that would be a violation of protocol. I wonder now if that was the truth, or if there were other reasons.

Out of pure malevolence, I promoted Karjan troop guide, but was disappointed. He merely looked at me with a baleful glare, muttered something about all things coming around in time, and went to our quarters to pack. The others with me were Lance-Major Svalbard, the morose roughneck; the archer Lance-Major Curti, another Lancer whose talents I well respected; and Lance Manych, whose skills with the bow I remembered from Kallio. I made him lance-major, to his considerable astonishment. Then he realized he was still the lowest ranker, and grumbled to Karjan.

Karjan chuckled. "Since y're th' junior one amongst us, there'll be no need for searchin' about when someone orders a fire t' be built. An' th' reason y're promoted, you'll find, is m' master buries as many as he promotes. P'raps more. Y'r widow's death benefits'll be greater. A kindly man, m' master." I withdrew, grinning, before Karjan could realize he was spied upon.

We would get horses and remounts in Renan, ride south and west, until we crossed into the Border Lands just west of the Urshi Highlands, and then strike for Yonge's secret track.

Yonge and I had spent four days going over and over the route, not only using the sketchy maps of the areas around the Highlands, but also Yonge's commentary, which was exact, in its way: "Turn off that trail when you come to the third fork of the creek. There'll be a tall tree at the fork, with a limb near as big as the trunk, that hangs off to the left. You'll know which one it is, because there'll be remnants of a rope around the limb. I hanged an old friend of mine there for being discourteous in a business matter. Might still be some bones around the tree, if the jackals haven't scattered them by now."

Yonge grudgingly gave up the trail's secrets, since he had meant to go with us, for flatlanders would never be able to find the trail's beginnings, let alone hold to it over the mountains. I said no, flatly, and he argued, threatened, and even begged. But I held firm. He knew better than to think I'd allow a tribune, head of all Imperial scouts and skirmishers, to ride off into the unknown, no matter how important the emperor considered my mission.

He glared, then nodded once. "I hear your command, Numantian. Very well." He appeared to drop the matter. I should have known.

I didn't leave my cabin for the first two days after sailing from Nicias, having about three hundredweight of orders to read and sign. But at last there was nothing left to remind me of Nicias, desks, or paperwork, and I went on deck. It was misting, not quite rain, and I let the moisture wash my face, my mind, and my soul, putting everything behind me.

We were still in the Latane River's delta, and the banks sometimes came quite close, although the channel was dredged deep. I was watching a particularly vivid waterfowl, marveling at its wonderful plumage, paying no heed to someone I took to be a sailor lounging nearby, back to me.

"That bird's lucky, Numantian. If you were ashore, with a bow and arrow, it'd no doubt end up as plumage for one of your hats." It was, of course, Yonge.

I started to ask questions, but caught myself. That would only increase the Kaiti's glee. I remembered my drill instructor days and painted anger on my face. "How dare you, Tribune! You've broken my explicit orders!"

"This is true," Yonge said.

"I could put you under close arrest, have you taken back to Nicias in chains."

"You could try," he agreed dangerously. "Or you could take what is done as done, and buy me a drink."

At last I had him. "There's none on board," I said. "Since I don't drink, and since we're on imperial business, I specifically ordered the purser to bring no alcohol aboard."

"You . . . you evil snake!" Yonge hissed. "You must've known! You must've guessed!" I put one finger beside my nose and looked wise.

We disembarked at a small dock on the far side of Renan, not particularly wanting to attract notice and lose a week being feted by every politician and officer in Urey. Our horses were waiting. We loaded our gear and rode through the beautiful city's outskirts and into the rain-drenched countryside. The farther from civilization and the closer to the unknown and danger, the happier I became.

The trail was wide, inviting, and all of us, without orders or comment, loosened our weapons in their sheaths. "You flatlanders can learn, sometimes," Yonge said. "This is an ambush route, for fools. Wise men use it as a marker, to reassure themselves they're on the right track."

I paid no attention to his insults, for I was intent on following the instructions I'd memorized. I spotted the cone-shaped rock, waited until it was aligned with the dimly seen grove of trees halfway up a slope, then looked for the turnoff. "Here," I announced, and pulled my horse's reins toward what looked like nothing more than a crevice. The crevice widened into the real trail, and Yonge grunted approval.

Ahead, the hills grew into treeless, forbidding mountains.

The temple loomed out of the blowing snowstorm quite suddenly, overhanging the narrow valley like a brooding eagle. It was built of dark wood, elaborately worked, and there were great stone statues of fabulous creatures unknown to any myth I'd heard. Statues of demons ornamented the uptilting eaves of the roofs. I wondered who'd built this temple, and when, for there was no way, even with an eternity to work in, the men and women who peopled the few dozen huts below it could have performed the labor, even with the strength of gods. I looked at the blank empty spaces of windows, innocent of glass or curtains, and shivered, without knowing why.

Yonge was staring at the huge building, or rather connected series of buildings, with an expression of baleful hatred. His instructions had said nothing about this place, other than that here was where we'd trade our horses for more surefooted animals. I dropped back beside him and began to ask what was wrong.

He shook his head. "No words," he said. "Not now."

I said no more, but signaled to my men, a tap on the pommel of my sword, and another on my gloved right hand. The signal went down the line, and we were ready for any surprise. A gong boomed across the valley as we rode up to the temple steps, and huge doors swung open. A man came toward us. He was very young, barely out of his teens, slender, shaved-headed, and wore, in spite of the storm, nothing but a light robe, shimmering with all the colors of summer. He walked as if he were royalty, surrounded by an invisible entourage.

He stopped, waiting, arms folded. "I greet you," he said in highly accented Numantian, voice soft, almost feminine.

"We greet you, Speaker," Yonge said.

"You know my title," the man said. "You have been here before."

"I have, but my friends have not."

The young man looked carefully at each of us, and I felt his gaze like a wind more piercing, more chill, than the unheeded storm. "You travel light for merchants," the Speaker said. "Or do you carry gold in your bags, to make purchases in Maisir?"

"We are on a different errand."

"Ah," the Speaker said. "I should have sensed that. You are soldiers. I can tell by your dress, by the way you sit your saddles. You desire . . . ?"

"Pack animals," Yonge said. "A resting place for the night. Perhaps food. We are prepared to pay."

"You know the custom?"

"I do." Yonge had said each of us must make a gift when we reached this village, a gift of warm clothing. I thought this more than reasonable.

"Then you are welcome," the Speaker said. "But only until dawn. Then you must move on."

"We shall obey," Yonge said. "But why do you put limits on our visit? This did not happen the last time I was here."

"I was not the Speaker then, nor do I remember you," the young man said. "But I sense blood. Blood is about you, blood is behind you, far greater blood is before. I do not wish you to linger, lest you leave your mark on us." He pointed at the village, and I saw two doors standing open, one of a hut, the other a stable. "Go now," he said, not harshly, not kindly, and walked back inside the temple.

Two men helped us curry our horses and three women fed us, a thick stew of lentils, tomatoes, onions, and other vegetables, highly seasoned with spices I'd never tasted before. After we ate, we unrolled our bedrolls on the wooden benches we'd eaten on. Even though there was a thick wooden bar, I put my bench across the door, so no one could enter, and had my sword ready.

I slept poorly, and had bad, barely remembered dreams, dreams of strange monsters, snowy battlefields strewn with dead, rivers that ran red with blood, even redder flame, and the echoing screams of dying women. I awoke intermittently, listened dumbly for a time to the storm raging outside as if drugged, then fell asleep once more.

The night lasted an eternity before there was a thudding at the door. I slid the bar away. The three women were there, one with a steaming basin of water, the second with towels, the third with a great bowl of steamed oats. We washed, ate hastily, and as we finished, heard the stamp of hooves and the snort of animals.

There were ten zebu outside, long-haired, snow-frosted, with wooden X-shaped pack frames already strapped on, and firewood lashed below each pack. Each of their horn tips was protected with a bright red metal ball, which would lessen our chances of getting gored. We approached them cautiously, and they seemed to eye us with equal suspicion. But they were quite tractable, and responded well to a nose rub or a scratch behind the ears. Captain Lasta, in fact, seemed quite at home with these strange animals, and I wondered if he'd been a teamster in another life, and then wondered whether being reborn a soldier was a reward or a punishment.

We lashed our gear onto the frames and were ready to march, each man leading one zebu, a second tied by long reins to the saddle of the first. We offered silver to the male villagers, gold to the women, but they would have nothing more than the garments we'd already given them.

The Speaker was standing in the middle of the path out of the village. "You are content," he said, and it was not a question.

"We are," I said. "I thank you for your hospitality."

"This is a duty given us by our god, who must not be

named," he said. "It needs no thanks. But you behaved well last night, offering no arrogances to my men, no insults to my women. For this, I shall grant you a gift, a riddle for you to work at as you travel. Last night, I cast certain spells. Our god permits us curiosity. Now I shall pique yours:

"The god you think you serve, you do not serve. The goddess you fear is not the one who is your enemy, but your enemy is one who seeks to become more, to become a god, yet, in the end, shall be no more than a demon, for demons are already his true masters. The final part of the riddle is this: Serve who you may, serve who you might, you serve but one, and that one will grant you naught."

He bowed his head, and I swear a smile flickered, then he strode off into the temple.

"What th' hells does *that* mean?" Karjan growled.

"Who knows," I said finally. "But have you ever known a priest who didn't try to keep you fuddled?"

Someone managed a chuckle, but when we went on, we were silent, full of unease.

"Who were those people?" I asked Yonge.

"I don't know . . . but there's tales of the village—and that temple—being there forever. From my grandfather's time it was known as a place of ancient mystery."

"What god do they worship?"

"I don't know that, either."

"Why do you hate them? They fed us, gave us shelter, traded for our horses."

"Because," Yonge said carefully, "I hate those who know more than I do, and refuse to teach it. I hate those who have more power than I do, with no reason for having it. I hate those who know someone will be betrayed, but stand back and let it happen. And I hate those who have some sort of tin god whispering in their ear and think they've been adopted into his son-of-a-bitching family!

"There was once a time when I, and three of my men, came here, sore hurt, and were turned away by this sanctimonious little snot's bastard father, for reasons I still do not understand, and for which I hope he was reborn as a slime-worm. Now, Numantian, are those reasons enough?"

I left Yonge alone for the rest of the day.

"Tribune, it's starting to feel like a storm coming on," Captain Lasta said. The wind was building, chill and wet.

"The trail goes down toward the rising ground as I recall," Yonge said. "We can take shelter—"

"Great gods!" The exclamation came from Manych. He pointed up the slope rising above us. For an instant, I could make out nothing, then the snow blew away, and I saw, standing perfectly motionless on a crag, a leopard, but a leopard marked as none I'd ever seen in a jungle. Its rosettes were very dark, and the fur around them pure white. It was huge, almost the size of a tiger. It gazed at us unmoving, curious.

"Will it attack?" Manych whispered.

"I'll not take th' chance," Curti said, moving slowly toward his zebu and cased bow. He froze as a man came out of the blowing storm and walked up to the huge cat. He was big, and had long hair, longer even than mine, and a full beard, dark as his hair. He wore a sleeveless fur vest, fur pants and boots, with a woolen shirt under the vest. He stood as still as the leopard, studying us with interest. The man's hand stretched out and stroked the leopard's head, and the beast preened under the touch. Snow flurried around the rocks, and when it cleared, neither man nor beast could be seen.

We reached the head of the pass. On our right was a nearly vertical cliff, on our left a bare mountain slope, deep with snow. I heard a clear, distinct voice: "Stop. Go back." It was a gentle voice, a woman's I thought, coming from nowhere.

"What?" My voice was very loud in the crisp, frozen stillness.

"What is it, sir?" Lasta asked. I heard the voice again, and knew I must obey.

"Get the animals back," I ordered. "Now! Move!"

There was confusion, but my men obeyed, turning our tiny formation in its tracks. I swore, knowing somehow we must move fast, faster. The men looked at me as if I'd gone mad. Then a rumbling began, a low drumroll that came from everywhere.

"Look! Up there!"

At the top of the slope a cloud of snow boiled, growing larger and larger as it moved. The mountain was coming down in an avalanche, boiling, smoking as it came. There was no more need to hurry the men, no need to shout orders, and even the zebu seemed to know how close death was, and they broke into a clumsy near-gallop through the withers-deep drifts.

We were moving slowly, far too slowly, and the roaring was louder, very close, and I dared not look back, dared not see the death that was coming. It took me, hurling me forward, and I was buried in a cloud of stinging ice and soft down, cold, spinning, buried alive and choking, soft, gentle, killing snow filling my mouth, my nostrils.

Then all was still. I could see nothing. I tried to move my arms, found I could, and flailed wildly, close to panic. I saw the sky then—gray, sullen—and realized I'd been buried in less than a foot of snow, at the very edge of the avalanche. I lay still, thinking I'd never seen a sky so pretty as that gray storm-bringer, feeling icy water trickle down my back.

I stumbled to my feet, realizing I'd been the last to run and the only one buried. My men gathered around me and I gaped at the mountain slope. Where there'd been thick drifts, there was nothing but gray rock. High up, where the avalanche had begun, I saw tiny dots moving, dancing around, and faintly heard screeches of disappointment and anger. I knew the emotion, but the voices were not human.

"What are they?"

"Dunno," Karjan said. "They're movin' on two legs . . . but not like men do."

The dots grouped together, went over the crest, and were gone.

"Sir? What made you stop us?"

"I don't know," I said. "Maybe I saw something out of the corner of my eye. Hells, maybe I'm just lucky."

There were nods—Damastes á Cimabue was known to be most lucky. Any other explanation would have been most worrisome.

We calmed the animals and went on, over the crest to begin the long descent into Maisir. And every step of the way I wondered who that woman's voice was. I wonder if it was even a woman. The man who called himself the Speaker had a very soft voice. Was it he? If so, why did he warn me . . . warn us? I have no answers.

We came to a narrow defile, and saw a narrow draw leading to one side.

"Will you stop for a moment?" Yonge said.

"Of course," I said, and ordered a halt.

"Come with me, if you would," the Kaiti said. I obeyed. "Leave us alone," Yonge told the others.

I followed him into the draw, to where it was blocked by a chest-high wall of boulders. Yonge stood at the wall, waiting. I peered over it. The draw continued for no more than another fifty yards, and was closed by vertical cliffs. The walls sheltered the draw from snow, and there was no more than powder on the rocks. Bones, human bones, littered the ground. In and around them I saw rusting armor, broken bows, a shattered sword, and animal bones.

"Fifty men," Yonge said. "Good, honest smugglers. They had five new members in their party when they made this crossing. The new men betrayed them."

Yonge pointed to a skull that was still encased in a half-helm. "That was their leader. Juin. A good man. He had time to cut down four of the traitors, then ordered his men back here, to fight to the death. Before they were slain, they fired and despoiled their goods, so the raiders gained nothing. He was the last to die, and his sword sang a deathsong for many

of those who came to him." Yonge stopped talking. There was silence, but for the whisper of the wind.

"How do you know what happened?" I asked. "Were you here?"

"No."

"Then . . ."

"I knew," Yonge said. "The last traitor told me before he, too, died." He looked again at the helmeted skull. "A good man," he said once more. "My brother."

I jolted. "Why . . . why didn't you bury the corpse? Or give it to the flames?"

Yonge's cold eyes met mine. "You mourn in your manner, Numantian, I mourn in mine."

He started toward the column, then turned back.

"None of the men who lay in wait for Juin now live," he said. "Not one." He smiled terribly, and his hand instinctively touched his sword's pommel.

Yonge's mood passed, and he reverted to his usual cheerily roistering self as we moved lower and lower toward the flatlands. Now we were truly in Maisir.

Everything smelled and felt different. Kait had been foreign, but very like the crags and ravines of the Urshi Highlands or the borders of Urey itself.

Trees rose around us, but now instead of the jungled growth of Numantia, these were high conifers, pines, cedars, whose branches whispered secrets of this unknown land as the wind blew through them. We saw bears, some larger than any I'd hunted in my own country, and the tracks of huge cats. The air was crisp, clean, and Nicias and my own problems seemed a world away.

Yonge, who normally walked slack—last man—in the column, came up beside me.

"It's a pretty land, Numantian," he said.

"It is that."

"And do you know why?" He didn't wait for an answer.

"It's because there are no people." We grinned at each other equably. "I've dreamed of building a little hut somewhere around here," Yonge went on. "Pack in what few supplies I'd need—corn, salt, arrowheads, some seeds for the winter—then live on what I could fish and hunt."

"A nice dream," I said.

"And there's only one thing wrong with it," he said.

"Which is?"

"This is Maisir."

"So? I doubt if any of them would begrudge you the odd bearskin or salmon."

"Perhaps there's more to the story than that," he said, looking mysterious. He clapped me on the back. "At any rate, Tribune Damastes á Cimabue, you've done well under my leadership, and I want to tell you that, perhaps, especially in view of the shortage of truly qualified men, you might, just might, be able to lead a patrol of your own. You can call yourself a scout, if you wish."

He was joking, but I was touched, and took the title to heart. "I thank you, Tribune."

He, too, turned serious. "So should I be suddenly called away, I know everything will be in good— well, perhaps not good, but at least not-too-palsied hands."

"And what does that mean?"

"Aren't you tired of asking me that question?" he said, and dropped back to his normal position.

The fog was thick, and we moved slowly along the trail. We walked quietly, boots and hooves muffled by the thick needles along the path. We rounded a bend, and they were waiting for us.

Fifteen men sat astride matching black horses. All wore dark armor. Spread out to either side was a rank of archers, shafts steadily aimed. I knew the men from engravings at Irrigon. These were Negaret, the border guards of Maisir.

"If you move, you will die," a heavily bearded man said.

"Keep your hands away from your weapons." He walked his horse forward.

My men stood as motionless as I did—but Yonge had vanished! His zebu's reins dangled to the ground.

"Give good report—or make your last prayers to whatever gods you have," the bearded man ordered.

The tip of his lance touched my chest.

SIXTEEN

The Negaret

I am Tribune Damastes á Cimabue," I announced boldly, "appointed ambassador plenipotentiary to the Court of King Bairan by the Emperor Laish Tenedos, in the name of Saionji the Goddess." I added the last because I wasn't sure these border guards had gotten word of who I was, and thought I'd invoke some protection, remembering the Maisirian's vaunted piety. Indeed, I saw two of the horsemen flinch at the dread mention of the destroyer goddess. The bearded man looked disappointed, and lowered the lance.

"And how did you come?" he demanded.

"By boat, horse, and foot," I retorted, and a Negaret snickered, getting a black look from his leader.

"I meant . . . But you will not tell me your route, eh?" I didn't reply. "Very well. Perhaps I know it. I am Jedaz Faquet Bakr. *Jedaz* is my title, and means—"

"Commander of the Threshold," I said. "What we call Frontier."

Bakr looked mildly pleased. "So you know of us Negaret, eh?"

"Not nearly enough."

"Come, then. Let us learn and grow together." He bellowed laughter. "I have been ordered by King Bairan, greatest of all monarchs, to await your arrival, to serve you in any way I can, and convey you to his officials at Oswy, where you will be greatly honored and taken to the capital of Jarrah. Allow me to be the first to welcome you to Maisir."

"I thank you," I said.

"You'll no longer need your horned beasts. Tell me, do your men ride, or are they *raelent*?" *Raelent* meant "less than men," and I guessed to the Negaret that meant anyone on foot.

"They ride," I said.

"Good. We brought horses." He waved to his men, and two led saddled but riderless horses toward us. "Tell me, Tribune Damastes," he asked, "what took you so long? We have been riding up and down picking our teeth for two weeks. Were the mountains harder than you expected?"

"Not at all," I said. "We found them so entrancing we stayed to frolic in the snow as a holiday. My apologies for letting you get bored."

Again Bakr shouted laughter. "Good. Very good. You are only the second Numantian I've met. I think you'll make very good enemies when we fight."

"But we aren't at war," I said.

"For how long?" Bakr said. "It's always the nature of the strong to test their strength, is it not?"

I shrugged.

"I would have expected a more soldierly answer," Bakr said. "We were told of your reputation as a warrior, and I expected someone far fiercer."

"When I'm among friends," I said, "there's no need for ferocity."

He looked impressed. "A warrior . . . and perhaps a man of words as well. Now, let us see how well you ride. Our camp is two hours distant, and let us see how much longer it takes us with our new baggage."

* * *

We moved lower and lower through the foothills. As we descended, the rain grew lighter and then stopped altogether.

I examined the manner, dress, and weaponry of the Negaret with great curiosity. They came from wildly varying stock. Some were dark haired, some were blond, one had long hair as fair as an albino's. They were tall, short, stocky, lean, and their complexions were equally varied. They wore dark armor, and under it a wild variation of clothing—fur vests, boots, leather pants, silks, heavy canvas—as if each man had outfitted himself at a different bazaar.

For weapons, each had a long steel-tipped lance. Their second weapon was either a curving saber carried sheathed on the back or scabbarded on the saddle, a short double-headed ax, or a hammer. They carried two daggers: one long and curved like a small saber, the second straight and single-edged, which was used for eating and close-in brawling. Some carried shields, from target-sized to conventional. The weapons were jeweled and their sheaths expensively worked, but their grips were well worn. All of the Negaret rode as if they'd been born on horseback.

We topped a rise and saw the Negaret camp. There were twenty huge tents scattered around a meadow with a pond in the center. The tents were octagonal, about sixty feet across, and made of heavy black felt. Above each tent was a second, circular dome of felt to absorb rain or snow.

The Negaret set up a great wailing cry as we drew closer, a cry that would carry for a league across the open prairies they called *suebi*. The cries were modulated in various subtle manners to convey simple messages.

As we rode up, men, women, children, came from the tents, looking at us curiously. The Negaret women wore multicolored garments of many styles. They were as weird in appearance as their men. They behaved boldly, as if the equal of the men, which I learned they were.

All was a babble of laughter, questions, and orders. Other

parties rode in, until there were about two hundred or more Negaret merrily boiling around the camp. There was to be a feast that night in our honor.

"Tribune Damastes," Bakr suddenly bellowed, "we have a problem, and I fear you, even though you are a great *shum*, are to blame."

I gathered he was intending for the entire clan to be audience to this conversation, so I raised my voice as well, as someone who'd been called lord—*shum*—should do.

"Far be it from me, great Jedaz, to feel anything but shame for having caused a problem for my new friends. How would you suggest I make amends?"

"If we were proper Maisirians, we would spend the rest of the day singing devotionals to various gods for your safe arrival," Bakr shouted. "And you and I would sit around complimenting each other on our charm and bravery. However, my people need meat, and, since it's early yet, we wish to hunt. Tell me, oh great Numantian, would this shame you?"

"Greatly," I said. "But you may make amends by letting us go with you. After we wash."

Bakr yipped. "Good! Good! Of course you're welcome. We'll leave as soon as we refresh."

Bakr came to me as I was making the acquaintance of the horse he'd given me. With him was a thin, white-haired and -bearded man. He was painfully thin and not particularly tall, but I thought his leanness was that of the greyhound, and that he might be well able to run with a horse until it foundered. "This is my *nevraid*, Levan Illey," he said. I knew *nevraid* was Maisirian for "magician."

"Will your men hunt with our riders?" he asked.

"Yes," I said. "At least until they sight something. Then they'll dismount and use their bows."

"Good," the *nevraid* said. "I have an idea to make their day more rewarding. We Negaret hunt from the saddle, but it will be easy to accommodate your soldiers. Perhaps, Faquet,

you could have a rider take them about half a league to the south of the herd? There's a rocky outcropping there, the one that looks like a fat man squatting, and the herd will run past it when we attack."

Without waiting for an answer, he bustled away.

"How does the *nevraid* know what path the animals will take?" I asked.

"Because he's a *nevraid*," Bakr said in some astonishment. "Can't *your* magicians perform such a task?"

I'd never heard of any.

"Tsk," Bakr said. "Hunting must be chancy in your land. Pardon me." He called for a lieutenant and gave him orders. A few minutes later, my five were mounted and rode off with three escorts.

"Now, as for you?" Bakr said when he returned.

"I'd prefer to ride out with you, then hunt on my own."

"As you wish." Bakr grinned. "You are a most unusual man for a diplomat, Tribune. Going hunting . . . letting your escort ride off . . . not worrying about being in danger."

I answered honestly. "I'm not a godling, nor are any of my men. If you intended us harm, do you think the six of us could do much more than worry you for a few minutes?"

Bakr nodded thoughtfully. "Since I've evidently proven I'm not an assassin, let us hunt."

We rode to where the antelope were supposed to be and dismounted below the hillcrest, and three men crept up to the top. Illey spread his map on the ground, holding it down with rocks marked with magical symbols. The scouts slipped back. The herd was there—about forty of them.

"Good," Bakr said. "Don't take the leader. Kill no yearlings, either. Take young bucks and any female without offspring. One per man."

We mounted. I unlimbered my hunting weapon, something I'd made from items borrowed at the camp, a weapon I thought the Negaret might find interesting.

"Now!" Bakr shouted, and we charged over the ridge at the gallop. The antelope saw us and stampeded. But then I heard a fierce roar, and two lions bounded over the far hillside. The antelope skittered aside, and for a moment I forgot them, cursing myself for having no better weapon to face charging man-killers. But the lions wavered and vanished and I realized it was Illey's magic.

I lashed my horse into a harder gallop, picked one buck, horns curving almost to his back, from the pack, and forgot the others. He ran hard, but my horse was running harder. I rose in my stirrups and readied the weapon I'd made. It was four iron balls, each in a tiny net, each net at the end of a leather thong. I whirled it twice about my head by one ball, then sent it spinning away.

I'd spent days and weeks learning how to do this, as a boy, after my father told me about the trick he'd seen used by desert tribesmen in Hailu. It looked easy, but wasn't, and I had gotten many rapped knuckles, a thumped head, and several lost snares before I felled my first guinea fowl.

The balls flew out, whirling at the ends of their thongs, and whipped about the antelope's back legs. It pinwheeled onto its back. I pulled my horse up and slid off, dagger out as my feet touched ground.

The antelope thrashed to its feet, but too late, as I was on it. It swept once at me with its curved horns, then I was inside its guard and slashed its throat. Blood spurted, I sprang back, and an instant later the animal was dead. I bled it out, cut out the musk glands on its inner thigh, gutted it, saving the liver and heart, and used grass to wipe out its body cavity. I managed to shoulder its bulk—I guess the dressed buck weighed just under a hundred pounds—and staggered toward my horse.

Hooves thudded, and Bakr reined in. He dismounted, took the beast's forequarters, and helped me load it. My horse neighed once, but didn't otherwise object.

"You hunt like a wild man, Numantian," Bakr said, and there was approval in his voice.

"I'm hungry," I replied.

"So are we all," he said, and pointed. Here and there, across the plain, were dismounted hunters, cleaning their kills. There was a rocky mount not far away, and I saw my men below it, busy at the same task.

"Not bad, Shum Damastes," Bakr said. "Perhaps the gods heard my jest and made it true. Perhaps there *are* things to be learned from you."

The meal that night was so memorable I can still name most of the dishes. It was chilly but clear, and several of the tents' rain covers had been pitched together for a long pavilion. A fire pit was dug to the windward side, and dry wood emitting no smoke laid, so we were quite warm. On the other side were cooking fires. I thought it admirable that, while the women cooked, the men served, and women sat as equals among us.

"You might be grateful for several things," Bakr announced at the beginning of the banquet. "First is we Negaret aren't addicted to constant toasts, unlike other Maisirians. So there's some possibility we may survive the evening and won't wake with the drummers of the gods behind our eyeballs. Secondly, our priest died last year, and as yet no man of the gods has joined us, so there won't be any long prayers to interfere with the gluttony. We feel terribly cursed." Bakr tried to look pious, failed. I noticed only a few Negaret frowned at his levity.

"Third is we're reprobates, every single one of us." He waited, like any good jokester, for my puzzlement, then went on. "We no longer swill what's supposedly the Negaret's favorite drink. Which is mare's milk, fermented in a treated stomach and mixed with fresh blood." He grimaced, then said quietly, "I've always wondered if every people must have some sort of dish that no one can tolerate, merely to prove how tough they are. At any rate, my men and women now drink like civilized folk."

He indicated a table laden with jugs. There were sweet wines and some brandies, but the favored tipple was *yasu*, which was made from grain fermented into a mash, then distilled. The clear liquor was flavored with various plants, such as citrus peel, fennel, dill, and anise. I'd gotten a gape of disbelief when I told Bakr I didn't drink. Again, he proclaimed I was unworthy to be a diplomat, but there'd be that much more for him.

The meal began with tiny fresh fish eggs spread on tiny, hot biscuits. With that went hard-boiled eggs, onions, small spicy berries, or a bit of lemon juice. The second course was the livers of the antelope we'd killed that afternoon, sautéed with wild mushrooms, wild onions, and spices. Next were prairie fowls, stuffed with seasoned marsh rice. The main course was roasted antelope, larded with bacon. Served between these courses were vegetables, including an assortment of various mushrooms in soured cream, and a watercress salad in sesame oil.

The finale was a dessert of goat cheese, egg yolks, nuts, currants, cream, and fresh and glazed fruit.

I could lie and say I was comfortably full, but in reality I felt as if I'd just been slopped, and now should go look for a mudhole to wallow in. Bakr belched resoundingly, and motioned me closer.

"You see the hard, austere life of a prairie nomad?" he said mournfully. "Do you not pity our harsh existence?"

We were roused the next morning for the journey to Oswy. The Negaret were civilized—there was little conversation on waking, and we were given a hard roll and strong tea after washing, then set to work. When the Negaret broke camp, or set it up for that matter, everyone worked, from the *jedaz* to the smaller children. Within the hour they were ready to move.

I saw how much they used magic. The tents, for instance, were in reality no more than a scrap of felt, various bits of rope, and some toothpick-sized pieces of wood, all ensorcelled. Illey bustled through the clamor. When a tent was struck, he'd stop, say a few words, and the heavily piled felt would vanish and someone would scrabble for the tiny bits that were its essence. Their sleeping robes, lamps, pillows—all were tiny items that might have come from a rich child's dollhouse.

"It's a pity," Bakr said, "nobody's found a way to magic chickens and such, so we could dispense with the wagons altogether." He turned to watch a goat being chased by two small boys and then, an instant later, two small boys being chased by the goat. "Yes. Goats especially," he mused, rubbing his thigh where he might have been butted once.

Then there was nothing left but the cooking fires and the pots and pans, the cooks bustling about them. Now we ate a real meal: eggs served with a sauce that would have cooked them if they hadn't already been hard-boiled, so it cooked my mouth instead, fresh-baked rye bread, sweet cakes, and more tea. The meal over, the kitchens were struck. Their iron pots were miniatures, as were the great iron plates for frying. Illey told me he didn't have the magic to create those to stand firm against fire, so they traded in the cities for them, built by magicians whose incantations were pleasing to the fire god, Shahriya.

And then we marched.

After two hours' ride, it began misting, but it was pleasant to ride down the last of the rolling foothills toward the plains that stretched far into the distance. Bakr moved up beside me and asked, "How many men, if it's not a secret, did you leave Numantia with?"

"No more than what I have now."

"That is very good," he said. "Most men who attempt the mountains leave some bones as they go."

"I guess we were lucky."

"Yes, lucky," Bakr said absently. "The reason I asked is that I've never heard of a diplomat traveling so light. They like to be surrounded with pomp and pissiness, I've observed from my encounters with the king's emissaries. Or is it different in Numantia?"

"It's no different," I said. "I guess politicians are the same everywhere."

We rode in silence, companionably, for a while. "Another odd thing," he said. "If you were Maisirian, holding a rank as high as you do, everyone in your party would be an officer."

"Who'd cut the wood and cook the meals?"

"The lowest-ranking *pydna*, of course," Bakr said. "The Maisirians don't like to be around the underclasses, the *calstors* and *devas*, except to order them to go out and die bravely. Soldiers aren't much more than animals."

"So I've read," I said. "And no officer who thinks like that can lead well. Maybe not at all."

"No," Bakr agreed. "Which is why so many soldiers desert to become Negaret.

"We're an outlet for the Maisirians, just like a covered pot on the fire must have a vent. A man or woman can't stand his lord, well, instead of waiting for him with an ax, he runs for the frontiers. If he makes it to us—he's Negaret."

"How do you know a runaway will make a good Negaret?" I asked.

"If he lives long enough to reach us, he'll be a good one," Bakr said. "He'll have had to elude his master's hounds, make his way through territory where a captured runaway's worth a bit of a reward, deal with wolves, bears, cataracts . . . He'll be tough when he reaches us. Or we'll find his bones in the spring."

Such a newcomer would then be assigned to a work group around one of the Negaret communities. When a column like Bakr's, which was called a *lanx*, came to trade, the runaway could join the *lanx* if he or she wished. "After a time," Bakr said, "the man or woman is a full Negaret, and allowed to speak in our *riets*, our assemblies. That was what happened to me." I was surprised. "Ah yes," Bakr said. "The lowliest can become the highest. At our *riets*, any man may become a candidate for leader, or others may name him. Every adult votes, and so the new *jedaz* is chosen. If someone doesn't like that *jedaz*, he's free to leave, and join another *lanx*. This is also good, for it lessens dissent, and also the blood in one *lanx* doesn't become too intertwined, so instead of warriors we might end with men who stumble around drooling and fucking chickens."

"Was there no supreme leader?"

"Of course. King Bairan."

"But no one great chieftain for the Negaret?"

"What do we need of them? Our towns have *kantibe*, mayors. They're chosen by the town *riets*. Lately the king has been sending his own men to our towns to administrate Maisirian interests."

"And do you like that?"

Bakr started to say something, then caught himself. "Of course we do, being all loyal servants of King Bairan," he said blandly. "And if we didn't, it's amazing the terrible accidents that can happen when a Maisirian *shum* goes for a walk by the riverside at night. Thus far, when a regrettable thing like that's happened, his replacement is far more gifted and sensible."

"At least about riverside walks."

We came out of the hills onto the *suebi*. It was just as the travelers had written, land that went on and on to an impossibly distant horizon. But it wasn't desert, or flat, and such a belief would deceive the unwary to their deaths. The *suebi* was riven with deep ravines a bandit column or a company of cavalry could set an ambush in.

Sometimes the land was marshy, sometimes dry, and a traveler had to pick his way carefully to avoid being mired or drowning. There were forests, not high pines such as we'd left, or the jungles of Numantia. The trees were low, twisted, bent, with thick brush between them. And always there was the wind—sometimes gently sighing, promising marvels just beyond, sometimes roaring fiercely.

I loved the *suebi* on first sight, loved the stretch and beckon of the sky, greater than any I'd known, any I could imagine. Some of us it made cautious, careful. Curti became even more wary than before, but wary of what, he couldn't say. At least one, Captain Lasta, was terrified by the grand reach. But being the brave man he was, he spoke of it but once, when we were musing about some clouds, and he said, harshly, he thought a demon was sitting up there, waiting to scoop up an unwary soldier, as a hawk hovers over a scurrying mouse.

In the days to come, that sky, and the *suebi*, would make many Numantians feel that way. And there would be more than enough hawks to provide deaths for poor mice.

It had grown colder while we traveled, and there was rime ice on the riverbanks, and my breath came frosty. Illey stood on a flat stone about fifty feet out into the huge river, which was almost a mile from bank to bank, with sandbanks rearing here and there. "Cast now," he shouted, pointing at what I thought was nothing more than a ripple.

I obeyed, hurling the long harpoon with all my might. The river exploded, and a great gray shape, coiling like a serpent, reared. Its face was an ancient evil, bewhiskered, fanged. My shaft was buried just behind its huge, water-drooling gills.

"We have him," Illey shrieked.

"Secure him well," Bakr ordered, and the men who held the end of the line ran to a nearby tree and whipped several lengths around its trunk.

The monstrous fish smashed to the end of the line, and the tree bent nearly double. The fish jumped, almost clear of the water, and I gasped, seeing how huge it was, almost thirty feet long. It ran hard downstream, trying to pull the spear out, trying to break the rope. But the line held firm. Again and again the fish tried to break free, but to no avail, and then it rolled on its back and was dead.

The Negaret cheered and dragged the carcass ashore.

I turned to Bakr. "You've honored me greatly," I said, "allowing me to cast that harpoon."

He nodded. "You and your men have been good companions to us. Good to travel with. We sought but to return a piece of that honor."

"I thank you, Jedaz Bakr," I said, bowing.

"Enough of such horseshit. We have fish to clean and egg pouches to cut away. We'll be awake half the night up to our crotches in fish guts," he said, as uncomfortable with sentiment as I.

Lightning erupted across the sky from horizon to horizon, and thunder slammed as if the gods were rolling stone bowls. Karjan and I had walked out from the camp after the evening meal. Behind us were lights from the guttering fires and, very dimly, from the tents. I was lost in my thoughts when Karjan suddenly said, "Y' know, wouldn't be bad, bein' like this always."

I blinked back to the present. My servant had been taken up by a slender woman about his own age, the widow, I learned, of one of the *lanx*'s best warriors.

"You mean, as a Negaret?"

He nodded.

"Not at all bad," I said. "No slaves, no masters. No jobs that make you do the same thing, day in, day out. Hunt, fish, ride—there're worse things than life like this."

"Guess I never was too good at bein' civilized," Karjan said. I saw his teeth flash behind his beard. "Best treat me well, Tribune. Or one day you'll commission me or do somethin' equally shitty, and I'll be gone."

"Run fast," I said. "For I might be right on your heels."

The next day, we saw a smudge of smoke on the horizon. The day after that, we rode into Oswy, and our time with the Negaret was over.

SEVENTEEN

Alegria

Oswy seemed to be two cities—one fairly clean, for a frontier town, the other shabby and mostly unpainted. The central street, very wide, very muddy, divided them. At first I thought one side held the well-to-do, such as they were, the other the poor, but Bakr corrected me. "On this side are the traders and those who give a shit about clean streets. On the other . . . the Negaret, who care more for the cleanliness of their souls and bodies, and spend as little time behind walls as they must." Proof that worldly injustice is rife was that the Negaret side sounded with music and laughter, and the Maisirian traders were pinched-faced and ill at ease.

Bakr had pitched his tents beyond the city walls, which he said was required for Negaret bands, then he and his warriors escorted me to the *balamb*, or military governor. Oswy, the first city within Maisir on the main trading route, was too important to be ruled by a civilian *kantibe*.

Balamb Bottalock Trembelie and his staff were waiting inside the gates of his sprawling compound. Trembelie was an odd-looking man. He must have been a fine bull of a soldier who'd spent too long at the trencher and not enough in the trenches. At one time he would have weighed 250, perhaps 300 pounds. But something had happened, perhaps a wasting disease he was only just recovering from, for his weight had fallen so quickly his skin hadn't had time to shrink to its proper size. His jowls drooped, and the skin of his hands sagged in folds. He should have worn a beard, for he looked like a dissipated, petulant baby. He wore jewel-crusted red suede breeches and vest, with a silk shirt that ended at his elbows. His forearms bulged, not with fat but muscle, and I knew he could handle a heavy sword without effort.

It was raining as we rode through the gates, but Trembelie paid no attention, striding down from the pavilion he and his courtiers were sheltering under. "Ambassador Damastes á Cimabue, Tribune and Baron," he said, and his voice was a flat, clear baritone well suited for the commands of the battlefield. "Welcome to Oswy. Welcome to Maisir."

I dismounted and greeted him. There was the usual babble of introductions.

"Balamb Trembelie," Bakr called. "My duty is finished, and I now give over this man to your keeping. Guard him well, as I have." He looked at me. "Take good care. When you return, come a-hunting with us. Or, if not, think fondly of the day when we'll be hunting each other."

I saluted with an open hand, and he wheeled his horse, kicked it into a gallop, and splashed out of the compound.

"May I ask what *that* was about?" Trembelie said.

"Jedaz Bakr has determined war between our kingdoms is inevitable," I said.

"That was rude."

"Not in his eyes," I said. "He thought it would be quite a wonderful time."

"And you?"

"My orders, my desires, and those of my emperor, are for peace. Let those who want war find another enemy than Numantia."

"Good," Trembelie said. "I feel the same. These bones of mine have seen enough of blood. I have no desire to scatter them on some forgotten ground. After what you've just said, I personally bid you another, fonder welcome to Oswy. Come inside, you and your men, and let us provide a proper—and dry—reception."

That night's banquet was interesting, if somewhat overspiced for my palate. The Maisirians love to give flowery names to their dishes, just as Varan cooks do. One dish, for instance, was called Heavenly Forest Log Bearing Scents of Spring. It was a haunch of venison with far too many spices, too much wine, and too much garlic, cooked with onions, scallions, shallots, and leeks. I foresaw that I'd better eat simple dishes when alone, if the Maisirians proposed to feed me like this in public.

Trembelie's eyebrows lifted when I told him I didn't drink, but within moments he'd ordered up various sorts of iced waters, some charged, others scented with flowers or fruit.

There were only a handful of women at the table, and these were the concubines of Trembelie and his highest aides. I don't know if any of these officials had wives in Oswy, but if they did, they were kept in seclusion.

Bakr had warned me about the interminable toasts, and so it went, beginning with one to the Emperor Tenedos, then to King Bairan, then to each other, then to the city of Oswy, and so on and so forth.

After dinner I gave out presents to Trembelie and four of his aides. These were clever cylinders that provided a different view of Numantia each time you turned and peered through them, tiny statues of strangely worked metals and semiprecious stones, and suchlike. For Trembelie, I had a dagger whose blade was skeletonized, with various-colored gems set within.

"We have gifts for you," he announced. "These come not from us, but from His Royal Majesty. I must say that our king, who does all things well, has outdone himself."

First were expensive, soft winter furs, then a jeweled and elaborately engraved sword.

"There is one more," and Trembelie sounded wistful. "The king has granted you a great honor, one which I hope, to be frank, to be worthy of if Irisu smiles and I serve my master well." He tapped a wooden clacker and a young woman walked into the room.

I don't know if I gasped, or if it was someone else. She was the most beautiful woman I'd ever seen. She was tall, four inches under six feet. She had straight black hair that fell below her waist and was pulled back and held with a jeweled clip. Her eyes were almond in shape, and green. She had a small, pert nose, equally small and inviting lips, and high cheekbones. Her complexion was a golden marvel, utterly clear, as if the finest lacquer had been laid over the finest hammered metal, and I knew her skin would be as velvet to my touch.

She was quite slender, but full-breasted. She wore a robe suitable for a bedchamber or an imperial audience—high-necked, close-fitting, and following the lines of her body to her ankles. It was light blue, with a raised pattern lighter blue. Her expression suggested someone who'd come quickly to laughter, curiosity, or passion.

"This is Alegria," Trembelie said. "She is a Dalriada." He said this as if I was expected to know what a Dalriada was, and to be suitably impressed.

She lifted her face and looked at me. I was shaken for an instant by an unknown emotion. It was lust, but more than lust. I yearned suddenly to take her in my arms, take off the robe she wore, and love her. I said, and meant *love*, not just lust.

"This is, as I've said, one of the highest honors our King can bestow," Trembelie said. "Alegria is given to you by our gracious king not only for your time here in Maisir, but to take back to Numantia if you wish." He paused, then said, "Unless, of course, there are . . . problematical circumstances."

Someone snickered, and I'm afraid I blushed, as much

with anger as anything, for a host of reasons. The most obvious was wondering why men behaved in such an utterly boorish manner. I thought, for an instant, a bit of amusement came and went on Alegria's face.

The clacker sounded again, and the spell was broken. Two servants appeared.

"Escort this woman to Tribune á Cimabue's chamber, along with his other presents."

Alegria bowed and walked out, as calmly as if she were royalty leaving an audience chamber.

We sat for another hour, perhaps two, mouthing platitudes of peace and brotherhood. I suppose I held up my end, but my mind was hardly present. I wasn't eager to have the evening come to an end, at least not until I determined what I'd do about the woman. But no ideas came.

Finally Trembelie yawned widely and suggested it was time to retire. "I assume you'd also like to . . . examine the gifts from our king." That got a laugh, but not from me. I forced a smile, rose, and a servant came.

My apartments were on three levels, on the highest floor of the building, and faced east, so the rising sun would illuminate them, with Oswy and the river it sat on below. Everything was silk, padded leather, and luxury, decorated in a rather feminine style.

Alegria was kneeling in the center of the main room. "Good evening, master." Her voice was as I'd expected, soft, gentle, purring but with the force of a tiger.

"Get up," I said.

She obeyed, rising with utter grace, hands not touching the floor.

"First, my name is Damastes. I'm not to be called master."

"As you wish, mas— As you wish."

"Sit down somewhere." She obeyed, curling herself in a round, backless chair. "Let's start over," I said. "Alegria, I am delighted to meet you."

"And I you," she murmured. She looked me up and down.

"I think I'm very lucky."

"Don't be so sure," I said, wondering why my voice was harsh, and forcing it to be gentle. "But why do you say that?"

"Forgive me for sounding arrogant," she said. "But those who my lord and master, King Bairan, deem worthy of a gift of Dalriada are generally, shall we say, not young, but of years commensurate with their station. Not to mention bulk," she said, a smile coming and going.

"Thanks for the compliment," I said. "But you should know that I'm married."

Alegria held out her hands, palms up. "That isn't important." She opened the first button of her robe and took out what looked like a small stone tablet. "My lord, would you do me a favor?"

"If I can," I said, eager for a new subject.

"Put this in your mouth for a moment." I took the lozenge. It was engraved with tiny symbols. I obeyed, and tasted perfume I knew was her body, her scent. "Now give it back to me."

I took it out of my mouth, then hesitated. "Sorcerers try to get a bit of spittle, blood . . . other substances from those they wish to control," I said. "Is there magic in this?"

"There is. But not concerning you. This is something all Dalriada are required to do when they meet their master for the first time."

"I said, I'm not your master! Please don't use that word any more. But what happens next?"

"Nothing to you, as I've said. I merely place this in my mouth for a moment. Then the tablet's spell is expended, and you may have it back, if you wish."

"What does the tablet do?" She hesitated. "Tell me!"

"It binds me to you. Forever."

"A love philter?"

"Of sorts. But one that's very skillfully woven. I . . . I will love you, certainly. But I won't be blind to your faults, so I won't moon over you, and drive you mad with doglike devotion. It makes what you do, your happiness, your success the most important thing to me."

"So if I said your death was necessary?"

She looked down, nodded slightly.

"Utter, complete, contemptible bullshit," I snarled, rage breaking into the open. I went to a window and hurled the tablet into the night. "Fuck *that* nonsense."

Alegria's face twisted, and she started to cry. I didn't know what to do, but finally sat beside her and put an arm about her shoulders. She found that of little comfort, and so I just sat there until the sobs stopped. She excused herself, went into the bath, and I heard water splashing. She came back out and sat down across from me.

"All this is quite beyond me, quite beyond anything I've learned," she said. "Forgive me."

"There's nothing to forgive."

"Your wife must be very fortunate to have someone who loves her that much."

The cheap and convenient lie I'd told suddenly came back up, acid in the back of my throat. "No," I confessed. "My wife has left me recently, and will divorce me, if she hasn't already."

Alegria's eyes searched me. "Oh," she said gently. "So now you hate women?"

"Of course not. I . . . just feel, well, dead."

"I've been taught ways my instructors said will open passion's gates to almost anyone."

"I don't mean in the flesh," I said, wondering why I was telling this woman so much. "But rather that there's no attraction."

Alegria stood, and slipped her robe off. Under it she wore a filmy wrap, tinged with red and green, growing darker around her waist and sex, then lighter once more. I saw the delicate brown of her nipples, the firm pertness of her breasts. "No?" she breathed. "Even without the tablet I'm drawn to you, wish to make you happy."

"No," I said flatly, honestly.

"Then what do you wish me to do? Do you want me to

leave?"

"If I did, I doubt if your lord and master would be pleased with me. But that's as may be. What would happen to you?"

"The same thing that'll happen when you leave Maisir, since obviously you'll have no interest in taking me back to your kingdom," she said. "I'll return to the Dalriada."

"Which is?"

"A place. An order. Where I grew up, where I learned what I know, where my friends are. Where I'll grow old and die. Probably they'll want me to teach the novices, although what I'll have to teach I surely don't know. Maybe that even the fair can fail."

"You haven't failed," I said. "Don't be silly. Don't you have, well, male friends?"

Alegria looked at me closely. "I see you're not making a joke. So you must've been told nothing about what I am. I was chosen to join the Dalriada when I was seven years old. From that time to this night, I was never permitted to be alone with a man."

"Oh." This was becoming troublesome. "But when you go back, surely you can do whatever you want. Your service to the king is complete. It's no fault of yours the situation is what it is."

"No. If I were to marry, or company a man, that would be considered a disgrace by the king. My life would be forfeit." She looked to either side reflexively, as if making sure she wouldn't be overheard. "I don't understand why that shames my lord and master, but then I'm not a man, not a king."

I almost blurted that neither was she a gods-damned fool, and I didn't understand that kind of thinking either, but caught myself. "Is this what happens to all Dalriada?" I asked.

"Most. But not all. Some of us are lucky. Some of us become mistresses of those who own us. There are tales of a few even becoming wives."

"What about being freed? Of no longer being . . ."

"A slave? That would be terrible," she said. "For who would protect me?"

"The first man you met," I said. "You are very beautiful."

She blushed. "Thank you. But you don't know the ways of Maisir."

"Evidently not. But I'll learn them. The question now is, what should you and I do?"

"Please don't shame me this night. Allow me to sleep on the floor. Then I'll do what I must do."

"That's not an option either," I said. "Let me ask you this—do the talents of a Dalriada go beyond the bed?"

"Of course! Why do you think we're as prized as we are?" she said indignantly. "I can sing. Dance. Balance accounts. Provide any sort of conversation you wish, from party chatter to talk about art or books or even diplomacy. We're very well trained in that," she said. "Perhaps because most of our mas—lords practice that craft, sometimes to the exclusion of all else. Or so I was told."

"Then there's a solution, at least for the moment," I said. "Alegria, would you travel with me as my companion? My teacher? For I desperately need to learn everything there is to know about your land." Needless to say, I didn't add that it would be for the purpose of conquest.

"Yes," she said. "Yes, of course. I am yours."

"Mmmh." I was still thinking. "I suppose that Trembelie will have my servants brought up and questioned, to see what happened this night, eh?"

"I would think so. He was quite interested in me."

"There's but one bed. Would it be better for everybody, I mean . . . I don't mean to be . . ." My stammer faded off.

"Thank you, Damastes."

I didn't meet her eyes as we went into the bedchamber. It was quite awkward, planning to sleep with someone who was a stranger, someone you weren't going to have sex with. I found a thick robe made of toweling, and that helped. I looked studiously in other directions as we washed, cleaned our teeth, and perfumed our bodies. I rather imagine it would have been roaringly funny to an observer, but it was only embarrassing to me.

We went into the bedroom, and she sat on one side of the bed. "One small favor," she said, without looking at me. "Have you a tiny knife?"

I did, a small folding blade, in my housewife, useful for cleaning nails and such. I gave it to her. "Be careful, it's sharp."

"Good," and before I could do anything she slashed the tip of her ring finger.

"What are you doing?" I exclaimed.

"The same thing you are. Preventing gossip." She pulled back the covers and allowed blood to drip onto the sheets in the bed's center. "Remember? I am . . . I was . . . a virgin." Alegria suddenly giggled. "Your face is red."

"I know," I said furiously.

"And your neck."

"No doubt."

"How far down *do* you blush, Damastes?"

"Stop it, woman. I meant what I said."

She leaned over and blew out the light. I took off the robe, lay back, and pulled the covers over me. She got into bed. It was utterly silent, save for the dim clatter of a cart somewhere beyond Trembelie's mansion.

Then she giggled once more. "Good night, lord."

"Good night, Alegria."

Given the strangeness of the situation, I thought, I'd toss and turn for hours. But I didn't. Sleep took me within moments. I don't remember what I dreamed. But when I awoke, just at dawn, I felt very happy, and had a smile on my lips. And my cock was as hard as an iron rod.

The next morning, we started south, toward Jarrah. We were escorted by two full companies of the Third Royal Taezli Cavalry. Their proper total strength should have been around four hundred men, the ranking captain and therefore man in charge of both formations, Shamb Alatyr Philaret said. But they'd never been able to muster more than two hundred fifty or so, and fifty of these men had recently been detached to "help train the new units," further indication the Maisirians were building up their armies.

The other *shamb* was named Kars Ak-Mechat, who, I was quickly informed, came from one of Maisir's oldest and "best" families. In truth, he reminded me of a certain arrogant fool of a subaltern named Nexo whose skull had thankfully been crushed by a peasant during the Tovieti rising. Ak-Mechat was a few years older than Nexo but no wiser at all. His favorite topic was himself, the second favorite how noble his family was. I tried to ignore him.

We had a caravan of five carriages, sprung on iron leaves. But the constant swaying on the Maisirian—I almost said roads, but rethought the matter—trails, rather, was as exhausting, as if I were on horseback or in a peasant's wooden cart. I often thought longingly of that huge piggish carriage I'd had designed and built to lug me about the reaches of Numantia in something resembling comfort, a word whose meaning I was gradually forgetting.

The carriages were big, I suspected converted charabancs, drawn by eight horses, and leather-upholstered, with oiled canvas screens at the side windows, to keep out the weather. I'm sure I was thought a lunatic for keeping the screens half-open, even in the worst weather. I know Alegria, though she never complained, must have muttered wryly to herself about her "luck," huddling in a huge fur robe with nothing but her eyes, the tip of her nose, and the ends of her fingers to be seen, even though we were still in the Time of Rains, and the Time of Change hadn't even begun.

I explained that when I was a child I'd once been shut in a tiny chamber, and I had suffered for it ever since. What I was really doing was surveying anything and everything an invader might need to know, from the depth of the fords to the provender to be gained from the countryside. Behind me, in the second carriage, my men were doing exactly the same. Every night we gathered, purportedly to pray, so no Maisirians, respectful of anything to do with gods, bothered us. Actually we were telling Captain Lasta everything of military value we'd seen, and he was keeping notes in minuscule script on a long roll he kept inside his shako. The other three carriages held emergency supplies and camping equipment, which we were forced to use too many times.

We ground on, day to day, moving south. I wish that I could say we moved steadily, but that was far from the case. All too often we were forced to wait until a raging river subsided, or blocking trees were cut away, or a severe storm passed. The Maisirian road system was an utter catastrophe. The current joke—and it wasn't much of one—was that it was easy to tell the road from the muck—the road was the one with the pair of ruts.

The Maisirian highways were alarming, for without good roads, our army, when and if we attacked, would crawl as slowly as in the old days when it was burdened with officers' mistresses, useless baggage, and camp followers.

We passed through tiny, grim towns, little more than shack villages with perhaps a stray cobble here and there to jolt the wheels—gray, dismal. The only solidly constructed buildings were the stone temples, invariably the most magnificent structure seen. Then we'd return to the *suebi*—gray sky, gray mud, gray rain, gray brush until the eye cried out for relief. The only color would be our uniforms and Alegria's bright clothes.

I never thought I would mind being wet, since I grew up in the jungles. But this grayness, this always being soaked, not freezing, but chilled, morning to night, then waking and donning clothes that hadn't dried—it worked on all of us. I was very proud of Alegria. She might have been born for palaces and luxury, but she was, indeed, a noble companion, always having a joke when we were tired, a tale of the road, or some bit of trivia about the river or hamlet we'd just passed. At night, when we were caught between cities, she'd have a tale for the camp fire, or a song.

When we readied ourselves for sleep, curled in our coach, I tried not to think of her, how close she was, and that she wouldn't object if I slipped across the foot or two between us. Of course that was like telling a man not to think of a green pig. Alegria was my green pig, and grew greener the farther south we went.

We were well and truly mired. Our coachman cursed and his whip lashed, and the horses neighed protest, but the carriage merely creaked from side to side. Officers shouted for their men to dismount, put their shoulders to the wheel, and give it everything. I jumped out the side door and joined them, another cursing, heaving, muddy trooper in the dusk.

Men were sitting their horses a few feet away, and I almost shouted to them to get their lazy asses down and work some muscles, but then realized they were officers.

Through the grunting and swearing I clearly heard Shamb Ak-Mechat's nasal sneer: "If that bathless barbarian and the slut he's obsessed about would deign to stop their futtering, get off their flabby asses, and dismount from . . ." I heard no more. I had Ak-Mechat's booted leg in my hands and yanked him from his saddle. He yelled, flailed at the air, and landed face-first in the mud.

"You . . . you fucking swine . . . I'll . . ." He rose, met my boot in his chest, and went back down into a puddle with a splash. Ak-Mechat rolled, and came to his feet, then recognized me. "You bastard, how dare you, you baseborn cocksucker, how fucking *dare* you lay hands on me," he hissed, out of control, hands yanking at his saber.

I was about to flatten him again when a bow thumped, and an arrow sprouted from the *shamb*'s stomach. He screamed once, grabbed at the arrow and tried to pull it free, and then three other arrows thudded into his chest, one impaling his hand. Ak-Mechat was very dead when he went into the mire for the third time.

Behind me was a grim Shamb Philaret, archers behind him. He looked at the corpse without pity. "Stupid bastard. Thought his gods-damned family would let him do anything to anybody he . . ." Philaret broke off. "*Calstor*," he shouted.

A warrant waded up. "You order me, sir," the standard response to any officer's call.

"Take this bag of shit to the nearest tree and hang him there. Put a notice on him: 'This Dog Disobeyed His Ruler.'"

"You order me, sir," the man said mechanically, as if he'd just been told to make sure a *deva* cleaned his equipment before the next inspection.

"That fughpig has shamed us," Philaret said to me. "My utter apologies. If you care to report this to the king, I would understand."

"What would happen if I did?"

"The unit would likely be decimated," he said. "The officers would be the first to die. Most likely Ak-Mechat's family would be required to pay blood-bond. He has a son and a daughter, so their lives would be forfeit. The king might also decide Ak-Mechat's father's life belonged in the balance." Philaret's voice was completely calm, as calm as the *calstor*'s had been.

"I don't see the need to bring this matter up again, Shamb. A fool's idiocies should be forgotten as soon as possible."

"I thank you, sir." Without further acknowledgment, the officer rode back down the column. I returned to my wheel, and about half an hour later, after we'd gotten the spades out, the carriage was free.

I could have said what I was thinking—how utterly unnecessary that death had been, for his saber would never have been drawn before he would have been hammered back into the mire and given a thorough hiding, which might have taught a lesson—but I didn't.

What I'd read was true—the officers of the Maisirian army thought their men no better than barnyard animals, and treated them the same. Shamb Philaret and his junior *pydnas* were shocked when I insisted on making sure my men were quartered and fed before I ate. For them, enlisted men were servants. I remember one night there was no shelter to be found, and so we pitched tents. Once the officers had their cover up, and servants making dinner for them, it was as if the poor enlisted swine no longer existed. How they cooked their ration of barley and raw bacon, where they slept, was no matter.

But Isa help the soldier who wasn't turned out smartly in the morning and ready to ride on. It didn't matter, by the way, if he'd bathed since last year, or if he was soaking wet, so long as his sopping uniform showed no traces of the previous day's muddy travel. But the *devas* and *calstors* never complained, at least not within my hearing.

One night, we camped next to a group of merchants, and before dinner I wandered over to chat with them. Like most traders, they were careful about what they said in even casual conversation, especially with a soldier. But I learned a bit more about the country, helping to fill out the map I was building in my mind, and I got to spend some time with people not in uniform. When I returned, I had a tiny present for Alegria. It was a pin of a kitten, batting at a butterfly, and was quite cunningly cast and polished. It was made of various alloys of gold, so variations of the precious metal swirled through it—yellow, red, white. Held in the palm, the kitten took on the hues of a real animal, and mewed and swatted, without ever coming close to the playful insect darting about its head. When I gave the pin to Alegria, tears welled in her eyes. I asked her why—it had been fairly inexpensive and was a very minor sorcerous bauble compared to what she must have seen around the rich and mighty.

"This is the first thing that's ever been mine," she said. "Truly mine."

"What about your clothes, all the jewels in your chest?"

"The king's. Or they belong to my order. They're only mine so long as I'm with you." She snuffled. "I'm sorry, my lord. I don't mean to be always leaking tears like a rain cloud. But . . ." She let her voice trail off.

"I think this is as good a time as any to also forget about the 'my lord,'" I said briskly. "Shall we make it Damastes?"

"Very well. Damastes." She started to say something further, then stopped and concentrated on the tiny kitten frolicking in her hand.

We stayed in village inns when we could, which gave me a chance to wander the streets and meet people. There weren't many tradesmen, artisans, or people of the middle class. Or many rich, either. The peasants were dirty, cheerful, friendly, and exceedingly religious. Cheerful, but with little use for soldiers, even though the enlisted men were of their own class.

Two examples of why, which came from the same incident: We'd been forced to shelter in a farmer's yard, pitching our tents from the eaves of his ramshackle barn. The farmer grudged us fresh, warm milk from one of his two cows, and two chickens plus a smattering of wizened vegetables for a very thin soup. The next morning he watched as we got ready to move. I realized no one had offered to pay the farmer for his favors. They were rude, but the best he could have done. I hastily got out of our coach, went to the man, and gave him three gold coins. He was incoherent in his gratitude, which embarrassed me to excess.

We set out. I don't know what made me do it—perhaps I'd seen something out of the corner of my eye to make me suspicious—but a mile down the road I shouted for a halt, and asked Shamb Philaret to loan me a horse. I had to ride back to the farm, where I'd forgotten something. He said he'd have a *pydna* go, but I refused. Karjan was looking at me skeptically, knowing me full well by now, probably angry that I was going to do some piece of idiocy without an escort. I rode back, pulling my horse down to a walk before the gates. Then I heard screams. I slid from my horse, sword in hand, and ran forward.

Three of our soldiers, one *calstor* and two *devas*, had the farmer trussed to one of his wagon's huge wheels, and the *calstor* had improvised a whip out of an unwoven rope with knotted ends. "Y'll tell us where th' rest of y'r gold an' silver is, or y'll show us your bones," he shouted, and the whip slashed down once more. I guess the three were outriders, and thought they'd be able to accomplish their villainy and rejoin us before they were missed. I was across the yard and behind the warden before he heard me. I smashed the pommel of my sword into the back of his head, and he gurgled and fell into the muck. The two *devas* saw my ready blade and screamed in fear.

"Cut him loose." They hastened to obey, then one of them, knife in hand, looked calculatingly at me. I put four inches of steel through his forearm before his thoughts became action.

"Find the rest of that rope," I ordered, and when they brought it, a length of about fifty feet, I had the three tie loops, five feet apart, at one end and then put their heads through. The farmer was blubbering something about "great lord," "great father," but he owed me nothing. I gave him more gold. I took the far end of the rope and started back toward the caravan. I kept the pace just below a trot, so the men had to run, stumbling along the muddy track. All fell more than once, and I'd ride for another few yards, dragging them, kicking, flailing, before pulling up long enough to let them regain their feet. By the time we caught up with the others, the three were no more than mud-men.

Philaret demanded to know what had happened, only I made no reply, but tossed him the end of the rope, gave the *pydna* back his horse, and reentered the carriage. I don't know what happened to the three would-be thieves, but I don't remember seeing them on the rest of our journey.

The Maisirian soldiery weren't all idiots and thugs. Crossing one swollen river, a man was swept off his horse and carried downstream. Without thinking, without hesitating for an instant, four *devas* dove after him. We never recovered the first man, and three of his four would-be rescuers drowned as well.

Noble, but Shamb Philaret would have ridden on without ever acknowledging the bravery of those three men.

I asked for a moment and said a prayer, a speech more to the other Maisirian enlisted men than an invocation to any gods. We went on, and the sound of a nameless river that had just killed four men died away gradually.

We reached the Anker River, about two-thirds of the way from the border to Jarrah. This east-west tributary was wide, almost two miles from shore to shore. But it ran the wrong way for commerce, and was heavily silted, so only small boats could navigate it. Here, at the village of Sidor, it broke into many courses, with sandbars and small islands between each of them. Some of the islands had a few ragged fishermen living on them.

There were two long bridges across the Anker, about twenty yards apart. Each was about thirty feet wide, made of wood, with low railings, like long causeways from islet to islet. Philaret said it was quite common for one or more sections to be destroyed in the spring melt, and for traffic to be held up for weeks or people forced to use boats to reach the next, intact, section.

Sidor, mostly built of stone, was a bit more solid than other villages we'd passed through. We admired the tall, six-sided stone granary that was the local landmark, bought smoked, salted, and sorcery-preserved fish to improve our impossibly dull rations, crossed the bridge, and went on up the low hill on the far side.

There was something even worse than the *suebi*—the marshlands. The swamps weren't as deep on our route as they were to the east—the enormous Kiot Marshes, actually a closely connected series of swamps, with thin peninsulas running through them. But the world was still gray, and it wasn't from the now-hidden sky, but gray moss hanging from colorless, rain-dripping, twisting trees that looked as if they never lived, never died. And there were few hamlets—Philaret said only the hardiest Maisirian ventured through these lands, although there were tales of mysterious people who lived in the swamps, paying no heed to King Bairan or anyone else of the government.

The road was, simultaneously, better and worse. It was no longer a rut, but rather corduroyed with logs—trimmed, laid beside each other, and lashed in place—and crude bridges over the many streamlets. We didn't mire the carriages as often, but our way was a constant jolting from log to log to log. I asked Philaret about how many men it took to keep this road up, and he told me the king's magicians helped, laying spells of preservation on the green wood and rawhide lashings, but it was still necessary to send soldiers through with axes and shovels every year, after the ice melted in the Time of Births.

There were creatures out there in the dimness. Karjan and I spotted, about a hundred yards from the road, what appeared to be an ape, but with two pairs of arms and legs and an elongated, nearly headless body, so it resembled a spider larger than a man more than any monkey. It gibbered angrily, then was gone. I was told no one knew, or wanted to know, much about these creatures. Supposedly they were intelligent, almost as intelligent as a man, lived in rude communities, and stole the children of the peasants living on the fringes of the marsh. "Either stole them," Captain Lasta reported, since he was the one who'd heard the tale, "or had them for dinner. There're two ways of thinking."

At least there were few insects in this late season. But I would rather have dealt with a thousand buzzing bloodsuckers than the terrible fear that hung over us, a dread of something unknown, unseen. I felt as if something, or somethings, was watching us, perhaps hidden in this hummock or cleverly concealed behind that gnarled, tortured tree trunk. Sometimes we heard noises, but no one saw anything.

We reached a section where the corduroyed logs were rotting, dismounted, and went on afoot, drivers leading their teams. We put dismounted scouts ahead of the column, to give warning if the road had been washed out from beneath. I was wondering where we'd find a place to camp when a terror-stricken scream rang. Swords snicked from scabbards, and arrows were fumbled onto bowstrings.

Running toward the caravan was one of the scouts, howling in complete, mindless panic. But no one could call him craven, for rushing toward him, moving parallel with the road, was an impossible nightmare. Conceive of a slug, speckled, slime-yellow, shit-brown, a slug with no eyes, but a score or more gaping mouths along its slime-bubbling snout, a slug thirty or more feet long. It moved soundlessly, faster than the scout could run. It was almost on him, and the man looked over his shoulder once, shrieked again, and darted off the road, toward a clump of trees. Perhaps he thought he could outclimb the nightmare.

Philaret and another officer bellowed at the man, shouting for him to get back to the road, get back or die, which made no sense.

The slug reared as it moved, then collapsed wetly on the soldier, burying him under its disgusting bulk. Arrows spat, and buried themselves in the creature, and spears studded its flanks. But the monstrosity took no hurt. It slid away as quickly as it had come, back into the dimness, back into the shadows. There was no sign of the scout, no sign at all.

"That stupid bastard," Philaret swore. I asked what the man had done wrong, what we should do if one of us were attacked.

"I don't know if it's a secret or not . . . but no one said not to say anything," he said. "I told you the logs had words said over them, to keep them from rotting as fast as they would otherwise. There's another spell, something supposed to keep any of the swamp creatures from crossing the road, or even going on it. Stay on the road and you're safe. Move off it . . ." He didn't need to say more.

We went on for another hour, then stopped where we were, on the road. We slept in the carriages, and the Maisirian soldiers spread canvas from the carriage tops to the roadway for shelter. It was uncomfortable, but I don't think anyone slept very much. I certainly didn't. Not so much out of fear of the slug's return, but because I was pondering what Philaret had said. As far as I knew, no magician, not even the Chare Brethren, had the power to create a spell like the one Shamb Philaret had described. The emperor had been right—Maisirian magic appeared to be far in advance of our own.

Eventually we came to the end of the swamps, and entered woodlands, part of the immense Belaya Forest that ringed Jarrah and was its final protection. The hills were low, rolling. The ground was poor, sandy. The trees were tall conifers, and the constant wind touched them, moved them, night and day, sometimes a whisper, sometimes a roar.

The track improved until it was actually a road, even graveled from small town to town, and in the towns the ways were cobbled. We were getting close to Jarrah.

We came on the great estates of the Maisirian nobility, which stretched for leagues. But as often as not the great houses needed work, the surrounding villages were shabby, and the land poor and unyielding. We were greeted joyously at these estates, since we were, in many cases, the first visitors "of their class" to be seen in half a year, and they were eager for what they called news.

Actually all they wanted was gossip about what the rich and powerful were doing and wearing in Numantia, in Oswy, or on other estates. Real news, such as the tension between our two countries, bored them. They were lonely, they said, but I noticed none would have considered inviting any of the merchant caravans to be their guests. Boredom was better than having to deal with a lower class.

We stopped outside a village, and a peasant came out with buckets of milk, which he sold by the dipper. We drank all he had and wanted more. I went back to his farmhouse with him, this time sensibly allowing Karjan and Svalbard to accompany me. I asked questions about the land, the farm, the growing seasons, what kind of help he needed to work the land, but the man grunted monosyllables. I'd hoped to ask what he thought of the king, of his rulers, but I realized I'd get nothing from this stone.

His farmhouse was a bit neater than most we'd seen, although very small by Numantian standards. Painted over the door was an interesting symbol. It was yellow, and looked like an upside-down, curving letter U. The ends were thicker, like knots in a rope.

"What's that?" I asked, keeping my voice innocent.

The peasant looked at me hard, a threatening expression that was strange from a man of his station.

"'Tis an' old family sign f'r luck an' good weather," he muttered. "No more."

The drawing looked very much like the yellow silk strangling cord used by the Tovieti.

"Let me ask something," I said, keeping my voice casual. "Does this mean anything to you? It'd be in red."

With my sword tip I sketched a circle in the mud, a circle with lines curling from it, the main Tovieti emblem, of murderous snakes rising for revenge from the pooled blood of the cult's martyrs.

"No," the peasant said quickly. "Means naught." But he wouldn't meet my eyes.

So the Tovieti were in Maisir, as well.

The mansion gaped at the gray heavens, stonework still scarred from the flames that had consumed it. It might have been just an unfortunate accident, but an hour earlier we'd passed through what had been a tiny village and was now a similar ruin. I asked Shamb Philaret if he knew what had happened, and he nodded. I had to prod him for the story, but eventually he told me the peasants had risen against their masters.

I remembered the horror of Irrigon—the flames and Amiel's death—and held back a shudder. "Why?"

"The usual reasons, I suppose," he said and shrugged. "Sometimes peasants forget their lot's nothing but a crust and the whip, and their master's got the right to do what he wants—and they go mad. It's like a plague," he said. "None of them think about what they're doing, about what'll happen, and they tear and kill, like a bear among the dogs."

"So the army burned that village putting down the insurrection?"

"Not the army," he said grimly. "The king's magicians sent firewinds against the killers, and let Shahriya's fire take them all—men, women, children. The king proclaimed these lands outcast, and forbade anyone to live here or plant the lands. This was to be an example that would live forever for man to know his station, and his duties."

"When did this happen?" I said, thinking such utter barbarism must've been a generation or more ago.

"Five, no six, years past."

We rode on, through other shattered villages, still-scorched lands. I felt the dark hand of the gods overhanging us.

The inn, only a day beyond Jarrah, sat on a hill overlooking a lake, and was a delight. It was frequently used for holidays by Maisirian nobility and was quite luxurious. There were stables, covered areas for the carriages to be washed, and barracks for servants of the guests. As with other Maisirian buildings, the lower story of the huge main building was of stone, framed in wood, and the upper stories were wooden. My men were on the second level, each with a room to himself. Captain Lasta was used to such luxury, as was Karjan, but the others were as delighted as children at their day-of-birth celebration.

I was utterly exhausted, and asked to have a simple meal served in our rooms. Alegria and I had three huge rooms on the top level, lit by gas piped from a nearby fault, which was a great rarity in Maisir. We'd barely examined the bedchamber or the main room, for this inn had that most precious of all things, something we'd barely seen since leaving Oswy—a bath. The room was hand-rubbed wood and stone, with controllable vents bringing heat up from the lower floors. Now I learned the Maisirian nobility's way of cleanliness.

Stone monsters were set on the walls, chain-pulls below each, which allowed spouts of water, in various temperatures, to gush out of the pipes into wooden buckets. You wet yourself, soaped, and rinsed clean at least twice. Then you went to the tub, a twenty-foot-wide wine barrel cut in half. You never sullied this water with dirt or soap, but used it for relaxation, Alegria told me. There were other carved monster heads with chains overhead, and when the chains were pulled, the heads would tilt and dump down hot or cold water.

Alegria went into the bathroom first, while I tried to keep awake. Every muscle in my body whined about the moil and toil inflicted over the last time and a half.

"You may come in now," she said, and I obeyed. Alegria floated on her back in the tub, eyes closed. I was too tired, too worn, to give a hang if she chose to watch. I hung the robe on a hook, filled a bucket, found the soap and a huge sea sponge, and began scrubbing. It took three complete baths before I felt the filth of the journey dissipating, and my skin was pink as a baby's. A hairy baby's, and I took out my razor and polished steel and shaved, amazingly without slashing my exhausted throat.

Alegria splashed happily, singing to herself. She, at least, was awake and alert. I considered drowning her. I thought about putting the robe back on, then thought myself foolish, went to the tub, and lowered myself into it. It was just above blood-warm, about three feet deep. Submerged, I felt my hair float like seaweed about my head. Finally I had to surface to breathe, and I stretched out on my back, my head resting on the tub's rim.

The water was unusual, bubbling, caressing my skin, soothing it, but without the usual stink of a mineral hot springs. Alegria lay as I did across from me, peering at me through toes she wriggled from time to time.

"Are you happy, Damastes?" she said.

I realized, somewhat to my surprise, that at least I wasn't unhappy. The leaden misery that had companioned me since

Marán had discarded me was still there, but far distant, almost a memory. "Pretty much," I said.

"I am, too."

I yawned.

"None of that, sir," she said. "You will be awake to dine. We have been eating slugs and snails and worms and grain and things I wouldn't feed a duck for ages."

"Well, we better not wait too long, then," I said. "Or I'll drown in the soup." Oddly, as I spoke, I felt fatigue draining, as if the bath had rejuvenating powers.

"Of course not," Alegria said. "These tubs are dangerous, I've learned."

"How so? Too warm and you melt to death?"

"No," she said, putting a worried look on her face. "It's the wood the casks are made out of. I read that it harbors small creatures that slip out after a time."

I raised an eyebrow.

"I'm telling the truth," she said. "They're somewhat dangerous, since they have a single claw, and dearly love to bite."

"I'm deeply concerned," I said.

"Oooh. I just felt one," she yelped. "It's down on the bottom, and it's moving toward you."

At that moment a pair of pinchers closed on my cock, and I found the power of levitation. Then I realized the "claw" was Alegria's toes.

I stood, streaming water. "Wench! Hoyden! Liar!" My outrage might have been more convincing if my cock hadn't been rising in front of me. "I told you not to do things like that," I said, again failing at dignified outrage.

"I'm *very* sorry, Damastes," Alegria said. "Especially since I hear the sound of our table being set outside. Shall we dine?"

* * *

We did, on freshly baked warm bread, tubs of country butter, a wonderful salad of many different kinds of greens, and tiny shrimp Alegria swore came from the inn's tubs, and were just like the one that had bitten me, sans claws. We could have had meat or fish, but both of us lusted after vegetables, and so we had quickly fried bitter melon with black beans and assorted mushrooms. Alegria had two glasses of wine; I drank mineral water. I summoned a servant and had him remove the ruins of the meal.

"And now to bed, my lord?"

"And now to bed," I said and yawned.

"Actually," she said, as she rose and went into the bedchamber, "I'm quite grateful we have the arrangement we do."

"Oh?"

"Were we anything other than what we are, we might be losing valuable sleep, which we need to build our bodies for the morrow."

"You sound like my mother," I said.

"But do I look like her?" She dropped her robe as she spoke. I caught a glimpse of her lithe, nude body, then she closed the gas valve, and we were in darkness, except for the tiny fringe of a moon through racing clouds. "Come to bed," she whispered, and I heard the creak of the springs.

I obeyed. It was huge, soft, warm, and wonderful, although, at the moment, I was having a bit of trouble thinking about the bed and sleep. Alegria was on her side, back to me. I took several deep breaths, but that didn't help matters.

"I'm almost asleep," Alegria said, but she didn't sound sleepy. "Tell me something, Damastes. Do Numantians kiss?"

"Of course, silly."

"Why is that silly? I've never been kissed by one. Least of all by you. I thought maybe your people thought it was evil or something."

"Alegria, you're not being good."

"No? What's the harm in one little kiss? I mean, just to satisfy scholarly curiosity and things like that."

"All right."

She rolled on her back and stretched her hands above her head. "Do Numantians kiss with their mouths open or closed?"

"This one does it with his mouth closed, because he's trying to stay out of trouble," I muttered. I leaned over and kissed her gently. Her lips moved under mine a little. I kissed the corners of her mouth, and it opened slightly. But I held to my resolve and kissed her cheeks, then, gently, her eyelids. There seemed no harm in caressing her eyelids with my tongue, however.

"Numantians are very gentle," she murmured. "Do that again."

I did, and somehow my mouth opened a little, and her tongue slid into it. Alegria sighed and lowered her arms around me. The kiss went on, and became less gentle. Her arms moved up and down my back. It seemed appropriate to run my tongue back and forth across her neck, and her breathing came faster. She took one arm from around me and pulled the sheet away. Her breasts were against me, tight nipples hard.

I kissed one, then the other, teased them with my teeth, then came back to her mouth. One of my arms was around her back, pulling her close, and the other caressed her, moving down, just over the swell of her buttocks.

She lifted a leg, curled it around me, and I felt dampness and a curly tickle on my upper thigh.

Then she yelped, pulled away, and rolled out of bed to her feet.

"What the—"

"Something bit me! Ouch! Son of a palsied—find the light, quickly!"

I fumbled on the bedside table for the covered slow match, opened it, and relit the gas.

Alegria stood naked in the middle of the floor, warily looking at the bed. "I'm not getting back in there—pull the blankets back, my lord."

I obeyed, and a black spider scuttled across the sheet. I crushed it with the heel of my hand.

"Where did it bite you?"

"Here," she said. "On the back of my arm."

There was a red area, rapidly swelling. I found the bellpull and clanged for a servant. One arrived in minutes, and I ordered vinegar and baking soda. When they arrived, I mixed the two together, then laved the back of her arm again and again. As I did, the innkeeper appeared. She was appalled that such a thing could happen in her inn, especially to such a noble visitor, and insisted on having the entire bed removed and replaced. She wanted to have the chamber smoke-filled—to make sure the spider was dead—to move us to another room, even though it wasn't her best like this one—and so on and so forth. But eventually I got rid of her and went back to Alegria. After about half an hour, she said the pain was gone.

"But when we reach Jarrah," I said, "I want you to visit a seer. Spider bites can turn nasty."

"I'll be fine," she said. She looked at me wryly. "I'm starting to believe Irisu wishes me to remain a maiden forever, though."

I managed a wan smile. My mood of romance, gentle lust, was gone. Now I wanted . . .

I didn't know what I wanted.

Alegria correctly read my expression. "Come, Damastes. Let us sleep. For real." Once more she shut off the lights, and once more we got into bed.

"Good night," she said, and her voice was dull, flat.

"Would you mind if I kissed you good night?" I asked.

After a moment, she said, "No," and there was a breath of life to her tone. We kissed, and it was very tender, very gentle, with no heat. She turned over, and I yawned. Her breathing gentled, became the tiniest snore.

I felt myself sinking, but as I did, she moved toward me, her behind warm against my stomach. She fitted her legs against mine until we were nestled together, her head just below and in front of mine. I kissed the tip of her ear.

I cupped her breast with my right hand, and she made a contented sound. It precisely filled my grasp.

Then sleep took me.

I don't know what might have happened if we'd stayed another day or two at the inn . . . or perhaps I do.

But the next day we moved on, and by dusk we were in Jarrah.

EIGHTEEN

KING BAIRAN

Jarrah sprawled for leagues, its symmetrically laid streets broken by parks and small lakes, even more than graced Nicias. The boulevards were wide and tree-lined, and a river wound lazily through the city, from east to west. The city was walled, but in a rather haphazard manner. It had been planned as an octagon, with siege-proof walls nearly thirty feet thick, and onion-shaped guard towers at the angles. But the city had sprawled beyond, and each time it did, another set of walls was built. These walls, when the metropolis devoured them, had arches driven through them, so commerce could pass through.

Farther south were rolling hills, and here were the palaces of the mighty. One held the Numantian Embassy, where we were going. Beyond these estates, each set off by parklands, was Moriton, the King's Own, a fortress enclosing many more elaborate mansions, barracks, and administration centers. Here dwelt King Bairan, and his satraps, servants, slaves, and administrators in their thousands.

Shamb Philaret had sent riders ahead the night before, so we were expected. A pavilion was raised beyond the city gates, against the occasionally spattering rain, and richly garbed dignitaries waited under it.

I wore a waist-length red cloak against the weather, black knee-high boots, white riding breeches, a white tunic with red trim, and a shako. I was armed with the sword King Bairan had given me.

Alegria wore a dark brown, almost black, silk garment with needlework, high-necked. At the waist, the suit flared into wide-legged pants, and she wore short boots underneath it. For protection against the weather, she had a hooded cloak that appeared to be no more than translucent cloth with exotic embroidery. But the garment was spellbound, so it cast off the rain and was windproof as well.

The first to greet me was Baron Sala, sad-eyed as ever. I wasn't sure if I outranked him, but there was little harm in being the first to bow, especially since the emperor wanted peace, and a peaceful man is never arrogant. Sala looked a little surprised, bowed as well, first to me, then, to my surprise and pleasure, to Alegria, whom he greeted by name and gave the title of *woizera*—noble lady. She might have been no more than property, but Sala had decency.

"Baron," I said. "You told me once you doubted if my emperor would allow me to visit your land. I'm delighted you were wrong, even though I'm deeply unhappy about the circumstances."

"As am I, as is my king," Sala said. "And by the way, my title is now *ligaba*. My king has honored me greatly."

"And wisely," I said honestly. *Ligaba* was the title of the court's highest chancellor.

"Thank you, Ambassador. I hope to prove you right. The king has also named me to represent Maisir in our negotiations."

"That is truly excellent," I said, a little less truthfully. It might be good I'd be dealing with someone familiar with Nicias, the emperor, and Numantia, but on the other hand it would make it very hard to run any sort of bluff.

Another man came toward us, dressed in a very dignified dark gray tunic and pants, with many decorations on a sash over one shoulder. I knew him by portrait, although we'd never met. He was Lord Susa Boconnoc, Numantian ambassador to Maisir. He came from a very old family that had been well rewarded when they declared loyalty to the emperor a day after the Rule of Ten had given in to Tenedos's demands. Boconnoc had always been a diplomat, and so he was named to the extraordinarily important post in Jarrah. I'd read his file, talked discreetly to others in our Foreign Service, and found he was considered no more than averagely bright, and not particularly creative. He was very good with people, particularly high-ranking ones, and moved easily among them.

One person said, frankly, that most people thought him somewhat thicker than sand, and I wondered why the emperor had chosen him. Then I realized Tenedos thought Maisir too important for anyone but himself to deal with, and had picked the ideal man for the job, someone who would obey any instructions to the letter but no further, someone who would report exactly what was going on without interpretations, someone who was utterly loyal.

Boconnoc was in his fifties, had a distinguished, carefully shaped gray beard and short hair, and carried himself with dignity. He could, depending on his choice of expressions, look like a favorite, if a bit stern, grandsire, or, when angry, or simulating that emotion—as all diplomats, commanders, and parents must learn to do—like the embodiment of Aharhel the God Who Speaks to Kings.

"Ambassador á Cimabue," he said, "there's a bit of a surprise. Originally you were to be quartered in our embassy. But the king determined otherwise, and requested you lodge within Moriton. This is a great honor, Ambassador, one which no other Numantian has ever been granted. I'll see your men are well provided for."

"The king made this decision," Sala broke in, "not merely as an honor, but to show how seriously he takes this dispute, and how quickly he hopes to have the matter resolved . . . before other alternatives are forced on him. He and I both hope a peaceful solution is possible."

"It is," I said. "Quickly and immediately. I have explicit orders from my emperor."

Both professionals looked surprised and a little shocked. Sala suddenly smiled. "Well . . . I wondered why you were chosen for this task, since I hadn't been aware of your talents in subtle negotiations."

"I have none," I said. "That's exactly why I was picked."

"This," Sala said musingly, "may be a *very* interesting time." He hesitated. "Ambassador á Cimabue," he asked, "may I inquire as to the state of your vitality?"

I was perplexed, then grinned. "Are you challenging me to a footrace, perhaps?"

Sala laughed. "I was instructed to ask the question, because if you feel up to it, there is someone who wishes to meet you immediately, even before you refresh yourself."

Both Boconnoc's and my eyes widened. There could only be one such person. And one such response.

"I am at your command, sir."

I climbed into a ceremonial coach with Sala, and we proceeded to enter Jarrah. The streets were filled with people, cheering, singing. I admired King Bairan for being able to mount a spectacle so readily. The people were chanting, in somewhat rehearsed unison, for their king, for the Emperor Tenedos, for Maisir, for Numantia, and every now and then, for me.

I waved graciously and kept a smile on my face. I noted that as many faces were looking up as at our small procession, and I peered out myself. Overhead was a horde of magical figures that came and went, twisting like kites in a strong breeze. Some were mythic beings, some monsters I guessed were native to Maisir, and I even saw the swamp-slug and that spiderlike ape.

As in Oswy, the buildings were frequently stone for lower stories, fantastically worked wood on the upper, and overall garishly painted and decorated. Unlike Oswy, roofs were often metal, and as loudly painted as the wooden walls. But Oswy had few tall buildings, and Jarrah had many. Some were even eight or nine floors tall, tipped with fantastically configured domes. They appeared to be apartments, and Sala confirmed this. "Generally of the poor," he said. "We are always building, but the people seem to have children faster than we can nail wood together. I suppose it's because making babies is a deal more interesting than pounding nails."

I commented on how well laid out Jarrah was. "That's a hidden blessing Shahriya gives us with her fire," Sala said, and explained that the city had burned three times in the last two hundred years—once by arson, once in a great fire that sprang from the forests around to devour Jarrah, once for unknown reasons.

The people dressed a bit better than in other villages and towns we'd passed through, but not much. Other than in its size, architecture, and lavish use of paint, Jarrah wasn't as spectacular as I'd dreamed.

I heard screams of fear and shouts of wonder, and looked up again. In the sky were legions of warriors, some marching, some riding. All were fiercely armed, and their armor was worked to cause terror. They were silently shouting and waving their weapons. Who were these magical warriors supposed to impress? The crowds? Or me?

We passed an enormous temple, and I heard a chorale rising and falling from within, ever-changing. There must have been at least a couple of thousand men and women in the congregation. "What is being celebrated?"

"Nothing," Sala said, "at least as far as I know."

I realized they were praying to Umar the withdrawn Creator. "We've always worshiped him," Sala said. "The oldest, the wisest, the one who gave all of us, men and gods, life. Perhaps, if we pray hard enough, he'll return."

He said this as if he actually believed it.

There were no crowds at the gates of Moriton. The grim black walls that rose before us would have discouraged anyone's presence. There were no visible guards, no challenges, and the gates swung wide with never a sound. There was an inner courtyard half an army could have assembled in, then a second set of gates. These opened, and we were inside the King's Own. Moriton was huge, a city within a city, except that few cities are composed entirely of palaces. Some were enormous, others merely huge, and they were interspersed with barracks and unobtrusive buildings Sala told me were the offices of the diplomatic corps and other administrators. Everyone seemed intent on his business, and no one bothered to look when we passed.

Our carriage turned onto a long drive, cobbled with stones of many colors. That led to a immense building with flanking buttresses, wings to sweep you into its stone heart.

The carriage drew up, and I waited for a servitor. None came. "Go ahead," Sala said. "You'll not get lost."

I obeyed, and walked up the steps. At each step a great gong sounded, and my heart trembled as I approached. The rain hesitated, as if it, too, were afraid. Half-crescent doors more than fifty feet high opened as I approached, and I walked into a long antechamber, arching high into gloom. There were tapestries of the richest silk, gold- and silver-worked, some abstract, some showing fabulous creatures of, I hoped, myth.

Another set of doors opened, and I walked into another huge room. Its windows were covered by translucent shades against the rain and chill, and fires roared at the four corners. The room was perhaps two hundred feet long, fifty or more feet wide, and seventy-five feet high. It was evenly lit, but I saw no torches, no tapers. At the far end of the room, on a great circular rug of red and gold, stood a man whose size was almost equal to this chamber. There was a curtained alcove behind him.

I am tall, but King Bairan was a head taller. He was in his late forties, or early fifties, lean, hard, with a hawklike, clean-shaven face and a predator's expression. He wore a simple gold diadem, with a gem the size of his fist in its center, gray pants and tunic, with thin gray leather pads outlining his muscled shoulders, upper chest, and lean waist and thighs, suggesting armor. At his waist was a simple leather belt, with an equally plain dagger on it.

He could not have chosen his costume better to suggest he was a man of war. *Approach in peace,* it said, *or be prepared for what you shall face.*

I knelt on one knee and bowed my head. I might have been familiar with one grand ruler, but this was different. I'd known the Emperor Tenedos as a young wizard, and so there was familiarity, knowledge Tenedos was all too human. King Bairan was the last in a line that had held the throne for centuries, and his kingdom dwarfed Numantia.

"Welcome to Maisir, to Jarrah," he said. His voice was chill, firm.

I rose. "I thank you, Your Highness, for the greeting and for honoring me by welcoming me into your presence so quickly."

"We have great business," he said. "I assume that you, like I, wish to reach a settlement . . . of one sort or another . . . so our two kingdoms may either find a new course or continue the old one."

"Your Majesty," I said, "may I be so bold as to suggest a third alternative? One which my master devised?"

"Which is?" King Bairan's voice was even colder.

"Peace, sir. A peace that will end any troubles between us, and guarantee amity forever."

"I would settle, Ambassador á Cimabue, for something that would last your emperor's and my lifetimes. Approach me, if you will. If we are to discuss important business, I dislike having to bellow it about." I obeyed. "So your master wishes peace?"

"With all his heart."

"Then I must say that I'm perplexed by certain signs from Numantia," he went on. "For some time, there's been growing tension. I felt we were coming to the brink of . . . unfortunate events, and so ordered certain measures taken. Now you say your emperor wishes peace. I *am* puzzled."

"That is why I am here, Your Majesty. The emperor has granted me full powers to negotiate a full and complete treaty between Numantia and Maisir, one that will, indeed, give us the peace and tranquillity both nations want."

The king was silent, looking hard into my eyes. "Ligaba Sala said you are a man of direct means."

"So I would like to be thought."

"He further advised me that you are the emperor's closest friend, and most trusted confidant."

"Such would be my proudest claim, sir. But I cannot know for sure that's true."

"Until very recently, I thought events between our two countries were on an unchangeable collision course," Bairan went on. "But when I received word you were appointed ambassador plenipotentiary, I allowed myself a bit of hope. For know this, Ambassador Baron Damastes of Ghazi," he said, his voice crisp, firm, each word a clear chisel stroke carving law into stone. "I do not wish war. Maisir does not wish war. I would hope you and I might reach an understanding to ensure peace."

"Your Majesty, you have my word that I can, and will, do anything to reach that same end."

"Then I truly bid you welcome to Jarrah," and he extended his hand. It was the firm clasp of a warrior.

I stepped out of the carriage in front of the estate I'd been told was mine for the duration of my stay. It was certainly private—its stone walls, topped with razored metal bills facing outward, reached almost thirty feet high. There was a door in one wall, with a large ring for a knocker. I lifted it, and heard the sonorous blast of trumpets. An instant later it was opened, and Alegria stood there, in a small anteroom, whose walls, floors, and ceiling were exotically inlaid wood. The room's back wall opened into a sprawling garden.

Alegria wore a floor-length purple gown with a low neckline, and a black floral pattern that ran asymmetrically from her navel to her right hip and shoulder. I could almost, but not quite, see through it.

"You're damned lucky it was me," I said, a bit acidly.

"Oh, but I could see. Look." She bade me lift the door's knocker once more, and I obeyed. As I did, it was as if a sorcerous porthole opened in the door's blank exterior. "If it wasn't you, I had this heavy robe to pull on, so no one would get any ideas."

"By the way," I asked, "where's our staff, where are our retainers, if we're such terribly honored guests?"

"I shocked the gateman by sending him away, saying I wanted to wait for you."

"A good thing King Bairan wasn't in the mood for all-night drinking," I said.

She sighed theatrically and muttered, "Men!"

I looked beyond the anteroom into the garden, and saw that it was in the first bloom of spring, instead of the dankness of the last of the Time of Rains.

Alegria started laughing.

"What's so funny?"

"You'll see."

As she spoke, I did see. In the center of the garden was the house. But it wasn't exactly a house. It appeared to be a huge, square tent. I didn't believe it. "This is a sorry jest," I muttered. "We've been living under canvas for almost sixty days, I've been sleeping in the open for longer than that, and by the king's kindness, we're going to do it again? This is a high honor? Better we should go back to that inn beyond Jarrah. At least they gave us a bed, even if it really belonged to a creepy-crawly."

"I know," Alegria gurgled, and now she started laughing hard. "But it isn't really canvas. Look harder."

I saw that the "tent" was actually elaborately worked wood, built to exactly resemble a campaign tent with its flies tied up for good weather. "This is what King Bairan calls his Warrior's Retreat," Alegria said.

"Lucky, lucky us," I muttered.

"Actually, it's wonderful. Come, let me show you."

Actually, it was quite wonderful, a work of art in both wood and magic. The "tent" was enormous. The outer areas were for us to live and eat in. In the center was an area we never entered, where our servants readied meals and waited for a summons. They came and went through an underground tunnel to kitchens, stables, and quarters hidden at the estate's rear wall.

Each side of the "tent" had four rooms—a study, a washroom, a dining area, and a bedchamber, each decorated in different, rich styles. On each side was the garden, exactly the same on all four sides, except that on one side it was in spring, the next summer, the third fall, and the last the depths of a snowy winter. It appeared as if each garden went on forever, with no high wall to end it. There were no walls, no windows, but a spell kept the rooms balmy, summerlike, with a gentle breeze coming from nowhere. When the lights were shut down, the temperature lowered as well, and a light wrap felt wonderful. Alegria showed me this marvel as proudly as if it were hers.

"How far do the gardens actually go?" I asked.

"Not as far as it appears. When you walk toward the end, all of a sudden you lose all desire to go farther, and find yourself turning back."

"All right," I conceded. "It's wonderful. But a gods-damned *tent*!?"

"I quite like it," Alegria murmured. "Each night we can sleep in a different time. That way, it'll seem as if we're being together for a very, very long time, instead of . . ." She didn't finish the sentence, but turned, and looked out as a bird splashed down in a fountain.

I put my arms around her, nuzzled her hair.

"And," she said softly after a while, "I can pretend there's no world beyond ours."

I said nothing, not knowing what to say. I was beginning to come alive, but there was still the shadow of the past, the shadow of Marán, between us. Sooner or later . . . but I wasn't here to worry about one man or one woman; I was here to worry about my country. Sooner could come later. First was King Bairan.

The next day, with Ambassador Boconnoc, I began preparations at our embassy. It was almost deserted. When the troubles began, Boconnoc had sent all Numantian women and children north to Renan, to safety.

Boconnoc was full of ideas about diplomatic niceties, and how we should spend the first day discussing what we should discuss. I was a bit—well, more than a bit—rude to him.

"The king said he wished to discuss peace, and to settle matters as rapidly as possible. This was also what the emperor ordered me," I said in a I-wish-no-discussion tone.

Boconnoc looked down his nose at me and said, "Very well then, Ambassador. What *shall* we begin with?"

I told him, and his eyebrows crawled toward the top of his head. He dearly wished to call me either a young fool or an idiot, perhaps worse. But whole generations of terribly discreet ancestors cried out. He finally heaved a great sigh and said, "Very well. This is hardly regular . . . but it will serve as an interesting lesson." He couldn't resist adding a jab, though: "For one or another of us." He sighed again. "Do you wish me to ask if there's a representative from that kingdom here in the capital?"

"If you wish," I said. "But if there's no one . . . so be it."

I think the walls moved out a bit on that second gust of wind.

"Where shall we start?" King Bairan asked, with some bemusement at my lack of ceremony. We were in a small conference chamber in his palace. There were six of us—the king, Ligaba Sala, Ambassador Boconnoc, myself, and a small, worried-looking man introduced as the Patriarch of Ebissa.

"At the beginning, Your Highness," I said. "You said two days ago you were confused by the signals Numantia is sending. First war, then peace."

"Yes. We are."

"Let us begin, then, by not only clearing the table a bit, but possibly showing our sincerity," I said. The Patriarch, hardly looking like a representative of his warlike and barbaric people, was sitting very straight. "The country of Ebissa has announced claims on a certain amount of Maisirian soil," I said. "Some time ago, the Emperor Tenedos announced that Numantia would support those claims. I now affirm that the emperor was misunderstood. In fact, all he wished to say was that he hoped you, King Bairan, would deal with their claims in an honorable manner, as the benevolent monarch you're considered."

"And if I simply renounce them?"

"You have never dictated to the emperor how he should rule," I said. "How, then, should we have any right to presume?"

The king regarded me solemnly. "Continue."

"There's nothing more to be said, at least not from the viewpoint of Numantia," I said coldly. "Ebissa is, and remains, an independent kingdom, with well-defined borders that have been agreed upon by mutual treaty between your two lands. If you wish to change them, that is a matter between you and Ebissa."

The Patriarch was goggling. "Perhaps, Ambassador," I said to Boconnoc, "you would assist the Patriarch from this chamber, as the matters to be brought up next no longer concern him." The man rose by himself and, trembling, shambled from the room. For an instant I felt a twinge, but steeled myself. Ebissa, an unknown jungle, or Numantia? There was not even the shadow of a choice.

The king sat quietly for a time. "You've certainly cleared a bit of air," he observed.

"I'd like to deal with more, in just as direct a manner, in the days and weeks to come," I said. "First is the matter of our mutual borders. Second is the always-vexing matter of the Wild Country on your borders, and the Border Lands on ours. Some time ago, you suggested we should reach some sort of mutual agreement and possibly jointly deal with the bandits of those lands."

"That's a complex issue," he said.

"It is. Perhaps, though, it's only complex because we've allowed it to be so. Your Majesty, I've spent time in those lands, and with those people. They are not fit subjects for Numantia or, if you will allow me the liberty, for Maisir. They prefer to spend time cutting each other's throat when they're not slitting the weasands and purses of any merchant or wayfarer passing through their domain."

"True."

"This is foolish, and expensive," I went on. "It seems there should be an easy solution, if two great nations wish there to be one." The king nodded. "Thirdly is a very old matter, but I might as well bring it up. For centuries, since before your father, before your father's father, Maisir has claimed a certain part of Urey, which is generally considered a state of Numantia," I said. "When you consider that Urey has the kingdom of Kait between it and Maisir, not to mention the most rugged mountains in the world, it seems this claim should be questioned by all parties."

"I've heard Urey is very beautiful," the king said.

"It is," I said. "But what are the chances of you taking a summer sojourn there any time in the near future?"

The king looked hard at me, then a smile moved under the beak of his nose. "Very well," he said. "Let us concede I'm not likely to go, what, three hundred leagues, then weave my way through a trap of bandits, to see any countryside, no matter how lovely. I'd say the matter of Urey could be resolved." He went to a window, then turned. "This brief meeting has been very interesting. I'm starting to feel that something other than words will be exchanged, Ambassador."

"Such is my hope as well."

"This is a beginning," the king mused. "A good beginning indeed. The future is starting to brighten in my eyes."

* * *

The signals went north, somehow made it across Kait in record time, then were heliographed on to Nicias. We had a reply within sixteen days. The emperor agreed Numantia had no reason to support Ebissa, and papers to that effect were being drawn up. He also said the Border Lands should be settled at once, in whatever manner King Bairan and I deemed fit.

He'd announced two feast days throughout Numantia, when sacrifices and prayers would be made for peace.

To further ensure his good faith, he was ordering the staff of the embassy to return to Jarrah.

The best thing was last: The units in Urey that had been built up to wartime footing were to be reduced to peacetime strength. All recently formed units were to begin demobilizing as rapidly as possible.

In a personally coded message for me, he said:

You've done it, Damastes, or so it appears.
Both Numantia and I owe you the greatest debt.
Peace now, peace forever.
T

"There was an incident some time ago," Ligaba Sala began delicately, "between some of our soldiery, supposedly in the province of Dumyat." He'd asked for a private meeting, and I'd wondered what it would be about. Now I knew, and decided to use truth as my first weapon.

"You're somewhat incorrect, Ligaba," I said. "There was great confusion in Nicias about the matter. We investigated, and found our patrol was across the border, well into Maisir, not far from the Maisirian town of Zante."

Sala hid surprise. "That was not what we thought you believed. We understood you thought your forces were ambushed."

"As I said, there was confusion. I'm sorry, but to speak personally, your soldiers were punished for defending their terrain, although perhaps they might've reacted too quickly."

"Such might be the case," Sala said. "None of their officers are alive to debate the matter, however."

"Might I ask why you chose to bring it up? I thought the matter was settled."

"The king wanted me to ask about it and, depending on what you said, either to have no response or to make the one I'm about to present: It is terribly early in the proceedings to sound optimistic, but King Bairan wishes there to be no impediments to the process of peace. For this reason, he's once again withdrawing all Maisirian troops three days' travel from the border until negotiations are complete. This should ensure that no new problems, whether overreaction or whatever, occur in the next few times.

"I can also assure you that, if negotiations continue as begun, the king will be releasing the classes we recently called up for military training. If there's to be no . . . trouble, what these men cost the state could be best spent elsewhere."

I felt happiness and, yes, pride swell within me. In spite of my fears, perhaps I would do a great service for my country. "Thank you, Ligaba."

"If things continue at this rate," Sala said, "we'll be quickly back to Damastes and Khwaja, eh?"

"Let us hope."

Word of this also went north, and, in fifteen days, the emperor responded: He, too, would withdraw Numantian units from the border. The only soldiery allowed in these lands until a treaty was made would be those on hot trod, pursuing bandits. We'd taken another step back from the chasm.

Waiting for two to three weeks between each step, as messages went back and forth between Nicias and Jarrah, could have been maddening, but it wasn't as if there was nothing to do. Alegria and I became the center of the Jarrah social whirl, Something New.

The nobility in the capital were as stultified as their country cousins. Everyone knew, and was somewhat related to, almost everyone else, and they'd gone to the same parties with the same people, and ended up drunk and in bed with the same wrong people, year after year, decade after decade. It was no wonder the grand balls presenting the pubescent noblewomen and -men were so well attended. I went to one, and it reminded me of a pack of vultures, waiting around a dying gaur to swoop on her calf.

It became fashionable to grow one's hair long and even, in some cases, to use harsh minerals to bleach it as blond as mine. Alegria suggested that I should be ashamed of myself, being responsible for a new spurt of baldness among the older men who miscalculated the strength of the bleaching potions. I said I was no more guilty than she, for the women were dressing as she did, in clinging, body-revealing garments. This was fine when the woman was younger. But when she was a waddling behemoth, I had to repress the urge to wince and turn away.

The Time of Change ended, the Time of Storms began, and arctic tempests crashed in from the south.

There'd been a party planned, a masked rout, that had to be canceled because of the weather. Jarrah was paralyzed by the storm, so there was nothing to do but fall back on our own resources. I was quite content, lying on pillows in our "tent." We were on the "summer" side, and birds were chirping in the garden, bees buzzing in the warm stillness.

I was studying maps of the Border Lands, trying to determine if an idea of mine made any sense at all.

Alegria lay on the floor on three gigantic pillows. She wore no more than a tie around her breasts and another around her loins, and was reading some very fat tome, a work that portrayed the gods and goddesses as being as goatish as the men and women they created. Of course the work was banned by the Maisirian priesthood, so naturally those who could read couldn't get copies fast enough.

She saw I was looking at her, smiled at me, and returned to her reading.

Suddenly I realized something. I was falling in love, perhaps was even *in* love, with her. Now I wonder why it took me so long to recognize this, but I know the answer. It was of course Marán.

There were still unfinished feelings, words I longed to say to my wife, or ex-wife, whichever she was by now. But why did that matter? The past was past, dead and gone. Why didn't I get up, go to Alegria, kiss her, and let what should have happened happen? I didn't know, and I don't now.

I finished a dispatch and the courier took it away. I suddenly realized I was exhausted, and could stand neither the embassy, my quarters, nor a city any longer. I needed to get out, to spend a few hours in the country. I told Alegria, and she winced, then bore up bravely. "Very well, my lord. We'll go out into the tempest, and if I freeze anything off, you're to blame."

An hour later we were muffled, cloaked, and shivering in the stables. Alegria mounted her horse and looked down plaintively. "So where are we going to go to die?"

"Hells if I know. You're the Maisirian, not me."

"Permitted out of my order into the capital no more than a dozen times. This is idiotic," Alegria said.

"I know . . . but isn't it fun?" Indeed, the sharp wind from the north was freshening my mind, my spirit.

"Shall we go to the embassy and get some outriders for security?" she asked.

"Why bother? Doesn't everybody in Maisir love us? No, I don't need any other company than what I've got," I replied.

Alegria sat indecisively on her horse for a moment. "I have an idea. But it's an hour, maybe more, away. And I'll have to ask the way."

"I am yours to obey, *woizera*."

"So when we're found as frozen corpses, it'll be all my fault in the eyes of the gods."

"Of course. Don't you understand men by now?" I offered. She hmmphed, and off we went.

No one paid us the slightest notice in the streets, intent as they all were on finishing their own business before the storm made the streets impassable. No one but one—and the well-aimed snowball smacked into the back of my neck and sent my shako flying into the ditch. I cursed, turned, and saw an urchin dash into an alley.

"How dare he," Alegria said, trying to keep a grim countenance. I didn't answer, but dismounted and picked up my helmet—and something else. The boy, and his three coconspirators, stuck their heads out as I remounted—and hurled the wad of snow I'd surreptitiously molded. It struck the wall next to them, but was close enough to spatter the boys with icy fragments. They yelped surprise and fled.

"If you mess with the bull," I said, quoting an old Cimabuen proverb, "you shall get the horns."

Alegria shook her head in despair, and we rode on.

We stopped twice, while Alegria asked directions from passersby, then went on. We reached the outskirts of Jarrah in an hour.

"Now what?"

"Ride on, you weakling," she said. "We've only just begun."

In truth, I was feeling a bit chill, and dreams of our nice summer garden were floating in front of me. "This woman's going to feed me to the wolves for neglect," I said mournfully, but I obeyed. The snow grew deeper, but the road was wide. We passed through open country, then a small village, then were in the country once more. I was about to whine again, when we rounded a bend.

Sitting on a high bluff was a dark stone castle, walls carved from the solid rock. It wasn't the largest I'd seen, but one of the most forbidding, with tiny barred windows and a gate with guard towers on either side. A road curved up the bluff to the gate.

"Here we are," Alegria announced.

"Which is where?"

"My home. This is the place of the Dalriada."

"Great gods," I mused. "How could something this grim produce anything but muttering monks and sourpusses?"

"Come on. I'll show you." We made our way up the winding road, and were challenged by four guards, two in each tower. Alegria identified herself, and me, and one guard went inside.

I leaned over to her. "A question, milady. If you—and the rest of the Dalriada—are as, well, pure as you say, what keeps the guards honest? Or did they have an unfortunate encounter with a very sharp knife and now sing in upper registers?"

"You mean are they eunuchs? No. They used to be, but the order stopped that." She giggled. "We girls heard stories that sometimes the eunuchs weren't as eunuched as they were supposed to be. Now volunteers from the army serve for two years here. There's maybe three hundred of them, and they guard all approaches to the Dalriada. They're quartered beyond the walls on the far side. During their service, they're under a spell that renders them not only incapable, but not interested."

"What a wonderful life," I said. "Let's spend two years sitting around talking about . . . about turnip planting and shining our armor."

"Better than dying on the border with a bandit's arrow in your chest."

"Maybe," I said. "Maybe not."

The guard came back, saluted, and said we were welcome. He would take our horses. We dismounted and went through the gates. A woman was waiting. She was in her forties, and very beautiful, almost as lovely as Alegria. Alegria yipped with glee and fell into her arms. The two babbled happily for a time, then I was introduced. The woman, whose name was Zelen, bowed.

"Alegria has indeed been given great fortune," she said. "And we are honored by your presence." She led us through a courtyard. A door came open, and seven little girls tumbled out, shrieking laughter. All were unutterably lovely, little dolls of various hair and skin color. They pelted snowballs at one another, saw me, screamed in mock horror, and darted away through another door. We entered a building and started up a long flight of stairs. Zelen was about ten steps above us.

"Zelen," Alegria explained quietly, "was one of my teachers."

"Teaching what?"

"Muscle control," Alegria said, and her face turned even redder than the icy wind had made it.

"Ah."

"She was very lucky, and very unlucky," Alegria said as we climbed. "She was given to a *lij*, a prince, who'd been recently widowed. They fell in love, and he proposed marriage to her. Before they could wed, he was killed in a hunting accident. So Zelen came back here."

The next few hours I found very interesting. There were perhaps a hundred, maybe a hundred fifty girls and young women being trained, and about an equal number of Dalriada who'd returned to the castle to teach and serve them. It was like an exclusive girls lycée. Sort of. I saw girls being taught to speak correctly, to sew, to do mathematics. One group listened to a woman poet read, then discussed, as skillfully as any scholarly gathering, what they'd just heard.

There were other rooms I was forbidden to enter, and neither woman told me what the course of instruction within was. I glanced into one deserted room as we passed. Inside, instead of study tables there were cots, and reposing on each of them was a dummy of a naked man with a full erection. I pretended I'd seen nothing.

We ended by having herbal tea and some freshly baked buns with the mistress of the Dalriada. She was in her sixties and, while lovely, was somewhat forbidding. She must have gained that manner after she returned, or else her "master" had been one of those who prefered to take orders rather than give them. It was interesting, but I was very glad to walk out of the gates.

"So that's where you came from," I mused, looking back after we'd reached level ground.

"Yes." Alegria waited for a time. "What do you think?"

"What is there to think? I wouldn't want to live there," I said, trying to choose my words carefully.

"Ah. But you have a choice," Alegria said. "I did not. And," she said, bitterness in her voice, "there are worse places."

"You said you came here when you were seven," I said. "Do you remember anything of your life before that?"

"I do," she said, her voice fierce. "I remember being hungry. I remember being cold. I remember being hit by one or another of the drunks my gods-damned mother stumbled back to our hut with. I remember when she sold me to the Dalriada."

I felt like taking her in my arms, but wisely didn't.

"Now do you see," she asked. "Now do you understand?"

It was a question that didn't want a response. We rode on in silence. I should have known most of the girls and young women would've come from situations like Alegria's. All of them would be from the poorest, or unwanted in other ways. I remembered, years earlier, when I was a legate on my way to his first post, a peasant had tried to sell me his waif of a daughter, a starveling who couldn't have seen her tenth birthday. People complain about the evils the gods wreak on man, and wonder how they can be so cruel. But when I think of the cruelties man does to his fellow man, particularly if she's woman or weaker, sometimes I wonder why our creators and lords don't permit even greater barbarisms.

By the time we returned to Moriton, Alegria had regained her blitheness. Or, more likely, painted the mask back on. I, however, was in the blackest of moods, but had the sense to cover my bleak humor.

* * *

A few days later, to everyone's surprise, the embassy staff

returned. They'd left Renan as soon as word reached them, and made swift passage through Kait. The last of the Time of Change had been mild, and storms had passed them by as they traveled through Maisir. They'd thought they were trapped by the winter twice, but those tempests passed quickly, after freezing the roads but not burying them in snow, so they made good speed.

Now the dark embassy was filled with the chatter of women and the laughter of young men, which lightened everyone's mood considerably. I noted—but said nothing—that none of the wives had brought their children back. Peace portended, but wasn't guaranteed by any means, and the women of the diplomatic corps were at least as perceptive as their husbands or lovers.

Almost as welcome was what they'd brought with them: preserved Numantian delicacies, letters from friends, and as wrappers, broadsheets for news from home. These were ironed, and passed from hand to hand. Here in a distant land, it was warming to find out how much Varan wine was selling for, what merchant had a special order on Wakhijr lace, and so forth. I was spending an idle hour reading these meaninglessnesses, and picked up a new sheet.

The leading story was the marriage of Tribune Aguin Guil, commander of the First Imperial Guard, to the emperor's sister, Dalny. I thought it must've been quite a ceremony, and indeed, scanning the list of notables, I saw that I was correct.

Then my mood shattered:

> Our Imperial Highness not only graced the occasion with his presence, but generously chose to officiate at the ceremony itself. He looked perfectly splendid in imperial scarlet with black leather. He was accompanied by Marán, Countess Agramónte, equally stunning in a green and white lace gown, as exciting as it was gorgeous . . .

* * *

A man is a gods-damned fool to pursue certain matters when he should leave things alone and accept the black doubt instead of looking for the certainty. I was, perhaps am, such a fool. I asked, and found that one of the secretaries had newly joined the embassy staff in Urey, having come upriver from Nicias. As were most diplomats, he was of minor nobility, and his duties would be to handle Ambassador Boconnoc's social calendar. I asked for a moment of the man's time.

"Of course. How may I serve you, Ambassador?" the young man, smoothed by many generations of nobility and behind-the-arras service, asked.

"This is in the nature of a personal favor."

"You have but to ask, sir."

"You probably know my wife petitioned for divorce some time ago."

"Y-yes, sir. I do."

"Do you happen to know if that was granted? I've heard nothing."

"It was, sir. Very quickly, sir. Since you were absent, and had lodged no protest, it seemed expedient . . . or so I heard, at any rate."

"I see."

So I had no claims whatsoever on what Marán did. Nor did I have any reason to be certain of my suspicions.

"I understand," I went on, "she accompanied the emperor to his sister's marriage."

"Yes, sir. Or, so I was told. I don't have sufficient stature as yet to have warranted an invitation. But one of my uncles went, and said it was truly the affair . . . of the season."

If I hadn't been listening closely, I might've missed the way he hesitated after using the word affair. As if it were a poor choice of words, considering the context?

"As a matter of curiosity," I said, in as dry a tone as I could manage, "and since I wish my ex-wife as well as could be expected, did the emperor honor her with any more such invitations to other events?"

"I . . . I really can't say, sir. I wasn't paying that much attention to what was going on in Nicias before I left. I was busy studying Maisir and its customs." If this man were going to continue as a diplomat, he'd have to learn to lie better than that.

I thanked and dismissed him, and sent for all the broadsheets that had come in. I arranged them in order, and read all of the gossip sections carefully. Marán and the emperor at this review . . . at that costumed ball . . . and then, a separate item that Marán, Countess Agramónte, had canceled her plans for the remainder of the season, including two masquerades, and would return immediately to Irrigon and busy herself rebuilding the ancestral home.

From first mention of the two to the last—just about a full time. Long enough for a seer to realize a woman wasn't pregnant and send her away, as he'd sent others.

I was red with foolish rage and barely held myself under control. Questions boiled within me. Did the bitch do it deliberately? I tried to give her the benefit of the doubt—she'd always idolized the emperor. With the divorce, what reason did she have not to . . . to see him? I stepped back for a moment. Could I be imagining things? Maybe, but I didn't think so. Perhaps it wasn't betrayal, but it was certainly a shitty thing to do.

Next I thought of the emperor. How in the hells could he do that to me? Didn't he know? Or didn't he care? Again I remembered the line, "Kings may do what others only dream of," but it was no comfort. I'd thought Tenedos a friend as well as my ruler. Friends, at least where I came from, didn't fuck each other's lady. Or did they?

I came back to myself and realized the short winter day was coming to an end. Now what? There was nothing to do but go on, I thought dully.

I went out to my carriage, barely seeing and returning the salutes of the guards. I didn't want to return to the mansion and Alegria, but there was no place else. I ordered my driver to go straight to the stables, and went through the underground passage to the servants' area, and slipped into the house. I didn't see Alegria.

I wondered if drink would numb me, let some of the pain wash over. Perhaps it would let me sleep, or at least find some ease. I found a bottle of wine, opened it, and went to the winter portion of the tent. I sat on the floor, staring at the magically created gale outside in the garden, and felt the echoing storm within.

I lifted the bottle, then set it back down. Maybe I'd have a drink in a moment or two.

The snow blew hard against the flickering stone lanterns, and ice grew on the reeds of the ponds. The door behind me opened.

"Damastes?" It was Alegria.

"Yes."

"What is the matter?"

I didn't answer. She walked up beside me, and I smelled the sweetness of her perfume. She sat down, cross-legged in front of me, looking into my eyes. "Something is the matter. Something big," she said.

I've always practiced the rule that a warrior stands on his own. But I didn't this time. I couldn't. I told Alegria what I'd discovered—or what I thought I'd discovered. Halfway through, I realized I was blinded with tears. She went into the bath chamber and came back with a soft, moist rag.

"Hells," I said. "Maybe I'm just imagining . . . maybe it never happened."

Alegria began to say something, then stopped.

"What?"

She took a deep breath. "May I tell you something?" I nodded. "Three days ago, when you took me to the embassy and introduced me to the newcomers, you left me for a meeting?" I remembered. "Well, I roamed around, talking to people, making sure I'd remember their names. I know they say that people who eavesdrop deserve to hear what they hear." Alegria gulped and started crying. She made herself stop, then went on: "I'd just left one woman—I won't say who she is—then remembered there was something I wished to ask her. I went back and was about to knock on her door, when I heard her talking to a man.

"They were talking about me. The man said something about how pretty I was, and the woman said she guessed I was attractive enough. Then she said, and these are her precise words, 'This certainly shows the high and mighty do things different than we do. Guess they don't take life as seriously as I do, anyway. Damastes's wife tells him to go away, and he bounces back with this lovely almost as fast as his countess crept up the emperor's back stairs.'

"The man laughed and said that you seemed to be a decent sort, so he hoped I'd be in your bed longer than your wife was allowed to pleasure the emperor.

"Someone came along the corridor then, and I hurried away. Oh, Damastes, Damastes, I'm so sorry." Tears welled once more in her eyes, but she held them back.

The emperor *had* betrayed me.

NINETEEN

THE SECOND BETRAYAL

I did not sleep that night. Alegria wanted to sit with me, but I refused her. "Are you sure I can't do something . . . make you feel a little better? Any way I can?"

I shook my head. Eventually dawn came. Alegria tiptoed into the room, started to say something, then went back out. I forced myself to bathe, shave, and put on fresh clothes. I was trying to decide what to do when a messenger arrived from the embassy.

There'd been a signal from Nicias. The emperor approved my plan, and told me to proceed at once. His message was full of praise for me, which seemed the cruelest sort of sneering.

The meeting with King Bairan was very odd. There was the king, Ligaba Sala, Boconnoc, myself, and the secretary. I had my maps and charts on easels and spoke easily, most familiar with my ideas. But it was as if I were standing or, better, floating above myself, just watching. I smiled, made mild clevernesses at the right time, but felt nothing.

My idea, laboriously worked out, was to combine the Wild Country and the Border Lands into a single administrative region. This region would be jointly ruled by Numantia and Maisir. It would be divided into separate subregions following the generally-agreed-upon borders of those bandit kingdoms within the region.

The first stage would be complete military pacification. This would be done by combined Maisirian and Numantian forces. I proposed new corps be established, with officers and men from both countries mingled. It would take two years or so to set these units up and train them, but then we could move through the wild lands, step by step. It would be expensive, very expensive. But would the loss be any less than that from the raids and caravan attacks by these bandits? The cities would be the first to be taken. If they were governed wisely and well, using, whenever possible, the native rulers, the outlying areas might see the advantages of peace.

"So the wolves will become sheep, eh?" Bairan said skeptically.

"No. First we'll make them into tame wolves, and send them out after their wilder brothers. Then we'll change them into sheepdogs, for I don't believe those mountains will ever be truly peaceful. The best we can hope for is that these sheepdogs will be grudgingly obedient under their shepherds from Maisir and Numantia."

"You've studied this well, I see," Sala said, looking at the maps.

"I didn't wish to make a total idiot of myself if the plan was completely impossible," I said. "Now it merely looks like a grandiose unlikelihood."

Both the king and Ligaba Sala smiled.

"If peace, or something sort of resembling that, came to these regions, Numantia and Maisir wouldn't have any excuse for war, either," the king said. "Would they, Ambassador?"

"Not as long as both nations truly wanted peace. But if someone truly wanted war, well, all this would be so much bum fodder," I said. "A man who wants a brawl can generally find one, even in the calmest tavern."

"Equal armies, equal governments?" the king said, with a question mark.

"Yes, sir," I said. "With frequent conferences between the emperor and yourself, or between your emissaries. So no misunderstandings can develop."

"Interesting," mused Bairan. "Now, if you'd said you'd just had this idea, I would've laughed and thought you mad, or a dreamer, and I'm nervous in the company of either. But since your emperor's endorsed this plan . . . hmm. Interesting. Either this has merit, or there's two madmen about. I don't know, Ambassador á Cimabue. Perhaps we could set up a couple of regiments and see what develops. Start at one end of the frontier, with one state."

"Excellent change, Your Majesty," I said hastily. Of course I'd planned we would begin slowly, rather than jump in everywhere at once, but an idea is always more digestible when one thinks it one's own.

"Very well. Let's try this out. Ligaba, would you and the Numantians work out a scheme?"

"Gladly, sir."

King Bairan stood. "Your emperor chose wisely when he sent you, Ambassador á Cimabue. I think you've done both countries a true service, and in time to come, perhaps your name will ring greater than either mine or your emperor's."

"I thank you, sir." I bowed deeply.

Bairan moved toward the door, then stopped and touched my sleeve. "Damastes, you seem disturbed. Is there aught the matter? If so . . ."

"No, Your Majesty," I managed to say. "I just didn't get much rest last night making sure I'd not make any blunders today."

He looked in my eyes. "Very well," he said, voice skeptical. "But don't forget my offer. A matter this imposing must be judged by calm minds."

Now there was little for me to do. Sala and Boconnoc began hammering out the details, and it was well for me to stay in the background. I could wallow, I could drown, in my anger and depression.

But there was Alegria.

Thinking of her, thinking of the shabby way I'd treated her, calmed my rage, my hurt, and I forced myself to behave less like a child, and worry about something beyond myself.

I had an idea, and determined to carry it out. Perhaps the setting would inspire the change.

"At least when I take you out of Jarrah, it's to a great castle," Alegria said skeptically.

"A depressing great castle."

"You *are* the picky sort. Besides, how could it be depressing, if it's where your favorite . . . favorite . . . whatever I am came from? Damastes, just what am I to you? You don't have to answer that honestly."

"Then I won't," I said. "Quit yammering, and help me unpack the sleigh. You're behaving like a nervous bride on her wedding night."

"Aaah?" Alegria looked innocently around. I threw her into a snowbank. She sputtered, flailed, and I, like a genteel oaf, extended a hand. She grabbed it and yanked. I yelped and fell, face-first, into the snow beside her.

"That was unfair," I managed to sputter when I surfaced.

"You're right," Alegria said. "I'll pay the penalty and let you kiss me."

"That sounds like a proposition."

"Of sorts," she murmured, and I did as she asked. The kiss lasted for some time.

"Mmmmh," she said softly when our lips came apart. "I'd say do it again, but I don't know how snowproof these furs are."

"Snowproof," I said. "I had six spells cast to make sure."

"Then kiss me again." I did. She ran her gloved fingers across my lips. "Congratulations," she said.

"For what?"

"For not being a gloomy-mug like you've been since . . . since you know."

"I got tired of feeling sorry for myself," I said truthfully.

"Then get up. You were lying again. This snow's seeping through." I helped her up, and again she looked at the rather ramshackle low wooden building. "What is it?" she asked.

"It's the meeting place Numantian envoys use when they want to meet Maisirian traitors in secret."

"How'd you hear about it?"

"I asked Ligaba Sala where a quiet lonely place was I could take someone."

"I guess," Alegria said, "Maisirian traitors don't last too long if Sala knows about this place."

"Guess not. Now, help me carry provisions."

I handed her two net bags of groceries. She looked once more at the building. "Quaint," she said. "I guess that's what you're supposed to call a building with a tree growing through its roof."

"Two of them," I said. "There's another down there."

"Wonderful. I wonder if there's a fire. It's going to snow."

"You go investigate. The embassy said there's a charm-pole that works as a key hung in that little box beside the door."

I carried the rest of our supplies onto the porch, then led the horses to the nearby barn. There was an unfrozen spring nearby, and I fed, watered, and curried the animals. By the time I finished, a gentle snowstorm had begun. It was nearly the end of the Time of Storms, and the weather was lightening. But it was still cold, especially for a tropic lad, and I entered the house chilled through.

The house actually was a retreat for members of the embassy, although Sala was the one who'd told me about it, saying it had once been used for clandestine meetings, until King Bairan got tired of that foolishness and had a certain diplomat—he didn't say if it was Boconnoc or not—greeted by a company of cavalry when he arrived to meet an agent. That ended the political uses for the lodge.

It overhung a frozen lake, with porches all around. There were eight bedrooms, half branching off a hall on one side of the main rooms, four on the other side. The center room was low-ceilinged, but huge. I could've almost stood in the riverstone fireplace, and the firewood racks on either side reached the ceiling. Around it were thick fur rugs of various animals. Everything was rough-worked wood, including the furniture. The chairs and couches looked as if they'd swallow you if you got near them, and the nap you'd be forced into might last an eternity.

To one side was a dining room and next to it the kitchen, the larder of which was filled with every sort of bottled or preserved viand imaginable. Heating was by wood, each bedroom having its own fireplace. A hot spring rose on the hill above the house, and the water was diverted into the plumbing system, the cold water for which came from a creek.

Two trees rose through the house, each in one hallway. They were supposedly trees of luck and had been blessed when the lodge was built. The place was utterly unpretentious, utterly charming, and a world of its own.

Exactly what I had hoped.

"Well?" Alegria asked. In the minutes I'd been gone, she'd lit two lamps, found kindling, and started it burning with crumpled paper. Three small logs were set in a pyramid over the crackling flames and were smoking into fire.

"Well what?"

"Aren't you surprised a woman, especially a Dalriada, can build a fire out here in the *suebi*, amid the wolves and dragons?"

"Not at all. You already told me Dalriada can do anything."

"I may have oversold the proposition. Come, Damastes. Admire me."

"I always do."

"Do you?" She rose from where she'd been sitting, cross-legged on a white bearskin in front of the fire. She'd taken off her furs and wore a soft, loose pair of pants, with a robe top that dipped low and tied at the side in matching leopard-skin-like material. She turned, letting the firelight silhouette her body, and once again murmured "Do you?" She unfastened the tie and slipped out of the top. Her body was firm, nipples hard.

She came to me, and I tried to take her in my arms. "No," she said softly. "There is no hurry, no haste."

I lowered my arms, and slowly she unbuttoned my heavy fur coat, undid the ties of my fur pants, and let them drop around my ankles. I kicked off my boots and stepped out of my pants, wearing only a loincloth.

"You're very pretty," she said.

"Not as pretty as you."

She bent and kissed my nipples. I ran my fingers down her sleekness.

"I would like to kiss you," she said, and her lips parted as she spoke. Our tongues wove together, and my arms came around her, pulling her against me. She pulled away, breathing hard.

"I was taught . . . the first time should be done slowly," she said. "But I swear I cannot stand it for long."

"Nor I," I said hoarsely, and picked her up in my arms. Her knees folded as if she'd lost all strength, and I laid her down on the rug.

"I want you to love me now, please love me now," she whispered. "All my places want you, Damastes. Do not stop until they're satisfied."

I kissed her tiny navel, ran my tongue inside it, and her fingers fumbled with the ties to her pants. She raised her hips and I slipped her pants off, and she lifted one leg and let it fall to the side. She had but a tiny tuft of hair around her sex, and I kissed it, then moved between her legs, and let my tongue move back and forth down there, caressing the small hardness between her lips.

Her hands moved in my hair as I loved her with my mouth, and her breathing grew faster, harsher. She gasped, jerked against me, groaned, but I didn't stop. "Come to me now, please now," she said, and I obeyed, moving up between her legs, rubbing her sex with my cock, back and forth. She was wet with her own juices, wet with my saliva. I pushed slowly, firmly against resistance, and it broke, and she cried out. I didn't push farther, but moved gently back and forth, fractions of an inch, and then she moved with me, moaning. I moved deeper within her, and her legs came up around me, and she pulled at me. I kissed her, and her tongue searched my mouth frantically. I moved back, almost out of her, then thrust deeply and she cried out again, this time in joy, and I repeated the motion and paid for my long months of stupidity and denial—I gushed inside her.

"Hells," I muttered.

"Hush," she ordered, and her fingers moved down, around the back of her thighs, touching my balls, the base of my cock, here, there, and suddenly I grew firm again. Now we moved together, first lovers, but it was as if we'd done it time and again, partners in a long-rehearsed dance, and then she shouted aloud, her head rolling, and her muscles spasmed around me, and I came for the second time. Her face was contorted, eyes closed, and I stroked her wet body for long moments until her eyes opened.

"I was right those long months ago when I said I was lucky."

"No," I said. "I am the one who's lucky."

"In time, that may be true," she whispered, and rolled me over onto my back.

"That was once," she said, and rose to her knees. She knelt and caressed my cock. "Ah, little one, you have not been doing your exercises, or you'd not be tired. You need some encouragement." She used her tongue on the tip of my cock, then pulled my foreskin back and slid her teeth back and forth on the head. Her tongue touched me here, there, while her fingers stroked my balls, my ass, my abdomen. I was firm once more, and she moved back and forth, taking my entire cock into her mouth, her tongue flat underneath it, and once more the world spun. It was my turn to cry out. She lifted her head and swallowed.

"The real thing tastes better than any of the compounds

they gave us," she said. "Or at least yours does."

I pulled her up beside me and kissed her.

"Twice," she said.

We lay contentedly together, caressing each other, feeling the warmth of the fire, and the greater warmth of another, invisible fire about us.

"Would I sound like a fool if I said I love you?" I said.

Her eyes snapped open in surprise. "N-no. Of course not. But . . ."

"But what?"

"I . . . This isn't supposed to . . . Oh, hells, I'm confused!" Tears started, but she rubbed them away.

"I'm sorry," I joked badly. "I'll never say that again."

"Don't be an ass."

She took a deep breath. "I love you, Damastes."

"Nice that we agree on things."

We kissed.

"Do you know when I fell for you?" I shook my head. "It was that very first night, when you threw that tablet off the balcony."

"Now, wait a moment," I protested. "That doesn't make any sense. I said no chains, so—"

"So I put them on. But who said love is a chain?"

I made a face, didn't answer.

"Forget about her," Alegria said. "That's gone. That's over. Think about something else."

"All right," I said slowly, a bit embarrassed, but still curious. "I've got a question, but you don't have to answer it. That first night, you cut yourself, so that people wouldn't talk about what didn't happen."

"Yes?"

"And tonight it seemed, it felt, like the first time you'd made love."

"I thought you said you were a country boy."

"I am," I said. "You're confusing me."

"Haven't you heard any of the old jokes about the poor girl who's been known to like the haystacks and the bumpkins she finds there, and then some old rich farmer decides he's got to marry her? But only if she's a virgin?"

I did remember those ancient jests that invariably finished with some young lad ending up in a place the old farmer thought exclusively his. "I do." This could have been embarrassing, as Alegria said. But suddenly it struck me as funny. "So as part of your graduation ceremony, when you became a full-fledged Dalriada, you stood in line while a midwife put a certain stitch somewhere?"

"No, you idiot! It was done sorcerously."

"Ah-ha. Now it's explained, for certainly you have certain talents I've never known in a virgin before."

"That was part of my training," Alegria admitted, blushing a bit. "I saw you peep into that room with the . . . what we called hobby horses. At a certain age, we were introduced to them and required to memorize many positions. As many positions as you lecherous men have been able to devise, and two more."

It was my turn to turn red.

"Yes," she went on. "They were used exactly as you thought. And there were other simulacra we were required to be familiar with, some large, some small. The small ones we called *lij* 's, princes, since we learned the older and more powerful the man, the tinier the toy."

"That sounds sort of mechanical, and pretty damned unromantic. Not to mention a little painful."

"Oh, the sisters of the Dalriada aren't brutal," she said. "First we learned to pleasure ourselves, when we were little more than babes. Then we were skillfully taught other techniques. Some of this was done in dreams. I remember one sequence well. I would've been thirteen, I suppose. He was tall, with a wonderful black beard that tickled when he lay atop me. He gave me great pleasure, and when I awoke, almost as damp between my legs as if I'd really known a man, and realized there was no one there, my heart broke, and wasn't repaired until the next night, when the wizards of Dalriada sent him to me again.

"I was foolish enough to be shocked and even jealous

when I told one of my friends about him, and she started laughing and said she, too, had been loved by him that night. The dreams were sent in cycles, so all of us learned the same things at the same time. There were other men in other dreams. Men and women. Sometimes more than one.

"Most of us had real lovers from time to time. The older women, or our friends. There is a tradition with the Dalriada that older girls take younger ones to teach. For a few weeks that woman you met, Zelen, and I were lovers. I didn't and don't feel it was bad, because I read most people will find pleasure where they can. Prisoners slake their lusts on each other, don't they?"

"I don't know," I said. "I haven't been one yet."

"And I've read that soldiers, when they don't have any virgins to despoil or whores, will secretly turn to their brothers, paying no heed to the punishment they could face."

"They do," I said. "But in Numantia there's no need to be secretive about it. I can't imagine anyone making something natural against the law."

"It is here in Maisir," Alegria said. "Although it's not enforced unless it's the only way someone can destroy his foe.

"To change the subject," she went on, "you realize I'm not supposed to tell you any of this."

"Why not?"

"Remember, I am— I was a virgin, and that's an important part of being a Dalriada."

"You mean the man a Dalriada is . . . given to," and the words still came hard, "is supposed to think all her talents, all the things she can do with her body, have been a gift of the gods?"

"Exactly. Specifically from Jaen."

"By my monkey god Vachan, men are dumb," I said.

"Maybe, but I think they're sweet. And worth taking care of."

Alegria was almost perfect, I thought, as I fell more deeply in love each day. Her biggest flaw was that she simply could not cook. Not because she didn't understand the nature of foods—she'd been well taught by the Dalriada, but because she simply didn't think it was necessary to be precise. A bit too much salt, a bit too few spices, a bit too long in the oven, a bit less kneading than specified—these didn't seem to matter at the time.

"But after all," she told me, "cooking isn't important to a Dalriada. The noblemen we're with have cooks and bakers and stewards and servants to bring us our meals in bed. Only barbarians would take a delicate flower like myself into the *suebi* by herself and require her to commit truly unnatural acts such as washing pots!"

"My humblest apologies," I said, bowing low. "For I am truly a barbarian, Woizera Alegria, and a foreign one at that. Perhaps this task would be more to your taste. Would you be so kind as to attempt to fit your ankles into my ears?"

She mock-saluted and lay back on the bed. "You order me, sir."

Not that it mattered—she had, as a dutiful student, memorized many recipes, and would recite them to me as I cheerily banged pots and kettles about. I can't say I was or am a good cook. But I was better than Alegria. Not that we spent all that much time eating, however. At least not in the strict sense of the word.

I wished it had been five weeks instead of five days, but the time ended, and we returned to Jarrah. There was an invitation waiting, one for that very night, one I couldn't have refused.

I showed it to Alegria, and she shivered, and her face paled with fear.

"What does *he* want?"

"I don't know. But I'm sure he'll tell me."

"Be careful, my love. Be very, very careful."

"You may call me *azaz*, my title," the small man said softly. "For I permit no one my name. I'm sure you appreciate that knowledge of a sorcerer's name can give power over that wizard, and even though I fear no one, I cannot see the reason to ever grant the slightest advantage."

The *azaz* was the mysterious master of ceremonies, the Maisirian chief sorcerer and most powerful magician. No one in the embassy knew anything about the man who held the post, other than that he was utterly feared. No Numantian, including Ambassador Boconnoc, had ever met him. The *azaz*, like his predecessor, preferred the isolation of his castle, a five-sided black stone monolith at the very end of Moriton, next to the high wall that held out the Belaya Forest.

When he attended court, he sat in an anteroom or cubicle with a heavy curtain across it. And when he called someone to his presence, he or she always came, even though there might well be no return.

The *azaz* was a small man, in his early forties, I guessed, balding and clean-shaven. He was sharp-featured and reminded me of another retiring man to be feared, Kutulu, the Serpent Who Never Sleeps. But where Kutulu's eyes were careful recorders of all they saw, the *azaz*'s were ice-blue, nearly colorless lances of power and authority.

It might sound as if they had the same blaze as the emperor's. The emperor's eyes drew you in, held you, and commanded obedience. The *azaz*'s glare was almost that of a madman's. He didn't need to give you orders, for his power was so much mightier he'd simply crush you if you stood in his way—or if the *azaz* thought for one moment you might.

He wore pants and shirt of a heavy, rich, dark brown silk, and held a wonderfully carved wand of ivory in one hand, that he toyed with as he spoke.

He met me just inside the anteroom of the castle. It was bare stone, with no decoration except a black banner hanging on one wall, with a symbol on it in red I didn't recognize. I bowed, introduced myself. Then he said, without niceties:

"I do not like you, Damastes á Cimabue," and his tone was as casual as if he'd mentioned the weather.

I blinked, recovered. "Why? Because I am a Numantian?"

"I have little love for your people, true, but my dislike is more personal. Do you recollect a man you would have known as Mikael of the Spirits?"

Mikael Yanthlus, Chardin Sher's supreme magician. I'd gone into the castle he and his master were sheltering in, and laid the Seer Tenedos's spell, then fled moments before some great demon rose from the earth and destroyed the castle and the rebels it sheltered. Here was yet another link to the past.

"Of course."

"Mikael and I were friends, or as much as any wizard permits himself friends, when we were boys. He decided he could learn more, faster, by wandering. He did gain much, but was hurled back to the Wheel by you and your emperor. I've tried to reach his spirit, or to find where he was reborn, but none of the demons I've summoned have knowledge of him. Perhaps he's still with the gods. Or perhaps he was destroyed unutterably. So I love you but little, Numantian."

Honesty, I think, requires its mate. "He was assisting a rebel in a foreign land against that man's rightful rulers," I said coldly. "He met the fate he deserved, as did the traitor he served."

"I see your bluntness, which I witnessed at your first meeting with my king, extends to all things," the *azaz* said, with a bleak smile. I remembered that curtained alcove behind the king.

"As for Mikael, I can't say I agree that he got what he deserved, but I won't argue that his doom was unjust. He was always more ambitious than I. If he'd lived, by the way, I don't doubt that he would have overthrown Chardin Sher, and then there would have been a contest of wizards to make the gods gape in astonishment."

I didn't reply.

"But that didn't happen. So I'll have to be the one who tests your great Seer Tenedos," the *azaz* said. "If for no other reason than to see if your emperor was able to steal Mikael's powers when he died. Myself and the War Magicians against Tenedos and his Chare Brethren."

"I can't see how this contest can happen, if there's to be

peace between our kingdoms," I said. "Which there will be. Or are you going to ruin the negotiations?"

"Not at all," the *azaz* said. "My king does want peace, and I serve him precisely. As I said, I'm not as ambitious as Mikael was. In fact, I'm a bit suspicious of those who reach toward the stars. I refer to both you and your emperor. I mean no disrespect, but, what, ten years ago or so, he was a disgraced magician sent into exile, and you were the youngest cavalry legate in the army."

"You know a great deal about both of us," I replied. "And while I have nothing to say about my emperor's goals, I can truthfully say that all of my achievements came as a surprise. They still do, to be frank."

The *azaz* looked skeptical.

"And," I went on, feeling a bit angry, "for a man who says he means no disrespect, you've certainly gone a very long ways in that direction for my comfort. If all you wanted was to have me here for a slanging match, then may I request your permission to leave?"

"Calm down, my cockerel," the *azaz* said calmly. "There was a definite purpose in wanting to speak to you alone. If what I'm about to say came from my master, it would be very easy to misunderstand as a threat. It is not. It is, rather, a warning. As I said, I mistrust those with overweening ambition, which I feel you, your emperor, and even your nation may be guilty of.

"If I'm correct, then there's a great likelihood this wonderful peace we're all so enamored of won't last for more than a few years.

"I'll give you another reason for my suspicions: The Emperor Tenedos has frequently cited his devotion to Saionji the Destroyer Goddess."

"Destroyer and creator," I said, parroting something the emperor had said time and again. "For it's sometimes necessary to tear things down to rebuild them."

"True. Your emperor mostly talks of the creator aspect of

the goddess. But most priests say Saionji's creative powers extend only to her control of the Wheel, and regulating how and when each of us is allowed to return to earth. There's no mention of her being creative as Umar was. But maybe your emperor is in Saionji's personal keeping and knows more of her attributes than the rest of us."

"Perhaps," I said impatiently. "But I'm no priest, nor do I have much interest in the gods or their aspects."

"Of course not. Soldiers seldom do, except in their dying agonies," the *azaz* said. "But this is part of my warning, so take heed. Your emperor may worship Saionji. But it's my belief such worship draws undue attention from the goddess. Perhaps it already has. In that event, I'd be surprised for her not to demand some sort of blood price.

"Such as declaring war on Maisir," he said, and now there was anger and threat in his voice.

"You're wrong, sir," I said, forcing calm.

"Am I? Perhaps. I hope I am, in spite of my interest in testing your emperor's magical thews. But if I'm not, take this as a second warning. I know you're a man of heat and the tropics, and this Maisirian clime is something new. So take the opportunity to immerse a bit of ice in water. See how little of it is above the water. That is Numantia, Damastes á Cimabue, and Maisir is as vast to your kingdom as a mighty ocean berg is to your bit of ice.

"Challenge us at your own peril—yours, your emperor's, and your country's."

I bowed, holding back anger.

"We can both feel relieved, sir," I said. "For I can give you my solemn word, my oath, which if you know anything of me or my family is one which has never been broken, that Numantia has no desire for war, for any piece of Maisirian soil, or for the death of one soldier, man, woman, or child, whether Maisirian or Numantian."

The *azaz*'s cold eyes held me. Neither of us dropped his gaze. Suddenly he nodded, and I was dismissed. I stalked out of the palace to my sleigh.

Riding away from the *azaz*'s dark estate, I pondered what he'd said. I thought that we had a very deadly enemy in the *azaz*, but at least he'd shown his feelings.

Three days later, on the eighth day of the Time of Dews, we met with King Bairan, to discuss the final outline of the preliminary treaty. I'd actually learned to think in contradictions like that. All went well, and the draft would go off to the emperor immediately. I wondered from where the *azaz* was listening, but set aside the thought.

Peace was in our hands, and as soon as we closed our fingers, it would be ours. Ours for this time, and, I hoped, with the borders brought under control, for all time to come.

"This is a much better way to celebrate than eating and drinking too much and shouting and singing," Alegria said breathily. "Is it not?"

She knelt over me, guided my cock into her, then sank down, lying on me, moaning as I lifted my hips, driving into her, our lips mashed together. After a time she sat up, her body twisting as I moved inside her. She slid her legs forward until she was sitting on me, her feet near my head, then swung, lifting one leg across my body.

Her breath rasped as she ground her hips against me, squeezing me with her inner muscles as she did. I almost came, and had to force control as she moved her leg back until it touched mine. She swung around until her back was to me, lifted her legs to either side of mine, leaned forward, hands on my ankles, then stretched her legs out slowly, and I was in a soft, tight vise and jerked upward, no longer able to hold myself. She lifted herself off my cock, slid back up, took me in her mouth as I caressed her with my tongue, and then we both rolled as our bodies convulsed and my mind drowned in warm wetness.

Sometime later, I came back. "Great gods," I managed to

say. "That's too much like work. I think I need a splint. What do you think I am, a gymnast?"

"Shut up," she said. "I was the one who had to do all the work."

"If my cock ever gets hard again, which I don't think it's going to," I said, "I'm going to show you one of *my* favorite positions. All it requires is a winch, twelve feet of timber, two hundred yards of rope, and sixteen sheep."

"Bluffer," she said. "But I do know where there's some very soft silk cord. If you're interested."

It was three weeks before we heard from Nicias, and I'd begun to be concerned, although I shouldn't have been, knowing the still-vile weather and the other problems communicating with Numantia presented. But there'd been so few problems thus far, and I've always believed luck is a fixed sum, and there is only so much to be spent.

I fretted, and the Time of Dews dragged past.

It was the fortieth day of the time when we finally received word. The emperor had approved the treaty. He'd have a few of the most minor changes to make, and then we could make arrangements for his trip to the border and the grand meeting between the two rulers.

I think everyone in Jarrah went a little mad. There were parties from the highest to the lowest, and no one seemed to have anything for anyone other than a smile and a cheery greeting. The temples were packed, and thankful prayers went up to Umar, Irisu, the special gods of Numantia and Maisir, and almost any deity worth praying to.

Except Saionji. Her flashing swords, her pale horse, would not be called upon.

Three more weeks passed, and a hasty message came from Nicias. The pirates who roved the coast around Ticao, the province bordering my own Cimabue, had joined together and landed in several places, not as simple raiders, but as conquerors, declaring themselves the founders of an independent country. They had two powerful sorcerers, and the emperor himself had to take charge of the expedition sent there.

The message was full of apologies, reassuring us nothing had gone wrong. As soon as he destroyed these villains, he'd return to Nicias and sign the treaty, and couriers would carry the document south.

I conveyed the message to King Bairan and Ligaba Sala, letting them read the decoded raw text to make sure no one was suspicious, although there wasn't any cause for wariness. Even a Time shouldn't cause any problems.

Lord Boconnoc announced that the fourth day of the Time of Births would be an embassy holiday, and anyone wishing to sample Numantian cooking was welcome. It was merely a pretext to be mildly homesick, and attempt to construct some Numantian dishes from Maisirian materials and long-hoarded delicacies.

There were no more than ten or fifteen Maisirian guests at the embassy that night. Everyone was gathered in the main ballroom, having a glass of good Varan wine before dinner. I, of course, was drinking water. Alegria found the wine a bit tart for her tastes—Maisirian wine was far sweeter than any Numantian vintage, but asked if she could have another glass.

I grinned, and was about to get it for her when the ballroom doors smashed, and a dozen armored soldiers stormed through. Behind them twenty archers trotted in and formed lines along the walls, arrows nocked, bows half-raised. There was utter, complete silence, then a woman sobbed once.

King Bairan stalked into the room. He wore black armor and held a naked sword.

"What . . . what is . . ." Ambassador Boconnoc stammered.

"Seven days ago, the army of Numantia crossed the Maisirian border, without any declaration of war," he boomed. "We received word of this treachery today, and a message the

Maisirian town of Zante has fallen and been sacked by your barbarians.

"This is a deed of the greatest infamy. You Numantians betrayed us, with your soft words of treaties, especially you, Damastes á Cimabue, falsely swearing you and your dog of an emperor ever intended peace.

"This was the act of bandits, not warriors, not diplomats, not civilized men. I therefore declare all Numantians beyond the law. As outlaws, you shall be judged, just as your foul emperor shall be judged after his army is destroyed.

"But none of you shall live to see that day. Take them away."

TWENTY

THE AZAZ'S CURSE

If it weren't for the barred windows and balconies, my cell could've been taken for a luxurious, if threadbare, apartment.

At the king's order, all of us in the embassy, Numantians and our Maisirian servants, were manhandled, not gentled, into wagons, and rushed through the streets of Jarrah. I don't know who had told the populace, but they were out in force, shouting obscenities and threats and pelting us with garbage. Twice they tried to charge the carts, screaming for our deaths, and were driven back by our escorts' whips. I was grateful for my love of finery, for I'd slipped my belt from my trousers, and held its slack end doubled about my fist. The buckle was about a pound of solid gold, and the belt set with heavy gold reliefs. The first madman that leapt onto our cart would've needed a new face. But the soldiers held them back until we reached Moriton.

Jarrah had many prisons, even more than Nicias, and we were taken to the most dreaded. It was the Octagon, and was completely impregnable. Outside the eight high walls of the cells was a spear-wall no one could break through, a spear-wall of exotically curved glass spikes. Next was a vertically walled ditch, more than thirty feet deep, with ten feet of muck to drown in at the bottom. There were pacing guards on the outer wall every fifty feet, and their watch was changed every two hours. Few who entered the Octagon's gates left. This was where the king's most infamous enemies were mewed up, until Bairan decided what agonies would best serve to show his displeasure.

We went through a gate in the outer wall and, surrounded by guards, were prodded off the carts. They herded us over a slender bridge that reached across the ditch and curved up and over the glass spikes, then down into the Octagon itself. I paid little mind, because I was looking for Alegria. I hoped she'd been able to hide or flee in the frenzy, but feared the worst—that the king had decided to make her an example because of her involvement with me.

The Octagon's chief warder, a thin, white-haired man with a smile suited for a skull, whose name was Shikao, told us the rules, which were quite simple, in spite of the half-hour drone it took to recite them: Obey any guard instantly or be very sorry you hadn't.

I was asked if I had a servant. I didn't know if it would be a good idea to name one, but before I could decide, Karjan stepped out and shouted, "I am the one." Shikao motioned, and a warder shoved Karjan toward me. Then we were pushed and harried to our cells. I was on the top floor of the five-story prison. The other Numantians were on the same floor and the one immediately below. "Our" Maisirians were imprisoned on a lower floor across the courtyard.

By now, my wits were returning, and I paid close attention, for a prisoner should always be planning his escape. But since I wasn't exactly a hardened lag, I saw no opportunity, nor do I know what I would've done had I spotted one, with only a city of enraged people and three hundred leagues of enemy territory between me and safety, not to mention what would happen to my fellows.

There was an inner and an outer door to my cell, with a ten-foot-long archway between them. The warders opened one, escorted Karjan and me through, locked it, then opened the inner door. There was a long main room, two small bedchambers off it, a jakes, and an alcove, for Karjan. The bathroom and the servant's alcove were curtained. The rooms were lavishly furnished, with battered, once-expensive furniture. Faded tapestries clung to the walls. There were three barred windows and two balconies opening onto the inner courtyard. The balconies could be closed off with folding wooden doors in bad weather. This would be my world until King Bairan ruled it was time for me to leave it.

I should have sent for pen and paper and immediately fired off a protest to the king about our unjust and, by the usage of diplomacy, illegal handling. But there were other matters concerning me, such as the Emperor Tenedos's second betrayal. Unlike the first, this needed little thought to comprehend.

What he'd done made quite a bit of sense, although understanding didn't lessen my rage. The Emperor Laish Tenedos had, quite deliberately, played me as a fool, to take in King Bairan, Ligaba Sala, and even the *azaz.*

Everyone knew I was irretrievably honest, not known for dissembling or being a good liar. So Tenedos said he wanted peace over all else, and I believed him, believed him as my friend and my emperor. Also, I was his most senior tribune, his best cavalry commander, head of his entire army. Only a fool would send such a man into the hands of the enemy if he intended war. And so the ambush was laid for Maisir to stumble into.

Not that I couldn't blame my own stupidity. Why hadn't I wondered why the emperor had suddenly changed direction after he'd saber-rattled for months about Ebissa, and his agents and broadsheets had made the Maisirians into demons incarnate? Shouldn't I have found that single night of magic, that great discovery, a little suspicious coming from a man who was the master of spells and caution?

I reluctantly recognized Tenedos's cunning in discovering a new invasion route, where he would find supplies for the army among the Maisirian settlers being moved into the *suebi*. That hand he'd played masterfully, especially after the Twentieth Hussars were attacked scouting that path into Maisir.

He'd built up units in Urey, so King Bairan paid more mind to the traditional path war and commerce took through Kait than to what was going on in Dumyat and Rova. My sincerity played into King Bairan's desire for peace, and he'd moved his soldiers back from the borders, so no Maisirian patrols witnessed Tenedos's preparations for war.

All Tenedos's moves, from pretending to echo the king's withdrawal of forces to hesitating over the niceties of the treaty, to the "pirates" of Ticao, were meant to give him time to assemble our armies for the invasion.

I wondered bitterly what final service I was expected to perform for my emperor next? Of course, to die as a noble symbol, here in the dungeons of Jarrah. I would die fulfilling my oath to Tenedos, the oath my family had never broken: We Hold True.

After all, there was little else but my pride left, since the only one who knew my honor was still inviolate was a thousand leagues distant, weaving a new web.

Again, I was grateful for my love of flashy garb. I pried one of the gold carvings from my belt and gave it to Karjan. He bribed a guard, and found out Alegria had been taken back to the Dalriada. Her moment of "freedom" was over. Now all that was left was the company of her sisters and the dark stone walls of the castle. But at least she would live.

They marched our Maisirian servants into the inner courtyard an hour after the morning meal. The thirty or so men and women huddled together, eyes darting about fearfully. But nothing happened, and they began to relax, and I heard their wondering voices.

Gates clanged open, and some forty armored men trotted into the courtyard. A servant walked toward them, asking something. Steel flashed, and a sword drove into his belly. Then the screams and the pleas for mercy began. But none were heard, and the swords and axes rose and fell.

From the balconies around me I heard Numantians shout curses, raging that our servants had nothing to do with what happened. But the killing went on, and none of the murderers bothered to look up. The screams softened to moans, tears. The killers went from body to body with daggers, and after that I heard nothing but their laughter and jokes. They dragged the bodies out, and all that was left was the spatters and pools of blood against the courtyard stones, scarlet darkening to black.

We waited for more horrors, but it seemed the king's rage had been satiated for the moment. Or else, more likely, what was happening far to the north filled his mind.

We settled into prison routine—waking, eating, pacing the courtyard, eating, trying to find something to fill the mind in the long, numb afternoons, eating, and then lying down and praying for sleep.

The food was acceptable, but monotonous: bread and tea in the mornings, a weak vegetable stew at midday, and the same at night with bits of meat or fish in it. Karjan and I entertained ourselves for a while remembering, precisely, course by course, the finest meals we'd ever consumed. But that grew too painful as the weeks dragged by.

We exercised hard, pacing our cell endlessly, wrestling, straining our muscles, each man against the other's pull, in improvised drills. We exerted our minds with a game Karjan contrived. Since we'd campaigned so long together, one would begin a description of a place, a fight, a parade, a person, and go on until the other caught him in an error. Penalty—a beer for Karjan when we were freed, an exotic sweetmeat for me. Then it would be the other's turn to talk about the same subject, until he made an error. In this simple and stupid manner, we kept our minds supple.

The war was always a presence. We heard the dim sounds

of marching men, army bands, clattering wagons, the neigh of horses and the clash of their hooves.

Even behind these stone walls, we were still able to hear news of the war. Karjan cultivated a friendship with one of the Maisirian prisoner-cooks, and he obligingly collected all the tales of the fighting.

At first the war went well for Numantia, as our huge armies swept south through the Wild Country and the developing farmlands.

It was hard to determine how well the Maisirians fought. Of course the tales were of incredible heroisms, but certain formations would be touted for a while, then never be mentioned again. I was grateful for my memory, because the penalty for keeping a diary would no doubt have been awful.

Karjan was told casualties were enormous on both sides, but more terrible for Maisir. Sometimes their soldiers fought like demons; sometimes it needed but one Numantian soldier on the horizon to make them throw down their arms in surrender. Of war magic, I heard nothing and could find out nothing.

Jarrah went into mourning when Penda, a district capital, fell. It had been a brutal battle with no quarter on either side, and the Maisirians were slowly driven back through the streets. But driven back they were, and then the city was ours.

Some Numantians rejoiced, but I didn't, for our army was moving far too slowly. No one—not the emperor, not my fellow tribunes, not the generals—seemed aware that the greatest enemy was the terrible Maisirian weather. The army held in Penda for too long. Perhaps the bitter fighting had taken something out of it. Then we heard that the emperor himself had taken command, and Numantia was on the march again. But this country was different from anything they were used to. Beyond Penda the new farmlands ended, and the *suebi* began.

The summer heat broke, and the Time of Rains began. Numantia floundered in the mire as the Maisirians counterattacked. Our army fell back on Penda, was surrounded on three sides, and the Octagon became a place of complete despair. I was more angry than depressed. The emperor must attack, for there was only one time left before winter. But Numantia stayed in Penda, fighting bloody but inconclusive battles around the broken city's perimeter.

The first Numantian to die was Lord Susa Boconnoc. He did not die well, but then, a politician isn't expected to have the same fearlessness as a soldier. Boconnoc had withdrawn, turned grayer and aged. When I tried to cheer him, when we walked in the courtyard, all he talked about was his estate in the Latane Delta and his plans for renovating it when the war ended.

The drumroll started at dawn and thundered for hours. Anything out of the ordinary in the Octagon was never good. As the midday flag was raised over the prison, a portable scaffold was rolled into the courtyard. Two warders came in behind it, one bent under a heavy wooden block, the other carrying a black case. A man wearing a red cloak and a black half-mask strode in and stopped at the scaffold steps, standing utterly motionless.

The windows of the cells had been full since the drums started, everyone waiting to see what terror would come next. I faintly heard shouts and protests from outside my cell, from my corridor. A Numantian was doomed. A courtyard door slammed open below, and a pair of warders dragged out Lord Boconnoc. He was limp with fear, hardly able to walk. He saw the headsman and keened wordlessly, tried to struggle, but the warders held him firmly. They half-carried him up the steps and threw him across the block.

The executioner opened the case and took out a great, evilly horned single-bitted ax. He went slowly up the steps. Boconnoc pled for mercy, but there was none this day.

A warder grabbed Boconnoc's hair, pulled it hard, and stretched his neck across the block. The ax came up, and Boconnoc squirmed frantically as it fell. The blade missed its mark, and thudded into Boconnoc's skull with the dull sound of a melon being hacked open. The ambassador's body writhed, and the headsman jerked his ax free and smashed it down again. This time his aim was true, and Boconnoc's mutilated head fell away, blood fountaining.

There had been no trial, no proclamation of sentence. Just death. I would be next.

But I wasn't. The next, for reasons I do not know, was Captain Athelny Lasta, my aide, and commander of my Red Lancers. He died a hero. Not the way an aristocrat would "die well," with a noble speech to ring down the ages, but as a warrior.

Again, two warders brought in the scaffold; again the headsman waited. The door to our wing banged open, and Lasta came out, arms bound above his waist, two more guards flanking him. But he walked proudly, as a brave man should.

He broke away from the warders and bounded up the scaffold steps like a man eager to embrace his doom. He boomed "Long live the emperor!" and the prison walls shook with our cheering. The purpling warders started up the steps to pin him to the block. The first one, instead of facing a meek victim, was met with a head-butt that sent him sprawling. Lasta knelt, fumbled the warder's dagger from his belt, and awkwardly drove it into the man's throat.

One.

The second warder jumped toward Lasta, drawing his own blade. But he was facing a well-trained soldier, and Lasta dropped to his side, spun his legs like sweeps, and tumbled the warder from the scaffold to crash headfirst against the cobbles and lie motionless.

Two.

The executioner, bellowing like the bull he was, grabbed his case and tore it open. Ax ready, he started toward the steps, looked up, and shrieked in horror. Lasta had cut away his ropes, and his dagger was ready. The ax clanged to the cobbles, and the executioner stepped back, mewling fear, hands trying to push away death.

I've never been able to throw a knife well, but Lasta used to amuse himself and others by tossing almost any edged weapon at almost any distance to thunk precisely on the named mark. The warder's dagger flipped once in the air and buried itself to the hilt in the headsman's gut where his cloak came open, just below his ribs. The man howled agony, and pulled the dagger free. His guts spilled, reddish-gray coils falling to the cobbles. Writhing, the executioner went down in his own gore and moved no more.

Three.

Lasta leapt from the scaffold and had the murderer's ax in his hand as the other two warders ran for the barred gate. They were shouting for assistance, scrabbling at the locked panels, and Lasta pitilessly cut them down from behind.

Four and Five.

The door smashed open, and ten or more jailers crashed into the courtyard, armed with spears and swords. Lasta brushed a spear aside, smashed a man's side in, parried, and rolled another's head across the stones.

Six and Seven.

I was bellowing cheers, unfelt tears runneling down my face as Lasta dropped an eighth victim, then cried out as a swordsman slashed his thigh open.

The ninth man died as another blade lanced into Lasta's chest. He stumbled back, pulling the sword out of his attacker's hands, found the strength to pitch his ax full into that man's face, then went to his knees. Then the warders were on him, and we saw nothing but swords rising and falling in a frenzy.

An officer ran into the courtyard, yelling for order, and slowly his men pulled themselves away from the roiling mass.

Lasta's body sprawled on the body of his ninth victim, and his hands were clawed in the throat of a tenth. That man tore himself up and staggered away. Shikao was in the courtyard, screaming, out of control, making no sense at all.

Our cheers died away. Karjan turned to me. "Nine of 'em," he said harshly. "Th' man's set us a hard goal."

But a goal it was, and I resolved I'd die no more readily than had Captain Lasta, and vowed that if I ever bore a son, he'd carry the captain's name.

They came for me at dawn. I woke, rolling out of my bunk, and there were a dozen black-clad men in my cell. Two rushed me, and I smashed them down. Karjan came awake fighting as well. I heard blows land, grunts of pain, then a truncheon hit with a thud, and I heard Karjan fall.

I thrust my thumb into one's eye, another struck me hard in the stomach, and I bent for a moment, but managed to kick his kneecap into fragments, and he yelped and hopped away. A club smashed across my shoulders, and I almost went down, but then turned, and tore the club out of my assailant's hands. I drove its butt into his groin, and started to slash it up across another's face, but then a knotted fist took me on the base of the neck and I knew nothing.

I groggily came back to myself, had a moment to realize I was lashed in a chair, then vomited rackingly all over myself, head spinning. A bucket of water smashed over me, and I heaved once more, and again I was drenched. The world, and my stomach, slowly ceased turning, and I forced my eyes open. There was a heavy wooden table across the room. Behind it, lit by two white wax tapers in floor stands, sat the *azaz*.

On the floor between us were chalked symbols, and braziers sent smoke coiling into the dank air. It felt as if we were underground, far underground.

The *azaz* looked at me unblinkingly, no expression whatever on his face. "There has been considerable discussion, Damastes á Cimabue, between the king and myself as to what your punishment might be."

"Punishment for what?" I managed. "For serving my emperor?" There was certainly no way I'd ever tell an enemy of my ruler's dishonesty and betrayal.

"For causing the deaths of many thousands, perhaps a million, Maisirians," the *azaz* replied. "Common murder, if you like."

"By that rule, any of your soldiers, any of your generals, might be guilty of the same 'crime.'"

"Perhaps," the *azaz* said. "However, there is a difference. You are in our hands, and therefore we're permitted to make the rules."

"Enough debate," a voice rumbled, and King Bairan stepped from behind me. "It's enough to know this bastard did evil to Maisir, and that he must pay for that evil."

"My apologies, Your Majesty. Of course." The king walked to the table and stood with his arms folded. He wore dark robes and had a dagger sheathed at his waist.

"A simple death would be far too easy," the *azaz* said. "Of course we could give you a death by torture that would be so protracted men would whisper of its horror for a thousand years."

He was speaking foolishly. A man can only be tortured until he gains the courage—or hopelessness—to bite through his tongue and bleed to death quietly.

"But that," King Bairan put in, "would accomplish nothing except to make me feel a bit better."

"We therefore devised a more . . . interesting fate," the *azaz* said. "Prepare him!"

Two men, wearing cowled robes so I couldn't make out their faces—if they were men at all—tore my tunic open and held me motionless. The *azaz* picked up an odd instrument from the table and came toward me. It looked like a small, thin knife, but one made of glass. He whipped it suddenly across my chest from shoulder to thigh, then again, so blood welled in an X shape.

The *azaz* moved the knife over the cut, its point but touching me, and it was as if he held a burning torch. I tried to keep from writhing, but failed. He showed no interest in my pain, but concentrated on keeping the knife's edge on the cut. As he moved the blade, it became red, until the entire weapon was blood-scarlet. He stepped back, but the burning agony remained.

"Your Majesty," the *azaz* said. "It would be better for the kingdom if you removed yourself for a moment. I don't think there's much risk, but there's some. And we could hardly do without you in these times."

The king walked past me, and a door opened, then closed.

The *azaz* moved around the room to tall tapers of multi-colored waxes in wall mounts. He reached up with that strange knife, and the taper would light. Five flamed when he had finished. He walked to the center of the room and spoke a phrase. The tapers boiled smoke—white, blue, green, black, red—but the chamber never filled, nor did I choke on the fumes.

Again the *azaz* spoke, and the world changed. Everything became gray or black, and what was the blackest should have been the lightest. Now the *azaz* began chanting, but I couldn't make out his words. His words droned on.

The *azaz* touched that odd knife to the stone floor, and blood, my blood, pooled out. A fire blazed where the *azaz* was, reaching almost to the ceiling. He stepped out of the flames, unharmed, and moved to one side. He said a single word, and the flames gathered themselves and reached toward me. As they came, the flames changed from red and yellow to the purest black.

A finger of fire touched my slashes, and pain roared through me again. The finger traced my wounds twice, and I almost passed out from the agony.

Now I could understand the *azaz*'s words:

"Now you are his
Now you are mine
Like clay
Like putty
I command
You obey
I command
You obey"

* * *

Those last two sentences were repeated over and over, growing louder, until they filled my universe, became my universe, then faded down, echoing into silence. I was cast in glass, a fly in amber. There was a distance between me and everything else, though I still looked through my own eyes. But I was also looking at myself from a distance at the same time. Noises, smells, came, but remotely.

"Stand, Damastes," he said, and the bonds were gone and I obeyed. I felt as if I were under water, moving slowly through a clear mire.

"Very good," the *azaz* said. "Summon the king."

Again, a door opened and closed, and King Bairan was in front of me. He came very close, inspecting me as if I were a rare specimen. "Did it take?"

"It did."

"I would like a demonstration."

"Certainly." The *azaz* thought. "What about that Dalriada you gave him?"

The king snorted. "That would mean nothing. No man values a whore, especially when she's nothing but a slave."

I felt rage, but it was distant, almost as if another's emotion were being described to me.

"I have it," the *azaz* said. He beckoned, and one of the robed men came. The *azaz* spoke quietly, and the man nodded and went out. The three of us stood for some time. I felt nothing, not worried, not bored. I could have been stone.

The door opened, and the robed man returned. With him was Karjan.

"Go to your master," the *azaz* ordered.

Karjan looked suspicious, but obeyed. He gazed intently at me. "Tribune," he asked, as if sensing something was wrong.

"Yes?"

"Are you—"

"Be silent," the king barked, and Karjan jerked, obeyed.

"You two," the king went on. "Hold that man."

The two cowled men pinned Karjan's arms. The king drew his dagger and held it butt-first toward me.

"Damastes," the *azaz* said, almost in a croon, and for the first time I saw excitement in his eyes. "Take the knife."

I obeyed.

"Kill that man."

Karjan's eyes went wide in surprise. I drew the knife back carefully, and his mouth opened, perhaps to scream in horror. I plunged the dagger into Karjan's chest, angling upward to skewer his heart. Blood spurted and ran down the knife's hilt, across my fingers.

Karjan, my servant, my friend, my savior in a score of battles, grunted, and his eyes were dead, his knees folded. The two men let him fall.

"Give the king back his dagger," the *azaz* ordered, and I obeyed.

King Bairan knelt, wiped the blade clean on Karjan's shirt, and resheathed the knife. "Give him his orders," the king said, and his voice was hoarse with passion.

"Damastes, do you hear me?"

"I do."

"Will you obey me?"

"I will."

"We are going to set you free. You and the other Numantians. We will give you safe passage to Penda, where your army, your emperor, wait. You will go to him and say you must speak to him alone.

"Then you will kill him."

TWENTY-ONE

THE HEALING FIRE

Two days later, all surviving Numantians left the Octagon for the Numantian lines around Penda, for a prisoner exchange. I remember little of the journey, except that it was cold and wet, but I didn't care. We were escorted again by the Royal Taezli Cavalry, for I recollect familiarly uniformed horsemen.

I was a tiny Damastes, floating in the amniotic sea of the greater Damastes the *azaz* and King Bairan had created. I could watch, I could listen, I could even participate, so long as I never allowed any thought of the task set me to surface.

Svalbard asked what had happened to Karjan. I can't remember what I replied. He gazed at me oddly and asked if something was the matter. I—the real I—managed to snap that nothing was amiss, and for him to go about his duties. He clapped his fist to his shoulder and obeyed, and as he left, I felt the other, false Damastes's rage. I'd saved Svalbard's life, for if he'd persisted, he would have died. I would have killed another friend with as little hesitation as I had Karjan.

That instant gave me, the real me, a bit of hope. I was not completely in that other's power. I remembered yeast bubbles rising in my family's cook's bread sour. Such tiny thoughts were permitted. If they ever surfaced, ever broke, then the other Damastes, the assassin, would realize it wasn't as much in control as it thought, and would drive me deeper, perhaps until I drowned and was no more. Then the emperor's doom would be certain.

As we traveled, as more days passed, tiny pieces of an idea came, and were hidden from that other Damastes. Actually, it was less an idea than a desperate hope, most likely useless. But I clung to it, clung as hard as I could, without ever letting those "bubbles" be noticed by the Damastes whose body I drifted in. That Damastes ate, slept, gave orders when they seemed necessary, but in its own way was drifting as I was, not to come fully alive until it faced the emperor.

I dully noted that there were always soldiers around us—new recruits, old hands—all moving north toward Penda and the battlegrounds. The other memory I have is of the people of Maisir moving against this uniformed tide, moving south, deeper and deeper into Maisir, away from the fighting, away from the soldiers. They traveled on horse, heavily laden cart, and on foot, carrying what little they could, hoping for some haven.

We were almost in the Time of Storms, and rain, then snow and wind, smashed into these poor wanderers, and there were sprawled bodies beside the rude tracks we followed, bodies thankfully covered with fast-falling snow.

I was not cold, was not wet, was like a baby about to be born, yet not wanting to come into the harsh world. I'd be born to instant death, for the minute I slew the emperor I'd be cut down myself.

What of it? I thought dully. This life was burdensome. I'd lost all—my loves, my ruler, my respect, my friend—and now my honor was doomed, for who would ever believe I was under a spell when I committed the ultimate sin and slew the father of my nation? The whispers would be how Damastes had been wooed by the evil Maisirian king to slaughter his best friend and ruler. Perhaps I'd be permitted a bit of rest when I returned to the Wheel, before Saionji judged me harshly, as I knew she would, a regicide, traitor, and monster, and spewed me forth to begin life again in some horrid low form to expiate my evil.

I was still alive enough to sense when we approached Penda and the fighting. I felt blood, the sharp feel of danger, and stirred, coming a bit awake. The other Damastes felt me and forced me back down. I pretended to obey, and spread a blanket of nothingness over myself. Then we were on the front lines—dirty gray snow, strewn bodies, shattered trees, and broken buildings.

Negotiations began to allow us to enter Penda. I paid little attention. The other Damastes was coming more and more alive as its senses sparked to full alert, ready for the greatest, the only, task of its brief life.

Maisirian uniforms were replaced with Numantian uniforms, and there was great rejoicing that we were finally safe, among friends. The other Damastes pretended joy, then told the leader of the prisoner exchange, my friend Tribune Linerges, that Damastes had a vital message for the emperor.

"Your wishes match my orders," Linerges said. "For you're to be brought immediately into his presence."

The other Damastes expressed pleasure, and we went through the lines, through the fighting positions, through the ruined streets and torn buildings of Penda, into its heart, to a palace where the emperor's headquarters were.

I was unarmed, but what did that matter? I could kill a slight man like Tenedos in a hundred ways with my bare hands before anyone could stop me.

My vision cleared somewhat, but it was as if I viewed everything in the reflection of a brightly polished copper mirror. All was red, yellow, orange. I was beginning to panic, seeking my chance, my only chance, but as yet I saw none, and the time was growing shorter.

We entered a big room, filled with tables covered with maps. Fire blazed in a great hearth, and next to it stood the Emperor Tenedos. He was dressed simply, as a private soldier, but his uniform was made of the finest heavy silk, and his boots were polished as mirrors.

I started to kneel, but Tenedos held up a hand. "No, no,

Damastes, my greatest friend. Welcome home, welcome to safety."

I rose and stepped toward him, moving a little faster at each step. Alarm flared across his face, and my hands were up, clawed, ready to tear out his throat, and somewhere behind me I dimly heard Linerges shout in horror.

But I, the real I, was too cunning for that other Damastes, and his creator, the *azaz,* and his master, King Bairan of Maisir. Before my hands reached the emperor, I hurled myself sideways, toward that searing fire with its high-roaring flames.

I felt the other Damastes scream in terror, and then the friendly flames reached out, held me, took me, embraced me, and there was nothing but red agony and then nothing at all.

I'd expected to awake finally seeing Saionji's face, or one of her manifestations or ghouls, or, perhaps best of all, to not wake at all, to have slipped through her talons into the joy of utter oblivion. Instead, I felt soft linen under and over me, the warmth of a blanket, a perfumed wind touching my nostrils.

I opened my eyes and saw I was in a large bedchamber, in a palatial bed. Sitting next to me was the Emperor Tenedos.

"Welcome back, Damastes my friend," he said gently.

Perhaps I was . . .

"You are not dreaming," he said. "Nor are you dead."

But I remembered that fire, that searing agony around me, and felt a great fear, one any soldier will admit to. There are worse fates than being killed: being maimed, crippled, emasculated, scarred so that your own mother shudders and shrinks away in horror. I'd seen men and women taken in Shahriya's embrace, who yet lived, their flesh twisted, warped like water-smoothed driftwood, pain rending them at every movement. But there was no pain. Involuntarily my hand came up and touched my face. I felt soft, warm, healthy, unscarred flesh.

"No," the emperor went on. "You have no scars, either." He smiled grimly. "My magic saw to that."

"How?"

"Do you wish to know? Do you really wish?" I should not have nodded. "There were three prisoners. Noble, or so they styled themselves, Maisirians. They pretended passion for two of my dominas, who were foolish enough to call on them. The feast was poisoned, and my soldiers found death instead of love.

"I had intended a terrible death for them, a death such as I've given to any civilian who dares harm one of my officers. Then another thought came, after you'd tried . . . after you'd done what Maisirian magic forced you to try. Certain spells were cast, and the three women were flayed alive. Their skin replaced yours, and some of their blood flows in your veins.

"It was a dark deed—but one I felt no compunction about. There was a darker price attached for me, but one I paid gladly, not only as your emperor, but as your friend. I need you, Damastes. And I owe you a great debt."

Part of me shuddered at what the emperor had said, but another part boiled in rage. He needed me again? How was I to be betrayed this time?

But the emperor spoke on:

"You have lain like a corpse for fifty days of this Time of Storms, barely breathing, eating only broth, and that seldom, but it is a true miracle you have come back so quickly. I know all, Damastes á Cimabue. While you were drifting between worlds, between life and death, I made other magic, and discovered the terrible curse King Bairan and his lackey laid, and how you slew the faithful Karjan and were supposed to assassinate me.

"That was monstrous, and both of those swine shall pay in a monstrous manner. For this war has only begun. Welcome back, Damastes. Now I'll call on you for your greatest deeds, and we, together, will find our greatest triumph." Tenedos rose.

"Yes," he went on. "I need you to lead my army to victory. For we're impossibly mired here in Penda. But there is no turning back. There can be but one end—either Maisir or Numantia shall be destroyed.

"And you will be the one to ensure it is not Numantia." He didn't wait for a response, but swept out of the room.

What emotions came then? A better question might be what ones did not. For hours my thoughts boiled. I was alive, and for this I should be grateful. But I still felt the pain, and part of me still wanted oblivion instead of a return to life. I was grateful to Tenedos, yet another part growled that there was no end to serving him, that he would—and had—brought me back from the grave to ensure that more of his visions, visions beyond reality into madness, would become real.

But I had no choice, and so concentrated on regaining full strength. I was whole, but weak. Whole—but when I found a mirror, there were changes. The most obvious was my hair, now only a bare stubble, that had burned like a torch in the fire and, I feared, would never grow back in its former profusion. My skin was, indeed, lustrous, and I shuddered away from the obscene joke that it was "just like a woman's." But there were wrinkles at the corners of my eyes, and I thought my expression was different: harder, colder.

I still felt numb, uncaring about anyone or anything. There was but one spark, and that was the dim hope that I might somehow find Alegria. That brought another realization. The only chance I had to find her was to do just what the emperor wished: Win this war.

I didn't and don't know if the emperor was aware of Alegria, and how my love would sway me. Perhaps so, for he was more than subtle enough to find out what had happened in Jarrah, and to use that knowledge as, I was realizing, he would use any tool, any man, to accomplish his ends.

And I had sworn an oath. That did as much as anything to return me to life.

We Hold True.

Very well. I was not permitted death, I was not permitted oblivion. Then I would deal it out to others, I vowed grimly.

That appeared to be what Irisu wished. Irisu—or, more likely, Saionji, and her manifestation as Death.

Very well, I'd take that manifestation for my bride, for my avatar, and welcome Death on her pale horse, swords held high, skull grin shining through her dark cloak.

Now there would be three of us: the emperor, myself, and Saionji.

And let the world scream long in terror and agony.

TWENTY-TWO

The Breakout

On the thirteenth day of the Time of Births, the Numantian Army smashed out of the perimeter around Penda, striking south. We had three objectives: to destroy the army of Maisir; to seize and occupy Jarrah; and, although this was unstated and somewhat nebulous, to either seize King Bairan's throne or make him the emperor's vassal.

It had been almost a year since the war had started, more than half of that spent mewed up in Penda. When I was able to totter beyond my hospital bed, I was inundated with problems and their causes. First I obeyed my own commandment and ordered all my subordinates, buzzing like mosquitoes, to leave me the hells alone unless I summoned them or it was a true emergency.

Then, with the emperor's permission, I summoned all of the tribunes and generals. My speech to them was very short and very pointed: We were fighting a war. We would win that war. If necessary, I would win it myself, killing the last Maisirian with the clubbed head of the last general who'd had the insolence to question my orders. That brought grins from the ones

I wished to smile, and blank expressions from some others. Those were the ones I noted as being worthy of attention.

Yonge and Le Balafre lingered behind. "Are we finally going to fight?" Yonge asked. "Or should I tell my men to plan yet another season's crops beside the holes they live in?"

Le Balafre answered for me. "We're going to fight."

"Good," Yonge said, and smiled twistedly. "But are we going to win?"

"I don't think we have any other choice," I said.

"There's always a choice," the Kaiti said. "It just might be one that no one likes."

"Defeatist," Le Balafre said, grinning.

"No," Yonge said. "A realist."

"Get out of here," I ordered. "It's time for us all to get to work."

Time and time past for that. The problems were simple and, not unexpectedly, began at the top, with the emperor. It is one thing to order a squad to charge a hilltop that's conveniently in view, or even command a corps to attack a crossroads that can be seen from the general's comfortable hilltop post. It's quite another to control an army that's sprawling for fifteen miles around a shabby, half-ruined city, an army and its hangers-on. The emperor had lost control, ironically just as he'd snarled at his new brother-in-law, Aguin Guil, for doing in maneuvers.

All efforts to regain control. When he attacked, his maneuver would violate the most basic rule: Pick a single objective and strike with all your strength. The emperor vacillated, without ever making a firm commitment to any plan, and so none succeeded. All his plans killed Numantian soldiers more than they slew Maisirians. They had the men to sacrifice, and we did not.

I'd been afraid of this when I'd heard of our army's inertia back in the Octagon. But all that could be done was to swear I'd never permit my emperor to place himself in such an impossible situation again. That was what we were for, his tribunes and generals, and I considered the emperor's failure more ours than his. He was, after all, the emperor, the ruler, not a general, even though that was one of his dreams. But we all have dreams that can't be fulfilled.

I knew better than most, for most of mine lay dead in a burned-out castle called Irrigon, and the one left was in the heart of the enemy. I tried to keep from thinking of Alegria, and continued collecting problems.

The emperor, and this I saw from personal observation, had another flaw I'd been vaguely aware of. He chose favorites, as does any king, but the favorites might only remain so for an hour or a day. Then another would be anointed, and the first's dreams of glory vanish. I thought Tenedos a vacillator, but realized he behaved this way deliberately, although I could never decide if it was conscious or not. As long as he had a courtier worried about his moment of splendor, that man wouldn't be plotting. There was of course no conspiracy, but I suppose those who wear crowns can never be sure when a smile conceals a dagger. Once more, I was glad I had never dreamed of being more than a simple soldier.

This problem was insoluble but, once recognized, easily dealt with. I merely pursued my own plans, checked them regularly with the emperor, and paid no mind as to which general had dined at the imperial table last night, and why I hadn't been invited.

Other personal matters were dealt with. My three warrants—Svalbard, Curti, and Manych—were commissioned legates, and the hells with anyone who gasped about their "unofficerlike manners." We needed warriors, not dancing instructors. I also promoted Balkh, that once overeager young legate from Kallio, to command my Red Lancers, and had the Lancers brought back to full strength by coldly raiding other formations.

As long as I allowed myself to think of personal matters, I wanted to know more of my ex-wife, but knew no matter how subtly I'd bring the matter up, it would be noted, and someone would shake his head about poor Damastes, still mooning over *her*. So I kept from asking, and only learned that, as far as anyone knew, she was still exiled to Irrigon and considered somewhat of a laughingstock for her cold-bloodedly unsuccessful pursuit of the emperor.

My most secret problem was my murder of Karjan. In spite of my mind's telling me that I was under another's control, that I had no will of my own, I still was shamed, fouled. I wondered if blood could wash the matter clean, and resolved I'd try to make it so. But little by little, that faded into the back of my mind, as I buried myself in other worries.

Numantia had had a terrible harvest that previous year, and it was taking forever for supplies to reach us, and all too often they were spoiled in transit.

The same with our replacements. We'd crossed the border with almost two million men and lost—killed, wounded, missing—almost 150,000. We needed not only replacements to build the army back up, but more soldiers to break out of Penda. The new Guard Corps had to end their training, no matter what stage it was in, and march south to us, taking casualties as they did. The army had made little effort to befriend the Maisirian peasants when it crossed the border, and, in accordance with imperial policy, had "resupplied" from the surrounding countryside.

Now, to our rear, where there should have been a cowed and complaisant populace, there were "bandits" aplenty, for what else can a man become when his cattle are driven off, his fields stripped, his larder emptied, and all too often, to my great shame, his women ravished? Numantia had laws forbidding such barbarisms, but how readily were they to be enforced, especially when the army itself survived by organized looting?

These crimes created partisans, reinforced by the Negaret, who were far too sensible to face our soldiers in open warfare. Instead, they mounted nibbling raids and cut off and looted supply trains. As for a straggler—if he were an officer and visibly rich, he might be ransomed. Sometimes. But a common soldier was doomed. The lucky ones were sold as slaves.

New units, inexperienced at real fighting, would take countless tiny pinpricks, each time losing one or more men. Like a horse driven nearly mad by summer flies, they'd lash out in any direction as they marched, and the peasants they savaged quickly became banditry.

The best solution I found was detaching cavalry units—thereby breaking another commandment about keeping my horsemen as a single cohesive force—to escort the new soldiers and the supplies from point to point, each point garrisoned by infantry. These behind-the-lines forces drained what I was thinking of as "my" army. But the increased flow of supplies and fresh men compensated, and we slowly rebuilt our strength.

I made personal reconnaissances along our lines, looking for a weak point. The emperor wanted a frontal assault all along the line, which was guaranteed to be as unsuccessful as his other forays. Our arguments reached the shouting stage on several occasions, and at last, pushed beyond common sense, my notorious Cimabuean temper flared and I snapped, "What the hells do you want? Your whole fucking army lockstepping back to the Wheel? If that's so, find another gods-damned tribune to be your corps master," and stalked out. Tenedos stopped me before I reached my horse, and soothed me back into his chamber.

His manner changed, as if he were no more than a common magician and I his chief aide, reminiscent of time long past. He poured himself a brandy, and me a glass of juice that didn't taste completely of dried fruit boiled and soaked in well water, then said, the steel in his voice buried under velvet, "So where *shall* we attack, then?"

Staring at the map of Penda, I remembered a hill that jutted into Maisirian positions that were no more than hastily dug breastworks. Behind that hill, I could mass any number of men, if the emperor's magic was enough to hide them from the Maisirian sorcerers. "Here," I said, tapping the spot.

"Then make it so," he said.

"As the Maisirians say, 'You order me,'" I replied. The endless planning began, always in secret for fear of discovery by either spies, for there were still Maisirians in Penda, or by sorcery. The emperor swore that he, and the Chare Brethren, were able to thwart all such attempts, although he wryly added that if a truly effective spell were cast, it would be so hidden no one could unveil it.

Once the plan was complete, the highest commanders were briefed, and sworn to complete secrecy. Then the units began moving, shifting positions on the line. I took a chance and pulled the cavalry units on the lines of support into Penda, making sure every man, every horse, was ready.

My plan was simple: First skirmishers, then three Imperial Guard Corps to attack through that outpost into the Maisirian lines. Smash the line, then turn right, and attempt to roll up the Maisirian front. Through that hole I'd send half my, or rather Nilt Safdur's, cavalry, curving left and then back, to take the Maisirians in the rear. The infantry would have already deployed through that hole, and turned, reinforcing the First Guard Corps elements. Then the army's main force would deploy through the hole, and follow the lead of the first elements, hopefully shattering the entire Maisirian line.

I gave Yonge his orders: Strike straight through the hole, and go as deep as you can. There'll be heavy cavalry and mounted infantry behind you. Keep the attack moving until you start taking real casualties, then let the stronger units attack through you. Then concentrate on causing as much trouble as possible.

"You mean you're actually going to let some of us skirmishers live, and not order us to destroy ourselves against the Maisirian positions? What an original plan."

"It's not that I care about you," I said. "It's just too expensive to train new skulkers."

"At last," Yonge said. "At long last a bit of wisdom enters the high command. World, ready yourself. Soon will be the ending. Umar will awake, Irisu will take his head from his arse, and Saionji will have a new manifestation as goddess of baby lambs and flowers."

I started laughing. "You're dismissed."

The Chare Brethren sent out their spells. If magic had been visible, our front would've looked as if smokepots were boiling behind it, with heavy clouds rolling forward over the Maisirians, so their wizards could sense nothing.

The attack began just before the noon meal.

It must have been terrible to see solid formations of Numantians come over the hill—endless waves of death. Arrows arched in storms, spears drilled the air, and our men went down. But the gaps in our lines were quickly filled, and the juggernaut rolled on, smashing the Maisirian line open.

The emperor and I stood in a small outpost, watching our army stream down into the blood-wallow. The first of our colors broke into the open on the far side of the Maisirian line. I signaled a courier. "Go to Tribune Safdur, and request him, with my compliments, to begin his attack!"

"Sir!"

Svalbard stood nearby, holding my horse. "Your Majesty, I'll ride forward now," I said.

"I thought you might," Tenedos said dryly. "Leaving me to wander around here, with nothing to do but cast a few spells."

"That's me, Your Highness. Always the selfish sort." We grinned at each other, and for a single instance it was as if the betrayals had not happened. But memory reminded, and I turned hastily away and climbed into the saddle. My mount was excellent, a fifteen-year-old chestnut stallion with a blaze face that had been a budding racer for a Maisirian nobleman. But he was still unaccustomed to battle, and pranced nervously. An excellent mount, but he wasn't Lucan, he wasn't Rabbit. I named him Brigstock.

Back of the outpost were my Red Lancers, wearing

infantry cloaks to conceal my presence in the front lines. At my signal, Captain Balkh shouted orders, and they mounted, casting aside their drab camouflage. Perhaps I should've stayed behind, and attempted to nitpick the course of the battle. But I would have been fooling myself. I—or rather the emperor—had competent tribunes and generals. Now was the time to trust them.

I wanted to see blood and feel the shudder of my sword meeting bone. Or perhaps I was looking for something else. Perhaps.

We went down the hill at the trot, Lancers forming a line abreast on my flanks.

Behind us came the Numantian cavalry, fierce behind banners, trumpets blasting. More than a hundred thousand cavalrymen went down that hill to battle.

Our Guardsmen were still in formation, although the battle was beginning to break up into swirling brawls. Then the Maisirians saw the cavalry, and over the shouts of the victors, the howls of the dying, I heard their screams.

Lances snapped down. The enemy hesitated, then ran. First a few, then more and more, and the wavering Maisirian line broke. We went through the ruins of the front line toward the rear. Soldiers braver and smarter—for a horse will not charge a solid wall—formed a square. I cried for the gallop, and we charged it. Brigstock drew ahead of my Lancers, as I'd intended.

Twenty feet away—then ten—was that spear-wall, and just before we reached it, I stood in the stirrups and pulled back on my horse's reins. Like the jumper I'd found him to be, he took flight, arcing gracefully over the spears into the formation's center, and in front of me was the Maisirian officer. My lance took him in the chest, and he clutched it and stumbled back, tearing it from my grasp. I drew my sword, wheeling Brigstock back into the square's line. But there was no line left. As their leader went down, the formation broke, men dropping their weapons and pelting away into the fleeing shambles.

Captain Balkh was beside me, eyes wide in admiration. I let him think me glorious—if he thought about what had just happened, he would realize I'd done the only thing possible, which is the furthest thing from what I deem heroism.

We trotted on at the front of this invincible mass, paying little mind to the Maisirians retreating around us unless they tried to fight or stand—at least most of us did. I saw a legate, not one of my Lancers, spear a running man full in the back and send the corpse whirling away. He shouted in pure glee, and I grimaced, hearing a man who thought killing a man was sport like boar-sticking. But the next man he charged was far wiser, and whirled just before the lance took him, and pulled its point down into the muck. The lance pole-vaulted the legate over his horse's head to the ground. Before he could recover the Maisirian was on him, and I saw a dagger rise and fall twice. Then an arrow took the soldier and sprawled him dead across the Numantian cavalryman he'd killed, and we rode on.

Here and there Maisirian officers and *calstors* rallied their men, and bows thwacked as archers sent arrows spitting. A mounted man can't fire accurately, but my canny bowmen waited until we were bare yards away and then shot for the group, not the man. There were men on horseback, and we fought, and I killed some, and we went on, my eyes, my mind, welcoming the red blur of combat.

We crested a hill and saw the tents of the Maisirian rear lines. Men and women scrawked when they saw us, and fled. The cavalry struck the encampment like a whirlwind, lances discarded, sabers flashing against people, tents, tent ropes—and chaos spread. Here and there I saw men dismounting and beginning to loot. A man trotted past into a still-standing tent and came out a moment later with a screaming young girl over his shoulder.

I pulled Brigstock around, leaned over his neck, and crashed the flat of my sword over the Numantian's leather helm and he dropped. The girl ran away into the confusion. I hoped she found a captor with different ideas.

Then we were beyond the tents, and officers were shouting to form up, form up, and horsemen found control and obeyed. We swirled back into something resembling a formation and were ready to strike back through the lines and join the Guard Corps. I could smell victory.

There was an instant to look around and see how many casualties we'd taken: not many, and no more than a man or two from my Lancers.

Tribune Safdur galloped his horse out, flanked by two buglers and a standard bearer, ready to order the charge. I saw something then, or rather didn't see something, and spurred Brigstock hard for Safdur. The buglers had their horns raised, and he shouted at them to hold. I reined in.

"Sir!" He clapped fist to shoulder. "Is something wrong?"

"Yes," I snapped. "Look," and pointed at the battle lines.

"I see nothing," he said.

"Exactly," I said. "Where's the smoke, the dust? Where's the fighting?"

He peered through the haze. "I see nothing! What's wrong? What happened? The Guards should be—"

"Should be," I said. "But aren't. And we're well behind the lines. With no gods-damned support!"

Safdur's eyes widened as he realized we were in the jaws of what could shortly become a trap. "Your orders?"

I should have growled for *his* orders. I wasn't in charge of his gods-damned cavalry. But there was no time for niceties. "The Maisirians don't seem to realize they've got us—or almost got us, at any rate," I said. "We've got to get back to our own lines before they do."

"Right, sir. I'll sound the retreat."

"No, you won't," I said. "Not and panic the men. Because we're not going to retreat. We're going straight back through them. Aim," and I pointed toward one of Penda's shattered church towers in the distance, "in that direction. The ground's fairly flat, fairly level. Put your regiments in a wide V. We won't stop till we're back in Penda."

Safdur nodded hastily. He wasn't a bad officer, provided he didn't get too far from his superiors.

The buglers blew a new call, and the dominas of the cavalry regiments galloped toward us. Safdur snapped orders, and the officers went back. Time was running short—dust clouds of infantry units were on the march, solid, deadly beetles coming to surround and destroy us. But we moved first, at the walk, and as we moved, the regiments spread into the ordered disposition. I saw this smooth machinery, moving like geared cogs, and confidence surged within me. The hells with millions of the enemy. Each of us was worth ten—no fifty of them.

Again we struck at the front lines, and there were Maisirian soldiers rallying, ready for us. But we sent them flying, cutting our way to safety. I looked for our army, for our Guard Corps. I saw them, to the right of the breach they'd made in the lines, but little farther toward the center of the Maisirians than they'd been when we rode through them an hour—hell, I realized, looking up at the sun, half a day ago.

They were stopped, holding in place. Why? But that was a question for later, as fifty Maisirian Heavy Cavalrymen attacked, intending to smash the lightly armed Lancers. But we went to the gallop, spreading out, and we were among them, sabers clashing steel against their blades. I brushed an armored man's blade away, my own sword flicked under his helmet, and he gagged in death, spraying blood.

There was movement to the side, half-seen, mostly sensed, and I ducked and a war hammer almost brained me. But its user overbalanced, there was an unarmored gap behind his shoulder for my point, and he rolled off his horse. That animal, panicked, butted Brigstock, and my stallion screamed rage, reared, and smashed a hoof into the other animal's skull, and it staggered away. I was standing in my stirrups, and almost fell backward, but kept the saddle as Brigstock came back down. Steel slammed into me, and I was inches from a scarred, grinning Maisirian. He had a dagger in one hand, but

I took it on my arm shield, slashed the sharpened edge of the shield across the man's face, and he was gone.

Svalbard was fighting two men, their backs to me, and I swung once, then again, and he was clear.

Sweat blinded me, and my breath was rasping in my lungs, and our infantrymen were sortieing, and the broad V of cavalry swept through, and back into Penda, back into safety.

I left Safdur to tend to the recovery, and went looking for an answer.

"Yes," Tenedos said firmly. "Yes, I ordered the halt."

"Why?" I was holding tight to my anger. Behind me were Le Balafre, Petre, Herne, and Linerges.

"The time was not right," he said.

Somehow I kept from insubordination. "Sir," I said, hoping my voice was level, "may I ask for an explanation?"

"You may," Tenedos said. "You deserve one. I felt magic building, and I couldn't determine what spell the Maisirians were attempting. Second, and this is the most important, I could see, from my position, that all we were doing was breaking up the Maisirian ranks."

"And what is the matter with that?" Le Balafre demanded. Linerges nodded involuntarily in agreement.

"I want their whole damned army destroyed. In one stroke," the emperor said. "I don't want to cut them here, cut them there. Those bastards seem to be able to rebuild instantly. We hurt them, but the next day the wound is healed, and it seems as if they're stronger."

"That's true," Linerges grudged. "It would be best to break them once and for all if we can."

"Of course the emperor's right," Herne said firmly, as always agreeing with authority.

"There was another problem none of you gentlemen were aware of," the emperor went on, "since you were well forward. We were having Isa's own time bringing the third and fourth waves forward, and I was afraid I'd only be able to fight with half my forces. But that won't happen on the morrow. I've made sure of that," he said grimly, "since I made certain . . . adjustments to my support elements. Even a quartermaster had better learn to follow my orders when and as they're given, if he wishes to continue to serve. Now we have the Maisirians," the emperor said. "We've hurt them hard. Look."

He pointed down from the slope, into the gathering dusk. It was easy to see the two army's positions. Here were the camp fires of our forces, holding Penda and a great bulge outward from the day's fighting. Then darkness between the lines. Then began the fires of the enemy, stretching over the hills and out of sight.

"We've driven them back, broken them out of their nice, comfortable positions. They're binding their wounds, shocked, scared, desperately afraid of what will greet them on the morrow. We know what that will be, don't we, gentlemen?"

Tenedos waited, and Herne, naturally, was nodding enthusiastically. Le Balafre and Linerges smiled, the hard smiles of wolves as they look down on the flock and see no shepherd. Only Petre's face still showed doubt.

"Tribune?" Tenedos asked.

"I'm not sure, Your Majesty," he said. "It's well to think of destroying Maisir in detail. But I think you were wrong. I think we should have taken our share today—and worried about the rest tomorrow."

I expected anger, but there was none. "No, Mercia," Tenedos said softly. "This time, I see farther than you. Tomorrow will be the greatest disaster Maisir has ever known. We'll go forward, all along the line, when they're expecting us to attack from the advantage we made today. When they turn, the cavalry will go in once more and mop up. By nightfall, it will be all over, except for the shouting. I promise you this."

His eyes met Petre's and held them with that gleam that bent men like willows, and Petre smiled, the same killer's grimace that Le Balafre and Linerges had shown. "Yes, sir. I'm sure you're right."

The four saluted, and I did the same, even though I was still unsatisfied. "Tribune Damastes," the emperor said. "Remain a moment, if you would."

"Of course, sir."

He waited until the others had left, then took me by the arm and led me away from his aides. "Did you feel abandoned, Damastes? Abandoned yet again?"

A bit of my anger became perplexity. "Yes, sir."

"Did it ever occur to you that I never doubted your ability to come back—with all of your men—once I was forced to change my plans? There's a reason you are my first tribune, remember."

He stared at me, his expression blank. All at once, the remainder of my anger vanished. I bellowed laughter, and Tenedos smiled, then laughed as well. "Very well then," he said. "Stop complaining, soldier. By the way, would you have the time to dine with me?"

"No, sir. I'd best see to the dispositions—"

"See to shit," he said rudely. "It's too late to make major changes, and all the minor ones should already have been made by your subordinates. Am I not correct?"

"You are, sir," I admitted grudgingly.

"Very well then. The matter's settled. Besides, you're looking a bit scrawny, and I suspect you're still not as healthy as you'd like to think. But instead of broth, I offer the finest roast to be had in this starved land. Fresh vegetables. The grandest of cream pies. Instead of milk-soaked bread . . . well, you won't drink wine. But I've learned to make a concoction of various juices that would make a saint bellow for music and maidens.

"Come, Damastes. Walk with me until dinner."

We did just that, as if we were strolling beside one of Hyder Park's lakes in Nicias. We heard the cries of the wounded, still untreated, the challenge and response of sentries, the shout of orders, but none of these registered on our soldiers' minds. Silence, rather, would have sounded alarms. We talked of this and that, the past and the present, and then something occurred to me.

"Majesty? May I ask a possibly rude question?"

"Why not? I may give it a rude answer," Damastes said lightly.

"What happens next?"

"We destroy Maisir."

"And then?"

Tenedos gazed at me, his expression suddenly chill. "I don't understand."

"Do we have peace?" I asked. "Is that the end of the wars?"

Tenedos sighed. "I'll give you the answer my divinations have provided, but I don't know if you'll like it. No. There won't be peace. There'll always be another enemy. Maisir had foes on its borders, and they'll become ours. Besides," he went on, "we *have* to keep on conquering."

"Why?" I wondered, shocked.

"Because if we don't . . . we'll die," the emperor said. "You are either growing, or dying. A nation grows by expanding its borders. A man grows by never turning from challenge, from danger, from glory, but always welcoming those cold, hard friends to his company. Isn't that so?"

I looked out at the flickering lights, a million stars, of the Maisirian camp fires, knowing my answer could not be his.

I guess he tired of waiting.

"Come," Tenedos said. "Let's see what my cooks have devised."

"Yes," I said slowly. "Let's do that."

In the morning, the Maisirians were gone. By magic, by stealth, by skill, they'd broken camp, using those unaccompanied fires to lull us, and retreated south. South toward Jarrah.

TWENTY-THREE

BLOODY ROADS SOUTH

Shaken to our souls, we formed up and went in pursuit of the Maisirian army. Less than two hours from Penda, we found it. Or rather, we found a company of mounted archers. They lofted two volleys into the column, then fled before the cavalry screen could pursue them. In the tumult, two companies of Negaret darted against a supply train and seized half a dozen wagons, losing only one man.

That began the long bloodletting. Every day we were hit in the rear, flanks, seldom from the front. The retreating Maisirians seldom stood to battle. When they did, they were an impossibly brave unit that would fight to the last. But these "famous victories" added no noble names to the streamers on regimental colors, fought as they were where two dirt lanes crossed, or over an abandoned and burning village of a dozen huts. Each time we fought, we took casualties.

As did the Maisirians. Petre estimated we killed four Maisirians for every Numantian death. But there were always more Maisirians streaming to serve, ready to die. Sometimes they fought well, more often they surrendered or fled. But they still fought, and none of our prisoners had any doubt King

Bairan would destroy us in the end. Strangely enough, many of them wanted to enter our service in spite of this. One prisoner shrugged and said it was enough to live the day as best you could. Tomorrow would bring its own evil.

The peasants' courage was in spite of their officers. When we captured one, he hardly ever asked about his men, but about his ransom. In the meantime, they insisted on being treated like the great lords they imagined themselves to be.

We hoped for some communication with the Maisirian army, for prisoners were draining our resources faster than the ever-lengthening supply chain could replenish them. But no answer came to our sorcerous or truce-flagged inquiries.

Consider the Numantian Army on its triumphant march through Maisir. It's all too easy to envision a proud phalanx of brightly armored horsemen, courageous infantrymen tramping in even ranks behind them. Of course in the vanguard would be the Emperor Tenedos and his most noble Tribune Damastes á Cimabue.

Here is the reality: a seething mass three leagues wide if the countryside was flat enough to permit our locust march to spread out, trailing all the way back to the previous day's encampment. There were more than just the almost two million men we had under arms. There were the sutlers who peddled their wares from a pack or a wagon. There were the women, some Numantian from every province—and how they reached Penda I'll never know—and more Maisirians that had joined us along the march.

There were the prisoners, shambling along, barely guarded. Sometimes one or a dozen would break away and run for a concealing ravine. Sometimes we let them go, sometimes archers or lancers would hunt them down, more to relieve the boredom of the march than out of any fear they'd rejoin their army.

We had horses, oxen, half-tame camels from the Rovan deserts, and who knows what. But most of us traveled on foot. Wagons were everything from the emperor's palatial coach, to ambulances, to supply wagons, to mobile bakeries, to looted carriages, farm carts, and traps.

Under the Rule of Ten the Numantian Army on the march had looked like a city being evacuated. Petre and I had stripped matters to one rule: Everyone who marches fights. No exceptions. But that was too hard, too strenuous, and certainly an officer, especially a ranking one, deserved a few privileges, did he not? So first it was a packhorse, then a wagon, then a small train, and now a rolling madhouse of cooks, bearers, servants, and so on and so forth. I heard that the officers of one regiment had ten horses supposedly to carry their iron rations but which actually transported the regimental wines. I know for a fact—I didn't discover it until much later—that one general had fifty camels with gear for himself and his aides. Needless to say, none of these luxuries were offered to the rankers.

Only one thing was left of the reformation: We still moved hard, and we still moved fast. We started at dawn, stopped for five minutes every hour, and took a full day's rest every fifth day. When we halted, an hour before dusk, we took ten-foot-long stakes that we carried with us, each six inches or so in diameter and sharpened on both ends, and built stockades against attack.

We covered four leagues every marching day, and gave no allowances for the occasional ambush. Those who straggled could catch up when we made camp. But all too often they didn't. Some were taken by the Negaret and partisans harrying our flanks, but more became deserters, hovering on the outskirts, living by their wits and knives. It was these who generally committed the most terrible depredations against the Maisirian peasants. Generally.

Slowly, but very steadily, as steadily as the Wheel turns, we marched south through Maisir.

The Time of Births ended and we were in the Time of Heat. This was hard, dry heat, the heat of the desert, baking down. Dust boiled and hung in the thick, still air. It caked our horses, our bodies, our souls. Those of us in the vanguard weren't daring so much as we preferred the occasional arrow to choking in the dry, heavy, dust-laden air, seeing nothing but the arse of the man in front of us.

When I rode beyond the main column, I'd see a horseman or six here and there, watching, waiting for a chance to swoop in and cut a throat or rob a wagon. Chase them, and they'd retreat. Chase them too far, and you'd run into an ambush.

It was the Time of Heat, but the weather was strange. It would be bakingly dry, then clouds would flash across the sky and icy rain drench us. Moments later, the rain would stop, and we'd slog through mud until it dried to bricklike hardness, and the dust would float up once more.

The Negaret would mass half a hundred men, and the cavalry would be ready for a counterattack. But the attack would never come. Eventually the cavalry would stand down, only to be shouted to horse the next time a Negaret was seen. Day after day of this, and our horses began dying, drained from never being unsaddled.

Other horses also died because all we could find for fodder was the greenest of rye and harsh grasses. A staple of our diet became roasted or boiled horseflesh. The flankers began looking for either of two herbs—a garliclike root and a low, broad-leafed bush the leaves of which were like searing pepper. Both served to disguise how rotten the meat of our dinner stew was. On our fifth day stops, the army's bakers labored mightily, but seldom did fresh loaves get completely distributed, especially to the fighting soldiers at the front and flanks of the formation, although imperial headquarters had its share and more.

The sky, impossibly blue or gray, the waiting enemy, and always the *suebi*, stretched on, beyond the eye's reach, beyond the mind's recall. Men became solitary, melancholic, walked beyond the picket fires, and someone would hear a strangled cry. His mates would run out, and find a dying or dead soldier, sword or spear stained with his own blood. As I'd seen before, it was generally the young men who died so readily. Most of the recruits hit this point of despair, but if they had the strength to push through it, or if their squad-mates kept close watch, they'd be on the way to becoming warriors.

As for our sick and wounded, those who could still stumble marched on with their units. No one wanted to go to the ambulance train. Soldiers felt their only chance was staying with their mates. We sent heavily guarded convoys to the rear when we could, and established garrisons in the villages. Too often these tiny garrisons, manned by the sick and halt, would be attacked by partisans who gave no man an easy death.

One day, the emperor was in a cold rage, and no one, including Domina Othman, could determine why. I eventually found out. A coded, sealed message had come by courier from Nicias. Its contents couldn't be trusted to the heliograph, but had to be hand-carried.

I only learned of them, and the reply, because I used Tenedos's code clerk for my own secret commands, and he was like many who deal in cryptic matters: He couldn't bear not telling at least one person the terrible secrets he held. Since I told no one anything, he frequently confided in me.

The message had come from Kutulu. He notified the emperor that dissidents were newly active in and around the capital, with two former members of the Rule of Ten, Scopas and Barthou, for their leaders. They hadn't considered active rebellion yet, but were talking about whether the emperor needed a supreme council to take some of the burden of ruling from his shoulders, particularly regarding "commonplace matters" of state. They weren't a threat thus far, but Kutulu was keeping everyone involved under surveillance.

The emperor, I was told, flew into a grand rage and dispatched a courier within the hour back to Nicias. Kutulu had been warned before to stop coming up with nonexistent conspiracies and worrying about senile dribblers of the past, and to concentrate on the real threat—the Tovieti. Since he'd disobeyed this order again and again, he was relieved from his duties in Nicias.

He was ordered to one of the farthest provinces—possibly Chalt, possibly Bala Hissar, my man couldn't remember exactly—in disgrace.

So while the emperor's finest were dying in Maisir, another of his best was destroyed for doing no more than his duty. But by doing so, Kutulu might have saved his own life. I don't know for sure, for I've heard nothing more of the man.

Even the tribunes' morale was affected by the day-after-day shambling across the *suebi*. I was surprised to hear Herne, the most politically careful of all the tribunes, express admiration for how skillfully the Maisirians were managing their retreat, almost as if it were a planned campaign. The emperor raged at him, ending with a snarl that if Herne was so impressed by the Maisirians, perhaps he should consider joining them.

Then he stormed out of the mess tent. Herne looked after him quizzically and murmured, "I can only hope our own retreat shall be as well handled."

Fire-breathing Myrus Le Balafre overheard his comment, and instead of losing his own temper about the tribune's defeatism, made a wry face and said nothing.

We finally left the loathed *suebi* for farmland. We were able to find livestock for our dinners, rail fences to tear apart for cooking fires, and, at least for the officers, houses to commandeer for shelter. But with more peasants to despoil, there were more partisans in our wake, and so casualties began mounting.

We paused long enough to cut hay and let it dry for animal fodder, but an army can never halt for long. Within two days, we would consume all provender within two leagues, a day later within four, and so forth, so we were always at the center of a widening circle of desolation.

The sudden rainstorms never ceased, and we wondered if the Maisirians had mastered weather magic, and why our own wizards couldn't find counterspells.

Then the Maisirians found a new weapon: laying waste to their land as they retreated. Even the green fields of grass were fired, and this could only be done by magic.

Every village would be aflame or have been reduced to blackened waste. But this wasn't done by magic, but by fierce, determined men and women, who so loved their land they'd destroy it rather than see it held by another. The Maisirians killed what livestock they couldn't flee with, and spoiled the carcasses with the animals' own shit. They caved in the wells, except for a few, and those they poisoned. The Chare Brethren were able to counteract some of those poisons, but few of us trusted their magic, so we drank from streams and ponds.

I left the emperor's tent after a briefing late one night, and it was like day. Ahead of us was blood-red cloud, and flames flared around it. Light shot up in pillars on our flanks, reaching toward the sky, as if the rising lights were columns, supporting the vaults of the heavens.

The soldiers began to dread the Maisirians. They were never sure if the enemy would fight or run, surrender and vow eternal servitude, or smile and cut your throat from the rear. Soldiers must respect and be wary of their foe, or else risk being destroyed through overconfidence. But they must never dread them.

There was also growing respect, for the Maisirians could march on nothing but a handful of grain and a splash of muddy water for day after day, and still fight. When they did fight, they could be incredibly brave. There was the true story of the soldier who'd been badly wounded when his outpost fell to our cavalry. He lay motionless in his own gore for two days, pretending death, never moving, until a supply unit set up its tents around him. He slaughtered fifteen men and women before being cut down.

There were impossible tales of horror: partisan women pretending lust with sharp steel hidden in their bodies; peasants who, when a soldier's back was turned, changed into wolves or wild oxen.

In revenge, we wreaked horrors on the Maisirians as we went. These weren't legend, however, but too awfully real.

The farmland's end was demarcated by the Anker River. When I'd crossed it, to the west, it had been broad and fairly shallow, with many islets. Here it was deep enough to be navigable, and there was a small port named Irthing. It was about half the size of Penda, and was unburned. I went forward, determined to be with the first elements to enter the town. It seemed deserted, although I could see smoke wisping from chimneys. A messenger came from the emperor saying to be most cautious, for he sensed jeopardy.

I rode with Domina Bikaner, at the head of the Seventeenth Ureyan Lancers, augmented by my Red Lancers. Supporting us was the Twentieth Heavy Cavalry. I planned to strike through the city to the river, take the bridges, which were movable wooden floating structures, and then secure the far shore.

The town was narrow, twisting, cobbled streets with close-leaning buildings and small squares, ideal for ambush—but I didn't plan to be trapped. We rode into the city at the trot, and funneled, in separate columns, through the winding streets. In my column were the Red Lancers, Domina Bikaner and his command group, plus Sambar and Tiger Troops of the Seventeenth.

I wore a breastplate with an armored right sleeve, an open helm, a small circular shield on my left forearm, the dagger Yonge had given me long ago that had saved my life on many occasions, and a plain double-edged straight sword, plus heavy leather boots with knee-pieces. I carried no device, for the only one I wanted was Alegria's—and I had no symbol of hers but memories.

We were about to cross an empty square when smoke boiled from the road as if the cobbles were lying over a fire. Men shouted, horses whinnied, and no one could see his mate, then the smoke vanished. The square's far side was blocked with a thick wooden barricade, and the roofs were alive with men and women. Some had bows and spears; others hurled down paving stones. We were trapped as surely as the Tovieti had trapped and obliterated a troop of the Golden Helms during the rising in Nicias.

I seized the bow that was tied to my saddle, hastily strung it, and pulled a shaft from the quiver behind my left leg. An arrow thudded past me and found a target. I spotted the bowman on the roof, and put my arrow into his chest. Arrows and spears clashed against cobbles or struck home, and men and horses screamed. I sent another Maisirian toppling to his death, and then doors crashed open and men charged out, armed with long knives and bills. A Maisirian would fix his hook in a horseman's clothes, yank him from his mount, and then a knifeman would finish him.

I hung my bow across my cantle and drew my sword. I slashed a reaching bill in half, and with my return stroke took half its owner's skull away. A knifeman ran at me, trying to gut Brigstock; I kicked his face in and my mount trampled him as he fell. Someone shouted "Tribune," I automatically ducked, and an arrow hissed past. A second later another shaft struck someone's armor, bounced free, and fixed itself half an inch deep in my arm. I barely felt the pain; I seized the arrow and pulled it free, ignoring the blood.

More and more Maisirians poured into the square, and I wondered where the hells they were coming from. Then, by purest chance, I saw something. A mislaunched spear flew toward the barricade. But instead of burying itself in the wood, the spear sailed through it. I shouted, "Charge the barricade," an absurd command, but the Lancers, trained to obey any order, kicked their horses forward.

I prepared to slide from Brigstock and attack that obviously magical block, for none of the horses would rush it, but I didn't have to. Like the smoke, the high gate shivered, then was gone, and our way was clear. We went out of the square at a gallop, and I spotted a man on a rooftop, his arms moving as he chanted. I went for my bow, but Curti was quicker and his aim far better, and a long gray arrow grew between the Maisirian wizard's ribs. He shouted agony and reached for it with one hand, but was dead before his fingers touched the feathered shaft.

We entered another larger square, and I shouted for Bikaner to order a halt. "To the rooftops," I shouted. "Kill anyone who's not of us." Doors were bashed down, and archers clattered up the stairs onto the flat roofs. From the heights it was easy to see our enemies, and arrows went out, and partisans—and the occasional magician—fell.

We went back the way we'd come, taking the city building by building. We weren't infantrymen, but my arrogance in wanting to be the first to conquer this pissant little city had forced us to be like them. Guards and other infantry units found us, and then the battle became easier. But it was still house by house, street by street. It wasn't as grim as some city fighting I'd known, but it was bad.

Irthing was ours by nightfall, but the battle had cost the Seventeenth Lancers almost two hundred dead, nearly half of their already-reduced strength. Among them was Manych, another of the brave soldiers who'd gone over the mountains to Jarrah with me. That burned worse than the arrow that had scored my chest.

We didn't tarry in Irthing, and that was a blessing, for the last elements of the army had no sooner crossed the Anker when a storm rose. Wind waves tore at the bridges, and the river rose as if it were heavy with the spring melt. If they'd been laden with our soldiery, the bridges could well have been torn from the banks, and the losses would've been terrible. Maisirian magic was great, but this time it was too slow.

We stopped on the far side of the Anker, in a great meadow, to rebuild and rest, for ahead were the feared Kiot Marshes. I'd just finished sacrificing in Manych's name, praying to Saionji to grant him a good next life, for he'd been a good warrior, when Yonge came with an idea.

I cursed for not seeing what he had, and told Yonge we must take this to the emperor at once. Yonge didn't have a ready speech—he was a fighter, not a diplomat. Nor was he a theoretician like Mercia Petre. But his enthusiasm flamed high as he spoke. He became so aroused that, without permission, he took a glass from a table, poured himself a brandy from the emperor's own decanter, and chased it with another glass.

The emperor should declare all Maisirians free. Free the peasant from his land-slavery to his lord, free the aristocrat from his generations-old debts to his king. Give them the right to become Numantians, to own their own land, to leave the land for the cities if they wished. Let them take up any trade they wished. Tell the women they didn't have to stay in a marriage unless they wanted to. Proclaim that no one had any privilege other than that granted by his new lord, the Emperor Laish Tenedos.

"That'll bring them in," Yonge said. "Then let them join the army. Hells, even levy them in. Bairan does that, so they're used to it and won't object much. That'll help get rid of those gods-damned bandits that are eating our ass alive, and build up our forces as well. We can go after the partisans that're left with their own countrymen, who know their hiding places better than we do.

"I can testify the Maisirians'll fight well for us, for I've been salting them in with my skirmishers, using hunters, trappers, and the like, and I like them well enough, as long as you don't let them knot up, and remember they're being a little traitorous. Seems to me this is an everybody-wins-but-the-Maisirians sort of thing. Sir."

He beamed at the emperor, expecting to be praised to the skies. Instead, Tenedos just stared. He turned to me. "Since you've already heard this proposal, obviously you endorse it."

"Of course, Your Majesty. Yonge didn't mention one advantage I saw. It seems to me if you declared freedom for the peasantry, their army'd melt away. Once we take Jarrah, that'd mean Maisir would be ours in perpetuity. They'd have good reason to remain loyal to you. It wouldn't be one of those always-rebelling states like, well, like Kallio."

"I see." The emperor stood. "Are you two quite mad?"

"I beg your pardon, Highness?"

"I spoke quite clearly. Do you realize what would happen if I were idiot enough to do what you suggest? There would be instant chaos throughout Maisir. No laws, no rules, no one to obey."

"Fine," Yonge said with enthusiasm. "That'll give their army and their king something to occupy their time with besides us."

"Anarchy," Tenedos said again, this time in a hiss like a serpent's. "Once a country falls into chaos, who can say whether it can be brought back? Obviously neither of you realize how closely run the civil war was, with the Tovieti and Chardin Sher behind it. I—we—almost lost everything!

"Now you propose we cast the die again, with the smug hope that everything will somehow come out all right. Do you two happen to remember that the Tovieti are active in Maisir, as well? Don't you think this piece of imbecility would encourage them? And what would it do to certain classes back in Numantia? Don't you think such a proclamation would stir *them* up again? We could well have another rebellion at home, while we're fighting in this terrible country. I have no urge at all to suddenly wear a yellow silk cord around my neck.

"I didn't think either of you were fools. I'm not at all sure of that anymore. Now, leave me. And do not ever mention that idea to anyone again, on pain of facing my wrath and most severe punishment. Go!"

Yonge walked out. I came to attention and saluted before leaving. The emperor didn't return it.

Yonge waited outside the tent. I expected him to be blind with rage, knowing his hillman's temper. I was more than slightly angry myself. But Yonge was pale with what could only be fear, and I'd thought that emotion completely unknown to the Kaiti.

"What's the matter?"

"Not here. Come."

He led me to a spot on a low knoll, away from the camp, where the only men we could see were two sentries on their rounds several dozen yards distant.

"I'm sorry for what the emperor said," I began. "He was wrong. I still think your plan is—"

Yonge waved his hand. "Forget about my idea. The emperor will one day learn that a man who readily calls another a fool is generally staring into his own pier glass. Numantian, we are in desperate trouble."

"I don't understand," I said.

"I'm no sorcerer or priest," Yonge said. "But let me ask you something: The emperor has said, often, that he serves Saionji, has he not? Goddess of chaos, correct?"

"Chaos, war, the Wheel, rebirth."

"But mostly death and destruction, eh?"

"Yes," I said.

"He's said that it's necessary to destroy before you can rebuild, hasn't he?"

I nodded.

"I think it's pretty obvious he's served his goddess well. Now he's told us he fears chaos, did he not? What do you think Saionji is thinking, if she exists, if she heard those words? What does she think of her finest servant now, eh?"

I never claimed to be much of a believer, nor a student of theology, but a sudden chill of fear struck me and, involuntarily, I glanced up at the dark, distant heavens.

"Curse chaos, curse the goddess," Yonge said. "I think we just heard Saionji's servant declare his own freedom, declare he's no longer her vassal, without ever realizing what he said. Don't you think she'll seek revenge, revenge as great as her rewards were?"

"Come on, Yonge," I tried. "The gods are distant, and seldom hear the stupidities of man."

"Perhaps," Yonge said. "Or perhaps we just heard our doom being prophesied."

"That's enough," I said, a bit testily. "Besides, what is there to do about it?"

"If I'm right, only three things. One I will not speak of, for I am not prepared to offer violence to a man I swore an oath to. Not yet, anyway. The other is to leave the service of this madman who thinks he can dictate to the gods."

"Nice choices," I said, trying not to show shock at how casually Yonge could talk of royal assassination. "And the third?"

"You can come watch me get drunk, Cimabuean. Drunk and dangerous. And if you were anything but the fool the emperor has named you, after what we've heard, you'd be the first to empty the bottle."

When I woke the next morning, it was if I'd not slept at all, for Yonge's words had made me remember what that magician who'd called himself the Speaker had said, long ago as we left his village with the colossal temple, high in the mountains between Numantia and Maisir: *The god you think you serve, you do not serve. The goddess you fear is not the one who is your enemy, but your enemy is one who seeks to become more, to become a god, yet, in the end, shall be no more than a demon, for demons are already his true masters.*

I pondered that man's words, trying to put meanings to them: The god I thought I served? Irisu? Isa the War God? But he is no more than a manifestation of Saionji. Was Saionji the goddess I feared that he spoke of? That made sense. So then who was my enemy? King Bairan? Hardly.

There could only be one answer: the emperor himself. I could well believe he sought to become a god. But my enemy? No, that I couldn't believe, in spite of the wrongs he'd done me. And that he served a demon or demons? In spite of Yonge's words, I doubted if he'd forsaken Saionji, or been forsaken by her.

In fact, could it be that he himself was a manifestation of Saionji? Just as Death, with her skull, swords, and pale horse, was a manifestation of the destroyer and creator goddess? Certainly he—and I—had sent enough people to the Wheel for Saionji to remember us well.

But the man I served a direct manifestation of that nightmare? The terrible thought brought me sitting up and completely awake. I shivered and once again reminded myself of my oath.

But as I got off my cot and went to my canvas wash basin, the Speaker's final words still rang: *Serve who you may, serve who you might, you serve but one, and that one will grant you naught.*

We moved into the Kiot Marshes on the last day of the Time of Heat. We could've cut due west and then marched along the traditional trading route to Jarrah, but we would've faced more *suebi*, and Tenedos was very aware of the corrosive effect the desolation had on our soldiers.

The emperor had used magic to discover where the marshes narrowed above Irthing. It would take no more than a week to reach the forests that bordered Jarrah, and the city was another week's march away, according to our rather unreliable maps. Finally, the emperor reasoned that since the marshes were as ominous to the Maisirians, we would be on equal ground there. After the army splashed into the mire, several people wondered, What ground?

There were roads—not much more than paths through the wasteland—but not many. Most were animal-made, but the better ones we thought had been made by the marsh people. Prisoners had told us the same thing Shamb Philaret had said: Those who lived in the Kiot never acknowledged King Bairan. So we hoped there'd be less trouble with partisans.

The emperor issued orders that the people of the marshes were to be treated as prospective allies, not looted or molested. This got a wry smile from Yonge and laughter from most of the other officers, who couldn't imagine a Numantian soldier confronted with a fat pullet or its mistress and merely smiling and touching his helmet. But the marsh people were, in fact, left mostly alone after the first time we encountered one of their villages.

I was riding behind the forward cavalry screen when our advance stopped. I went ahead with the Red Lancers to investigate. I found half a regiment of horsemen, with a milling crowd of Guardsmen behind, and a wide fen. In its center was an unwalled village of two dozen long thatch-roofed huts—each two-storied—with a roofed, raised platform in the middle. I saw a scattering of pigs and chickens rooting about, but no humans. "What's the problem?" I asked the domina in charge of the cavalry. I noticed that he, and five or more of his men, were soaking wet, even though the day was dry, if overcast and gray. "What's holding up the advance?"

"We came on this village, and started to ride into it," the domina explained a bit sheepishly. "None of my scouts could find a path, so we rode directly forward."

"And started sinking," I added. "I assume no one drowned."

"No, sir. But we were well and truly stuck. Had to be dragged out with ropes, sir. I sent other scouts to find the path into the village, so we could, er, negotiate for supplies."

"I see." I wondered if we should skirt the village, but curiosity suggested otherwise. Besides, I rationalized, it would be well for me to know these people, since we'd be encountering others like them.

A figure came out of one hut. He was not tall, but very very heavy, waddling as he came. He carried a carved wand under one arm, had a dagger sheathed at his belt, and wore a loincloth and what looked like the remains of a Maisirian officer's tunic. Atop that he had on some strange sort of armor that, the closer he got, looked more and more like the tanned and sewn-together scales of some enormous snake or crocodile. I wondered if he was drunk, for he went hither and thither across the swampland, from one grassy hummock to another, then, sometimes, walking across open water.

He stopped when he was two long spear-casts distant, and stared for a very long time. Finally he cupped his hands and shouted in accented Maisirian: "Go away."

I dismounted and walked to the edge of the swamp, and shouted back that we were not Maisirians, but their enemies, and wished to speak of peace, since we had heard that the people of the marsh had no use for Maisirians, and the enemy of our enemy was our friend.

The response came back: "Go away."

"That is impossible."

The fat man stared for a while longer, then, without saying more, walked back to his hut, using the same erratic path as before. He disappeared into his hut, and further shouts brought no other signs of life.

"Yes, sir?" the domina asked. He was keeping his lips quite firm, but I heard buried laughter from the ranks.

I thought I had the situation in hand. "The reason he thinks he's safe," I said, "is that the way to his village is under water. It zigs and zags and unless you're familiar with the path, you'll go over your head."

"Yes, sir?"

"I was watching where he put his feet," I said. "Put men out on line. Swimmers all. Have other men behind them with ropes. Walk forward until you find the beginnings of the path. Once we find that, I'll lead us into the village, and we'll see what song he wishes to sing."

"Yes, sir."

And so it was done and, after a very wet, very muddy hour, the beginnings of the path were found. Men paced ahead carefully, probing with saplings, and it was as I said—there was a path just under the water, graveled and wide enough for four men to walk abreast. We put stakes on either side of the path so we wouldn't lose it, and eventually it wound to where the man had stood.

"Very well," I said. "Svalbard . . . Curti . . . Domina, give me half a dozen other men. Behind me." I splashed forward, with perhaps five hundred or so soldiers watching. I felt a bit foolish, but remembered that a leader had to be willing to wade in the shit as well as ride in the parades. Without mishap we made it to where the track ended.

"Very good," I said, feeling confident. "Now, he was standing here, and when he left, he went . . ."

And four paces forward I went into water well over my head. I surfaced, spluttering, and Svalbard hauled me back to the path. There was real laughter from the bank.

"Let me try, sir," and the big man waded out in a different direction and promptly stuck himself in quicksand. It took Curti and another soldier to drag him free. After that, I was willing to be a little less a leader, and let others probe for the path. Another hour, and we still hadn't found it.

I saw a galloper back at the bank, and the domina waving, and knew the messenger was from the emperor, who was wondering what the hells was holding up the advance. Very well, I decided. These marsh people could have their gods-damned swamp and piss on 'em. I went back to shore and ordered the march to continue, avoiding the village.

As we moved away, I swear I could hear laughter echoing across the dismal waters from the village.

The Time of Rains began, and travel was as it had been a year ago—a good day was when it only drizzled, and a bad one when you couldn't see your squad leader through the downpour. The rivers and creeks rose, and the way was always muddy.

One night, the army was waiting for our pioneers to throw bridges across a swollen river, when a galloper found me and said the emperor wondered if I cared to dine with him at the headquarters of Tribune Aguin Guil. I said I'd be more than delighted and, as dusk rose, rode back to Guil's headquarters.

He had pitched a huge pavilion that must've taken half a dozen carts to carry, and great fires roared around it. Magic must have dried the wood, for I hadn't been able to build more than a smoldering smudge pot for four days, and had had no hot food for the same time. I licked my lips, smelling wonderful odors—of roast beef, freshly baked bread, and spices. Quite suddenly fatigue slammed me, and I felt like what I was—a very wet, very hungry soldier, not a little discouraged and feeling near the end of his rope.

I saw servants wearing fresh, clean, dry uniforms, laying out plates on linen-clad tables, and the plates winked gold reflections of the crystal lamps hanging above the comfortable chairs. I heard laughter, some of it women's, and the clinking of glasses, and I saw the emperor's carriage drawn up outside.

I reined Brigstock in and slid from the saddle. A man came up and saluted. He wore a legate's sash. When tribunes entertain emperors, horsemen or even lances are too low-ranking to be horse holders.

"Tribune á Cimabue. The emperor is delighted you were able to make an appearance."

"Not nearly as delighted as I am," I said, and started toward the pavilion. I turned back to the legate, to ask if it was possible to find some grain for Brigstock, and saw, just at the fringes of the firelight, twenty or so men. They were all footsoldiers, none with a higher rank than private or axman, and all were wet, ragged, and dirty. Their beards and hair looked as if they'd been plucked from scarecrows. None of the men appeared to have eaten for a day or more. All that was clean about them was their swords and spears.

I knew all of them, for these were the men who'd followed me from the terrible retreat at Sayana through the ghastliness of the Tovieti suppression and the Kallian campaign. After that they'd been with me in a hundred nameless skirmishes and confrontations on our borders. They were slovenly, crude, mostly uneducated. They smelled and swore and couldn't be trusted around taverns or bordellos.

But they'd always been there, and when I'd ordered them forward they'd cursed me for a murdering son of a bitch—and gone. Men from their ranks died as often as not, sometimes screaming, sometimes quietly, sometimes with a rough jest on their lips.

Now they stared at that golden pavilion, faces quite blank.

I walked back to the legate.

"Sir?" His expression was a little fearful, as if the first tribune had found him doing something wrong.

"Those men there?"

"Yessir?"

"Were they there when the emperor arrived?"

"I don't know, sir. I suppose so."

"Did he see them?"

"I couldn't say, sir."

He glanced over at the ragged warriors. "Is there something wrong, sir? Should I order them away?"

"No. But you might be good enough to tell the emperor I was called away on urgent business. Be sure and extend my apologies."

I no longer felt the rain, or my creaking bones. I remounted, and rode back forward, and spent the rest of the night with the pioneers, up to my chest in icy currents, lashing together crudely cut logs.

At dawn, someone gave me a cup of barely warm tea and a scrap of bread, and I found it a banquet. I mounted Brigstock and rode across the creaking bridge, shouting for the army to move out.

The marshes never stopped; they just slowly grew shallower and dryer, and there were more hummocks and trees growing from solid ground. Now we were in the Belaya Forest, and a vast feeling of relief ran through the ranks that the worst was over. At last we could see, through the light rain—actually more of a mist—the ground rise toward a series of rolling almost-foothills. The army was marching toward them on a series of tiny peninsulas that wound together. To our left and right—west and east—was the last of the swamp. We quickened our pace, wanting dry feet, dry fodder, and the chance to build a fire on the rising ground ahead.

Our last elements were clearing the fingers when the Maisirian army attacked from the marsh.

Their magicians laid spells of confusion, of indifference, of a kind of invisibility, so no one would trouble about what lay to the west, believing, without ever investigating, that there was nothing but mud and dankness. There the Maisirians had concealed themselves and waited.

They charged without even a signal and surged out of the swamp, ululating battle cries as they came.

They should've left us room for panicked flight. If the ground to the right had been forest or *suebi*, the troops might have broken. But with swamp on all sides except the front, there was nowhere to run.

The Maisirians still hadn't learned that our army marched with fighting men scattered throughout the column, so they weren't hitting just support units. After they'd butchered the stragglers and hangers-on, they slammed into corps led by Mercia Petre and Myrus Le Balafre.

These two reacted instantly, calmly if loudly, ordering all elements to turn left and prepare for the attack. Their officers and warrants bellowed terrible punishments for anyone who didn't kill his Maisirian or six, and Saionji herself help the one who hesitated or dreamed of flight. The truth of the training was there: Make a soldier more afraid of his leaders than the enemy, and he'll fight hard and long.

There was also a rage, long-buried, simmering, that the Maisirians wouldn't stand and fight, but keep on with their endless back-stabbing. Now they were before us in the open, and we wanted blood.

The column turned on its left flank and went on line. Supply and other "soft" units were shouted to the right, to the new rear. I won't pretend all this happened smoothly, or even happened in all columns. But there were enough soldiers who'd dropped their packs and had swords ready, and enough archers who'd grabbed a handful of shafts from quivers and sent them arcing toward the enemy, to stop the Maisirian first wave.

Before the second wave could attack through the hesitating first, other soldiers seized the stakes carried below our wagons for the bivouac stockades, and rammed them into the soft ground, angled toward the enemy. Then the second wave slammed into our lines.

I was well forward with the Twentieth Heavy Cavalry, the emperor's carriage not far behind me, when a rider galloped up—although I'd already guessed what must be happening from the din.

Officers were shouting orders, and men were shrugging off packs and knocking bedrolls off their horses, lances and swords coming into their hands.

I slid from the mare I'd been riding, to mount the already-saddled Brigstock. I kicked him into a gallop, back to the emperor's carriage. Tenedos had his wagons drawn into a circle, his bodyguard dismounted and ringing the site. He was ordering robed Brethren about, and the area was a scurry of staff officers and acolytes. An acolyte was sprinkling colored powder on the wet grass in arcane patterns, since there was no other way to mark the meadowland, and braziers were being lit. Magicians were ordering herbs mixed and dumped into the braziers, and unrolling bundles and sorting through their contents.

"Damastes, take charge of the cavalry," the emperor ordered. His voice was completely calm. "Take 'em out and try to hit these bastards on their flank. I'm going to bother them a bit myself. I've already sent reinforcements back down the line to Le Balafre and Petre."

I saluted, and rode Brigstock back to the Twentieth. My gallopers and the Red Lancers were waiting. I sent quick commands to the dominas commanding the screen on the army's former front: We'd march out to the right, then swing back to the fighting. After we turned, we'd go on line and take them. At the walk, we moved out.

I felt a sort of shimmering, a crawl and shiver on my muscles and nerves. Magic was about. The emperor's spell was being cast. I was on the fringes, and saw trees and vines twist and lean, and felt malevolence, until we were "recognized" as friendly. This was the spell Tenedos had cast against Chardin Sher's army, in the forest around the village of Dabormida. I'd thanked Tanis back then that I hadn't witnessed such an evil. But now I would. The trees would come alive and reach for their foes. Branches would strangle, trees would fall and crush, roots would rise to trip and tear. Men would go mad in this horror, seeing things that must not be, and run screaming, to be crushed by another terror or cut down by the oncoming soldiers.

The trees were moving, coming alive, as if a gale were twisting them, but there was no wind and the rain fell straight from the sky. Men turned, looked at me, and their faces were white, afraid. I pretended laughter and shouted something about the emperor's magic striking hard, and they forced courage. Then the crawling sensation was gone, and all was normal. I didn't know what had happened, but logic said the Maisirian wizards had broken Tenedos's spell.

Now it would be their turn, unless the emperor could rebuild his power quickly. He wasn't quite fast enough, and red splashes flickered through the rain. It was as if fireflies were attacking, or perhaps those tiny redbirds that flocked through Cimabue's jungles in the Time of Births. Then they were on us, and they weren't anything sensate or friendly, but bits of pure flame, straight from Shahriya's realm, unquenched by rain, drawing close. They found, clung, and flared, and screams began.

One touched my forearm, and a fiery brand seared. The flame grew bigger, feeding on me, on my energy, and my mind reeled in agony and fear, remembering that greater fire I'd flung myself into not long ago. My other hand scrabbled at my waist, and Yonge's dagger was in it. I scraped frantically, and the flame fell away, and the pain was gone, though my sleeve was scorched through. At first I thought it was the silver of the knife's pommel and hilt, but then I realized I'd touched the flame with bare steel.

Other men made the same discovery, and scraped swords, knives, even arrowheads across the tiny killers, and they vanished. But there were those who hadn't been quick enough, or who panicked. Their bodies became flame, and they fell, writhing, and were dead. Horses reared, neighing in terror and pain as they burned. The formations nearly broke, and then the flames were gone, as if the rain instead of a counterspell had quenched them.

The emperor sent an order down the line for Le Balafre and Petre to attack. But those two hadn't needed orders, knowing as they did that the best counterattack is immediate, and the best way to break an ambush is straight into it. The two tribunes were the first to charge, swords high, beside their banners. Our men shouted loud for Numantia, and attacked.

They cut down the second wave and the remnants of the first wave, and moved on, lines wavering, then firming, rain washing blood from their spears and swords as they rolled inexorably toward the Maisirian lines.

Now it was time for me to put my cavalry on line, strike for the Maisirian left flank, and rip them apart. Except that . . .

I make no claims to having the slightest ability in magic or any sense beyond a normal man's. So perhaps I heard something, far distant. Or possibly there might've been the gleam of armor, or a flag, or even a fire.

But I found myself staring to my right, away from the Maisirian lines, toward that tempting, rolling high ground we'd been hurrying for. A fine place to camp. Or mount an attack from, using the slope to add weight to the charge. And I'd seen no Maisirian cavalry other than outriders . . .

I called for my gallopers and snapped orders. Some goggled, and I shouted "Yes, yes," and said "Now, ride out, damn your eyes" and they obeyed. Tribune Safdur, nominally in charge of the cavalry, gaped, but said nothing. I sent two of my staff officers back to the army, one to tell the emperor of my stupidity and disobedience, the other asking Linerges, commanding the corps just behind mine, to attack with us.

Slowly the great mass of the Numantian cavalry swung right, away from the Maisirian attack, toward the high ground, as stupid a thing as I've ever done, and so I signaled for the trot. Bugles rang, and the monstrous mailed fist reached out. I kicked Brigstock to the gallop, and we swept through the flankers until we were at the cavalry's head, my Red Lancers close behind.

Men and horses one tempered weapon, we hurtled up the gentle slope, over its crest, into the Maisirian cavalry. They were drawn up, waiting to make their surprise attack as we smashed into their flank as a lance rips into a soldier's unarmored side. They tried to turn, but were too slow, and we shattered them as a hammer smashes crystal.

A man swung a morningstar, and I let the weapon's chain wrap around my lance, then yanked it from his grip. He flailed, not knowing what to do next, and Curti killed him. I threw the now-useless lance into another Maisirian's face, and let Svalbard finish him. I had my sword in one hand, Yonge's long dagger in the other, as I parried a sword stroke, swung at my attacker, missed, and he vanished into the fray.

A spear darted toward my face. I flinched away, and the spearman grew an arrow from his eye and went down. A riderless horse pawed at Brigstock, and he screamed and smashed the animal with an iron shoe, as I gutted a man running at me swinging a sword over his head. There were two men attacking me, getting in each other's way, swearing at each other, and I put my blade in one's stomach and let him roll back, screaming, into his fellow, then slashed that man's thigh open and he lost interest in me.

The battle went on . . . and on . . . and we broke their lines, re-formed, came back, and again butchered our way through their ranks. I looked for banners that might mark King Bairan or, better yet, the *azaz*, hoping to find an easy way to end this battle, this war, letting red anger touch me, but I saw nothing.

I saw fifty men on identical white stallions, all wearing black, with a yellow banner at their head. At their head was an armored man with an open helm. I recognized him, Rauri Rewald, commander of their cavalry, whom I'd met in Jarrah, and he knew me at the same instant, and we cried orders that were the same:

"Take that man!"

"Kill him!"

My Red Lancers and his bodyguard surged together, and all was demoniac madness. A man slashed at my leg, and I felt a bit of pain, saw a bit of blood as I slashed and his sword—and arm—went spinning into the air, and then I forgot about him.

Another Maisirian reeled from some unseen blow, and I smashed my blade into his helmet and sent him tumbling. I may have killed another man, perhaps two, maybe three, but I don't remember precisely.

I do remember the sudden open space in this roiling slaughter, with no one in it but Rewald on his prancing white horse and myself. Rewald's two-handed sword struck, and I knocked it away, and then chanced a thrust that clanged harmlessly against his breastplate. He swung with all his might, and my arm went numb as I took his power on my shield.

He opened his mouth to shout something, no doubt a great challenge to ring down the years, and I had no reply but a darting thrust that took him in the face and went up into his brain, through his skull, sent his helmet spinning away. His eyes gaped, then he fell away, off my blade, and I heard a great wailing.

But his men didn't stop fighting. The swirl of their death went on, and on, and then there were blood-drenched horses pawing in death, and piled, black-armored bodies moaning as they tried to deny Saionji's summons. But all too many of my Lancers were down as well. I gasped for air, not remembering having breathed for hours, days, and saw, across the bloody field, weapons being flung down, riders galloping away, men holding their hands up in surrender, and I realized we'd taken the field.

Then the emperor's final spell was sent against the Maisirians in the swamps. No Numantian knew what to make of it for an instant, but the Maisirians appeared to have gone mad, suddenly swinging at nothing, clawing at their eyes, screaming in pain, having no mind for war—and then our soldiers cut into them.

The spell was simple, nothing more than deerflies. Of a sort. Deerflies that were invisible, whose bites burned like the Maisirian fire, whose searing agony shattered a fighter's thoughts—and let his attacker end the contest. The magic lasted for brief seconds, but that was enough. The wavering Maisirian line broke, and soldiers in their thousands were surrendering or fleeing.

We'd finally met the Maisirian army, and shattered it. But there was no formal surrender. Nothing came from King Bairan, nothing from the *jedaz*, the leaders of his army. The remains of the Maisirian army fled north once more.

But the emperor was content. "We have them," he said. "Their king can't allow this war to continue. Not after this." Then he said something strange. "And the price has been met. Now the power is on my side. Now the way is open to Jarrah."

But the cost was terrible. Almost thirty thousand of our finest—infantry, cavalry, skirmishers—were dead, dying, or desperately injured on this nameless field. Our sorcerers and chirurgeons did what they could to help the wounded, but all too often there was nothing but a moment's prayer and finding a bit of cloth to lay across newly empty eyes. Among the dead were Mercia Petre and his aide, Phillack Herton, who I truly hope had been more than just a companion and servant, had given my friend love.

That night, we built pyres and sacrificed.

I watched the fires rage and remembered Mercia, that unemotional, dry, sometimes slovenly man, whose only life was the army.

There was a man beside me, and I saw that it was Le Balafre. His leg was bandaged, and he had his arm in a sling. He stared long at Petre's flaming memorial, then said, so quietly I barely heard his words:

"It was a good death. Our kind of death." Then he walked away, into darkness.

The way was open to Jarrah.

TWENTY-FOUR

THE EMPTY CITY

Once again I looked down at Jarrah's sprawl, and this time my skin crept. It's one thing to see a small town like Irthing abandoned; it's quite another to see a metropolis like Jarrah in a misting rain with never a horse or man about, not a chimney puffing smoke or any sound but the wind whistling down empty avenues.

We'd made the march to Jarrah in barely six days, and our scouts and skirmishers had entered the city's outskirts on the morning of the seventh. They found nothing, and had the good sense to take defensive positions and send word to the emperor. He'd gone forward with an entire corps for his bodyguard, and taken the Chare Brethren with him. They laid spell after spell to see if Jarrah had been turned into one great sorcerous trap, but they discovered nothing.

I tried to imagine a people so obedient they'd march into the wilderness at their king's orders, and thought of how many helpless people were doomed to return to the Wheel in those harsh forests to the south. What was Bairan's plan? What did he intend? Had he gone insane?

The emperor ordered the army to set up camp outside the city. He wanted Jarrah intact, not as a looted ruin. The disappointed grumbles from the army were muted, since no one knew what snares had been laid.

Two regiments of cavalry were to reconnoiter the city, and I'd "suggested" to Safdur that it be the Seventeenth and the Twentieth, my favorites among the elite formations, and said I'd lead them.

The sound of our horses' hooves was very loud on the cobbles as we entered the city. This time, I did it by the book, posting squads at each crossroads, never committing my forces until an area was cleared. My goal was Moriton and Bairan's palace. Halfway through the city I ran short of men and sent for two infantry regiments to replace my vedettes, then continued my leapfrogging advance.

We found a few Maisirians, mostly ancients or those who were beyond anyone's law. They scuttled for hiding places, and we made no move to stop them.

The gates of Moriton were barred. We cast grapnels over them, and half a dozen volunteers went up the ropes. Minutes later, the gates swung open. We rode past the Octagon, and the gates yawned. With three men I went inside. The cells were empty. I saw a body, impaled on one of the tall glass spikes of the inner wall. It was the skull-smiling Chief Warder, Shikao. That was a puzzle—certainly King Bairan's soldiers wouldn't have permitted that. So what *did* happen to the prisoners? Where were they?

We went up the many-colored drive to King Bairan's palace. I went in, saw my breath fogging in the empty, unheated corridors and audience chambers, and heard my boots clatter in the emptiness.

I made one further incursion, to the end of Moriton, where the walls brooded against the Belaya Forest, to the dark castle of the *azaz*. We saw no one, and its gates were sealed. We didn't enter. The *azaz* would certainly have left wards against visitors.

We made our report to the emperor.

Tenedos exploded. "How dare this barbaric bastard call himself a king? And these damned people who're his subjects—fucking idiot peasants! What are they doing? Are they too gods-damned dumb to realize they've lost? Where the hells is Bairan's peace delegation? Where the hells are the white flags?"

I was far too wise to voice my thoughts: Suppose King Bairan and the Maisirians don't think they're beat at all? Suppose Jarrah doesn't matter to them, any more than the rest of Maisir they've given up? There're still thousands of leagues to the south, north, and west where no one has ever heard of Numantians. For them, has the war barely begun? Are they still confident, thinking it can still be won?

That brought a chill, for anyone who could believe that, with their capital and hundreds of leagues of their country in enemy hands, and never a battle won, was as alien as any wizard-summoned demon.

"Not that it matters," Tenedos said, forcing a lighter tone. "I— We have his capital, which means we hold Maisir. We'll invest the city tomorrow, at first light."

I wondered what sort of triumph that would be, but smiled, agreed, saluted, and asked to be dismissed. I should've busied myself preparing for the morrow, which units should march where and so forth. But I had a staff, and so I let my heart decide, something I perhaps should have done more often. I told Svalbard to find Captain Balkh and have the Lancers ready to ride in ten minutes.

I set forth on my fool's errand, knowing how hopeless was my dream. We rode quickly through Jarrah to the southern outskirts, then continued on into the country. It was late, getting on toward nightfall, and the misting rain grew heavier.

There was a tiny village ahead, and Svalbard pulled his horse beside mine. "Beggin' your pardon, sir. But would y' do me the favor of lookin' in my eyes?" I was astounded, especially that this came from a closemouthed old soldier like Svalbard, but I obeyed.

"Right," he muttered. "I guess you're not bewitched. Though how I'd know for sure's beyond me . . ." He let his horse trail back into formation. My worries vanished, my dark mood ended, and I roared laughter. This no doubt made my Red Lancers even more unsettled.

The village was not only abandoned, but had been looted and burned to the ground as well. We rode through into deep country, then rounded a bend, and the bluff with the gloom-ridden castle of the Dalriada reared above us.

I saw movement at the castle's base, and we went up the curving road at the trot, weapons ready. There were sixteen men a bowshot beyond the gate, men dressed in everything from tattered Numantian uniform to woodsmen's motley to a couple in Maisirian tunics. My archers had bows drawn and arrows nocked, when one man ran toward me, waving his arms wildly. "Wait," he shouted. "Don't shoot. We're your'n's. We're Yonge's men."

Their leader managed what I'm sure he thought was a very military salute. "Scout-Major Lanbay," he said. "With Third Hun'erd, Yonge's skirmishers."

"What the hells are you doing this far from the army?"

Lanbay shifted and looked extraordinarily uncomfortable. "Uh . . . we was, well, sort of trying to see what'd happened to . . . to things."

One of my men snickered.

"You mean you were looting?"

"Nossir." Lanbay searched his inventory of expressions, couldn't find one for injured innocence, and settled for rounding his eyes, which made him look like a village imbecile. "Wouldn't dream of doing something like that. Sir. Hangin' offense, isn't it?"

There was more than one laugh.

"Set that aside, Scout-Major, but be advised you're a truly shitty liar," I said. "Now, what were you doing out here at Dalriada? Try the truth. It might not poison you."

Lanbay took a deep breath, examined my expression, remembered I'd hanged more than a few Numantian soldiers for crimes of war, and decided to do what I'd suggested. "We was afraid of bein' in the city, sir. Didn't know what magics c'd be waitin'. Thought we'd find somethin' beyond Jarrah, then mebbe work back toward our lines."

His men came up beside him, relieved that I evidently wasn't going to hang them in the next minute or so. "Thought we might find somethin' in that village back yon," one of his men volunteered. "But it'd already been combed through an' torched. We spied this castle. Castle's allus got things worth takin'. But it's defended."

"Irisu on a rope," I near-shouted, and I looked for cover as I saw a line of helmeted, grim-visaged men at the battlements. I was aghast at my, and my men's, unbelievable carelessness. My Lancers scrabbled for cover, archers fumbling arrows to bowstrings.

"Don't fret, sir. They ain't attackin'. Guess there maybe ain't enough of 'em to muster a good defense, an' they're waitin' to see what we're doin', eh?"

I stared up, and realized there was something wrong. One face then another somehow touched a chord in my mind. I searched for the memory, then heard the creak of machinery, and the gates slowly swung up. A slender figure wearing a soldier's greatcoat came out.

A woman. She came toward us, and I recognized her, and I was out of the saddle and we were both running, tears pouring from my eyes and I quite unashamed. I caught Alegria in my arms and held her for a disbelieving eternity. I guess we kissed, I don't remember, for my heart was too full, is too full now at the recollection.

"How . . ." I managed to gasp.

Alegria, too, was crying. She managed a smile. "Aren't I supposed to say I knew you would come to me?"

I pulled her close again, my mind stammering thanks to Irisu, Isa, Vachan, Tanis, even Saionji—gods I knew, gods unknown—for this.

"Would you, and your men, care to enter my castle?" Alegria said.

I tried to shout an order, but found my throat was clogged. "We'll go inside," I finally said, sounding less like my army's first tribune than like a mewling adolescent. Then I recollected. "Warn your guards, please."

"My guards need no warning," Alegria said. "They know my every thought." She giggled.

Heedless of my men, of anything except wanting, needing, to be alone with my love in a room with an enormous bed, I numbly walked through the gates.

"My men, sir," she said with a curtsy. "Perhaps you remember them for being known for . . . other duties." I looked up at the battlements, and snorted in shock. All of the guards I saw were dressed for battle, wearing helmets and mailed shirts. Spears were propped beside them. But all were naked from the waist down, and none turned from their watchfulness to stare curiously at us. Even more oddly, all had cocks of various sizes, each very erect.

Then I remembered where I'd seen them—when I'd peered through a door that shouldn't have been open, and saw them lying on cots, cocks sticking straight up, waiting for the next group of students. Then I remembered what Alegria said the Dalriada called them: hobby horses.

"The king's soldiers came," Alegria said, "and said we'd all have to leave, leave Jarrah, for the evil northerners were coming, and we must not be present for their savageries. All was a scurry and a frenzy, and in it, I hid in a place I knew no one would find me. For I knew you'd be with the savages, and I had nothing to fear.

"But I realized it might be some time before you'd come, and didn't want to . . . become acquainted with any Numantian soldiers who might not listen to my story. The guards, of course, marched off with the Dalriada. But the hobby horses were still here, and since they were perpetually boasting of their manhood, I thought I'd give them a chance to prove themselves. I found weapons and armor in one of the magazines, and used kohl to give some beards and mustaches, since the artisans that built them gave them all the same face. I'd say my men did quite well for themselves, wouldn't you?"

But my ears were barely listening. "Alegria," I said hoarsely, my mind swirling. "I need you. Gods but I need you. Now!"

"You order me, sir," she said demurely.

"If I'd known you were planning to come *that* quickly, I would've loved you with my mouth," Alegria said. "And I didn't know any man could have that much in him."

"That and more," I said. "For I've been with no one since you."

"I note you're still as hard as any of my men on the battlements, sir, so there's no loss." Alegria's light voice changed, grew throaty. "Now, come love me again, for gods but I love you."

Our clothes scattered about us, we lay on a throw rug in front of a fire flickering into life. Still inside her, I picked her up by the waist. She wrapped her long legs about my hips, and I carried her toward the small bed. I saw something better—a long, knee-high padded bench to one side of the tapestry-hung room—and laid her down on it, her hips just at the end.

"You came out," she said, in disappointment. "And I'm leaking you."

"Not for long," I said, going to my knees and sliding my cock back into wetness. I moved in and out steadily, almost coming out of her at each stroke, and she moaned and moved her legs up and down along mine.

Her gasps grew louder, and she called words, obscenities, my name. Her legs lifted to my shoulders, and I held them tightly, deep inside her, moving her thighs around and about as she screamed in release.

"Would it not be wonderful," she said dreamily, "if this night gives me your child?"

Her words brought me back to reality for an instant. "Do you want that?"

"Certainly," she said. "I've become utterly shameless, Damastes, and anything I can devise to bond me more closely to you . . . well, that I'll do."

"You need do nothing more than what you've already done," I said truthfully. "For I'm yours, for as long as you wish."

"How long is forever?" she whispered.

Sometime before dawn, sanity returned, and I realized I'd had no concern for my men, or for anyone's safety. Muttering about my stupidity, I got out of bed without waking Alegria, dragged a cloak over my shoulders, and went to a window, fearing what I might see. There was a Red Lancer pacing the nearest battlement, and down below in the courtyard, a pair of guards were walking their rounds.

No, they hadn't needed me, and had granted me a few hours' comfort. I knew none would ever say a word about my malfeasance, or about the favor they'd done. I swore these men would have the finest rewards for this fine favor as soon as I was able.

Now I think how hollow, how useless, that vow was, for all I was able to give them was pain, death, and a desolate grave far from their homelands.

A second bit of coherence reminded me that the emperor was entering Jarrah in a few hours, and if his first tribune wasn't present, there'd be words said. I prodded Alegria awake, and we dressed. She already had her few possessions ready. She smiled shyly and showed me the kitten pin I'd gotten her so long ago.

Then, Alegria behind me, we rode back to Jarrah at a hard gallop.

The Grand Army of Numantia's entrance into Jarrah was less a triumph than a dirge. Long lines of shabby men strode through the dripping rain, and there were none to cheer on the sidewalks. Half of our cavalry was dismounted now, and our wagons were motley and paint-worn. Our bands' finery was tired and bedraggled, and too many musicians had died or gone sick, so the music was thin and shrill as it echoed against the dark-eyed buildings.

But our heads were high, and our boots crashed against the pavement in ominous rhythm. Battered we may have been, but we were still ready to fight.

But where was the enemy?

Tenedos's lips were pursed, and his face flushed. "Not a candle to Numantia," he muttered. "Bah. This city is the best they have? All that it is is big. And where the hells is King Bairan? He ought to be waiting, his colors reversed to present me with this muddy-assed bleak kingdom.

"Very well. If there's little to be gained by taking Jarrah, I'll at least ensure my soldiers have the best. Domina Othman!"

His always-present aide pulled his horse closer. "Sir?"

"Issue the following order, and make sure it's understood:

"Good soldiers of Numantia, you have bled and died for long. But your sacrifice has not been in vain. I grant you the city of Jarrah. In time, it shall be renamed, a name I'll select to reflect your glory. Now billet yourselves in its finest mansions, and rebuild your bodies with the good meat and wine your quartermasters will secure.

"But you are forbidden to loot, on pain of death. Jarrah is to remain as fair as it is today. Guard Jarrah well, for it is yours, and it shall reflect the glory of the Numantian Army for as long as it stands.

"That's not bad, now is it?" Tenedos said. "And, Othman, I want every commander who receives my order to realize I mean every word. I'll hang any man, be he private, warrant, officer, or general, who breaks my commandment."

And so the army invested Jarrah. Every officer had a mansion, and almost every man his own house. Streets were given new names to fit the occasion, and there was Varan Guards Avenue, First Guards Street, and so forth. City squares stabled the units' horses, and their wagons would be parked all askew along the curbs.

Of course there was some looting, but it was fairly circumspect, especially after Tenedos proved he was quite serious and hanged two sergeants and a captain within hours of our sad parade into the city.

We found a few Maisirians, for not everyone had obeyed the order to abandon Jarrah. Mostly they were older people, although there were some who'd thought they could profit from emptiness or from Numantia. Some, generally the women, were proved correct, and were absorbed into the army's camp followers.

Soldiers bathed, and found new apparel, and silk or the softest wool was none too good for the lowliest private. And every man had a hidden pouch or even pack stuffed with real riches—at first silver, then gold, then only the choicest gems. Certain sutlers who knew a bit about stones became very popular and charged hard cash for their opinions.

Riding the streets, or even finding a spot out of the chill wind and rain and watching the army's antics, was well worthwhile. Here a band would be playing from a covered stand in a park, there soldiers were cleaning equipment while the best storyteller held forth. Officers strolled here and there as if we were at peace. But there were few people to be seen not in uniform, and fewer women.

No one seemed to grudge me Alegria, however.

Those were not the only lacks I noted. There were wine, candies, exotic teas, brandies, and jarred morsels of the rarest sort. But there was no fresh meat, or animals on the hoof, to butcher. There was no bread, only dry crackerlike loaves in sealed containers. We set up our mobile bakeries, but then we encountered another problem: There was almost no grain, either for bread or, more importantly, for fodder.

The weather worsened as the Time of Change began and winter drew near.

Tenedos was struck with some sort of inertia, and spent hours in King Bairan's libraries, although what he studied no one knew. I guessed he was waiting for word from King

Bairan, word of a truce, word of a surrender. But nothing came.

I asked his plans, and he said we'd be forced to continue our pursuit of the quick-heeled Maisirians, and to chase them to the farthest sea if necessary. I suggested the army was hardly in the best shape to continue the campaign, particularly with winter coming on. He said I was being deceived by its motley appearance. Warm Maisirian clothes would do as well as Numantian uniforms, even if the ranks did look somewhat mottled. Besides, replacements were reaching us every day.

Tenedos was right, but he hadn't gone to the depots and seen the new men. For every hundred men who crossed the Numantian border into Maisir, fifteen would die at the hands of the bandits or the Negaret. Another eighteen would succumb to sickness. Another twenty-eight would hobble into Jarrah sick or wounded, fit only to further fill up the mansions we'd converted to hospitals.

Word came from our rear of disaster. Bandits, partisans, who'd massed in the Kiot Marshes, crossed the Anker River secretly and attacked the garrison in Irthing. They wiped them out to the last man, and held the city for two days.

Only by great fortune did a newly formed Guard Corps, headed by an experienced general, send scouts forward before entering the city. He attacked, and Irthing was ours once more—but that Guard Corps was forced to become the city's garrison, instead of reinforcing our ranks.

Alegria straddled me on the long dining bench, tongue moving on mine as she ground against me, then gasped as I grabbed her buttocks, yanked her hard to me, and came. She collapsed, head on my shoulder, and her body throbbed around my cock. After a time, she lifted her head. "Am I heavy?"

"Not at all."

"You're just saying that to be polite."

"No. I like the feel of your breasts all squashed like that."

"What a charming way to put it." She sat up, yawning. "I suppose we should think about sleep."

"We should," I agreed. "I've got to get up early, and find out why those gods-damned Guards seem to think the army's bakeries are exclusively for them. And then I've got the court-martial of an idiotic young captain who not only broke all regulations by challenging his domina to a duel, but had the utter bad taste to kill him as well."

We'd been in the middle of a very late supper, no more than a thin soup and biscuit, which should give an idea of how scarce food was becoming, when passion took us.

She went to a window and looked out at the night. We occupied an enormous palace, which had belonged to the Maisirian *rauri*—commander of cavalry—and my occupying it seemed appropriate.

"What comes next?" she said, her mood changing abruptly, something characteristic of many Maisirians.

"I don't know," I said.

"Captain Balkh said something today about our wintering here in Jarrah, then continuing the war in the spring."

"I don't see how that can be," I said. "What will we eat? What will we feed our horses? If we remain here, all that'll happen is we'll grow weaker and weaker."

"You know, Damastes," she said carefully. "Don't misunderstand me for what I'm going to say. I love you, and I'll stay with you as long as you want, do whatever you wish and go anywhere you do. But don't think I'll ever be a Numantian."

I didn't respond.

"I'm still Maisirian," she went on, not turning. "This is still my country and, deep in my heart, I'll still think of King Bairan as my ruler, even though the emperor orders my life now. Don't expect me to be glad at what's happened to my country, even though your coming has changed my whole world, granted me a life I'd never dreamed of."

"I didn't think otherwise," I said, truthfully.

"That doesn't bother you?"

"It's not good to let things bother you that can't be changed, is it?"

She turned to me. "Thank you. I do love you."

"And I do love you." Hand in hand, we went up to the bedroom we'd chosen for that night.

Alegria's declaration of inner fealty hadn't bothered me. But one thing had: What *was* to come next? We couldn't abandon Jarrah and pursue Bairan farther into the wastelands, especially not with the country alive behind us. We couldn't winter here in Jarrah, not unless we found a magical source of foodstuffs. I could see but one option. And I'd have to go to the emperor with it.

"Damastes, are you exhausted?"

"No, sir. Nor am I mad, dispirited, traitorous, or foolish."

"I'll accept all but the last," the emperor said. Surprisingly, he hadn't raged at me. "It's absurd to suggest we've got to retreat when we've done nothing but win battles since we entered Numantia."

"I can see nothing else," I replied. "The army's being drained of its strength every day we're in Jarrah. Sooner or later the Maisirians will recognize that, and then—"

"Then we'll smash them for good," Tenedos said. "Consider this, my friend. How could I go to the army and say we're falling back? How could they continue to hold me in the regard they do? And something else that might not have occurred to you," he went on. "The Numantian Army has never known defeat. Never. Do you realize how few of us even know how to retreat? You . . . me . . . some of those thugs you keep around who were with us when we were driven out of Kait, and that's all. And I don't see any way to rehearse things, either, do you?

"No, no, my friend," he said, grasping my shoulder firmly. "Retreat is not a word that exists for Numantians. Sooner or later King Bairan will come to his senses, and then the war will be over. Leave me to take care of the grand strategy, and you do what you do best—making sure what I order comes to happen."

* * *

So I said, and did, nothing. But as the days grew shorter and the nights colder, the army recognized its peril. Valuables were still traded, but now the most desirable were the most portable, as were imperishable foodstuffs, winter clothes, and heavy footwear. I was part of this black market, using my rank shamelessly. I acquired two sturdy closed carriages abandoned by the Maisirians, and eight horses for each. If we left Jarrah, they'd carry not only Alegria, but the baggage we'd need for a winter march.

I asked Svalbard and Curti if they'd mind new duties. They laughed uproariously and said it was a terrible thing I was asking, but they'd find a way to live with the disgrace. I wanted preserved meats, twice-baked bread, stimulant teas, hard candies for provender, and brandy, and bagged oats for the horses. I further asked my rogues to look for gold curios to be stuffed in a pocket or bottom of a pack, things peasants might think valuable enough to cooperate with the giver for.

I wanted furs and good heavy boots for me and for Alegria and my two men as well. Finally, I told them to prepare four packs that, if we lost the carriages, we could still carry or sling on our horses.

I ordered Captain Balkh to search for the same items for my Red Lancers. If I couldn't help everyone, I would help those closest to me.

Then there was nothing to do but wait. The next step would be taken by the emperor. Or the Maisirians.

Domina Othman sent a messenger, saying that, with the emperor's compliments, I might wish to ride to the Octagon, speak to the person who'd been found there, and possibly provide the emperor with an explanation.

At the prison was a captain I vaguely remembered from the emperor's intelligence staff, and half a dozen Guardsmen. A scouting party had discovered that the prison still had one resident, cowering in a distant cell. He was a bearded man, perhaps thirty, perhaps sixty, quite mad.

"Alone . . . yes . . . now alone," he said, unquestioned, "for I wouldn't go with the others . . . even though the cage was open . . . Knew, I knew it was a trap . . . outside was death . . . my death, and I could be safey-safe as long as I stayed within . . . safe in my womb . . . I crept out, mousey mousey . . . There was bread, there was wine . . . the guards' wine . . . I saw Shaoki's body . . . spat on the bastard . . . He put me to the torture once . . . laughed, laughed . . ."

"Old man," the captain said, "tell this man what you told me."

"Oh no, no no no, for he's too fine, too pretty."

"No he's not. He's a friend of yours."

"A friend?" the loon said skeptically.

"You have my word."

"Word . . . word . . . There weren't any words . . . no one . . . just wonderful silence when they were gone."

"The other prisoners?"

The man nodded.

"Where did they go?"

"Ah . . ." The man's eyes gleamed like a rat's. "Gone out . . . gone below."

"Did they leave the city?"

"Oh no, no, no. They had a task, they were told. They were to wait, then do what they were told."

"Why?"

The man's expression changed, became almost normal.

"Because," he whispered, "they were given a promise. A promise from"—he looked about to make sure he wouldn't be overheard—"from the *azaz*. One task, one job, and they'd be forgiven all. They'd be free men when the king comes back to Jarrah."

"What were they to do?"

"Not yet, not yet, not yet," and the man cackled.

"What *are* they to do?"

"Ah, but that's the secret, and if I give you the secret, then the *azaz* will know, and he will strike at me."

"No, he won't. You're safe now. You're in Numantian hands," I said.

The madman laughed long and hard, as if I'd told him the best jest ever. "No, no, no, no. Not safe, not from him, not ever."

"Tell me what these prisoners are to do. Are they still here in the city? Where are they hiding?" the captain demanded. "Sir," he added, turning to me, "we've had bits and pieces from him, and there's something going on, or about to happen, but he won't tell us. I'd question him with . . . other means, but I don't know if that would be successful."

"No, no, no, no," the man cackled. "Torture doesn't work. It didn't work for the king's bastards, didn't work for the *azaz*'s nail-pullers, won't work for you."

He sounded momentarily sane, and I seized the moment. "Tell us what the captain wants to know, and you'll be free. Free and rich."

"And then dead. Oh no, no, no. But I'll tell you this. They're there. They're here. And you'll see them soon.

"Very, very soon."

The man slumped to the stone floor of the prison, and his eyes gazed far out, far beyond the walls.

I shook my head. "I don't have the slightest idea what he's talking about. Send my apologies to the emperor."

I pulled my greatcoat and helmet on and adjusted my sword belt. The movement caught the prisoner's eyes.

"Oh yes. You'll see them," he said once more. "See them, see them, see them. Soon. Very, very soon."

TWENTY-FIVE

The Doom That Came to Jarrah

I came groggily awake, puzzling why the world was orange, orange flaring red, and it was hard to breathe. Fire! I ran to a window, naked, and opened the sash, heedless of the cold wind.

The fire came from the still-sealed, never-investigated palace of the *azaz*. Flames shot up to touch the bottoms of the lowering storm clouds, and choking smoke boiled toward us.

Alegria was awake, and I told her to dress warmly and for travel, for nothing happens by accident around a magician. I pulled on thick pants and tunic, knee-high boots, and a heavy jacket. I armed myself with my straight sword and, on the other side belt, Yonge's silver-mounted dagger. I took gauntleted gloves and a close-fitting helmet, and ran down the stairs, shouting for the Red Lancers. They were already up, buckling on their weapons as they clattered toward the stables.

The fire was the signal, and throughout Jarrah, men and women scurried out of their hiding places. Each had a bundle of oil-soaked clothes for tinder, and steel and flint. Tiny fires flickered in basements, in stores, in magazines, then built and built. Other fires came from inhuman sources, as a horde of the fire flecks the War Magicians had created spurted into life and caressed old dry wood, baled cloth, brandy-soaked warehouses. Jarrah, mostly wood, embraced the fire like a lover.

The clamor of the spreading flames grew louder, so I had to shout. "Captain Balkh!"

"Sir?"

"Take Svalbard, Curti, two others. Make sure my lady is taken to a place of safety. I'll take command of the Lancers."

"Sir," he said, but his lips were pursed, little liking what he'd been ordered. But I paid no mind.

"The emperor! To the emperor!" Horses, neighing, whinnying in fear, were brought out, and we swung into our saddles and galloped for King Bairan's palace. But the fire had gotten there first, and some of the towers, wood with metal covering, were smoking, and flames flickered.

The halls were madness as courtiers and staff ran here and there, shouting orders and obeying none. I grabbed one oaf and shook him into a measure of calmness.

"The emperor! Where is he?"

"He left his quarters . . . He's in that big study."

I ran for it, Lancers behind me, and crashed into the room. There was fire here—a small, comfortable fire behind a grate. The emperor wore seer's robes and had the huge map tables pushed back. Two acolytes were drawing symbols on the red-purple porphyry floor. Tenedos was quite placid. "Good morning, Damastes. The Maisirians have finally woken up."

"Yes, sir. And you're to leave now. You must get to a place of safety."

"In good time," he said. "If I can't manage to force out this fire spirit that's seized Jarrah."

"Sir?!"

"Be silent, Tribune! I've given you my orders."

So I paced and fumed, trying to stay silent and not disturb the imperial magic. He chanted, muttered, and his attendants and half a dozen Chare Brethren tried spells. But the light through the great windows grew brighter and brighter. "It would seem," the emperor said, still calm, "that the *azaz*'s magic, which I'm guessing is primal, has taken strong root. The fire shall have to burn for a time."

I shouted to Othman to get the imperial carriage ready, the emperor's chests into it, and chivvied Tenedos into dressing. His staff members needed no encouragement, and by the time we ran out of the palace, most had vanished. I half-shoved the emperor into his carriage, and told the driver to take it directly toward the *azaz*'s palace, open the nearby gate in the wall, and get outside the city.

"But . . . there's likely enemy soldiers waitin'."

"Soldiers are maybe—the fire's for certain! Move, man!" Reluctantly, he obeyed, and the carriage lurched away. I sent all my Lancers with the emperor. I wouldn't need to be there to command them if there were Maisirians outside.

I swung into Brigstock's saddle and rode for the nearest Guard Corps headquarters. I passed a mansion Alegria and I had visited three nights earlier to see a most amusing dance put on by the Varan Guards, in which the younger legates, undismayed by the absence of suitable partners, had shown us native dances, so wild and abandoned the Negaret in the wilderness would've been jealous. Now the mansion's windows were yellow and red eyes, the walls bulging. The house exploded, and the metal roof spun high, reflecting the flames. It pinwheeled, and slammed into the ground a few yards away. Cinders, sparks, flames cascaded, and Brigstock pranced in fear—but we were safely past.

I found Aguin Guil and told him where the emperor was, and that he'd best send several regiments out to make sure of Tenedos's safety. For once, he didn't hesitate, or ask for further orders. I forgot about him, about the emperor, and tried to think of a way to fight the fire. I could find none. No one knew where the Maisirians hid their fire-fighting mechanisms. I didn't even know if they had them, and remembered what I'd heard of thrice-burned Jarrah. Even if we could've found such devices, we wouldn't have been skilled in their use. Soldiers are meant to kill people and break things, not save them.

I ordered guard patrols to stop the incendiaries by any

means necessary. The soldiers, grim-faced and afraid, seeing their sole refuge against the Maisirian winter vanishing, needed no specifics. At first, anyone with fire-making materials or close to a fresh fire was hanged. But that took too long, and a sword or spear thrust was all that was necessary. But the fires still grew, and so anyone who moved in the fire-dancing streets and wasn't wearing Numantian uniform might be cut down.

I remembered, from when I was a boy in Cimabue, that we used to set counter-fires when we burned the rice fields after harvest, and I tried that. But the winds were wrong, or else the *azaz*'s spells very strong, for the fires intended to create safety zones merely added to the catastrophe.

Dawn came eventually, black clouds swirling over the city so it was no more than dim twilight, and the fires grew. I rode into a square with a huge fountain in its center. Fire had taken all the buildings around, and the soldiers quartered in them had fled to what they thought must be safety, immersing themselves like so many terrified frogs in the fountain. But the fire had been too hot, and the soldiers were boiled alive. I saw other corpses on other streets, black like potatoes left too long in the fire, so charred they bore no resemblance to men or women.

The dead were the fortunate ones. The others, seared beyond recognition, were lucky if they were so shocked as to be beyond pain, but all too many could still scream. I'd never known a man could howl, in dying, more loudly than a horse. Yonge's silver dagger saw dark work that morning, and helped many with the only blessing I could give: quick return to the Wheel.

I saw Alegria once—she'd convinced Balkh to let her back into the city, then found one of our chirurgeons and become a nurse.

Jarrah burned on. The only buildings that were safe, that wouldn't burn, were the stone temples, and so we seized them for hospitals, for billets, for headquarters. I knew this would be termed desecration by the pious Maisirians, but there was no other choice.

The firestorm raged for three days, and then, as if other elemental spirits were angered by Shahriya's indulgence, winds screamed, and the skies opened.

On this third day, I encountered the emperor. He strode through the ashes, looking curiously about. I managed a salute, numb with fatigue. He returned it. "Thank you for perhaps saving my life," he said. "This is terrible. I can't conceive of a man . . . a people . . . so barbaric they'd burn their own capital. Although it'll no doubt be blamed on the savage Numantians.

"There was beauty lost here," he said softly. "Splendor. But when I rebuild, Jarrah, if that will still be its name, will be a thousand times more glorious."

I was shaken that Tenedos could see any good in this disaster. He seemed to read my thought. "Yes, Damastes. It is terrible. But it is also a great reward."

A reward? I thought he was being incredibly cynical, darkly jesting. But then another, darker thought came. Suppose there was no jest intended?

The blackened ruins stretched for miles. Jarrah had only a scattering of buildings left. Every now and then one would inexplicably flare up or explode. All was rubble, broken up by open spaces that had been streets. Now we had no choice at all.

"I have decided," the emperor said, "on our course of action." His words echoed against the temple's high stone walls. There were several hundred of us gathered around him—tribunes, generals, a few of the highest-ranking dominas. "King Bairan has refused to see reason and negotiate or even ask for a truce," Tenedos said. "It is obvious that he's quite mad, and imagines he can fight on.

"He's clearly not aware of the power of his enemy, and that Numantia has never—not ever—surrendered the field. We must continue to press him. I have word the king's army is to the south and west of Jarrah. We shall march out to fight him. I am sure we'll confront him on a field of our choosing.

"If not, we shall continue to march on, to the north, following the traditional trading route, until we reach a suitable city for wintering and resupply. My goals include a return to Jarrah in the spring, if we haven't destroyed Bairan before then.

"He's decided, in his infinite arrogance, that Maisir is only himself, himself and his corrupt nobles, and has not the slightest concern for his people. If that is the war he wishes, then that is the war he shall have.

"Our righteous anger shall be pitiless. We'll destroy Bairan and his army unutterably, until, two generations hence, no one in Numantia or Maisir will remember his name. Prepare your men for the march."

There was a cheer, but not a very strong one, and the officers dispersed to their commands. The emperor hadn't met my eyes once during his speech. Nor had he used the word "retreat." But that was what he'd ordered.

It was deemed simpler for the army to simply reverse itself on the march out, so the elite units that had spearheaded the attack would now bring up the rear. At the head of the column would be Le Balafre's units, which had been the army's rear guard, mostly straggling or lost combat units and support elements. Not that it mattered, we were assured. We'd have more than enough time to regroup before we met the Maisirians.

Officially, Jarrah was never abandoned. There was a tiny garrison left to hold the city until spring, and the hospitals were full of our sick and wounded. As for the other garrisons along our invasion path, gallopers were supposedly sent out to order them to withdraw along the column of march toward Penda.

But none of those couriers reached the garrisons. Perhaps they were ambushed by Negaret or murdered by the partisans. My belief is no such couriers were sent. The emperor couldn't admit his terrible defeat.

Regardless of intent, all of these units, garrisons, supply depots, most terribly hospitals full of casualties—perhaps a hundred thousand men, I believe more—were abandoned. To the best of my knowledge, not one man, from Irthing to Penda, ever returned to Numantia. Thus the Emperor Tenedos betrayed his army.

"How bad will it be?" Alegria asked.

"I don't know," I said truthfully, helping her into our carriage.

"But we'll be all right. Won't we?"

"We will," I said honestly, remembering the horrors of the flight from Kait. But even though more than half our army had become casualties, we still had nearly a million men, the finest army the world had ever known, led by the greatest magician of history. And the gods were certainly on our side.

The emperor asked if I'd take command of the rear guard instead of leading the army. I guessed he had no more idea of where the Maisirian army really was than I did, and feared the worst. I said I would, provided I could have the three best units—my elite frontier regiments the Tenth Hussars, the Twentieth Heavy Cavalry, and my own Seventeenth Ureyan Lancers. He frowned, then said I could. I pressed my luck and asked for two hundred of Yonge's skirmishers for support, and he said I'd have to ask Yonge personally.

Sometimes I wondered if the emperor wasn't a little afraid of the Kaiti. I knew I was. Yonge scowled, said I wasn't leaving him but a scattering of men, but at least they'd be in the best position to scavenge the best of the loot as it was abandoned. And so we marched.

I was told the Emperor Tenedos stood beside the great northern gate he'd entered Jarrah through less than a time ago. Behind him the ruins of the city still smoked, demarcated by the streets that now led from nothingness to nothingness. Bugles sang, and the stark cadences of the salute rang into emptiness. Regimental standards and lances dipped, soldiers stiffened, trying to keep in some kind of step, and their officers sat rigid in their saddles, fists clapped to shoulders.

Tenedos was regal, calm, confident, and took the honor as if the army were passing in Grand Review.

As for us in the rear, we didn't reach the city gates until late afternoon, and by then the emperor had long taken his place in the column. We traveled but four or five miles before a chilly dusk fell, and we made camp.

I'd already noted trouble. Abandoned gear had been strewn along the road, but not the prized items Yonge dreamed of. There were enormous carriages barely suitable for the smoothest of city streets, which had cast a wheel or had their teams founder, and they'd been stripped and in many cases burned.

Strange items lay beside or in the road. I saw a smashed harp; a statue of some god or goddess that would've filled an entire wagon; women's silk clothes hanging amid the tall trees as if they'd been cast there by a playful giantess; huge paintings slashed with sabers before being abandoned; several hundred books, uniformly bound in red leather, scattered in the muck; and, even after this short distance, bodies.

Svalbard and Curti had done some carpentry on our first coach so the seats could be moved to create a bed, and Alegria and I were out of the wet. Sometime after midnight, I was called awake. Both of us were fully dressed, and I had only to pull my sword belt and boots on.

Domina Bikaner of the Seventeenth had a tent for his headquarters, and was waiting with one of the most shattered men it's been my misfortune to see. His arm had been amputated, and the bandages were filthy black and blood-soaked. Drops of blood spattered the straw flooring of the tent. He wore only ragged breeches and a torn shirt, and was barefoot, in spite of the weather. He was a Guard color-sergeant, who'd been badly wounded in a skirmish with Negaret, so badly the chirurgeons hadn't been able to restore his arm, but rather had to amputate it. He hadn't been healing well, and had been left in one of the hospitals that had once been temples.

He'd been drowsing, coming out of a delirium, when he

heard a strange sound, somewhere between a snake's hiss and the wind. He opened his eyes to see dark gray, almost black, wraiths float down the ward. "An' ever' now and again," he said, "th' mist'd solid up, and I swear I saw an eye peerin' at me. I acted like I was dead, or unconscious. Din't know what else to do."

"And then?" Bikaner prodded.

What came next was much worse, especially because it was entirely human. Into the ward rushed half a hundred men and women. They wore rags, and most were drunk. All were armed, some with our discarded or broken weapons, others with the tools of their trade—scythes, long knives, sharpened spades. They were howling in rage.

"They started killin' right off," the color-sergeant whispered. "A chirurgeon tried t' stop 'em, and they cut him down. Then they went from bed t' bed, killin' as they went, laughin', slashin', givin' no mercy, no matter how y' pled. Nobody lived. Th' only reason I'm alive is there was a window behin' me, an' I smashed it and leapt for m' life. There were more of th' bastards below, but I hit on m' legs, thank Isa, an' started runnin'.

"They come after, but I lost 'em someways. I could feel th' blood leakin' out've my arm, but I'd rather run myself t' death than stay there. Once, maybe twice, I saw th' black mist wi' th' eyes, an' dropped flat, and it went on, I guess without seein' me. I dunno, sir, whether th' mist, or whatever it was, was guidin' those sonsabitches or if it was just watchin'. I dunno. I just dunno."

He stared down at his blood-soaked bandages, his near-nakedness, and swayed. "It . . . was a long run. But I had t' get someplace safe. 'Tis safe now. Isn't it?" He looked at me hopefully, then his eyes rolled back, and I barely caught him as he fell.

We called for a chirurgeon and told him to stay with the color-sergeant and do anything necessary to keep this brave man alive.

"So what's left in Jarrah?" Bikaner said. I didn't answer. I didn't need to. "About what I thought," he said. "I'll make sure th' guards're alert. An' we'd best march on at first light."

The color-sergeant died as we were striking camp.

At midday, we came to the inn where Alegria and I had almost made love for the first time. It was a shattered, burned ruin. "Sure am grateful," Svalbard said, "those up front're thinkin' of their brothers back here in th' rear. Think we'll ever see anything but horse turds an' ruins, Tribune?"

I managed a laugh, and we slogged on, slowly, ever so slowly, but when I glanced over at our carriage, I saw Alegria staring back at the ruined inn. Our eyes met, and she smiled wistfully.

It didn't take long for the days of our retreat to blend together. Rain, mud, sleet; abandoned, shattered wagons and bodies. We were traveling through the charred region of the peasants' revolt, and so there was little to scavenge. Every now and then the Negaret or the partisans would dart out, seize a wagon or two, kill anyone within reach, and flee back into the forest before a cavalry troop could respond.

Horses died even faster than they did in the advance, and we saw more and more abandoned saddles. The animals were rough-butchered, and kept their riders alive for another day or two.

Once more I was grateful for the harsh training I'd forced down the throat of every cavalryman under my orders: first your mount, then yourself. The horses of my three regiments died, certainly, but not nearly as fast as other, more slovenly units.

On the far side of the desolation was a village I remembered, though now it was smoldering wreckage. There was a certain farm beyond the settlement, and I asked Domina Bikaner for a troop of cavalry to accompany me there. The farm was, strangely, unburned, and seemed to have suffered no damage. In the walled yard were ten bodies.

One was the farmer who'd told me the yellow emblem over his door, the upside-down letter U that looked like a knotted silk cord, was no more than a family sign.

He'd been spitted on a soldier's sword. The other nine

bodies were Guardsmen, and all had been strangled. Strangled with yellow silk cords, strangled by the Tovieti.

But how could the stranglers have crept up on alert soldiery? What sorcery must the farmer—or someone—have worked? And why hadn't the Guardsmen's superiors gone after them, found the slaughter, and fired the farmhouse? Were the Tovieti going to rise against us again? Or had they already?

What would, what could, the Tovieti do to take full advantage, now that we were in retreat? Here—and in Numantia? I had no answers, and ordered my men back to the column. I felt eyes on my back as I did.

Each day saw more skirmishes, more casualties. The dead weren't given last rites or burned any longer. No one had the time, or the makings of a fire, at least not to waste on the dead. Occasionally a high-ranking officer might have one of the Chare Brethren in attendance, and magic would leave his body smoldering after a few quick words, and the stink of burned mutton would spread along the column.

The wounded would be put on any cart that would hold them, for our ambulances were always full, even though men died hourly. These wounded were almost surely doomed, for the wagoneers, mostly civilians, sutlers, or quartermasters, saw no gain in hauling bleeding men instead of loot or food that could be sold, and so "accidents" happened, and men were tipped into ditches or, worst of all, dumped into the track, to lie a moment in gasping horror before the oncoming wagon crushed them.

Alegria now rode atop our carriage, for it was full of dying men.

It was easy to track the army's route—flocks of dark carrion crows hung over our march, Saionji's death-birds, growing fatter by the league.

I didn't notice the first snowflake, or the tenth, but then they were falling softly all about us. The snow, after an hour, turned to rain, and the mire grew deeper and deeper. The Time of Storms was here.

Captain Balkh grimly pointed out a corpse beside the road. It was stripped naked, which wasn't uncommon—the dead hardly needed warm clothing. It lay facedown, and its buttocks were raw, wounded, and there were other wounds on the body's upper thighs.

"Somebody cut steaks off that one," Balkh said. My stomach turned.

Svalbard, riding behind me with Curti, muttered, "Least someone'll eat good t'night."

Curti laughed harshly. "Best be on y'r guard, big man. More n' more you're lookin' like a steak t' me."

As the days passed, that horror became more and more common.

"Officer . . . officer . . . a boon? For Isa's sake, for the love of Panoan?" I tried not to look at the man sprawled against the tree. "Officer . . . kill me! Return me to the Wheel. Please?" I couldn't grant that wish, even though I'd managed to do so for the burned victims in Jarrah. But there were others marching with me who could, thank Saionji.

Then the moans, the pleas, became too many, too often, and we heard their plaints no more and stumbled on, through the brown muck, seeing only the drifting snow and the back of the soldier in front of us.

Again and again the Negaret or bandits struck, hurting us a little with each pinprick. Sometimes it was more than a pinprick, as the Maisirians grew bolder.

Men died by the sword, but more died of the cold, the wind, hunger, exhaustion. There was one sure way to tell if a soldier was doomed: He gave up hope. Those of us who survived had one thing in common: Each knew, absolutely, that he, at least, would see his homeland, even if he were the only Numantian soldier to do so. The minute one of us let go of that determination, he died.

Officers would trail back, saying that their company—their troop, even, most awfully, their regiment—had been cut apart again and again, and then their domina had fallen, and there was no longer anyone to give orders, and no one to take them, either. Officers without soldiers, soldiers without officers.

Two men were talking as I rode past: "Come on, Kirat! Come on! You can't just stop. Not here."

"No, comrade . . . no. I think it's time to go."

The second man stumbled off the track, into a copse of trees. The first man shrugged and shambled forward. Little by little, my army was dying.

I was leading a flank patrol, and had ridden far ahead with three others when the Negaret came out of the silence, long white cloaks wrapped around them, shouting battle cries. I heard shrieks of fear from my men, then they were on us, and all was a seethe of steel and blood. A long-bearded Negaret started to cut at me, but I heard a shout of "No!" and he turned his saber and tried to club me down.

I put the point of my blade into his chest, and I let him fall off my sword, and spun before another could take me from behind. But instead, I was ringed by Negaret riders, and there was merriment on their faces, and they shouted gleefully, "He's the one!" "Take him! He's worth gold!" "That's their *rauri*!"

"There'll be no ransom for me," I shouted, and started to gig Brigstock into them.

Then I saw their chieftain. It was Jedaz Bakr, the Negaret who'd led my escort from the mountains to Oswy. "Greetings, Numantian," he cried, and his riders pulled up. "Will you surrender?"

"Greetings, oh great *jedaz*," and for some idiotic reason the gloom that had haunted me for so many days fell away, and I felt the merriment of a warrior facing his last moments. "Did you come to try to kill me?"

"There'll be no death for you, Shum á Cimabue. Not unless you stay with these other fools and freeze your balls off in some snowbank or starve. Surrender, and I'll teach you how to be a Negaret. There'll be rich work when you Numantians are destroyed."

"Not a chance."

"You can even bring that woman with you, the one those bastards gave you. Marry her in our tents, Damastes. She won't be a slave with us, but your princess."

"No! You know who I am . . . what I am."

Bakr's smile vanished. "I do. And I know you'll likely die with these others. But I thought I should make an offer, since I've seen your face every day now. You're always the last to fall back, and I'm the first in our advance. Come, join us.

"I sense there is a time coming for the Negaret, time when we shall be more than we ever dreamed, more than King Bairan ever wished."

I shook my head. Bakr grimaced, then shrugged. "Then try not to die," he said, then shouted an order, and his riders swirled and were gone.

Captain Balkh, Svalbard, and the other Red Lancers galloped up. "Tribune, we lost you for a moment, and—"

"Never mind," I said shortly. "For there's no damage done. Let's return to the column."

"Yes, sir," Balkh muttered, too ashamed of his failure to meet my eyes. Svalbard and Curti looked at me most strangely as we rode back, but said nothing.

The forest was gone, and we entered the Kiot Marshes. It was even worse than before, because the log roads were smashed, and the way was nothing but mud. Horses bogged down and couldn't be freed. They were left to die, or butchered for steaks while they still lived. Their carriages blocked the track and further slowed us.

Even so, those who could stay on the roadways were fortunate, for many of us were forced into the swamp itself. I thought we might be swallowed here, and never be seen again, but, very slowly, we moved on.

I took the Seventeenth forward, toward the head of the column, and checked every wagon we came on. I set an arbitrary rule: one wagon per officer. Any others—we turned our backs while the marching men looted them, then, at my orders, tipped them into the swamp.

A wagon claimed by the infantry, and filled with their gear, if it was roadworthy, I ignored. They needed any assistance to be found in this nightmare.

Dominas, generals, even a couple of tribunes complained, and I told them to shut up. Some reached for their swords, then saw the archers with half-drawn bows and stalked away.

One fat captain, who had five wagons stuffed with wine and the finest foods, broke into tears when I ordered his supplies handed out to the starving men he rode beside and ignored. I laughed at his tears and rode on.

Some officers complained to the emperor, who rode near the head of the column. Three times imperial staff gallopers came back with handwritten orders from Tenedos that I was to immediately stop this nonsense. I thanked these officers, told them to return to the emperor with my respects, then continued my ruthless clearing. I had sworn an oath to Tenedos, but not one that required me to croak like a frog if he said "green."

We saw the ape-like beings many times, but they offered no harm. Men asked permission to hunt them for the pot, but I forbade it. Perhaps they weren't men at all, but I already had enough sins to concern myself with. Twice we encountered the terrible sluglike monsters, but I'd been thinking about them and had devised a weapon. I wished that I could've had one of the Chare Brethren create a spell, but I also wished for a warm, sunny day, dry breeches, a bath, and a feather bed with nothing but Alegria in it and nowhere to go for days, and I hadn't seen that, either.

For my weapons I had the archers carry five or six arrows daubed in pitch and, in their pouches, flint and steel or a bit of smoldering tinder. As the slugs slid out of the gloom, the bowmen would strike fire and light their arrows. The flaming arrow would then be whipped into the monsters.

That caused pain or at least discomfort, for they bubbled, turned, and fled. But not everyone knew of my weapon, and so the slugs fed well, sometimes on horses, more often on men.

The swamps came to an end, and we reached the small stone village of Sidor.

Waiting across the Anker River's curling, half-frozen tributaries, in a great crescent that reached for leagues, was the Maisirian Army, two and a half million strong.

TWENTY-SIX

THE BRIDGES AT SIDOR

The enemy held the far bank and had outposted both bridges on our side. The bridges were piled with flammables, and the moment we attacked, the outposts would pull back, spreading flame as they went. For additional security, they'd also stationed men on the islets that split the river.

The Maisirian forces were drawn up in three lines in an arc around the village of Sidor, and behind them were massed reserves.

Our army was a mess. Units had become mingled on the march; no one knew who was at point and who was supporting, and every officer was bickering about it at the top of his lungs.

Yonge's skirmishers held positions between the road head and the bridges, and arrows flickered back and forth.

The Emperor Tenedos stood on a tiny hillcrest, a tight, confident smile on his face. His staff surrounded him, waiting for orders.

"We have them now, Tribune," he said in greeting to me.

"So it appears."

"You've crossed here, correct?"

"Yes, sir. On my journey to Jarrah."

"How deep is it? Is it fordable?"

"Not really. A horseman could swim it, and we could span

it with ropes in the summer or fall. But not now." I pointed at the racing water, and the occasional ice floes bobbing past. "If it'd only freeze . . ."

"Or if we grew wings," the emperor said. "Very well. There's no use in subtlety. We'll spend the rest of the day sorting out this mishmash, and attack at first light. We'll have to assume they'll burn the bridges before we can take them.

"Put the skirmishers across first, swimming, with light cavalry, then pioneers behind them. Have them run ropes, and we'll have strong swimmers posted. They'll have to gain a foothold immediately, or we'll be doomed. Send for Yonge." An aide scurried away.

"Other pioneer units should start cutting logs for a floating bridge, for the main force. I'll bring the Guard on line, and we'll make a frontal crossing and attack. Perhaps a diversion up- or downstream.

"We'll hit them as hard as we can in their center, and watch them fold up on themselves." It was a simple plan, and it might work, although the cost would be terrible.

"Comments, General of the Armies á Cimabue?"

I studied the village and the bridges. "It's a good plan," I said, being politic since there were aides within hearing. "But perhaps I could make a suggestion?"

"Go ahead." Tenedos's voice was as frosty as the air.

"Perhaps, my Emperor, we could move over here, so I could show you a few salient points I noticed?"

Tenedos looked skeptical, but came down from his knoll. Domina Othman tried to accompany him, but I sent him reeling back with a hard stare. "All right, Damastes," the emperor said. "What did I miss?"

"Nothing, sir. But perhaps there's, well, a way that might increase the odds in our favor."

"Go ahead."

My ideas were brief and made only a few changes in the emperor's tactics. Tenedos's face went from doubtful, to interested, to enthusiastic. When I finished, he was nodding excitedly.

"Good. Good. And I'm an utter dolt for not devising a similar plan. But I can't believe the Maisirians don't have more guards posted. How many men will you need?"

"Ten men, the absolute best, for each attack group. Twenty others behind them. Ten of your Brethren with those, then another fifty, and fifty more to remain on each bridge and deal with those below. They should be archers. We'll need skirmishers for the first thirty, Guardsmen for the rest. Volunteers by squad, to keep unit discipline."

"That hardly seems enough."

"It isn't—but six hundred wouldn't be any better," I said, "and would be a hundred times as noisy."

"While this is going on . . . ?" the emperor asked.

"The pioneers will be hacking away, the units will be scuffling back and forth showing lights every now and then, and the Maisirians will be waiting for daybreak and our attack. I hope."

Tenedos smiled slyly. "I notice you've included yourself in the party."

"Of course." I could hardly ask someone to do what I drew back from.

Tenedos's grin grew broader. "So, of course, you know what follows."

"No . . . oh, shit. Sir, you simply cannot—"

"But I shall. And haven't we gone through this before? Remember what happened the last time?"

I realized the impossibility of argument. "And if things go wrong?" I tried.

"Then neither of us will know about them, will we? Now, let's put the others moving. I have spells to prepare."

Sometimes I wonder what it would be like to serve in an army where tribunes and emperors knew their place. A bit saner than being a Numantian warrior, I'd wager. Yonge said, just as flatly as the emperor, that he'd be with the first ten. I argued halfheartedly, not because I knew I'd lose, which I would, but rather because I wanted his skill with a knife.

Svalbard and Curti also volunteered. I hesitated, for I wanted to keep Curti with the second twenty, given his keen eye, but I relented.

I spent the last two hours before sundown crouched behind an ice-hung bush, watching those two bridges and the islets through the snow flurries, memorizing landmarks I'd recognize in the dark.

Behind me, the army prepared for a grand crossing. Pioneers could be seen here and there, cutting trees and dragging them to the river's edge, preparing for battle on the morrow or the day after. About two hundred and fifty men—all that remained of the Varan Guard, Myrus Le Balafre's old command, which had marched across the border with three thousand—moved east, about a mile downstream, not quite able to conceal their movement from the Maisirians.

I saw a small fishing boat overturned beside the river, and had pioneers drag it up from the water's edge.

When it grew dark, I returned to the emperor's headquarters. A large tent had been put up, with wood heaters inside, and tables were set with smoked hams, preserved fish, freshly cooked bacon, freshly baked white bread, even oysters and cheese—foods I hadn't seen since Jarrah.

I grew angry, then realized they weren't for the staff officers, but for the soldiers inside, my first thirty, plus another ten magicians. Farther back, the two hundred Guardsmen were being fed, if not as sumptuously as we were, better rations than they'd seen for many leagues. All had their faces, hands, and necks darkened with mud, and any shiny medals, buttons, or frogs removed. They carried knives, in addition to their swords or sabers, and some had lead-weighted sandbags as well.

I laid a slab of ham on a piece of bread, cut a wedge of cheese atop that, slathered the cheese with bitterroot relish, and gnawed it while I turned myself from a dashing tribune into a gob of invisible earth.

The emperor joined us as I was giving my orders, which only took a few seconds. He, too, was mud-daubed and wore black. It took a moment for the men to recognize him, and some of the Guardsmen instinctively went to their knees.

"Up," he said brusquely. "Tonight I'm but one of you. Tomorrow will be time for ceremony. Tonight is for silence—and death. Death for the Maisirians."

He pulled me aside. "There *were* wards, as I thought," he said. "Notice I said 'were.' But they'll never realize I countered them, not even if their gods-damned *azaz* is hanging over their shoulders."

All the men were experienced fighters, so there was no need for a rousing speech, and we waited as patiently as we could, some pretending mirth, some sleep, until the emperor ordered us up. The snow flurries had become a full storm, which was all to the good. I said a brief prayer to Isa and Tanis, wished I'd had time to kiss Alegria, whom I'd left at the rear of the march with Domina Bikaner and the Seventeenth, and we slipped into the night.

"Halt! Who comes?" The challenge was in a hoarse whisper.

"Calstor Nevia, with a ten-man patrol," I answered in Maisirian, using one of the country dialects I'd learned centuries ago at Irrigon.

"Advance one to be recognized."

Yonge moved past, and two shadows came toward him. The first Maisirian jerked backward as Yonge's knife went in under his chin. The second, too close to use his spear, jumped away, twisting, and my sword took him in the side. He died a bit more noisily, gurgling, but it didn't matter, as eight Numantians rushed the outpost, boots silenced with cut-up sheepskin laced to their soles. We waited tensely, then a black-faced soldier came from behind. He held his palm up. The outpost at the other bridge had been silenced. A moment later, that team joined us.

"All right," I said in a low voice. "Remember, march like you own the damned bridge. You do. But don't sound too smart, eh? You are Maisirians, after all." In tight formation, we went into the heart of the enemy, boot heels smashing against wet wood as if we were on parade. I saw teeth flash, saw Tenedos in the dimness. I wonder if our thoughts were the same: Long years ago, we'd attempted something as daring, and carried it off.

Isa—or, hells, why not pray to the emperor's own goddess, Saionji—be with us this night as well, I prayed.

Behind us came the rest of our raiders, half-crouched, walking softly, and keeping to the middle of the bridge. Six carried what I hoped would be the center of my deception—that abandoned boat. I counted paces, recognized landmarks, and knew we were over the Anker's islets. At each, I motioned and squads fell out.

The Maisirians couldn't have had that much faith in their magic, and only had one set of guards on either bridge. I was right. They didn't. A man came out of the darkness, spear thrusting. But Curti had seen him, and an arrow thunked into the man's face. He tore at it, his spear clattering away. I flung myself on him, one hand clawing at wetness, clamping his mouth closed while my dagger drove again and again into his chest. When I picked myself up, four other bodies sprawled—but one was Numantian.

We went on and on, across that endless bridge. Eventually we saw greater blackness looming, and the long causeway came to an end. Here was another post, manned by at least thirty men. Our bravado let us get within ten yards, and then someone scented danger and shouted an alarm. We swarmed over them, cutting, thrusting, and most were down, but some were screaking and running.

I called for the six men carrying the boat, had them drop it on the beach, and drop a Maisirian corpse nearby, as if he'd been killed when the raiders put ashore.

"At the run," I ordered, seeing torches flare in the stone village, and the men were running after me, east toward the other bridge. Midway between the two was the three-story, six-sided stone granary. The door was closed, but it smashed open to my boot heel, and three Maisirian officers stood, befuddled, and Svalbard, Curti, and I slashed them down. Numantians poured into the room.

"Brethren to the stairs," the emperor shouted. "All the way to the top floor."

"Balkh," I ordered. "Take charge of this floor, and block the door."

"Sir."

I went up the broad stairs to the second floor, a tall-ceilinged single room, sweet-smelling of grains and summer. There were only four windows here, so I sent half my men downstairs to reinforce Captain Balkh, and took the rest up to the top story. It was like the first, and two magicians teetered on a ladder, trying to push open a trapdoor.

"Get down," Svalbard growled, and they obeyed hastily. Curti and I braced the ladder, and the big man shot up the rungs, curving his head as his shoulders thudded into the weather-jammed hatch. It banged open, and we were on the roof, the emperor and his magicians behind us.

Sidor was a-clamor—their defenses had been sprung! I heard nothing from the bridges, though, and hoped the Maisirians would convince themselves the tiny boat I'd brought along carried all of the murderers. That might give my raiders time enough to kill the outposts on the islets.

The magicians took out their gear. The first two spells had been prepared before we set out. One was a conventional spell of blindness, so hopefully the Maisirians wouldn't be able to see the granary's doors. Timbers thudded from below as the Guardsmen barricaded them.

The second spell was one of binding, of strength. Bits of wood were cut from the timbers blocking the door, and piled atop a tiny iron rod that had symbols cut into the surface. Around it was piled, I learned later, dried herbs such as pepper plant seeds, lavender, fenugreek, quassia chips, and others. These were burned, with a purple flame that never flickered when snowflakes fell into it, while two sorcerers muttered a spell in unison. This was intended to—and did—give those timbers the strength of iron bars. I remembered the tower at Irrigon, and wished my seer, Sinait, had been with me. If she had been . . . perhaps . . . perhaps . . .

I forced the thought away, and peered over the edge of the balcony and saw hordes of Maisirians crowding into the square around. But no one showed himself at the windows, so the Maisirians didn't know what to do.

"I sense their magicians awakening," Tenedos said. "Be wary." One of the Chare Brethren began a counterspell.

I saw three officers organizing an assault team below. "Archers," I shouted, and those three dropped. We had, I estimated, about two hours until daylight, when Tenedos had ordered the main attack.

Men lugged a long stone column into the square, while other soldiers held shields over their heads against the arrow storm.

I suddenly felt sick, my head swimming, and saw others sway and curse. Our magicians drew symbols on the roof, sprinkled foul-smelling potions about, and the War Magicians' spell was broken. "That was a new one," the emperor said. "Usually it's just various sorts of fear and confusion. I'll enjoy learning that from their *azaz* when I'm pulling him apart after the war." He sounded as if staying alive for a few hours in the middle of the Maisirian army were less than a problem. He and the other wizards began casting small, harassing spells as the Maisirians below readied their attack.

Tenedos said he had a Great Spell ready, but it couldn't be cast until the time was right. Which would be when? I asked, and he gave me a dark look and said he would know the time full well, and all I should do was keep him healthy until then.

The Maisirians ran forward with their ram, twenty men on a side, and crashed it into the side of the granary. I sent Svalbard below, and he returned saying there was no damage. Again the ram smashed into the stone walls.

"This is beginning to annoy me," Tenedos said. "But at

least the confusion spell seems to be working, since they're not attacking the doors. But still . . ." He drew his dagger and used its butt to chip a bit of stone from the parapet. "I don't know if this will work . . ." and his voice trailed off as he chanted under his breath, frequently glancing over the side as the ram smashed again and again into the stone. "Hells!" he said, and cast the chip aside. "I was hoping they quarried all their rock from the same place, but I suppose not. No similarity, no damage. Damastes, would you care to attempt a more prosaic solution?"

The shield holders had grown careless; carefully aimed spears sailed down, and six men fell. The rammers lost their balance, and the column slammed to the cobbles of the square, trapping five more soldiers under it.

"Archers," I ordered. "Kill me every man that tries to help the men who're pinned. But don't strike them, or I'll have your asses." Cruel to use wounded men, crueler to kill those who had the courage and bowels to try to help them? Of course. But what do you suppose war is?

A lookout shouted a warning, and I saw a party of men moving toward the bridges. "*That* can be dealt with," Tenedos said, and motioned to three magicians. A brazier flared. One wizard uncorked a vial and sprinkled dark fluid over the flames, and I smelled the stink of human blood burning. Tenedos and one other began chanting:

"Take the fuel
Feed your strength
Grow and be fecund
Give birth
Give birth
Your children dance around you."

There were smaller flames around the brazier.

"Scent your food
Scent your prey

Go forth
Go forth
As I bid you
Find water
Cross over water
Your prey awaits
Go and feed
Go and feed."

Tenedos dropped into the brazier a bit of cloth from a Maisirian uniform, a shard of bone taken from a frozen corpse, a bit of hair from another body, and the tiny flames darted out. They hovered, seeking direction, and Tenedos put his hand into the fire and picked up a bit of flame, yet remained unburned. He stretched his hand, the fire dancing on it, toward the bridge.

"Go and feed
Go and feed
Go and feed,"

he chanted monotonously, and the flames sped away. As they moved, they grew larger and larger, to nearly the height of a man. They swirled and swept over the river, then swooped as one, as a swallow dives in the summer dusk. The Maisirians had reached the bridge when the flames caught them, and over the shouts from the square I heard screams. The flames grew as they fed, and Maisirians twisted, died, or leapt over the railings to end the agony.

"I wonder how they like the taste of their own magic," Tenedos muttered. "Especially since I've added a touch." As the men died, the flames lifted away, unlike the Maisirian fire, which had died with its victims. Stronger, larger, they came back toward the granary.

"Find others," Tenedos cried. "Find others and feed, feed, my children," and the flames obediently dropped toward the square.

I saw something against the driving snow, a huge cupped hand. It reached down from nowhere and, just as I pinch out a candle when I'm ready for sleep, this enormous, half-visible hand closed, and the flames were gone.

"A little late," the emperor said. "But still effective. Let's see what this *azaz* thinks of my next."

He bent over his equipment. But the *azaz* cast first, and I heard a keening begin, and the wind buffeted us. We knelt and braced, and one sorcerer made the mistake of grabbing for a tripod the wind was pushing toward the parapet. As he stood, the wind screamed in triumph and sent him spinning over the edge. The gale whirled about us, and we were the center of a vortex.

The emperor dropped his potion and hurriedly scrawled symbols on the stone. The wind vanished, and snow fell straight in the stillness. "I'll wager," Tenedos said, "he's never heard of that one, for it was taught me in far-off Jaferite. He should learn the virtues of travel." Tenedos chuckled at his jest, then went back to his casting.

"Why aren't they sending more men to the bridges?" someone asked. I didn't—and don't—know. Perhaps the officer who'd thought to reinforce his guards was burned by Tenedos's fires. Or perhaps Maisir's attention was held by the magicians' battle. Perhaps they only forgot for half an hour, but that's an eternity in battle.

Lights flashed across the river, about a mile downstream, and the Varan Guard began their diversionary attack. The emperor stared into the blackness as if he could see what was happening, and I realized, from his words, that he could. "They've taken one of the islands. Brave men," he said. "There's ice in the damned river, and they're pushing through it like it's not even there. Shit. The Maisirians had soldiers on that island—as many as the Varans." He was silent, then nodded approvingly. "Good. Now the Varans have re-formed and are attacking again." Tenedos returned to his spell.

Archers in perfect formation marched into the square, opened ranks, and volleyed up arrows. Two men on the parapet went down. One was a wizard, the other a spearman. One writhed in pain, the other lay motionless. "You," Tenedos said to another archer. "Give me one of your arrows." The man obeyed. The emperor considered it for a second. "Now, if I only had a bit more of their blood," he said. "But this will have to do." He closed his eyes, touched the point to the lids, and then to the ground, while chanting in a language I didn't know.

"Get down," someone shouted. "They're firing again!" We went flat, which was nonsensical, for we would've been better off standing up, presenting a smaller target to the arrows as they plunged down from the peak of their arc. But none of the arrows landed on the roof; they wavered, as if a wind had taken them, then dropped back.

Tenedos called over a wizard. "You know how to do that?"

"I think so, Your Majesty."

"Recast the spell every time they start to shoot at us. They'll tire before we will."

He looked across the river. "They've sent cavalry downriver against the Varans," he said. "Two, no three regiments."

"Don't you have a spell to stop them?" I said. The Varan Guard would be outnumbered at least eight to one.

"I have a spell in the making already," Tenedos said. "I cannot chance it. Besides . . ." He let his voice trail off and said no more.

I remember these events as if they were happening in a quiet room, and there were no distractions. In reality there were screams, shouts, the keening of the wounded and the dying, and the blare of the Maisirian bugles.

"Now the cavalry is on them," Tenedos announced. He bowed his head, and everyone on the parapet was silent. I swallowed hard. Tenedos grimaced, looked up. "They died well," he announced. "They'll be remembered." Then he added, "The Great Spell may now be cast."

That should have been my final clue, but I barely heard him, for false dawn was at hand.

Across the river our main attack began. Guardsmen in

close formation trotted over the hillcrest and down onto the bridges. Our army was completely vulnerable, and the Maisirians closed their lines into and through Sidor. Arrows lofted in sheets against the men on the bridges. Other Numantians fell, but I'd seen no weapon take their lives. The War Magicians were doing their part.

Our front ranks went down to the man, and the next wave had to step over their bodies. They, too, died, and there was a parapet of corpses to shelter behind. But pitiless officers ordered the Guardsmen on, and bodies were pitched over the railings as the Guard advanced. This was when the pretty uniforms, the young girls' fluttering eyebrows, and the parade honors were paid for. The Guardsmen knew it, and forged on, heads bowed as if pushing into a strong wind.

The Maisirians were whooping in glee—this would be the deathblow to the usurpers. All of us, from the emperor to the lowest soldier, would die in this village.

I'd hoped the enemy would forget about the granary, but men ran into the square with scaling ladders. Other soldiers held shields over their heads and set the ladders against the walls. My soldiers tried to kick the ladders away, but the ends must've been treated with something sorcerously sticky, and they refused to move. Maisirians swarmed up. Arrows, spears went down, and climbers fell. But others, baying for blood, replaced them.

Maisirian bowmen volleyed arrows, and the blocking spell must have been gone, for the shafts sped accurately through the granary's windows. Two Maisirians reached the top of one ladder, bounded into the upper story, and killed a man before Yonge cut them down. There was a small battle at the ladder head before we drove them back and an ax-man smashed the rungs of their ladder. More climbers were at another window, and the battle raged on.

Unless our forces crossed the river, we were doomed. And they were being driven back, hesitating, then reluctantly pushed forward by the officers they feared more than the enemy. Bodies littered the bridge and the islets, and corpses floated in the river between small floes of ice.

The emperor quietly watched all of this. I almost said something, but stopped myself. He was the seer king; he would know the time. "Very well," he said, and whispered a single phrase. I heard a great roaring, like the wind, like a fire, and my palms dampened, and I felt a chill that had nothing to do with the icy wind.

I saw something. Some *things*. They came from our side of the river, moving steadily across the water, needing no bridge, no land. They were mostly stark white, and I peered closely, trying to see what they were. Someone with better eyes than mine screamed, and I could see what the emperor's spell had brought forth: A hundred, five hundred, perhaps a thousand horses, of the palest white, with a black-cloaked rider on each, swept toward us. Every rider held a curved sword in each hand, swords that glittered, though there was no sunlight to reflect; they shone not silver, but blood red. I couldn't see into the cloaks' hoods, but knew the riders' faces would be naught but skulls.

This, finally, was the Great Spell. Tenedos, in his arrogance, his supreme confidence, had dared summon Death, or her minions, the final manifestation of Saionji, to fight with us. Some Maisirians had the bravery to shoot at the riders, some cast spears. The weapons sometimes hit the cloaks, but fell away as if they'd struck plate armor, and the riders came on. Then they were amid the warriors on the waterfront, swords flashing and red gouts spraying high.

Now I heard laughter, hard maniacal laughter filling my mind, filling the universe, and the Death demons killed on. It was the Maisirians' turn to waver, then turn to run. But their own lines blocked retreat, and panic struck, and men tossed their weapons away and ran, running in utter fear, looking back, knowing they must not look at Death closing, but afraid not to.

Death—many Deaths—rode on, for this blood-soaked place in no way was their home. Their swords scythed and Saionji laughed harder.

Our soldiers, nearly as frightened as the Maisirians, attacked, pushing across the bridge and cutting out a foothold on either side of the granary, and we were safe.

The first squadron of cavalry trotted onto one of the bridges. Another sound boomed across the skies, the roar of a man's rage. The air became solid, and a huge Maisirian warrior bestrode the village, five hundred feet or more tall. It swung a hand, and half the Death demons vanished, and the rage became a war cry. The demon's hand closed about a rider, and a high, womanly scream came from him. Again the warrior killed, and our soldiers keened in fear as loudly as the Maisirians had.

The demon saw the cavalry, reached out, and as its hand came near, horses screamed, and the hand swept the squadron—horses, officers, men—into the Anker River. The warrior looked for more prey, but then its eyes widened as if it had been struck, and it stumbled back, crushing Maisirian soldiers as he did. Its mouth gaped, but no sound came, and it flailed at the air, as if choking.

Its hands grasped its throat, and it staggered. Its voice changed, flowed, and it became something awful, not man, not ape, as its cheekbones widened and great fangs grew from its mouth. Its jawline dropped and elongated, the face stretching like putty. Its body warped as well, became misshapen. Its hands became pinchers, and its arms grew and grew, almost brushing the ground. The demon's eyes were green fire, and it turned against its own, and slashed at the Maisirians. One blow smashed down a village street, and stone buildings shattered like rotten wood. Again the panic shifted as the *azaz*'s demon killed and killed—always its own men. I heard the emperor shouting in triumph at his counterspell.

Then the demon howled and dropped to its knees, holding its head in agony, and my bones shook. Quite suddenly, it vanished, and there was nothing but a broken village, and warriors trying to fight, trying to flee, and all confusion.

Numantian units poured across the bridges, and the

Maisirian rear line broke, and their army was shattered, falling back, away, into the *suebi*.

We had won a great victory, perhaps the greatest in Numantian history.

The Emperor Tenedos's face was utter, unholy glee. Yonge stood beside him, completely expressionless.

The price was terrible. The river was dark red as far downstream as I could see, and the bridge, the islets were choked with our dead. The streets of the village were blocked with dead Maisirians, and there were more beyond. Cavalry pushed through them after the fleeing Maisirians, and more blood soaked the land.

We lost nearly forty thousand, and the Maisirians twice that, although no Numantian counted their bodies.

We had won a great victory. But ahead lay the wasteland, the endless *suebi*.

TWENTY-SEVEN

DEATH ON THE *SUEBI*

Among the Numantians who died at Sidor were a dozen dominas, five generals, and three tribunes, including Nilt Safdur, commander of the cavalry, and the emperor's brother-in-law, Aguin Guil.

Safdur was killed when the demon swept the cavalry squadron from the bridge, leading from the front.

Guil didn't return to the Wheel in nearly as heroic a fashion, but was cut down inside Sidor, surrounded by his bodyguards. A Maisirian wasn't as dead as he looked, and took one more Numantian with him into death.

For me, their deaths diminished Numantia not at all, but the single worst casualty was one who still walked—Myrus Le Balafre.

I'd encountered him just after the battle, while I was scurrying to the rear to make sure Alegria was safe. I'd congratulated him on our victory and gone on.

Alegria was safe, having been treated as if she were in lamb's wool by the Ureyan Lancers. She looked pale, drawn, and I vowed she'd have a proper meal before we marched on, and a magician's spell or a chirurgeon's potion to let her sleep around the clock.

Le Balafre's face kept returning. It was gray, haggard, and that famous fire in his eyes was gone. I sought him out as soon as possible, two days after we'd burned our dead and marched away from that gods-damned charnel house of Sidor. He looked no better than before, and I asked what was the matter. Was one of his old wounds bothering him?

"No, Damastes. I'm just tired."

"There'll be time enough to sleep in the grave," I jested crudely.

"That thought has come more than once," he said, without smiling. Now I was truly concerned. I took a minute, through my own fatigue, to find what I hoped were the right words.

"Come on, man. You're too long without Nechia," I said.

"I'm afraid the absence has only begun."

I sought for another jest, but couldn't think of one. He nodded, tried to smile, and asked if I'd excuse him, for he had pressing duties. I felt helpless, but couldn't hold the hand of every soldier, even one as vital as Myrus.

The emperor told me I'd be in command of the cavalry, as well as my regular duties. He asked me to lead the march, which he still insisted was an "advance," never a retreat. I said I would if he insisted. But I thought Linerges more suited for point. I could better serve Numantia by bringing up the rear, as he'd first commanded me.

I assumed the Maisirians were behind us, and would mount an attack at any time. I asked if his magic had shown otherwise. Tenedos looked upset, and said he could see nothing. I was astonished, and he explained: "It's not that they have so many great magicians. The *azaz* seems to be the only one I should concern myself with. But they've got many, many of these War Magicians, and each seems to have some favorite spell to fog the mind. Break one, and there's another. Break that, and there's a third. I don't have the time or the energy. So your idea of where the Maisirians are is as good as any. Better than most," he said grudgingly.

It would have been very easy to accept the emperor's command, for then I'd have been in the vanguard, not seeing the gore and filth of the army as it crawled onward. But I knew where my duty was, and evidently so did the emperor, for he merely growled and said I could do what I wished, and perhaps I knew best.

We hadn't moved far beyond Sidor when the Negaret returned, snapping at our flanks. Stragglers and outriders were easy prey for them, or for the ever-increasing partisans. Patrols reported something disturbing: The partisans had been reinforced with squads of regulars from the Maisirian Army. Prisoners said King Bairan had sent a general order out requesting volunteers, something unheard of in their army. He promised that anyone who came forward would, when the war was over and we were driven out, be freed of any and all debts and burdens, including those that were hereditary. Not quite freeing the peasants, but very close.

I cursed, thinking how Tenedos could have done the same, or better.

The horses drawing my coaches, though they were given as much care as any of my Red Lancers, were wearing out. We stripped and abandoned one carriage after four horses died eating some sort of half-frozen prairie brush. We went on, with twelve horses slowly pulling what eight had easily galloped with.

As the winter grew worse, so the war became grimmer. We took no prisoners, having no way to keep or hold them.

The Maisirians were almost as brutal, but they did take a few. The lucky ones were officers who shouted they could ransom themselves, although this only saved them if they were faced by the greedy Negaret. A few more became slaves, and still labor in the heart of the *suebi* as far as I know. Others met a harsher doom. The Negaret learned they could sell Numantians for a few coppers to peasants. These prisoners were slowly and cunningly tortured to death, an evening's entertainment for an entire village.

The eye, the mind, grew numb to brutality. I saw so many corpses, so much evil, that my memory blurs over much. Only the extraordinary remains.

One incident can serve for all: A Guard victualling party vanished, and I rode with the Twentieth's patrol to see if there were any survivors. There weren't. Half a day's march from the trading route the Guardsmen had come on a small village that hadn't been looted or abandoned. They'd found supplies—and women.

After the village men had either been slain or fled, the Guardsmen enjoyed themselves heartily. Children were slaughtered before the Guards turned to the women, eldest to child. Then they were killed, not quickly.

In the midst of the blood orgy, they were surprised, and it was the Guardsmen's turn to die slowly. Their mutilated, naked bodies were lined up on blood-soaked ice, cocks and balls severed and stuffed into their mouths.

I thought it had been partisans, for the Maisirian women were not buried or cremated, but the troop guide with me offered another possibility: It could well have been Numantians. I was shocked, and he reminded me of the deserters, stragglers who marched along the army's flanks like jackals, and like jackals fed on what they could, when they could.

I had the women's bodies burned, and said a prayer, but would not permit any honorable disposal to the Guardsmen. We rode away from the dead village, leaving their bodies for the wolves, four- or two-legged.

The cavalry I commanded was a bitter joke. I should've had a million men, two million horses. But instead, I had far fewer men still mounted than when we'd first campaigned against Chardin Sher so many years ago.

Most of our horses were dead, and more were dying. We had no ice nails for the horse's shoes, and so they'd slip and go down on the icy tracks. Even if limbs remained unbroken, an animal wouldn't have the strength to get to his feet, and was left to die.

The cavalryman would curse, hurl his heavy saber into some bushes, abandon his saddle where it lay, and lurch onward as an infantryman, but one who had no more idea of how to form a line or attack a redoubt than of how to fly. A cavalryman thinks of himself as better than his unmounted fellows, and so, afoot with the commoners, it was easy for him to give up hope. And that was something, in those terrible days, no one had very much of.

But some lived. Strong men did, and I do not mean those with bulging muscles, for many of them saw yet another icy hill to clamber up, whimpered, and slumped to the roadside as not, while a puny, scrawny boy from Nicias' gutters gritted his rotten teeth and went on—another foot, another league, another day.

Men with faith lived, and it didn't seem to matter what they believed. Some were religious, which is a rarity in Numantia, insofar as true religion goes. Or they had faith in family, wife, even, I suppose, although I know of none, in themselves. A man's friends, his squad-mates, if he still had any, would be his strongest bower, chivvying him on when he wanted to stop, cursing him, even striking him when his soul weakened. A league farther it would be turnabout, and his turn to scream, swear, and cry at one of them, and together another league would creep past.

I lived, I think, because my oath would not let me die as long as men who depended on me still lived.

And because of Alegria.

Beyond that, beyond her, I lived because Saionji had not yet tired of japing with me.

I woke, without knowing what woke me. Alegria coughed, a deep, racking cough. I sat up in our blankets, scrabbling for flint and steel.

"What's the matter?"

"Nothing," she said. "I'm sorry I woke you. Go back to sleep."

"Are you sick?"

"No. I've just got a cough."

My heart turned. "How long have you had it? Why haven't you told me? Why haven't I noticed?"

"Because you've had other things to worry about. And it's only been . . . a couple of days or so."

I struck the steel.

"Don't bother with a light," she said hastily.

But I persisted, and our tiny lantern flared, illuminating the cave-like interior of our carriage, blankets hung over the windows to try to hold in some warmth. Alegria hid something under the covers.

"What's that?"

"Just a handkerchief."

I pulled her face close, saw its utter paleness in the flickering candlelight, then saw something worse. There was a hint of blood at the corner of her mouth.

"Let me see that handkerchief."

"No!"

"Dammit, show it to me!"

Reluctantly, she did. It was wet with blood.

At dawn, I took her to the imperial caravan, before the army began to move. The emperor's own chirurgeon examined Alegria, against her protests of good health.

"Yes," he said, and his tones were artificially hearty. "Not the first such I've seen. I'll mix up some herbs, and I want you to make tea three times daily. That'll give you some relief from the coughing."

I followed him to his carriage.

"What is it?"

He shook his head. "I don't know. It's been going around for about a week now. The first case I noticed was after we had that little set-to last week. In that village."

I tried to remember. But there was always fighting.

"The one with two temples," he said. "We used both for hospitals for the two days we were there, before Tribune Linerges broke through."

I vaguely remembered it.

"That's when it materialized."

"How long does it take to recover?"

The chirurgeon gnawed at his lip, looked away.

"I asked a question," I said sharply.

"Sorry, Tribune," he said, unused to being commanded. "I don't know. I really haven't had the time to follow up on things like that. There's far worse matters to fill my hours."

"How much worse can it get?" I asked.

The man looked around the encampment—the dirty snow, the bundled men, the dark sky—then at me. "I'm sure your lady will recover," he said. "Keep her in a carriage, and make certain she eats. She'll have as good a chance as anyone."

I was afraid to press him, afraid I had my answer.

* * *

We marched on, bodies strewn in our path like a carpet. They'd always be stripped, and now it was commonplace for them to be half-butchered. I made sure, when I was invited to eat something in my rounds, that I inquired about the source of any meat offered. But most didn't. They couldn't—there simply wasn't that much food.

Even I, the highest tribune in the army, went hungry. One or two days at a time wasn't worth a single complaint around a fire, and was sure to elicit a sympathetic reply such as "you overfed fat bastard."

I came back from a long patrol, out in the cutting snow for almost a week trying to find the gods-damned Maisirian Army, and almost cried when someone handed me a blackened, half-roasted, half-burned potato he'd dug from a farmer's field and roasted in a tiny fire. It tasted better than a many-coursed banquet.

Some of the Maisirian women who'd become bed partners of soldiers stayed with their lovers where they fell. Others found new mates within the hour. I remember one general who'd happened on a very pretty girl in Jarrah and seduced her. She'd foolishly gone with him when we retreated, fearing her countrymen would kill her when they reoccupied the city.

When the general found the girl to be pregnant, he threw her out of his carriage and said if he saw her again, he'd put her to the sword. The man who told me the story said she'd stood beside the line of march like a statue, eyes staring in disbelief, tears in a frozen runnel down her cheeks.

The rear guard came on her half a day later, crouched beside the trail. Her face, dead eyes still wide, stared up the roadway, after her lover.

The first sign of catastrophe was the high shrill of our lead horse, as he lost his footing on the curve. He pulled the pair behind off the icy road, and the carriage slid gracefully with them and tumbled into the deep ravine.

At the top of the low hill we were climbing I planned to have the carriage pull over, unsaddle Brigstock, tie him to the rear of the coach, and slip inside for an hour's sleep. It was snowing, getting worse, and I dreamed of holding Alegria and the warmth around me in a few moments.

Instead, I watched a wooden box holding all I held precious go a-tumble down the rocky slope. I was out of the saddle and scrambling down the icy rocks, somehow not losing my footing. The carriage hit the bottom of the ravine, smashed through a frozen rivulet, and lay still, on its side. The body of one teamster was impaled on the winter-frozen spear of a tree stump, and the other lay crushed under the wagon itself, screaming. His screams stopped just before I reached him.

I jumped atop the shattered box and pulled at the door. It came off in my hands. There was no movement in the darkness, then a pile of blankets stirred, and Alegria's tousled head peered out.

"Am I alive?" Alegria asked, then spasmed in coughing.

"Yes. Oh, gods, yes," and I was down in the carriage, holding her close.

Please, gods, I prayed. Name your price, name your sacrifice. But don't let her die. Please. I've seldom prayed to you, feeling that if I went to you in good times, you'd never listen when things were bad. Take me if you wish, but let her live.

The Lancers helped us take what was salvageable and clamber back to the top of the hill.

A gust of wind hit Alegria, and she shivered. "It's . . . good to be out," she said, attempting good cheer. "Stuffy in that coach. It's time I got some exercise, anyway."

I paid no attention, but looked down the trail, through the now-heavy snow. An ambulance creaked toward us. I waved it down.

The driver didn't recognize me in my filthy greatcoat and my long-unburnished helmet. "Full up," he shouted. "No room for nobody, not officer, not man. Out'n the way."

Svalbard jumped in front of the horses, grabbed one's halter and pulled it to a halt. "For th' First Tribune, you'll fucking stop!" he shouted.

"Sir! Sorry, sir. What do you need?" the man stammered, coming out of his frozen stupor.

"We lost our carriage. Is there room for my lady?"

"Sir . . . she'd be more'n welcome, but there's no room for her to fit. Sir, I wasn't lyin'," the man said, knowing I could kill him if I wished and no one would stop me. He clambered down and yanked open the door of the low carriage. I flinched, smelling drying blood and sickness. There were half a dozen men packed in the interior, which was more like a coffin than anything else.

"Go on, driver," Alegria ordered. "I'm healthier than any of these men. I can walk." Then she promptly disproved it by bending double in a spasm.

"Here," a man said, and pulled himself from the carriage. "I'll not ride when a great lady is on foot." His uniform was in tatters, and he wore a Maisirian cloak, cut at the waist so he could walk. He had the emblem of the Seventh Guard Corps pinned to the cloak's side, and a bandaged left leg. He put weight experimentally on the leg, fought back a wince, tried again, and managed a smile.

"Hells, sir. I'm ready to go back to my comp'ny. If there's a comp'ny to go back to."

I knew what I wanted to order, but could not.

"Driver, I said move on," Alegria ordered.

The man climbed back to his seat.

"Now, you," she said, turning to the Guardsman. "Get back in."

But he wasn't there.

"Where . . ."

Svalbard pointed to the edge of the road, where it dropped off into the ravine. I ran to it and looked down. I saw, dimly through the snow, a man, limping as quickly as he could, away from the road into the darkening *suebi*.

"Stop!" I called.

But he never turned, never looked back, and a moment later was lost in the storm.

I never even learned his name.

The ambulance, with its sick and wounded, and Alegria, became part of our formation. The men in it were given some treatment by two of my Lancers, who knew a bit about herbalism.

We'd just pulled off to the side of the road, circled the half-dozen open wagons we had, set out pickets, and considered our miserable rations for the night, when the emperor's galloper found me.

"How dare they!" Tenedos shouted, and spun a wand against the tent wall in rage. It wasn't a question. "Gutless back-stabbing bastards! How in the hells could they betray their country so?"

The emperor had tried time and again to use his Seeing Bowl to reach Nicias, but without success. Finally he'd used seven of the most skilled Chare Brethren to force his spell. With that power, he'd successfully contacted one of the Brethren at the palace. They'd been trying to contact him as well, but without success, until the seer thought of summoning his two sisters, Dalny and Leh, "blood touching blood," Tenedos explained.

The news from both sides was bad. There'd been an attempted revolt. Scopas and Barthou, the former members of the Rule of Ten Kutulu had warned of, had led it, backed by those same barons that had come to me for help and approval in setting up a private army, with Marán's brother Praen. The group was now headed by Lord Drumceat, and had no more loyalty to Numantia or the emperor than before. I held back rage. I should've done what I'd threatened and had those traitorous sons of bitches arrested.

They'd gotten two of the parade units in Nicias on their side, and seized about half of the government's buildings. But they'd made two errors, Tenedos explained: They hadn't arrested the magicians, and they hadn't bothered with two regular units camped outside Nicias awaiting ships to take them south to the war.

"There was a third mistake," Tenedos finished. "They didn't have any real leaders. So when they called for the people to rise up, the people went home."

A day later, the revolt collapsed. But neither Scopas, Barthou, or Drumceat had been taken. They were in hiding, although every warden in the country sought them. Nicias, however, was safe. "At least for the moment," Tenedos said.

"What did they want? What could they . . ." I'm afraid I was sputtering like an old fool.

"What did they want? Power, of course. How could they consider such an action? Easily. When the lion weakens, the others in his pack stalk him. Things aren't going . . . as they should here. I assume rumors have gotten through. And not hearing anything from me since Jarrah could only have made matters worse."

I gathered myself. "What of the Tovieti? Were they involved?"

Tenedos gave me a hard look, then grudgingly admitted: "No one mentioned them. Perhaps they had sense enough to realize only a fool would follow Scopas."

I thought of how Tenedos had constantly ridden Kutulu

about the men and women of the yellow cord, and told him to ignore anything else, and Kutulu's warnings about Scopas and Barthou, but realized only an idiot would bring that up, or mention Kutulu's name, although I desperately wanted to suggest that the Serpent Who Never Sleeps should be brought back from exile and given a free hand. Brutal though he might be, he'd at least guarantee the emperor's back was safe. But, as I said, I wasn't in the mood for imbecility.

"What can we do about it?" I asked.

"Nothing, now. Dalny broke down when I told her of her husband's death. I suppose she might've actually loved the man. I ordered my Brethren to bring whatever Guard Corps that are anywhere close to trained from Amur and garrison Nicias." Tenedos growled. "As if we won't need them when we reach the frontiers. Leh will be named regent."

I kept my expression blank, remembering the last time I'd seen the emperor's sister—half-naked, being serviced by several Guardsmen.

"That's not good," the emperor went on, "but in these times we have to do with what we have. Hopefully I'll be able to keep in touch, and the Chare Brethren won't let her do anything completely absurd. *Damn* it, but I wish Reufern hadn't been killed!"

I pointedly looked aside, and there was silence in the tent except for the wind whipping at the canvas.

"Oh well," Tenedos said. "He would've insisted on coming with me, so it wouldn't have made any difference."

"Sir, you really didn't answer my question. What do *we* do?"

"All we can do is move as quickly as we can," Tenedos said. "As soon as possible, I'll have to leave the army and get to Nicias. I can't fight a war if my kingdom is slipping from under me. You'll have to take charge of holding the Maisirians at the frontier, if they're foolish enough to follow us through Kait."

I barely understood his last words. Abandon the army? How could he even think that? Didn't the oath all of us had sworn require an equal duty from the emperor?

Tenedos must have read my face.

"There are no good decisions, Tribune. Not when everything is falling apart around us. This is the best that I can devise. Perhaps *you* have a better plan, not just for your so-loved army, but for all Numantia?" He waited, lip curling a bit.

I didn't.

"Very well," he said. "This is some time away. You're forbidden to speak of this to anyone, including your woman. That's all."

I think I managed a salute. I stormed outside the tent for an hour, rage seething, paying no heed to the storm, or the curious glances of staff officers, before I was capable of riding back to my post.

This would be the emperor's second betrayal of his army.

I wonder, if I'd not been in such a black mood at the emperor's unbelievable callousness, if I would have behaved in another manner to Herne, and if I had, if that would have changed anything? Probably not, for Herne always had an eye out for his own welfare.

We were pushing our way back through the darkness when we came to a roadblock. Six freight wagons made up a small caravan before us, with an enormous carriage in front. Two horses on the first wagon had gone down, creating a cursing, shouting jam. Infantrymen were pushing past on either side, still far from wherever their officers had planned to stop for the night.

Imperial orders were very clear.

"Captain Balkh! Find this infantry column's officer and, with my compliments, have him detail men to strip that wreck and push it off the road!"

Before Balkh could answer, there came a scream of rage from inside the carriage: "In a pig's arse! This is a tribune's property, and there'll be no interference! Lend a hand, you big-mouthed shit out there, instead of playing like you're a god!"

I slid from the saddle, went to the carriage, and saw Tribune Herne, fuming and mud-covered. He recognized me in the dim light from the carriage's sidelamps. "Oh," he said weakly.

"Oh, my ass," I snapped, giving rein to my temper. "What the hells is going on?"

"This is my . . . my staff's supplies," he said. "I'll send one of my officers down the column and commandeer a pair of horses. We'll be moving as soon as possible."

"Captain Balkh," I said. "Follow my orders!"

"Sir!"

"You cannot do this, á Cimabue," Herne snarled. "I have my rights!"

"Sir, you will stand at attention when you speak to me," I half-shouted. "You may be a tribune, but I am general of the armies, am I not? Do you wish to be placed under close arrest?"

I dimly realized this was a threat I was using a lot these days.

"This is absurd," Herne said, his face reddening to match his elaborately worked uniform.

"Two men," I ordered. Svalbard and Curti were beside me, fighting to keep their faces expressionless. "Tear the canvas off that first wagon."

"Sir!"

"Dammit, Tribune . . ." Herne said, then fell silent.

My two men were atop the wagon, daggers out. Ropes were slashed, and the heavy canvas dragged away. Of course the "staff supplies" were barrels of wine, hams, bags of bread, sides of beef well frozen by the cold, and other fineries. The marchers had stopped, and were staring at these goods they hadn't seen for weeks. I heard a low growl, as an unfed tiger makes.

There was an officer beside me. "Sir, Captain of the Upper Half Newent. At your command."

"I want this wagon off the road," I ordered. I thought of propriety, then red rage made me discard it. "Here are my orders. I want them followed precisely. This man is Tribune Herne."

"I know, sir. We're part of his corps."

"Very well. He is to be allowed to fill one wagon, and one wagon only, with whatever he wishes from this wreck and from the others. Then he is to go on his way. Everything else—horses, wagons, and what they hold—are now the property of your unit. They are to be shared out equally between officers and men. Use them well, use them fairly. If I hear of any favoritism, I vow I'll have you hanged, and when I return to Nicias, your family will be notified of your having shamed your uniform."

"You won't have any cause for that," Captain Newent said flatly.

"I hope not. If Tribune Herne attempts to interfere, I want him held here until my rear guard reaches this point. At that time, I'll take charge of the prisoner and deal with him as necessary."

"Yes, sir."

Herne was glaring at both of us.

"Tribune," I told him, "those are my orders. You are to obey them absolutely or face imperial justice. Do you understand?" Herne muttered something. I used an old drill instructor's trick, and spoke to Herne again, my face almost against his, but as if he were across a parade ground. "I said, do you understand?"

Herne opened his mouth to bluster, finally had brains enough to realize my mood, and said only, "Yes."

"Sir!"

"Yes, sir."

"Very well," I said. "Further, if I hear of any attempts to revenge yourself on this officer or on his unit, I'll have you relieved and your entire staff and servants assigned elsewhere." His face whitened, for this would be a death sentence. He'd be no better than the crookedest sutler, regardless of his high rank.

"That's all!" I strode back to my horse, remounted, and we forced our way through the mass of soldiers. As we rode off, there came cheers and, for the first time in recent memory, laughter.

Captain Balkh drew my attention to a corpse beside the road.

It was a giant of a man, perhaps in his fifties. His right hand had been amputated earlier, and the bandages had come away from the stump. His features were hard and lined, and he wore the insignia of a regimental guide. An old soldier, but the bodies of old soldiers weren't uncommon. Then I noted what had made Balkh point. The man's coat had come open, and there was a flag wrapped around the warrant's stomach.

The guide was the last of his regiment, and had torn the colors from the staff, and tried to carry on, tried to carry them back to Numantia.

I thought the flight from Kait had been terrible enough, but this was worse. This was the slow death of my army, my emperor, my country.

There were soldiers without units, and officers as well. Tenedos ordered all officers who had no command to his headquarters, established a "Sacred Squadron," and ordered them to concern themselves with only one thing—his safety.

He already had bodyguards, but at least this gave these men something to worry about, something to occupy their minds on the march. That was good enough for some, but not others, who were beyond even his reach.

One was Tribune Myrus Le Balafre. Curti told me he was riding with the Twentieth, without servants, guards, or staff, no more than a common soldier. I sent one of my officers to find him and ask him to join my staff. The officer returned saying he couldn't find Myrus.

I sent again, and once more the tribune couldn't be found. I would have to go myself, winkle him out and kick him until he was ready to try to stay alive again. But before I could find the time, his troop was sent out against some Negaret.

The enemy turned out to be stronger than anticipated—

two full companies, almost two hundred men. The cavalrymen reined in, ready to pull back to our lines for reinforcements.

Le Balafre shouted something, someone said a battle cry from a regiment twenty years disbanded, spurred his horse, and, at a full gallop, charged the two hundred. They sat befuddled as this madman came, saber pointed, standing in his stirrups.

Then he was among them, and his blade flashed, and there was a frenzy and they lost sight of him. Seconds later the Negaret rode away, as if fleeing a regiment. They left six dead or dying in the snow.

Next to them sprawled Le Balafre. His body had more than a dozen wounds. When they turned his corpse over, there was a contented smile on his face.

I remembered what he'd said when Mercia Petre's body was burned: "A good death. Our kind of death."

I hope Saionji granted him the greatest boon, and released him from his debt to the Wheel. For I cannot conceive there could ever be another warrior like him.

The day was clear for once, and the way was straight and level, the *suebi* reaching to the horizon. If there were any Negaret about, they were harrying another part of the army. If it hadn't been for the solid, dark mass of staggering, dying humanity, and the scatter of bodies for three miles on either side of the main road, the day might have been almost enjoyable.

Brigstock stumbled and went down, pitching me into a snowbank. He tried to get up, failed, then tried to find his legs. He looked at me, expression infinitely apologetic.

I looked at this ruin of a magnificent stallion, ribs showing, mane and tail scraggly and long, his coat mangy, only rough-groomed. His tack, once so splendid in many-colored leather, was cracked and rotting. His eyes were dull, his gums dark and diseased-looking when he tried to nicker and managed only a faint wheeze.

I should have found a quartermaster and given him up, but

I couldn't.

There was a narrow draw about a quarter mile away, and I took Brigstock's bridle and gently, slowly, led him to it. The draw was only about fifty feet long, and the snow was thigh-deep, but anything in it would be hidden from the road.

Brigstock followed me into it and stood dumbly, as if waiting for what he knew would happen.

I scrabbled in one saddlebag, found a few scraps of sugar at the bottom, and let the horse lick it from my glove.

I held his eyes with mine so he wouldn't see what my right hand was drawing; caressed and lifted his head gently with my left. I slashed his throat cleanly with Yonge's gift dagger, and blood spurted.

Brigstock tried to rear, but couldn't. He fell to his side, quivered once, and was dead. I sheathed the knife, turned, and stumbled back toward the column.

The sun was dark and the sky was the deepest black.

The Seventeenth had found a tent for Alegria and myself. It was a gaily colored thing, intended for a baron's summer lawn, perhaps so his children could pretend they were explorers in distant lands. A soldier talented with a needle sewed blankets inside for a lining, so it was cozy in spite of its summer look. We'd laid canvas for floor, had our sleeping furs, and were warm. Normally we slept fully clothed and I only allowed myself one luxury—slipping out of my boots before I moved in next to Alegria.

She hadn't gotten any better, but rather had grown paler, and her coughing fits made her shudder in pain. I was about to come to bed, thinking she was already asleep, when Alegria opened her eyes.

"Damastes. Please make love to me."

I didn't know if I could, being utterly fatigued, but I didn't protest; I slipped out of my clothes.

Alegria was naked under the furs, and I took her in my arms, kissed her deeply, stroked her, trying not to notice how thin she'd gotten, how coarse her always silken hair had become. Surprisingly, as her breathing came faster, I found myself hard, and then she rolled onto her back and raised and parted her legs. I moved over her, and slid my cock into her, moving gently, rhythmically, to her sighs of pleasure.

Alegria's body shuddered under mine, and then I spasmed for a moment. "There," she said, when her breathing slowed. "Thank you."

"Thank *you*."

"I love you."

"And I'll always love you," I said.

"There's a better place," she whispered. "Isn't there?"

"Of course," I said, although in truth I doubted it.

"We'll be very happy there," she said.

"What do you mean?"

She didn't answer, but her breathing became regular, and she slept. Thank whatever gods there are, gods I'm no longer able to worship, I didn't follow her into sleep. Instead I lay there, holding her close, still inside her, trying to keep from crying.

Sometime during the night, without outcry, without any sign at all, Alegria stopped breathing.

And my life came to an end.

TWENTY-EIGHT

BETRAYAL AND FLIGHT

Yet I lived on. If Saionji had taken everything I had, then I would become truly hers. I would go in harm's way until she allowed me relief and forgetfulness in my return to the Wheel.

My Red Lancers found wood for a pyre, and Tenedos himself held the ceremony, a great honor that was, like all else to me, totally meaningless.

The retreat continued. The gods should have had mercy on any Negaret, any partisan, any Maisirian regular who came within range of my rear guard, for I had none. We struck hard, and stayed on their trail until we brought them to bay, and then killed them to a man.

We lost soldiers, but what of that? All men die, and all of us would perish in this vast desert, and it was better to die with a sword in your hand, spitting blood, than to slowly freeze in your filth.

Prisoners said the Negaret called me a demon and unkillable, and so it seemed, for men were brought down on my left and right, but I never received a scratch. Svalbard and Curti fought on either side of me, and they, too, remained unscathed.

The army plodded on, leaving bodies, wagons, horses in the snow. The Time of Storms had ended, and the Time of Dews begun, but the weather did not break.

Yet slowly a bit of hope came. The city of Oswy could not be far, and beyond that was the border. At last we'd be quit of this hellish country. There was no reason King Bairan would pursue the shattered remains of the army into Numantia, or so they hoped.

Only Svalbard, Curti, and I, and a handful of others, realized peace wouldn't be at hand, but rather the savage mountains of Kait, the murderous hillmen and their evil Achim Baber Fergana. Every rock would hide death, every pass an ambush. But I said nothing.

On a clear morning, we saw the walls of Oswy.

And, in a great arc to the east of them, the Maisirian army, ready once more for battle.

"I know of no other army capable of such a feat," Tenedos said. "Which is why the Maisirians will be utterly bewildered when we pull it off."

The emperor had proposed a bold tactic to the tribunes and generals assembled in his tent: We should turn right, or east, as if preparing for frontal battle. But, masked by sorcery and the weather, we would continue moving, marching parallel with the enemy lines until we were about to attack Oswy instead of the Maisirian army. If we took the city, we could resupply, and hold the Maisirians off until the weather broke and we were able to march on.

Such a flank-exposing maneuver is terribly hazardous, but such maneuvers had been rehearsed in peacetime, and carried off. The question was whether we were still capable of such cleverness.

"If we do not succeed?" Herne asked skeptically.

"Then we're no worse than if we'd stood and fought," Linerges said.

"Not true," Herne said. "For if we form battle lines now, we'll have our reserves properly positioned. And Your Highness's plan, with all due respect, will leave our support elements open to attack from the west, from what the Maisirians will think to be our rear."

"The Negaret to the west will be busy," the emperor said. "I'll have certain sorceries for them to concern themselves with."

"It's terribly chancy," Herne said, still unconvinced.

"Not for you," Linerges said, half-smiling. "Your units are just ahead of Damastes's in the line of march, and I doubt if any Maisirians will dare hit the demon Cimabuen, or even strike close to him. Most likely, if they scent our plan, they'll smash into me."

"I'm worried about our entire army," Herne said sourly. "Hit us anywhere in the column, and the army's cut in two, leaving me and *General* of the *Armies* and *First Tribune* á Cimabue surrounded." I noted the sarcastic emphasis he put on my rank, and knew he had neither forgiven nor forgotten my redistribution of his wealth.

"Perhaps *you* have a plan," the emperor said.

Herne hesitated, took a deep breath. "I do. But you will not like it, Your Highness."

"I like very little these days," Tenedos said. "Try me."

"I suggest we attempt to negotiate with King Bairan." Everyone looked at him in amazement.

"He's shown little interest in talking," a general in the rear said bitterly, "only in slaughter. And I can't blame him, since he's got us on the run. So why talk?"

"Because no one, not even the Maisirian king, could want any war to go on to annihilation," Herne said.

"Who makes that guarantee?" Yonge muttered. Herne ignored him.

"Let me surprise you," Tenedos said. "I have tried to contact the king, but his sorcerers keep blocking any attempt I make." There was a shocked murmur, and I came out of my glumness long enough to wonder what terms Tenedos had devised, and why no one had heard of this before.

"Try another route," Herne said. "Not magical, but direct. Our First Tribune's dealt with him. Send him out under a flag of truce."

"The hells," I spat. "The only way I want to see that bastard is at the end of a lance. I'll not—" I caught myself, seeing the emperor's look. "—Play diplomat. Unless the emperor orders me," I finished weakly.

"And I'll give no such order," Tenedos said. "Tribune Herne. Don't slacken now. We're almost clear of Maisir. Bear up, man. Once we cross the border, and have time to take a breath and regroup—then you'll realize how weak your idea is." Strangely, his tone was almost pleading.

Herne stared at Tenedos for a long moment, then nodded abruptly. "I hear and understand what you've told me, Your Highness, and withdraw my suggestion," he said, suddenly formal.

"Very well," Tenedos said. "Gentlemen, return to your units and order them for the march. And remember . . . the end is very near."

Linerges drew me aside as we left the tent. I feared he was trying to do for me what I'd failed to do for Myrus, and, frankly, I wanted no bucking up, thank you, I was quite content following the weird I'd chosen. Sooner or later death would take me in this monstrous land, and I'd find rest for a time before Saionji summoned me to be judged for my evils and cast back into the world's muck. I thought I might make the first move.

"I hope, Cyrillos, you aren't planning to tell me you've realized The End Is Near, and are giving me the ownership of your stores, for I've no sense at all when it comes to commerce, and they're better left to your wife."

He surveyed me wryly. "I was going to try to cheer you up," he said. "But if you're capable of even wormy sallies such as that one, the hells with you. Go on and die. As for me, I'm immortal, in case you haven't figured it out by this time."

I looked closely at him, and couldn't tell if he was still trying to be funny or had gone mad. "Careful," I said, "the gods might be listening."

"No," he said seriously. "No, they're not. Or, anyway, the gods that give a shit about us aren't. The only one who might be is the emperor's prized whore Saionji, and who cares, for she intends nothing but evil for us anyway."

And I thought I was becoming an unbeliever, or, rather, a non-worshiper.

"Careful," Yonge said, coming up from behind us. "Your curse might change things."

"For what? The worse?" Linerges laughed boisterously, the harsh laughter of a warrior beyond fear, beyond hope. "Anyway, Damastes, do me a favor and don't die tomorrow. We're running short of tribunes, and I'm afraid the crop the emperor might name next would be terrible drinking company." Linerges barely drank at all. He smiled once more, clapped me on the back, and hurried toward his horse.

"So he thinks he's immortal," Yonge mused. "Why not? Someone has to be, sooner or later."

"What do you think?" I asked, making sure no one was within earshot.

"About what? The emperor's plan? It's possible. Maybe even good. Not that I care," Yonge said. "For I came to bid you farewell, Numantian."

"Come on, Yonge. This sort of claptrap only works for mummers. You're too devious, sly, and duplicitous to die, at least honorably in battle."

"Thank you for the compliment, my friend, and I hope you're right. I mean I'm leaving the army."

"What?"

"I said, long ago, in Sayana, when you were a legate and I was a native levy, I wished to learn about Ureyan women, and whether they were more interesting if they had a choice as to bed or no. I'm content with my knowledge that they are.

"I also said I wished to study honor. Now I know all I wish to on the subject. And on its opposite." He turned, looked back at the emperor's tent, and spat scornfully. "So I'm quit of my sash and the army tonight."

"You can't!"

"I can," he said firmly. "My command is either dead or parceled out to other officers, so there's no one to care whether I shout orders or put my thumbs up my arse and walk on my elbows."

"Where'll you go?"

"Back to Kait, of course. And I doubt if there's anyone, either Numantian or these dogs from Maisir, who'll even see me, let alone be able to stop me." I knew he was right there. "So I came to say good-bye, and to thank you for what we might call an interesting time. Perhaps I'll see you once more, although I doubt it, this side of the Wheel.

"So I'll give you two favors now. The first shall be a surprise, when you find out about it, in the fullness of time.

"The second requires some meditation, so imagine you're some sort of dirty holy man with fleas, an unwiped arse, and able to think of great things and tell us peasants what they mean."

"All I've got is the shitty ass and fleas," I said, suspicious of all this.

"Then think harder than you have before. Remember, long ago, after my skirmishers were almost destroyed at Dabormida, when I came to you, drunk, and said my men were sacrificed, and I didn't know why?"

I was about to snap something about that being many corpses and campaigns ago, but I saw Yonge's deadly seriousness. "Yes," I said. "I remember."

"Well, now I think I know the answer," he said. "And I suspect you can come up with it as well. I'll give you one clue: Why did the emperor, back at Sidor, insist on the Varan Guard's sacrifice? He called it a diversion, but what was it diverting? We had already crossed the river, and were known to the Maisirians. Why did he let them die without sending a spell? Why, come to think about it, did he send such a small unit out in the first place? Why didn't he send more men with them?

"More questions," he said, holding up a hand for my continued silence. "Why did he wait to cast his Great Spell until the Guardsmen were already on the bridge? Already on it, already dying? There, I think that's more than enough, so I'll leave you.

"One other thing that just came to me as I talked. Remember the demon that destroyed Chardin Sher?"

I shuddered. In spite of all the horrors I'd seen, that mountainous four-armed V-mouthed demon was the worst.

"I'll make a wager I'll never be around to collect," Yonge said. "I'll wager you'll see that fiend again. Not now. But later. When all seems lost. Now, Numantian, good-bye. And take good care."

Before I could clasp him in my arms, try to argue or even say anything, he slipped away, around the imperial bodyguards' warming tent. I went after him. But he wasn't in the tent, or, when I circled it, anywhere around it.

So passed Yonge the Kaiti, by far the strangest of all the tribunes of Numantia.

I was in my blankets, pretending sleep as a calm, confident commander should, actually trying to blank my mind, trying to avoid thinking of the past two years of unrelenting sorrow and pain, when Captain Balkh woke me.

The news was as disastrous as it was shocking. The Twentieth Heavy Cavalry had lost contact with the rearmost elements of the five Guard Corps and their supporting elements, which Herne commanded, and had sent out a patrol. They found nothing—Herne's positions had been abandoned.

He'd marched his entire force, almost twenty thousand men, due east, into the enemy lines. Herne, we learned later, had ridden in front with a white flag, shouting his surrender. I don't know how he fooled his officers, whether he said he'd gotten imperial orders to take positions to the east before dawn, or if the *azaz* seized the moment and used his magic to fog the minds of our soldiers.

All that mattered was the gaping hole between my rear guard and the rest of the army. Minutes after I was roused, I heard the sounds of battle. The Maisirians had discovered the hole and were attacking through it. Herne's treason was about to destroy us all.

I had to do something, and it couldn't be anything predictable. An idea came, which at best might mean we'd be on our own in the *suebi* for several days, at worst . . . But I refused to think about that.

I sent Captain Balkh, wearing my helmet and with the Red Lancers, to the Twentieth Heavy, ordering them to fake an attack toward the Maisirians, as if I were leading an assault to link up with the rest of the army.

They were to strike until they hit real resistance, then fall back on the Seventeenth, which was to be an assembly point for our support units, the ragtag men who'd fallen to the rear, and those civilians prepared for a hard march instead of slavery or death. Then the entire formation would strike due west, away from the Maisirians, away from Oswy, with the Tenth Hussars leading the formation.

We would turn north after I'd broken contact with the Maisirians, circle east-northeast and rejoin the army at Oswy. It was a desperate hope, but the best we had.

The Twentieth Heavy Cavalry, even though they were decimated, their horses barely able to manage a trot, smashed into the Maisirians. The enemy had rushed forward with vast glee, looting what little there was to steal, and were swarming about, not yet re-formed, when the cavalry hit them. They fell back in amazement, shocked that the Numantians were able to mount a counterattack so quickly.

Before they could recover, the Twentieth withdrew as quickly as it had come. By the time they rejoined the Seventeenth, the Lancers were ready to move, and the column pushed out, away from the road, into the open *suebi*.

It was hard going, and again men and horses went down, and civilian carts weren't able to keep up, and so the panicked sutlers and camp followers had to grab what they could and trundle on afoot.

But this wasn't the worst. The ambulances filled with our sick and wounded bogged or overturned as they tried to cross the deep ravines that intersected our path.

I gave hard orders: Abandon the train. Even Domina Bikaner gave me a shocked look before he saluted and went to see my orders were obeyed. But it was simple in my mind: Either they would fall into the hands of the Maisirians, or we all would. A handful of chirurgeons volunteered to stay with them, and while I admired their bravery and dedication, I refused to allow it. We'd need every one of them on the march. Men and not a few women cursed, screamed at us, as they saw men cutting the trails of the horses pulling the ambulances, but their anger was to no avail. An hour later, we marched away, leaving some of our honor and our hearts as we did. But compassion had no place in this wasteland.

Two hours later, as I was hoping my ruse had succeeded, our outriders reported Negaret patrols. I cursed—our movement would be followed and reported to King Bairan, giving him more than enough time to move troops between us and Oswy. But I had to continue the attempt, and ordered the Tenth to swing north.

Then came horror. The snow ahead of the Tenth's screen heaved as though it were alive, as if great burrowing creatures were under it. The hillocks sped toward our men, then buried the lead elements as they screamed and tried to run, nightmarishly slow through the waist-deep snow. But no one saw or felt anything under the snow.

This was the surprise Tenedos had planned for the Negaret, a horror weapon that had turned against us. The snow-burrowers—snow-worms if that's what they were—smashed men down, broke them like frozen twigs.

The Tenth fell back, and the snow-worms turned away, not interested in anything moving away from Oswy.

Now we were doomed. South and east was the empty, man-destroying *suebi*, west were the Maisirians, north were the snow creatures. Then something came, an utterly foolish notion, as I realized we were out of contact for the moment—the Negaret patrols following us had fled even faster from the nightmares than we had.

I summoned my three dominas and the tough regimental guide who was the most senior of Yonge's skirmishers, and told them we were about to make a one-day forced march, and to put the strongest men at the rear, not to guard against attack, but to make sure everyone kept moving and that we left as few tracks as we could. Put the weakest on horseback, I said, and everyone else afoot.

We had two Chare Brethren, and I ordered them to summon flames to consume any corpses. We were going to try to vanish. This might give us a slight, very slight, chance of life. Otherwise, we might as well start thinking of ourselves as either Maisirian slaves or frozen corpses.

"What direction will we march?" Bikaner asked.

"East," I answered. "East by northeast."

Almost directly away from the emperor and our army. The only chance we had was to break contact with the enemy, and then attempt an impossibility: to cross the mountains into Numantia as I'd done once before.

But then I'd had only a handful of men in prime condition to worry about; now I'd cross with several hundred shattered, starving men and some camp followers.

I should have ordered an attack, back the way we came so we could die nobly and uselessly for the emperor.

But I stood by my foolishness.

Two hours later we stumbled off into the empty *suebi*. I put my Red Lancers at the rear of the formation and told them to obey my command with no bowels, no mercy. No man was allowed the privilege of dying, not until nightfall. I was the last of all, screaming, shouting until my voice sounded as if it were drawn across broken glass.

I swore at men, and they swore at me. I struck them, and

they tried, feebly, to hit me. But I always sidestepped the blows, and then taunted them to try again, or were they weak worms? I said I'd call them women, but that would shame the sex, for women were ahead of them—sutlers, laundry maids, whores, who knew, who cared.

I felt no fatigue, no exhaustion, no hunger. I'd become a creature of the snows, of the wilderness, and drew my strength from the wilds around me.

We went on, and on, and slowly the smoke of Oswy's warm fires slipped back over the horizon, and there was nothing but empty prairie in front of us. It began to snow, and for the first time the storm was the blessing of Isa, of Nicias, of Irisu the Preserver, for it hid our path, and blinded any enemies who might've pursued.

Eventually I called for a halt. We collapsed in our tracks, and the long frozen night dragged past.

I commandeered Balkh's horse and pushed ahead before dawn. About half an hour distant was a tiny valley surrounded by twisted low trees. A frozen stream ran along one side. I rode back and told my officers to get everyone moving.

An hour later, they did, but there were twenty-three bodies in the snow. I had my Lancers drag them together, but forbade my sorcerers to try to burn them. We could afford neither the smoke, the loss of the magical energies, nor the possibility the *azaz*'s War Magicians might pick up our scent.

It took almost two hours to reach the valley, but we did. I had the men assemble in whatever formations they had left, and it was a pathetic sight. Bikaner and his adjutant did a fast count and reported. We had forty-six of my Red Lancers, one hundred fifty of the Seventeenth, about two hundred of the Tenth Hussars, the same number of the Twentieth, some of Yonge's skirmishers, three hundred fifty or so odds and sods from other formations, forty-nine women, and even a scattering of children. I tried to hide a wince. Ration strength of the Seventeenth Lancers was over seven hundred, the

Tenth Hussars and Twentieth Heavy Cavalry nine hundred each.

I had to do something to make people believe there was the slightest chance of life. I told the men to break ranks and form up around me. The wind blew cold, but it was over our heads, whispering across the *suebi* beyond the valley.

"Well," I started, knowing better than to sound inspirational, "I don't know about *you*, but I'm glad to be away from the army." That brought a shock.

"At least we aren't wallowing along in their shit and ashes," I said, and there were a few snickers. "That's what I like, to be out here where someone can breathe, where there's plenty of fresh air." There were a few open laughs.

"All right. We've been cut off from the emperor," I said. "And that fucking Bairan is rubbing his hands together, thinking that he's got us on toast. I'm going to prove him full of horseshit, and anyone who wants to do the same is welcome to take a little walk with me."

"Where we goin', Tribune?" somebody shouted.

"We're going to stroll across the *suebi* until we come to some mountains," I said. "Then we'll go up 'em, and down the other side, and we'll be right at the borders of Numantia. We ought to be home sometime in the Time of Births, so the weather'll be fine. Anybody want to go with me?"

Again, mutters, some laughter. But most faces still looked empty, hopeless. "Or do you want to see how many ways a Maisirian clod-knocker has to keep you screaming before you go to the Wheel?"

A hard-faced warrant stepped forward. "Ain't gonna happen to me, Tribune. I ain't plannin' on bein' taken alive. And they'll know they been in a pissin' match when they come for me."

"Good," I said. "But wouldn't you rather stay alive and get your own back another day?"

"Hells yes! But—"

"But nothing, man. Now, shut the fuck up and listen!"

"Sir!" And he fell back into the formation.

"That's the spirit we need," I said. "Because all of us are going to try to stay alive. Look at the man—or woman—on your left. Do you know him? You'd better, because he's going to get your sorry ass over those mountains. Tell him your name. Go ahead. Right now."

Silence, then a babble as some, then more, obeyed.

"We're going to spend the rest of the day here. First we're going to put everyone into a formation. If you're already part of one, you're going to get reinforced. Friends stay with friends when we divide up. That'll help.

"I'm going to make some men officers, others warrants today. Maybe you've never held any rank, and don't want it, don't think you can carry the weight. Tough shit. You'll do it, and you'll do a damned good job of it. Another thing we'll do is divide up all supplies. There'll be no more fat bastards eating while others starve. We all eat or none of us. That goes for officers, warrants, men, civilians.

"Now, I want the Tenth, Seventeenth, and Twentieth on that side of the valley. The rest of you, see if there's anybody else from your old unit. Get moving. I want to be on the road before any Maisirians wander across our tracks."

That put people in motion.

There were a surprising number of Yonge's skirmishers still alive. In spite of their hazardous duties, I had ninety-two of my original two hundred. I took them to one side and told them they were all promoted sergeant.

"The reason I'm promoting you isn't that I think you're heroes. Yonge told me better. I know you're thieves, sneaks, back-stabbers. Like your leader. And I'm damned proud he tried to train me to be like you."

I waited until the laughter died.

"I'm not promoting you because you're good, just because you're still alive. Now I want you to help all these others stay the same. But there'll be one change. There's no more of just worrying about your own flea-bitten hides. Each of you'll have at least a squad, some more. If you don't like it, my piles bleed for you. You're welcome to see if the other side can use you."

There was louder laughter, for the skirmishers were thought bandits, lawless murderers for whom there was no mercy, even from their counterparts in the Negaret. "Now, all of you report to Domina Bikaner of the Seventeenth for your new posts."

Late in the day, we gathered in our new formations.

"Good," I shouted. "You almost look like soldiers again." Even though they were bearded and ragged, and I could smell them from where I stood, they held their weapons ready, and I knew they could use them. "Look again at the man on your left. Now you know his name. You're mates, whether you like it or not. And my first order is that you're to make sure that man beside you lives to see Numantia. Because if he doesn't, most likely you won't, either. There'll be no more of this pull for yourself and let the other bastard sweat.

"We're all in this sewer together, and we'll all get out of it together. We're an army again, and warriors once more. No more of this hobbling along, letting any shitty-dicked Maisirian do whatever he wants. From now on, we'll fight them if they find us, and make them sorry they ever came on our trail.

"You know me, you know how I smashed the bastards every time they hit us. If they find us now, we'll do the same. Let them get their fingers lopped off to the knuckle, and they'll go somewhere else, looking for easier targets.

"That's enough words," I finished. "Let's take our walk."

I still wished for death, for oblivion. But not yet. First I must try to cross those great mountains. Most likely I'd fail, and we'd all die, for I didn't believe a thousand soldiers could manage that smuggler's track.

But I wouldn't let myself be killed. Ironically, I found myself praying, empty words, but still saying them, prayers to Vachan, my monkey god of wisdom, and to Tanis, asking for the boon of life.

Twice now I'd sworn fealty to Saionji, after Tenedos had brought me back from the fire, and when Alegria had died, and promptly tried to renege on my vows.

The goddess couldn't be thinking very much of me as a mad juggernaut, I thought, and had to laugh. With the laughter, I felt myself coming alive a bit, coming from under my woe cloak.

Again, I remembered the wizard's prophesy when I was born, and prayed I had been savaged enough by the tiger, and that again it was my turn to ride him, and that the thread of my life would run on. At least for a while.

I had my warrants and officers up and down the ranks constantly, shouting orders as they'd always done, but now doing something different—showing they deserved their tabs, their sashes. They swore at a man who dropped his weapon, but if he couldn't lift it, they carried it for him until he got some strength back. If he went down, they bullied two of his comrades into draping the man's arms over their shoulders and going on.

If they didn't do this, and thought my words were as empty as the wind—that first day I reduced seven officers and thirteen warrants to the ranks.

Compared to the pace I'd made with Bakr and his Negaret, we were crawling. But we were moving, every day farther away from Bairan and his army.

I asked the two Chare Brethren to try a spell to contact the other magicians in our army. They'd barely made marks in the snow for their symbols and burned a few herbs when one shouted in fear and kicked the markings into nothingness.

"He's out there," he managed to say. "Somebody is. Somebody looking for us."

We made no more attempts to communicate with the emperor.

A man fell to his knees, moaning. I was on him and jerked him to his feet.

"Please. Please. Just let me die," he begged.

"I will, you bastard. But in Numantia. Not here. Get up, you piece of shit! No wonder you're down, you asshole! Your whore of a mother didn't have time to give you any heart, did she! Nor did any of the pimps who could be your father," I raved.

The man's eyes sparked life, and he swung at me.

"Not close," I jeered. "Come on. Try again."

He did, and I let the blow land against my chest.

"I've been hit harder by babies," I laughed, and stalked away. He shouted a curse at me, and I hid my smile. He might make it across the mountains, if for no other reason than to kill me.

The last two horses died, and were consigned to the pots. Two horses and perhaps a dozen sackfuls of roots we'd scrabbled from the frozen ground, to feed nearly a thousand.

We reached the great river, and Isa was with us, for it was frozen solid. We hastily crossed.

Another miracle—one of the skirmishers found a shallow backwater, and in it were three of the bewhiskered, evil-faced fish, seemingly asleep. We cut a hole in the ice, spears went down, and the fish awoke to lashing agony. But as they wriggled, smashing the ice about them, arrows flicked into their hides, and we had fresh food.

Two were over twenty feet long, the third almost forty, and we devoured them eagerly, half-cooked or even raw. Other fish were found sleeping close to the banks and we broke the ice and killed them as well.

We made several meals from those fish, enough so everyone was heartened. Perhaps it was possible to live in this spare land after all.

Men still died, but not as often. When they did, we carried their bodies until the night's camp, and then our wizards said the words and tried to summon the flames. All too often they failed, and we had to bury them under mounds of rock. But this was better than letting them lie where they fell. And there was no more cannibalism.

* * *

The country looked slightly familiar, and I thought the weather was becoming milder. We were coming to where Bakr's Negaret had been camped. It might have been a hundred years ago. I remembered how good that antelope tasted we'd hunted, and if Isa was truly on our side, perhaps there'd be game wintering over here, and who cared if it was a bit gaunt. We could rough-tan their hides, and that would give us better footwear and coats for the icy mountain passes. I put scouts far ahead of the formation to make sure we saw any game before it saw us.

We found better meat than I'd hoped. Our scouts reported seventy black, circular tents in a large hollow: Negaret. I guessed they might be having one of their gatherings, their *riets*.

My Brethren sensed no magical wards, so the Negaret weren't on their guard, never imagining there'd be any enemy this deep in the *suebi*. I sent the Ureyan Lancers to sweep wide around them and attack from the rear.

I had the former skirmishers, such men as they recommended, and the dismounted Hussars move forward as my main attack element, and held the rest of my column about a mile in the rear, guarded by the Heavy Cavalry.

It wasn't a *riet*, I learned from the scouts who'd crept close, but a camp of Negaret women and children, safe while their men harried the outlanders.

There were only a handful of sentries, just boys, and they were quickly silenced. We swept down from the heights around the camp screaming battle cries.

The Negaret women and even children poured out with what weapons they had, sometimes swords, more often butcher's implements or even sticks. They fought bravely, but we vastly outnumbered them. They fell back through their tents, and the Ureyan Lancers took them from behind.

Some fled into the *suebi*, others tried to fight on and were cut down or disarmed; still more held up their hands, knowing what horrors were about to come.

I saw a man reach for a woman, who struck him down and kicked him. Other officers and warrants were shouting, screaming, and the bloodlust died, a little. Before it could rise again, we beat the men back into ranks and began the systematic looting of the camp, working in squads, for a man alone is more likely to murder and rape than when he's with his fellows under tight control.

We took food, drink, weapons, heavy clothes, all the boots that fit, blankets, packs, horses. I wanted the cook pots, sleeping robes, and tents that could be made small through magic, but one of the women said their *nevraids* were at the battle, and none knew how to work the magic. Of course she was lying, but what was I to do? Put her, or others, to torture?

It was almost dusk when I ordered the men to march on. We could have, should have, stayed the night in the comfort of the tents. But I doubted I could keep control of my soldiers with enemy women, particularly those of the loathed Negaret, close. Not that I was, or am, innocent of crimes of war. Perhaps the Negaret still had their tents and cookware. But what could they prepare in them? And how would they hunt for game? I refused to admit pity, any more than I permitted that weakness when I abandoned our sick.

At least, I thought to console myself, the women and children of Jedaz Bakr and the other Negaret who'd befriended us hadn't been at this camp. Not that it would have mattered if they had.

The plains became foothills, and the mountains drew closer, dark shadows through the clouds. The weather was warmer, and it rained constantly. The rivers beside the rough trail were in full flood, and fording the creeks crisscrossing our track became a challenge.

One day we reached a clearing I thought I remembered, where men in dark armor had been waiting for me. But if not, it was as good a place as any to announce we'd crossed the border. Maisir was behind us. We were in the Border Lands, which Numantia had long claimed for its own.

Cheers rang, and I ordered an extra ration of the Negaret's grain, which we ground and added hot water to.

Over us hung the silent mountains.

The climb went on and on. Once more we were surrounded by snow, but it didn't matter as much, for that signified we were farther away from Maisir, closer to our homeland.

It stormed, and we found shelter in a canyon for a day? A week? Time became meaningless in the grayness. Our sturdy Negaret horses could go no more, and we slaughtered and rough-butchered them. Most of the meat we froze, but I permitted one great feast.

Soon enough all around us would be nothing but cold, and the memory of that meal would have to warm.

The storm ended, and we went on.

We heated snow water in whatever served as a canteen, mixed that with grain we'd mashed up, and ate it as we marched. The way was now narrow, with high cliffs to one side and emptiness on the other. Men began dying again, of the cold, or a stupid fall they wouldn't have taken if they had had proper strength.

Sometimes, scrabbling for a hold as they fell, they found another man's leg, and pulled him over the edge with them, to tumble screaming into white nothingness.

We reached the head of the pass and started downhill, and again we rejoiced. I was happier than most, for I'd been certain no body of soldiers could make this passing without being destroyed. I'd been wrong, and humbly swore I'd never forget this triumph of the spirit. Men, properly led or leading themselves with a strong will and heart, can storm the very heavens.

A day was simple: Wake from the shivering half-sleep you'd passed the night in. Hope someone nearby had found enough wood for a fire, so you could melt snow water for your "tea." Pick up your pack and weapon and stumble on, one foot in front of the other, over and over, sucking air, not letting yourself fall, then another step, and another, and another. When a warrant shouted stop near dark, eat whatever scraps you and your mess-mates had, or whatever had been doled out. Try to find a place out of the wind, close to a fire if you were very fortunate, and spread whatever blanket or canvas you had, and slip into a nightmare-ridden drowse. Wake when you were kicked for guard duty, or to tend a fire, and pray for dawn. Again and again, over and over.

On this dreary trek, I had time to brood about the past, then to do something I was most uncertain at: think. About who I was, *why* I was, and consider coldly the endless disasters, from Kallio to the present. Catastrophes, in various shapes, had been constant since I'd helped the Emperor Tenedos seize the throne.

I couldn't believe we'd gone against nature when we overthrew the stumbling morons of the Council of Ten. But why had there been nothing but tragedies ever since?

The strongest memory that kept returning, and I kept trying to push away, was of Yonge's questions before he vanished. Reluctantly, for there was nothing else to hold my mind but the dirty snow I was plodding through, the wind down my back, and my sodden clothing, I considered Yonge's sardonic queries.

Quite suddenly, the answer came, an answer that should've been obvious. Evidence assembled itself, things Yonge hadn't been privy to.

I began with the night the emperor had gotten me to volunteer to enter Chardin Sher's fortress, spill a certain potion, and say certain words that brought up that nightmare demon from the burning hells under the earth.

Tenedos had said that for the spell to work, the powers he'd contacted wanted someone Tenedos loved to willingly perform a great service that could cost his life. Of course that meant me, and of course I volunteered.

But there had been more. He'd said this "power," which I thought to be that terrible monster from under the mountain, had another price, and Tenedos's words came clearly: *You may not ask what its price is, but it is terrible, but not to be paid for some time to come, fortunately.*

A price. A sacrifice? That word sprang into my mind. This was appalling. My thoughts were traitors to the country I served.

No, I reminded myself. My inner oath, the oath of my proud generations, was to Numantia. But the oath I had sworn was to the Emperor Tenedos. Very well then. I was being disloyal to him.

I returned once again to Yonge's questions.

Why *had* Tenedos waited so long to cast the spell that made the trees become stranglers at Dabormida, wait until heavy cavalry units and Yonge's skirmishers had spent themselves bloodily against the Kallian defenses?

Did the casting of *that* spell also require a price? A price not in gold or in servitude, but in blood? Of course, my mind said contemptuously. What sort of debt do you think a man who loudly espouses vassalship to Saionji the Destroyer would incur?

I remembered the conversation I'd had in Polycittara, in the seer scholar Arimondi Hami's cell, and his words came back very precisely. A friend of Chardin Sher's mage Mikael Yanthlus, Hami asked if I thought one man could pay a high enough price to call forth the demon that destroyed Yanthlus, Sher, and their mountaintop citadel.

I also remembered when I'd tried to ask the emperor about Hami's conjecture and was forbidden to mention the subject. There *had* been a price the emperor couldn't discuss, not with the person who was the nearest thing he had to a friend.

Price . . . I thought of how nervous the emperor had been the longer war took to come, and then the sudden inexplicable plague that had appeared in Hermonassa, slain a half a million, then vanished as strangely as it had come.

Blood. Could blood—enough blood—satisfy any demon, make it do anything its summoner wished? Was this Laish

Tenedos's great secret, something he'd deduced in his far wanderings and studies with dark sages?

If his spells required blood, did that mean he must be willing to sacrifice anything, including his own army, for eventual victory? To feed a mountainous, V-shaped demon? Or to feed Saionji herself?

Must the emperor make constant blood sacrifice to the dark Destroyer to hold his power, either magical or temporal?

Yonge had warned me after Tenedos had rejected our idea to free the Maisirian peasants.

But why these disasters, then? After all this slaughter, all this destruction in Maisir, wouldn't the goddess be well pleased with her servant?

Again, Yonge's voice came, saying that when Tenedos rejected chaos, rejected unleashing the peasants against their masters, Saionji turned away from him. Certainly she must have welcomed the slaughter, but just as a drunkard who is grateful for a pint of wine at first soon thinks it's his due, the goddess of destruction wanted more: utter chaos, with each man's hand turned against his better.

Was Tenedos scrabbling to regain her favor? Or had he gone beyond that? Was his power now completely grounded in blood, in disaster?

And I'd sworn an oath, an oath to help in whatever he endeavored, my mind ironically reminded me. Did that include helping him destroy Numantia, if it came to that?

Thank Irisu that Domina Bikaner came with a problem requiring my immediate attention, so I wasn't forced to answer that question. For the moment.

Now we moved faster, for we were marching downhill, and I swear I could smell Numantia's welcome warmth. But almost a third of us who'd marched away from Oswy were dead.

I stared downslope at the huge temple and the small village where we'd been fed and sheltered, and where we'd obtained our zebus. I remembered that young Speaker who wore no more than a summer robe against the snow, and the riddle he'd told me. I also remembered Yonge's fear and hatred, and wondered what demoniac curses might be brought against us, six hundred men who surely wouldn't be welcome.

But there was no choice, and so I went ahead, flanked by Svalbard and Curti, gathering my stuporous wits, trying to think of words that might grant us safe passage.

But I needed none. Before, the temple had been dark, foreboding. Now it gleamed with bright lights, and soft music floated toward me. There was a huge, winding stone staircase, with fabulous beasts on the balustrades and, at the top, enormous stone doors. I should have felt fear, trepidation, after Yonge's snarl of how he hated these villagers, their temple, and most especially *those who have some sort of tin god whispering in their ear and think they've been adopted into his son-of-a-bitching family*. I recalled, too, him saying that he and three of his men, all wounded, had been turned away by the Speaker's father.

The doors swung open as I approached, and I knew they couldn't be of stone to have moved so easily. A man came out, a big man, but old, bearded, with still-dark waist-length hair, floating like silk in the wind. I thought I knew him, but that was impossible.

"I bid you and your soldiers welcome, Numantian."

I bowed. "Thank you. But there are far more than we three."

"I know. I counted them as they came across the glacier. Five hundred ninety-three warriors, women, and children, by my figuring."

"You're correct," I said, covering amazement. "We accept, gratefully. We ask only a night's lodging, and perhaps a place to prepare our rations, and we'll march on at first light, without disturbing anyone."

"I bade you welcome, and it would be a poor host who wasn't prepared to feed his guests. Summon your command, if you would."

I nodded to Curti, who saluted and trotted back down the staircase. The big man looked at Svalbard and me.

"Your companion may be harboring suspicious thoughts of my intent, although how one man could harm as many soldiers as you lead seems hard to imagine. Does it not, great Svalbard?"

The big man jolted, looked afraid, then forced resolve. "Not f'r a magician like you, which I know you to be, knowin' my name an' such."

The man inclined his head. "It might be possible. If I were a wizard. You're welcome to post guards if you wish, and those two men with you who're students of magic, even if they're not quite sages, may wish to lay any spells they care to. It matters not."

"I don't see any purpose in guards," I said. "You *are* a sorcerer, and if you think my two men nothing but acolytes, then we're in your power anyway. I'd rather my soldiers come in out of the weather. If you have evil intent, at least we die together. And warm."

Of course I had no intention of putting myself completely in this man's powers. But there wasn't any reason not to let him think I'd lowered my guard.

"I'm honored at the trust," he said. "You and your men will be more than warm. Please enter."

"I thank you," I said, bowing once more. "I am First Tribune Damastes á Cimabue, General of—"

"I know you," the man said. "And I know your army. All of it. Come inside." He made no move to give me his name.

I looked up the hill, saw my men coming toward me, less an army than a ruin, and walked inside, feeling no fear at all. I touched the doors as I passed. They were the heaviest stone.

The temple was even larger than I'd thought, extending for many levels underground, stone ramps curving down and down. There were floors of nothing but small one-man stone cells, perhaps thousands of them, which we were offered as bedrooms. There was an oil lantern and a straw mat in each, and they were spotlessly clean, but smelled old, disused.

"These were for your monks?" I guessed.

"You might have called them that," the man said.

"How many live here now?"

The man smiled, but didn't answer. He said for my men to leave their weapons, packs, and outerwear in their cells, unless they felt particularly fearful, and to go down one more level. They would come to two doors. Men were to take the one on the left, our few women the one on the right. He said a clean man would be even hungrier.

Those chambers were high-ceilinged, solid stone, and had changing rooms with stone benches, where we left our clothes, and one great room with stone tubs four feet deep and twenty feet across. Naked, I felt my skin burn, as it always did when I came inside after spending a long time out of doors. I stepped down into a tub and let the bubbling water, just uncomfortably hot, lave me. There was no soap, but bars of sandstone we could scrub with.

I ran my fingers through my hair and beard again and again, trying to comb them, but not making a very good job of it. As I did, tangles, knots of hair came away, and I was reminded once more of how I was aging.

If it weren't for my howling gut, I could've spent the rest of my life in that stone tub, but I was forced out.

As I walked back to the changing room, a blast of hot, perfumed air caught me, and I was dry. More than dry, I realized, as I reflexively started to scratch, a habit we all had, then realized there was nothing biting me.

A greater marvel was our clothes. Ashamed of our rags, we'd tried to stack them neatly when we stripped. Now they were folded as if a laundress had been at them, and so someone invisible had, for they were clean, rips and tears not just mended, but the cloth seamlessly joined together. They were still stained and battered, but lice-free.

We dressed and went up the ramps. The women, chattering as gaily as we, came streaming out to join us.

We entered a huge dining room, with tables and benches of heavy, ancient wood. The tables were laden with brass bowls, filled with food. Taking little heed of formation or rank, we rushed them.

Our host entered as we sat down. We caught ourselves, expecting some kind of prayer.

"Go ahead," he said. "The gods look with disfavor on hungry people."

We needed no more encouragement. There was rice, spiced hot with Numantian herbs none of us had tasted since we left our country, and sprinkled with melted butter; aubergines sliced and fried in an egg batter; lentils so spicy tears ran from our eyes, fresh tomatoes with grated cheese from buffalo milk; rice pudding with mangoes, jackfruit, and herbal teas of many varieties.

Svalbard leaned close. "Wonder how long it takes t' train a demon t' cook?" he whispered.

The bearded man had preternatural hearing, for he smiled broadly. "So you're still suspicious," he said. "Let me ask you something. What are demons?"

Svalbard frowned. "Evil. Spirits that'll do you harm."

"But these beings you're worried about are feeding you. So they can't be demons."

"Poison," Svalbard said, not giving an inch.

"Poison? Then you will die. Die nobly, opposing evil forces, which will advance you on the Wheel, am I not right? Since their deed would have done good for you, they could not be demons, for demons are incapable of good work, by your definition."

"Words!" Svalbard snorted. He looked for a place to spit, couldn't see one, and buried his nose in his food.

The man smiled once more, and walked down the rows of tables, for all the world like the genial host of a country tavern.

Perhaps I dreamed, but I think not. I seemed to wake and

walked out of my cell into the corridor. The lamps that had been burning when we came away from dinner were flickering low, and my sentries were pacing their rounds, trying to stay awake, at each end. No one saw me.

I knew exactly where to go, and went up the ramps to the main level, and walked assuredly down one hall whose ceiling was lost in gloom. There was a small door, and then I was in the temple's heart, a vast polyhedronic room with silk hangings on the walls in blazing colors. But there were no idols, no paintings of any gods, or benches for worshipers, not even an altar.

In the center of the room the old man sat cross-legged on a purple silk pillow. There was a circular straw mat in front of him. I knelt awkwardly on it. He looked at me calmly, expectantly.

"Why did you welcome us?" I asked, without preamble.

"Why not? If I hadn't, you would have tried to take what you needed from the villagers, and I feel duty toward them."

"Who are you? Their priest? Their king?"

"Neither. All."

"What god—or gods—do you serve?"

"None. All."

"There was a young man here the last time I passed," I said. "He called himself the Speaker."

"And so he is. My son."

"Why haven't we seen him?"

"He disagreed with the manner in which you should be greeted. I decided to overrule him."

"What would he have done?"

"You need not know. But it would not have been the best. He is young and has much to learn."

"He told me a riddle."

"I know," the man said, then quoted exactly: "'The god you think you serve, you do not serve. The goddess you fear is not the one who is your enemy, but your enemy is one who seeks to become more, to become a god, yet in the end shall be no more than a demon, for demons are his true master.' Am I not correct?"

"You are."

"The riddle went on," the man continued. "'Serve who you may, serve who you might, you serve but one, and that one will grant you naught.'

"Can you answer any of its questions now?"

I could, although my mind tried to shudder away:

The god I thought I served . . . Isa, god of war. Or perhaps Irisu.

The goddess I feared . . . Saionji, obviously. But if I didn't fear her, then:

My enemy, he who seeks to become more, become a god?

It could be but one.

Laish Tenedos.

The emperor.

The demon king.

If this was true, he could and would grant me nothing, for demons never give more than they must, and I'd sworn an oath of loyalty and servitude of my own free will.

The things he'd given me in the past—riches, titles, power—all of those things had bound me closer to him, made me serve him better, more loyally.

Yes, I had the answer to the riddle. But would I tell it to this man? No. Not ever. He waited. A smile came and went, and he nodded, as if he'd heard someone—myself?—speak, and he'd approved.

"Good," he said. "Very good indeed. Now, since you've suffered much, perhaps you'd like me to give you something."

"Why should you?"

He shrugged. "Because it amuses me. Because it's my duty. Does it matter?"

"I suppose not."

"Very well then," he said. "Of course, being who I am, or what I am, perhaps a man, perhaps a demon as your Svalbard fears, I shall speak in another riddle."

"Naturally."

Both of us laughed, and the sound echoed in the huge

room. Now I remembered him, him and the great leopard who'd watched us climb toward Maisir so long ago.

"You were the boy who rode the tiger," he said, and paused as I started. I began to blurt a question, but realized he wouldn't answer it, wouldn't explain how he could know what a jungle sorcerer had told my parents on my name day. "Now the tiger has turned on you. You've felt great pain, and there will be greater pain to come. But the thread of your life goes on.

"The boon I grant is to tell you that it shall continue far longer than you think now, or shall think soon.

"Some time from this moment, your thread shall change color.

"Perhaps the color I sense has meaning to you. It is a bright yellow, and is now made of silk."

Yellow? Silk?

"The Tovieti's strangling cord," I growled.

"I know of them," the man said.

"They've tried to kill me several times," I said. "I'm their sworn enemy."

"Indeed," the man said. "But all things change. The one you serve, for instance, may become your most bitter enemy. Why shouldn't evil become good, if perceived good is evil?" The man rose. "I think I've satisfied both my duty and my sense of humor, and added confusion, just as my son did. Sleep well, sleep long."

He walked away. The chamber was huge, but he walked away from me forever, growing smaller and smaller, as if it were miles long.

I was back in my cell, and the straw was rubbing into my bare shoulder for an instant, and then I fell back into sleep.

I awoke feeling as if I had slept for ages—fresh, eager, although when my dream, if dream it was, returned, I shivered, not knowing what to think. But I didn't have to, for there was work to be done.

The men were cheerful and loud, dressing in the corridors like so many schoolboys. We formed up outside the temple, while I sought the one who'd guested us.

My calls echoed against stone, without an answer. After a time, I gave up and went out.

It was bright, clear, and a warm wind blew up from the lowlands. Without looking back, we marched away.

Into our homeland, into Numantia, into the fairest land I'd ever known: Urey.

TWENTY-NINE

CAMBIASO

Urey was once bright flowers lining blue lakes, marble and gold, laughter and love. We came into fire, death, and desolation. The armies of the night had already passed on, leaving nothing but black ashes and emptiness.

Still-terrified peasants said the Numantian Army had stumbled out of Sulem Pass, with the ravening hordes of Maisir close behind. The Maisirians had been told by their king and court magician that Numantia was theirs to do with as they wished. The tales of atrocity were heartrending, unlistenable. But as my guts churned in rage and revulsion, a cool part of me reminded that we'd done no better when we invaded Maisir. What else could be expected?

But how had our army moved so fast? I'd expected it still to be entangled in Kait, slowly being butchered by the Men of the Hills. We found a wounded soldier who'd fallen behind and somehow not been captured by the Maisirians.

Oswy had declared itself an open city, which had done no good at all. Our army, beyond mercy, beyond the law, had torn it apart, taking everything when it had nothing. They left the city in flames, its streets filled with the torn bodies of innocents, and marched on north.

By the time they reached Kait, they'd heard from their officers and warrants what they could really expect from the Men of the Hills, and were ready for the worst. But nothing happened. There'd been only isolated ambushes by small groups of bandits. Most of the hillmen were afraid to face so big a force, even one as ruined as the army.

The soldier said he'd heard stories that the ruler of Kait, some pig named Fergle or Foogle, had been killed, and a new man sat the throne, and the hill tribes were frantically making new alliances, settling old feuds, and had no time for outsiders.

Achim Baber Fergana, my old enemy, had finally met someone more ruthless, more cunning?

Who . . . And then a strange thought struck and I knew, without any facts, who his assassin had been, and knew what Yonge's last favor was to the army he'd served.

I grinned. Yonge would make a very good *achim* for Kait, and give the Men of the Hills more than enough to concern themselves with instead of raiding Numantia or Maisir. Or perhaps he'd lead the raids himself.

Anyway, the soldier went on, when they'd reached Kait's main city—Sayana, I told him it was named—its gates were closed, and when the emperor ordered them opened, there came nothing but mocking laughter. There was no time to mount a siege, for the Maisirians were in close pursuit, and so our army went on through Sulem Pass into Urey.

"I heard we wuz supposed to make for th' river, where there'd be reinforcements. But they wuz on our butts through th' pass, then cut around us, usin' Negaret, an' took Renan, I think it's called. We went west, intendin' to hook around 'em, an' come back t' th' river further north.

"But I took this spear when we wuz bringin' some cattle back, crawled away, an' dunno what's happening now."

Both armies then were north of us, deeper into Numantia.

I summoned my officers and told them we had one duty: to rejoin the army as fast as we could, bypassing the Maisirians. Sooner or later, we'd be able to link up with the emperor.

Perhaps he *was* the demon king. But I remembered my oath, and that invaders were laying waste to my land, and that was a rock in a tempestuous sea for this drowning man. I would, I *must*, hold true.

My officers, warriors all, didn't argue. Their units had been stationed in Urey, and it was considered by most their home, and they wanted revenge. The Maisirians had to be stopped, or else all Numantia would be like Urey—ashes and despair.

We moved north, and we were no better than the Maisirians, except we didn't murder or rape. Stand against us and you met the sword. We took what we needed as we went: horses, and eventually we were all mounted; food, until we were all fed; clothes, and we were clean once more. There was nothing to be done about our haunted eyes that had seen too much death and our weary bodies that'd done too much killing. All of us realized that the only peace we'd know would be death.

At least most of us, those of us who were regulars. But there were those who weren't, and each night some would slip away. Domina Bikaner wanted to send out patrols to bring back and hang a few deserters for an example. I forbade it. Let them seek out their homes, far from war and blood, I thought, and wished them luck.

There would be a great battle to come, and why would we want the fainthearted, the cowardly? There was no room for anything but the most carefully forged steel.

Wars—armies—have a certain sound, a certain smell. Blood, fire, even fear have scents. We'd left Urey, and were riding through the poor farming province of Tagil. Smoke pillared in the skies, and we were very close, and rode farther east, then hard north, and then west, looping in a wide semicircle around the Maisirian Army.

My scouts were challenged by Numantians, even more ragged, more weary, more desperate than we were. We'd rejoined our brothers, and reached safety. Such as it was.

* * *

"I should have guessed Damastes the Fair would find a way around those bastards," Tenedos said, trying to sound hearty. "So Yonge's smuggler's route is passable for soldiers, eh? That'll be useful when we invade Maisir next year or the year after."

It was good the emperor was babbling nonsense, for it gave me a moment to cover the shock. I thought I was battered by time. But I was nothing compared to the emperor. He was only a few years older than I, but looked as if he were of another generation. His black hair was almost gone on top, and the round face I'd once thought boyish was lined, harsh.

His eyes still blazed, but they were different, a disturbing gleam to them.

"Yes, sir. I've four hundred fifty cavalry. What's left of the Seventeenth, Twentieth, and Tenth. I'll be frank, sir. We're not in good shape, but we're in better mettle than the soldiers we saw riding through the camp."

"Good. For the great battle that'll send those ants scurrying back to their hill is close." He forced a smile, and the corner of his mouth twitched a little. "Since you're being realistic, I'll do the same. This battle will settle everything. Either the Maisirians and Bairan will be destroyed, or we will.

"It's that simple. They have the numbers, but we have the spirit. We're fighting for freedom now. I know my soldiers will put every bit of their soul, their blood into play."

His words sounded less as if they came from the heart than like tired phrases he'd used again and again until they had no meaning at all for him, and therefore none for his audiences. No wonder the army appeared so dispirited if this was the best their emperor could do.

"Spirit's all well and good," I said. "But it's generally swords, and how many of them there are, that win battles."

"Swords, yes. Or magic. There's our greatest secret strength, for when we fight them next, I have a weapon that will utterly destroy the Maisirians. They won't be able to retreat, but must either surrender where they stand or die."

I wondered how much of our blood this secret magic would require, pushed that thought away, and asked for a briefing on where everyone was positioned.

"One thing before that," he said. "Remember I told you before that once we reached Renan I must leave the army for a time and return to Nicias? That still holds true, even though those traitors were suppressed. I don't want to do it, but I must, to guarantee a final triumph that will ensure the safety of Numantia for all time."

I made no response, but he didn't seem to require one. He called Domina Othman and led me to another tent, where a huge, newly drawn map lay across three pushed-together tables looted from farmhouses. He told the other staff officers to leave, then told me our situation. It was grim. We had no more than a hundred thousand men ready to fight.

I didn't hear what he said next, for my world rocked about me. We'd lost how many men in Maisir? Two million? More, counting replacements? Gods. Even if Tenedos's secret weapon worked, and we destroyed the Maisirians, it would be generations before Numantia recovered.

I forced myself back to the present as Othman continued. Some reinforcements had come in, marching overland from Amur, but they were hastily formed units of fresh recruits and the training depots' cadre.

"There're more, though," the emperor interjected. "I've heard there're at least ten Guard Corps from all across Numantia who assembled at Nicias and sailed upriver to Amur. Link up with them, and that'll give the army a new backbone, and after that there'll be even more reinforcements, once our lines to the river are reopened. So Amur and the Latane must be our obvious immediate goal.

"We'll break through the Maisirians, let them chase and not catch us, which they're good at, then turn and destroy them at the Latane."

I stared at the map without replying. The army held hasty positions just north of the small, now-ruined trading city of

Cambiaso. Amur's border was about twenty miles distant, but then it was a hundred miles to the Latane River.

And the Maisirian Army was between.

I wondered where these Guard Corps, over a hundred thousand men if they were at full strength, had come from. Tenedos had stripped Numantia almost bare for the invasion, and all new units had been fed into that cauldron as soon as they were formed. Did these units really exist? Perhaps there'd been a great rush to the colors, and various border units had been amalgamated and given Guard designation to bolster their morale. I wanted, I needed, to believe this.

I returned to the map.

The emperor wanted another frontal attack for his breakthrough. That appeared suicidal. But farther south was wasteland, near-desert, except for a great semicircular series of peaks on rising ground, nearly ten miles from horn to horn.

"Sir," I suggested. "Instead of striking straight into the Maisirians, what prevents us from feinting north, as if we're moving into the desert, then hitting their flank while they're organizing to come after us? Hit it hard enough, knock it back, and in the confusion we'll have at least a day, maybe more, to break contact. They've got to be almost as exhausted as we are."

"No," Tenedos said firmly. "We can't do that. Not now. Not the way the army is. We don't have the strong backbone we used to. I left too many of my best tribunes and generals, my best thrusters, on the *suebi*.

"The confusion would be too much, and the Maisirians would smash us while we were moiling about.

"My army will fight, though, and fight hard, if we give them a target. That's what we're giving them, right in front of them, something to smash at, smash at hard, and once they break through, break into open country, then the river's in front of them—the river, home, and the end of the war!"

Tenedos's eyes were searing, willing me to believe. But the map was there, too, with its hundred miles of scrubland before the Latane.

"What magic will you use?"

"Once the battle is joined, there will be awesome spells, dreadful demons sent against the Maisirians. But I want to make sure their War Magicians are fully involved before we cast our spells."

I realized I didn't believe a word he'd said. Yes, there'd be magic. But only after a great deal of blood was shed. And the army, like a sickly man, had little to give before complete collapse. "Sir, I think—"

Tenedos's face colored. "That's enough, Tribune! Perhaps you've been on your own too long, and forget you must obey orders like any other soldier! I've given my instructions, and my plans are well under way.

"Now, I have other matters to attend to. My staff will brief you thoroughly as to your role."

He gave me a harsh look, didn't wait for a response, but hurried from the tent. My temper flashed. I certainly didn't need him to remind me I was a soldier, and that soldiers obeyed orders. Hadn't I brought nearly four hundred men through impassable terrain, and—I forced my mind and anger back under control. There wasn't time for infighting. The emperor had made his plan, and it was not a good one. But it was the one which must be followed.

"Domina Othman," I said. "You heard the emperor."

The attack was even more disastrous than I'd feared. The Guard units had barely left our positions when Maisirian infantry struck, twin-pronged like snake fangs, and stopped them cold. Solid waves of Maisirians counterattacked and sent the assault formations reeling back. The Maisirians didn't stop at our front lines, but attacked all along our front line.

We fell back and back, out of our positions, and in two days of brutal fighting, most confused and hand-to-hand, we were driven almost into the desert. But we stopped with that nameless rock formation at our backs, counterattacked, and stopped the Maisirians. Before, we would have hit them again—before they recovered—broken them in half, and had a great victory.

But all we'd done was buy a bit of time, and lost twenty thousand men and our positions.

As for the emperor's magic—nothing happened, except the usual minor spells of confusion and fear, which only the rankest private would let affect him.

"Very well," the emperor said grimly, "we are in disastrous straits."

The tribunes in his tent were silent. There was nothing to be said.

"But we are *not*, I repeat *not*, doomed. In fact, now we are able to utterly destroy the Maisirians. There is a Great Spell I used once before. Some of you older soldiers may know it, for it was the one I used against Chardin Sher to destroy his rebels and win Numantia."

I started. Yonge's prediction would come true, and the monstrous demon would rise from this desert to wreak havoc once more.

"This spell is costly," he went on. "But we paid its price once—and we must be willing to pay it again."

His next words were lost in my shock. It had taken all this blood, all this slaughter, the loss of an entire generation of Numantia's finest youth, for that one moment of destruction? What would be the demon's price now?

"It will take three days, perhaps more, to assemble the . . . forces for this spell. Tell your units we're getting ready for battle. Do not mention what I told you.

"Our battle plan will be very simple. Once the . . . force has been unleashed, after it's wreaked its destruction, then we shall attack. All that will be necessary is to mop up the few remnants of their army, so there's no need for elaborate tactics.

"General of the Armies á Cimabue will command the physical attack, for I shall be unable, for various reasons, to lead you myself for a time. I'll caution you on one matter, and this you should pass along to your troops. Until their War Magicians have been silenced, the Maisirians may try all sorts of deceptions. Therefore, obey only Tribune á Cimabue or myself, and obey us absolutely, no matter what we order. I have wards around myself, and will cast equal ones for the tribune, so no false image may be summoned. Remember this well.

"Be of good heart, of good cheer, gentlemen. This is our greatest hour, this is when we are almost gods. We hold the fate of millions in our hands—those already born, and those who've not yet come from the Wheel.

"This shall be the deciding moment, and only one great nation shall go forward into the bright future.

"Numantia!" His voice rose into a shout: "Now and forever! Numantia and Tenedos!"

The tribunes, wounded, battle-weary, cheered wildly, and it seemed the entire army cheered with them.

If I'd been in command of the Maisirian Army, I would have attacked us immediately, giving no chance to recover. Perhaps King Bairan was afraid of the casualties he'd take, storming the heights we held, or perhaps he needed time to regroup—he was fighting a long way from his homeland, with long supply lines and in a desolate country. But his troops were more used to hardship than ours.

Regardless of the reasons, the Maisirians, vastly outnumbering us, only half-surrounded our rocky citadel, leaving the dry plains behind us free of their forces. It seemed as if they were preparing a siege, planning to starve us out.

I made sure our positions were properly outposted, so we'd have warning if the Maisirians struck first, then made endless rounds, cheering some, cursing others, reminding them what they fought for and that this would be the greatest battle of history, secretly dreading the day.

But what else could Tenedos have done? Surrender? I saw no other way. Numantia would have another horrible debt with demons, one far greater than the last. And that was if we won. What would happen if the *azaz* and his War Magicians cast a spell greater than the emperor's? What would happen then?

I caught myself. That was impossible. The emperor was the most powerful magician in the world. His mistakes in Maisir happened because he underestimated the enemy, as did the army. I was certain no such arrogance existed any more.

The emperor's headquarters was a bustle of Chare Brethren, and tribunes and generals concerned with temporal matters were snapped at and sent to me. I hoped the wizards were successful in camouflaging our plan, and that the *azaz* was as complacent as we'd been long ago.

On the morning of the third day, I was about to make another set of rounds, then caught myself. I was like a young legate, so worried about his first command he spends endless hours harrying them, and, instead of turning them into better soldiers, makes them into twitching wrecks.

I ordered my own plans for the day of battle. I'd ride at the head of the cavalry once again. My handful of Red Lancers, augmented with the rest of the Seventeenth Ureyan Lancers, would have the honor of riding at the fore.

Late that afternoon Domina Othman came, and said the attack would begin two hours after dawn the next day. By dusk, Numantia's fate would be settled.

I forced myself to sleep from two hours before midnight until perhaps an hour afterward, then woke. I lay there, feeling the army stir around me, flexing its thews.

I remembered a little prayer I'd said as a child, a prayer to Tanis, our family's godling. It was like the prayers most babes are taught by their mothers, to give them strength in the loneliness of the night and to make them think of the welfare of others instead of themselves.

I whispered the words, although what good a small jungle deity like Tanis could bring on this battlefield, when gods as mighty as Saionji and Isa, her manifestation, would stalk the land, and demons carry out wizards' terrible commands, was beyond me.

I got up and dressed. I'd washed and shaved before I lay down, and put on clean, almost dry underclothing I'd scrubbed out myself the afternoon before. I remembered the vast wardrobes I'd once had, and ruefully looked at my possessions. I donned the cleaner of my two shirts, this one as red as my Lancers' tunics, laced on a boiled leather vest battle-stained almost black, and tucked that into tight black breeches that matched the boots someone had polished until they almost glowed, as if they were new, and the worn-through soles wouldn't be seen. For armor I wore only a breastplate and my helmet, whose roached plume was beginning to shed.

I buckled on my sword belt, a straight blade on one side and Yonge's silver dagger on the other.

I went to my command tent and once more went over the map. I studied the latest patrol reports on the enemy dispositions. There were no changes, so the Maisirians had not been alerted. I hoped.

It was close to dawn when Domina Othman rushed into the tent, and for the first time since I'd known the always-calm, always-prescient aide, he was clearly rattled. He stammered that the emperor wanted me, must see me immediately! I must come at once!

What could have happened? Had the Maisirians learned of his spell? Or perhaps, magic being what it was, would he be unable to summon that dreadful thing from wherever it laired?

A terrified captain of the Lower Half, his uniform torn and travel-stained, stumbled out of the emperor's tent as I approached.

As I came in, Tenedos sent a brazier spinning, its smoldering incenses scattering unheeded. Another brazier, a single broad flame rising motionless from its center, sat in the middle of an elaborately inscribed figure drawn in blood-red chalk. I remembered that figure—I'd drawn a simpler version of it again and again before I climbed the walls of Chardin Sher's stronghold, chalked it one final time on the stone inside, then poured a potion and fled for my life as the demon came into our world.

The emperor's field desk and chair were overturned, and ancient scrolls and musty books thrown about, hurled in blind rage.

I clapped my boot heels, snapped as perfect a salute as I'd ever managed as a prospective legate at the lycée. "Sir! First Tribune Damastes á Cimabue."

"Those bastards! Shitheels! Traitors! Back-stabbers!" he raved.

I held my silence, and looked at Othman, who was as broken as the emperor. Tenedos went to a sideboard and picked up a crystal decanter of brandy. He found a glass, unstoppered the decanter, then, rage boiling once more, hurled it against a map cabinet. The crystal shattered, brandy sprayed into the brazier, and perfumed flames shot up.

He fought for control, found it, and turned to me. "That man who left," he said, quite calmly, "is a brave officer. He's ridden all the way from Amur, from the Guard's depot. Killed three horses on the way. How he managed to snake through the Maisirian positions I don't know. But thank Saionji he did. We've been betrayed, Damastes, betrayed by those we're fighting for!"

Scopas and Barthou had learned from their first failure. Somewhere outside Nicias, they'd made careful plans that included real soldiery. They'd used any and all troops they could rally, units evidently terrified they'd be sent south to be torn apart in the grinder.

They'd marched on Nicias, and there wasn't a Guard Corps at hand to save the day. Trusted units garrisoning the capital mutinied and joined the revolt. The final blow, Tenedos said, was that this time the commoners had listened to the simple message Scopas and Barthou were preaching: Peace now, peace at any price. Surrender to the Maisirians, give them what they want so they'll leave Numantia. Bring down the usurper Tenedos and his people, for they've ruined Numantia with their insane war against a former good neighbor. Peace now, peace forever!

This had happened a week ago. Somehow the traitors had sealed off the river, and no word of the catastrophe came south. In that time they'd sent heliographs to other province capitals.

"Who knows what else they promised, what they threatened, what they said," Tenedos said. "By the time the news reached Amur, half my provinces were in open revolt. I suppose more have joined by now."

I was appalled. To be so betrayed was inconceivable. Without asking permission, I picked up Tenedos's chair and slumped into it.

"What now?" I finally managed.

The emperor and I stared at each other. Again I saw the corner of his mouth twitch. "I know what to do," he said, his voice a bit shaky. Then it firmed. "In fact, what just happened makes the decision even easier.

"Othman!"

"Sir!"

"Make sure my Brethren are aroused and ready! I shall be needing their services within the hour. Now leave us. There are still some secrets I can't share even with you." Othman saluted, and hurried out.

Tenedos smiled, a smile that was purely evil. "I have all of the devices, spells, herbs assembled to summon the demon that brought doom to Chardin Sher. All I need do is call the Chare Brethren, give them certain parts of the spell that'll prepare the ground, and I'll perform the rest of the ceremony.

"This day we'll destroy not one, but two of Numantia's enemies—one who attacks from without, the other who bores from within. The demon shall be called, and given permission to savage the Maisirians, as I'd planned. Then I'll grant him greater pleasure, and give him Nicias.

"I mentioned the cost of this summoning. What Scopas and Barthou have done is make it far cheaper, at least cheaper for honest Numantians.

"I shall give the demon Nicias," he repeated. "Let him do to that great city what he did to Chardin Sher's rocky citadel. Tear stone from stone until the City of Light explodes! Let him take everyone—men, women, babes—for his own, and let the raging fire consume anyone or anything he scorns. Let him tear the land so no one can live there again and it becomes a swamp darker than any in the Maisirian wilderness.

"Let Nicias become an example for future generations, who'll pass by the wasteland, home only to monsters and decay, and know what the price is to stand against the Seer Tenedos, the Emperor Tenedos!"

The emperor's voice had risen and gone shrill, and his eyes glazed as he raved. He calmed himself. "Yes. That is what we'll do. I know how to keep the demon from returning to his own plane. Before, I was worried about losing control, and so arranged that blue lightning that sent him back to his home of dark flames.

"Not now. Not this time. This time, I'll keep him here, and woe to anyone who stands against me, for they'll meet the same fate as the Maisirians, as the scum traitors of Nicias!

"After he destroys Nicias, we'll reach out once more. We'll retake Numantia, Maisir, then on, seizing lands no Numantian has known. We'll let the demon, and others I'll learn about, become our assault divisions, and few Numantian lives will be spent. The creature's pay will be the souls of those conquered, and when the land is empty, we'll resettle it with our own!

"Then, Damastes, we'll have *real* power. There'll be no need for altars, for prayers to fickle goddesses who betray you when they wish. I promised once, my friend, you and I would bestride the world.

"Thanks to Bairan, thanks to the *azaz*, full thanks to those bastards in Nicias, for they've opened a new way for me—for us—a way it perhaps would have taken us years to see, more years to have the courage to grasp.

"Desperate times breed desperate measures, don't they? They also breed greatness.

"They breed gods!"

His face was glowing, and the years had dropped away, and he looked as he had the day we met, long ago, in Sulem Pass, surrounded by bodies.

But now his eyes carried the fires of madness, not power.

He held out his hands, to seal the bargain. I rose, held out mine, and he came forward.

I hit him once, very hard, just below the chin. He dropped without a sound.

I made sure he was unconscious, then rummaged through his magical chests until I found strong cord. I tied the emperor's hands and feet, gagged and blindfolded him, then hid his body in the rear of the tent, in his private sleeping area, pulling sleeping furs over him. I was crying soundlessly all the while, nearly blinded by my tears.

I fed the books piled near the symbol into the flaming brazier, and it ate without a flare the dark knowledge Tenedos had worked so hard to obtain. Then the set out herbs and materials were cast into the fire. I scrubbed at the red chalked symbol until it was gone.

I saw a flagon, uncorked it, and the stench of that same potion I'd poured out in Chardin Sher's castle came back. I put the flagon in my sabertache and left the tent.

I ran to my horse, pulled myself into the saddle, and kicked my mount into a hard gallop. Somewhere in the gray dawn, I uncorked the flagon and hurled it as far away from me as I could.

Captain Balkh was waiting outside my tent.

"Alert the buglers," I ordered. "Sound the attack!"

We rode out from our lines at the trot, bugles singing bright songs of death. Drums thundered, and the infantry, crouched in their positions, came to their feet and charged into the open, cheering.

I signaled, and the bugles called again, and we went to the gallop, Red Lancers in the fore, behind me all that was left of the proud host that had ridden across the border so long ago, a steel-tipped lance now aimed for the heart of Maisir.

Our banners, all the colors of Numantia, rippled in the morning breeze as we rode, and the thunder of our horses' hooves was louder than drums.

I looked back, and my vision blurred, seeing the great army of Numantia I'd spent my life serving, building, and commanding go forward—never hesitating, terrible under its banners—into its last battle.

I felt blood rage, let it build.

We smashed through the Maisirian lines as if there were no one against us, going hard for the center of their army. Men rose in front of me and were cut down screaming, and we smashed on, killing everything in our way.

I felt a flicker of foolish hope that there was a chance we might carry the day, that the Maisirians might break and run. We crushed their second and third lines, and before us was their headquarters.

Then we were hit from the flank by line after line of elite infantry, to whom a man on a horse was an easy target, not a figure of terror. They ducked under our lances and went for our horses. Other soldiers were in front, holding firm, and our charge was broken, and all was a swirling whirlwind of stabbing, slashing, killing, dying men.

Ahead of me, not a hundred yards away, were huge, lavishly colored tents, flags floating over them. Here was the king, and I shouted to the Lancers to follow me, and we pushed on, foot by bloody foot.

Then the demons came from nowhere. They were horrible insects, scarabs perhaps, larger than a horse. But, terribly, they bore above their slashing mandibles the faces of men, and I gasped, recognizing, even through the bloody eyes of battle, one.

Myrus Le Balafre.

I heard someone else scream, as he knew another monster's countenance, and then I saw Mercia Petre's solemn face. I hope in the name of all the gods that these were just devices the *azaz* had summoned to terrify us, and he'd not been able to call the souls of these men back from the Wheel. I cannot believe Saionji would let anyone usurp her domain so.

One horror slashed at my horse, nearly severing its head, and it reared and sent me sprawling. I rolled to my feet, and the horror loomed over me, snapping with its scissorslike jaws, and I lunged, burying my sword in its body. It collapsed, snapping at the wound as I pulled my blade free, and howled, an eerie high screech, and green ichor sprayed me, and then it was motionless.

"They can be killed," I shouted, and saw one rip Captain Balkh nearly in half as Curti sent an arrow into the center of its human face.

The *azaz*'s magic was almost as deadly for his own soldiers, striking as much terror into them as it did us, and they were yelling in panic and running. Another monster came, and Svalbard cut two legs from under it, drove his long sword through its carapace, and it, too, died.

Three men attacked, one armed with an ax, and I opened his guts for him, ducked the sword thrust of the second, and hacked his side open. The third screamed and ran.

There was no one close then except a pair of wounded, dying demons, and I ran for the flag-draped tents, hearing my breath rasp in my lungs, hardly realizing I was muttering that childish prayer to Tanis.

I saw a man standing in the doorway to a tent. He wore dark robes and held a strange wand, not solid as every other one I'd seen, but made of twisted silver, woven like tree branches.

The *azaz*.

Everything in the world vanished, and I was moving toward him, and all was very slow, very blurry. His wand moved, and a demon came from nowhere, and it had Alegria's face. But I was beyond life, beyond caring, and my sword had come back for a thrust, when one of Curti's arrows thudded into the demon's body and it snapped at the shaft, and was gone.

Again the *azaz*'s wand moved, but I was closer, still not within sword striking distance. I think I was still running, but perhaps not.

My free hand, without my willing it, fumbled at my belt, and Yonge's wedding gift, the silver dagger that had killed far more than its share, came out of its sheath, and I hurled it underhand. The blade turned lazily in midair, then took the *azaz* just under his ribs, and he contorted, screaming, and his scream filled my life, my world, with joy, and I thought I could hear Karjan laugh as well, from wherever Saionji had cast him. The wizard's face was agonized, and my sword went into his open mouth and he was dead.

Again hope shot through me, and I turned.

"Now the king," I bellowed, but there were only three men behind me. I saw Curti down with a spear through his thigh, not moving, and a scatter of dead or dying Lancers amid a welter of bodies.

But there was Bikaner, Svalbard, and another man, a Lancer I didn't know. All were blood- and ichor-drenched, but all bore that same twisted death-giving, death-embracing smile I knew was on my own face.

I went for what must have been King Bairan's tent, and there were two men, big men, bigger even than Svalbard, coming. I blocked the first's slash, but the second man's lunge cut me along the ribs.

Svalbard slashed, and the man's head bounced free, then Svalbard turned to me, his expression that of a child, wondering why he hurt, what had struck him, and I saw he no longer had an arm, but a stub that sprayed blood.

He fell, and there was only Domina Bikaner and myself, and there were many men around us, and all wore the brown of Maisir.

Bikaner killed two more, and then an arrow grew from his chest, and he shouted and fell.

An instant later hot pain took me from behind, and I stumbled. But there was a Maisirian still alive in front of me, and just behind him I knew I would see King Bairan, and take him with me.

But my sword was far too heavy to lift, and the pain was fire roaring over me, and I stumbled, feeling another sword bite into my side.

Then there was nothing at all.

THIRTY

EXILE

I didn't regain consciousness for several weeks, and by then the war was over. When I fell, most of our army had either been killed or was trying to surrender.

Few officers, especially anyone with real authority, were permitted to live. All tribunes, all generals, died at Cambiaso.

All but two.

Cyrillos Linerges fought to the very last, until there were no more than a handful of his bodyguards around his standard. Then everyone was down. But when the Maisirians looked for the dead tribune, to loot his corpse, there was no Linerges to be found.

Later the story came that he'd somehow escaped the battlefield, made his way to the Latane River, and from there out of Numantia, to a foreign land, where he lives to this day. Good. There should be at least one of us able to tell of the demon king's rise and fall.

Tenedos survived. I'd hit him harder than I'd thought, for when the Chare Brethren found and untied him, he was in deep shock, unable to remember any spells whatsoever. He didn't return to normal until the battle was over and he was a prisoner. Why the first Maisirian to encounter his most hated enemy didn't put him to the sword I'll never know. But he was taken, and the War Magicians made sure he was kept from attempting any magic.

When I returned from my sweet dreams of death and nothingness, I found King Bairan standing over my bed.

He stared for a long time, saying nothing. I stared back.

He nodded once and was gone. That was the last I saw of him.

Surprisingly, the peace terms he dictated were extraordinarily liberal. What he'd vowed turned out to be true: He *was* content with his own kingdom, and wished nothing to do with Numantia. Not being a fool, however, he made sure we could never threaten him again.

He went to Nicias and visited the treasuries. His words were simple: "They are mine." In addition, he levied penalties against every city and every province in the country, enough to bankrupt Numantia. There were few protests, especially after he said any argument and he'd loose his army with orders to make all Numantia as desolate as Urey.

He confirmed Barthou and Scopas as lawful rulers of Numantia, knowing neither had military ambitions, although he required them to make obeisance to him.

To make sure there'd be no threat from the north, he created a new title—guardian of the peace—and named the traitor Herne to the post, with orders to suppress any nationalist aggression and report frequently to Jarrah.

Herne was authorized to raise a unit as large as two Guard Corps, to be headquartered in Nicias. Of course there were more than enough bullies to fill its ranks who cared little about treason and wished legitimacy from a uniform.

King Bairan ordered that the Numantian Army was never to re-form, on pain of immediate invasion. The largest forces permitted to bear arms, beside Herne's Guardians, were local police forces and border patrols.

The Chare Brethren were also dissolved.

Bairan considered Tenedos's sisters, decided they were no

threat, and mercifully allowed them to return to their childhood home of Palmeras.

As for myself and the emperor:

King Bairan said he would take no measures against us, leaving "proper punishment" to Numantia's new rulers. Actually, as someone explained to me, he was canny enough not to make a martyr of either of us. Neither Barthou nor Scopas could decide what to do, ditherers now as they had been with the Rule of Ten, and so we were exiled.

The Emperor Tenedos was sent to an island not that many leagues distant from Palmeras.

I was sent many miles to the east, to a tiny islet a week's sail from the Latane River's mouth.

Escape was impossible, even if I'd wanted it, even if there'd been somewhere to go.

The Tovieti must have rejoiced—their two greatest enemies had been destroyed by another. But perhaps our destruction rendered them pointless, for I've heard nothing of the cult since.

Sullen time ground past—a year, then more. I recovered my strength, exercised, read, thought about the years with the Emperor Tenedos.

I wondered what would happen to me, assumed I'd either die in decent obscurity or, more likely, be assassinated at some appropriate time.

Then word came:

The emperor was dead. How he died, no one would or could tell me. I assume he was murdered, and so think my own death near.

I will welcome it, for I realize that, even though I intended nothing but good, I brought the greatest evil possible to my beloved country. Perhaps I made small recompense for my crimes when I stopped the emperor from his last, mad attempt to tear apart the world as he fell.

I felt and feel no guilt for what I did, no sense that I violated my oath, for isn't it the duty of an officer to keep his ruler from destroying himself or his land?

Duty, honor flow both up and down.

The emperor never learned this, never knew it. But he *was* the emperor.

Sometimes I think woefully that it would have been better, easier, if I'd been an hour late, years and years ago, arriving at that battlefield in Sulem Pass. Would that we'd both died before we sacrificed Numantia on the altar of Maisir.

But then I would never have met Marán, never have known her love, or that of Amiel and Alegria.

I slowly realized one truth. It may be good to have lived, but it is better to have never lived at all.

Perhaps, when I finally come face-to-face with Saionji, I can beg a boon—for after all I sent uncounted thousands, perhaps millions, into her embrace—and she will free me from the Wheel.

But I'm being foolish, feeling childishly sorry for myself, and Saionji shall have other lives, other deaths, harsh punishment waiting.

So I continue with the drab life of a prisoner.

All I want is the embrace of my last friend.

Death.

THIRTY-ONE

THE MESSAGE

All has changed.

All is chaos.

This morning, I sighted a fast courier boat, the same one that had brought the news of the emperor's death. This time there was no bunting, no banners.

The message it carried was even more shocking than the first.

Laish Tenedos is alive. Alive and free.

He'd prepared a clever spell or potion in his island prison that gave him the semblance of death, enough to fool chirurgeons and the sorcerers set to guard him.

His dying request was to be carried to his native island of Palmeras and his family permitted to hold funeral rites. This was granted, provided no stone was raised to his memory, no memorial built as a rallying point for malcontents.

Somehow the coffin vanished, and Tenedos reappeared in his native town, alive as ever.

At first no one believed it wasn't a ghost, or an impostor. The Peace Guardian detachment on Palmeras sent soldiers and their most skilled wizard to investigate and end the nonsense.

The wizard died horribly, as did the soldiers.

The man claiming to be Tenedos vanished.

A week later, he reappeared on the mainland, in the capital of Hermonassa Province.

He cast certain spells, said certain words, and there was no more foolishness about him being an impostor.

Hermonassa revolted against Barthou and Scopas, and declared for Tenedos. Two Corps of Peace Guardians were sent to Hermonassa, and they also mutinied and swore the old imperial oath to Tenedos.

No one on my prison isle knew what to make of it, but I noted with cold amusement that my warders began calling me sir.

The day passed in a haze of bewilderment and questions.

At nightfall I stood on the gray stone battlements, not feeling the cold wind and rain batter my face.

The emperor still lived.

I know he will summon me, whether to punish me or use me once more to retake his empire.

The oath I swore rings through my mind:

We Hold True.

ABOUT THE AUTHOR

CHRIS BUNCH is the coauthor (with Allan Cole) of the Sten series and the Anteros trilogy for Del Rey. As a solo writer, he is the author of the Shadow Warrior science fiction series, also from Del Rey. Both Ranger and airborne-qualified, he was part of the first troop commitment into Vietnam, a patrol commander, and a combat correspondent for *Stars & Stripes*. Later, he edited outlaw motorcycle magazines and wrote for everything from the underground press to *Look* magazine, *Rolling Stone*, and prime-time television. He is now a full-time novelist.